About the Author

The author is a retired teacher who spent many years teaching Psychology and Criminology, after having worked in several different careers. He has travelled extensively and gained a fascination for other cultures and beliefs, which has led to the writing of this book. He currently lives in the UK with his wife and a house full of rescued cats and dogs.

Worlds of the Jinn

I. L. Darby

Worlds of the Jinn

Olympia Publishers
London

www.olympiapublishers.com
OLYMPIA PAPERBACK EDITION

A CIP catalogue record for this title is
available from the British Library.

ISBN: 978-1-78830-877-9

First Published in 2021

Olympia Publishers
Tallis House
2 Tallis Street
London
EC4Y 0AB

Printed in Great Britain

Dedication

I dedicate this book to my recently deceased older sister, Ann, and to the marvellous NHS for their sterling work.

Acknowledgements

I would like to acknowledge and thank my wife, Gillian Darby, without whose help, this book may not have been completed. She continued working to enable me to retire from teaching to focus on my writing and singing. She has also regularly agreed to read over the work as it progressed, to check for continuity errors and typos which, in my eagerness to complete the book, I sometimes overlooked. I'd also like to thank Olympia Publishers for agreeing to publish this work and their production team for their hard work.

CHAPTER 1
1240 A.D.
The Beginning

"There's a cave near the top of that hill, sir. Do you want us to search it?"

Seated upon a black stallion, the officer glanced at the hill. His chain mail glistened in the hot afternoon sun and his sword hilt shone like an evening star. He, like so many of the European knights, found the heat of Palestine almost unbearable. Clearly irritated by the humidity, he wiped the sweat from his brow with a grubby white cloth.

"They're long gone by now and I fear the Saracens may discover our presence here. Our treaty with the Emir in Jerusalem forbids us to venture this far inland." He paused, discarding the rag with an angry fling to the ground. "But the traitors must be caught, for by God they could do far more than merely wreck a treaty… Search the cave! They may have stored something there!"

Just then, the two men saw movement near the cave entrance. With the sun in their eyes, it was difficult to make out anything clearly.

"Could it be them?" The other knight asked.

"Perhaps. We should check it out."

As they kicked their horses on towards the hillside, they were oblivious of the three young children playing near the cave.

Ahmed and Abbas often played near what they called 'the secret cave of Sulayman', just outside Jerusalem. It lay halfway up the small hillside, away from the belligerent adults, their own brothers, fathers, uncles and cousins among them. The children had never entered the cave itself, believing that its dark, foreboding entrance hid all kinds of imagined things that they preferred not to encounter. They had heard stories of Jinn and ghouls since their infancy and they could never be sure whether they were true or not.

With them was Hassan. He was almost sixteen years old, the only son of a Turkish officer in the service of the Emir in Jerusalem. His father was Abbas' tutor, or Atabeg, and in that role, he held considerable influence. Although originally slaves and servants, the Mamluk Atabegs had gradually become key players in the region's politics. Their descendants would make great strides in the power struggles that would ensue over following centuries. Hassan had taken the youngsters to the cave and he felt responsible for them, particularly for Abbas, the Emir's son who only months earlier had been made Hassan's ward.

On this day, Hassan was dressed in a loose Turkish tunic that comprised of baggy blue trousers, tucked into soft leather boots, and a thin but warm, light blue cotton shirt. The colours seemed to clash with his bronzed skin and deep brown eyes but could never detract from his handsome good looks. Everyone who knew him teased him about them. *"You'll have the women begging to make them your wives"*, they would say. His hair was long, shoulder length, straight; a subtle blend of dark brown and red that shone whenever the sunlight struck it.

Abbas was darker than Hassan, shorter and two years younger. He stood chest height to the older boy. His hair was short and, unlike Hassan's, was tucked neatly beneath a loosely worn black turban. Like his father, Abbas often dressed in black, the colour of the family of the Prophet Muhammad. On this day, he wore a black cotton shirt and trousers, the latter held up with a grey leather belt, securely fastened with a gold buckle.

Ahmed, the smallest of the three at only six years of age, was the son of the leader of Jerusalem's garrison of troops. Abbas enjoyed teasing the younger boy and today was no different.

"The cave is full of Jinn and if you annoy me, I'll throw you in, Ahmed," he said.

Ahmed glanced at the cave entrance, dark and foreboding. Noises emanated from within, caused by the circulation of the desert wind that entered and swirled around inside.

"Hear that, Ahmed? They're waiting for you. They eat little boys, you know."

Hassan rebuked the prince. "Leave the boy alone," he said, "and we'll investigate the inside of the cave ourselves. Ahmed can wait outside."

Despite his bravado when teasing the younger boy, Abbas had no intention of entering the cave himself, fearful of the very things he tormented Ahmed with. He sat down next to Ahmed and reached out for the younger child, but Ahmed, afraid now of Abbas' intents, ran around the hill to a safe place.

Tucked behind a small boulder some yards away from his friends, he saw the two soldiers riding towards them; soldiers he immediately recognised as being from the enemy army—two Crusaders from Europe. His heart was pounding more, and his head felt as if it were about to explode. This was real fear; something tangible that was truly worthy of his dread. He had to keep out of their line of sight, but he knew he also had to rush back to the other boys.

As the soldiers reached the base of the hill, Ahmed started to make his way across the gravelly earth towards them. He had almost reached the other boys, who were standing at the face of the cave, looking in, when his tiny legs began sliding on loose rocks. Two of the pebbles dislodged and one of them flew from the hillside and struck one of the soldiers' horses. The horse veered sharply to one side and the soldier looked up again. He could see the three boys in silhouette against the sun but, at first, was unable to make out whether the figures were those of men. Were these the men they had been chasing, or were they young goat herders who often wandered far from the cities?

He squinted to get a more focused picture, but the sunlight was too strong, too blinding. He raised his roughened right hand and placed it, visor-like above his eyes just as a rare cloud passed in front of the sun, clarifying their forms at the top of the hill. It was then that he realised that they were only children.

Wishing to speak to them, to enquire as to why they were here and find out whether they had seen the men he sought, he yelled out in broken Arabic. He called to them to stop and come down, but the boys were too frightened to obey him; their only thought was escape. Hassan and Abbas were both sweating and shaking, the blood rushing to their heads. Instinct had taken over from conscious decision-making, and they reached for their little friend. Hassan caught hold of Ahmed's arm, lifting him effortlessly to where he was standing with Abbas. As Ahmed dangled from his friend's hands, his tiny legs like two pendulums swinging in the light desert breeze, one of the soldiers dismounted his hefty, grey horse, and called out to his colleague.

"We must get them! We have to get them! They have seen us Amalric, and if we let them get away, the Emir's army will think our forces are on their way to attack Jerusalem!"

He still had hold of his horse's reins, even though the animal was exceptionally well trained and stood stock still, apart from the odd shake of its head and occasional snort. The soldier finally released the reins and ripped his sword from its sheath. The sun caught it fleetingly and the light bounced, intricately, across his buckles and braids. A warm breeze blew, increasing the discomfort he was experiencing. Sweat trickled down his face and neck, irritating him. Ants gathered near his feet and biting insects seemed to have targeted him in an all-out onslaught. He pulled at his tunic with his free hand and wafted the material in a vain attempt to create a cool breeze.

The boys could hear the men talking, but the sound of medieval European languages was just babble to their ears. Nevertheless, it increased their levels of apprehension. Nothing is more fearsome, particularly to a child, than something that is not understood.

The second soldier, Amalric, the officer, a man who oozed status and authority, climbed slowly from his horse. He was slightly shorter than his comrade. He thought for a moment, and then gently nodded in agreement with his companion. "Regrettably, Bohemond, you're right. I fear, however, that talking, explaining, may be difficult, so then, we'll have a decision to make."

He sighed and pointed at Bohemond's sword. "Sheath your weapon. They are children and already afraid." He thought for a moment. *What are we to do with them if we're unable to convince them that our motives are pure?*

Bohemond sheathed his sword and both men glanced up at the children. Without speaking, they began to make their way up the hill. Their progress was slow and cumbersome, with their suits of chain mail and heavy European swords weighing them down.

The boys were panic-stricken, and in their confusion, Abbas lost his footing at the entrance of the cave. He fell into the dark, cold, emptiness, losing his turban which fell from his head and unravelled in the darkness.

Although the other children called after him, there was no reply. He rolled down a small incline, just inside the cave entrance and ended his cascade with the strike of his head on a large boulder.

Hassan acted quickly. He knew that in the eyes of the Muslim world he was a man now and he realised that this was the time to act like one. He looked hard at Ahmed. He knew that to send such a young child for help would be taking an almighty risk, but he had to stay to help Abbas.

CHAPTER 2
Al-Baahita: The Shadow World

In a brightly lit, jewel-studded cave in another world, a small man sat gazing at the floor before him, seemingly mesmerized by what he saw. This was Zaman, an unusual looking character, and not at all what you would expect the Overseer and leader of half the Jinn world to be like. Short and thin, with a pale, sickly-looking face, he sat in a chair so large that he looked like a doll on a king's throne. His clothes were plain, not at all king-like, but anyone stood before him would quickly realise they were in the presence of power and authority.

Beneath him and in front of him was a giant hologram containing vivid images of the three Arab boys. They looked so real, yet so small and vulnerable. He watched as Abbas fell into the cave and waited, knowing that something lay ahead of them of which they were completely unaware and for which they were wholly unprepared.

The jewels on the cave walls around him glittered. With the intensity of the light emitted from the gemstones, it was surprising that the hologram was visible. Yet it was. It was clear, the sharp images appearing almost real, albeit tiny.

As he surveyed this scene a tiny man, no bigger than a small boy's hand, ran through the hologram image and rushed up to Zaman, waiting for a moment at the Overseer's feet; waiting for permission to speak. The man was elf-like in appearance, with ears forming to a point and a small, goatee beard and moustache. He sighed but said nothing and occasionally he shuffled his bare feet and twiddled with a leather belt that seemed to be holding a single piece, beige tunic to his minute body.

The Overseer continued to monitor the images before him, never once making eye contact with the tiny Jinni. He waited a few more seconds and then said, "Speak".

"Master, I have news about the humans, the ones that the children belong to; they are searching for them and are heading towards the cave of Sulayman."

Zaman thanked the tiny man who then turned to leave. He began to walk again towards the hologram when his leader motioned a hand at him.

"Ahem," the Overseer coughed, attracting the man's attention. Zaman wagged his finger and the little servant walked *around* the image.

"Sorry Master," he said, smiling and carefully sidestepping the shimmering borders of the image; then he left.

The Overseer waved a hand over the hologram and it changed. No longer were there miniature images of Ahmed, Hassan and Abbas on the floor before him, but Saracen knights, Muslim warriors on horseback, on the outskirts of Jerusalem. Even their voices could be heard clearly, and Zaman watched their every move. A troop of seven men on horseback had left the city of Jerusalem and were riding, at a gallop, towards the nearby hills that housed the children's secret cave. One of the men, the commander of this small unit, was a Saracen knight. The others were Turkish warriors; light cavalry of the type the Muslims used very effectively against the rather cumbersome European horse soldiers and infantry.

Zaman watched them for a while and then shifted the holographic image to that of the boys again. All around him the cave fell into darkness, not suddenly but gradually, the light growing steadily dimmer and the picture before him growing, both in intensity and in size. After a minute or so, the hologram was actual size and the only light in the cavern came from within that image.

Zaman clicked the fingers of his right hand and a tall Jinni appeared from behind him. This man, if he could be called a man, was resplendent in fine white, almost transparent clothes and armed with a sword that must have been crafted by the finest blacksmiths anywhere in the universe. The Overseer did not speak. He did not need to. The Jinni understood what he was to do. He stepped forward, into the hologram and for a moment in time, the image faded from view before returning as a miniature world laid out on the floor before Zaman. The Jinni had gone—sent on an errand of utmost importance.

Zaman began flicking the image from one scene to another,

monitoring the Crusader knights, the children, the Muslim horseman and his faithful servant who had just appeared in a dark cavern in another place; a place no human had ever seen or heard of. The Jinni made his way along a dark corridor of wet rock that seemed to have been carved out of the innards of a mountain. There was no light in the corridor and no light at the end of it, but all around the Jinni himself was illumination. There was clearly a long way to go, but he had been unable to enter where he needed to be. Something, some force, had prevented him from doing so. So, he walked.

Eventually, the corridor opened out into a cavernous area, like the belly of an enormous beast, from which other corridors reached out like fingers. He needed no time to decide which one to take. He knew exactly where the boys were and which of the corridors would take him there. Time, however, was not on his side. There were forces in play that had opened a portal in the cave where the boys played, and those forces had done so for a reason. Zaman was sure the boys were in peril and it was his duty to reach them and keep them safe.

CHAPTER 3
1240 A.D.
The Crossing of Worlds

"I know you're the youngest of us Ahmed," Hassan said, heaving a big sigh afterwards. "This is not an easy thing for me to ask a six-year-old, but I have to stay to help Abbas, so I want you to run around the hill and back to the Garrison at Jerusalem. Alert your father and bring him here."

Ahmed's father was the Emir's General, Abdul Qadoos Al-Harawi. He oversaw the Emir's Garrison in Jerusalem and Hassan knew that he needed to be told that the Crusaders were scouting nearby. He watched Ahmed for a few seconds and then he entered the cave to search for Abbas, a frail child, only eight years older than Ahmed, but considerably less independent.

Ahmed, crying and wiping the tears from his eyes and face, hesitated so Hassan caught him by the shoulders and looked him in the eye.

"If you keep low until you are on the other side of the hill, you can run towards the city, with the hill between you and these men. You can do it, Ahmed. Now move!"

Ahmed did as Hassan ordered him to and headed off towards the garrison. As he moved along the dirt path that led around the peak of the hill, he crouched low, his long jelabiya occasionally tripping him over as he did so. Once on the other side of the hill, he caught hold of the tunic with both hands, lifted it to almost waist height and ran for his life but one of the soldiers had seen him and gave chase. He was taller than any man Ahmed had ever seen, and clean-shaven with exceptionally long, straggly, red hair. His arms were course, freckled and covered in hair and a deep red scar sat menacingly beneath his right eye. The small boy's heart was pounding and as the 'giant'—for that is how this Frankish warrior appeared to him—caught hold of him, he let out a piercing scream.

It may as well have been a whisper, however, for the garrison that housed the Emir's army was too far away for anyone there to hear him and the other boys were unable to help him, even if they had heard his shriek. Ahmed shook with fright; he felt sick to his stomach, and he fainted as soon as the soldier grabbed him.

Meanwhile, Amalric, a blonde man with piercing blue eyes, had reached the cave entrance. Although shorter, he was more muscular than his colleague. Some people might have mistaken him for an unthinking thug. He was, however, an officer in an elite troop of Acre's Christian army.

Total blackness greeted him at the cave entrance, and it seemed that both the other boys had completely disappeared. He returned to his horse to fetch a torch and then climbed back up the hill where he waited outside the cave for his associate to reach him. He then lit a fire, so that the torch could be lit when needed.

He was a fearsome looking man. His hair was carefully fixed in plaits, hanging well below the middle of his back. He sported a drooping, sun-bleached moustache, the ends of which hung below his jowls. Untrimmed, the moustache covered the whole of his top lip and hopped up and down whenever he spoke. At certain key moments, the sun and the flames of the fire seemed to glisten off his pale skin and his eyes appeared to shimmer like the water on a pool in which a small pebble has recently been dropped.

Minutes later, his colleague arrived, climbing up the hill carrying Ahmed like a small Persian rug slung over his left arm. The boy had fainted with fear and Bohemond laid him on the ground and tied his hands and feet to prevent him from running again.

"They're inside", Amalric said.

Inside the cave, Hassan had found that Abbas was just a yard or so in but, having struck his head on a rock, was lying unconscious alongside a cold, stone slab. He dragged him behind another rock, took some water from a flask on his belt and began dabbing it gently on his face and lips until, gradually, the younger child awoke. The cave stank of damp and animal urine and the smell was making Hassan gag, so he covered his nose and mouth with his left hand. Abbas was dazed and confused at first, but gradually regained his senses and began to panic.

"Stay calm," Hassan whispered, his voice barely audible through his hand.

Neither of the boys could see anything inside the blackened hole— their secret cave. They could see the outlines of the men outside. They could hear their voices and just about hear the soft whimpering of their little friend Ahmed as he began to stir from his brief slumber. The shorter of the two men was talking.

"The other two are in there, Bohemond", he repeated, "Light the torch and we'll search for them. I doubt the cave is that big?"

They entered and began to search but Bohemond called to his commander. "The light is fading out there and the other boy is stirring. We can't waste time looking for them."

Amalric sighed and nodded. "We'll take that one with us. We may be able to prevent the Emir from getting news of our presence some other way, and in case we do not, we at least have something to bargain with."

Bohemond was right. Daylight was beginning to fade with the steady drawing on of night, so the two soldiers moved away down the hill and out of sight of the two boys, who remained snuggled together in the chilly, damp cave. The knights' voices were still audible, but just barely, and the children certainly could not understand them.

As the knights moved away from the hillside, Bohemond spoke. "His clothes are very fine Amalric. Do you think these are just ordinary children?" Amalric shrugged and pulled on his reins, enticing his steed into a canter.

When the men's voices had faded away, Hassan whispered to Abbas. "It's all right," he said, soothingly, "we're safe in here… I hope."

Then he murmured to himself, "If they only knew who they have…"

He waited for the sound of the soldiers' horses to disappear before speaking again to Abbas.

"We have to tell our fathers what has happened and warn them that the Christians are coming, the Franj are coming, and probably with an army… They must be planning to march on Jerusalem."

The boys planned to leave the cave and return quickly to Jerusalem but, unfortunately, with the onset of nightfall they found themselves surrounded by a blanket of darkness, as black as pitch. Not even a star in the sky was visible to enable them to distinguish the entrance from the walls of the murky cave, let alone to guide them home. They were trapped in a cold and gloomy den of unusual sounds and unfamiliar smells, and their fear was indescribable. Bats fluttered past their heads periodically, and Abbas insisted that they try to find their way out. So, holding each other's hands, they moved to their left around the large rock that had hidden them so well from the soldiers.

They stepped forward, in what they believed to be the direction of the cave doorway, but three steps are all Abbas took before falling. He was dropping like a stone, while apparently still in contact with something firm on all sides. It felt like the walls of a long shaft, full of unexpected twists and turns. Above him, following closely behind, was Hassan; his muffled and barely audible shouts vibrating off the tunnel's inner surface.

The youngsters were wondering if this long drop would ever end and, if so, what lay at the bottom. Hassan's mind conjured images of the two of them smashing into the ground once they finally came to it. *If the impact doesn't kill Abbas, I'm sure I will when I come crashing down on top of him,* he thought to himself.

He was sweating profusely and on the verge of sheer terror when suddenly the tube levelled off and they found themselves soaring along horizontally at extremely high speeds. Abbas too had begun to wonder whether their ordeal would ever end, or whether it would end in death or terrifying injury. He was screaming and his howls echoed like a siren. Hassan's ears were assaulted by the echoes of Abbas' screams, making his own ordeal worse.

They were thinking about where they might find themselves at the end of this tunnel, when they were suddenly thrown out of it into a brightly lit cavern, the ceiling of which shone with jewels and glistened with traces of gold. Abbas flew out of the tunnel first and found himself thrust across the cavern, only to land against a cold, but soft, moss-covered wall. By now, cuts covered his hands, legs and face and he was more than a little shocked. He had an urge to sob but stopped when Hassan too shot from the tube and landed with a dull thud against the wall, barely missing his young companion by inches. The Emir's son shook violently as Hassan, nervous and startled, tried desperately to calm him without revealing to him his own fearful state.

"Lay your head on my lap and rest Abbas," he said, panting and puffing between each word. He whispered softly to the young boy, who slowly drifted off to sleep in his arms. "There is... no point going anywhere now..."

Hassan glanced down at the now sleeping child in his arms before staring, disbelievingly, at the jewels and gold around him. The opening, through which they had entered the cave, was gone. There was not even a trace of it. With a sigh, Hassan muttered to himself, "In fact, I'm not even sure that we *could* go anywhere, even if we wanted to..." he paused and smiled wryly, "... and with all these riches here too—just our luck!"

Once again, he glanced across to where they had entered this cavern but there was just rock face. No entrance, no tunnel, nothing. He looked again at the sleeping child in his arms, at his sun-bronzed skin and shiny black hair. He tried his hardest not to, but he too began to drift into a deep sleep as he wondered whether they had stumbled into an Aladdin's cave or a demon's dungeon.

In his sleep, his mind was cast back to when he first moved into the Emir's palace in Jerusalem. He was just ten and the city was daunting; the palace was terrifying. He spoke no Arabic back then and his Father was seldom around, busy as he was in his duties with the Emir. Hassan's mother had died during childbirth and his early years involved care by a nanny who also served as a wet nurse. He had had few friends and constantly found himself in trouble for fighting, but year by year, he hardened, learned Arabic and became determined to make something of himself. His father's move to the palace was like a gift from heaven. Opportunities would appear, of that he was sure.

In his mind, he stood in the main hall of the palace, the Emir introducing his son, Abbas, to him and coaxing them both towards the garden. Hide and seek was the game they ended up playing but Abbas was poor at it and Hassan found himself sitting behind a bush for what seemed like a lifetime. Waiting patiently for Abbas to find him, he nodded off. So, now he dreamed a dream within a dream, of water and boats and his nanny's hands gentle upon his brow...

CHAPTER 4
1240 A.D.
The Town of Acre

In our world, Ahmed, his hands and feet tied, his mouth gagged, was lying across the lap of one of the riders, being carried north east to the coastal town of Acre. The town had been occupied for many years by the crusaders, the knights of Europe. Much of the coastal regions of Palestine and Lebanon were still under European occupation, as well as a few cities in Syria. Crusaders, led by King Richard the Lionheart of England, and Philip Augustus of France, had recaptured Acre in 1191. Many of the key towns along the coast, together with the Syrian strongholds of Aleppo, Damascus and Homs, plus Jerusalem in Palestine, had been wrested back from the Christians several years earlier. The man who had achieved that was Salah ad-Din Yusuf ibn Ayyub, known to the West as Saladin the Saracen, although he was from a Kurdish family in Mesopotamia.

He had taken Jerusalem from the Christians and, with extraordinary magnanimity, had spared thousands of lives, even allowing crusader soldiers to leave the city fully armed. This contrasted in the extreme with Richard's brutal and savage slaughter of Jews and Muslims in Jaffa. Saladin, however, never hated Richard for his act of barbarism. On the contrary, he respected his foe as a fearsome and skilled fighter on the field of battle, but he pitied Richard's woeful inability to control his pride, anger and prejudices once victory was his.

Saladin had built a battery of enemies across the region, including members of the Ismaili sect who had run Egypt until Saladin's conquest of the country. He had not been as magnanimous in victory there, as he had been in Jerusalem. He showed little mercy for the Ismailis of Egypt and found himself beset on all sides by enemies that were both domestic and foreign. Acre had been lost because of this and was now firmly back in the hands of the Europeans.

Halfway through their journey, Bohemond brought his horse to a halt.

"Why have you stopped?" Amalric asked.

Bohemond glanced back in the direction of Jerusalem and breathed a heavy sigh. "Something is very wrong, my friend. We know that messages have been sent from traitors in Acre to the Templars in Syria. We know also, because we have intercepted them, that the Templars, or at least some of them, are communicating with the Hashisheen. Why, then, were the men we were chasing today heading towards Jerusalem?"

"Or Bethlehem," Amalric said. "We can't be sure they were heading to Jerusalem."

Bethlehem was an Arab Christian town, lying South of Jerusalem and Bohemond shook his head at that suggestion. "The Templars and Hashisheen hate the Arab Christians of Bethlehem more than they hate anyone else. I doubt there is anyone there who would work with them."

He paused and shook his head again. "No, my friend, they were headed to Jerusalem and my question is this; who among our people in Acre is known to have an affinity for the Templars, while also voicing his opposition to the truce with Jerusalem?"

Amalric's expression was stern. "Cedric."

"Cedric," replied Bohemond. "I've never trusted that man."

Amalric kicked his horse forward. "We've dawdled enough. Now, we ride." Bohemond followed.

The ride was long and tiring, but eventually, the two knights reached the city of Acre. As they approached its gates, the first rain for months fell. A brief flash of lightning appeared in the distance, followed by a burst of thunder.

They entered Acre with Ahmed still slung face down across Bohemond's horse's back, like a sack of rice. The child was awake, but neither moved nor spoke. Terrified that he might fall from the horse, he clung to the front of the leather saddle, as well as he could with his hands tied. He looked up just once, as the two riders approached a prominent white building. It housed the quarters of the Frankish commander who, for many years, had led this army of fearsome fighters across most of Europe, through Turkey, and into the land of the Arabs. Now, this army stood guard over a sizable portion of the Holy Land of Palestine and prayed that one day all of it would once again be theirs. The journey from Jerusalem must have felt like a brisk canter, compared with the staggering trek these hardened warriors had made from England, France and Germany. The journey from Europe to this far off land had been beset by constant battles against Arab, Kurdish and Turkish warriors, each supposedly in the service of the Khaliph of Baghdad. In truth, however, loyalty was bestowed only to an assortment of sultans and emirs.

Bohemond and Amalric left their horses and walked through the corridors of the magnificent Arab palace to two massive brass doors that led to a large and spacious room. Inside, and seated opposite them, was another tall man, dressed in baggy Turkish trousers and sporting a fine silk shirt. A waistcoat of chain mail hung over the back of a huge chair and at the man's side hung a jewel-studded leather sheath. Protruding from it was the carved bone, cross-shaped handle of a giant sword.

From his rather uncomfortable position in the arms of Bohemond, Ahmed caught sight of this impressive weapon. It reminded him of the crosses that he had seen the Christians carrying through the streets of Jerusalem on their festival days. For several minutes, he was captivated by its ornate splendour, but eventually his eyes wandered upwards, to the man himself. His hair, black and unkempt, dangled knotted, twisted and in parts plaited, down to his broad shoulders. Beneath his red nose and covering most of his mouth, was a bushy moustache and around his chin, a black beard. This man was so covered in hair that his face was almost invisible. Had Ahmed been less terrified, it may even have made him laugh, but frightened he was, and his anxiety increased as the man before them rose to his feet.

Bohemond stepped forward a couple of paces and dropped Ahmed on the stone floor. His head struck the cold surface and he winced as a shot of pain registered in his brain. He began to cry, but restrained himself, choking back the tears and, in a manner that was way beyond his years, pulled himself to his feet, lifted his head high and stared ferociously at the wall ahead of him. Briefly, he stared in shock at the grazes on his hands and arms that had gone unnoticed since his capture, but which must have been caused as he tried to scrabble away from the two crusaders. Cat-like, he wiped his eyes. It was not clear to the soldiers whether it was bravery or shock that had stopped him crying, but once he caught sight of the blood on his fingers, he let out a yelp. The blood had oozed from a small cut above his right eye and it appeared far worse than it was. He wiped his eye again and his crying worsened as more and more blood covered his hands.

"You've cut me, you've cut me!" he kept calling out in Arabic.

The lone figure on the other side of the room was a senior Commander of the Franks, or Franj, as the Muslim Turks and Arabs called the invading European knights. He was Raymond of Saint-Gilles. Only André de Chauvigny, one of King Richard's strongest allies, held more power in the region.

To the men around him Ahmed's screams sounded like the wailing of a cat in heat and Raymond in particular, was becoming increasingly irritated. When he finally broke his silence, it was with great authority.

"Shut that boy up!"

Bohemond took a leather belt from his waist and struck Ahmed across the back with it. The child stumbled forwards but remained on his feet. He turned sharply and stared up at the soldier, who replaced his belt and removed his helmet, revealing the full body of his long ginger hair. Ahmed had never seen a man with skin so white and hair so red before, and such a tall man as well! He looked more like a Jinni than a man, with arms like the thick branches of a tree and hands the size of plates. The terror that overcame this poor six-year-old, dark-eyed son of the Saracens sealed his vocal cords momentarily, and a shiver rippled throughout his entire body.

Raymond stood up and moved around his desk to stand in front of Ahmed.

"Bring the boy to me Amalric and explain to me the reasons for your arriving back from the mission with nothing, or so it would seem, but a small Saracen urchin."

Amalric caught hold of Ahmed by the hand and lifted him clear off the ground, almost throwing him to Raymond, who stood as still as before, emotionless, stern. The Franj commander looked down at Ahmed, placed his right forefinger under the boy's chin and forced his head back. Ahmed resisted looking at Raymond for as long as he was able. He tried with all his might to face the floor, but with his head pressed backwards so far by the strong hand of the French knight, eye contact was soon unavoidable.

Saint-Gilles snapped at him. "Look at me boy!"

His words were meaningless to a child whose only language was Arabic, but Ahmed understood from the tone of Raymond's voice, what was required of him. His eyes slowly peered upwards into the dark eyes of Saint-Gilles, who proceeded to speak to the boy in very poor Arabic.

"What your name boy?" His poor command of Arabic made Ahmed giggle.

Saint-Gilles let go of him and then stepped around him. Ahmed, meanwhile, tried to follow with his eyes, but dared not move his body.

"Why you laugh? What funny?" Raymond enquired of his tiny prisoner.

Ahmed began to laugh aloud, which angered the Frankish commander intensely.

"Speak me boy!"

Raymond shouted so loudly that his booming voice echoed around the voluminous room, returning to Ahmed repeatedly. The boy stopped laughing and stood, terrified and motionless, his bladder becoming more and more uncomfortable and his legs began shaking uncontrollably. As a trickle of urine ran down his leg, forming a small puddle on the floor, he turned slowly to face the enormous table before him.

"I frighten you?" Saint-Gilles asked, a calm having come over his voice.

Ahmed nodded tentatively.

"And yet you laugh me."

Ahmed's puppy-like eyes pleaded with his captor for understanding. "You... you... you speak in a funny way," he said softly.

At this the commander let out a bellowing laugh, slapped Ahmed on the back of his head, in a gentle, almost friendly way and looked over at Amalric and Bohemond, who were both smiling, cautiously. Raymond took a deep breath and then asked the boy again, "What your name?"

"Ahmed bin Abdul Qadoos al-Harawi!" he answered firmly and decisively, turning to face the two 'giants', Raymond and Bohemond. "And I'm not really afraid of any of you!" he shouted.

Saint-Gilles became very sombre. "You are the son of Abdul Qadoos?" he asked.

Ahmed nodded, and the commander turned to Bohemond, beckoning the knight towards him. "Do you know who this young fox is?" he asked.

Bohemond looked confused and slowly shook his head to indicate that he did not know, but that he had realised that he obviously should know. That was made manifest to him by the expression on Saint-Gilles' face and the tone of his voice. The commander turned the boy around and gently pushed him towards Amalric, who was fully aware now of who the boy was.

Raymond continued; "This is the son of the Saracen Commander in Jerusalem. Take care of him, hand him to the interpreter, and find out as much as you can about anything he knows, as soon as you can." He paused briefly and then added, "The Saracens will be searching high and low for him very soon. They will not be easily convinced that we never intended to kidnap him, so we must keep him until we have ways of convincing them. At all costs we must keep his presence here a secret."

Bohemond glanced at Amalric, waiting for him to tell Raymond of the other boys and knowing that they would be sure to tell Abdul Qadoos that two crusaders took his son away. Amalric, however, remained silent and Raymond waved them away with the boy.

CHAPTER 5
Al-Baahita: The Appearance of Zenith

"Strange little creatures, warm and soft to touch."

Hassan dreamed that he could hear whispering and giggling but his nanny's hands were gone, replaced by something harsh and rough, rubbing across his forehead, waking him with a start. Looming over him, but not much taller than a very small child, were two diminutive creatures eyeing the boys curiously, studying them with intent and talking about them in some unfamiliar tongue. The little beings were incredibly fearsome in appearance, their skin thick and dark and their features not dissimilar to those of a hairless baboon. They had short, thick hair on the top of their heads, and only three fingers and a thumb on each hand. Despite their primate appearance, they had hooves instead of feet. As one of them moved, Hassan witnessed a long, sturdy tail and soon became aware that they were wearing no clothes. Despite this, their form failed to embarrass him in any way. Their ugliness, however, was beguiling.

Both creatures held long spears, almost twice their own height, and Hassan was torn between believing he was still asleep, regarding himself as insane, and fearing the worst—that these things were real!

"I'm dreaming... I must be dreaming," said Hassan, closing and reopening his eyes at least three times, until one of the creatures touched them, quickly withdrawing his hand. "Who... er... who are you?" asked Hassan, "am I dreaming?"

Surprisingly, one of the creatures replied in Arabic. "You are not dreaming little boy... little human." Each word seemed to be carefully chosen. "You have entered a world in which you do not belong. You have made a grave error."

The creature's voice was chilling and intimidating, giving Hassan great cause for concern. He began to shake, partly with fear but also with cold, as the cavern's temperature had dropped somewhat since their arrival. Carefully, he pulled at Abbas' tunic. Meanwhile, the second creature stalked them like a hunter approaching prey, seemingly unable to pause for even a second. He walked back and forth, scrutinising the boys, eyeing them up and down and occasionally approaching them to sniff them, dog-like.

Hassan shook Abbas and whispered, forcefully in his ear.

"Abbas, wake up! Wake up! But be careful and try not to panic!"

"What? What... where am I?" Abbas mumbled to himself as he lifted his head off Hassan's lap. He began rubbing the sleep from his eyes until Hassan took hold of his hands and pulled them away from his face. That was when Abbas found himself face-to-face with the little beings.

"Oh no! Oh no, no!" he shouted, "Aootha billah himinal Shaytaan Ar-Rajeem—I seek help from Allah against the cursed devil."

He kept screaming this—twice, three times, four times, on and on. Each time he sounded more anxious than the time before, until finally all that was intelligible was "Shaytaan Ar-Rajeem,—cursed devil, cursed devil" being repeated, over and over again.

Hassan held him and calmed his nerves.

"In the Name of Allah, what are you? We ask Allah for help", he whispered softly, before looking down at Abbas. "Master Abbas," he said, "I don't know where we are or what is happening, but I also don't think we should antagonise them, at least for the time being. They are armed, and they do look pretty nasty."

Tears flowed from Abbas' eyes and ran down his face, but it was the urine in his trousers that captured his attention. He looked away from the creatures for a moment, as one of them reached out to touch the tears.

"What's that?" the creature asked, but as the teardrop touched his finger it burned him, scorching his skin, which began to hiss and smoke. "Ouch, curses on these humans; their eyes produce this poisonous, burning fluid."

The creature stepped back, its face transforming into something even more horrific than it had been originally. It poked Abbas in the chest with its spear, not hard, but with enough force to make the young prince wince and stop crying. The foreboding entity was angry and as it spoke to them, a long scar on its left cheek throbbed.

"You will come with us," it said, stepping back once more. "Stand up!"

Abbas was frozen with terror. His whole body began to shake and his heart pounded in his chest, pumping blood around his body, forcing it ultimately to his brain, until he almost passed out. Light-headed and woozy, he tried to calm himself and meet any impending peril with valour. He re-focused his attention on the creatures, who were chattering, like animals.

"Maybe we should use them now for our amusement. The Master will forgive us for they are very pretty humans and difficult for us to resist."

"No! We must take them with us. Maybe later he'll let us have them as our personal pets or perhaps even more."

The creatures laughed aloud for a while before prodding the boys again.

"Come on pets, move!"

"Wait!" Hassan called out loudly, "who… or rather, what… well, er, who and what are you and how is it you speak our language, and why do our tears burn you, and…"

"Enough! What are we? We are ghouls, rebel genies, Jinn; the offspring of the one to whom we are taking you—our Master, Iblis." He paused for a second, rubbing the scar on his face. "Your tears, as you call them, burn us because you are children and not soiled by sin; we, you see, are workers of the Evil One, Iblis, Shaytaan, Satan; call him what you will."

He signalled again for the two boys to stand up and then he turned to the older child.

"And you are Hassan bin Arslan."

"How do you know my…"

"Your name? Ah, we come and go in your world, although we lurk unnoticed in the darkness and you are unlikely to see us unless we wish it. We take many forms and we meet some of you in your dreams. We know you Hassan, and all about you. We also know of your little friend, Abbas bin al-Afdal, the son of the man some say is the Emir of Jerusalem, the Sultan of Damascus, a descendant of Salahuddin." He paused momentarily. "Of course, no history writer will ever record your existence young Abbas, being as you are the bastard product of one of

Al-Afdal's drunken orgies." He smiled and nodded; his self-satisfaction was evident to all. "Ah yes, our Master will be most pleased to meet you two."

After another brief pause, he grabbed Hassan by the arm, pulling him sharply to his feet. The creature's claws dug into the back of Hassan's arm, drawing blood, the smell of which seemed to arouse the two demons further.

"Now move! That way!" he ordered, pointing to his left.

"Wait," Hassan shouted in desperation. "Abbas is not fully fit and only partially conscious. Give me a moment to prepare him for whatever journey you intend for us."

The ghoul snarled and poked at Hassan again with his spear. "No!" he said, angrily, "if he can't walk, you'll have to carry him", but just as Hassan was about to bend to lift the young lad, Abbas snapped out of his stupor and stood up, a little uneasy on his feet at first, but able to catch hold of his friend's arm.

"I'm okay," he said. "I can walk."

"Good." The demons stepped back slightly and then directed the boys towards what seemed to be a solid wall of brightly shining jewels.

"Where are we supposed to go to? There's nothing here but rock!" stated Hassan.

One of the Jinn prodded him in the back with the spear.

"Just walk!" he ordered, as he nudged the boys again.

Both children were sweating heavily, despite the cold chill of the chamber, and as Hassan wiped some of the perspiration from his brow, he forced a smile in Abbas' direction and slowly nodded; then they did as they had been so forcefully told to do. They walked towards the wall and were astonished to see it shimmer like water in a sunlit pond as they approached it. All of them passed right through it to a far darker place.

On the other side, everything smelled damp and foul. No longer were there jewels and crystals shining all around them. Here, there was the foul stench of decay and a maze of eerie underground tunnels branching off in a variety of directions from where the four of them now stood. Each tunnel seemed to slope downwards and not one of them was silent. Emanating from each passageway were whispers, a strange hullabaloo, and languages completely unrecognisable to the two human children.

Hassan knew he had to find a way of escaping from these Jinn, but all ideas had deserted him. Where would they go? Wherever they ran, they would probably end up somewhere just as bad, or maybe even worse. So, reluctantly, he remained.

"Down the third lane on your left", the ghouls ordered, nudging Hassan firmly in the back with the flattened side of their spearheads. Hassan stumbled forward, grazing his legs on the stony ground. Now he was not just tense from fear, but out of anger. He leapt to his feet and launched himself at the Jinni, grabbing hold of the spear and attempting to wrest it from him. The second creature reacted instantly. He caught hold of Hassan's shoulder, pulled him away from the weapon and hurled him against a wall. A jagged piece of granite struck the boy's back, just below his ribcage and sharp pain shot upwards, triggering every neuron on its rapid path to his brain. He gritted his teeth and clenched his fists, partly as a response to the agonising pain and partly in preparation for a fight.

The ghoul who had thrown him against the cave wall approached him. His eyes red, he stared at Hassan as if trying to burn his way deep into the young man's soul. Hassan trembled, his heart raced, and his tightly clenched knuckles turned white as he prepared to strike the leathery skin of the demon. The ghoul sniffed the air, again sensing the boy's blood. Hassan was preparing himself mentally for a fight that he was unlikely to win, when a flash of light temporarily blinded all of them. It was so intense that the entire cavern remained illuminated after the effect of its initial appearance had worn off.

The boys rubbed their eyes and looked at the two Jinn who were now cowering beside the cavern wall. In front of them, as if pressing the little ghouls against the cold rock by some unseen force, there was a being not wholly unlike a human. A haze of shimmering light surrounded his near perfect features and his deep voice reverberated around the whole cave. The whispers from the tunnels had ceased.

He turned to face the two boys and his hold on the ghouls was lost for a second. One of the ghouls lunged at him with his spear, more out of desperation than with any sense of purpose. It was a mistake, however. The being of light wrenched the weapon from his grasp and launched it back at the attacker. The steel point entered the ghoul's neck, severing

34

the jugular and forcing deep brown blood from his throat in a gush. The ghoul slumped to the ground, his blood-filled mouth and throat gurgling and spluttering as he died.

The being of light pointed a finger at the remaining demon.

"Go, Evil One! Return to your master and warn him that the innocent ones he so desired are in our care now. We are their protectors and will be until we can return them safely to their own world."

The ghoul turned and ran through one of the tunnels, while the being of light stepped over to the boys, bent down and picked up Abbas, who eyed him suspiciously. Surprisingly, neither child showed any fear or resistance. Although a little wary, they felt surprisingly secure and safe for the first time since their ordeal began.

"Who are you?" Hassan asked nervously.

The creature returned Abbas carefully to the ground and the aura surrounding his body faded, revealing his full features. He wore the clothes of a Saracen warrior, and had a sword strapped to his back. The handle was studded with jewels and shone as bright as the sun. He was a muscular person, a man of obvious power, both physical and mystical and when he spoke, a tranquil atmosphere flooded the cavern.

"I am Zenith, messenger and soldier of the army of Zaydussia. Don't be scared, little ones; I'm a friend. You have entered our world, a hidden world; you have entered Al-Baahita but fret not. You really are under our protection now." He smiled softly and reassuringly as he spoke.

"Are you an Angel or are you a Jinni too?" asked Abbas.

"My dear little friend," replied Zenith, laughing a little, "you have entered the world of the Jinn. Almost every being here, almost every living thing you come across now will be Jinn of some kind or another. Although there are animals here, there is no guarantee that every animal or person you come across will be what they appear to be. The Jinn can come in many forms and some are indeed Angels."

"So, are you an Angel?" Hassan asked.

Zenith did not answer the question. He could see that the boys were somewhat confused and perhaps slightly perturbed.

"Do you know your Holy Book?" he asked, and the boys nodded, or at least Hassan did, and he nudged Abbas who followed suit.

"Of course!" the prince shouted, indignantly.

Zenith lifted his hand and in it appeared a manuscript, which he unfolded. He read aloud from the paper and the boys listened.

"Say, it has been revealed to me that a company of Jinn listened and said, 'we have heard a wonderful Recital, giving guidance to the right, and we have believed in it'."

He blew softly on the document and it vanished as mystically as it had come forth in the first place. Then he studied their bewildered faces for a moment, and after a brief pause, he spoke again.

"Do you recognise that verse?"

The children nodded.

"You see my young ones, some of us, some of the Jinn are followers of The Upright One, The Gracious. Different people call Him many different names, but you call Him Allah."

He paused momentarily and crouched in front of the children so that he was at eye level with them.

"It is fortunate for you that I appeared when I did, for the two who had captured you are servants of..."

"...the Evil One, Iblis," interrupted Hassan. "We know. They told us."

He turned away from Zenith for a second and stared at the dark tunnels before him. Then he caught hold of Abbas by the shoulder and pulled him close to him.

"What would have happened to us if you had not come?" He asked. "They said they wanted us as their pets."

Zenith frowned. "Pets indeed," he replied. "You've seen a cat playing with a mouse?"

The boys nodded.

"Well, you may well have become rodents for these two to play with."

Hassan looked at the body of the dead ghoul, its face and chest now covered in blood.

"But cats eat mice... would they have eaten us?" Abbas asked.

Zenith glanced at the body and took a deep breath.

"It is most likely, eventually, yes. That is if you could not provide what Iblis wants."

"And that would be?" Asked Hassan.

Zenith sighed and frowned. "We don't know." He shook his head and eyed the ground for a moment. "We just don't know".

The cave was cold and both children shivered while staring at the Jinni, apparently hanging on his every word, but Hassan's thoughts were on home.

"We have to get back to our world," he said, desperately.

Zenith waited, as if he were aware that Hassan had more to say, and the boy continued, "you see… our friend Ahmed…" Hassan's voice was becoming more distressed as he spoke, "well, er… he's been taken by the Franj. Our parents are going to be so worried, but that's not all…"

There was another pause. Hassan pulled Abbas even closer to him and placed a consoling hand on each of his shoulders. The faces of both children were beginning to show signs of understandable alarm.

"The Franj must be planning an attack on Jerusalem and our people are not prepared because of the treaty, so we must get back to warn them!"

He was raising his voice and becoming quite emotional, so Zenith took hold of both boys' hands, asked them to keep calm, to trust him and to stay close. Then he led them towards the last tunnel on their right.

"Be steadfast," he said, "things are not always as bad as they seem. We will help you to return home, but you can't go back the way you came. You have to reach the Ridge of Fertheron and from there you can return easily."

CHAPTER 6
The Drakon

"Why can't we go back that way?" Hassan asked, pointing behind him, and when he received no answer, he repeated his question, more impatiently.

Zenith remained unruffled. "I will explain later, Hassan. All you need to know now is that to reach the Ridge is very dangerous, and a long journey lies ahead of us. Plus, all the while, the dark Jinn will be striving to get you from us."

As they approached the tunnel, Hassan and Abbas shivered with cold. They were wearing only thin baggy trousers and light shirts, and the wind whistled through the long passageway. Abbas was wet with urine and as the wind struck him, the smell wafted behind him, meeting Hassan's nose with the force of a hurricane. Zenith walked in front of them and as they followed cautiously, he once again became illuminated. He gave off both heat and light, which protected them from the worst of the biting wind and lit the way for them. His entire being seemed to burn like a flaming torch, and yet he remained cool enough to touch. Abbas turned to look behind them, but saw nothing but pitch darkness, a blackness that he had only ever seen twice before; in the Cave of Suleyman and in one of his father's prisons. Ahead of them, however, was a glow that was brighter than that found in the desert at mid-day, when the sun is at its highest and most illuminating. When it is at its zenith.

It seemed that only a very short time had passed when the three travellers emerged from the tunnel onto a ledge overhanging a giant cliff-face, which stretched upwards maybe fourteen yards to a cloud-filled sky. The blue and white of daylight was visible between two gaps in the puffs of white steam slowly blowing by. Beneath them, the cliff went further, perhaps thirty or forty yards. Its face was sheer and at its base was a river, wild and turbulent; white water crashed against colossal rocks, forming rapids the like of which few Arabs had seen before that day. The Jinni placed his arms around Hassan and Abbas, pulling one boy to each side of his huge body.

"Hold on tightly around my waist and don't be afraid" he said, and as they latched on to him, he lifted himself off the ledge, carrying them through the air. At first, Abbas closed his eyes and muttered quiet prayers under his breath, but ultimately his curiosity got the better of him. He opened his eyes and stared in awe at the beauty that surrounded them. Hassan's gaze was already transfixed on the Jinni, awesome in appearance, strength and power.

As the light shone on Zenith, the boys could see two barely visible, translucent wings on his back, carrying them across the air. He flew downwards, down, down, down, until at last the children were as close as was safely possible to the masses of dark blue water and pure white froth of the violent rapids. They turned left and flew along the river for maybe a mile. Then they veered right, crossing the mighty rapids and heading towards a giant forest on the river's far bank. Zenith landed and placed the children on the serene, grass-covered ground, beyond which lay the seemingly endless forest of peculiar trees and other extraordinary plants. The trees were huge; so tall that when Abbas looked up, he could see no end to them. After a few seconds of staring skywards, dizziness overcame him, and he fell backwards onto the soft turf of the riverbank. Hassan sat down opposite his friend and laughed. His thoughts again wandered to times at home when they were younger and would often play together. He thought of his father and of Ahmed, now holed up in some Christian dungeon, he mused. Their new guardian, however, quickly interrupted his reflections.

"There is no time to rest now my young children," he said insistently, "we have far to go and no time to waste. From here, we must travel through the forest on foot. I can't fly above the trees. The air above the forest is lethal to me."

The three travellers made their way into the murky depths of the virtually impenetrable forest and, after only a few minutes, an overpowering presence of huge trees and vegetation surrounded them. Their senses were overwhelmed by unknown smells, the strange feel of the damp forest air and by the sounds of the bizarre creatures of the wood, lurking ominously in the midst of the undergrowth. Owls, nightingales and cuckoos were among the birds heard overhead, but other animals, some unknown to man, were also present. Many of the sounds were eerie, giving the children Goosebumps and shivers.

As the Jinni and his wards carried on deeper and deeper into the gloomy forest, the noises increased to a deafening pitch and the children were forced to cover their ears. Some of the creatures were becoming frantic at the presence of the three travelers.

"Stick to the path and stay close to me," Zenith whispered but for some reason he felt the urge to look behind him, upon which he noticed that Hassan had stopped. "What are you waiting for Hassan?" he asked, impatiently.

"You must tell us where we're going and explain how we can get back home, or I'm not going anywhere, and neither is Abbas!"

"We don't have time for this Hassan," the Jinni responded, edgily.

Hassan refused to budge. Stubbornly, he folded his arms and stared indignantly at Zenith. Seconds later Abbas, who copied the older boy's stance precisely, joined him.

Zenith stepped back a few spaces and once again crouched down in front of them. For the first time, they saw the flawlessness of his features and they noticed that his skin, like his wings, was translucent. He appeared to transmit light from his face and hands, and the details of his features were not easy to make out. He took hold of both boys' hands and drew them towards him.

"You cannot return to your world the way you entered ours. There is no return by that route. Only at the Ridge, the Ridge of Fertheron, can you cross the dimensions from our realm into yours."

Hassan looked confused. "How is it we could enter but can't return that way?" he asked, with some mistrust.

Zenith paused for a second and sighed. He looked down at the floor and then at the boys. His speech was soft and measured. "When you entered the cave, the dark Jinn were waiting for you. They created a doorway between our worlds. It opened near to you and closed again after you had entered. That door is lost forever, but at the Ridge there is a permanent way through."

He paused again and sighed again. "Unfortunately," he continued, "I don't have the mastery to open the gateway there. Only my master can do that."

He turned to his right and pointed along the dusty pathway that stretched out before them. It was narrow and arched by overhanging trees and it seemed to vanish into oblivion in the near distance. The chill of a cold wind blew across the forest, biting through the boys' meagre clothing, increasing their shivering.

"At the end of this forest," the Jinni said, "we have a journey equivalent to seventeen of your days, through mystical caverns and across magical valleys. If Allah wills it, we will reach Zaydussia and our leader, Zaman, and he will assist us from there."

"Zaydussia?" Hassan queried.

"The holy city, from which Zaman monitors the worlds, both yours and ours."

The Jinni stood up and moved off again.

"Now, let's move. Yallah! We have wasted enough time!" he said, his voice raised for the first time since the boys had met him. "And touch nothing. Many of the plants here are noxious, toxic and some can kill a human in seconds".

The boys sighed in resignation and the travellers trekked on through the wilderness, past bogs and marshes, and under overhanging trees. The vegetation was unusual, the smell was almost unbearable and a mood in the air sent chills up and down the boys' spines.

"I'm really scared Hassan," Abbas whispered, eager to keep his feelings securely between Hassan and himself.

"I know," Hassan said, sympathetically, clasping the younger child's shoulder as he did so. "I'm scared too. I don't know what lies ahead of us. I keep thinking I'm dreaming and will soon wake up, but I'm sure we're not and this Jinni seems to have our welfare at heart, don't you think?"

Abbas sighed and nodded in agreement. Then he yawned. Both children were tired, their legs weary and their eyes heavy. Hassan was about ready to collapse with fatigue when Abbas began tugging hard at his shirtsleeve.

"What now?" he replied, a hint of irritation creeping into his voice.

"I need to go to the toilet, and I need some new clothes. These stink!"

Hassan looked ahead towards Zenith. The Jinni was about seven or eight yards in front of them and the young Turk felt they could easily catch him up.

"Quickly! Go there, by that bush," he said, ushering his young friend towards an area of thick undergrowth, and wild bushes. "Clothes will have to wait though."

A few minutes later, just as he was calling to Abbas to be quick, so they could run and catch Zenith, Hassan thought he saw something out of the corner of his eye. He wasn't sure what it was, but thought it was a lizard, a grotesque giant reptile. He looked across to his right and saw it flash before him. It *was* a lizard, a large, scaly lizard, but it was standing on two legs.

"What was that?" he called out.

"What was what?" replied Abbas.

Zenith was walking back towards the boys, to find out what was keeping them, when he heard Hassan shouting. As he got closer, he saw the boys running like crazed animals in his direction. He reached out and caught hold of Hassan, fearing that he may run right past them and into greater danger, and demanded to know what he was running for.

"I saw a demon. It was ugly, wet, and slimy and it was over there in the marsh. It looked like a giant lizard."

Zenith seemed concerned. For the first time since meeting him, the boys felt that he might not be as invulnerable as they had thought or hoped. He grabbed hold of both boys and began to draw them away in a hurry.

"That's the Drakon, a beast of great fury and power. We must hasten, for it has a taste for warm animal blood and it won't distinguish between a goat and you two," Zenith replied.

The boys started to run, but Abbas tripped and rolled towards the marsh. He rolled twice and then his feet touched the thick, marsh water and he thought he was going to topple in. The Drakon must have sensed his presence, or maybe smelt him, for it turned sharply towards him. Abbas screamed and clutched at some reeds as Hassan rushed towards him, stretching out his arm to him. He was too late. Unable to reach him in time, Hassan let out a loud yell, a panic-stricken plea for assistance, for his friend was in great peril and he was unable to assist him. The lizard seized Abbas' leg, wrenching him away from the reeds, a bunch of which remained tightly clasped in the small boy's frail little hands.

The Drakon was about ten feet tall when it stood on its hind legs. Its scaly, green skin rippled as it pulled the boy high into the air. Red, demonic eyes glared at Abbas and it let out a bloodcurdling, ear-piercing screech. With its mouth wide open, its horrific teeth were visible. They were not unlike those of an alligator or a crocodile, but so much greater in size. Abbas tried to wriggle, attempting to escape, but the Drakon began to salivate in anticipation of its meal. It exhaled a foul-smelling breath towards its victim but paused to monitor the possible threat from the approaching Jinni.

Zenith drew his sword as he ran towards the beast. He wrenched it from a sheath on his back and wielded it over his shoulder to challenge the reptilian, and a rush of air whistled past Hassan's ear. The sword sparkled. It had a handle cast from silver and gold, and its blade curved to a fine point, as sharp as a needle. Sunlight, or those flashes of whatever light source existed in this place, seeped through the thick, dense trees and glistened off the smooth blade.

"Release the human!" he demanded, and the Drakon spun round to confront him, lowering the child slightly as he turned. The children were food for this beast, but Zenith was a Jinni from the light side. The reptile wanted to kill this one just for the sheer pleasure it would bring him. First, however, he would tease the Jinni. Without warning, he lifted Abbas sharply towards his mouth, his vast, sharp teeth reaching out for the boy's throat, the pupils of his red eyes dilating in anticipation of the pleasure to come. Zenith, just as quickly, rushed forward and thrust his sword deep into the monster's chest. The boy dropped into the marsh and the Drakon collapsed into the water behind him, sending vast ripples through the marsh, which pushed Abbas towards Hassan. The Drakon slumped backwards, yellow blood pouring from his mouth and from the gash in his chest where the Jinni's weapon had struck him with such immense force.

Without warning, the giant reptile staggered once more to its feet and then lurched forward. It was collapsing into the water again and Abbas, thrashing about in the marsh, was lying right in the path of the toppling demon. The boy reached out to grab Hassan's hand, which by now was stretching out from the bank of the grimy pool. Lying on his stomach and clutching a large reed with his left hand, the older youth grabbed his friend and began to drag him up to the bank as the animal's massive torso smashed into the marsh and sank. Hassan was too late. The force of the sinking reptile sucked Abbas' shoes from his feet and then wrenched him from Hassan's grip. He was pulled down with the Drakon as it disappeared beneath the thick murky waters of the bog.

Hassan was toppling forwards but had managed to draw in a massive breath before he hit the water. Abbas, however, was not so fortunate. Liquid rushed into his lungs and his life began to slip away. Hassan managed to reach, and grab hold of the younger boy and desperately tried to pull him away from the suction that was threatening to drag them both deeper and deeper into the shadowy depths. Alas, it was too late. Abbas entered another world as images of home flitted in and out of his mind and then there was darkness, ink-like and silent. Finally, there was nothing.

Meanwhile, Zenith stepped into the marshy pool and disappeared beneath its surface. Within seconds, he had found the boys. He caught hold of Hassan, who still had hold of Abbas, and with an effortless tug, he pulled them both to the surface. After placing them safely away from the pool, he returned to it and dived beneath the surface of the murky water once again. Hassan shook in terror, wondering about their fate, but then he remembered Abbas. What should he do? The younger child was no longer breathing. He cast his fears aside, though, as the Jinni stood up, the marshy water up to his waist, and Abbas' shoes clasped firmly in his hands. On his face, he wore a smile. It was the first time the boy had seen him smile and it had an instant calming effect upon him. Zenith called out to Hassan to breath into Abbas' mouth, short but strong breaths, followed by a pause, during which he should press, with regular motions, on the boy's chest.

Hassan began. He was crying the whole time, fearful that it was too late but after what seemed like an age, Abbas spluttered and coughed, anxious to rid his lungs of some of the filthy marsh water he had swallowed. He was alive but may not be well enough to travel any further for some time.

The chilly air was now freezing the boys' wet clothes, and Zenith wrapped them in huge leaves that he had pulled from a nearby bush. The leaves were thick and furry and once they were enveloped by them, the boys began to feel warmth emerging once more in their chilled bodies.

Perhaps now they could rest a while, Hassan thought to himself. Perhaps now they could persuade Zenith that they needed to stop.

"Hey, Abbas, at least your clothes have had a wash!" He called.

CHAPTER 7
The Journey to Brillar

Hassan was calmer now, but it was a serenity that was not to last. Zenith had taken them away from the reed-laden bank, settled them down and then gone to seek food. Minutes later, he parted the branches of a bush, behind which he had left the boys. He placed the food, a selection of fruit, on the ground and was about to sit with them, when the Drakon suddenly lurched out of the water. It rushed through the undergrowth and grabbed Zenith's sword with both hands. Then, it held the blade against the ripped skin in its chest, producing a flash of intense light. The weapon vanished, the creature's wound healed in an instant and the Drakon's eyes turned once more to the one that had wounded him.

Zenith did not delay. He lifted his arms across his face to create a shield of shimmering light, which the reptile struck with great force. As he did so, the radiating shield began to absorb him, firstly pulling in his fist and then his arm. It let out an ear-splitting roar as terror and alarm overtook it. The Drakon's face became disfigured and contorted as the gleaming shield began to slowly draw it deeper and deeper into another dimension, another time, another world, until ultimately both shield and beast annihilated each other. In an instant, they were gone, the creature and the shield. The three travellers found themselves surrounded by silence, darkness and an uncanny stillness. The noise of every living thing in the forest had ceased, and for a moment, it felt as if they were standing in a vacuum. Zenith's sword had reappeared on the far side of the marsh and the Jinni waded across to retrieve it.

By now, Hassan was starting to take some of the remarkable happenings a little more in his stride. He stood up as Zenith stepped from the water onto the bank and Abbas sat up with a start, a serious frown across his brow; the type of frown only a young child displays if he is obviously very perplexed. The little boy whispered softly to his servant

Hassan. "He…he's dry; how can he be so dry Hassan?"

"Master," Hassan replied reassuringly, "you've just seen a gargoyle disappear, you've flown on a man's back and you've met ghouls, yet you ask how Zenith can stay so dry in water." Abbas forced a painful laugh. It was perhaps the first sign of happiness from either boy since their ordeal began and it made Hassan giggle too. "My young prince, I think we must learn to expect all things in this world. It's not our world and things, as Zenith said, are not always how they seem, or as we would expect them to be." He placed a comforting arm around Abbas and continued; "the rules and laws of our world, which we have grown accustomed to, appear not to apply here."

Abbas sniggered even more loudly. "So," he said between giggles, "if the rules of our world don't apply, does that mean we can stay up late and eat what we like?"

Hassan smiled and lifted Abbas to his feet. They walked across to the Jinni and he surrounded them with his great arms. Clearly, using so much power to defeat the Drakon, had weakened him. He looked and sounded very tired and, like the children, he needed rest.

"Your friend is right," he said softly to Abbas. "On your journey you will come across many things that are not known to your people. For example, we have soon to cross the vast crystal desert of Brillar, but first we must rest, for my fight with the Drakon has weakened me and in the desert, we will be much more open to attack by our enemies. I must regain my strength and power before we enter there. We'll walk on to the Forest edge and rest there."

"Ghouls", mused Hassan, "and I always thought they were things made up by our parents and… well then again I suppose we really should be ready to just believe in anything now."

"That's correct," replied Zenith and they walked on for two more hours until just before them the forest end came into sight. Shafts of blinding light pierced the trees at the edge of the forest. The crystal desert, a desolate area of crystalline rocks, through which ran sparkling streams of the purest water, created the light. A warm breeze entered the forest from Brillar and about twenty yards from the forest edge, Zenith called his companions to a halt.

"Here," he said, "we rest here, and I will tell you more of this world."

He pulled apart a large bush, behind which was a cliff-face. Zenith closed his eyes and the rock-face gradually vanished before them, revealing a cave entrance—not a very large one, but big enough for them to crawl through—and in they went. Inside was a round room with smooth marble walls and a carpet of dark green moss. They entered, and the entrance sealed itself behind them.

"Wow!" exclaimed Hassan in astonishment. He slumped down onto the soft, cushion-like floor.

The cave was unlit, except for the parts that were illuminated by Zenith, and the boys could see that it was small, empty and silent. The sounds of the outside world remained firmly outside, while within the cavern, the only sound they could hear was that of their own breathing, movement and voices.

Zenith, like Abbas, had remained standing after Hassan had lain on the mossy cave floor. He appeared to be about to say something when Abbas' little voice stopped him short.

"Well?"

"Well what?" asked the Jinni.

"Well, how did you know this was here? I mean it's not every day you come across a marble room hiding behind an old bush, is it? Not even here, I bet."

Zenith laughed. "No, I suppose it is not and to tell you the truth, I knew this was here because I built and prepared it many aeons ago and use it whenever I am in the forest." He seated himself beside Hassan and slapped his hand on the floor, indicating to Abbas to sit down with them.

"In a short while you must sleep, both of you, but first I will tell you about Brillar, the Crystal desert, and warn you of some of its dangerous characteristics. In Brillar, there are many miraculous things, but you must beware! For every miracle, there is a nasty by-product. Whatever temptation appears before you when we enter Brillar, you must be sure to seek my guidance and advice before submitting to it."

He looked at the boys, one-by-one, firstly at Hassan and then at Abbas. Their wide eyes exposed simultaneous feelings of trepidation and awe. Hassan was lighter skinned than Abbas, the result of his Turkish ancestry. His reddish-brown hair and dark, brown eyes offset his pale face delightfully. He was a very handsome boy with a smile that might, one day, soften and captivate even the hardest of hearts. Abbas, on the other hand, was very dark. His father had taken a woman from Egypt as a second wife and he had those mixed-race features that always seem to be eternally appealing. His hair was darker than Hassan's; it was close to black, but it was wavy and long, hanging to his shoulders at the back. He had the look of someone who was not only important but knew it too. It was a sort of acceptable arrogance, unusual in a child so young.

"Do you understand what I said?" Zenith asked them. They both nodded. "And do you promise to do nothing without my permission?"

They answered with a nervous 'yes' and then he laid them down beside him, perhaps aware that a child's word is easily broken. They asked him for a story about Brillar and he related one from a thousand years before.

Brillar had not always been a desert of crystals. At one time green vegetation and wildlife had thrived there. Zenith was a young Jinni back then, born of two farmers who had worked the land for thousands of years before his birth.

Their home was modest. A house created from the earth, raised up by his father and moulded into the shape he desired. They worked, and they were happy. Their bond with nature was deep rooted and their loyalty to Zaman was unquestionable. It was this loyalty, however, that had brought an end to their idyllic lives. Iblis, the Evil One, determined that no followers of the Overseer should be allowed to live away from the safety of Zaydussia. So, he sent a plague of locust-like demons to ravage the land and kill the Jinn that lived there.

Animals were butchered, plant life was torn from the earth and Zenith's parents fled with their son to Zaydussia. It was a frighteningly long journey, beset with dangers; hunters sent by Iblis tracked the family and finally, Zenith's father made the decision to stand and fight. He sent the boy with his mother to Zaman's city, high above the world. His smile was the last thing Zenith saw and the only clear image he had now of his father. He heard stories in the days to come of a Jinni who had been killed and eaten by ghouls and, although he was sure it was his father, he forced that image out of his mind. He remembered his father as a strong man, a brave man, who smiled at him that day a thousand years ago.

Brillar, meanwhile, was left barren. It was a dead zone, and the demon Jinn were starting to move in. Zaman had to act, and he did. He cast a spell over the entire area, turning it into crystals, so bright that while lit, no demon could bear to be near them. The brightness would last several hours but would fade for several more. The desert had an artificial day and night and during the night, the demons returned. The few of the light Jinn that remained in the desert protected themselves with oils and spells but were always prisoners in their homes at night. Zenith, however, had been raised to a higher status by Allah. He was then trained by Zaman, in Zaydussia, to harness his natural abilities. Consequently, he developed speedily into the master Jinni the boys now saw before them.

Zenith looked down at the boys and smiled. "That's all for now," he said. "We really must rest."

Within seconds, they were all asleep.

CHAPTER 8
1240 A.D.
The Emir's General

"Sir, we have found the boys' tracks near an old cave a short ride from here," a young Mamluk Turkish soldier said to the rather dignified and authoritative figure seated on a glorious black mare. The horseman's right fist gripped a fine leather saddle, which was raised high in front of and behind him.

"Show me!" he ordered. This was Abdul Qadoos Al-Harawi, the Emir's most senior General and Ahmed's father. His skin was darker than the other man's and his face was rough, yet handsome. Born in Jeddah, Arabia, he was a true son of the desert with features carved by the fierce winds of the Sahara. A thick, dark beard covered much of his face and upon his head was a small, but dignified turban, a part of which hung down his back and unintentionally wound around the sheath of his curved Arab sword. The hilt of the weapon was visible above his right shoulder and matched the hilt of a small knife that nestled comfortably at his waist. The markings on these weapons were distinctive, composed as they were of his family name, carved elaborately in fine Arabic calligraphy into dark wood. He waited patiently while the Turkish soldier mounted his own horse.

"I can certainly show you sir," the Turkish officer said obediently, "but with your permission I would like to inform you that we found other tracks near those of the children, sir."

"What other tracks?" Abdul Qadoos shifted in his saddle, clearly irritated.

"Horses and men sir and, judging by the depth of the horse prints and by the size of the men's footprints, I would have to say they were Crusaders sir. Big men they were, with large heavy horses, obviously weighed down; probably with chain mail sir."

"Then let us go Arslan, for I fear danger greater than just our missing children."

Arslan was guide and tracker for the Emir's army, but he was also Hassan's father, and was Atabeg, or tutor, to Abbas until Hassan had taken over that role. In recent months, many of Arslan's tutoring duties had been handed over to his son. Arslan's horse was an elegant grey Arab mare, beautifully groomed and highly decorated, its white hair glowing in the sunlight, its mane plaited ornately. Arslan was one of the most fearsome looking men one could ever come across. Bearded, but light-skinned, his dark, deep-set eyes were piercing in their intensity. Impassively, he sat majestically upon his steed, his hand set almost permanently upon his sword, which hung not in the Arab fashion across the back, but purposefully at his side. His hair was short and black and from his left temple, down past his ear, ran a scar acquired in battle.

Before long, the two men were riding with great haste to the Cave of Sulayman, accompanied by ten cavalrymen. Once there, they searched the cave with lighted torches. It was empty, chilly and clammy and they found there was no way out, except for the one opening at the top of the hill, through which they had entered.

"The children's prints seem to end here," Arslan said, pointing at the ground where the day before the vortex had opened. Now there was only rocky ground. "Over here," he continued, turning towards the cave entrance, "we have the Europeans' prints again, and it is safe to assume that they picked up the boys and carried them out of the cave. This is the only explanation for the sudden disappearance of the children's prints sir."

Abdul Qadoos glanced around the cave and then stormed out, throwing his torch to the ground. The flaming stick rolled down the hill and landed so close to one of the horses that it reared up on its hind legs with a start.

Arslan followed him out and looked in the direction of Jerusalem. "Only two of the children were in the cave sir," he said, somewhat nervously.

His commander turned sharply and Arslan continued; "the third, Ahmed we believe because the prints are the smallest, was caught by the Franks while running down the hill there." He pointed to the place where

Bohemond had lifted Ahmed into his arms the day before.

Abdul Qadoos started to walk in that direction, down the hill towards the dirt track that led to Jerusalem. Arslan stayed where he was but called out to the General.

"Once again sir, the boy's tracks suddenly stop, signifying that he too was picked up and carried off." For a second, he paused as Abdul Qadoos returned up the hill. "They most likely rode that way sir, towards the coast... possibly towards the town of Acre."

He paused for a second, waiting for Abdul Qadoos to arrive alongside him again.

As they pondered the situation, one of Arslan's soldiers approached them, dragging a young European man with him. He threw the man to the ground at Arslan's feet. "Found him cowering among those trees," the soldier said, pointing south. "He says he saw two Franj soldiers carrying a child but didn't see anything else."

Arslan put his foot on the man's chest. "Why are you so far from Acre, Franji?" He asked.

The man was clearly frightened and unable to answer immediately, so Arslan took a knife from its sheath on his belt and knelt beside the man. He held the knife threateningly at the man's throat and asked again.

Stuttering and shaking with fear, the man finally answered.

"I was sent with a message for someone in Jerusalem. There are plans to start a war."

Arslan pressed the knife into the man's throat, drawing blood, which ran down the man's neck. "Were you sent alone?"

The man shook his head. "No," he said. "But my colleague fell from his horse a short time after we left Acre and broke his neck. I hid his body and continued alone."

Arslan pulled the knife away, sheathed it and stood up. "Tie him up and bring him with us!" he ordered.

"There's no blood anywhere, sir—no sign of any real struggle," Arslan said. "I believe the children are still alive, or at least were when they were taken, but the only way to be sure is for someone to go to Acre."

"Then we must go there and get them back, one way or another," the commander answered, resolutely, causing Arslan to stare at the officer for a moment before responding.

"Do you think that's wise sir?"

"Do we have any choice?" came the raised voice response. "You said yourself that someone has to go there. What else would you suggest Arslan?"

"Send in an agent sir, a Christian from Jerusalem. He could find the boys and, if possible, bring them out. He may also be able to uncover more information about this plot to start a war."

The two men stood in silent thought for a moment and then the Turk continued; "I have the perfect man for the job and can arrange it as soon as we arrive back in Jerusalem… if you agree."

The commander took a deep breath and glanced around for a few seconds before looking down at the ground for a little while longer. Sunset was fast approaching, and the air was growing noticeably colder. A biting wind was building from the North and both men were beginning to shiver. Abdul Qadoos looked up and ordered one of the cavalrymen to bring him a hooded black cloak from behind his horse's saddle. Upon receiving it, he threw it around his shoulders and pulled it around himself. Then he turned towards the now shivering Arslan, stared at him momentarily and asked whom the agent was.

"Jemal Habash. He is very calm, very trustworthy, a first-class spy; he speaks the Frank's language and he even looks like a European. His mother was Armenian, and his father is Sayeed Habash, the Vizier of the Christian sector of Jerusalem." By now, Arslan's shivering was very noticeable with the air growing colder as the night fell. "May I go to my horse and fetch my cloak sir?" he asked, and when his commander nodded his permission, Arslan respectfully suggested that they should return to Jerusalem.

Abdul Qadoos sighed, threw back his cloak and nodded again. "Yes!" he said, as he began walking down the hill towards the horses, "yes, we should."

They half ran to the horses and mounted up immediately. Arslan quickly thrust his cloak around his shivering body and grabbed hold of his horse's reins. As Abdul Qadoos kicked his horse forward, he turned and called out to his fellow warrior.

"Do it! Get your man Habash and arrange for him to enter Acre. If he can get out safely with the children, then he should do so without hesitation, but if their lives can't be guaranteed I want him to gather information for us. I want to know what the situation is like in Acre. What are the Franj up to? Do you understand Arslan?"

"Yes sir, perfectly sir."

"He is in no way to put the children's lives at risk. Is that understood?" He paused then added: "And tie up that prisoner. He's coming with us."

"Absolutely sir."

Dust filled the air as the horse's hooves thundered away from the base of the hill and in the face of the cave a man appeared. He watched them ride away, nodded and smiled. From behind him, a ghoul appeared, its red eyes shining in the low light as the sun fell sharply.

"It seems to be working Master Iblis," the creature muttered, menacingly.

"I need the boy; the younger of the two who fell into our world. I am tired of Zaman and his self-righteous followers interfering with my plans."

He turned, re-entered the cave and dematerialised, the ghoul following.

CHAPTER 9
Brillar, The Crystal Desert

The three travellers stood at the edge of the forest and looked out at the vast expanse of the Crystal Desert, the surface of which glistened, glints of light flashing in phases, sometimes from the left, sometimes from the right. The sky was the deepest blue and the ice-white crystal slabs and pillars plus the masses of snow-like drifts, stood starkly against the rich azure of the air above them.

No sun was visible and all the light around them seemed to be coming from the desert itself, an apparently everlasting stretch of luminous crystal. First impressions would indicate a cold environment, but as Zenith had said, first impressions must be treated with skepticism here. In fact, as the travellers stepped into the barren solitude of the desert, the first thing that became evident was the warmth. A hot breeze blew gently across their faces and the crystal floor beneath their feet thrust warmth high into the air. Overhead, the rising heat evaporated the clouds the instant they began to form, and yet the temperature was by no means uncomfortable to the human children.

As the light caught the jagged edges of the landscape, it reflected and refracted through prisms of crystal peaks and troughs. Colours filled the air, an aurora piercing the vivid white of the sky and illuminating the crystal desert until the entire region shone like part of a celestial dream.

Zenith spoke quietly to the two boys. "After about twenty of your Earth hours, the heat and light of the crystals will die down and a cold, mystical gloom will beset Brillar for a further two hours," He paused, momentarily and then continued; "Each period of heat and cold is known as one Zura and we will be just over eight Zuran in Brillar before we reach the Path of Fortune that leads ultimately to Zaydussia."

"Where do we sleep when the cold sets in?" asked Hassan.

Zenith paused for a second and then placed his hands on the boys' shoulders.

"Before nightfall we must reach the town of Al-Bahira, which is situated on a great lake. If we get there, the inhabitants will feed us and give us a place to sleep, if we are polite and obey their rules while we are there. Then, in the morning, we can use one of their floating vessels to…"

"A boat you mean?"

Zenith paused temporarily. "Er, yes Abbas, a boat. With it we will cross the lake to the River Rahan and, God willing, we will follow that river for five Zuran to the other side of Brillar and the town of Slegna. From there, it will take us a further one Zura to reach the Path of Fortune."

"Well I suppose we'd better get going then," remarked Abbas, smiling and full of energy after his first good night's sleep since this ordeal began. They began to walk towards the brightest part of the desert and found the shining crystals surprisingly easy to walk on.

"I thought we would slide like I did once on the ice in Lebanon," Hassan said.

"Ah, first impressions Hassan, first impressions." Before Zenith could say much more, he was distracted by a sharp tug on his cloak. Looking down, the Jinni saw Abbas pulling hard at him, desperate to gain his attention.

"Why can't we fly like we did before?"

Zenith stopped and for a moment that seemed, to Abbas, to last forever, he stared out across Brillar. Then, in a soft tone that revealed concern or perhaps anxiety, he spoke.

"There are a number of reasons why," he said, and pointing up at the sky he continued, "from up there this desert's light is blinding. I would be unable to see any dangers ahead of us and the crystals interfere with my ability to navigate from the air."

"What dangers could lie ahead of us now?" asked Hassan.

"Oh, there are many, including the evil ones you met earlier."

The Jinni hesitated briefly.

"Just remember what I said before; beware of first impressions and trust no-one without checking with me first. Now come, let us hurry, for time is not on our side!"

By the end of the first Zura, as the light faded, they had walked more than the boys had ever walked in their lives. Hassan was not looking forward to a further six periods of travel, even if the bulk of it was to be by boat. He was also concerned about Abbas. Presently, this was an adventure for the young child, but it was an adventure fraught with danger. Nevertheless, he saw no alternative but to trust Zenith and continue and now, ahead of them, they could see the outline of the town of Al-Bahira.

CHAPTER 10
Zaman, The Overseer

Zaman the Overseer watched the three travellers on their trek to Al-Bahira. He mused quietly to himself about their journey.

"You'll make it to Al-Bahira before nightfall... yes, yes... I'm certain you'll do that, but beware my friends, for the second stage of your journey will be riddled with pitfalls."

He leaned over the hologram and watched Zenith looking skywards, almost as if he had heard what his ruler had said. Perhaps he had. The Jinni nodded slowly, caught hold of the children, and moved on.

Zaman, meanwhile, passed a hand over the image. It glistened and then shimmered before altering shape and form. It appeared like a pool of blue water rippling from the effect of a stone having been dropped into its centre. Seconds later a new image began to materialise. It was the Palace in Jerusalem and, in a large and ornately decorated room, there stood two men arguing. One was Abdul Qadoos who, upon removing two curved Arab swords from the sheaths on his back, smashed them down in anger on the table before him. He turned to face the younger man and although he was shouting, there was still obvious control in his voice.

"You will not go! And I care little for the fact that you are the Emir's first-born son!" He paced up and down the room for a few seconds and then turned to face the young man again.

"We will find the boys. We will deal with the Franj! We... the military, and not some jumped up little prince!"

Abdul Qadoos continued pacing the room while the prince stood impassively, apparently listening, but with an air of carelessness about him. Prince Sieffuddeen was a young and handsome man, with shoulder length, black, curly hair that bounced whenever he moved his head, and a full, black beard that was neatly trimmed. The officer pointed his finger at him.

"I have already spoken to your father and he has agreed that you are to stay here in Jerusalem! We have a captive who has informed us that he was to deliver a message to someone unknown who will meet him tonight at Al-Aqsa Mosque. He will be there, and we will be there too. We will catch the traitor in our midst. You, your Highness, will keep out of our way. Your father has put me in complete charge of this situation. Is that understood?"

The prince did not reply. Instead, he walked towards the door and Abdul Qadoos called out to him again.

"If you have not understood, or if you allow your insolence and pride to get the better of your intelligence, may God Almighty teach you the lesson which I am not in a position to do." There was a pause before he added, sarcastically, "Your Highness."

This made the prince turn. He charged across the room and shoved the officer against the wall. Abdul-Qadoos, initially unprepared for the attack, found himself pinned against the cold wall, the prince's arm across his throat. He quickly composed himself, however, and swept the prince's feet from under him, with an arching kick. Sieffuddeen fell, face first, onto the hard, stone floor, breaking his nose in the process. He wiped blood from his face with the back of his hand and launched himself to his feet, keen to show no fear. He moved forward to attack the officer again, but Abdul-Qadoos was ready for him. He caught the prince by his shirt and dragged him to his large wooden desk. There, he held him in place. A far stronger man than the prince, he knew he was now in control of the situation. He leant forward, close to the prince's ear.

"I don't like you, Sieffuddeen. I don't trust you and your father is my master, not you. So, heed my warning boy. If you do anything to undermine your father's position, anything that puts Jerusalem at risk, I will not hesitate to kill you. Now, get out!"

He let go and Prince Sieffuddeen marched out of the room, slamming the large carved wooden door behind him. The force with which he closed it was so great that the room shook, and the bang echoed for a full twenty seconds afterwards. Outside, he called to three members of his personal bodyguard. These were no ordinary warriors. They were former members of the highly secretive sect based in Syria and Egypt. Called Hashisheen, rumoured to be because of their use of the drug,

Hashish, they were effectively hired killers, Assassins. They often performed suicide assassination missions for their leaders. These three, however, now fought only for money; brutal and merciless, these mercenaries were also skilled trackers and excellent guerrilla fighters, and many people in Jerusalem wondered why the prince would seek protection from such as these. However, use them he did, and without even casting a glance in their direction he wrenched his broken nose back into position without making a sound. Then he spoke to them as all four marched across the Palace courtyard.

"Prepare the four best horses in Jerusalem and provisions, enough to last the journey to Acre and back. Then meet me at the Damascus gate immediately after sunset prayers! It seems I will not be meeting the messenger from Acre after all."

The men left his side and he continued to walk across the courtyard when suddenly, as if out of nowhere, another man stepped in front of him. Like Sieffuddeen, this man was young, in his early twenties, but perhaps a year or two younger than the prince was. Both had similar length hair and golden-brown skin, although the second of the two wore a turban, raised high above his head. Their features were also similar, but Sieffuddeen's were starker and more statue-like. Nevertheless, one could still have been forgiven for mistaking them for twins. Yet, their builds were so different. Sieffuddeen was a strong man, with broad shoulders. He was unmistakably a fighter, a pugilist, someone not to be toyed with. The other man, though, was rather less muscular, quite slim, and had the air of an artist about him.

As they stood face-to-face in the courtyard, the light from a nearby burning torchlight gleamed off the face of the man who had obstructed Sieffuddeen's path. Legend has it that these two were the Emir's sons, although no written testament to their existence has ever been discovered. The younger man stepped forwards.

"I know what you're up to brother of mine. I know, and I advise you to stop!" the man insisted.

Sieffuddeen laughed and pushed past his younger brother. "My dear Jawad; return to your poetry. You have no place in a man's world."

He marched off sharply towards his residence, while Jawad bowed his head, ashamed of his inability to halt his brother, and acknowledging some truth in Sieffuddeen's remark. Although only a year younger than his brother, Jawad was almost half his size. He was unlike the Emir's heir in many ways, and certainly had no knowledge of fighting. He dressed in the intricate fineries of one of high status, with the end of his silk turban trailing down his back. Unlike his brother he wore no weapons and, despite being in his twenties, his face possessed the prickly stubble of a youth in his earliest attempts at growing a beard.

For a moment, his thoughts drifted back to their childhood. Jawad was a sickly child, frequently ill and never one for physical activity. His older brother, on the other hand, was an aggressive individual; some might say a bully. He persecuted anyone he regarded as beneath him and that included his younger siblings. Unlike their half-brother, Abbas, who would resist Sieffuddeen's intimidation, Jawad had quite early on resigned himself to a life of physical and psychological torment from Sieffuddeen. With most of life's activities, Jawad had adopted a state of learned helplessness, but there was one thing he was good at and he pursued it with a passion. He had found that writing down his feelings as poems was a comfort and with the Arabs' love of good poetry, he also found that it was a way of increasing his acceptance among his people. He would publicly recite his words to vast crowds and their applause and acclaim elevated him, cutting away at his depression.

Now, however, was probably not the time for poems. It was a time for action, although he doubted whether he could master his fears enough to act.

After Sieffuddeen had gone, Jawad raised his hands, palms upward, and prayed; "Allah help us. If my brother has his way, we will be plunged into deadly war again with the foreigners. Give me strength and grant me the opportunity to prevent it."

Abdul Qadoos had watched them arguing. He could not hear what they were saying but could see that Sieffuddeen was agitated. Jawad also seemed more anxious and jittery than normal and Abdul Qadoos was clearly concerned. He was deep in thought when Arslan entered the room. The General snapped out of his abstraction and left the window to greet his visitor, inviting him to take a seat on a rather grand, velvet-covered couch.

"I'm worried about Sieffuddeen. I don't trust him, I don't much care for his pompous attitude and I am concerned that he surrounds himself with those murderous, treacherous Assassins," he said.

Arslan nodded in agreement. "The trouble is that Sieffuddeen is a fine orator and he speaks in words that the people understand. He talks of war and conquest, he says what many people want to hear, and he is popular among many in the city. He has built for himself quite a considerable reputation as a pious and forthright man. The people like his brother's poetry, but they take heed of Sieffuddeen's words."

Abdul Qadoos slammed his right fist into the palm of his left hand. His face showed signs of anger and frustration and this was shown by his tone of voice.

"Ha! Forthright indeed! Pious? Pious? The very thought would be laughable if it were not so disconcerting."

He paused for a moment and glanced back across the courtyard.

"The people are too quick to judge by superficial qualities," he said. "Oh yes, young Sieffuddeen appears to be a fine young Muslim. He is a passionate speaker who calls for a holy war against the Franj and he cleverly spends his wealth on others when he thinks it will produce a good return in the form of praise or support. But he is dangerous, Arslan, very, very dangerous."

The General paused, eyed his desk and sighed quite heavily.

"Poor Jawad," he mused. "He is but a romantic fool in the people's eyes; a crazed poet, who talks not of that which is right and wrong, just and unjust, but of each person's rights and justice for all. The intellectuals and the women like him, but he is an idealist who annoys the peasants with his open-minded thinking, for unlike him they refuse to accept the possibility that not all Muslims are good and not all the Franj are bad... He is beyond their simple lives. To him the world is grey; to them it is always black and white."

He nodded his head and smiled to himself.

"You know, I often think it is we the people who are the fools... for not listening to him."

Arslan smiled and nodded in agreement.

"I have even heard some calling him a heretic sir. He is not well liked by many of the common people at all, perhaps because he challenges the very structure of our society's belief system with all his questions and his mystical philosophy."

Abdul Qadoos' smile suddenly faded. He took a deep breath, stood up, and walked back to the window.

"Yes," he said, "but that brother of his will most likely inflict far greater damage upon our society with his scheming and hypocrisy. He's using religion to manipulate the peasants. His prostrations are like the performances of minstrels or travelling actors or even trained animals; a show for a willing audience, lacking sincerity."

CHAPTER 11
Al-Bahira

Zenith and his travelling companions arrived in Al-Bahira just before nightfall. The town at first appeared deserted. Its crystal buildings were in darkness and its streets were empty, but faint noises emerged from within the houses.

"Where is everyone then?" asked Hassan, a little annoyed.

"We must join them inside. We have to get indoors before the light fades." Zenith's voice sounded a little eerie and apprehensive. He virtually dragged the children into one of the odd-shaped buildings and slammed the door hurriedly behind them.

"We're safe now," he said, "as long as we remain inside until daybreak."

"Safe? What do you mean, safe?" enquired the children in unison. "If the demons are coming, how can such flimsy-looking buildings keep us safe?"

"I'll explain later, but first let's arrange our sleeping accommodation."

Inside, the building bore an uncanny resemblance to the maze of tunnels the children had encountered after their fall into the cave of Sulayman. In this building, glass-like tunnels ran in all directions from the hallway where they were standing. It reminded Hassan of the inside of a beehive he had seen once. They could see that from each transparent tunnel there emerged several octagon-shaped rooms, each secluded by what appeared to be curtains, fitted so that they were flush with the oddly moulded walls. Zenith led them to one of the rooms where, instead of a doorway, there was a shimmering veil of light, purple in colour. The Jinni and his two human companions passed through the veil. Hassan was the last to enter the room and he glanced at the doorway behind him after he had stepped through it. The shimmering veil of light faded and transformed into a solid wall, indistinguishable from the rest of the walls. The children also noticed that the walls were not shielded by curtains at all. In fact, down the inside walls ran a dark liquid, which flowed, into a shallow guttering. Inside the room, were beds of soft feathers and robes of silk. The children clasped the silken robes and stared, open-mouthed, at the 'black water', as they kept calling it.

"Not black water", explained Zenith, smiling. "Those are perfumed oils. There is no end to the supply of them here and their smell, together with the sound of the flowing liquids, are known to ease a traveller's mind and help a tired visitor to sleep. The fluids relax the mind and calm the brain. And since your brain manages and operates your body, once *it* is relaxed your entire being relaxes too."

He caught hold of their shoulders and led them to their beds.

"By morning you will feel like new boys and then I will begin to explain more fully the realities of Brillar."

"You still have not explained how such a weak-looking building can keep the demons out," Hassan interjected.

"An invisible shield, created eons ago by a Master Jinni, covers each building. I enabled our entrance to this one by whispering a word, known only to those entrusted with it. I can tell you no more. Now, you must rest."

The exhausted boys quickly fell off to sleep and Zenith covered them before retiring himself.

Outside, the streets of Al-Bahira were now in total darkness. The crystal desert had lost its light and warmth. Screams and wails echoed throughout the entire region, banshees screeched, and small demons cackled and laughed. All forms of evil and depravity were taking place; murder, sexual depravity and theft flourished throughout the night.

In a street not far from where the three travellers lay sleeping, a young Christian Arab suddenly materialised, dressed as a monk. He seemed confused and frightened but made no attempt to leave until confronted by a being so hideous it made his heart jump. The creature had the form of a man, but his head was like that of a bear and his hands too, with long sharp claws. The Christian took a step backwards but tripped. He did not fall, however. He seemed to float on air temporarily. He blinked and when his eyes reopened, his surroundings had changed and so had his behaviour. He found himself running, chased by the half man half bear until he reached a small, crystal building. His heart pounded, and his tongue and mouth were dry as sawdust and all the while, the creature drew closer.

Without thinking twice, he began to bang on the outside of the building, shouting for someone to come and help him.

"Please, let me in, let me in."

His calls were heard by Zenith, who emerged at a doorway to the young man's right; a doorway that did not seem to exist a moment earlier. The wailing of demons stopped the moment Zenith emerged into the darkness.

"Awaken Jemal Habash. Awaken."

Habash glanced behind him, sure that the bear man would have reached him by now, but there was nothing there and when he turned again to the door, that too was gone, as was Zenith. In his place was a crusader knight, a Templar knight, clothed in chain mail and covered with a white apron, upon which was adorned a large red cross. His sword was sheathed but he held a dagger in his hand.

Habash blinked, felt the blade enter his side and made a grab for the hand that held it, but the hand was gone and so was the knife. A silence filled the air and, as instantly as he had appeared in this world, Habash left it. Zenith, meanwhile, returned to his slumber and the noises of the night began again, polluting the air with evil and hatred.

Then, as the first shimmers of light began to crack open the shroud of blackness that had covered the town, the sounds died away, and the evil ones retreated.

When the children awoke, they found Zenith sitting cross-legged in the air, playing a chess-like game consisting of tiny animals—real, live animals that moved around a hexagonal board. As the children stirred, the Jinni blinked, and the game disappeared.

"Ah! You are awake... good!" he said jauntily. "It's time to eat and breakfast is prepared behind you."

The boys turned around to discover a feast fit for an army, nestled on silver trays, spread neatly upon the floor behind their beds.

"Where on earth did this lot come from?" asked Hassan.

Zenith laughed. "Actually, it didn't come from anywhere on earth at all. It came from another world altogether." The Jinni lowered his feet to the ground. "Some of the Jinn of Al-Bahira spend a lifetime travelling the universe to gather provisions for the townspeople and their guests… and a lifetime for a Jinni is an exceedingly long time."

The boys just shrugged their shoulders and plunged into the food. It had always amazed Zenith just how quickly children come to terms with the new, the unusual. They adapt to change rapidly. Unfortunately, the adults they had left behind were less adaptable and the consequence of that was often war. Of course, he knew that Hassan, at 16, was an adult in the human world, but he was young for his age—something that would have to change if he were to survive the future ordeals that would confront him.

"This is delicious," they both kept saying, over and over again, and it was not until some moments later that Hassan stopped to ask Zenith why he was not eating.

Zenith shook his head.

"I have taken all that I need already. Please eat well my children, for it may be your last meal for quite some time."

After they had finished, he began to explain about the Crystal Desert.

"I warned you to beware of first impressions. Beware also of the night in Brillar. The fading light results from the dying of the crystals for the night. It also brings about a kind of death among those of us who have chosen not to follow Iblis. The fading of the crystals saps us of much of our energy, and we are forced to rest. We have to wait for the light to return and while we wait, the evil ones come out to rule."

He sat down beside the children, took a piece of meat from a plate, divided it into two and offered the pieces to the boys.

"Please, continue eating while I talk to you."

With a little hesitation, they took the food and he continued.

"The rules here will also apply in Slegna. Remember that anyone outside after nightfall will fall prey to them, but they approach with deceit. Inside, the shield protects us. The demons hate it. They can't pass through it and they are unable to destroy it, so they will not approach us inside. But outside, after dark, they cannot be beaten, except by Zaman… and he is not here."

Hassan took a mouthful of food, chewed it a little and then tried to talk with his mouth full. It was impossible to understand a word he was saying, and the sight of half-chewed food, churning around inside his mouth was making Zenith feel quite uncomfortable. He leant forward and indicated to the child to keep his mouth closed, so the boy hastily finished chewing and then swallowed with a gulp.

"Why can't Zaman just come here and take us away if he is so powerful?"

"The Overseer must protect Zaydussia. If he leaves his castle, he risks leaving an opening through which the Evil One might enter Zaydussia and occupy it; that must not happen, for it is the last remaining stronghold of those of us who worship the Almighty One and oppose the Evil One."

Zenith paused for a moment, looked carefully at the children, and then continued.

"Remember; don't let first impressions fool you. If we are, by some misfortune, left out at night in Brillar, beware the approach of what is not, for it may win your confidence and force you into error."

He sighed before continuing. "Sedu is a particularly violent spirit. It is the evil spirit of the wind and it is ruler of Brillar at night. But you must also beware of the Rakshasas. They are shape shifting demons who usually take on animal form, but they can also appear human if that is what is required for them to get what they want."

He stared briefly at their white faces, their blank expressions, their innocence, and as he did so Abbas started to sob. He quickly became quite distraught.

"I'm scared," he murmured, "I want to go home."

"You are on your way home, my child. Your fear is something you must learn to deal with. That is part of growing up, so prepare yourselves. The brave man is not the one who has no fear, but the one who keeps his fear under control. Remember this and you will show courage too."

He waited for a moment before speaking again. "Finish eating, for we leave now, for the boat."

CHAPTER 12
1240 A.D.
Acre and the arrival of Marie

The port of Acre bustled with traders and sailors, and with local womenfolk purchasing seafood from the incoming fishermen. Although European Christians now controlled the town, many of the locals, Muslims, Jews and Christians, remained there. In fact, some had sought refuge in Acre from two opposing, marauding bands of thugs and killers. Many towns and cities in Palestine, Lebanon, Egypt and Syria had fallen prey to one of two heretical factions. The Hashisheen were responsible for the murders of as many Muslims as they were Europeans, while the fanatical Knights Templar had slaughtered thousands of Jews, Muslims and even local Christians, during their own personal crusade in the Holy Land. The Templars had secured themselves in Syria, in vast castles, many of which were impregnable and fear provoking.

However, it was widely believed that some soldiers of the Knights Templar had entered Acre, just as the Hashisheen had manipulated their way into Jerusalem by way of the corrupt Prince Sieffuddeen. The people of Acre were nervous and suspicious of all strangers, so Raymond's troops carried out a thorough search of all newly arriving vessels and each docking ship.

It was just before midday, a hot and humid midday, when the French ship arrived, a warship flying the flag of the house of Saint-Gilles. Waiting at the dockside was a company of twenty men, led by Cedric and his second-in-command, André. The plank was lowered, and the two men walked aboard to be greeted by the ship's Captain, a Spaniard named Miguel Alvarez. He was a large man—in fact rather obese—and his short-cropped hair seemed to clash with his straggly moustache.

"Welcome Miguel," said Cedric, smiling. "There is good beer in the officer's quarters on shore, but first we must attend to routine."

Cedric was a tall man, muscular and authoritative. His long hair was sun-bleached, and his skin was well tanned. The roughly trimmed beard and moustache he sported, made his unusually large nose appear far smaller than it was. He was wearing European clothing, which seemed far too warm for the type of weather he was enduring in the Middle East, and yet he showed no signs of discomfort. His clothes were dusty, though, and drab. It did not look as if they had seen water or soap for several weeks. Yet, overall, he appeared to be a clean and well-groomed man, the roughness of his beard and hair due only to the use of a knife to trim them.

His hands were enormous, with muscular fingers that bestowed on him a grip of iron. It was certainly a grip he would need, to wield his sword with any skill. It hung, threateningly, at his side. The sheer weight of this mighty beast would have prevented most men from using it with any achievement in battle. For Cedric, however, it was like a child. He nurtured it, cleaned it, sharpened it and could use it with ease; he had lost count of the number of people he had killed with it, but his reputation in battle was known far and wide. Friends and enemies respected his prowess and stories of his swordsmanship had become legendary. Keeping your head when faced with Cedric on the battlefield was literally of major concern to anyone who stood up to him.

Now, however, he was with an old friend. He was relaxed and in high spirits as he had not seen him for several years.

Miguel reached out and grabbed Cedric by his enormous upper arms.

"My dear friend Cedric. How are things in Acre?" He let go of the Frenchman's arms and placed his left arm around Cedric's shoulders. The two men then paced the deck together, before heading towards the Captain's cabin.

"Acre is tense these days Miguel. Our checks of incoming vessels must be undertaken far more rigorously now. It is not just contraband either, or the odd stowaway. The problem now is spies and fifth columnists." Cedric paused for a moment and then turned to André.

"Take everyone ashore. Take them to the holding station and then search the ship!" he shouted.

"Right you are sir," replied André, obediently.

André could not have been more different in appearance from his superior officer. He was weasel-like and he scurried around, always appearing to be in an immense hurry. His face was thin and clean-shaven, with a long, pointed chin, a thin nose and pockmarked cheeks. His eyebrows, which were jet black like his hair, met firmly in the middle, just beneath a deep furrow on his brow. One could be forgiven for thinking he was always cross, but in truth, he was a light-hearted man who loved to amuse the people around him with humorous stories. He wore no sword but did carry a small yet deadly knife. André was a bowman and had never felt at ease wielding cumbersome 'lumps of iron' around. The unwieldy Crusader broadsword, like most European swords, weighed almost as much as he did. He was far more suited to the skilful art of archery.

Once Cedric and Miguel had entered the cabin and seated themselves, the Frenchman continued his conversation with his old friend.

"The Templars are a bigger nuisance to us than the Saracens," he said, shaking his head in despair. Miguel nodded in agreement but something about the expression on Cedric's face hinted that the knight did not agree with his own words.

The Knights Templar, or Knights of the Order of the Temple of Solomon, had begun as a small, but effective force of fighting monks who had set out to be 'protectors of the faithful' in the land of the 'infidel'. They had won many victories in earlier Crusades for the European Christians, and had established, for over a hundred years, a Crusader stronghold along the coastlines of Palestine and Lebanon. Saladin finally removed their grip on the Mediterranean. He quickly realised that the Templars' main offensive strategies consisted of a reputation of fear, backed up by fearsome cavalry charges. Saladin had formulated tactics that made such offensives ineffective. The Templars were forced away from Palestine and retreated to Europe, except for small pockets of knights who had secured themselves in large castles, such as those in Syria, or had taken refuge with other secretive societies.

Many people believed that by now the Templars had transformed from an idealistic body of warrior knights, into a secretive and elusive religious cult, led by a single Grand Master and held together by massive donations from its initiates, and from interest earned through a complex network of banking and accountancy.

Cedric continued; "There are some who believe we would be better off forming alliances with the Emir in Jerusalem, instead of trying to form a united Christian front with some of the factions that are calling themselves 'Christian'." Again, he seemed to be saying what was expected of him, rather than what he truly believed.

"But you don't subscribe to that view, do you Cedric?"

His heart suddenly jumped at the sound of André's voice behind him and for a split second, he regretted having said that. André was out of breath but did not wait for a reply. He held the door open and took on a more formal air.

"I think you should see this sir," he half shouted, "there's a boy, dirty and thin… must have been there ages…"

"Hold fast André!" shouted Cedric. "Catch your breath and tell me where this boy is."

"He's on the dockside now, sir. We took him there after we found him. He's a stowaway sir and that's a certainty; sleeping with the stores he was and smelling like sin… but sir, he was wearing this around his neck."

He handed Cedric a medallion, bearing the crest of the family of Saint-Gilles. At this point, the ship's Spanish captain began shouting angrily.

"Not on my ship! I don't believe that! No thieving stowaway could remain undetected on my ship!"

"But it is true sir, and he's a wild one—scratching and clawing like a cat he was. He put two of our best men in the infirmary with bleeding eyes and cheeks and it took five of us to restrain him. I think you'd better come and see him sir."

Cedric nodded, clenched his fist around the medallion and followed André to the dockside. There, trussed up with strong rope, sat a boy, maybe eighteen or nineteen years old and dressed in a loose, Turkish, cloth suit. His hair was short and sandy brown, although blackened in part from months on board ship without access to soap or water. His skin was mud brown, but that too was more dirt than pigmentation. He was clean shaven. In fact, he looked like someone who had not yet begun growing hair on his face.

Cedric looked at him with disdain, partly because he was a stowaway, but mainly because he detested weak men. Cedric lifted him from the ground and began removing the rope from his hands, upon which the boy spat, forcefully, in his face. Then, without warning, his right hand came free and he scratched Cedric across the face, just below his left eye. The wound began to weep, and blood slowly trickled down Cedric's face. The soldier immediately struck the boy across the face with the back of his hand, knocking him back to the floor and, for the first time, the lad spoke. His voice, however, was not that of a male youth in his late teens, but more akin to the unbroken voice of a small child.

Cedric smiled, picked up the stowaway again, and then laughed very loudly.

"Ha…! This is no boy!"

Without any further hesitation, he ripped off the tatty, loose shirt the stowaway was wearing, and the youth instinctively tried to cover her revealed breasts. Cedric threw the shirt back at her, upon which she used it to hide herself from the prying eyes of all the men who surrounded her on the dockside, many of whom were now smiling or laughing.

"A girl! A stupid, irresponsible female… and filthy with it," Cedric said, disdainfully.

"I'm no girl, you dog! I'm a lady!" She screamed, hurriedly pulling her torn blouse around her.

"Well, you're a thief and no mistake! Where did you steal this medallion from, eh?" Cedric asked, as he turned to face all the men. Miguel was transfixed, staring in almost total disbelief at the young girl.

"What is it, Miguel? You look as if you've seen a ghost," he was asked by Cedric.

The Spaniard approached his friend and whispered in his ear.

"Do you not know who this is? Do you not see the resemblance?"

Cedric shook his head.

"Then I suggest you look again."

Cedric glanced once more at the girl, but still responded in the negative, and Miguel shook his head, but out of disbelief that the soldier had failed to recognise her.

"Oh, she looks a little different from the way we remember her, Cedric, with her hair so short and her skin so dirty, but this is Marie, daughter of Raymond of Saint-Gilles. That's who this is!"

The girl pushed past André and marched up to Cedric and Miguel, scowling and snorting.

"That's right!" she stormed, "and when my father finds out what you did, you'll wish you hadn't! Mark my words!"

Cedric called André to his side and whispered to him.

"Go to Raymond and tell him we have a female stowaway here, dressed as a boy, who claims she is his daughter. Oh, and give him this medallion."

André left, returning some thirty or forty minutes later with instructions that Cedric and the girl should take audience with their commander-in-chief immediately.

CHAPTER 13
1250 A.D.
Cedric and Bohemond in Acre

When Cedric entered Raymond's room with the girl, the Frankish Commander was seated behind a large desk, bent over a copy of the Bible. Cedric dragged the girl to within two yards of the desk and she continued to shower the officer with abusive language. André followed them into the room and closed the door.

"You third son of a wart hog, unhand me in the presence of my father!" Marie screamed.

Raymond lifted his eyes and stared coldly at the girl.

"I will not allow a young vagabond to speak in such a manner to one of my officers!" he said, sternly. "Especially a youth who is a thief, a liar and probably also a whore!"

"But father, it is I, Marie. It is I, your daughter. Please order this brute to let me go and then punish him for his ill-treatment of your only daughter."

Raymond continued to stare, glancing ever so briefly at Cedric once or twice. He said nothing, and Marie started to rant at him.

"This man had the audacity to call me filthy, stupid and irresponsible... *and* he tore off my blouse in front of his men, bringing shame and dishonour to our family!"

Raymond sat up, closing the book and brushing his moustache.

"Filthy, stupid and irresponsible?" he said, glancing across at Cedric. "You called her this Cedric?"

"Well, yes sir, but..."

Raymond interrupted Cedric as he stumbled to find an acceptable excuse.

"Yes, I do believe these are accurately descriptive words to use in reference to you, dear child."

Shocked that her father was clearly not well pleased with her, Marie frowned but remained silent and Raymond stood up, forcing his chair backwards so quickly that it screeched on the marble floor and crashed against the wall behind him.

"Now, let us deal with your claim that you are my daughter." He shook his head. "My daughter is at home in France, with her step-mother and step-brother."

Marie looked down at the floor before her as Raymond walked around the desk and approached her. He stood directly in front of her, eyed her up and down, and then placed his finger under her chin, lifting her head until their eyes met.

"Dressed like this, girl, and so disgustingly dirty, I do not recognise you at all! Perhaps it is you, girl, who has brought shame on your family!"

Saint-Gilles waved his right hand towards André and spoke one more time to Marie.

"I am going to give you some time to think about what you have done," he said, and as André stepped towards them, Raymond turned his back to Marie and spoke to the soldier.

"Call Bohemond to take her away and lock her up, and go with them André," he said. "Cedric, you remain here."

Once Bohemond arrived, the girl was dragged, kicking and screaming from the room and when the door was closed, Raymond spoke to a rather surprised Cedric.

"Let my daughter sweat for twenty-four hours and then have some of the Turkish maids clean her up before bringing her back to me. I will see her in private then."

Cedric questioned nothing, despite his surprise.

"Of course, sir," he said, before departing from the room.

Later that day, Bohemond approached Cedric to enquire after the young girl he had thrown into a positively miserable cell.

"Is it true Cedric? Is she Saint-Gilles' daughter?"

"If such rumours were true, I would not be the man to tell you Bohemond. And I would suggest you spend less time concerning yourself with gossip and more time trying to trace those two spies who escaped last week. Apart from the Arab child, what exactly did you find the other day, you and Amalric?"

"I don't understand why Saint-Gilles trusts you Cedric. I would never have told you about the boy if I were commander here."

"I'm sure you would not have, but you're not commander are you. So, tell me, what did you find?"

Bohemond began gesticulating with his hands as he spoke, attempting to convey more clearly to Cedric what had occurred. As he did so, his sword knocked against the wall, just now and again, but enough to become a distraction to Cedric.

"I can only tell you what you must already know. We found the tracks of the three Arab boys... Are you listening to me Cedric?"

Cedric looked up with a bit of a start.

"Er, yes. Er, Bohemond, can you stand away from the wall?"

"What? Oh, easily distracted then, are you?" he said, realising that his sword had become the focus of Cedric's attention. "Well, I hope your focus is not that easily thrown off when you're in battle."

Cedric grunted and frowned. "So," he said, eager not to be drawn into such petty bickering with Bohemond, "you were saying about the boy you found, the son of Abdul Qadoos."

"Not one! Three! You see, I knew you weren't listening to me."

"Three? But you only brought one boy with you. Where are the other two?"

"They escaped... Anyway, as I was saying..."

Bohemond was clearly agitated at having been interrupted so rudely. He disliked Cedric and had done for many years. The feeling was mutual though. Something about these two men always produced tension. On several occasions, they had come to blows and many of those around them were convinced that sooner or later one would kill the other.

Bohemond hailed from Normandy and so was a descendent of the Norse warriors who had settled in that region of France and taken French women as their wives and mistresses. Cedric, on the other hand, believed himself to be of pure French stock. Bohemond, to him, was no more than a savage. Descended from barbarians, he was, in the eyes of many of his French comrades-in-arms, just another barbarian.

Bohemond took a deep intake of breath and continued, half wondering why he was even bothering to tell his adversary so much. The

Norman was, however, a man who liked to talk. He relished telling anyone about anything he had done. Cedric regarded him as a bit of a bore but, on this occasion, he wanted to listen. He wanted to know what had happened and now that the distraction of the clanging sword was gone, he was ready to. So Bohemond continued.

"The boys' tracks had almost, but not entirely, covered the tracks of our escapees. By chance, and just before the boys spotted us, we happened upon half a horse print; one of our horses, not an Arab."

Bohemond paused for thought. He seemed both confused and concerned about something and, despite his hatred and mistrust of the other man, he knew that Cedric might be able to provide answers to some of his questions.

"What is it? What's wrong?" The way Cedric asked the question indicated that he was more irritated than concerned.

"Well, here's what I'm still having trouble understanding. The spies seemed to have been heading straight for the Saracen's garrison at Jerusalem."

"That would make sense. They're spies so isn't it obvious that they would be in alliance with the Musalmen?"

Bohemond was cautious in his response.

"No, no I don't think that is very likely. No, my fear is that the spies, both of whom seem to be connected to the Templars, may be in league with a faction within the Saracen ranks. Perhaps they are hoping to create a confrontation between the Emir and us."

"Oh, I see, another of your conspiracy theories, eh Bohemond?"

Cedric's laugh irritated Bohemond, who paced up and down with his hand placed firmly on the grip of his sword—a sword that hung menacingly at his side.

"Don't mock me Cedric! Remember that I know what you are. I have seen your savagery first-hand. I should have killed you that day and have regretted not doing so, every day since."

Cedric smiled. "Try if you wish. What I did, had to be done. Our commanders accepted that I acted in accordance with their orders. So, let it go, Bohemond."

"Our commanders were fools. We had no orders to slaughter the innocent, to rape, to mutilate both the living and the dead."

79

"Let it go, Bohemond."

"I will never let it go. I also care not whether you believe me about my views on the Templars. Nor do I care if you think me a liar. I believe I'm right and that's why I brought the boy here. I felt we needed something that we could use to enforce dialogue between Saint-Gilles and the Saracens, before the Templars and their allies could ferment trouble between us!"

"Oh, come now Bohemond. You didn't know the importance of that young lad until your arrival here. You took him because you just didn't know what to do with him. And besides, bringing the Saracen Commander's son here could ferment the very trouble you wish to avoid."

At this, Bohemond stormed off and Cedric called after him. What he said intrigued Bohemond.

"For what it's worth, Bohemond, I think you did the right thing. I believe we will soon be contacting the Emir and now we have his Commander's son. I don't think your theory about factions working together is worthy of consideration, however."

Bohemond wondered what he had meant by his comments. *We will soon be making contact with the Emir?* Did he know that for sure, or was he surmising?

"There is subterfuge afoot and no denying it," he muttered to himself as he walked away.

CHAPTER 14
1240 A.D.
Marie's Story

Twenty-four hours passed slowly for the young French girl and most of it had been spent awash the tears she had shed in that time. By the time Amalric came to take her to her father, she had become quite numb with fear and cold. The cell in which she had been placed was dark and dank and infested with cockroaches, some of which had flown around her head during the night. Her first two hours of captivity were spent screaming and yelling, but her anger had gradually turned to despair and then grudging acceptance of her fate.

What hurt most was not the conditions in the cell, for they were no worse than those she had experienced for many months as a stowaway on Miguel's ship. It was her father's rejection that had bitten so deeply into her soul and, if truth be known, most of her tears were shed because of that.

Amalric stood silently in the doorway after he had flung open the heavy iron door. He did not need to say anything, for the prisoner knew she was expected to go with him. She lifted herself off the floor and walked out of the cell, her eyes constantly staring at those of the soldier. He, however, stared right through her. Once out of the cell he shoved her gently along the corridor and then handed her to a maid, who took her to be cleaned up before the second audience with her father.

Raymond was standing by an ornate window when his daughter entered. The light reflected off two ornate candelabra that stood either side of the window, and created a shine in his normally dull, brown hair. The door closed behind the girl and, as it clicked shut, she looked behind her, perhaps unsure as to why she was not followed into the room by Amalric.

She stood in silence, her head down, gazing at the ground, although occasionally she would glance at her father, who continued to look out of the window even when he began to speak to her. All the passion and anger she had displayed twenty-four hours earlier, was gone. She was a beaten woman—beaten mentally and half-wishing she had never set out on the journey to Palestine all those many months ago.

"If you were my son, and not my daughter, you would have suffered a far worse punishment for what you did," Raymond said emphatically. Marie said nothing. Instead, she began to weep.

"Weep not Marie," her father said, "just tell me why you came and perhaps suggest to me what we should do with you now child."

"With all due respect father, I am no longer a child, but I am perfectly aware that this fact has escaped you, since you are never at home to see me."

Raymond turned from the window abruptly and angrily, raising his voice as he approached his daughter.

"Impudent talk like this, Marie, will only force me to return you on the next ship sailing back to Europe!"

"I'm sorry father," she whispered softly, bowing her head at the same time.

Then, without warning, Raymond approached her, hugged her, kissed the top of her head and then stood back slightly, still with his hands on her shoulders.

"You're right, though. I have neglected my family, my country, even my people, but I believe it is necessary." He hugged her again and then spoke quietly in her ear. "Anyway, right now I just want to know why you came."

He led her to a fine couch covered with hand-embroidered material and cushions. The exotic dress, which the young lady was wearing, blended beautifully with the satin couch covers and cushions as she seated herself. Raymond sat down beside her and Marie sighed, before deliberating briefly and then talking again.

"As I'm sure you know, father, my step-mother died following her illness four months ago." Marie waited for her father to compose himself before continuing. "Then Antoine took control of everything."

She stopped to wipe back her tears and her father took hold of her hand. It was obvious she was very distressed, not from her journey, or even from her twenty-four hours in solitude, but from something that was clearly far worse.

"Look at me my princess," Raymond said sternly. "What exactly has my step-son done?

"Oh father, he has taken control of your entire estate. He is proud and arrogant and is creating enemies for our family every day, but that's not all… he…" There was a long pause while she choked back some tears. "He assaulted me father… repeatedly. I'm so ashamed, I'm so sorry, I really am sorry… I had to flee. I would rather die, or rot in one of your prison cells, than live another moment with that man, that savage!"

Raymond pulled his daughter's head onto his chest and comforted her.

"You will remain here as long as I do my daughter, so fear not and don't be ashamed. You have nothing to be ashamed about." He shouted to Amalric who was waiting outside the room, and the soldier entered.

"Amalric, take my daughter to my quarters, get her a maid and ensure she gets anything she wants. Then ask Cedric to report to me at once."

Within half an hour Cedric appeared and Raymond handed the knight some papers.

"Cedric, I have a task for you. These papers show that you have been appointed by me personally to arrest and seek the execution of Antoine Le Tort, my stepson, on charges of attempting to usurp my estate from my rightful heirs and myself. You will then remain in France to protect my interests there until my return."

Cedric was shocked but failed to show it. He nodded, tied the papers to his belt and saluted. Return to France was, in some ways, welcome to him, for he had been away from his family for four years. On the other hand, it would interfere with his work in the Holy Land and could place his own life at risk because of that.

"Take forty men of your choice, Cedric, and Godspeed your journey home."

Raymond trusted Cedric to undertake such a task with total loyalty, although he was also secretly pleased that the soldier would no longer be in Acre. He, like Bohemond, believed Cedric possessed undisclosed sympathies with the Templar cause. He was also sure that Cedric was aware of his intention to begin negotiations with the Emir in Jerusalem and he did not want to risk him notifying the Templars or their allies, whomever they should be. Sending him to France would kill two birds with one stone. To Raymond, Cedric seemed ferocious in his loyalty to the Saint-Gilles family and he had little doubt that he would ruthlessly punish any attempt by Antoine to resist arrest. However, he would also send word to some men of law in France, to ensure that he wasn't replacing one usurper with another. They would ensure that Cedric could do no more than he had been asked to do.

Outside the stables, Cedric prepared his company of men but just before they were to set off, he called to one of them, a man he knew from his hometown in France. The soldier dismounted and walked away from the rest of the men, saluted Cedric and waited in silence for his commanding officer to speak. Cedric pulled a note from his tunic and handed it to the soldier.

"Take this to Syria by the fastest but safest route you know. It must reach Martin urgently. Our cause depends upon it, Pierre. Our cause. Is that understood?"

The soldier nodded. "May the Temple of Solomon rise from the rubble of a recaptured Jerusalem!" He said, passionately, but not loudly enough for any of the other men to hear.

The soldier returned to his horse, mounted and galloped out of the city, leaving a cloud of yellow dust in his wake.

Cedric swung himself onto his own horse and ordered his troop of forty men towards the Port where Miguel's ship waited for them. He considered his position. All the antagonistic chatter with Miguel against the Templars was a distraction and he had successfully diverted attention from his affiliation with the Order of the Temple for many years. Now, out of the blue, he was being sent away, sent to France, sent to safeguard the estate and the affairs of a man he loathed. *How had Marie got here?* He wondered, and *why had Raymond chosen him to complete this task now?* Then, he relaxed as it dawned on him that to be in such a position of responsibility and power in France, would benefit not just him, but also the Templars. His only regret was that he had failed to goad Bohemond into revealing anything about Raymond's plans. *Was there contact between Acre and Jerusalem? Why had the boy been brought to Acre?* Too many questions. No answers.

CHAPTER 15
1240 A.D.
Acre: The Prince and the Spy

Several days after Arslan and Abdul Qadoos had found the boys' tracks near the Cave of Sulayman, Jemal Habash arrived at the port of Acre dressed as a nomadic trader. The Arab Christian, sent by the Saracens to trace the three missing boys, had with him six camels, fully laden with goods to trade in the town markets.

He was unaware, however, that when he entered the town someone was watching him from a nearby hillside; five men, one of whom was Prince Sieffuddeen. Two of the others were the Hashisheen who had prepared the prince's horses for him in Jerusalem. The other two were Templars.

"Let him find the boys for us and leave the city. Then we'll take them off his hands," Sieffuddeen said calmly to his companions.

"What shall we do with Habash?" one of the Hashisheen asked, smiling, as if he already knew the answer.

Sieffuddeen also smiled, before coolly answering.

"Kill him of course... but make it look as if he was found out and executed by the Franj." The others waited, realising he had more to say. "And if he has the boys with him, kill them also and dump the bodies near enough to Jerusalem to be found but far enough out to suggest the Franj did it."

Inside Acre, life was busy. Market traders in the local Souk bartered eagerly with crowds of men and women all desperate for a bargain. In the air, hung the smell of lamb, roasting on an open flame, but that aroma was periodically dispersed by the pungent whiff of spices and perfumes. Habash lingered a while in the Souk, enquiring about the price of a hand carved knife handle, but the whole time he was scouting the area, trying to get his bearings and locate likely buildings where the Franks might hide some young Arab boys. The dream he had had a few days earlier still weighed heavily on his mind. He kept telling himself it was just a dream, but something about it gave him cause for concern. Was it an omen? He would keep his eyes peeled for Templars, he thought to himself.

Hanging over his left arm was a leather bag, containing a variety of objects that he intended to use for bartering. He reached inside, pulled out an ornately decorated jewellery box, and attempted to offer it in trade for the knife handle. As he inspected the handle and haggled with the market trader, he occasionally took a fleeting look around him, trying his hardest not to look too out of place. It was during one of these moments of surveillance that a young man approached him. He was dressed in a hooded priest's robe with the hood obscuring most of his face. He took hold of the small wooden box and asked him the price. The trader paid little attention to the priest but Habash recognised the voice immediately and turned sharply towards him, before whispering excitedly to him.

"Your Highness, what are you doing here?" he asked, clearly concerned for the other man's safety.

The priest replied quickly.

"My brother, Sieffuddeen, is here somewhere. I am sure of it and I am sure he is plotting something with the Hashisheen and the Templars. I don't know their exact plans, but I believe he aims to take the boys away, perhaps to kill them and to then convince our father that the Franj did it."

"Come with me, Your Highness," Habash said, leading Prince Jawad to a darkened alley. "Change clothes with me and take care of my goods. I will nose around and find the boys. It will be easier for me dressed as a priest."

They changed clothes and Habash gave the prince his sword, keeping an easily concealed dagger beneath his robe in case his disguise turned out to be less successful than he hoped. He pulled the hood over his head and made to leave but paused momentarily. He stared, curiously, at the priest's robe he was wearing.

"Where on earth did you get these clothes?"

"I, er, stole them… from a church in Jerusalem. May Allah forgive me."

Habash smiled.

"There's more to you than people think," he said, shaking his head and walking out of the alley.

Jawad called softly after him.

"If you happen upon my brother, beware."

CHAPTER 16
1240 A.D.
Acre: The Search

Zaman was watching the happenings in and around Acre with ever-increasing interest. He called to his side two formidable-looking warriors and referred them to the hologram, and specifically to Habash.

"He must find the boy. He must learn that the Franj have no desire or plans for war against Jerusalem at this time, and that they do not have the other boys."

He sighed and gently shook his head before continuing.

"I dislike interfering in earthly affairs, but if we do not on this occasion, war will be inevitable and Iblis' final inroad into the human world will be secured."

He paused again and then smashed his somewhat petite fist down on the arms of his oversized throne.

"War is not right in such circumstances!" he shouted, "War is not just, if the corrupt win and injustice rules thereafter! It is bad enough that the agents of Iblis have tried to hide God's true message under a mountain of bureaucracy, false traditions and petty dogmas, rules and regulations."

The Overseer glanced at the hologram and at Habash, fumbling around Acre without so much as a clue of where the boys he sought, might be held. The young Arab had tried desperately to find them. He had been to the prisons but had found nothing there, and to make matters worse for him, several prisoners, thinking him to be a real priest, had held him up for hours offering their confessions to him.

"Look at this silly human," moaned Zaman. "The world will be at an end before he finds the boy."

He waved his hand irritably towards the image in front of him, but then calmed down briefly, leant on his elbow and spoke to the two Jinn.

"You are messengers of the Highest One. The humans call you guardian angels and the Almighty One has issued an order that you assist this human in finding the boy. But you are to remain discreet… elusive… and are to give no indication at all that those from our world are helping him. Just make things easy for him."

They nodded, stepped into the hologram and vanished.

Zaman, meanwhile, continued to watch the dithering of Habash as he moved from corridor to corridor and room to room. Guards were patrolling the Palace and it was only a matter of time before one of them saw him.

The hologram shifted, and the Overseer watched Jawad, waiting in the shadows beyond the entrance to the Palace where, sometime earlier, Habash had entered. The prince was afraid. Of that, there was no doubt. The sweat forming on his brow was beginning to trickle towards his eyes, his heart rate was so high he was sure it would be heard by passers-by and his bladder felt as if it was pressed beneath the weight of a horse. He had to concentrate. He had to keep himself calm and above all he had to pray for the safe deliverance of the Christian and the boys he sought.

Hidden in the darkness of the shaded area at the side of the Palace, he was confident that nobody would detect his presence, but still the fear held its grip on him and all the time he wondered where his brother was.

CHAPTER 17
1250 A.D.
Acre: The Rescue

Ahmed, meanwhile, was locked in a room near Raymond's quarters, in conditions that could only be described as luxurious. With him were two other children, Turkish servants, or the children of servants, together with a small dog. The Frank Commander had ordered that the son of the Saracen's Chief Officer be given every luxury, including companions of his own age, although Ahmed was stubbornly resisting making himself at home. He had hardly spoken a word to the Turkish children and rejected all the dog's attempts to gain his attention.

Outside the locked door, seated in a long-carpeted corridor, was a single guard, an elderly man armed only with a rather decrepit-looking sword. His face was craggy and thin, and mostly covered by a long, grey beard. Most of the time, he was snoozing, unless startled by the sound of approaching feet or the occasional knock on the door whenever Ahmed sought something from him.

Meanwhile, Habash had reached the fort, but was unsure of where to begin his search. The priest's clothes were cumbersome and itchy, and he was considering finding some alternative clothing. As he pondered this, while walking one way but looking the other, he bumped into a tall man dressed in a crusader's uniform of chain mail and a cotton tabard.

"Excuse me, I apologise," said Habash, nervously, as he quickly stood back from the man.

"The boy you seek is in the chambers of Saint-Gilles, in the room reserved for his second concubine," the stranger said softly.

"I'm sorry… who are you?"

"My identity is of no consequence to you Jemal. Just listen and act."

Habash was quite unnerved by the fact that the stranger obviously knew who he was and knew his reason for being there.

"I am a humble priest, serving God. I don't know anything about a boy." He wondered why the stranger had referred to 'boy', rather than 'boys', but that thought passed quickly.

Habash felt for his dagger and prepared himself for a fight, but something told him that it was unlikely to come to that. His mind was telling him to show caution, but his heart felt he might have to trust this man. Nevertheless, he wanted to know more.

"And why would you want to help me?" he continued.

"It is sometimes best not to know the reasons why. Listen carefully and follow my instructions precisely".

Habash said nothing. He was deeply suspicious, but nevertheless stood impassively and listened as the stranger continued.

"Enter the door to your right, climb the stairs to the second level, and along the corridor you will find an old man. He will be speaking apparent nonsense about spirits and devils, ghosts and ghouls, and you are to tell him that, as a priest, you can chase them away."

The Jinni placed an odd-shaped leaf in Habash's right hand.

"Tell the old man to close his eyes and then rub the leaf over his forehead. He will sleep for ten minutes. That will be all the time you have to enter the chamber and free the boy."

"Boy…? You mean boys, don't you?"

The stranger said nothing.

"Are you one of the magi? Who are you?"

He was wasting his breath. The stranger turned and walked away and, as he moved further from Habash, he was caught by a shadow and seemed to fade into nothing. The Arab clutched the leaf, shrugged his shoulders and entered the building. Not entirely convinced that the man had told the truth, and concerned that he may be walking into trouble, his steps were slow and deliberate as he tried to remain as silent as possible. His hand gripped the dagger tightly.

His heart rate was up, and his mind was awash with thoughts.

It could be a trap, he thought, *but why set a trap if they already know who I am? Why not just come and get me? A few well-armed soldiers could have made short shrift of arresting me.*

He continued, up the unlit wooden staircase to the second level. His steps were even more carefully placed now. He couldn't see the stairs in the dark and the last thing he wanted now was to lose his footing and find himself tumbling back down them.

Meanwhile, upstairs, the old man was being teased by the second of Zaman's beings. Remaining invisible, he nudged the elderly guard and whispered his name in his ear repeatedly.

"Who's that?" the guard kept asking, the sweat running through the ridges of his aged, screwed up face. He looked up just as a black vase lifted off a small table and flew towards him. "Ghosts, poltergeists, devils!" he began shouting, and as he did so the being, still unseen, lifted the old man's keys from his belt and took them across to the door.

All the while Ahmed was banging furiously on the door and screaming for someone to let him know what was happening outside the room. As the guard stood by his chair, white-faced, his eyes wide open, gawking at the keys floating through the air and into the door, Habash arrived to hear him mumbling about demons, just as the stranger had foretold.

"Fear not old man," he called out. "I am a priest who is well-versed in the way of the spirits, so close your eyes and recite the Lord's Prayer, and I will make all things well again."

The old man seemed to be in a trance. He simply stood and stared at the keys, forcing Habash to repeat his instructions.

"It is the only way to rid you of the devil's agents," he said.

Slowly, the old man's eyes closed, and Habash gently rubbed his forehead with the leaf. The guard, his grey beard so long that it rested upon his chest, slumped back into his chair. Jemal knew that he now had just ten minutes to enter the room, grab the boys and leave. As he opened the door, he could see the boys huddled together under the covers of a giant bed. At first, he was unable to see their faces as they were burying them in their pillows, but he pulled away the silk covers and called out, "Ahmed! Hassan! Abbas! Come along now! I am here to rescue you, but time is truly short!"

He was greatly taken aback when the boys looked up and only Ahmed was recognisable among them. The spy frowned. He was clearly confused but, with no time to lose, he grabbed Ahmed.

"Where are Hassan and Abbas?" he asked, impatiently.

Ahmed pulled himself loose from Jemal's grasp and ran around to the other side of the bed.

"They're not here!" he shrieked, fearfully. "They were never here and for all I know they may be dead!"

As tears began to roll down the child's cheeks, he sniffed and then shouted again at Habash.

"Now go away or I'll set the dog on you!"

Habash began to plead with the child to listen and to trust him but his appeals went unheeded and it was not long before the spy realised that his ten minutes were almost up.

"You must come with me, Ahmed. I was sent by your father to take you home."

"How do I know that? You could be anyone... The Franj told me the Templars might try to kill me or kidnap me, and for all I know you could be one of them."

As he spoke, Ahmed carefully reached under his pillow and caught hold of a small knife. Once within his grasp he pulled it out and began waving it in front of Habash's face.

"Now get out or I'll kill you."

The spy's time was up. He shook his head in a display of annoyance and disbelief, knocked the knife from Ahmed's grasp, grabbed the boy and turned towards the door.

"I pray God that you don't get us both killed," he said as he ran from the room, the child screaming his protests as they fled along the corridor, down the stairs and out of the building.

Habash stopped, forced the boy into silence with a large hand, held firmly over his mouth and told him in no uncertain terms to behave. Realising the boy believed he was a dangerous enemy, he used that to gain the advantage, although hated himself for doing it.

"Stay silent child, or I will cut out your tongue and you will never speak again."

When the old man regained consciousness, he noticed the door of the chambers was wide open. The keys were still hanging from the lock and he feared that the boy in his charge had escaped. Cautiously, he peered into the room and was more than a little surprised to find the three boys sitting on the bed, staring at the open door. For a second, he felt a shiver come over him as it dawned on him that someone else might still be in the room, and so he nervously tried to peer around the open door.

"It's all right, he's gone," one of the boys called out in Turkish.

The old man didn't understand what the boy had said but guessed by the tone of his voice that it was safe to enter.

"I don't know what's happened here, but I'm not staying here a minute longer!" he shouted, his voice shaky and faint.

As he left the room, he slammed the door shut. The noise it made echoed around the empty corridor and made him jump. As he tried to turn the key in the lock, his hand shook so much that the bunch of keys rattled against each other and knocked against the wooden door panels. After a few minutes of this, he finally managed to secure the door and then stormed off down the corridor, mumbling incoherently to himself.

In the room, the two servant children were in shock as the unearthly being who had taken Ahmed's place, evaporated before their eyes.

CHAPTER 18
1240 A.D.
Acre: The Betrayal

When Habash left the city with Ahmed, Prince Jawad followed him at a distance without attracting his attention. Less than a mile from the city gate the prince sought cover when he saw none other than Prince Sieffuddeen, accompanied by two Hashisheen bodyguards. They were approaching the Arab Christian so Jawad moved in as close as he could, to listen to their conversation without being detected.

"Your Highness, what are you doing near Acre?" Habash asked, eyeing the two bodyguards warily, as the prince replied.

"I see you found one of the boys" he replied, coldly.

The young Christian was unsure about whether he should say anything to Sieffuddeen or not. He remembered that the prince's brother had told him to beware, but he was also concerned about disobeying one of the Emir's sons, so nervously, he answered.

"Er… yes, the son of Abdul Qadoos. He was being held by the Franj in Raymond's chambers within the city of Acre… but the other two boys, er… your own brother included, are, erm, well Ahmed thinks they may be dead."

Habash lowered his head but then looked up quickly, surprised by the coldness of the prince's reply.

"He is only my half-brother!" There was an uncomfortable silence before he spoke again. "Abbas is only a half-brother, not my brother."

Habash swallowed and took a deep breath before speaking again. Momentarily, he glanced at Ahmed who said nothing. The boy listened intently, but in the presence of Sieffuddeen, he remained quiet as a mouse.

"Of course, Your Highness, my mistake," Habash replied, apologetically.

He stared at the two bodyguards and began to sweat; his breathing grew steadily heavier as he noticed that one of them had begun to walk around behind him.

"Is that all?"

"Yes, Your Highness, that is all."

The prince nodded towards his bodyguard and suddenly Habash felt the thrust of cold metal in his back as one of the Assassins forced home a short-bladed knife. As the sharp pain rushed up his spine, he felt the life draining out of him and he looked the prince straight in the eye, as if questioning him as to the reason for such treachery. The pain burned inside him, and he felt himself gradually losing consciousness, until seconds later he slumped helplessly to the ground, where he lay dying, blood seeping through his priest's robe, onto the dry ground beneath him.

The Christian's grip on Ahmed was gone and the boy stared, unmoving, at the body lying before him. He wanted to scream but could not. He wanted to say something to Sieffuddeen but dared not. He wanted to move but his feet seemed fastened to the earth until he noticed a Templar knight, making a move towards him. Where this man had come from, he did not know, but he was spurred into action and raced away from all of them, back towards Acre.

Sieffuddeen nodded at the second Assassin, a crossbowman. He lifted his weapon, aimed at Ahmed and fired, the bolt leaving after a click. As Jawad watched, he almost cried out, but fear overtook him. In seconds, the bolt reached its target, but the entire scene appeared as if in slow motion and then the bolt struck. It entered Ahmed's back beneath the left shoulder blade, towards the centre of his back, slicing through bone and piercing the child's heart. Ahmed made no sound and, in an instant, his tiny body collapsed to the ground. He died instantly.

Prince Jawad, so shocked by what he had witnessed, almost gave away his presence nearby with a yelp. The killers turned in his direction, but he stayed motionless, holding his breath and forcing back his tears. As he sat praying for their departure, he began to sweat, and he felt sick to his stomach, but the longer he waited the more his shock turned to anger and rage. However, as he contemplated his next move, he caught sight of someone creeping about just beyond his brother and the Assassins. He soon realised that it was a girl, perhaps sixteen or seventeen years old. At first, he thought she was a boy for her hair was short. She appeared to have witnessed the murder and it became painfully obvious that she was desperately trying to make her escape before the killers saw her.

Unfortunately, in her haste, she stumbled and fell, and the noise she made alerted Sieffuddeen to her presence. Shocked, she half screamed; then, realising she had been spotted, she started to run again, back towards the town. Jawad could not understand why nobody was giving chase, but seconds later the reason became all too evident. Looking back briefly as she ran, the girl bumped into a tall Crusader dressed in full chain mail armour and covered with a white tabard, upon which was painted a bright red cross. This symbol stared the girl in the face and at first, she thought she was safe in the arms of a Christian knight. However, as she began to explain to him what she had seen, he grabbed her arms, thrust his hand viciously over her mouth, and began dragging her back to Sieffuddeen. She struggled to free herself, every so often digging her heels into the ground, but it was far too hard and dry for it to have any effect and the more she wriggled the more the knight strengthened his grip, almost cutting off her oxygen.

Jawad continued to watch everything, desperately wanting to rush over and help the girl, but so fearful of the consequences that he felt glued to the spot. His brother was right, he thought; he was merely a poet and not a fighter. As the Crusader came closer to Sieffuddeen with the girl, however, Jawad could see what he was.

"A Templar with my brother," he whispered to himself.

His brother gave instructions to the knight. His voice was icy cold and heartless. He ordered the knight to take the girl to the Citadel of Salah Ed-Din in Syria, where an exiled group of the Knights of the Temple of Solomon, The Knights Templar, were secured under the protection of the Hashisheen. Jawad had never understood why two factions of deadly enemies had decided to work together and now his confusion increased, with the inclusion of his brother. He had to find out what was going on and that would mean following them to the Citadel. It was a formidable fortress, he knew, built in ancient times, possibly during the rule of the Phoenicians in the early first millennium BC. They had surrendered it to Alexander the Great in around 334 BC and it changed hands many times more, with Salah Ed-Din finally taking it from Crusaders in July 1188.

"My father will believe Habash was killed by Raymond's men," Sieffuddeen said triumphantly, "and Raymond will believe the girl was taken by the Emir's men. Then it won't be too much longer, Jean, before they'll be at each other's throats and Jerusalem will be yours, Syria mine."

The Templar spoke to Sieffuddeen in fluent Arabic; "This is more than just a girl, though. This is Raymond's daughter, a very worthy prize."

Sieffuddeen smiled, touched the girl on the cheek and then repeated his orders.

"I leave for Jerusalem," he added, "and then on to Syria. I will meet you there and question the girl".

Jawad was still whispering to himself, unsure of what to do.

Raymond's daughter? he thought. *I have to do something.*

By now, he was pouring with sweat. He was scared and very confused, but nervously he reached behind his back and grabbed the hilt of the sword Habash had given him, gripping it with all his might. He had never used a sword, even in training. His hand was trembling and, as he licked his lips, the salt of his sweat dried his tongue.

He prepared himself mentally to act, but his brother left on horseback with his Assassin bodyguards. The Templar then dragged his feisty female captive towards a horse-and-cart. She was struggling, trying to free herself from his grip, but to no avail. Jawad had to act now. He pulled his sword from its sheath and ran up behind the kidnapper, but the Templar must have heard the swish of the blade as it slid from its cover, for almost immediately he shoved the girl to the ground and reached for his own sword, turning to face the approaching Saracen. He was too late, though, and the prince thrust his sword into him, the blade smashing through his ribs and slicing through his heart. The Templar slumped over the metal blade, his weight drawing the sword and the arm that held it towards the ground. Jawad struggled to pull the bloodstained weapon from the man's chest, pushing the soldier's body one way while twisting the sword and tugging it in the opposite direction. When he finally pulled it free, he watched his victim crumble into a lifeless heap in front of him and at that point, he felt quite sick and a little faint. Blood fell from the blade onto his shoes and tunic and he dropped the weapon to the ground. He took one last look at the corpse and vomited uncontrollably before regaining his composure and turning to the girl, who had pulled herself up and was running away.

Jawad, amassing all his available strength, picked up his sword and chased after her. He caught hold of her tunic and pulled her to the ground with his left hand, his right one still clasping his blood-soaked sword. Breathing heavily and sweating, he looked hard at her, quite taken aback by her outstanding beauty, and he slowly ran his fingers through her soft, albeit short-cropped, fair hair.

"Your hair is soft and yet short like a man's," he said, as his hand wandered down to her warm cheeks. "And your skin is so…"

He was cut short as she slapped his face and tried desperately to wriggle free.

"Wait!" he shouted, first in Arabic and then in broken French. "I'm trying to help you! We have to work together; we need to help each other and let our people know what is happening."

She was not listening, though. Her only thought was escape. This was her first encounter with an Arab. She did not understand his language and she made no effort to listen to his attempt to speak hers. His dark skin frightened her; although his sombre, dark brown eyes threatened to captivate her. As she wondered what to do, something behind him drew her attention.

"What is it?" he asked, "what are you staring at?"

CHAPTER 19
1240 A.D.
Left for Dead

He turned around, but the last thing he saw was a brief glimpse of a large fist that pummelled into his face. The prince lost consciousness and Marie was lifted violently to her feet by another Templar. Despite her struggles, he was too strong for her and he lent down, ripped a scarf from Jawad's neck, and used it to gag the young girl. He was about to pull her towards the cart when Jawad began to come around. He moved, and the Templar was momentarily distracted, upon which Marie, anxious and afraid, almost twisted free. Her efforts were to no avail, however, and she soon felt the angry slap of the Templar's hand across her face that would finally force her to submit.

I have to kill him, the knight muttered to himself as he looked angrily at Jawad. *He killed my friend.* He turned to face Marie and he smiled. It was not a comforting smile, but rather one of self-satisfaction and his eyes were murderous. "Besides, we want your father's forces to blame the Emir in Jerusalem for your disappearance, so what better than to leave a Saracen's corpse here as evidence? Dead men don't talk, do they?"

Clasping Marie's arm with one hand, the Templar wrenched a small European dagger from his belt. The handle of this knife carried the symbol of the Knights Templar, a circular church with a dome. Unmercifully, he thrust the blade into Jawad's chest, but as he began to remove it again, his prisoner pulled her arm free and once again tried to run away. The knight gave chase immediately, but in his haste, he left his knife protruding from Jawad's chest. The knight caught the girl surprisingly quickly, considering that he was clothed in chain mail and carrying a weighty sword at his side. She was so afraid, though, that her legs seemed to have turned to mush. She was trying to run but could not.

He tugged at her shoulder as he drew level with her, and then punched her viciously in the side of the head, knocking her unconscious. He needed hardly any effort then to lift her onto his shoulders and carry her to the cart. Once there he threw her in, bound her feet and hands with rope, and covered her over with a large tarpaulin. Finally, he returned for his friend's blood-drenched body, Habash's corpse and the lifeless body of Ahmed. All of these were to be Marie's travelling companions, but the two Saracens would be dumped near to Jerusalem. The other, his friend, would accompany Marie for the entire journey to Syria. He pulled half of the tarpaulin over the bodies and then set off.

Jawad was fortunate that the knife remained embedded in his chest for it stemmed much of the bleeding. Nevertheless, without help, he would most definitely bleed out and die. As the horse and cart disappeared into the distance, there was movement near where the incident had taken place. Minutes later, two monks, out gathering berries, spotted something alongside some shrubs near the Damascus road. They were cautious at first in case it was a wild animal, but they soon recognised it as a person.

"Is he dead?" One of them asked.

The other threw down his basket of berries and rushed to the prone body. He felt for a pulse and found one. "He's alive but won't be for long if we don't get help for him. Quickly, fetch a horse and cart and inform the guards. Tell them a Saracen is dying here and we need help to get him to Amalric. If we can keep this man alive, he might be able to explain what has been happening in Acre lately."

His brother monk lifted his cassock and ran back to Acre to get help.

Meanwhile, en route to Syria, Marie came around. She was dazed, but gradually started to remember what had happened. Unable to move, bound up and tied to the side of the cart, she stared up at the sky. She wondered about who the Saracen was who had tried to save her. She thought about what he had said, and she recalled the touch of his hand through her hair. Although she may never have publicly admitted it, she found him quite attractive, and she wondered about his fate. Was he dead? Would she see him again? God alone knew what their fate would be.

CHAPTER 20
Arrival in Slegna

Zenith and his two human travelling companions arrived in Slegna later than they had expected, and this was unfortunate, for it was now night again. The boat, a white vessel shaped like a giant fish with a huge, white square sail, floated silently into port. After disembarking, Zenith ordered the children to stay close by him and they set about their main task, which was to get indoors as quickly as possible.

The town of Slegna sat above the pier where the boat had docked. To reach safety, they had to climb a path, which wound its way up a steep cliff. It was an exhausting climb. About halfway up, Hassan noticed that Abbas was trailing quite a way behind them. Without telling Zenith he went back to help him and found the younger boy sitting on the ground, weeping. Hassan was about to bend over him when another boy, a grey-skinned child of around 14 years of age, suddenly emerged out of the shadows.

"What the..." said Hassan, clearly startled by the stranger's appearance.

The boy smiled. "It's all right, I'm a friend," he said reassuringly. "I'll help you carry him."

"But... who are you?" Hassan asked, obviously troubled by the presence of this stranger and thinking about Zenith's many warnings. "Zenith told me to beware of..." he began to mutter, before being interrupted by the visitor.

"Who's Zenith?"

Abbas was clinging to Hassan's trousers and slowly creeping around behind him. He was comforted when his friend and defender touched his hand reassuringly.

"Er... well, Zenith's our protector. He's helping us to get home," he finally replied, before pausing and glancing behind him up the path.

"He's just up there, ahead of us, and we really should be getting back to him now."

"Let me meet him," the stranger insisted.

His tone made Hassan even more suspicious. He sounded so insincere and although he smiled constantly, it was not a smile of compassion, but one of cunning and deception. His eyes were not smiling at all, but stared, maliciously, at the two humans. Hassan repeatedly thought about Zenith's warning. He kept staring at the ground and biting his lower lip, desperate not to look at the other boy.

What if this boy is one of those rakshasas things—those shape-shifters? he thought. *Zenith said they could take on human form.*

"Why won't you look at me?" the stranger asked, taking a few steps towards the other boys.

Hassan tried desperately to resist looking at him, but his will was finally broken and he slowly raised his eyes, only to have them transfixed momentarily by the boy's hypnotic gaze.

"Meet me at the cliff-top at the third hour of the morning, near the gateway to the Overseer's Kingdom," he told Hassan, who nodded compliantly. "I can help you all to…"

Just then, he was interrupted by Zenith who was calling Hassan and Abbas. The Jinni was returning down the path and his voice had broken the stranger's hold over Hassan, who blinked rapidly before turning towards his guide.

"Zenith!" Abbas shouted, "come and meet our new friend".

However, when he looked back to where the boy had been, he found that he was gone.

"Of what friend do you speak, Abbas? Have you ignored my advice?"

Afraid of being reprimanded, Hassan lifted Abbas into his arms and replied for both of them.

"No, of course not," he replied, "there's no friend really. Abbas was only joking."

"Well, it is not a very funny joke!" responded Zenith, angrily.

Abbas was too scared and weary to say anything more. In fact, he was now unsure whether there had ever been another boy with them. He presumed he had imagined it all and he never gave it another thought.

Gradually, he drifted off to sleep in Hassan's arms.

That night, they rested in a dwelling that resembled the ones in Al-Bahira. It was situated just yards from a cliff edge, overlooking a seemingly never-ending mass of blackness. Out there, somewhere in the dark, was the entrance to Zaman's Kingdom, although the children found it difficult to believe there could be anything in the suffocating gloom in front of them. Hassan had decided that he would meet the stranger near that entrance. So, it was into that shadowy darkness that he went, early the following morning. He tried to sneak out of the dwelling as quietly as he could, but Abbas spotted him and followed him out, tiptoeing silently behind him.

"Where are you going?" the small boy asked, once they were outside and out of earshot of Zenith.

Hassan was startled to hear the young prince's voice behind him, but rather than risk waking Zenith by taking Abbas back inside, he decided to take him with him. It seemed to take forever to reach the cliff edge. Two boys, puffing, panting, and fumbling around in the dark, repeatedly stumbled over what seemed to be rocks and mounds of earth obstructing their path. Suddenly, Hassan tripped. Falling headlong, he quickly discovered the true nature of the obstacles beneath their feet. As he lay on his stomach, muttering complaints about his grazed knee, his eyes fell on what could only be described as a dog's skull, staring up at him. For a moment, it was almost as if it were alive; its eyes shone momentarily, teasing the boy with their illusion of movement. He looked around and realised that the entire area was littered with the skulls of all manner of creatures, some of which even looked human. The shroud of darkness was lifting and the landscape that surrounded them became steadily clearer. A kind of dawn was emerging that brought with it a half light that is often associated with visions and hallucinations.

Sweating profusely, his heart was pounding so fast that its rapid beat had become the only sound he could hear. He jumped to his feet and began brushing himself down, as if he were trying to push away something horrible that was clinging to his body. He stared down at the skull, but once on his feet again, the ground appeared almost barren. He realised, to his great relief, that Abbas, therefore, would not have seen what he had seen.

"What is it? What's wrong?" asked Abbas, excitedly.

Hassan caught hold of his young ward and led him on towards their destination.

"Nothing," he replied, abruptly. "Nothing! Just a bit shaken up by the fall and my imagination running wild."

The boys continued, arriving at the cliff edge just before the third hour of the morning. The stranger was already there, sitting cross-legged on a huge boulder, and flinging pebbles into the black sky beyond. He waited for the boys to reach him before acknowledging their presence with a pat of his hand on the ground. They sat down beside him and looked briefly at each other, although neither of them said a word.

"You can come out now!" the boy shouted and, within seconds, about twelve other young lads surrounded them. All of them were untidy and unclean; none of them looked older than about twelve.

Hassan was growing a little nervous. The hypnotic control over him was evaporating. His suspicion was now aroused, and he began to wonder whether these boys might really be Jinn. As they gathered around, his fears subsided slightly, because they all looked so human and were so sociable. Their new friend stood up and indicated towards a tiny ledge, just beneath the cliff edge.

"On that ledge is the key to the entrance to Zaydussia, the land of the Overseer, but none of us can get it. We are too heavy to stand on the ledge." He turned at looked at Abbas. "But your friend here is perfect for the task," he continued, "we can lower him down and he can bring us the key."

Now Hassan's concerns escalated. Once again, his heart began to thump, and he began to regret ever meeting these boys. Automatically and instinctively, he pulled Abbas towards him, attempting to reassure the young lad that he was safe.

Why would they want the key? he thought to himself and then, warily, he spoke.

"Er, I don't know about this," he said, "I'm responsible for Abbas and I... er, I shouldn't really have come here. Zenith told us not to trust anyone". He began to walk away when the stranger spoke again.

"Oh, Zenith, Zenith. That's all you keep going on about. This damned Genie of yours. He is wasting your time, taking you on this long-winded journey to reach the Ridge of Fertheron, when all he has to do is use that key to take you straight through Zaydussia and up to the Ridge itself."

As he spoke, the other children moved towards them and began a slow chant, which grew louder and louder as they approached.

"Let him do it, let him do it," they called out, repeatedly.

Minute by minute the two humans were being urged to conform, firstly to the chants and then with taunts and teasing. Relentlessly, the group punished them psychologically for their non-conformity.

"You cowards! You weaklings!" they shouted repeatedly. "You're weird! You're not one of us," they shouted, pointing at Abbas. "You'll die here. You'll never get home."

The pressure to fall in with the pack overwhelmed Abbas and, without Zenith to pull him back from the brink, he finally succumbed to the attack. He weakened and submitted.

"I'll be all right," he kept saying, "I'll be fine," he added, pulling himself away from Hassan.

CHAPTER 21
The Rakshasas

When Zenith awoke, he became anxious and angry once he realised that the boys had gone. They had abandoned the protection of the dwelling and he feared the worst for them. He left in a hurry, clearly fretful about the prospect of searching in the half-light for such irresponsible children. Every step he took brought greater and greater fear and he sensed the presence of evil all around him; he knew that out there, somewhere, something harmful was lurking. He also knew that until the darkness receded and was replaced by light, he was in a weakened state. Then, without warning, his passage was halted by Hassan. The boy had been running but was looking behind him and he ran straight into the Jinni. The startled child let out an ear-piercing scream and Zenith grabbed him firmly by the upper arms.

"Hassan, don't you look where you are going when you run?"

"Oh my God. I'm so glad it's you. Abbas is stuck on a ledge. He tried to get the key to Zaydussia, and the other boys lowered him down and now he's stuck and…"

"Hold it, not so fast!" Zenith shouted. "I don't know what you children have been up to, nor do I understand why Abbas would be on a ledge looking for a key that does not exist."

Hassan frowned, clearly confused, and then he began to cry. It was the first time he had broken down like this since his ordeal had begun.

"I am also genuinely concerned at your mention of 'other boys'. There are no boys here, only Jinn. However, if Abbas is in trouble, then we must help him, so let's go. Show me where he is."

Abbas' wails could be heard when they were still yards away from the cliff edge.

"Stand back Hassan. The last thing I want is another boy going off the edge. Rescuing Abbas will weaken me quite considerably as it is."

The group of other boys had gone, and Zenith inched closer to the cliff edge. Once there, he looked over. Huddled on a tiny ledge some nine feet below them was Abbas, gripping the cliff-face, his knuckles white. He was staring up with expectation as Zenith leaned over. From where the boy stood, the Jinni looked like an angel from heaven.

"Just hold still child, I'm coming down," he heard him say.

Zenith raised himself gracefully into the air, floated out across the canyon and lowered himself down to the ledge. Abbas was trembling and weeping, so the Jinni reached out and lifted him into the air. He rose slowly to the summit and rested the boy gently on the grass. The two boys ran to each other and Hassan wrapped his arms around Abbas, so elated that he would not have to return home with the sad news of the loss of the Emir's son. The younger child was dishevelled, frightened and cold. He shivered in Hassan's arms and whimpered softly, his tears dropping to the ground in almost slow motion.

"It's all right master Abbas," Hassan said comfortingly, "you're safe now."

He relaxed, loosened himself from Hassan's arms and turned towards Zenith, who had landed near the cliff-edge, tired and weak. The Jinni smiled, and Abbas returned the greeting, wiping the tears from his eyes at the same time.

The shock of what happened next, stunned the boys. Just as they were about to walk towards him, a colossal spear came out of the darkness and slammed, brutally into the Jinni's chest. His hands grabbed it instinctively, his head rocked forward and then, without warning, a second spear tore into his right shoulder, thrusting him off the cliff and into the dense gloom of the canyon.

"No!" The children screamed in unison. Abbas broke free from Hassan's grasp and ran, as fast as he could, towards the cliff edge. He looked out at the dark sky but could see nothing. Hassan, however, turned around to see the source of the weapons that had so violently struck their dear friend. There was no one there—no one at all, and the fear which overcame him, was indescribable. Despite that, he approached Abbas and placed a reassuring hand upon his shoulder. As he looked out over the canyon he sighed, and then glanced down at the younger child.

"We should return to the town for help," he said, but before he could say any more a voice called out from the darkness behind them.

"No Hassaaaan! You must come with ussss."

The children's hearts jumped. They were startled, petrified, and they turned around with great trepidation, only to find the group of boys they were with earlier.

"Thank God it's you" Abbas remarked, perhaps a little hastily.

Hassan gripped the young lad's hand tightly. His face betrayed his bitterness, his anger.

"They're not our friends," he whispered. "They're demons, shape-shifters, murderers."

As the rakshasas moved towards them, their features transformed. Their faces distorted, their colour altered and within seconds, their true features were visible. They were ghouls, but not like those the children had met when they first fell into this netherworld. Some of these were yellow, some green, and others blue, with vertical slits for eyes, large bellies, and elongated feet with clawed toes. Despite his fear, or perhaps because of it, Hassan could control his passion no longer.

"You… you killed him. You murdered Zenith. You lied to me; you tricked us, you…"

"Silence!"

The one that shouted was an ugly brute, covered in warts, with blood dripping from his mouth. In his hand, he held an oval shield, decorated with a simple skull design. His fingernails were unusually long and pointed and his eyes were unblinking.

Two of the other ghouls grabbed the boys and began tying their hands to a long metallic pole, which they used to march them away. They had only taken a few strides, however, when they were stopped in their tracks by a tremendous blast. It was almost as if the air itself had exploded right in front of them and was now being sucked into a vortex. All sound disappeared, and the ghouls collapsed. The children wished they could have clasped their hands to their ears, but tied to the pole, they were unable. They felt the rush of wind roar right through them, and within seconds there was a flash of light, which brought with it the manifestation of a small being with human-like features.

Panic-stricken, one of the ghouls muttered something under his breath, but gradually a smile materialised on his face. He looked briefly at his companions and then at the newly arrived visitor.

"So... Zaman has left his Kingdom unattended, unprotected, to save these wretches," he whispered, eerily.

The Overseer was surrounded by light so dazzling that the two boys had difficulty keeping their eyes open. Gradually, its intensity decreased until the grey of the now misty morning returned. Zaman appeared less and less awesome with the fading of the aura and the stormy winds, and yet the ghouls became increasingly anxious. Their fear of him became progressively more evident the longer his impassive stare fixed upon them. He was, after all, preceded by a reputation powerful enough to frighten even the most truculent of the Evil One's devotees.

Hassan and Abbas stood motionless, unsure of what to do or say. Abbas fidgeted and then glanced down at his now wet trousers. He peered nervously at Hassan and the older boy offered him a comforting smile, before discretely taking hold of the young child's hand and squeezing it tightly.

"It's all right Abbas," he said.

CHAPTER 22
Zaman's Appearance

Zaman, although not much taller than Abbas, possessed the features of someone who was elderly, knowledgeable and experienced. His presence evidently disturbed the ghouls but hesitantly, the one in charge stepped forward, speaking as he went. The tone of his voice signalled his disdain, arrogance and disrespect, but its shakiness exposed his apprehension and alarm.

"You were foolish to leave your Kingdom unprotected for the sake of two such insignificant humans," he hissed. "Why, this very minute, my master, Iblis, will be preparing forces to attack Zaydussia, and you will need all your strength to resist my forces here in Brillar."

This superficial effrontery evaporated the instant Zaman moved towards him. The Overseer clutched the most impressive sword that either of the earthlings had ever seen and when Zaman spoke, all around them seemed to collapse into deadly silence.

"You muster a great many warriors and make considerable effort, oh ghoul, for two humans that you claim are insignificant."

The ghoul twitched, and Zaman continued.

"My Kingdom is adequately protected, and your master will attack at his own peril. I have been away for just a moment and shall now return, with these children, the way I entered Brillar in the first place."

He turned to the boys and stretched out his arms to them. "Come little ones, we must leave now."

Abbas raised an eyebrow and whispered to Hassan. "Who does he think he's calling 'little ones'? He's no bigger than I am!"

Hassan was not listening though. He had other things on his mind, and he moved free of Zaman's arm for a moment. "What about Zenith? You have to save him!"

Hassan looked out at the black sky hanging over the shrouded, misty canyon. In his heart, he knew there was nothing anyone could do now for the Jinni. Zaman lowered his arms and shook his head. He was about to speak when one of the ghouls cackled loudly.

"Yes, yes, you have to save him!", he began shrieking. "And that will drain you, weaken you and detain you, upon which we shall destroy you."

Zaman lifted his hand and pointed at the ghoul. The creature's mouth instantly vanished, and Zaman glanced down at the children. He sighed, noticeably aware of their concern for their friend.

"I cannot save Zenith," he said with understandable regret. "Granted, I am a being with great power, the Overseer, but only Allah has power over life and death."

"Is Zenith dead then?" Abbas asked in a whisper.

Zaman sighed.

"If he is not, it would surely be miraculous, and the Hand of Allah would undoubtedly have saved him."

He pulled his satin mantle around his shoulders and looked around him for a few seconds before continuing.

"And, if that is the case, we should leave his fate in the hands of Allah. If, on the other hand, he is dead, then we would only be risking our own lives and all we hold dear, for no constructive end. Now, we must go". To himself, he pondered the situation. *Despite what I told the ghouls*, he mused, *my kingdom is at risk, the longer I stay here.*

He stepped back, raised his arms and once again beckoned the children. They stepped across to him and snuggled close by his side. Zaman began to draw his cloak around them but one of the ghouls suddenly reached out, grabbed Abbas by the arm and endeavoured to wrench him away from the others. Zaman held the back of his right hand towards the ghoul and launched a shaft of light and heat at him. It tore through the beast like a knife through butter, removing his head from his shoulders and killing him instantly. The boys were frozen with shock and stared at the lifeless, headless cadaver on the ground before them. The ghoul's decapitated body had frozen, as if rigor mortis had already seized it. For Abbas it was all too much, and he fainted in Zaman's arms. Meanwhile, all the other ghouls fled in haste, occasionally stumbling over each other in the dark as they desperately sought self-preservation.

Zaman calmly caught hold of both boys by their waists and then closed his eyes.

"You must shut your eyes Hassan, or the light will blind you. I will leave Abbas in his present state until we arrive in Zaydussia."

Hassan did as he was told, and through his eyelids, he could see a glow, reminiscent of the midday desert sun. His body warmed up, his fingers tingled and all he could hear was a gentle hiss, akin to the sound of a summer breeze. It reminded him of the wind which breezed through the narrow streets of Jerusalem in the early morning, as the people arose from their slumber.

In the instant it took to leap from Brillar to Zaydussia, Hassan seemed to have seen his entire life go by. He remembered those empty Jerusalem streets before dawn, and the hundreds of early morning walks and runs he had made to the baker. Young Ali, a boy of about twelve years old, had always baked the family's bread for them in his father's large, clay oven. However, after Hassan's mother died when he was still quite young, his father took him to work with him at the Emir's palace and the bread runs were no longer made. As Atabeg to Abbas, Hassan's father was highly influential, despite his servant status. If the Emir and his older sons were to die before Abbas was old enough to rule alone, the boy prince would rely on his Atabeg for guidance and advice. Hassan's father would effectively take control and Hassan thought of all this, and of his friendship with the child in his protection. Then he remembered Ahmed, whose fate remained unknown to them.

Amid all these thoughts and feelings, the blinding illumination evaporated like a candle extinguished by a moistened finger. As it did so, Hassan opened his eyes to discover that the gloom of Brillar had also gone. He now stood with Zaman on a grassy plain, where there were trees and birds, a stream and blue sky. The bright light of day encircled them, even though there was no visible sun, and for a very short-lived moment, it felt to Hassan as if he were back on earth. Everything reminded him so much of Lebanon, a place he had visited once.

He began to relax and appreciate these new surroundings as Abbas returned to consciousness.

"Are we home?", he asked, as he searched for something recognisable—a landmark of some kind.

"No child, this is not *your* home, it's mine!" Zaman replied. "This is the Kingdom of Zaydussia. It is like Earth, yes, but that is because I feel affection for Earth and so designed my realm to be like it." He paused for a second and glanced around. "Once the clouds pass, if you look across the valley before you, you will see my castle. It is just above the peak of that hill, and we must make it there soon."

Hassan frowned. "Don't you mean over the peak of that hill, and not above it?"

Zaman smiled but did not answer the question.

"Let's hasten!" he said.

"But what's the rush?" asked Hassan, "I like it here and we're safe now... aren't we?"

"Perhaps, for a while, but you heard the ghouls. My absence has emboldened the Evil One."

He caught hold of the two boys, rather roughly Abbas thought, and began to lead them towards the hill, continuing to talk as he led them away.

"At this very moment, Iblis and an army of the most hideous of Jinn are attacking my troops, trying to capture my castle. Militarily, his forces are no match for my troops, but I fear that in my absence my warriors could lose heart. They are a fickle bunch and their morale needs to be constantly boosted."

Abbas laughed. "Ahmed's father says it's the same for him. He is always telling his men to rely on the Almighty, but most of them rely on the next man in charge. He says they are, er... oh, yes, weak willed, faint-hearted and timid. And he says they worship their heroes more than God. He gets very angry with them."

Zaman chuckled. "Good, I think you understand, so let's go now!"

"Wait!" Hassan stopped in his tracks. "Tell us more about this Evil One."

"In good time Hassan; in good time."

Hassan persisted, demanding that they could be told as they went but Zaman refused to be drawn.

"We must make haste and talk will slow us down, distract us from our goal."

Hassan's head dropped but he had one last question before he was willing to begin the trek.

"I suppose there is a good reason why you couldn't have taken us directly into your castle, is there?"

Zaman frowned. "Sometimes I like a challenge Hassan. Sometimes I just like to make things hard for myself."

CHAPTER 23
Zaydussia

The hill was a long hard climb and as they neared the summit, they could see the ghouls, thousands upon thousands of them, flying around a magnificent marble fortress some one hundred yards in the air. Zaman's citadel was under constant bombardment by bat-like creatures, their membrane wings several yards across.

On first inspection, their weapons seemed quite ordinary in appearance, like any other medieval armaments. Hassan scrutinized the fighting and what he saw captivated him. The ghouls' weapons fired bursts of fire, balls of flame and rays of burning light. The Jinn inside the fort's walls struggled to stop the barrage. Their firepower seemed to be dwindling and every ghoul attack exposed another part of the castle's defences.

As the three travellers looked on, a rupture appeared in the sky just beyond the castle and several hundred more Jinn warriors poured through, swarming onto the battle scene like a plague of locusts.

"You children remain here beneath this tree. Do not move and do not make a sound. I'll be back soon."

At this, Zaman blasted into the air like a bullet. Within seconds, all that could be seen of him was a streak of light, like a comet or a shooting star. He exploded onto the scene of the fighting and the sky around the fortress lit up. Zaman sent a fireball towards the rupture, sealing it and killing hundreds of the demons as they emerged from the fracture in space and time. The battle intensified, and with the arrival of Zaman, his forces strengthened, first in courage and then in physical prowess.

For almost an hour, the battle raged, and the sky shone like the sun on a sweltering summer day. The intensity of the light generated by the warring Jinn was so great that the two human children had to hide their eyes from it.

Then, without any warning, it stopped. Silence surrounded them, and the light dimmed. Cautiously, they peered up at Zaman's fortress, which stood motionless in a clear and bright, blue sky. There was not a soul in sight as the children emerged from beneath the tree that had shielded them so well. They gazed all around them but there was nothing to indicate what the outcome of the encounter had been.

"What's happened?" Abbas asked as he glanced up at Hassan who was staring unemotionally around them.

"I don't know. I don't know who won, who lost, or what to do." He paused, sighed and then, taking hold of Abbas, walked towards Zaman's stronghold. "I don't think we have any alternative but to go there and see what has happened," he said.

"But... what if the Evil One was victorious?"

"If he was then all is lost anyway."

It seemed to take hours before they reached the battle arena. Above them, the colossal castle cast a shadow over most of the surrounding area. The boys glanced up.

"Now what?" asked Abbas, somewhat disheartened.

Just then, they felt something gripping them, like giant hands around their vulnerable bodies. Whatever it was, it was lifting them towards the palace. They wanted to look up, but found they could not move a muscle, and as they neared the underside of the palace, they closed their eyes. To their great surprise, they passed right through it, like a hand immersed in water. The base of the structure rippled as they entered. Once inside, they were set down on a marble floor in an expansive, but empty, room. All the walls were bare, except the one immediately in front of them. There stood a tall mirror, reaching some ten feet from the floor and six feet wide. It was the only object in the room and the boys instinctively walked towards it.

They looked at themselves in the mirror but also the figure standing behind them. A tall warrior, with wings that were as white as those of a swan. Hassan turned around and began to ask the figure if he was an angel, but there was nobody there. He quickly looked back at the mirror and could see only himself and Abbas. For several minutes, they stood before the looking glass, staring at their reflections and trying to adjust their clothes, but Hassan noticed that the image had begun to shimmer.

Their hearts almost shot out of their bodies as Zaman stepped out of the mirror, almost as if he were a part of it, the undulating substance that was the looking glass, trailing behind him. In an instant, he had completely materialised, and the mirror had returned to its normal texture and shape. He smiled at them and held out his hands, upon which the boys rushed towards him and clung securely to his legs.

"You won, didn't you?" Abbas shouted, excitedly.

"How did you do it?" Hassan asked, impatient to hear Zaman's voice once again.

"Come my children. There is much to tell and much to do, but time is very short, very short indeed. Time, I am afraid, is not on our side."

Hassan screwed up his face. "Yeah, so we keep being told," he muttered under his breath.

Zaman took them to his throne, set in a magnificent marble room, around the walls of which stood elegantly dressed, and well-armed, Jinn guards. After seating them alongside him, Zaman began to tell them more about the Evil One.

"You may not be aware, children, that the words, Jinn and Jannah, come from the same Semitic root, meaning hidden or unseen. The Jinn are hidden. The Garden of paradise, Jannah, is hidden, but the Angels are also hidden, also unseen."

As he spoke, moving images of all that he narrated, appeared before them and the children were spellbound.

"There are some who claim we Jinn are spirits that are lower than angels, because we are made of fire, not light, and we are not immortal. But we can take on human and animal shapes to influence men to do good or evil and many of us are quick to punish anyone who is indebted to us but who do not follow our rules."

He paused for an instant and seemed to have drifted off into a kind of daydream. Then, without warning, he continued.

"Allah created Adam, but Adam was not a man. Adam means mankind, humans. In the beginning, Allah told the angels to prostrate themselves before humankind, because humans were favoured by Allah, to the detriment of angels and the Jinn."

"Favoured?" questioned the children in unison.

"Yes, for unlike the beings of light, humans were given the gift of

Free Will, and, unlike the Jinn, who do have free will, humans understand true love for each other and for their Creator.

"The Angels were Allah's closest servants, until the creation of humans and they were made up of beings of light and some beings of fire.

"The highest of all the beings of fire was Iblis. He is sometimes called Azazel , the Prince of Darkness, Satan, Shaytaan or the Devil. The Christians call him the Fallen Angel, but, although he had been chosen as an Angel, he has always been a Jinni, and he was the most favoured by Allah.

"So, all the angels prostrated themselves, but Iblis refused because he was a Jinni, made from fire. He was arrogant and disobedient to his Lord. He was cast out of Paradise by Allah but given virtual immortality, the chance to live until the end of time, until Judgement Day, when he would finally receive his punishment."

He shifted in his seat as if trying to get comfortable and he heaved an almighty sigh.

"Iblis, Satan, Belial, Azazal, call him what you will. He promised to spend the rest of time tormenting God's treasured humans, deceiving them, enticing them, and causing conflict on earth. All Jinn have magical powers, which we can bestow upon anyone who asks us, but Iblis' powers are matched only by mine and surpassed only by Allah's."

Zaman paused but neither child made a sound. They stood, mesmerised by the Overseer's narration.

"His powers are restricted, however. He remains trapped in Jahanam, Hell, until he can obtain a magical staff that would open the gateway to Earth. Without it, he can temporarily enter Earth's realm, but for no more than hours at a time. In the meantime, he releases his Jinn servants through temporary portals, to work on his behalf. They can remain on Earth far longer than he can. He believes, however, that if he possesses the staff, he will escape from the bounds Allah created for him. He is so arrogant that he genuinely believes he will then be able to challenge Allah. He is wrong, but the consequences of his misguided intentions will be catastrophic if he is not stopped."

Zaman leaned forward, waved his hand across the air in front of him and changed the holographic images before them. Within it, the image of

Sieffuddeen began to materialise. He was standing in a dimly lit room with his two Assassin guards and Abbas frowned heavily as he stared at his brother. Zaman was about to speak when Abbas, whose screwed-up forehead made him look like a little old man, rudely interrupted him.

"That's my brother!"

"Please listen Abbas."

Zaman leaned forward and stared at the hologram.

"Your brother, in league with the Templars, is plotting to overthrow your father. His plan is to destabilise the treaty which exists between the Crusaders and your father's empire, and so bring them to war with each other."

As he spoke, he noticed that Abbas was continuously shaking his head from side to side in apparent disbelief.

"He has forged a deal with the Templars, granting them control of Jerusalem in exchange for Syria falling under his direct rule."

"These are lies! I don't believe it! You're lying!" Abbas shouted, trying desperately to pull himself away from the Overseer.

Hassan prevented him from running off. The Turk had never trusted Sieffuddeen and he knew that what Zaman was suggesting was a highly likely state of affairs.

"Listen, Abbas," he said, "there is no reason for Zaman to lie to us, so let us hear him out before we make any rash decisions, eh?"

Abbas was still unhappy. His body language revealed this and if looks could kill, both Zaman and Hassan would have been lifeless cadavers by now. Nevertheless, his physical resistance abated, and he returned to his seat. Zaman waved a hand over the image and the voices of Abbas' brother and his cohorts became audible.

"In less than a week, Syria will be mine," Sieffuddeen muttered, smugly. "And it is all thanks to those fool Templars." He grinned and peered down at the floor. Then he nodded. "Once my dominance of Syria and Lebanon are complete and secure, we will take Jerusalem from the Knights and Egypt will be my next port of call after that."

His grin turned into a raucous laugh and, closely followed by his henchmen, he left the room.

Zaman put his hand gently on Abbas' shoulder to comfort him.

"I'm sorry Abbas. I realise that this must come as a great shock to you, but I'm afraid there's more and far worse news."

He explained to the boys about the murder of Habash, the kidnapping of Saint-Gilles' daughter and the stabbing of Abbas' other brother, Jawad. Then, he broke the sad news of Ahmed's murder, ordered by Sieffuddeen and witnessed by Jawad.

Both boys were stunned and distraught, but Abbas continued to deny it all. Yet, he cried. Meanwhile, Hassan remained silent, a strong feeling of anger and revenge building inside him, eager for the opportunity to be expressed. When he finally spoke, it was softly at first, a whisper that was barely audible.

"What of Jawad? You said stabbed, not killed."

"He was stabbed and left for dead by the Templars when he tried to stop them taking Marie away. Now he is locked in a Crusader dungeon in Acre," Zaman replied.

"They believe he may have conspired to kidnap Raymond's daughter. They also think he may have been stabbed by one of his co-conspirators for some personal gain or political motive that they could only speculate about."

He once again waved his hand over the hologram, creating a new image. It was Jawad, lying helplessly on a cold slab in a damp, windowless room.

"Of course, they are wrong. He tried to save the girl and now I must act to save him."

The Overseer caught hold of the boys by their shoulders and looked directly into their faces, his eyes unblinking and an air of determination they had not witnessed in anyone before.

"Time really *is* short my children. The longer Sieffuddeen and his accomplices continue to operate undetected, unabated, the stronger the Evil One becomes. His defeat here has weakened him in our domain. Of that there is no doubt. But with strong human allies, his armies could turn to fresh human pickings and his chances of finding the staff will increase."

The hologram gently faded away, Zaman stood up and began pacing the room, and the boys followed him. As he made his way across the vast chamber, he whipped his cloak around him in the manner of a king and, as he approached the room's only window, he stopped. The boys were one or two paces behind him, but they stopped when he did, and he turned to address them again.

"A battle of the scale envisioned between your people and the Christians, would present Satan with very rich rewards indeed," he said.

The children looked tired and emotionally drained. Hassan's face was drawn and haggard and Abbas was having great difficulty keeping his eyes open and in focus. Realising their tension, Zaman took hold of them and led them away to somewhere they could sleep. They walked along a plain, pale green corridor and, although he thought they might no longer be listening to him, he continued to talk to them.

"I will have to send forces, unseen forces, to fight against the Templars and Assassins if necessary, but first you two must escape to your world and try to warn both sides."

He rested one hand on Hassan's shoulder before continuing.

"To do this, you must reach the Ridge of Fertheron by mid-morning and that means you must leave here within twelve of your hours. You will need to take food and water with you too."

At the end of the corridor, they came to another room, ornately decorated and beautifully furnished. In one corner, there were two piles of children's garments. In the opposite corner, a counter overflowed with food and drink. In the middle of the room were two of the most comfortable looking beds the boys had ever seen. Thick mattresses were overlain with deep-filled quilts, soft as the deepest snow, and to one side of the beds were two canvass sacks, each draped over a thick, pile carpet.

"Take your pick of the clothes and whatever food you want. Pack it into those sacks and, in the morning, someone will collect you, Allah Willing."

Zaman was walking around in circles, staring at the floor as he spoke and clasping his hands in front of him. Occasionally, he came to a halt and looked at the boys, as they wandered across to the beds and sat themselves down. Abbas' drift into sleep was disturbed when Zaman continued talking.

"Two agents of mine are on their way to free Jawad, so fear not for your brother, young Abbas."

A pleasant smile appeared on Zaman's face and he added, "they will also help Jawad to track down Marie, but if Shaytaan's Jinn interfere, we will retaliate."

CHAPTER 24
1240 A.D.
Captive

In a depressingly dark, windowless room, Jawad awoke to find himself in the company of three men. Everything was blurred, but he could just make out that they were monks. The young prince attempted to sit up, but his chest felt as if a hot poker was wedged inside and the sudden pain forced him to remain on his back.

"Ya Allah!" he screamed.

One of the monks touched his forehead lightly with a wet cloth and gently lifted his head from the cold, stone slab.

"Where am I?" he asked. He was still weak from his injuries and his voice was shaky.

One of the monks placed a compassionate hand upon Jawad's shoulder and smiled at him. It was clear to him that they did not understand what he was saying, so he spoke in French and asked again.

"Relax my son," one of the monks replied. "You have suffered a vicious wound. You were stabbed in the chest and you need further rest to aid the healing process."

He offered the prince a sip of water, but Jawad pushed it aside, spilling some of it on the floor.

"WHERE AM I?!" he shouted, irately.

As the monk made to speak to him again, Jawad heard the creaking of a door opening behind him. He could not move and was unable to see who had entered, but behind him stood Bohemond. The soldier gestured commandingly to one of the monks, who stepped aside.

"This man has been identified by one of our agents as the Emir's second son, Prince Jawad."

He stepped forward and, as Jawad followed him with his eyes, Bohemond leaned his full weight upon his chest, forcing an agonising scream from the injured man.

"Where is the Lady Marie?" The Christian asked but there was no reply. Jawad simply winced. "What were you, a prince, doing so far from home?"

One of the monks tried to intervene, demanding that the prisoner be allowed to heal, but Bohemond ignored the plea and continued to press for information.

Again, there was no answer and Bohemond turned to the monks, pressing his forefinger into the chest of one of them.

"You are to nurse this man back to health and then hold him at the monastery until further notice," he ordered.

The monks nodded and Bohemond left, slamming the heavy iron door behind him, the sound echoing throughout the long, dank corridors of the monastery. It was a short walk from there to the Palace and within a quarter of an hour, Bohemond had arrived at Raymond's quarters. In the room with Raymond was Amalric. Raymond sat behind his desk, while Amalric stood against the wall to his right, some two or three yards away from the door. Bohemond wasted no time in reporting the findings of his investigation into the events of the previous three days. As he spoke, the light from a nearby window glistened off his belt buckle and highlighted the creases in his bright, blue, shirt.

"It is difficult to understand precisely what has happened sir. Someone entered this building unnoticed, moved about your private quarters and stole away with the boy."

He could feel the anger rising in Raymond but continued regardless.

"The guard has gone mad. He is raving about demons and spirits. I doubt whether we'll get much of any use out of him, but there is strangeness afoot."

"The captive is the Emir's second son and he was discovered lying near the area where the Lady Marie disappeared. He was, as far as we can make out, stabbed by a Templar knight, the knife still being in him when he was found, but we don't know who or where the knight is."

Bohemond paused and frowned.

"What we also don't understand is this; if the prince was part of a kidnap group, and if the rest of that group have got away with Lady Marie, then who stabbed him and why did the kidnappers not take him with them?"

Raymond leant back in his chair and glanced away from Bohemond. His mind was racing, and he was growing increasingly concerned over the whereabouts of his daughter. He took a deep breath to calm himself and pondered, for a short while, the situation. Something was telling him that the Arab prince was not involved in the kidnapping of his daughter. As Bohemond had just reasoned, why would the kidnappers leave behind one of their own. There was no chance that they would leave even a common soldier behind, let alone someone as important as Prince Jawad. Something strange truly was afoot and he was determined to get to the bottom of it all.

"The captive needs to be questioned further," he said, rather impatiently.

"Er, there is one other thing sir…" Bohemond continued. "When we showed the captive to our agent, he referred to the prince as 'the poet', which I felt was an unusual epithet for a fighter or a spy, don't you think?"

Raymond frowned and Bohemond continued.

"Oh, and the servant boys who were with the Arab child, spoke of an Arab sir and they said he wore a cross."

Raymond looked at Bohemond, took a deep breath and shook his head. He placed his palms together, his fingertips touching his lips.

"Something is clearly not right, not as it seems," he mused. "Whose knife was in the victim? Where is the assailant, or where is his body? Who was the Arab and was he a Christian, or just made to appear like one? Was he, perchance, the man who stabbed the prince; a Templar in disguise?"

He slammed both hands on the desk and then waved the two men away. "Find out!" he shouted as they exited, "and keep me informed!"

CHAPTER 25
1240 A.D.
The Celestial Visitors

For almost a week, Jawad had been incarcerated in the squalid cell. Some of the monks had been treating the knife wound in his chest, but it had become infected. That was hardly surprising, considering that he had been repeatedly tortured and questioned, beaten and sleep deprived. There was nothing he could tell them, other than what he had seen and experienced, but his tale seemed so far-fetched, that the interrogation had continued unabated.

Now, as all hope of escape had left him, things were about to get even more bizarre. Having slept for several hours, his first descent into sleep for some time, he was awoken by a man's shout. He looked up and saw two of his regular visitors, the monks, backed up against the wall opposite the cell door. Their faces were white with fear and sickly-looking; their eyes were transfixed, in an almost unblinking stare. The prince turned his head very slowly to see what it was that was terrifying these holy men to such a degree. As his head began to move, he noticed the side of the room to his left was drenched in light. His own heart began to pound, and he felt beads of sweat slowly dripping from his forehead, running down his face and clinging to his clothes. As the sweating continued, he began to shiver, and his heart thumped faster and faster. By the time he caught sight of the visitors he was struggling to breathe and was fighting to prevent himself from passing out as the blood went rushing to his head.

Suddenly, he saw the most awesome vision. Standing in front of the cell door, dressed in golden armour, and standing almost eight feet in height, were two beings that appeared to be made from the most intense light. Their faces could barely be made out, although they seemed to be human in both shape and form. Despite their brightness, however, they emitted no heat and Jawad knew all too well that his sweating was the product of immense terror. His hands were shaking and as he glanced to his right, he noticed that one of the monks was lying on the ground between the strangers and himself.

"Fear not Jawad," one of the creatures said in a voice that was concurrently soothing and authoritative.

Jawad looked at them, first one, then the other. He kept glancing at them quickly, but neither could be distinguished from the other one. They were identical, not only in appearance, but also in voice and mannerisms. Seconds had passed, although to Jawad and the monks, it seemed like an eternity. As they sat, transfixed, the second visitor spoke.

"We are Messengers of the Almighty One. We have only one purpose and that is to assist you prince. We have been granted all the powers necessary for us to achieve that."

He smiled at Jawad and then continued.

"Our role is to heal you, free you, direct you to the princess and advise you on how to free her. We have no other role so do not ask us for anything more than this unless you wish to be disappointed."

Jawad's eyes peered down at the motionless monk on the floor before him.

"Fear not Jawad; he is alive. He fainted when we entered the room. And be assured that before wc leave, we will calm all of these servants of God."

Jawad was still filled with anxiety and fear, so he was a little surprised by the question he then asked, since it seemed somewhat trivial in the circumstances.

"Pray, tell me, how do I distinguish between you?"

The being to his left stepped forwards, causing Jawad to shift backwards towards the wall behind him, and bringing on an agonising stab of pain in his chest. The stranger smiled and reached out a hand towards the prince.

"There is no need to know us, or to distinguish us from one another," he said. "Just take heed of whatever we say to you and please, stay calm."

His voice was comforting and as he spoke, he moved his hand closer to Jawad, who flinched.

"Please trust us Jawad. You are wounded, and we can heal you."

Warily, Jawad relaxed and nodded his willingness to trust them. Then, albeit rather submissively, he held out his own hand and took hold of the visitor, who continued to speak.

"I am going to remove your shirt and when I do so I want you to place your other hand upon the wound. Then, listen to what I say and believe it with all your heart."

After a brief pause, he pulled open the shirt, waited for Jawad to place his hand over the wound and then asked whether the prince was ready. After acknowledgement he continued.

"The human brain—your mind—is a wondrous piece of architecture. It controls your bodily functions and without conscious thought, you can walk, talk, eat and ride, simply because your brain orders your body to do so. However, it can be trained. It can be made to control other functions; other bodily behaviours."

Jawad was mesmerised by his words and the monks were equally captivated.

"It can also order the body to ward off attackers, such as bacteria, poisons and disease," he continued. "Thus, the brain can order the body to heal itself, so if the Almighty One desires that your brain should do this for you, so it shall be."

The messengers both closed their eyes and their brightness magnified.

"Now, Jawad, concentrate all your mind's energies on your wound. Exhaust your thoughts on that single task!"

The prince did so. For several minutes, he meditated and concentrated, while the monks, both now conscious and transfixed, sat like helpless rabbits caught in the glare of the beam of light. Their mouths dropped open in disbelief, as gradually, miraculously, the wound began to heal. Eventually, there was nothing but a small scar, but by then the prince was exhausted and could barely keep his eyes open.

"I must find the woman. She may have saved my life, for she distracted my assailant. If he had pulled the knife from my chest, I may have bled to death." He spoke in a whisper and staggered against the wall.

The two messengers caught hold of his arms and the three of them began to de-materialise until they were gone. The cell-like room was once again in darkness, save for the flickering light of a small candle nestled beside Jawad's now empty bed. The monks now lay unconscious on the floor of the cell and, by the time Bohemond would discover them, Jawad would be long gone and en route to Syria.

CHAPTER 26
1240 A.D.
The Mission Begins

The two extraordinary spirit creatures carried Jawad across space and time, reappearing outside Acre's city walls, not far from the spot where he had been stabbed and left for dead. Feeling quite perplexed after his ordeal, he stood impassively, statue-like, and waited for further instructions from his rescuers. By now, there was no doubt in his mind that these two beings were no apparition. They were very real, perfect examples of purity and immaculacy. They were virginal in their splendour, unadulterated, undefiled… without doubt, Holy!

Despite his initial reservations and fears, he now felt obliged to trust them implicitly. He found it impossible to doubt their word and felt that for them to be dishonourable was unthinkable.

As he pondered this, one of them pointed to a tiny dirt track, heavily marked with the traces of the horse and cart that had carried Marie away just two days earlier.

"If you follow those tracks, they will take you to the main route that runs from here to Syria. A number of weeks' ride and you will reach the Citadel of Salah Ed-Din, where the Knights Templar are holding the Lady Marie."

"Lady?" he said. "That vagabond?"

"She is Raymond's daughter."

As he listened to them, Jawad was startled by the unexpected appearance of a grey Arab stallion. Where it came from, he would probably never know, but there it was in all its glory, waiting for him to mount it and embark upon a labour of love—his quest.

"Syria is a dangerous place for a young poet," continued the messenger. "This horse will outrun any other in the known world and…"

At this moment, he produced a large, curved sword, gleaming at its diamond-studded hilt… "This weapon will protect you," he said. "The minute you clasp it with the intention of using it in battle, it will guide your arm, but that will not be enough. To make of you a fine swordsman, you must be trained."

He held out the sword to Jawad, who accepted it with humility, and with all the manners expected of royalty.

"I swear to do my duty," he said, "to free the princess and to slaughter those who have treacherously and malevolently abducted her!"

He began to swing the sword viciously around his head but one of the messengers quickly rebuked him.

"Hold fast your anger, young prince! Your mission will not succeed if it is based in any way upon your personal emotions. You must not undertake this task to satisfy your love of a woman, or your hatred of any man, but simply because justice must be done and be seen to be done."

Jawad lowered the sword and asked them what they meant by needing to be trained. The two messengers started to speak in unison.

"The sword we have given you will remain firmly in its sheath if your intention is to fight or kill out of anger, pain or humiliation. Serve the Powerful One, seek to remove injustice and prevent evil, and you will surely excel, for the truly conquering hero must first conquer himself. But, in Syria, you will meet someone who will give you the training you require."

They waved him away and he mounted his horse. Despite his reservations, he set off on his journey into the dragon's mouth. He pulled on the reins and moved off, turning to bid farewell to the two emissaries, but they were already gone. He was now alone. Ironically, perhaps, a greater, deeper fear overcame him; greater than he had experienced when the Seraphs had first appeared; greater than that he had felt as the dagger plunged into him on this scrubland outside of Acre—the fear of loneliness and the unknown. His thoughts wandered, finally resting upon the Franj girl who had so enamoured him.

"I will find you," he said, under his breath. "I am coming for you now."

CHAPTER 27
1240 A.D.
The Haunting

Tension was mounting in Jerusalem and Acre, as an increasing number of reports of paranormal experiences circulated in both cities. Sightings of ghouls, spectres, angels of light and howling devils, had reached almost epidemic proportions. One would have been excused for thinking that the whole of the Holy Land was being overrun by demons. There was talk, especially among the religious orders, that this was a punishment for secular ambitions in Palestine. This tension and rampant paranoia culminated in a young urchin boy calling out, from his corner of one of Jerusalem's narrow streets, that the holy men were forecasting the coming of the Antichrist and the Messiah.

"Save your soul and give me bread," he called, although most believed it was simply a cynical form of begging.

There was, in fact, a battle underway already in the Holy Land. The armies of Zaman and Iblis were vying for influence among the humans. Demons spent hours misleading them, enticing them, deceiving them, frightening them and destroying them, while those Jinn in the service of Zaman worked hard to eradicate the devils' influences.

At the heart of all this indiscernible activity, the military men refused to believe the stories of mysticism emanating from their holy men. Each side blamed the occurrences on their temporal enemies. The Muslim Saracens and Turks blamed the Franj and the Franj accused the Arabs and their allies.

In Acre Raymond was angry. Not only had he lost an important prisoner, and perhaps the only man who could reveal to him the whereabouts of his daughter, but the monks who had allowed him to escape spent all their hours babbling about angels. He banged his fist on the table, across which he then swept his hand, knocking a knife and candelabra to the floor.

"If we don't get a grip on this situation Bohemond," he shouted, "we will destroy ourselves from within!"

He began pacing up and down the room, stopping every few minutes and pounding his right fist into the now sweaty palm of his left hand. Then, suddenly, he stopped. He turned to face Bohemond and fixed a stare upon him—an elegant smile gradually appearing on his face.

"Tell me Bohemond, who is the most easily corruptible priest in Acre?" he asked, but before his right-hand man could answer he continued, "Which one of them can we most easily persuade?"

Bohemond looked a little confused and raised an enquiring eyebrow. Nevertheless, he answered, after a sigh.

"Probably Michael of York, sir, an Englishman of very weak character, but well-liked by the people."

Raymond nodded in satisfaction. "Perfect!" he said. "Order him to persuade the people of Acre that these mystical manifestations are the direct result of witchcraft practised by the Jews and the heathen Mohammedans. Once the people blame them for all their ills… well, then we will go to war against Jerusalem."

"But sir, what about the treaty?"

Raymond stared reproachfully at his officer. "Treaty?" he questioned, as he crossed back to his desk, picked up a small scroll and set it alight. "Do you mean this treaty?"

Bohemond blushed. "I'm sorry sir. I will of course proceed with your orders immediately."

The big man left the room, thinking to himself that his leader had responded impulsively, and perhaps irresponsibly. He began muttering these thoughts to himself as he left the building, but he felt somewhat constrained by rank to follow the orders he had received.

Later that day he met up with Amalric and they discussed all the events that had occurred since the escape of the prisoners they had so desperately sought in the hills around Jerusalem. They were seated in a dingy inn, close to the outskirts of Acre. Each had a container of ale and they planned to get increasingly drunk while they talked.

"Something's wrong." Bohemond looked his friend right in the eye. "Do you remember that raid on the gypsies in northern Spain?"

Amalric was slightly taken aback by Bohemond's question but nodded. "Of course."

"I said at the time that things weren't right. The raped girl accused the travellers and we fell upon them in the night like demons from Hell, slaughtering them all—men, women, children. My God man, I'll never rid those images from my mind. I still lose sleep over that raid."

Amalric's gaze dropped and his head followed but he tried to offer some level of comfort to his disturbed friend.

"We must keep reminding ourselves that the atrocities were committed by Cedric and his men, not us."

"But we did nothing to stop it."

"We cannot change what is done my friend."

"I said at the time that her story didn't sound right, remember?" Bohemond added.

Amalric nodded. "And who was it that brought her to us? Cedric. And who was it who mutilated the dead gypsies, raped their women, even raped young girls and butchered women who were pregnant, ripping the unborn child from their wombs?

Bohemond nodded again, then sighed. He stared at the floor. "Cedric," he muttered. "Then, after the camp was destroyed, we heard of a further rape and then another and another. We caught him, this monster who was raping and dishonouring our daughters and sisters and he wasn't even a traveller. He was one of us, a soldier."

"He was one of Cedric's men and you killed him. It's over Bohemond."

"I did, but he refused to point the finger at Cedric, yet I know he was involved. How he rose in the ranks after that day."

He paused and shook his head. "And the feelings I had then, I have now. Something's wrong. This Poet Prince is not the enemy and I don't believe the Emir or any of his loyal people have a part to play in Marie's kidnapping. Yet, we prepare for war against them."

Amalric said nothing. There was nothing that could be said, for Bohemond was just speaking his mind, not looking for a response. In fact, he did not give his colleague the chance to offer one. The conversation moved on, the two men got progressively worse for wear with ale and, at the end of the night, Bohemond left the inn, leaving Amalric to his thoughts.

CHAPTER 28
1240 A.D.
Arslan

In Jerusalem, tension was at fever pitch. While the haunting continued, Abdul Qadoos stood by his window, staring indifferently at a page of writing. It was clear from his vacant staring at one part of the page that he was not actually reading it. His thoughts lay elsewhere and the sudden unannounced entrance of Arslan snapped him disturbingly from his trance-like state. The Turk looked anxious and spoke without waiting for permission. As he did so his scar seemed to glow as the blood rushed around his face.

"Sir, we have received news concerning the Emir's son and Habash, but...

Abdul Qadoos looked up sharply at his visitor, visibly annoyed at being so brashly disturbed, but Arslan continued.

"I'm afraid it's not good news sir."

He proceeded to inform the General of the murder of Habash, adding that they had received word from a shepherd boy, who was unsure of the identity of the assailants. Abdul Qadoos, meanwhile, toyed with his beard and, while not appearing nervous, did seem more thoughtful and pensive than normal.

"You say there is news of the Emir's son. Do you mean Jawad or Abbas?" he asked quietly.

Arslan continued: "The boy arrived at the entrance to Acre as Franj soldiers were carrying an Arab man into the city. He couldn't be sure if it was a dead body or an injured man and..."

"What of the children, Arslan? What of Ahmed, my son; your son, Hassan, and the young prince, Abbas?"

The General's voice was not raised but was firm and commanding. Arslan, in turn, was not in the least flustered by Abdul Qadoos' growing impatience. His response was calm but cautious.

"Please bear with me sir, for the news of young Ahmed is not good" he replied, stepping towards the Saracen officer.

"You are concealing. If there is unwelcome news about my son, I wish to hear it, NOW!"

Arslan took a deep breath and then continued.

"The bodies of your son and Habash have been found on the outskirts of Jerusalem sir. I am so very sorry."

Arslan paused, rubbed his hand over his head and licked his very dry lips. Then, lowering his arms to his side he took a deep breath and spoke again.

"Clearly, the Franj have Jawad, either in a jail or in a morgue."

Abdul Qadoos stood up, put on his sword and clipped a small, curved knife to his belt. He showed no emotion upon hearing the fate of his youngest son, but Arslan could see beyond the façade. The warrior would not show his distress to Arslan or anyone else, not even his wife, to whom he would have to break the awful news later. In private, however, his grief would manifest itself in a flood of tears, followed by a display of utmost anger. The latter would spill beyond his private chambers and emerge in public.

He placed a hand on Arslan's shoulder, thanked him, and then stepped into an adjacent room. The door closed behind him and he remained there for several hours. The tears did come as he thought of his son, of those precious few hours they had spent together, of the boy's smile and of his voice. His voice, which now seemed to echo in the General's mind, lingering long after the actual memory had passed.

Arslan waited. He dared not to attempt to disturb Abdul Qadoos. He simply waited until the officer re-emerged from the room bringing his anger with him.

"I am losing patience with the entire situation," he said as he leaned on his huge, wooden table. "I want an army prepared by the end of this month, and that gives us fifteen days. Is that clear Arslan?"

"Yes sir, it is, but…"

"Don't argue with me Arslan. Remember your place." The officer's voice was calm, and his eyes stared coldly into Arslan's.

After a moment's hesitation the Turk saluted and left the room full of fear and apprehension of war. Sweat began to drip from his brow and an uneasy feeling came over him. His stomach began to turn in fearful anticipation and he recalled the last battle with the crusaders, in which his older brother fell and died. Tears welled up in his eyes as he pictured his brother's blood-soaked head resting in his arms, just before he lost his final grip on life. Arslan pondered the future. If he felt another war could be prevented, he would not feel this fear, but it all seemed so inevitable now, without the intervention of a miracle.

Not long after Arslan had left his quarters, Abdul Qadoos was summoned to the office of the Emir on the other side of Jerusalem. He arrived there within the hour, nervous and anxious as he had very little news for the Emir about his sons. He also knew that the Emir would be exhausted after his journey from Damascus, and he was usually cantankerous when tired. All of this would likely lead to an angry confrontation between the two men.

The officer entered the Emir's room and waited for permission to speak. Once given, he went over the background to the events of the past few days, and the Emir listened in silence. He sat on an elaborate and ornate couch, fiddling all the while with a set of pearl prayer beads, which clicked together in a steady rhythm. It was, however, the Emir's silence that Abdul Qadoos found most unsettling and soon he could stand it no longer.

"Sir, er, Your Highness? Please say something."

The Emir took a very deep breath and laid his beads carefully upon the couch. He was dressed in the finest white silk robe, around the waist of which was a belt, made from rope that had been plated with the most ornate cable of gold. His hair was short, although not out of choice, for he was clearly going bald. His beard was long, trailing over his chest as he reclined on the couch. Both hair and beard had been dyed with bright red henna to conceal the grey, which, together with his hair loss, would have revealed his advancing age. Looking at this man it would be easy to doubt that Abbas was his son, the child being so young. He was born out of wedlock, after the Emir took a liking to young and nubile woman. He had come across her during a raid on Christian forces a decade earlier. The woman had seemed lost and, perhaps through shock, would not speak. She said she was a slave and she seemed so vulnerable. Her beauty, however, was unquestionable. He wanted her from the moment he saw her and what he wanted, he usually got, but when her pregnancy was revealed, some months later, a sense of panic overcame him. He was not concerned about his wives, back in Jerusalem, but of his reputation for this was not another wife, which would be acceptable to Muslims. This was a mistress, which was not.

He took her to his palace in Jerusalem as a servant for one of his wives and when the child was born, that very wife took the baby and brought her up as her own. The servant girl was exiled and never seen again, and the secret was kept firmly within the family for several years. That was, until Sieffuddeen discovered the truth from a soldier who was being punished for drunkenness. The Emir's reputation suffered a blow, but his power never dwindled as a result. He would, however, endure the whisperings of people about his bastard son, Abbas, forevermore.

As the Emir pondered his son's fate, his expression was sullen, and it did not alter when he spoke.

"You have my deepest sympathy for the loss of your son, Abdul Qadoos, but I worry that your grief is driving your decisions. Are you saying that we should go to war? Please, sum up precisely what you are saying," he said sternly.

Abdul Qadoos breathed deeply and prayed that the Emir's apparent anger would gradually recede.

"We can only presume that Habash and my son were murdered by the Franj sir. It was, I believe, a Frankish knife that killed Habash, and a European crossbow bolt that was used to murder my boy. As for His Royal Highness, Prince Jawad, we know nothing more than that which we heard from the shepherd." He paused momentarily and then tried to shift the emphasis of the conversation. "With all due respect sir, I am more concerned that this city is at risk of tearing itself apart over these rumoured spiritual visitations."

"And so you should be!" the Emir retorted angrily.

He waited for a moment before continuing and leaned forward, placing his elbows on his thighs. Then he nodded.

"Very well! Prepare for war, but in the meantime, try negotiation and report back to me within forty-eight hours."

CHAPTER 29
1240 A.D.
The Premonition

The following morning, Ahmed was buried in the Islamic tradition, wrapped only in a white cloth and laid in the earth. There was no coffin, and the funeral was not a large affair. Excessive grieving was not what Abdul Qadoos wanted. He wanted his son to be buried, some prayers to be spoken and the chance to find the men responsible for his murder. He shed no tears and displayed no other emotions. He even seemed to filter out the screams and wails of Ahmed's mother and the other women who had attended the funeral.

When the last piece of earth was thrown over the grave, Abdul Qadoos returned to his quarters, walked to a small window and looked out onto the palace courtyard where some days earlier the Emir's sons had stood arguing. He could not help but wonder whether Sieffuddeen had some hand in all that was happening, but wonder was all he could do.

The courtyard was busy this day and on the opposite side people were teeming into a small Mosque, while to his left he could see the outline of the larger Al-Aqsa Mosque. All around he could hear the voices of the Imams, the religious leaders of the Muslims, preaching doom and calamity to the worshippers who had flocked into the Mosques since the visitations began.

His eyes returned to the courtyard and he listened to the mingling of the sounds of voices, church bells and singing birds. So absorbed was he in his thoughts that he failed to notice that Arslan had once again entered the room. The Atabeg coughed quietly to attract his commander's attention and Abdul Qadoos turned around slowly.

"Ah, it's you," he sighed, and then turned back to the window where he continued to stare down at the dusty courtyard. "The Emir will have to climb the steps of the pulpit at Al-Aqsa and speak to the people, I'm afraid. He will have to convince them that these apparitions are a punishment from God—a punishment because our people have allowed foreign armies to occupy parts of Palestine."

Arslan said nothing and Abdul Qadoos began pacing the room. His thoughts flittered from one idea to another and his pacing was becoming increasingly uncomfortable for Arslan. The Turkish Atabeg wondered whether his General should be left with decision-making of such immense importance, when he was so obviously racked with grief. As Arslan considered reporting his feelings to the Emir, Abdul Qadoos suddenly stopped pacing. He looked directly into Arslan's eyes.

"I remember the stories, Arslan, of a barbarian people from the northernmost regions of Europe, who devastated the Crusaders' lands. They left pain, death and misery in their wake."

He paused again, smiled, and then spoke with deliberation and with a certain degree of personal satisfaction.

"I have had a premonition which must be conveyed to our people, Arslan. It is of a worse enemy than these Northmen, an enemy that will burst through the barrier of Alexander the Great as hordes from Hell and wreak havoc, such as none have seen before in our lands". Abdul Qadoos analysed the reaction of his friend, but Arslan's face revealed nothing, so the General continued.

"We must convince the Emir to persuade the people of this. Then we can proceed to war against the Franj, for it is they who have weakened our defences against future enemies."

He turned and smiled at Arslan. The Turk knew there had been no vision and that Abdul Qadoos was merely referring to events that spies had reported on in the East; events that ordinary people knew nothing about. *Is he losing his mind?* He thought. *Does he believe he has had a premonition? Or is this a very cunning plan?*

His thoughts were interrupted, as the General placed a hand on his shoulder and said, "But first…" He paused briefly. "First, we will attempt negotiation, so send a letter to Raymond."

Arslan issued a sigh of relief and then acknowledged the command. He started to leave, when Abdul Qadoos added, wryly "Demand too much."

"I beg your pardon, sir?"

"In the letter, demand too much."

In Acre, Raymond was also arranging for a messenger to be sent. Hearing from his spies that the bodies of Ahmed and Habash had been found and that the Muslims believed they had been murdered by Christians, he wished to calm the situation. His messenger left Acre moments before Abdul Qadoos' messenger left Jerusalem.

CHAPTER 30
A Historical Account

Zaydussia was also full of tension and Zaman was clearly agitated. The peace was brief and now the war continued to rage. Zaman's forces were being depleted, slowly but surely. He looked out from a small window, at the expanse of land surrounding the citadel. Then his eyes moved to the Eastern sector, where the enemy was gaining the most ground. He shook his head in despair.

"Iblis is winning, my children. He is stirring the humans to war again. If we don't act quickly to return you to your world, I fear things will only get worse."

He turned away from the window, crossed the room and caught hold of the boys by their arms, half shaking them as he spoke.

"Listen carefully. You are men now and you have a mission; to seek out Jawad and Marie and let them know what is happening. They will have to go to the Emir and to Raymond and convince them that war against each other should be avoided at all costs. They need to be made aware of the identities of their true enemies. If that is not possible, you must warn your fathers in Jerusalem."

He eased his grip on the boys' clothes and continued.

"The Saracen General conjured a premonition from his own imagination, based loosely on intelligence information he had received from the lands East of Palestine. I am not convinced that he realised how accurate his statement was. Mongol hordes, Gog and Magog, are at this very moment in time ravaging Asia. They will, inevitably, turn their attention to Persia and the Arab lands."

Hassan stared at Zaman, refusing to take his eye from him for even a split second.

"What is it Hassan? What is on your mind?"

The teenager continued to stare, without blinking, and at first appeared reluctant to speak. Then, with some trepidation, he questioned the Overseer.

"You're not telling us everything are you? It is not just the Templars or the Hashisheen, or Sieffuddeen, is it? How did the European invasion succeed in the first place? I thought the Arab Empire was strong, so why are we in this mess?"

Zaman sighed. He knew that Hassan needed to know the answers to all these questions, but he felt that he still might not be ready to accept the fact that much of the blame rested with his own people. Nevertheless, the boy was growing increasingly impatient.

"Well?" he shouted. "Stop treating me like a child and tell me!"

The Overseer seated Hassan comfortably on two cushions and sent the younger boy away to play. Then he began to narrate the events that had led up to the European invasion of the Holy Land.

"The Jinn under my command are the descendants of Shesah, Masah, Alhamlakan, Marzeban, Mazeman, Nasah, Sahib, Hazib and Amer, who were the first group of Jinn that accepted the call to serve the Almighty One. Ever since, the events of the world have been carefully monitored and recorded, by those of us who reject the Evil One."

As he spoke, the hologram began to reveal the region's history in incredible detail.

"Your Prophet tried to take his people to a higher spiritual level of understanding, and it is certain that some of his followers were more spiritually aware than others. His son-in-law, Ali, and his grandsons, Hassan and Hussein, were given superior spiritual and mystical insight, and their descendants, plus their very close followers, continued in this vein. Unfortunately, most people were, and probably always will be, secularist empire-builders, more obsessed with material improvement than spiritual development."

Hassan was mesmerised. The holographic images, combined with Zaman's explanation, had brought the past to life for him. It was as if he were there, seeing history unfolding before his eyes and, as his mind was flooded with all these images, Zaman continued.

"Some of the Caliphs spend their spare time studying books on the unseen arts, the occult crafts and, as predicted by Abdul Qadoos, new hordes of Gog and Magog will tear into the Arab and Persian lands. First, they will set about destroying the material structure of society, but gradually they will convert to the Caliphs' religion, enabling them to tear it apart from within."

Zaman was endeavouring to be careful about what he was saying, for he knew it could be taken the wrong way by the Turkish youth who sat before him. He hesitated briefly, and Hassan looked up at him, urging him to continue.

"These hordes will come from the Steppes, north of the Oxus River and some of them will write lies about your Prophet almost two hundred years after his death. They will attack his family and create extremist schools of thought of varying persuasions."

Hassan looked disturbed, but Zaman continued.

"They will suck the spiritual heart out of the region until only a handful of mystics and pietists remain and your lands are in turmoil. Sultans will fight other sultans; brothers will kill brothers and invasion by new waves of foreigners is inevitable. The Seljuks were followed by the crusades of the European forces and their defeat will leave you weakened. The Caliphate will be subdued by a savage monster, led by the Khan."

Hassan's face had turned quite pale and he was shaking his head, his lips locked together, and his nostrils flared. In fact, he was snorting like a bull ready to charge.

"What are you saying? What on earth are you saying? I am a Turk! I am a descendent of those very steppe people you speak of! Are you saying we are Gog or Magog? Are you calling me an enemy of God?"

By now, the boy was on his feet and marching around the room like a soldier without a parade, banging his fist against any object that was within reach. Zaman approached him and tried to calm him down.

"Hassan. Of course, I am not saying that. All I am suggesting is that the Turkish hordes, the Seljuks, who smashed into the lands around Arabia and infiltrated life there, were of Gog and Magog, and that they weakened the Muslim Empire, and that *some* of them were corrupt. Their relations, the Mongols, led by the Khan, will wreak yet more havoc. I make no comment on individual descendants of those people, like you."

Hassan kept his distance from the Overseer and still seemed to lack trust.

"I don't know whether to believe you or not. I think I trust you; we both do, but I know how adults exaggerate stories of the past to strengthen their argument. I may be young, but my mind is not. Anyway, I thank you for your story."

Zaman smiled and asked Hassan to fetch Abbas.

"It is time you got some rest, for tomorrow you both leave for the Ridge of Fertheron. I will not speak of the past with you anymore, unless you ask me to. It is, after all, the future with which we must all concern ourselves now."

In another part of the Jinn world, Shaytaan was sending his own agent to stop Raymond's messenger. He called for a female Jinni called Niamh, a beautiful Succubus, whose job it was to carry men to the land of youth. Instructions were given, and Niamh left.

As Raymond's messenger rode hard towards Jerusalem, a fierce wind suddenly appeared in front of him, startling his horse, which then threw the messenger to the ground. He struck the ground hard, his head striking a rock, knocking him unconscious. In this altered state of consciousness, he found himself in the Jinn world, the realm of dreams. Awake and confused in this alien world, he was met by Niamh. She was naked, and he felt himself growing sexually aroused even before she touched him. Her hands reached for his crotch and then she kissed him, mesmerising him. Almost instantly, they were making love, no longer in the open expanse where they had been before, but in a soft bed, in a large chamber.

"Will you stay with me?" She asked. "Forever?"

The messenger, all memory of his mission gone, nodded and his fate was sealed. He would remain with Niamh, lost in a purgatory until the end of time. His earthly body, lying at the roadside, not far from Acre, was dead.

CHAPTER 31
Reappearance

Hassan's sleep was shattered in the morning by the sound of chatter, like that of apes or monkeys. Periodically, he heard what seemed to be words. He tiptoed across to the door to listen and it was perhaps this movement that had stirred Abbas. The younger boy sat up with a start.

"What's going on? Who's there?"

"Calm down and be quiet," Hassan replied, pressing his right ear to the door. "I can't make out what they're saying. It's just gibberish."

His eavesdropping was brought to an abrupt halt as the door burst open, knocking him to the marble floor. It felt like ice beneath him and he slid backwards until he struck the bed with his head.

"Ow!"

He was going to complain more, but his thoughts were interrupted by the vague outline of a man standing over him. At first the man's features were indiscernible; he seemed almost like an apparition. Then, gradually, his form was revealed, and the complexions of both boys paled. They looked quite ill; no... more than that. They appeared to be in a state of shock, fear and total disbelief.

"Th... this can't be... you can't be here."

Hassan's voice trembled, and he was sweating. His breathing was heavy, and it quickened until it was more akin to an exhausted pant, after a ten-mile run.

"It's just not possible. It's against nature. You're dead! I saw you fall! I saw you die! I don't believe..."

The man spliced through Hassan's mutterings as if slicing rope with a scimitar, and he nodded.

"You did see me fall, Hassan, I grant you that, but you did not see me die."

Abbas' shrill voice suddenly pierced the air and rather took the other

145

two by surprise.

"You can't die, can you, because you're a Jinni!"

Zenith laughed. He lifted Hassan off the floor and laid him gently on the bed beside Abbas. Then he sat down with them, carefully manoeuvring his sword as he did so, a heart-warming smile on his face.

"Oh Abbas, our lives are no more infinite in duration than your own. Granted, we live longer, and time here moves more slowly, but death still catches up with us eventually."

Abbas fidgeted nervously, and his irritability began to irritate the others.

"Oh, what is it Abbas?" asked Hassan, impatiently.

Zenith repeated the question in a more casual manner, as it was apparent to him that the boy was eager to say something.

"You won't punish me, will you?" he asked, timidly.

Zenith frowned, a little perturbed by the boy's question.

"For what?" he asked.

"For what I'm about to ask, that's what!"

"And why should I do that?"

"Well, my parents and the Imams always punish me when I ask this, so maybe you will too."

Zenith rested a comforting hand on Abbas' shoulder and pulled the child towards him.

"My child, you can only learn by asking questions. If your questions are answered with wisdom and honesty, without bigotry or flippancy, then you will surely gain in knowledge and wisdom. True knowledge, complete understanding, can only improve us, so please ask away."

Abbas sighed, and smiled, hesitantly.

"All right. Is it possible for anyone to know for sure what happens to us after we die?"

Zenith raised his eyebrows and sighed.

"All that is certain is that eventually we will all die, but the time and circumstances of our death are unknown to us, and the aftermath of death can only be assumed."

"What do you mean?" This time the question came from Hassan.

"Many of us believe in a life after death, but we cannot prove it. We can only try to explain our belief through logic and intellectual argument,

146

but ultimately all belief possesses personal understanding which differs from person to person and which cannot be explained."

Zenith shook his head and stood up.

"Look, I'm just confusing you. When you're older you can study it all for yourself. Then, perhaps, you will understand what I am saying to you now."

Moving towards the door, he clapped his hands together and then rubbed them, as if excited about something.

"Come on then. It's time to leave now. Zaydussia is a vast Kingdom and the Ridge of Fertheron is at its most easterly edge. The Dark One's forces continue to place us under considerable pressure and time does not favour us, even here."

"Yeah, so we keep being told," replied Hassan.

Zenith led the boys out of the room and down a long, dark corridor to a marble hall, in the centre of which, on a transparent table, were three suits of armour. Lifting two of them up and holding them out towards the boys, the Jinni asked them to put them on and they found them surprisingly light, despite their appearance. They were not at all like the chain mail worn by the European knights. They felt more like the silk robes of the Emir's wives and were no heavier than that. They were also soft to touch and, after sliding into them, the boys giggled as they did them up.

"What are these for?" asked Hassan, who seemed to think that wearing them would serve no purpose at all. "How can such thin pieces of cloth protect us from anything?"

"These suits will protect us from the weapons of the dark ones, because they generate a defensive field of energy, comprised of forces which will be unknown to humankind for thousands of years."

By this time, Hassan was parading around the room in his new clothes, like a peacock impressing its mate.

"Oh, yeah, it should be easy for Zaman's troops to defeat Iblis wearing these," he said, sarcastically. "Look at us boys, with our stunning suits; we'll kill you with envy."

Abbas giggled, but Zenith just sighed and shook his head. He did up his own suit and replaced his sword, sheath and belt.

"Unfortunately, the materials used in the construction of these clothes are in extremely short supply. We only have ten of these in the entire Kingdom. They are produced in an isolated city situated on another Jinn world far from here."

He led the boys by the hand, out of the hall, and along another dark corridor. This one was partly lit by flame-free lamps and carpeted with a thick pile. All along the walls, metallic panelling was half-covered by rich blue curtains that hung from ceiling to floor. At the end of the corridor, Zenith pushed open a heavy metal door. A hiss of released air accompanied the movement of the door and a rush of wind struck their faces, as it swung open.

Initially, the doorway appeared to lead nowhere. They were high above the ground and there seemed to be no way of descending from the Palace. The children edged cautiously towards the doorway and, nervously, they looked down. Clouds drifted across the sky beneath them and the occasional gap between the puffs of white revealed the terrifying drop from the Palace to the ground below.

Gently, Zenith pushed the boys apart to enable him to pass them. To their surprise, he stepped straight through the doorway into mid-air, without falling. He stood before them, defying gravity, floating effortlessly in the sky. Hassan naturally assumed he was flying again and that he would grab them before flying them gently down to the ground, as he did from the cliff beside the Forest of Traveller's Needs. However, Zenith turned away from them and started to walk off. He seemed to be stepping down an invisible staircase.

"Wait! What about us!" the boys shouted, in unison.

"Follow me," he replied, instantaneously.

They looked at each other and Hassan raised an eyebrow as if to say, *well here we go again*, and he was about to step out of the door when Abbas rushed towards it and shouted out at Zenith.

"Wait! Why can't you fly us down!?" he asked.

Zenith waved his hands up and down the protective suit he was wearing and shook his head.

"What, wearing this?" he called back.

It was then that Hassan noticed the Jinni's translucent wings were hidden inside the suit. He wasted no more time and took his first tentative step onto the invisible staircase. He half believed there would be no stairs there and that his first step would also be his last. Unsurprisingly, therefore, he yelped with joy when his foot met the unseen stairway.

"It's OK," he called out to Abbas, although he did not turn to face the smaller boy. He just kept on going, until he reached Zenith some six or seven steps down. Abbas' attempt was even more cautious than Hassan's. He held the doorframe firmly and then warily stretched out his right leg to try to feel the step. Hassan looked up at his friend who looked a little like someone carefully testing the temperature of bath water.

"Come on Abbas. You heard what Zaman said!"

Abbas called back. "Yes, I know, time is not with us."

Hassan laughed and then muttered quietly to himself, *I really meant that we are men now, so he should show courage, but what the heck.*

Zenith set off again, calling back to the boys as he plodded on down the steps.

"Keep directly behind me. The stairs are not very wide."

It seemed to take hours to reach the bottom, although they had actually completed their descent in less than ten minutes. At the base of the stairway was a lake, surrounded by trees and shrubs and on the far side of the deep, blue water, Hassan could just make out an outlet to a river.

"Is that where we're headed?" he asked, pointing to a path through a wooded area, across the lake.

"Yes, the path follows the river and will lead us to the Ridge of Fertheron. From there, you will be transported back to your own world, but we have less than two of your earth days in which to do it."

CHAPTER 32
Iblis

Iblis, the Prince of Darkness, gazed upon a large crystal the size of a horse. He sat on a purple throne, decorated with the carved heads of ogres and other macabre creatures. His spirit servants surrounded him, most of them standing silently, staring at him in awe.

Iblis, the being nicknamed, among other things, the Father of Lies, stared impassively at moving images of Zenith and his companions in the crystal.

Paradoxically, Iblis' appearance was extremely handsome and his obvious wealth, power and display of ostentation, gave him an impression of pre-eminence. This was highlighted by the obsequious nature of the spirit folk who gathered to kiss his hands and feet. His voice was neither harsh, nor terrifying and yet it was also not soft or beseeching. It was firm but in an unusual way, pleasant like that of a mesmerist. The creatures around him knew, however, that it concealed his ruthless and sadistic nature.

He tugged at a thick, red cloak that hung from his shoulders. His hands pulled the two corners of the cloak around his body and he watched the crystal thoughtfully. The ghouls and demons were chattering and cackling, while some even fought to get near to their Master. Their noise was steadily growing louder and louder until Iblis could stand it no longer.

"*SILENCE!*" he yelled.

His face had become contorted and hideous. His eyes were wide open, and he bared his teeth, sharp, with extended canines, like those of an angry dog. As he began to calm back down, his face shimmered between the ugliness that revealed his true character and the stunning good looks of his masque. Response to his order was immediate. A silence fell upon the cavern and all within its walls stood motionless as he rose out of his seat.

"That annoying Jinni continues to be a nuisance to me. Within two days he will have reached the Ridge of Fertheron with the humans, so we will have to move quickly."

His voice was now calm, although it disguised a trace of sadistic pleasure and he smiled wryly, lifted his cloak a little, and then sat back down.

"The younger boy is mine and I shall have him."

In fact, Abbas was his, in a roundabout way. The servant girl who had given birth to Abbas a decade earlier was, in fact, a Jinni; not just any Jinni, but the daughter of Iblis himself. But his daughter died from an unexpected illness and the boy was brought up by his human father's maid servants.

His plan was for the half Jinni, half human boy to be taken by his mother, into the depths of Iblis' domain, where he would be educated in the ways of the evil Jinn. As a man, he would find human women and father demon children, who would take positions of great power in the world. That, Iblis believed, would mark the beginning of the end of God's rule. Capturing Abbas was bound to happen, he thought to himself, but in the meantime, chaos and mayhem had to be fermented among the humans.

"The poet must be prevented from reaching Syria," he said, out loud. "And the princess' desires and attentions must be diverted… just in case he manages to arrive there."

For a few seconds he glanced around the cavern at the spirit folk before him, until his eyes settled on the most beautiful female form ever seen. Her skin was neither pale nor dark, but a light, russet colour and smooth as silk. Her eyes captivated the Prince of Darkness. They seemed to be calling him, inviting him into her life, and her hair, so dark, hung down her back in a long ponytail. The light of a nearby flaming torch glistened off every strand of hair. Yet, what he found most haunting was her shape. Every part of her represented perfection of the female form and she stood before him naked, a temptress of the most supreme order, a Succubus.

"My most sensual Sunev," he whispered to her softly, "I have a task for you."

The girl stepped forward, past several other creatures, some of whom fainted in the presence of her exquisiteness, until she was just inches from her master.

"I am a direct descendent of Lilith," she said, with a smile. "And I am here to serve you Master."

"You shall enter the dreams of the Poet Prince," Iblis continued. "You shall corrupt him, seduce him, manipulate his feelings, take control of his most basic desires, and thus delay his journey."

Her reply was swift. "Yes Master," she said, her eyes focusing firmly upon the floor as she spoke. "I live only to serve you," she added, waiting a moment before continuing. "Am I to go now, Master?"

Iblis nodded, but as she was about to leave, he leant forward and grabbed her arm. She turned in alarm. Her breathing had accelerated, her lips had turned a light shade of pink and her face was blushed red, despite her fear.

"You can only return to me successful. If you fail, do not return!"

Iblis' words cut through Sunev like a dagger. She closed her eyes, nodded, and then slowly began to de-materialise. Iblis then turned towards a tall, muscular young man whose perfection of features was not dissimilar to those of Sunev.

"O Incubus, what name do you use?" Iblis asked.

"Erif, Master," came the answer, without hesitation.

"Your task is like that of your sister. When the princess sleeps, you will reach her through her dreams. Make her fall in love with you. Make her want you more than anyone or anything in the world, and above all, make her believe you are real. She must forget that Saracen aristocrat!"

Erif nodded and bowed before leaving in the same way as Sunev had done and Iblis beckoned to a small, ugly, brown creature that waddled quickly to its master, with head bowed. The Prince of Darkness waved the rest away and a cold blackness descended on the cavern. He stared at the diminutive being, whose skin was shrivelled, as if it had been dried up in the hot sun like a date. Its squat little body was like that of a crushed old man, but its muscular frame, hideous features and long, black, greasy hair would strike terror in anyone who had the misfortune of meeting it.

The beast's head remained bowed for several minutes. It dared not raise it, or even its eyes, until permission to do so had been granted by the Dark One seated before it. Iblis' voice was slow, deliberate and without emotion.

"I'm going to need your great armies of the Northern Lands my faithful troll. I realise you are unaccustomed to the climate of the Mid-Eastern world, but your physical strength is urgently required."

He glanced for just an instant at the crystal—at Zenith and his two human companions—and then looked back at the troll.

"Look up troll!" he stated, forcefully. "Can you do this for me?"

The troll did not dare to reply in the negative. That would be more than his life was worth and by agreeing, at least he would have a chance to prove his worthiness. His voice quivered as he spoke, though.

"Most certainly Master. It will be our pleasure."

"And bring me the boy, the one they call Abbas. The other one you can kill or do with what you may."

The troll replied in the affirmative and then left. As he walked away from his master, another being entered the lair. He was tall, covered in battle scars and dressed in the way of a Persian warrior. He stood before Iblis but said nothing. He waited and waited, time ticking by until finally his master spoke.

"What is it Abigor?" He asked.

"A vision Your Excellence, of our future."

"Continue"

Abigor was a seer; one who could forecast future events, occasionally accurately to the extreme, but usually with a vagueness that required interpretation. He took a deep breath and smiled. "The boy, Abbas, will be yours, master. I have seen it and it will be so."

Iblis stood up from his throne and touched Abigor on the shoulder.

"You are sure about this?" He asked, with some doubt evident in his tone.

"Quite sure. I cannot say when, but he will be yours."

There was a moment of silence and Iblis looked away as he pondered the future of which Abigor had told him. His servant, who nervously plucked up enough courage to ask a question of his own, however, interrupted his thoughts.

"Why is this child of such importance master?" He asked.

Iblis pulled his cloak around himself and sat back down. His face shimmered, between the handsome, human features that were his masque, and the demonic features that revealed his true self.

"The Emir's mistress, the mother of the one called Abbas, was a Jinni. In fact, she was my daughter, my offspring and she has begun a new line for me. The boy is a half-Jinni and he must return to us here, where I can educate him in our ways, before returning him to the world where my line will continue until the time is right, when one of my progeny shall rule the world of humans."

He laughed. It was a self-satisfied, sadistic laugh that made even Abigor shudder. Iblis' eyes burned yellow and then red and his hands grew, the fingers elongating, the nails forming themselves into talons. His body shimmered, and the transformation continued until he stood before Abigor in full manifest appearance of his true self. Satan, he would be called for the rest of time, his deceitful schemes permeating human existence until the end of all things.

"My half-human offspring has the powers that humans fear in their own. He shall be a necromancer, able to bring forth demons at will, able to communicate with the dead and able to bring the spirits of the dead into human form by helping them to possess any hapless man or woman without their knowledge."

He raised his voice as he continued, until he was shouting his words, which echoed around his underground chamber.

"And he will bring forth more of my progeny. Their names shall be many; they shall be called shamans, witches, warlocks, mediums and even necromancers, and man will fear them, kill them and shun them for millennia.

"But there will come a day when the divining powers of my progeny will be loved and sought after, when it will be a subject of analysis, not hate, when it will be commended and utilised. By that time, the religion of the Creator will be dying or twisted beyond recognition and that time will be mine."

He paused, relaxed and allowed himself to change again, back to his more sombre form.

"Oh, the irony," he whispered, "that as science destroys religion, it merely opens the door for me, for my way is greed, selfishness, war, pestilence, corruption, hatred and lies."

He laughed again. "That is what the future holds for humans, Abigor, and I don't need your divining talents to tell me that."

CHAPTER 33
The Ridge of Fertheron

The Ridge of Fertheron towered above the three travellers at the top of a massive wall of white stone. Hassan's mouth hung open and his eyes stared upwards in disbelief. Abbas, meanwhile, lay in Zenith's arms, asleep. He had collapsed with exhaustion less than halfway from Zaman's castle. The Jinni gently laid the child on a mossy slope and covered him with a cloak. Then he sat down beside him, crossed his legs, and folded his arms. Hassan looked at them both carefully but said nothing. By now, he was as exhausted as Abbas. He dropped slowly to his knees and then collapsed in a heap in front of Zenith. The Jinni pulled the boy towards Abbas and stretched the cloak until it covered them both.

He looked down at the children and thought about all that they had been through, and then he prayed.

"Lord, this is a most difficult mission that you have decreed for me. These two humans have stumbled into a world without the logic or rationality that human minds can fathom, and yet I am constantly at pains to explain events to them in terms they might understand. They seek reasons for everything when there is little reason for much of what occurs here. Plus, that which has reason is so awful that to tell these humans would doubtless destroy them. I pray that upon return to their world they will only recall this as a dream or a vision, for otherwise I fear for their reputations and their sanity."

It was deathly quiet. There were no animal noises, no rushing water sounds, no wind, nothing. It was unnerving, as if time had stopped or life had been sucked from the world around him. He began to mull over the journey and wondered why so little had been done by Iblis' forces to stop them. There had been opportunities. The fight with the Drakon had weakened Zenith, making him a vulnerable target for attack. The incident with the rakshasas had threatened to leave the boys isolated and defenceless. Zaman had left Zaydussia to protect them, but no concerted attack by the enemy had occurred. Then, he began muttering to himself.

Something's wrong. We have not encountered a single enemy since leaving Zaman's castle. They must be waiting for us at the Ridge.

As he drifted off to sleep himself, he wondered whether the boys really had just 'stumbled', by mistake, into the world of the Jinn. Perhaps their disappearance sparked the human clashes, which in turn brought Iblis and his minions into the open.

He also pondered about the fate of Abbas, for he knew of the boy's lineage, both human and Jinn, and of Satan's plans. He also knew from Zaman that the future spoke of the boy's eventual possession by Iblis. Was it a fixed future, he wondered?

The boys slept for six hours while Zenith's sleep was sporadic. He awoke often, driven to keep watch over them. He knew that working their way up the path that led to the Ridge of Fertheron would not be easy. The Deceiver's servants would be there waiting to stop him from returning the boys to their own world. Fighting them was going to be inescapable and beating them would be impossible by himself. Now, it really was time for Hassan to mature. He would have to fight, to kill, and perhaps even die. The Jinni was racked with torment as he pondered having to break this to him but tell him he must.

He woke Hassan and immediately held his hand across the boy's mouth to silence him. Then, lifting him to his feet, he ushered him away from Abbas until they were out of earshot.

"When I remove my hand, do not speak. Just listen."

He pulled his hand away very slowly and Hassan stood, statue-like, waiting to hear whatever the Jinni was to say next.

"Do you remember when you thought to yourself that it was time for you to become a man?"

Hassan nodded, but remained silent. His knees trembled, and his lower lip twitched, although it was unclear whether this was the result of nerves or the cold, dawn air. A biting wind whistled through the rocks beneath the cliff face, blowing his clothes and hair forwards. Zenith pushed the hair away from the boy's eyes and then continued to speak. As he did so, he placed his powerful hands on the boy's shoulders.

"These shoulders are about to broaden. The time for you to stand tall is now. Independence is just around the corner."

He pointed skyward, towards the Ridge.

"Up there are the soldiers of Shaytaan, determined to prevent you from returning home; determined to take Abbas for himself and determined to stop you from reaching your people in time to prevent a catastrophe."

He began to walk away from the young lad when he suddenly halted and drew one of two curved swords he was wearing in sheaths on his back. For a moment, which seemed like a lifetime to Hassan, the Jinni stared at the fine blade and as a bright star began to rise behind them, a flash of light glanced off the sword and caught Hassan across the face. He blinked as the light reflected into his eyes, which he rubbed furiously with both hands, and as he took his fists away from his face, he saw Zenith presenting the sword to him.

"Take the weapon Hassan. It's yours."

The boy reached out and carefully took the sword by the hilt. The handle was a blend of carved silver and gold and the blade was unlike any he had seen before. Zenith removed the sheath from his back and hung it around Hassan's young body.

"The blade of this sword is made from a mineral not found on Earth and the sword has mystical power for the one who yields it. That person is the only one who can use this sword and that person is you, Hassan. This sword was destined to be yours."

He waited as Hassan studied the blade, his hands shaking as he held it in front of him.

"We will be forced to fight the demons, you and I", Zenith continued. "And we will have to kill to win your freedom."

He stopped and placed a comforting hand on Hassan's shoulder.

"We may also die. I can't say what our fate will be. That is for the Almighty to decide, but if it happens, we shall have died fighting for what is right and just. However, you need to be aware of what confronts us both. Our main priority is to at least get Abbas back to your world and back to his father."

He hesitated for a moment and then continued. "Iblis is desperate to take Abbas under his wing. I cannot disclose why yet but know this. It is not in your interest to let that happen."

Hassan was staring at the ground, the sword now hanging loosely from the fingers of his right hand. Gradually, his grip loosened, and it fell onto the rocky ground at his feet.

"I am sorry Hassan, but this has to be. It is unavoidable."

"But what of Abbas? Who will look after him if we both die?"

Zenith looked across to where Abbas still lay sleeping.

"We will take him as far as the trees which surround the summit of the path that leads to the Ridge. There, I will place him in a deep slumber for his own safety. I will place in his mind the means to get home once he awakens. Then, you and I will approach the Ridge itself. That is all I can say. That is all I can promise."

Hassan was sweating, despite the coldness of the dawn air. He stared, trance-like, right past Zenith as he pondered this situation for a moment. He rubbed his eyes briefly and then looked Zenith straight in the eye. The Jinni stared back, emotionless, impassive. His pupils seemed to dilate rapidly, and Hassan felt transfixed, unable to move away. Suddenly, he found himself hearing Zenith's voice, even though the Jinni's mouth remained firmly closed. The voice was within his head.

Fear not young man, it said, *your mind is very strong, and your psychic energy is extremely powerful. Were it not so, you would be unable to hear my thoughts right now.*

Hassan blinked and shook his head violently.

"Stop it! Stop it!" he shouted. "Stop this witchcraft you Shaman!"

Almost without thinking, he bent down, picked up the sword and began swinging it, uncontrollably, in front of him. Zenith never moved. He spoke calmly and slowly to the human, asking him to relax and listen, but Hassan continued to wave the weapon uncomfortably close to Zenith's face. The Jinni finally acted. He waved his hand and the sword wrenched itself out of Hassan's fist before flying across the air and into the Jinni's hand. Zenith reached out and grabbed Hassan before he had a chance to run away.

"Witchcraft?" he asked. "My dear boy, psychic power is not witchcraft, any more than the use of herbs to treat illnesses is witchcraft!"

He let go of Hassan, trusting that he would not now run off.

"If God has bestowed this ability upon you then use it in His service, against the armies of the Prince of Darkness."

The boy was still filled with doubt and Zenith was forced to argue and explain until the light of day was almost completely upon them.

Finally, Hassan conceded that Zenith was right, and he retrieved the sword from the Jinni. Then, they collected Abbas and headed up the path, towards the cluster of trees at the top of the white rock wall, near to the Ridge.

When they were three quarters of the way up the path, daylight appeared, slowly. The sounds of morning surrounded them gradually, as they reached the thicket. The trees swayed in the cool morning breeze and, for an instant in time, they seemed to chant and sing, as the wind whistled all around them. A pathway led through the grove of trees and they could see all the way to the Ridge itself. As Zenith had predicted, about a dozen warriors guarded the doorway at the Ridge of Fertheron. Some were trolls, some were giants and others were without obvious form, appearing only as empty grey-and-black armour. Within their helmets were no faces, and their weapons seemed to be floating beneath their arms. To Hassan, however, their invisibility seemed wasted when their armour clearly gave away their presence and position, providing him with a visible target.

The giants were grotesque. Their faces resembled that of a serpent, but they bore elephant-type tusks. They wore no armour, but their skin was scaled and extremely sturdy looking. Yet, despite their appearance, they were not the most frightening or awesome. The trolls were far more fearsome, warriors in the true sense. Not as huge as portrayed in legend, they were, nevertheless, formidable and bristled with weaponry and armour. Their faces and arms were inundated with the scars of battle. One of them had his left eye sewn up, and a massive scar ran across it from his forehead to his nose.

Abbas began to cry deliriously, and Hassan started to fret and panic. He caught hold of Abbas and dropped to his knees. Abbas stared unblinkingly at the enemy and started to scream loudly. The older boy shook him furiously, but to no avail, and he was worried that the enemy soldiers would hear the screaming. He looked up at Zenith, questioningly, and then back at Abbas.

"What can we do with you?" he asked. Then he turned back towards Zenith. "I'll have to stay with him, look after him. I thought you were going to put him to sleep!"

Zenith was deep in contemplation. Hassan was not too sure whether the Jinni was listening to him or not. He seemed to be totally preoccupied with the warriors lined up ahead of them. The young Turk scrutinised the Jinni with extreme care and Zenith began to draw his sword. It seemed to take forever. To Hassan it was as though time had slowed down. The weapon rang like a bell when it finally slid from its sheath and knocked against the silver emblem on Zenith's belt. The Jinni was prepared for battle.

Hassan turned towards Abbas again, only to find the youngster in a deep trance. Gradually, the ground around him began to move and within seconds, Abbas was absorbed. He had vanished. Hassan called to Zenith for an explanation, but it was too late. The trolls *had* heard Abbas' scream and they were moving towards them.

They looked as if they could taste victory, but they were soon to be disturbed. Into the copse stepped the largest man imaginable. He stood over eighteen feet tall and his unyielding frame stood stark against a clearing sky. He was wearing no body armour at all. In fact, he appeared to be wearing just a small piece of cloth draped around his waist and private parts. In his enormous hands were an axe and a shield, which he kept waving at the trolls, provocatively, while shouting threats at them. His skin was coated with blue oil—a deep marine blue and it shone like the noon sun off glass as the light of a new day reflected off it.

Suddenly, Zenith and Hassan had an ally. The battle could now begin. Hassan drew his sword and followed Zenith towards the trolls. In an instant, they were in the thick of it, swords clashing and creatures dying all around them. The stranger slashed with such ferocity that he brought down clusters of the enemy with single blows from his axe. Zenith and Hassan focused their minds on the task at hand. All thoughts of home, of Ahmed, even of Abbas, were absent from their minds and all their attention was focused on the goal of achieving victory over this immediate foe.

The fighting raged, and the air thickened with the smell of blood and the sounds of battle. Zenith tried to exercise his paranormal powers to force the enemy back, but Satan had protected them from all forms of enchantment. Only conventional weapons of war could break through this horde of demons.

Hassan moved towards the thick of the fighting but caught a glimpse of something approaching him from his right side. He turned quickly and found himself face-to-face with a gruesome, fearsome troll.

CHAPTER 34
Battle at the Ridge

Hassan stood his ground like someone way beyond his years. He lunged at the advancing troll, catching him in the side with his blade, but the boy lacked the strength of an experienced warrior, so the blade remained firmly planted in the creature's side. As the troll collapsed, Hassan fell with him. He found himself caught beneath the weight of the troll's legs and, as he struggled to free himself, one of the giants ran towards him with a spear. The boy closed his eyes and yelled, as loudly as he could. He was as certain as anyone could be, that death was upon him, but nothing happened. Cautiously, he opened one eye and saw the giant's headless body lying on the ground beside him. Standing over him was the stranger holding the giant's head in his hand. As he opened his other eye, he could see what remained of the enemy forces, some of whom were fleeing from the area. Bodies lay everywhere. The ground was soaked in blood and the smell of the dead and dying hung heavily in the air. There was something about the smell of blood in the thick of a battle that aroused the fighter in most men. Hassan felt it. His heart pumped faster, his pupils dilated, and bloodlust welled up in him, but the battle was over.

The stranger moved the troll's leg to one side and picked Hassan up by the scruff of his neck, like a mother cat moving one of her kittens. He lowered him to the ground and, as his feet settled on the moss-covered earth, Abbas came running towards them from the thicket. Zenith put forward a welcoming hand to the stranger and asked him his name.

"Odinike," came the answer. "I am the last of the race of Sintaata who were destroyed by an earthquake, visited upon us by the Evil One who then dragged our city to the depths of the ocean."

Zenith was about to speak when he noticed that Hassan was looking past the Ridge to a small clearing some thirty yards away from them. He started to walk away from the other three and the Jinni called him back, but to no avail. Hassan continued to walk away.

"No, Zenith," he called out. "I must go. It's Prince Jawad. He's over there on the grass."

Zenith looked across at the clearing where a young man was lying asleep. He rushed after Hassan and pulled him back, but the boy tugged himself loose.

"Let go of me!" he shouted. "That's Prince Jawad!"

"I know it is, but before you go rushing across to him, I need to explain something to you."

The Jinni waited for Hassan to indicate a willingness to listen before he continued.

"He is here and yet he is not really here," he said.

Hassan just shook his head.

"Oh, look, I've had enough of all your weird tales, silly excuses, and crazy riddles. That is Jawad and…"

Zenith interrupted him abruptly.

"Where do you go when you dream, my child?" he asked, glancing periodically towards the young man asleep in the grassy meadow nearby.

"What?" came Hassan's instant retort.

"Jawad is asleep in your world. In this world he is about to awaken into a dream."

Hassan was very cross. He waved his hand at Zenith in anger, and then paced around.

"You're confusing me with all this gibberish. How can anyone awaken into a dream?"

Zenith smiled, reassuringly, and then sat down upon a nearby rock.

"It is simple. You see, the world you stepped into is the world where we Jinn live, but it is also the world where the souls of the dead come, to wait for the Judgement Day, and it is one of many worlds which the souls of sleepers visit during their dreams…"

He paused, looked across at Jawad, and then nodded his head.

"In fact, this is a remarkable opportunity. If you meet Jawad here, in the right circumstances and in the correct manner, you can convince him that he has received a forewarning in a dream. That way, when you return to your world, you will be able to more easily convince him of your story, by reminding him of his private dream."

Jawad's stirrings interrupted the Jinni. He was waking up and slowly coming to his feet. As he did so, however, a beautiful, naked woman approached him. It was the Succubus, Sunev, and Zenith immediately grabbed Hassan, holding him back.

"I suspect that that woman has been sent by Iblis to seduce and tempt the young prince, so you must go to him quickly and warn him of her intention."

Hassan did not stop to think. He rushed across to Jawad just as he was about to step towards the woman, who had already held out her hand to the prince.

"Don't go with her!" he shouted, attempting to get between them.

The smile on the girl's face suddenly turned to a frown when she heard the child's voice. She scowled at him, warning him to keep his distance, and her features distorted temporarily, her beauty disappearing and her demonic soul manifesting itself before him. Jawad, his eyes not fully open having just awoken in this dream, did not notice her transformation. Nevertheless, the boy kept advancing towards them. Prince Jawad was obviously surprised by the appearance of Hassan, but before he could say anything to the boy, the woman had hit the teenager with a burst of energy that emanated from her palms, knocking him to the floor.

"What on earth are you doing?" cried Jawad at the girl, whose scowl had reverted to a pleasant and beguiling smile.

"I'm sorry," she said, her naked form shining in the daylight.

Jawad, however, ignored her. His thoughts were only for his young friend and the words he directed towards Sunev were far from gracious.

"Be gone harlot!" he shouted, as he shoved past her to reach Hassan, who lay unconscious and limp on the grass.

He was about to attempt to revive him when he felt the presence of other beings nearby. His heart began to beat faster but, after some hesitation, he plucked up the courage to turn around. Behind him, stood Zenith and Odinike. The size and appearance of the latter sent a shudder down his spine and, for a moment, he froze with shock.

"Fear not young prince," said Zenith. "I am a friend of this child."

As Jawad prepared to speak, Abbas came running over to him and grabbed for Jawad's shoulders, but the boy's hands and arms went right through the prince. Jawad watched with surprise as his younger brother stumbled forward and the boy fell through him, landing in a heap on the floor. A few tears trickled from the prince's eyes onto Abbas' shirt, but they passed through Abbas, as if he were not there. The prince again looked up at Zenith.

"What is going on?" he asked. "How on earth… I mean, where on earth am I, and why are you merely apparitions?"

Zenith leaned down and placed a hand upon Hassan's chest, upon which the boy took a deep gulp of air and regained consciousness. Just then, Jawad remembered the girl. He turned sharply in her direction, but she was gone. A confused frown appeared across his forehead, so Zenith explained things to him.

"You see, young prince, it is not we who are apparitions. It is you. You are here in soul only," Zenith said. "Your body lies far off from here in a small valley in Syria. It lies there asleep and you have come here; and here is where all souls visit, both during slumber, which is the lesser death, and during the greater death. Here, you see all of us, the dead, the sleeping, the Jinn and the angels."

The Jinni looked hard at Jawad, who had turned quite pale.

"You see, Jawad, you are dreaming. When your body awakens, you may remember this, but only as a dream. The girl, however, was a Jinni, a Succubus, sent to you by the Evil One to delay your mission."

Jawad kept shaking his head. "I'm very confused," he said, looking across at the two young boys. "What about them?" he asked. "Are they dreaming too? Or am I dreaming of them?"

Zenith let go of the prince's hand and placed an arm around Hassan's shoulder.

"No, the children are here in body and soul. There was an unfortunate interference with space and time, brought about by the servants of Iblis…"

He stopped suddenly and took a deep breath.

"Listen to me carefully, Oh prince," he continued, in a far more serious tone of voice. "You must take care in all future dreams. The girl you saw can lead you into great danger, and I don't doubt that she will try to seduce you again."

164

"But how can she harm me, if this is only a dream?" Jawad asked, impatiently.

"She will tempt you to stay with her, by influencing your desires and twisting your passions until your willingness to remain here with her is far greater than your wish to return to real life."

He paused briefly, and his eyes glanced down at the earth beneath their feet.

"At that point, Jawad, your soul will be trapped here, and your body will die. You will have chosen to accept the greater death and, as far as anyone finding your body will be concerned, you will have died in your sleep. Your soul-less, lifeless body will be taken and buried, and your mission will be over!"

Jawad nodded and clenched a fist.

"Then I must return and now!" he said, adamantly.

Zenith asked him to wait, while Hassan explained the plotting of Sieffuddeen and the Templars on Earth. Then, Zenith touched the prince on his forehead. Instantly, he vanished, and Zenith nodded. Then he smiled and gently touched the two boys upon their heads. Abbas' eyes were tear-filled, and Hassan's face looked sullen. Their ordeal was far from over and every new moment brought greater trauma. *How much more could they bear?* Zenith wondered, but his thoughts were interrupted by a sight he had hoped he would not see.

Abbas' eyes burned yellow, just for a second, but enough for the Jinni to know that Satan was reaching out for his grandson. If they did not leave this world and return to their own very soon, Abbas would find his mind infiltrated, controlled and manipulated. He will find his will sapped and his destiny changing forever.

"Now it is time for you to pass through the barrier at the Ridge of Fertheron," Zenith said, forcefully.

He signalled his thanks and appreciation to Odinike and then led the boys slowly towards their exit, which gradually materialised before them.

Meanwhile, Odinike walked, unnoticed, into the distance, disappearing into an approaching mist.

CHAPTER 35
1242 A.D.
Jerusalem

Hassan and Abbas emerged on the outskirts of Jerusalem and behind them, the vortex closed. They found themselves completely alone and for a moment in time, surrounded by a deafening silence that seemed to be endless. As they gradually came to terms with their new situation and the task that lay ahead of them, the bleating of goats on a distant hillside shattered the peace. The olive groves on the city's outskirts were a welcome sight for the boys, but Hassan knew that they could not dawdle. They had been in Al-Baahita for several months, but here on Earth, two years had passed. This would only become evident to them when they entered the city.

"We'd better go," he said, placing his hand on Abbas' shoulder, but as they walked off, he noticed that he no longer had the sword. It was a gift of a different world, given to him for a purpose now fulfilled and as that world had disappeared, so had the sword.

As they walked through one of the gates into Jerusalem, they entered a city steeped in an atmosphere of despair. The streets were empty, despite it being morning when most people would normally have been up and occupied in a variety of tasks. Market stalls lay vacant, of both goods and people, and the only sound the boys could hear was that of a few dogs barking. From street to street, the scene was the same. Occasionally, a person would appear in a doorway, but disappear back into their homes when they saw the boys passing by. As they approached the Emir's palace, a soldier stopped them. He was armed with a lance and he held it out in front of him to prevent the boys from passing.

"Stop where you are!" he shouted, his voice echoing around the narrow streets. "What are you doing out during curfew?" he then asked them.

"Curfew? We... er, we didn't know there was a curfew. We've only just arrived in Jerusalem," Hassan answered, humbly.

The soldier looked them up and down, suspicious of a youth with a young boy, arriving unaccompanied, in Jerusalem. The sarcasm was evident in his voice when he spoke next.

"Well, welcome to Jerusalem. You're now under arrest and you'll come with me."

Both boys tried to explain who they were, but the soldier was not in a listening mood. After ordering them, in no uncertain way, that they should be silent, he called for one of his compatriots to escort them to a holding area. They were led to a somewhat run-down area of the City's Arab quarter, which was the location of the soldiers' barracks. Once there, he led them into a small, damp room, lit by three dim candles. The soldier was about to shove them into the room when another soldier thought he recognised the younger of the two boys.

"Wait!" he shouted, as he reached over and grabbed the younger boy. "You're the Emir's son, Abbas."

Another soldier, waiting inside the room, stepped forwards, holding a lit torch in his hand. He lowered it towards the boys, looked hard at them and then back at his comrade.

"Are you sure? Which one?"

"I am!" shouted Abbas indignantly.

CHAPTER 36
Erif, the Incubus

Jawad's memory of the dream was hazy, which in a way was fortunate since his mind was now focused more upon his mission than it had been a day earlier. He prepared his horse and set off in the direction of the castle which held Marie.

Meanwhile, in that castle, she had drifted off to sleep herself. In her dreams, she found herself in the same clearing where Jawad had met the Succubus, Sunev. Marie was lying on the ground with a young man; both were naked, and the man was speaking softly to her.

Soon… soon, young child, you will be mine and when your desire to be with me is greater than your will to live, your soul will remain here, with me, forever.

His voice was mesmerising, and Marie's eyes remained closed, giving her the appearance of someone who was asleep in the dream itself. Once the man had ceased his whisperings, he woke her up. At first, she was startled, but he seemed to hold her in his power with his deep, dark, brown eyes.

I am Erif, he said gently. *I found you at the side of the road and brought you here to rest. I think you must have fallen from a horse.*

Being a dream, the idea that she had fallen from a horse and been found at the side of an unknown road by a compassionate stranger did not seem out of the ordinary to Marie. The castle in Syria and her capture by the Templars were nowhere in her mind right now. Reality for her was only what she could currently behold; that she was in the company of the most handsome man she had ever set eyes on. So, enraptured was she by his looks, his charm and his kindness, that she had not even noticed that they were both completely naked. As she smiled at him, he took hold of her hand and stood up, pulling her to her feet as he did so.

"Where are we going?" she enquired, as they walked away from the clearing, in the direction of the Ridge of Fertheron.

The man said nothing, but within a few seconds Marie caught sight of a small village ahead of them, which she was sure had not been there just moments earlier. She was about to ask where it had appeared from when she suddenly noticed their nakedness. Her arms rushed to cover herself and she closed her eyes.

There was no telling how much time had passed before her eyes re-opened. All she noticed was the kiss. He caressed her and kissed her again, and all her senses were magnified. The intensity of his touch threatened to bring her to a state of unrivalled pleasure when suddenly she found herself lying, still naked, on a large bed in a completely non-descript room. Standing above her, legs astride, Erif had his right hand on his enormous member. He knelt before her, and his left hand began working its way up the inside of her thighs, towards her most treasured area.

She seemed utterly seduced, but a voice wrenched her from the trance. It was Jawad's voice, although he was nowhere to be seen.

"I will find you," he said, and Marie's heart skipped a beat. "I am coming for you now" he continued.

"The Saracen," she said as she rushed back into awareness.

She looked at Erif, kneeling over her with his huge penis working its way towards her, and she screamed.

"Get away from me!" She shouted, pushing against his face, her fingers catching him in the eyes.

He flinched, and she saw the chance to run, so run she did, but found herself in a valley, running but getting nowhere. Ahead of her, the scenery seemed to be moving away from her and the faster she ran, the faster it receded. She glanced behind her and saw Erif a long way back, so she slowed her pace slightly. Another glance behind her brought an end to her futile efforts to advance, for there was no sign of him now. She stopped, tried to settle her breathing, and turned to face the still receding valley ahead of her, only to find Erif standing before her, his erect tool seeming far larger than it had before. She shrieked and considered running the other way, but he grabbed her, beginning what she imagined would be a terrifying assault. It started with the forceful tearing of her dress and, for a bizarre moment, she wondered when she had got dressed.

169

What is happening? She thought, and it was in the transition between that thought and her next that Erif was lifted off her and thrown some ten or twelve yards away.

The village stood behind them but now it sat in a field of corn. She had a kind of memory of each of these events, but somehow her mind treated each episode as if it were the only reality. She now stood alone in the clearing, and she noticed the silhouette of a man on the distant horizon, against the setting sun.

Who is that? she muttered to herself.

She turned towards where Erif had landed and prepared to repeat her question more loudly, but he was gone. A panic now set in and she began to run around the field calling after him. She begged him not to play such games with her. Why she would seek his help, she could not explain.

"Please Erif," she pleaded. "Don't do this."

Her speech was cracking, and her eyes were beginning to fill up with tears when suddenly, the appearance of another man startled her. In her rush to get away from him, she stumbled, and while she lay upon the ground, he stepped towards her. Frightened and confused, she covered her face with her hands and screamed, but the man merely held out a hand, took hold of hers and helped her to her feet.

Slowly, she opened her eyes and looked at him.

"What is happening?" She wondered.

"Don't be alarmed," the stranger said, quietly. "My name is Zenith and I am here to help you."

"Where's Erif? He said he would help me too," she shouted.

"Regrettably, he would not. In fact, he would have raped you and imprisoned you here in this unearthly world, had I not arrived."

Marie vaguely remembered the attempted assault. She looked down, expecting to see her torn dress, but found it immaculate, untouched. Confused, she frowned, so Zenith explained to Marie that she was in a dream. He told her about the incubus, Erif, and before long, he had gained her trust, as was his way.

"Now, it is time for you to wake child, but before you go, remember this; recite your 23rd Psalm often and particularly before you sleep. That way the Incubus will be kept at bay."

When she awoke, she was sweating, and her heart was racing. Parts of the dream were very vivid, very memorable. She was still in that half-sleep, half-awake state we experience when exiting suddenly from a powerful dream, and momentarily it felt real to her, but then she remembered some of what Zenith had told her.

"Oh, what else did he say?" she kept asking herself, repeatedly.

Then, as if put there by some unseen force, the words of the psalm began to echo through her mind. She whispered them to herself.

"Yea, though I walk through the valley of the shadow of death..."

She had remembered. She sat up in bed and smiled and was still smiling when the guard entered the room. This, he found a little perplexing since he saw nothing at all for her to smile about. The windowless room was cold, damp and malodorous, with only a single candle to light it. Mice scurried along the skirting of the walls and cockroaches infested the eastern corner, which she was forced to use as a toilet. The guard, finding her sitting on her wrought-iron bed, staring into space and smiling, assumed that she had gone completely insane or was possessed of some maleficent spirit. *It would not have been the first time that a prisoner here had lost their mind*, he thought to himself. He walked over to her and handed her a tray of rather miserable looking food, a bucket of warm water and a jug of milk. Then he left and, as the door slammed shut, the key turning slowly in the lock, Marie got down on her knees and began to pray.

Meanwhile, the Incubus and the Succubus were brought before their Master, Satan. The troll guards that brought them in, made them lie prostrate before their King and neither the temptress nor her brother dared lift their heads or make eye contact with him.

"You have failed me," he said, calmly, even reassuringly.

For a moment the siblings wondered if he might be ready to forgive them, but forgiving was not in Satan's nature. Vengeance, punishment and even torture, were far more his forte. He stepped over to them and lifted them both from the ground by their hair, hoisting them up and holding them out in front of him like two rag dolls. His face contorted, his skin changed from a golden brown to burning red, his pupils narrowed to snake-like slits and his iris' reddened. The two Jinn made to scream, but the attempt was forestalled. Satan opened his mouth, revealing his sabre-like eyeteeth and then he bit into them, first Sunev and then Erif. Their blood was sucked from them and their bodies dried like dates in the sun. Then, Iblis threw them towards the trolls, but in mid-flight they ignited and disappeared.

"I will not accept failure!" Iblis shouted, his face contorting and his voice echoing around the chambers.

He beckoned to Abigor to join him and waved the trolls away. As Iblis spoke, he gradually transformed from the grotesque devil into the handsome man that was his preferred facade.

"Do you know, my faithful Abigor, that I was there at the beginning, when Allah gave the Order for that wretched human species to come into existence?"

Abigor nodded but said nothing. He knew it was only his place to listen.

"The Angels, He had created from light, robotic creatures with no free will, who obey His commands without question and then He created us, the Jinn, from fire.

"We were given free will and a rebellious nature, but we are borrowers, users, destroyers. We build only what we copy, we wreak havoc and we produce turmoil, but we create nothing, nothing wondrous, nothing new anyway. And so, we lost our privileged place with God, to those humans.

"Some say He created them in His image, but of course that does not mean He looks like them or they look like Him, for none of us know of His true appearance. What it means is that He gave them the ability to create, to imagine, to build, to truly love and care... and to forgive; all things of which most of us who are Jinn are devoid.

"Some of us, some of the Jinn, had been raised to the status of Angel Jinn and I was one of those for a while. But my pride got the better of me, for pride I had in abundance. So, when He ordered the Angels and Jinn to bow to His newest creation, I refused. My neck stiffened, and I told Him that I would never lower myself to the level of mere Angels and I would not bow to a creature built from dust when I am of Fire!

"He could have destroyed me there and then, but I begged for a reprieve and He cast me down, the Fallen One, until the Day of Judgement. Could I control my pride? Of course not, for I am Jinn. I told Him I would tempt his human pets. I would mislead them, pull them from

Him and destroy them by working on the evil that lies within the breast of every human and every Jinni.

"For how could we have free will to choose right from wrong if we had no capacity for both? Of course, most Jinn were far more easily controlled than were the humans, although there are plenty among the Bani Adam who submit to me willingly.

"So, here I am, waiting for the inevitable, trapped by my own arrogance and my hasty threats and promises. What an irony, that in choosing free will, I should so easily let it slip away."

He shook his head and then stared at Abigor with snake-like eyes, piercing, cold and predatory. Then he stood, pulled his cloak around him and headed past his servant to the cavern exit, calling after Abigor as he went.

"Now, I am forced to do my own dirty work and retrieve the child in person, and somebody will pay for that."

CHAPTER 37
1242 A.D.
Jerusalem

It began to dawn on Hassan that, while he and Abbas had spent just months in Al-Baahita, two years had passed in Jerusalem. *Much has changed here,* Hassan thought to himself, *and there is clearly tension everywhere.* As the guards took the two boys to the Emir, Hassan wondered if they were too late. After bathing and obtaining fresh, clean clothes, they went to see the Emir and his entourage. The boys sat in the Emir's private quarters, gorging themselves on food from the feast that was prepared for them on the Emir's personal orders. They had not eaten properly for some days and this was evident by their noticeable lack of table manners. The Emir, however, chose to overlook their rather boorish and barbaric behaviour. He was grateful that his son and his servant had returned home alive and well. Nevertheless, he was concerned about Jawad. He would have to ask the other boys if they had news of him.

"I realise you are both tired and hungry, but there are things we need to know; things we need to be told… by you, and there are things, grave things, that we must tell you." He was half expecting a negative response and was a little taken aback by Hassan's reply.

"Your Highness, we have many things to discuss, many things to tell and no time to lose," Hassan called out, his mouth still full of food.

The Emir relaxed a little. He was never very comfortable around children, but he could see the change in Hassan. He had experienced an ordeal that had transformed him into quite a mature young man, and this encouraged his leader to give him an adult ear. He sat down beside the boys and listened carefully. Hassan, assisted occasionally by Abbas, started to explain their experiences, since they went missing. After a moment or two into the explanation, Abdul Qadoos entered the room. The Emir quietly and diplomatically ushered him to a seat. The Emir then placed a finger to his own lips as a request for silence while the boys spoke, and the two men listened to the most unbelievable tale they had ever heard. Although they made intermittent glances at each other, each of them raising eyebrows, or shaking their heads in turn, neither of them stopped the boys from talking. It was as though they felt the children needed to say all this, to get over their ordeal—a kind of therapy if you like. Finally, Hassan stopped speaking and the Emir took his General to one side for a private talk.

"I think the Franj must have drugged them," the Emir whispered. "These hallucinations of theirs can only have been drug-induced."

Abdul Qadoos breathed a deep sigh. "That maybe the case sir, but they know about your eldest son and the Assassins. How could they know that? Do you think they witnessed it?"

"I know, it is most certainly odd, and the Templars too; it is worrying for sure…"

The Emir looked at the boys sitting on the couch and then back at Abdul Qadoos. For an instant he was prepared to believe that they may be telling the truth, but then he shook his head and sighed.

"No, it's a Franj trick. They want to distract our attention—to drop our guard," he said.

"It is no trick!" Hassan shouted. Then he paused and looked around. "Perhaps I should also reveal to you that we know about Ahmed too. I am so sorry sir, for your loss," he said, glancing at Abdul Qadoos, "but we know that it was not the Franj who killed him; it was Sieffuddeen."

The atmosphere in the room changed. Silence drowned them, and a chill went through Hassan like a cold blade. He glanced from one man to another.

"What is it?"

Abdul Qadoos' face tightened as anger overtook pain. "Sieffuddeen," he whispered under his breath, but nobody heard him because just at that moment, a messenger arrived. Arslan, who had attended the Emir's palace with Abdul Qadoos, to see his son, ushered the messenger into the room.

The Emir called to the envoy to step forward, and ordered him to speak, while Abdul Qadoos gestured to Arslan to go to his son. The messenger, ragged, dusty, and tired after a hasty dash from Acre, hesitated. He was clearly very nervous and found it hard to get the words out. The Emir quickly lost his patience.

"Speak messenger!" he shouted sternly.

"Er, a Christian army is preparing to leave Acre within the month and a vanguard is marching, as we speak, towards Jerusalem, Your Highness."

The Emir thanked him and waved him away. He turned to Abbas and waved him over. "Come here, son," he said. Abbas ran to his father, who hugged him tightly, holding his head against his chest. While gripped in this embrace, he looked once more at Hassan, who had been approached by Abdul Qadoos.

Hassan, who had rushed across the room and into the arms of his own father, waited patiently for the General to speak.

"I don't know why", said Abdul Qadoos, "but something tells me you are right about Sieffuddeen. Do you know where he is?"

Hassan, nervous, as he always was in the presence of the Emir's General, mumbled his reply.

"He, er, no. He might be in Acre, or Syria."

Abdul Qadoos took a deep breath. His fists were clenched so tightly that his knuckles had become a sickly white. He nodded and crossed the room to the Emir.

"I don't like this," he said, shaking his head. "Someone is making a fool of us. I know we can't let the Franj army approach Jerusalem unheeded, but what if someone is trying to trick us into opening up our southern flank and leaving the northern one exposed?"

The General could not conceal his anger. He paced the room, slapping his thigh repeatedly with his fist. The Emir, however, just shook his head.

"We cannot base our tactics on the idle gossip and imaginings of these boys, particularly when they include such monstrous accusations against my eldest son." His voice was raised, and he was about to order everyone to leave the room, when his anger suddenly subsided. Calmly, but firmly, he said; "It is too late Abdul Qadoos, too late. Prepare to meet the Franj."

Hassan, meanwhile, pulled away from his father. He was, by now, extremely angry himself, just as angry as Abdul Qadoos and the Emir.

Now, however, the nerves which had subdued him so before, had dissipated.

"You don't believe us, do you?" he shouted, frowning all the while at the men around him. "Damn you all! You don't believe us…Well? do you?"

He began striding from man to man, his face screwed up in hostile animosity, and as he approached the Emir for a second time, the adult tried to place a reassuring hand on the child's shoulder. Hassan pulled away sharply.

"I'm sorry child," said the Emir, with a look of pity in his eyes, "but your story is just too incredible to believe, and we can't risk exposing Jerusalem to a European onslaught, based on a child's far-fetched tale."

The Emir sighed as Hassan stormed across the room to where Abbas had been sitting watching the entire incident.

"I am not a child!" Hassan screamed.

For a moment, the room was plunged into an immaculate silence. It was as though no one wanted to be the first to speak and shatter it. Everyone present was shocked that a servant should speak in such tones to the Emir. The Emir, meanwhile, studied the two boys, standing together against the far wall, Abbas with his hand firmly planted in Hassan's.

Turning to one of his aides, he requested that an urgent message be sent to the Sultan, a son of Saladin now controlling much of Syria. The message requested immediate assistance. However, the Emir was not optimistic that help would be forthcoming. He knew that to offer reinforcements would mean leaving Syria at the mercy of those to whom no mercy was shown when it was taken. Nevertheless, the Emir felt that, out of courtesy to the Sultan, he had to send the request.

Having dispatched his messenger, he thought to himself and then turned to the other men.

"The shepherd boy spoke of Templars, did he not?" he asked. He was greeted by silent nods. "And, so have these two," he continued, nodding towards Hassan and Abbas. "So, let us not burn all our bridges."

He turned to a tall Syrian officer who had been standing at the door the whole while. The soldier's battle-hardened face revealed his violent past and his eyes exposed an inner surety and discipline of a man of cunning and determination in the face of danger. However, both betrayed an inner compassion, unusual in those who had spent most of their lives in vicious combat.

"Take ten men of your choice. Ride to Syria and report back to me on anything untoward that you witness there. I mean anything that seems even remotely out of the ordinary. Do you understand Sami?"

The officer responded and left, upon which Abdul Qadoos, concerned about the current military situation that would soon be in the immediate vicinity of Jerusalem, reminded the Emir of the approaching Franj vanguard.

"Calm yourself, Abu Ahmed." The use of the familiar term, 'father of Ahmed', left Abdul Qadoos somewhat stunned, as it reminded him of the loss of his beloved son, but his thoughts were broken as the Emir continued. "I am not about to allow a siege of Jerusalem to take place. In two days, we will march out to meet the Franj. We will strive to forge a peaceful settlement but, if necessary, we will do battle on the plains outside Haifa."

The Emir's intention was to keep his General calm and focused by using the title Abu, the Arabic for 'father of'. To refer to a man as 'father of' his son, is an informal compliment. It worked.

Outside, Sami gathered a group of ten fearsome-looking fighters. They mounted their horses and rode out towards Syria. Sami was a professional soldier, a battle-hardened man who had spent the whole of his adult life, and part of his childhood, at war. He sported a short beard, and hair that was plaited. His face carried several scars, but none of them undermined his handsome looks. Despite his occupation, he was a man of vast knowledge, having read many magnificent books, in Arabic and French. He spoke with a slight, almost unnoticeable, lisp, because of some damage to his mouth, caused by a dagger. Yet, he displayed, in both his actions and his words, a cunning level of military intelligence. This was, in effect, the medieval equivalent of a Special Forces soldier and he was riding out with a team of crack troops, including a Syrian assassin, named Assad.

CHAPTER 38
1242 A.D.
The Citadel, Syria

Jawad's arrival in Syria had been delayed by a host of unforeseen incidents. He worried that in the two years since Marie had been taken, anything could have happened to her. She may not even be alive. Nevertheless, he persisted in his quest, and now his goal was within reach. Outside the Syrian Citadel lay a small village. It was one of the poorest in the region. The Angels had dressed the prince in clothes that befitted his rank and he knew that he would stand out like a sore thumb, dressed as he was in the fineries of a Saracen prince. He needed to pass through, or around the village, unnoticed, or at least unnoticeable. He removed all his clothes, except his trousers and sword and then buried the discarded items on the southern side of the village.

Creeping quietly among the small houses, he searched for clothes and a place to sleep. It was almost midnight and the only light available to him came from the dying embers of a blacksmith's fire. The first hut he came to, appeared to be empty, save for some pigeons in an old wooden box. A pile of clothes lay on the floor, almost certainly awaiting collection for washing at the nearby stream. Jawad could not see the clothes clearly and had to try distinguishing one item from another by touch. Eventually, he found a shirt and a woollen, hooded cloak, but as he pulled them on their smell almost knocked him senseless. At one point, he thought he was going to retch, and he let out a slight groan.

It was only then that he discovered that the house was not empty at all. On a rickety old bed in the corner of the room, a young man stirred.

"Who's there?" the sleeper asked, as he struggled to focus his eyes in the dark and reach beneath his bed for a large dagger. He spoke in Arabic, but with a foreign accent.

Jawad lunged at him, pressing the man's arm against the wall and clasping his hand across the villager's mouth.

"Stay silent and you will live," he said, menacingly, before slowly removing his hand from the frightened youngster's face.

"I'll not betray you sir," the man said in a whisper. "You are a Saracen, are you not, from Jerusalem if I'm not mistaken?"

Jawad frowned. How could this man know so much? However, the villager smiled, reassuringly.

"It's your accent," he said. He looked at Jawad's trousers, barely visible to him in the dark, but close enough to touch. "And that material, sir, it's far too fine for you to be a European."

Jawad released the man's arm, picked up the knife from beneath the bed, and held it towards the villager. "Your Arabic is unusual, young man," the prince said. "What are your origins?"

"I am a Farsi; I hail from Persia originally. I was sent here by the Khaliph in Baghdad three years ago, to spy on the Templars and report on their movements."

Jawad smiled and nodded. He looked straight into the man's eyes. "The pigeons are messengers then."

"Yes... now Saracen, you tell me what your business is here, so far away from Jerusalem."

Jawad moved away from the young man and sat himself down in a half-broken chair on the opposite side of the room, next to the pigeons.

"I am on a quest," he said. "To free a woman who is held captive in that fort." He pointed in the direction of the imposing stronghold standing proud on the cliffs above them.

The Persian raised an eyebrow with interest. "I saw a young girl brought to the castle by Templars about two years ago. But..." He paused and frowned a little before continuing. "She was not a Muslim—not even an Arab, and when she screamed, and boy did she scream, it was in French; a language I speak fluently, but alas, she was too far away for me to hear all that she was saying. However, I did get the clear impression that she felt her captor was a heathen son of a disease-infested dog."

Jawad's face beamed. The broadest smile ever seen on a man had spread across it and his eyes lit up like jewels. "And her skin, did it shine through the night, like satin?" he asked.

The Persian nodded. "It's her isn't it? But what does a young

Saracen want with a Franj female?"

"That is something I would prefer to keep to myself, for the time being." Jawad stood up and prepared to leave. "Now, I must go," he said, excitedly. "I trust you to keep safe the knowledge of my presence here, Farsi," he added, rather authoritatively.

Just then the Persian caught hold of his arm, not firmly enough to prevent him from leaving, but with enough pressure to indicate that he wished the Saracen to wait.

"Wait!" he said, "I'll come with you," he said, pausing briefly before continuing. "I work for the Khaliph in Baghdad and I too need to get into the castle. I've been trying for years, and I can't wait to see how you aim to do it. This should be very interesting. Besides, you need my help to get through this village. Apart from anything else, you need some clothes and judging by the way you carry yourself you'll need some training. You are most clearly not a fighting man."

"Interesting may not be the correct word to use my friend. There are some things I have not told you—some things are best left untold. Since you are obviously a spy, I'm sure you'll appreciate that."

The Persian smiled and nodded, but as Jawad looked away from him, towards the castle gates, the smile disappeared. He stared at the prince intensely. As a spy, albeit a young one, he had learned never to trust *anyone* unconditionally.

He was not lying when he said he had been trying for years to enter the Citadel. The security was immensely tight, and the fortress boasted only one entrance, the main gate. The young Persian had arrived in the village with a troop of actors and jugglers. For most of the journey from Iran, he had posed as a carpenter and, while with the carnival troop, he repaired their stage props and carts on a regular basis. When they left the village, a week later, he had remained, gaining employment once again as a carpenter. He repaired houses, built market stalls and regularly worked alongside the local wheelwright. One would build and repair the carts, while the other built and repaired their wheels. It was arduous work, but it paid well, and the locals soon accepted him.

He relayed all of this to Jawad, but the prince was convinced the Persian spy was keeping something from him; he considered that for a moment but decided that this was not the time to pursue it.

"What is your name Persian?" He asked, quickly changing the focus of conversation.

"Reza Ahvazi, and yours?"

"Jawad."

"And your family name?"

"At the appropriate time, Reza, if that is truly your name. At the appropriate time."

"And, in good time, we'll approach the castle, my Saracen friend. For now, we sleep. In the morning, I will go about my day's work, while you wait here and for the next few days, we will train."

Jawad's face revealed his unhappiness at this plan. He wanted to go now, but he restrained his youthful impetuousness and agreed to stay put.

Reza was currently working on a roof repair for the village blacksmith. It was not a problem during the dry, warm weather, but recently they had been beset with rainfall, and a blacksmith cannot operate effectively if his fire is constantly doused with water. Reza's work was almost finished. The gaping hole that had caused so much irritation to the blacksmith was now gone and he was applying the finishing touches to the inside of the roof.

As he replaced his tools in his bag, the smith entered the workshop. "A job well done Reza. Worth every coin you asked for." He handed the Persian a small bag and Reza took hold of it with his left hand, shaking the blacksmith's hand with the other.

"Thank you," he said, looking outside at some of the horseshoes hanging from nails on the workshop wall. "Now, my friend, you could help me. I need three horses, strong ones and fast. Can you find me some?"

The blacksmith squinted, thoughtfully and then nodded. "Are you going away?" he asked.

"For a while, yes," Reza responded. He did not want to give anything away and had to choose his words carefully. "I'm meeting up with two friends of mine and we're travelling to Jerusalem. I have relatives there."

CHAPTER 39
1242 A.D.
Inside the Citadel

It was past midnight, a week on, when Reza and a rejuvenated Jawad walked the three horses through the village in the direction of the castle. They kept to a soft, water-sodden stretch of the dirt path that ran through the centre of the hamlet, trying to keep the noise of their exit to a minimum. The occasional snort from the horses made Jawad's heart skip a beat, but it did not seem to have caught anyone's interest. So, they continued, down the track and out of the village.

The castle itself was a short walk away, set high in mountainous terrain, on an elevated hill, overlooking a deep ravine. Surrounded by thick forest, the castle imposed itself upon its surroundings. It was a formidable fortress of power that was seemingly physically impenetrable, while also being psychologically powerful. Reza needed the horses only to aid with their escape later, one for him, one for Jawad and one for Marie. He knew exactly where they could leave them without attracting any unwanted attention, either from inquisitive locals, or from opportunistic thieves; in a gully, running along the Eastern side of the cliff face that housed the daunting fortress. Trees and thick undergrowth shrouded the gully and few people, if any, would be likely to go there. The horses would be well shielded from view and there was ample grass there for them to eat. A small stream would provide them with water.

They tethered their steeds and climbed the short distance to the front face of the fortress. Its intimidating gates stared down at them as they crouched low behind a series of weathered rocks and uncut grass.

"What now?" asked the Persian, not looking at Jawad, but keeping his eyes securely focused on the gates, half-expecting to see evidence of guards on duty, but there were none. The occupants were so confident that this place, set in the side of a mountain, was impregnable, that there were no guards posted anywhere.

As Reza pondered that fact, Jawad lifted his sword, placed it vertically in front of them and began to chant in Arabic. The Persian watched in total disbelief as the castle gates began to ease open.

"Come on Reza!"

The young Persian's fair skin stood out in the moonlight against his jet-black hair. He was a most handsome man and for an instant, Jawad wondered whether bringing him to the princess was such a clever idea. Jawad had rather a weak-looking frame and his features were by no means as stark and masculine as those of his new compatriot. Furthermore, his slightly hooked nose and delicate features made him the least likely looking warrior. Yet, despite his artistic bent and his obvious insecurity regarding his appearance, he was an attractive man, with piercing dark eyes and a strong jaw.

Unlike the prince, Reza looked every bit the fighter. He was quite awe-inspiring, dressed in a fine European tunic and a large woollen cloak pulled securely around him. He was well armed too, with a threatening broadsword, a small recurve bow, a quiver of arrows and an assortment of knives. Despite his diminutive size, he was fearsome, the years of experience of violence etched on his face and arms, and apparent in his intimidating eyes. After a quick glance around, he followed the prince and together they made their way, stealthily, towards the opening gates.

Meanwhile, within the castle itself, Sieffuddeen received word that his brother may have journeyed to Syria and may be nearby. The prince walked across his room, opened a desk drawer and pulled out a note that had arrived two years' earlier. Unfolding it, he read it a few times.

The son of the Emir, your brother, was held at Acre. He survived and was imprisoned there but managed to escape some weeks ago. Raymond intends to strike a deal with the Emir. Act soon or your enemies will be united against you.

It was signed, *Cedric.*

Sieffuddeen stood and began pacing the room. He was agitated and repeatedly tapped his right hand against the hilt of his sword. He called out for the Templar who had originally taken receipt of the note from the messenger, two years before. Half an hour later, the Templar knight joined him. For a moment, there was silence, both men thinking but neither of them ready to make their thoughts known to the other. Finally, Sieffuddeen spoke.

"The bodies of the Christian spy and that snot-nosed brat were discovered by the Emir's men years ago, were they not?" He asked.

The Templar smiled. "Our sources informed us that the bodies were found and taken to Jerusalem, not long after they were left where you had asked us to leave them", he replied.

"And my brother? Does anyone know where, precisely, he is now? Why are we only finding out today that he may be here, right on our doorstep?"

He lifted a goblet from a large oak table and threw it against the wall. It bounced off the wall, onto the floor and came to rest almost at his feet. "It is time to pull all of our allies together and send people to find my damned brother. This time make sure they kill him."

CHAPTER 40
1242 A.D.
The Freeing of the Prisoners

"Who's that?"

Sami glanced in the direction in which his junior officer was pointing. Just North West of their position and beneath the castle walls, two men were scurrying, like rodents, through the undergrowth. Just beyond them, the bushes rustled, and Sami wondered if more men were there.

He was about to order a man round behind that position when he looked again at the two men running past them, towards the castle gates.

"Oh my God, it's Prince Jawad."

"Sorry Sir, what was that?"

"The man at the front, it's the Poet Prince. What in hell is he doing here and who is he with?"

There was another rustle in the bushes and his concentration was disturbed for a moment. Again, he prepared to send some men around behind the bushes, when he noticed a horse's tail.

"Horses…" He whispered. "Look Assad, they've left horses. They're expecting to be running soon."

Sami and his commandos waited and watched as the Gates of the Citadel opened. Jawad and Reza ran into the fortress and Assad fixed his eyes anxiously on Sami. Sami, however, did not break his concentration. Instead, he pulled himself to his feet and ran towards the gates. He said nothing. His men looked at each other, curious and confused, and then they took to their feet and followed.

The gates had opened just wide enough to allow a man to squeeze through. Jawad pulled his hood over his head and brought it forward over part of his face. He knew that his darker skin would soon stand out among the European knights housed within the castle.

The two men kept themselves hidden in the shadows by moving along the walls and away from any torch-lit areas. Somehow, Jawad knew the way to the castle dungeons. It was as though someone or something was guiding him there. For a while, Reza followed unquestioningly, but as they turned into a steep, dark stairwell, he caught hold of the prince's arm, stopping him in his tracks.

"Look, I don't know what magic you used to open the gates, but I'm a little concerned that you seem to know exactly where you're going."

Jawad was unable to see the young spy in the darkness of the stairwell, but he understood his concern.

"Trust me Reza, please," he said quietly. "I don't know how I know where to go. I just seem to know."

The Persian sighed but maintained his grip on the prince's arm.

"All right, but if you lead me into a trap, I'll kill you Saracen, so be warned!" He paused for a moment and stared ominously into Jawad's eyes, before continuing. "I suppose you're planning on bewitching the guards later, eh?"

Jawad placed his hand on Reza's shoulder and smiled. "Trust me Reza," he said, "please, trust me."

Reluctantly, the Persian relaxed his grip and followed as Jawad continued to make his way down the damp, stone, winding staircase. Reza could not understand why, but for some strange reason he did trust his new brother in arms. Something about him spoke of honour and sacrifice.

Within minutes, they were at the base of the staircase, situated at one end of a long, damp corridor. The flames of a dozen torches dimly illuminated it. Each one hung from the cold, stone, walls between the cell doors, several of which lined each side of the corridor; but there were no guards. Once again, the thought crossed Jawad's mind that the Templars were so sure their fortress and these cells were completely secure, they needed no guards. It was likely that the only time they ventured down here was to feed, move or torture the prisoners.

The two men looked along the walls of the corridor, wondering how the massive iron doors could be unlocked. Their ponderings were suddenly ended, however, as the entire passageway was bathed in a blindingly intense light. For a moment, the men were unable to see, but instinctively they shielded their eyes anyway. Then, as quickly as it had appeared, the glow vanished.

The bright light receptors had become attuned to the brightness, and a few seconds passed before their eyes re-adjusted to the dimly lit passage again. It was then that Jawad instinctively reached out and pulled on one of the cell door handles. Both men were astonished to see it open, but nowhere near as amazed as the occupant of the cell. As the two men entered, he backed himself into the corner of the room. Thinking it was time for food or another beating, he assumed the position the Templars had imposed upon him for such occasions.

Jawad and Reza burst into the cell, but the pitch-blackness within halted their progress instantly.

"Grab a torch from outside," Jawad shouted.

Seconds later, Reza re-entered the cell with one of the burning torches, enabling them to see who was inside, and giving the prisoner his first glimpse of light for several months. He was cowering in the corner of the room, a man of European appearance, possibly in his late twenties, although looking much older. His hair was long, hanging dirty and untidy well below his shoulders. A thick, long brown and ginger beard and moustache almost completely covered his face. He was unwashed, and his clothes were in tatters, but although thin and hungry looking, he still appeared to be strong. Jawad correctly presumed him to be a soldier, but he wanted to find out more. A realisation slowly dawned on the man that these were not guards and he, hesitantly, tried to speak to them.

"Who, er, who are you?" He asked.

"Reza, do you speak this European tongue? I speak the language of the Franj, but this language is not known to me."

Reza nodded. "He is speaking the Saxon language. I know it well."

In any other circumstance, Jawad might have asked how a Persian could possibly know the Saxon language, but there was no time for that now. He glanced at the man and asked Reza to speak to him.

"Good. Tell this man that he need not fear us. We are here to liberate him, and we need his help... oh, and ask him his name."

The Persian stepped forward and reached out a welcoming hand to the prisoner. While waiting for a response, he repeated, in broken Anglo-Saxon, what Jawad had said. The prisoner offered a cautious hand in return and stood up slowly, with great deliberation and some mistrust. After a pause, he answered.

"Most people call me Robin or refer to me by my surname, Hod," he said. "I am from England, from the village of Loxley in a beautiful part of the country called Warwickshire. I was captured by Assassins while fighting with King Richard many years ago and I was brought here." He paused briefly. "But I have seen Templar knights here too"

Both men nodded and responded simultaneously with a resigned 'we know' and Robin continued. "The Templars hold this castle now. The Assassins are all but defeated."

Robin looked confused, but continued; "Yet you are Saracens, are you not? So, what is going on? Are you Assassins? Are the Templars working with the Assassins?"

Reza paused before replying.

"We will explain soon enough, but first I must tell my friend what you have said."

Robin nodded in agreement.

"Oh, and by the way," Reza continued, "he is the only Saracen in this room. I am a Persian."

The air of pride in Reza's voice made the Crusader smile; he felt more at ease now and chose to sit on the only thing in the room resembling a bed or seat. It was a long, stone slab, raised about a foot above the ground, and exceptionally cold.

Jawad listened to Reza's translation and then went to try to find Marie, leaving Reza to continue in conversation with the tired-looking Englishman, who would become their new ally. The Persian was very keen to know how long the crusader had languished in this jail. He wanted to know everything he could tell them about the castle or its occupants.

"I think I've been here for more than two years, although I can't be sure, if the truth be known. Pray, tell me sir, what news is there of Richard?"

"The one called Lionheart is thought dead I'm afraid, although his body was never found so, like you, I can't be sure."

Robin's face sank.

"I feel it is time to return home, a free man."

Reza raised an eyebrow. "You look tired but otherwise fit and healthy, which is surprising, given your situation."

"I forced myself to eat the muck they gave me, and I exercised daily. I also created stories in my head to keep me sane."

Reza nodded but was curious to find out more about this man. "Why are you here? I don't mean here in this dungeon. I mean here in Palestine."

Robin took a deep breath, glanced down at the cold stone floor and then looked straight at the Persian.

"I was wrongly accused of being an outlaw in England. After my arrest, the King's army conscripted me, and my skill with a long bow secured me a place in Richard's personal guard. Before long, he grew to trust me. I explained about my false arrest and he promised me a full pardon upon our return."

He paused shortly and then continued.

"My belief, the thing that has kept me alive, I suppose, has always been that when I return to England, it will be as a loyal servant of King Richard." He stopped, frowned and glanced at Reza. "But if he's dead…" He shook his head and then shrugged his shoulders. "Well, whatever the situation with Richard, I just want to go home."

"Oh, I feel the same way, but first please tell me of the Templars. What do you know of them?"

"Nothing really. Personally, I see them as a curse on Christianity, with all their mysticism, secret meetings and evil pride. I've heard stories of sheer butchery, murder and treachery committed by these glorified bandits."

He looked down at the floor briefly, before continuing. "If it weren't for our need for their finance, we would never have allied ourselves with them."

He paused briefly and stood up. Reaching out and touching Reza on the arm, he continued.

"I will say this to you sir; if we have to fight our way out of here, you can trust me to stand side-by-side with you against them. Now, tell me more of your colleague."

"There is very little to tell. He has said nothing to me, except that he is searching for a woman, a French woman by all accounts."

He stopped talking and slipped into deep thought. His eyes surveyed the floor as though somewhere there he would find answers to a question that had been nagging him since the moment he met Jawad.

"He would not inform me of his family name, but I get the feeling that he is not a commoner. The way he acts, the way he speaks, and that sword he wears… they all point to royalty to me."

Reza moved to the door and glanced out. Jawad was at the far end of the corridor, which was now slowly filling with tired and emaciated prisoners. The prince stood in the doorway of one of the cells, sword in hand and eyes fixed in a rigid stare on an old man who was seated inside the cell, his back leaning against the cold, stone wall.

"She was never brought down here," the old man said in a half whisper. "She was far too important to them."

"So… so where is she then?"

"Locked in a chamber near the officers' quarters on the western side of the castle."

Jawad sighed with disappointment. He closed his eyes for a moment and then shook his head.

"Why should I believe you?" His question was asked with a considerable degree of agitation in his voice. "How could you possibly know where she is, if you're locked away down here?"

The old man raised an eyebrow and glanced at Jawad with a satisfied smirk on his face.

"Until a few days ago I worked as a servant in the officers' quarters. I served your princess food on a regular basis."

"And what happened a few days ago?"

The old man smiled openly now. His eyes had been previously hidden beneath his bushy, grey eyebrows and the furrows of his elderly skin, but they now opened wide enough for Jawad to see their deep brown colouring. They emerged like the first stars of night through the forest of silver hair that covered his head and most of his face.

"I tried to help her escape," he replied, his smile transforming into open laughter. "She was very captivating you know—so much so that I actually believed I could get her out. Ha! Me! This frail old man you see before you. I must have been crazy! Well, anyway, they caught us and put me down here."

Jawad smiled, held out an inviting hand to the man and then asked his name.

"Turgay," he replied as he grabbed hold of the prince's extended palm.

"Well Turgay, my new Turkish compatriot, now you can help me to help her escape. Show us where she is."

CHAPTER 41
1242 A.D.
Sami

Turgay certainly seemed to know his way around the compound. He took Jawad along a multitude of corridors, cleverly bypassing all the guards and any populated areas. Just minutes later, they arrived at an oak door, covered with intricate carvings, some religious, some abstract.

"She's in there," he whispered to the prince, who immediately tried to open the door. "But there is no key. I'm sorry, but I don't think we can get in there."

Jawad pushed the old man away with his left hand, while pulling his sword from its sheath with his right. Carefully, he held it in front of him, raised above the ground, curved blade facing downwards, and his hands locked together around its hilt. His eyes were vacant and unblinking, his concentration at maximum levels. His breathing had altered along with his state of consciousness. He stood like this, reflective and trance-like for almost a minute and then the blade began to glisten. Gradually, the light grew in intensity, until the door had been lit up like a thousand beacons. The old man shook with fear and tried to move away, so gripped by terror that he failed to hear the lock of the door clunk or see the oaken barrier swing open.

The light evaporated, and the corridor was plunged once more into relative darkness. The old man looked at the prince with an air of distrust. *Who is this man? What unnatural powers does he possess?* he pondered. His train of thought, his questions, were suddenly disturbed, however, when Jawad tugged on his sleeve and pulled him into the room.

"No time to daydream old man," he called out as he ran into the chamber.

Seated upon a comfortable looking couch was Marie. She peered at the men through tired and tearful eyes and it took a while for her to recognise Jawad. As she did, however, a soft and appealing smile slowly emerged, and the prince knew that she was pleased to see him. He tried his hardest not to reveal to her his own pleasure at finding her safe and well, but something stirred within him that he was going to find more and more difficult to control as time went on. For what seemed an eternity, he found himself staring at her, overwhelmed by her stunning beauty and her soulful, unrelenting blue eyes, which were accentuated by her now long, brown hair.

How on earth did he find me? She wondered. *And how did he get in here?* She wanted to ask him, but he had already caught hold of her, pulled her to her feet and begun dragging her out of the chamber. He could just about make out, in the dim light of the corridor, that she was dressed in a single, plain robe made of coarse fibres, dyed a pale yellow, most likely with saffron. It was hardly the most suitable attire to be wearing during a jailbreak and Jawad asked Turgay where they could find some men's clothes for her.

"Kill a guard," he replied, coldly. "There's no other way."

Jawad shook his head. "We'll make do for now. I only want to start killing when it's absolutely unavoidable."

Marie, meanwhile, had hoisted her robe up and tucked it into a cord belt. Jawad nodded in her direction and set off ahead of them. Turgay stared at the prince as they made their way back along the corridor, occasionally offering directions to the exit. He knew this was no warrior, but he instinctively felt he *was* a great leader, or could be.

Jawad, with Marie just behind him, made his way towards the steps that led from the castle's basement to the courtyard above them. In tow were Turgay, a few steps behind, followed at some distance by Reza, Robin and a handful of other freed prisoners. They could see the glint of torchlight as they approached the entrance to the courtyard, but before they had reached the top of the stairs, a sword, thrust against Jawad's throat, stopped him in his tracks and pinned him to the wall.

"Don't move and say nothing."

The words were Arabic and that, together with the sudden appearance of a cluster of armed men, took Jawad by surprise. The men seemed to be preventing his escape, but he recognised the voice, even though he could not place it.

Turgay remained in the shadows and signalled to the other men to wait. He waited and listened but remained as silent as a cat in search of its prey.

"Why are you here, my prince?" The swordsman asked.

Turgay, Reza and Marie simultaneously adopted the look of a surprised rabbit, caught in the glare of an extraordinarily strong light. Almost in unison, they muttered, questioningly, the word 'prince?'

"Who are you?" asked Jawad. "I shall not answer your question unless you identify yourself."

"It is I, Sami. We have been watching your brother and his allies and followed some of them here."

"Lower your sword Sami and I will explain everything..."

CHAPTER 42
1242 A.D.
The Parting

Sameer Al-Shami was a fearsome warrior whom Jawad had met on many occasions in Jerusalem. The Syrian was very fond of the Poet Prince and would often ask him to recite poetry to him. He said it was so that he could use it to woo a bride, but Jawad always felt the tough warrior enjoyed the verses himself. He was so very different from Jawad's brother. Sameer, known to everyone as Sami, was an honest, loyal, and kind-hearted man, with a heart of fury in battle, but compassion in social circumstances. A highly educated man, which one would never imagine could become such a fearsome warrior. Jawad clasped his friend on the shoulder and Sami immediately noticed a strength and confidence he had not seen before in the prince. He smiled and then listened astutely as Jawad explained the occurrences of the past few weeks.

"So, Sami, we must return to Jerusalem and warn my father of the impending danger. Marie must escape to Acre to warn her father, Raymond, of the same."

He then introduced Sami to the rest of his group and, once the introductions were over, the group of freed prisoners, Jawad, Marie and Reza, stood in the shadows with Sami and five of his soldiers, discussing their plans.

Jawad continued; "There is no time to lose. We must prevent war between our peoples. We have to unite against my brother and his wicked allies, or this land will be under their yoke."

They looked across the courtyard towards the castle gates, which seemed far more daunting now than they had upon entry to the fortress. It was clear that their only route of escape was blocked. Guards had found the open gates and raised the alarm and if they were to leave here now, they would have to fight their way out. It was only a matter of time before someone from the castle guard thought to check the jail cells.

Turgay grabbed hold of Jawad's sleeve to attract his attention. "There are very few guards in the castle sir, er, I mean, Your Highness."

"Jawad will suffice, old man," the prince replied.

Turgay nodded and continued. "The Templar knights and the Assassins are away on a campaign. Ten of us can hold off these guards so that you can escape."

Jawad nodded and breathed a deep and long sigh, but he wondered what campaign a force of Templars and Assassins could possibly have embarked upon. *Where are they headed to?* he pondered. *Jerusalem?*

Decision made; he began to issue orders. "Robin, Reza, Marie, you're all with me. We'll head towards the gates, but we need a diversion."

"That, Your Highness, is something we are adept at providing," Sami responded, confidently.

The prince looked at all the men who were staying to provide a diversion, and then he shook their hands.

"We will be forever in your debt. God help you all."

"And God speed your journey home Your Highness," answered Turgay, a half-smile penetrating his hair-covered face.

Sami, Assad and their commandos, together with the freed prisoners who were not travelling with Jawad, rushed from the doorway into the castle courtyard. Within minutes, they were absorbed in battle with the castle guards, while ordinary citizens screamed and ran to avoid the inevitable carnage. Sami struck first. His sword embedded itself in his assailant's shoulder, almost severing his arm from his body. The guard fell backwards, yelling in agony and trying desperately to clutch his wound. Within minutes, he would be dead. The endorphins would keep him alive for a while, but eventually the loss of blood and the toxic shock from the effects of Sami's not altogether clean blade, would get the better of him.

Behind him, and concealed in shadow, two other guards had taken one of the prisoners by surprise. The first the prisoner knew of it was when he felt the cold blade slice into his side. His insides were burning, but he still tried to wield his own weapon against his attacker. It was hopeless, though. The second guard hacked at his chest with a blunted axe and his life was over. As the axe blade struck, his blood spattered over the guard's face—a face that contorted with rage. Adrenalin flooded his body and after his victim lay dead on the ground, he took one final swing at him, slicing the top of his head clean off. He felt the excitement of victory, but it was short-lived. Sami's commandos attacked the enemy with a vengeance. They stabbed and chopped at the unfortunate guards, who had had no time to protect themselves with chain mail when the alarm was sounded. Their demise was inescapable.

With the sound of fighting behind them, Jawad, Marie, their two new friends and a handful of escapees, rushed to the castle gates. The guards had made some effort to close them, but they had to leave them unguarded to assist with quelling the prisoner rebellion. The gates stood open—seemingly rooted to the spot by unseen forces. So, with relative ease, they escaped. They gathered the horses and walked them down through one of the ravines, past the village and through the surrounding forest.

Warning their respective people in Acre and Jerusalem was now their priority. Avoiding war, at all costs, was crucial. At least, war between the Franks and the Muslims. They decided to split up. Jawad and Reza would travel towards Jerusalem, while Robin and Marie would take the road to Acre. The remaining escapees went their own way.

For the briefest of moments, Jawad glanced back at the castle, listening to the faint sounds of fighting and knowing that he was leaving behind some very brave men, Sami included. Then he turned to Reza.

"We'll pass through some of the poorer villages on our return to Jerusalem," he said, feeling in a small leather pouch that hung from the belt inside his tunic. "Firstly, I feel we'll be safer with the peasants, but also because it is time for me to pay my zakat tax to the poor. I have three gold coins here."

Robin, who was already walking away with Marie, stopped in his tracks.

"What did you just say?"

Jawad turned to face him and repeated what he had said to Reza. Both the prince and the Englishman looked as confused as the other.

"You're a rich man," Robin said, "a prince, and yet you speak of paying tax to the poor. What strange manner of behaviour is this?"

Jawad took a couple of steps towards him, placed a friendly hand upon his shoulder and explained that in the Islamic religion, all people were expected to pay a percentage of their net wealth as a tax to the poor.

"We call it Zakat," Reza interjected.

Robin shook his head and smiled. "What an extraordinary idea—to take from the rich and give to the poor." He laughed to himself. "I must try to introduce that in England. Unfortunately, there the custom is to tax the poor and give to the rich."

Marie was also fascinated by the conversation and found herself looking at the Arab prince, starry eyed. Jawad glanced across at the woman he had come so far to rescue. He was captivated by her beauty and, breaking away from Robin, walked over to her.

"Your Highness," she said, curtsying.

Jawad took her hand and kissed it. He then stood back and, without warning, began to recite a poem.

"From a faraway land, she came to be
A quest of love for me
Her eyes so blue, her skin so pale
That captured my heart in that faraway vale.
She..."

Marie interrupted and began to laugh. "Stop, please, just stop."

"Did you not enjoy my poem?"

"My dear prince, if you wish to woo me, serving up a soppy poem is not the way to do it."

"But I love you and wish to express that love to you in the best way that I know."

Marie laughed again. "Love?" She asked. "You hardly know me. How can you love me? You know full well that you are lusting after me, don't you? You're after my body. Isn't that true?"

"Most certainly not. You insult me. I am a good Muslim man and could not lower myself to such crass thoughts or feelings."

"You are a man and you can deny what you're truly feeling all you like, but I am right."

Jawad was about to speak again but decided to walk away instead. Marie stopped laughing and ran after him, grabbing hold of his arm to stop him.

"I am sorry, Your Highness. Perhaps I'm used only to uncouth men. Perhaps you do feel love. I don't know. What I do know is this. I have feelings for you too, not because you are handsome, although you are in a strange sort of way and not because of your poetry. I am attracted to your courage. You came so far to rescue me, and you fought alongside common men. You are an impressive man, dear prince."

"Then, will you marry me?"

"Is that your culture too? To rush into such an important event?"

Jawad sighed. "Now it is my turn to apologise. I…"

"Prince Jawad, if you want my hand in marriage, it is not I to whom you should be talking. It is my father. Do that, seek his approval. If he agrees, I will agree. Then we will see if there is love."

She smiled and walked past him to stand at Robin's side. The English archer was laughing. "She's a wild one, that one. A real handful. I'd think hard before committing yourself, Prince Jawad."

Jawad smiled, shook Robin's hand and left with Reza towards Jerusalem. The journey would be long for the Persian, with Jawad talking incessantly about the French woman.

CHAPTER 43
1242 A.D.
Marie's Return

Acre seemed bereft of normal activity. Nervous guards staffed the city walls and gates, while the people barricaded themselves in their homes, fearful of an attack by the Saracens. Robin and Marie approached the main gate to the city and were met by a knight who demanded to know their identities and their reasons for being there. It was a dark and chilly night, so both Marie and her escort wore woollen cloaks. Their heads were covered with hoods and their faces barely visible. Marie spoke first. She dropped her hood and called to the guard.

"It is I, Marie, daughter of Raymond. Take us to him. It's a matter of great urgency. Her hair had grown since she was last in the city, but this guard had never seen her before so had no idea if she was who she claimed to be."

He screwed up his eyes to get a better look, despite knowing that he would not have been able to identify her anyway. He pondered for a moment.

If I don't let her in and she is Raymond's daughter, then I'm in big trouble, he thought.

Hesitantly, he approached them, sword in hand.

"Disarm and you may enter," he called out.

They discarded their swords and he escorted them through the city towards the palace. The streets were deserted and there was an uncanny silence all around them. Even the birds had stopped singing. Nothing moved, all window shutters were closed, and all horses were locked inside their stables. The city even smelled different. The market traders, food sellers and spice merchants were absent, and the streets bore a musty smell, instead of the aroma of jasmine and rosemary, shawarma and warm soup.

They were handed over to Bohemond, who escorted them into the city's palace. By the time they reached Raymond's quarters, they were exhausted. Their clothes were dishevelled and dust-coated, their skin was weather-beaten, and their hair knotted and caked in dirt.

Raymond showed an uncharacteristic emotional response to the return of his daughter. He almost ran across the room and wrapped his muscular arms around her, squeezing her tightly and repeatedly kissing the top of her head.

"My God girl, where have you been?"

He caught hold of her shoulders and pushed her to arm's length from him, so that he could get a better look at her.

"Look at the state you're in! Tell me what happened."

Marie smiled but before she could speak, her father noticed Robin standing by the door.

"And who is this gentleman?"

Robin was unable to get a word in edgeways. Marie interjected. Her speech was hurried and full of excitement.

"This is Robin of Loxley father. He and some other men, including Saracens and a Persian, rescued me from a castle in Syria where I'd been taken against my will by Templars."

Raymond looked deeply into her eyes and then glanced up at Robin. He recognised the name and it did not take long before he recalled who he was, but he felt this was not the time to raise it with Robin.

"Come, both of you. Sit and tell me what the hell has been going on."

As Marie related the events of the past two years to her father, Robin remained silent, unless specifically questioned by Raymond. A servant entered a few minutes into Marie's dialogue. He placed a tray upon the table before them and then left the room, as discreetly as he had entered. Raymond took a small cup from the tray and handed it to Robin.

"Ah, Arabic coffee," Robin remarked. *Beer would have been more welcome,* he thought. "Perfect," he said, with a smile of gratitude and a nod of his head.

Marie and Raymond each took a cup and all three downed their beverages in one gulp, as was the tradition and necessity with the rich, thick and unbelievably sweet coffee drunk in these parts. Eventually,

Marie finished, and Raymond leaned back in his chair, his palms pushed firmly together, his fingers perched ponderously on his lips. He took a deep breath.

"What is going on?" he mused. "The Templars are involved in intrigue and conspiracy, but with whom?"

Marie glanced at Robin, then at her father.

"Father," she said, "a Saracen rescued us, a prince from Jerusalem." She paused to ascertain Raymond's reaction to this, but there was none, so she continued.

"Prince Jawad is convinced that his brother, Sieffuddeen, is in league with the Templars in Syria and some Ismaili Assassins in Egypt. Plotting is afoot, but to achieve their ends, they must force war between Acre and Jerusalem."

Raymond rose to his feet and strolled over to the window, his favourite place to be when he had a decision to make. He ran his right hand through his hair and leant his left against the windowpane. Robin looked at Marie. With body language alone, he enquired as to what her father was doing.

"Wait." She mouthed.

Raymond turned around and hailed Bohemond, who appeared from the corridor, post haste.

"Find someone to take a message to the Emir in Jerusalem."

He scribbled a note in Latin, requesting an urgent meeting between them, to find a way of avoiding bloodshed, of avoiding war. Bohemond took the note and left.

CHAPTER 44
1242 A.D.
Assad

Jerusalem was as a city besieged. The defensive walls had been bolstered with weaponry and human reinforcements. In this atmosphere of fear and animosity, Jawad could see that the slightest wrong move could result in an edgy bowman letting loose an arrow before the identity of the travellers could be made known to him. It was unsurprising to him that people were on edge. There had been multiple skirmishes over the past two years, as each side tested the other's defences.

While pondering his next act, movement and noise at the city gates disturbed his thoughts. The sound of creaking wood indicated that the gates had opened, just slightly. A huge, bearded soldier stepped out. He was lightly armoured and held a Roman-style short sword, rather than the traditional Arabic scimitar. His eyes squinting against the sun, he began calling the prince's name.

"We've been expecting you," he cried, shielding his eyes with his left hand.

"Assad?" Jawad murmured the question and his forehead creased in a frown of bewilderment. He hesitated and then stood up, signalling for his comrades to stay hidden.

"Assad!" he called, as he walked towards the gates. "How on earth did you get here so fast? The fighting must have been swift for sure."

They walked towards each other and Jawad offered a handshake.

"I've heard you Syrians are fierce in battle, but this has astounded me."

Assad half smiled and shook the prince's hand firmly.

"And where is my dear friend, Sami?" Jawad continued. "Is he not with you?"

Just then, two of Sami's commandos appeared through the gates, their heads bowed, but Jawad suspected that they were not, for a moment, showing reverence to him. He could see it in their posture; they bowed in shame. He looked again at Assad.

"Where is Sami?" he asked, more forcefully this time, eyeing the Syrians with some distrust, his gaze shifting from Assad to Sami's men and back again.

Jawad knew that Sami would not have remained behind, unless he was dead, and he could not bring himself to accept that Sami had been killed. He paused, waiting for a reply, waiting for some tell-tale sign in Assad's voice.

Assad looked away from the prince. "He's dead. We were fighting our way out of the fortress when an arrow struck him from behind."

Assad had come to Jerusalem only recently. He was a charming man and had convinced everyone in the circle of power in the city, of his loyalty to the Emir. Despite his Syrian lineage and his background as an assassin, Sami had been quick to trust him, but Jawad had always felt that he had been too quick to do so. The prince turned towards the two commandos who had served so loyally with Sami for several years.

"Is that what happened?"

They both shrugged their shoulders and spoke in unison. "We weren't there. Sami and Assad were behind us. We were making tracks from the gate towards the village. We were looking out for any trouble that may have been on its way to meet us from that direction. We didn't see what happened."

Jawad shook his head and eyed the ground.

"We must go inside the city," Assad urged, placing his hand upon the prince's arm and guiding him, protectively, towards the gates.

Jerusalem was deserted. Guards were on duty but were inconspicuous. Assad began to lead the three men towards the Palace, but suddenly took what he insisted was a short cut. He directed them through a wasteland of derelict houses and disused stables. Jawad's suspicions amplified but his thoughts were horrifically intruded upon when Assad suddenly thrust his sword into the back of one of the commandos. The other man reached for his weapon but was too slow. Assad pierced his throat and let his blood-soaked torso slump to the ground, nerves twitching uncontrollably.

Jawad's hand was drawing his own sword from its sheath when Assad struck him across the face with the handle of his weapon. The prince felt the energy of disturbed neurons firing. It flashed from the side that was hit to the opposite side of his head and continued downwards. He felt his right leg going numb and his grip on consciousness waning.

He awoke in a cold, damp cell. He had no idea how long he had been there, or what time of day it was. The cell was windowless and dark, and the walls were thick. The only noise he could hear came from a food grill and a ventilation hole in the cell door. There was no bed, no blankets and nothing that could be used as a toilet. Judging by the sickening smell, the previous occupier used the south-eastern corner of the cell as his latrine, and it had never been cleaned up.

Jawad sat up and leaned his back against the cold, stone, wall. His sword was gone and so were most of his clothes and jewellery, but his immediate thoughts were of the impending war. *How can I warn the Emir now?* he thought.

Just then, he heard Reza calling him from the neighbouring cell. "Nothing is ever easy, is it Your Highness?" He shouted.

"It is good to know you are still alive, my Persian friend," he replied. Then, they both fell silent.

CHAPTER 45
Misfortune

The Emir's army was fully prepared. Saracens stood side-by-side with Moors. The Berber North African warriors had originally been brought to the Holy Land as slaves, but since their conversion to Islam, fought as free men. Muslim men, alongside their Arab brothers. The army's ranks were also swelled by a large contingent of Turks, descendants largely of the Seljuks who had fought and killed their way to the Middle East from the Russian Steppes, but also some Mamluks. They too had converted to Islam and integrated with the Arabs, adopting their language and lifestyle. They had also introduced some of their cultural and political practices into Arab life. The Persians, too, had changed the Arab world. They had significantly influenced the political, military, and diplomatic systems in the Islamic world after the absorption of the remnants of the Persian Empire into the ever-developing Muslim one.

An army of weaponry readied for battle. Saracen, Persian, and Turkish knights straddled magnificent Arab mares. The Moors, however, rode camels into battle. Such a practice was unthinkable to the Arabs, who only ever used these beasts for burden.

The signal was given and the Emir, together with his General, Abdul Qadoos, led their warriors out of Jerusalem towards the open plain, not far from a small village called Megiddo, or Armageddon. Hassan watched the army leave. He had tried, in vain, to convince his father and the powers-that-be in Jerusalem, that this war was wrong. He was rebuked, ignored, and ordered to remain behind as part of the militia that stayed in Jerusalem. Their role, he was told, was to protect the women and children, mainly from opportunist bandits. He shook his head and sighed but wondered where Prince Jawad was. The prince never rode out with the army and, since Hassan's return to Jerusalem, he could not recall having seen Jawad. He decided to investigate his whereabouts.

His search began in the royal palace. It made sense to start there, in case the prince had left some clue as to where he was. He decided to avoid the open courtyard. Instead, he walked around the walls of the building, keeping under the cover of palm trees. Ahead of him, about 60 feet away, was the black hole of an open doorway. A stairwell led from there to the dungeons. *The doorway should be locked*, he thought to himself. Something was amiss here, and, for no apparent reason, he decided to investigate.

He pondered the situation, privately. *Is he there, locked away, held captive? But why would he be?* he asked himself. Yet, something was drawing him toward the door. Everywhere was quiet. There were no people around and the doorway beckoned, like a siren enticing ships to an untimely end upon a mass of sea-smothered rocks. He glanced behind him, making sure nobody was present. Nobody was, so he made his way to the dungeons. He turned, and his heart almost leapt from his chest as he came face-to-face with a middle-aged man who stared down at him, expressionless and wide-eyed. Hassan could not speak through fear and shock and he physically shook, his sweat running ice cold down the back of his neck, his face burning and his fingers tingling.

"You'll need a distraction," the man said, in a whisper.

"What, er who are…?"

"Find some boys, create a diversion and then enter the dungeons. The fourth cell houses Prince Jawad. The fifth holds his friend, a Persian. The keys hang upon the wall outside the cell and Jawad's sword lies prostrate on the floor by the cell door. Release him Hassan. Release him."

Hassan stared into the man's eyes. "Were you sent by Zaman?" He asked, nervously. The man nodded. "Why is his sword lying outside his cell? Why didn't they take it away and who are they anyway?"

"I placed his sword there, but I must go soon. The weapon cannot be lifted by anyone else but Jawad. His captors released the scabbard, let it fall to the ground and left it where it lay. I brought it here and it lies there still, outside his cell. I could not release him though, for my time in this world is limited and I must leave. Now go!"

Hassan ran back the way he had come, searching now for Abbas and some other boys to assist him. What would he say to other boys? How would he and Abbas explain all this without them thinking they were possessed? As he was about to leave the palace grounds he glanced back. The man had gone.

Hassan decided that there would be plenty of children in the palace to help him. He ran to find Abbas first. He knew the youngster would be with some of his friends. He found them sitting together on the Eastern side of the palace grounds, eating oranges that they had picked from one of the many trees that were scattered throughout the palace gardens. They were small children and unlikely to be of much use in creating any kind of diversion. For a moment, he waited, deep in thought and then an idea came to him.

"Rats," he said, more loudly than he had thought, because the children looked at him as he said it.

"What did you say?" one of them asked, rather condescendingly.

"Abbas," he called out, ignoring the child who had spoken. "I need your help and the help of all your friends, but we need some rats too; lots of them, bagged up and angry."

Abbas stood up and walked towards his friend and guardian. "Are you possessed Hassan? What on earth would you want rats for?"

"I can't explain right now, but just believe me. A Jinni told me to do this; a Jinni sent by Zaman."

The mere mention of the overseer's name kicked Abbas into action. "The stables, we'll get rats in the stables. I've seen loads there, but we'll need a heavy sack to catch them in."

It took far longer than Hassan had expected for them to catch any rats and, no sooner had they placed them in sacks than they gnawed their way out. Eventually, they realised that what was needed was bait, a trail of food leading away from the stables and off towards the castle dungeon. As they approached, they noticed that there was only one guard on duty at the cells. He sat at the foot of the stairwell, so the boys decided to lead the rats to the top of the stairs and then chase them down. Seeing about thirty rats scurrying around your feet at around midnight, when tiredness is throwing its weighty blanket over you, can produce a startled response in most people. For this guard it was his most horrifying nightmare. He yelped, like a small dog or a frightened child and then he began stamping his feet in a vain attempt to chase the rodents away. One of them clambered up his leg and as the rest of them ran along the corridor, the guard made a beeline for the stairwell. As he exited the building, he punched the rat, which had reached his waist, and it fell to the ground, hidden in the darkness of the night. The guard stepped away from the doorway and, panic-stricken, began beating his clothes to rid himself of what were now imaginary creatures clawing their way towards his face.

The boys took this opportunity to rush down the stairs towards the cells. Hassan found the keys right where he had been told they would be. He grabbed them and ran along the corridor until he found Jawad's sword. Filled with trepidation, he almost dropped the keys as he tried each one in the lock of the cell door. Finally, he found the right one, turned it and pushed on the door. Jawad was standing on the far side of the cell, looking tired, dirty, and cold. At first, he did not recognise Hassan, but slowly his eyes focused, and he rushed towards him, grabbing his arms.

"What are you doing here? Where's the guard?" he asked.

"Oh, he's otherwise engaged," Hassan replied, with a broad smile. "Quickly, we must get out of here."

"I need my sword," Jawad snapped.

"It's outside the cell. Is it a magical sword? Apparently, nobody except you can lift it."

Outside the cell, Jawad found his sword and his younger brother, whom he hugged and kissed on the top of his head. He picked up the sword and thrust it into the scabbard. Hassan, meanwhile, had freed Reza.

"Have the troops gone?" Jawad asked. Hassan nodded but said nothing. "Then I must get to them", Jawad continued. "If this war goes ahead, Jerusalem is lost. Hassan, Reza, let's go."

He slung his sword over his shoulder and left, the children following behind. At the top of the stairwell, the guard was incapacitated. Hassan turned to the other boys, ready to send them home but Abbas was not with them. The others were white, as if all their blood had been drained from their veins and arteries.

"Where is Abbas?" Hassan asked, anxiously.

"Gone," one of the boys replied, nervously.

"Gone? Gone? What do you mean, gone? Gone where?"

Suddenly, the courtyard was drenched in an unnerving silence and out of the shadows came a man, dressed all in red. He was extremely handsome and not at all a frightening sight, yet Hassan was afraid of him. Something about him was concerning. Jawad had stopped, turned, and was watching as the man took regimental steps towards the boys.

"Hey you!" he called. "Hey!"

The man said nothing. He raised his left hand, palm towards Jawad and thrust the prince against one of the nearby walls. Jawad was pinned there by an unseen force. The younger boys were crying, and Hassan was shaking. "Who are you?" he asked, cautiously.

"I am Iblis so fear me child. I have your little friend. He is mine now and will remain so. Do your worst earth-dwellers but whatever the outcome this day or this week, the child will be mine forever. I have had to leave my realm to come here in person and retrieve my child and for that, someone will pay, later."

Then he dematerialised. The sounds resurfaced, and Jawad rushed over to the boys.

"What does he mean?"

Hassan, man or not, began to cry. He took a deep breath and looked directly into the prince's eyes. His crying stopped, and he turned to the other boys.

"Go home."

They stood frozen, wet with their own urine; their faces were drenched in tears.

"Go home!" Hassan screamed it at them this time and they ran, almost instinctively, never once looking back.

He composed himself, grabbed the prince by the arm and made eye contact once again. "There is nothing we can do for Abbas, but there is much we can do to stop a disaster."

Jawad was somewhat surprised at Hassan's calm and unemotional approach. He was on the brink of tears, his younger brother snatched like that, right before his eyes. Doubt had begun to eat at his mind, but Hassan had chased it away. The prince nodded and led the way to the stables, where the two of them saddled and harnessed two fine stallions. They were walking the horses towards the stable door, when Assad appeared, blocking their exit. Hassan and Reza stepped forward to challenge the Syrian, but Jawad ordered them to stand back.

"He is mine. He murdered a man of honour, a man who was my friend and I will avenge him."

Hassan was relieved that he would not have to face the mountain of a man who stood before them, sword-in-hand. He stepped back and watched as Jawad pulled the magical sword from its sheath. Assad rushed towards the prince and swung his sword but missed his target. Jawad, the sword leading the way, thrust the blade into the stumbling man's side, pulled it loose and then followed with a slash across the man's neck. Assad's lifeless body slumped to the stable floor and Jawad turned back to the horses. He, Reza, and Hassan mounted them and headed out towards Megiddo.

CHAPTER 46
1242 A.D.
The Visitation

The Syrian castle was virtually embedded in the cliff face, on a ridge so high that vast swathes of the Syrian landscape could be viewed with ease. The only entrance was the gate through which Jawad had entered with Reza, weeks earlier. A portcullis guarded the opening that led into a small courtyard. However, it was only used when the castle was under attack and such an onslaught had not occurred for many years. The courtyard was bounded by a series of walls and doors. One of these doors, the most ornately decorated, opened into a great hall, at the far end of which stood two men. One was Pierre Lavelle, the Templar second-in-command. The other was Sieffuddeen, who held a metal goblet in his hand. He took one look at the other man and then threw the goblet against the wall.

"What curse has been bestowed on me, that I should be surrounded by so many fools?" he shouted, not expecting an answer. "How could all of them escape?" he asked, his voice booming around the hall, his face red and the knuckles of his now clenched fists, white.

Finally, one man plucked up the courage to respond. "Five of the escapees were killed before they could make it to the gates," he said, nervously. The others in the room glared at the man, as if to say, *there's your fool.*

Sieffuddeen also glared at the Templar, but with fierce and piercing eyes. "But the prince, my brother, he was here, you say? He came, he freed the female captive and then he escaped the castle, along with this Frankish girl. A damned poet made fools of you all!" He drew his sword and swung it angrily at a nearby vase. The men present flinched as the vase shattered.

The Templar nodded, his lips shaking along with his hands. He wanted to say, *the prince had help*, but he did not dare to do so. His head dropped, and he stared, forlornly, at the floor as the Saracen pushed past him. Sieffuddeen left the hall, muttering his disappointment in Arabic. As he entered the corridor leading away from the main hall, he slammed the heavy oak door behind him. The noise reverberated along the corridor and the echo seemed to continue, perhaps unconsciously, even after the sound had physically ceased.

Sieffuddeen marched along the corridor to a room at the end. There, lay his quarters. Another slamming door accompanied his entrance and then an unprovoked attack on a defenceless chair. Kicked across the room, it came to rest near the window. Sieffuddeen followed its path and stared out at the expanse of land situated beneath and beyond this mountain fortress. His anger was subsiding, and his thoughts turned to battle. His hope was that Jawad's escape would not hinder his plans, his brother's story sounding too far-fetched to be believed by anyone in Jerusalem.

A voice behind him shattered his thoughts and he turned to find a tall man, dressed in Assyrian armour, and armed with two swords.

"What? Who the hell are you and how dare you enter my private quarters without my perm—"

The force that hit him knocked the wind from him and threw him off his feet.

"SILENCE, FOOL!"

The stranger raised a hand and Sieffuddeen was lifted into the air and suspended there, paralysed.

"My name is Abigor and my Master has sent me to offer my assistance to your cause. You seem to need it."

He lowered his hand and Sieffuddeen collapsed in a heap on the floor. The prince's heart pounded and his ability to speak had vacated him. He slid away from the stranger and cowered.

"I thought you were more of a man, Oh prince," Abigor said, sarcastically. "My Master spoke so highly of you. You are one of his, he said, a man of greed, of lies, of murder."

Finally, Sieffuddeen spoke, his voice shaky and uncertain.

"Who, er, who is your Master?" he asked.

"My Master is your Master." Abigor laughed, a cold, self-satisfied laugh. "When you prayed for power, for wealth and for glory, surely you did not think Allah would answer you, did you? Oh no, Sieffuddeen, Allah was deaf to your selfish prayers, but my Master was not. He heard you and has been helping you ever since, and now he has sent me to assist you further, but first you must offer yourself to him."

"But who is he?" Sieffuddeen enquired.

"Shaytaan, Iblis. Now, do you want to win this campaign?"

Sieffuddeen shuddered. For an instant he had doubts, firstly about this information and then, once he accepted what Abigor had told him, whether he should seek help from the Master of Evil himself. However, this messenger was right; Sieffuddeen was motivated by greed, power and wealth and that was to drive his decision now.

"Yes, I want to win this campaign," he replied.

"Then do you accept Iblis as your Lord?"

"I do," came a more assertive reply from the prince.

"Then your fate is sealed, whatever happens here on earth. Your destiny beyond the grave is now decided," replied Abigor as he dematerialised right before the prince's eyes.

CHAPTER 47
1242 A.D.
Confrontation

The armies of Raymond and Emir Al-Afdal faced each other in the afternoon heat, which was having a far worse effect on the Crusaders than it was on the Muslim troops. Weighed down in chain mail, their horses covered in armour and their weapons huge and heavy, the European knights were struggling to remain focused. Many were fainting, and some were stripping their armour away and throwing it to the ground. Foot soldiers had marched a day and a half in this heat and water supplies were limited. The horses were restless, and the men were becoming increasingly disillusioned by the sight of jeering Muslim troops, not only ahead of them, but also on the high ground. There was no sign of tiredness or weakness among the Muslim soldiers. They looked formidable and confident. They were banging their shields and drums and shouting, in unison, Allahu Akbar—God is Greater!

Raymond rode forwards, a flag of truce raised high in his hand. The Emir watched him approach and placed a reassuring hand on Abdul Qadoos' left thigh.

"If we can avoid killing, we should," he said quietly. "Stay here."

Without any further talk, he kicked his horse forward and rode through his troops towards Raymond, arriving alongside the Crusader a few seconds later. There was no translator present, for Raymond knew the Emir spoke French and, as soon as his Arab counterpart halted his horse, he began to speak.

"Peace be unto you Emir and upon your family." The Emir smiled, nodded, and returned the greeting before Raymond continued. "I've been reliably informed that we are both being played for fools." He waited, expecting some reaction, but there was none, so he proceeded. "Tales of Templars and Assassins, uniting with some of your son's personal guard

216

are planning to usurp your authority over Jerusalem; these are the tales that I hear, my friend."

The Emir shifted in his saddle and his horse snorted then shook its head. Its front hooves scuffed at the soil and a plume of dust rose between the two men. The Emir waved it from his face and sighed.

"I too have heard such tales, but from a child, and I find them unconvincing."

Raymond was about to retort when the Emir pointed to the European force behind him. The Frenchman turned, to see some of his horsemen riding forwards.

"Do you break this truce before it has begun, Raymond?" The Emir turned his horse around, preparing to return to his own troops, when he saw two of his own horsemen advancing at pace towards him. One of them was shouting something, although it was lost in the air. It was Jawad, closely followed by Hassan. As they arrived alongside the Emir, their voices were audible.

"It is true, what you have been told," Jawad shouted. "I have been to Syria. I've seen them. I've heard them. While we're here, posturing, they're planning to march on Jerusalem".

Raymond raised a fist, a signal to his advancing men to halt. The Emir, however, frowned and stared into Jawad's eyes. He knew his poet son was one for flights of fancy, and was about to say so, but something in his son's eyes signalled that he spoke the truth. The Emir nodded and turned again to face Raymond who was unaware of what Jawad had said. Something told him that this was not the right time to spark the war. He waited, and the Emir asked his son to repeat his words to Raymond in the Frank's language. Still somewhat suspicious, however, the Emir began to question Raymond.

"What of Abdul-Qadoos' son? My sources say he was killed by a Crusader. He was a five-year-old boy, found with one of your arrows through his heart. Is it true? Is one of your soldiers responsible for this outrage?"

Raymond was impassive. "He was with us, but he was not a hostage and he escaped, helped apparently by an Arab Christian, or so I'm told."

Jawad stepped in again. "Ahmed was not killed by any Christian father. I witnessed his murder and it was at the hands of one of

Sieffuddeen's guards, on his direct orders. Your eldest son, that traitor I am dishonoured to say is my brother, is responsible for Ahmed's death. He issued the order to the Assassin, who fired a crossbow at a fleeing child. Shot in the back like a frightened deer."

The Emir's anger was evident, but Raymond remained calm. His rudimentary knowledge of Arabic helped him to pick up the gist of what the prince was saying. He spoke to Jawad in French.

"Are you the Saracen my daughter has spoken of?" he asked, and Jawad again nodded. "Then you shall dine with us in Acre when all of this is over, but now our armies should ride together against these traitors in Syria."

The Emir looked at his son, sighed and shook his head.

"You will return to Jerusalem, son. You are no fighter and I have already lost one son, a traitor to us all."

"No!" Jawad caught hold of his father's sleeve. "Father, I must join you on this campaign. I cannot be left useless in Acre, while my brother's army tries to steal our Emirate from us."

"I too, will be joining the fight," Hassan said.

Another sigh and the Emir called for Abdul-Qadoos to join them from the ranks of men. He explained everything to his General and advised him to relay the information to the men under his command.

"That settles it," said Raymond. "We go together, prepare our united force in Jerusalem and proceed to war."

The Emir shook his head, assertively and raised his voice at Raymond. "You shall go nowhere. We don't want a Franj army anywhere near Jerusalem. We go alone to Jerusalem."

Raymond called Bohemond, André, Robin and Amalric to his side. They kicked their horses forward and drew alongside him. "These men, plus three others of their choosing, will come with you. Any Templars taken prisoner will return to Acre with my men. Do we have an agreement?"

"Accept the terms, father," Jawad said.

The Emir nodded, suggested that Raymond remain as a defensive force, should his own army be overrun, and offered his hand to strike the deal. Raymond acknowledged, and the two men shook hands. The Arab-Turkish army headed back in the direction of Jerusalem, with seven

Frankish warriors in tow, Bohemond, Amalric, André, Robin and three others. Raymond led his troops back to Acre.

Jawad and Hassan rode alongside the Emir. They would march to Jerusalem, leave a significant force to guard the city and send the rest of the army to fight Sieffuddeen's forces. Part of the tactics would be the use of small commando units who would repeatedly attack Sieffuddeen's army where and when he would least expect it. Depletion of the enemy army before the main battle, was an important strategy.

As they left Megiddo, Jawad reached across to his father's reins and pulled him back.

"Father, I have further sad news, about Abbas."

The Emir pulled his horse to a halt and signalled the rest to continue. Looking his son straight in the eye, he brushed a fly from his face and waited for Jawad to continue. The prince took a deep breath. This was going to be the hardest thing he could say to his father and he needed to build himself up, choosing his words carefully. He could not mention Iblis. His father would think him insane, so he suggested that an unknown assailant kidnapped his younger brother.

Al-Afdal said nothing. He kicked his horse forward and moved to the front of the troop of soldiers ahead of them, to ride alongside Abdul-Qadoos. As Jawad pulled up alongside, his father placed his hand upon the prince's thigh.

"It is unlikely that they will launch their attack now. They will wait to see whether their plan, to force us into war with Acre, has worked."

He paused and felt a chill. Palestine in winter could be a miserable place. "I want you to prepare horses and supplies for a small, advanced unit. We will make it appear as if tensions are increasing here. Troop movements and skirmishes should suffice in forcing Sieffuddeen to wait.

"Then, in the new year, a few weeks away, you will go with Hassan, Arslan, these Franj warriors, my son and some crack troops," he said. "Gather intelligence, and only engage the enemy if absolutely necessary. Otherwise, wait for our army to arrive."

"With all due respect, my Emir," replied Abdul-Qadoos, "I feel we should disrupt the enemy, engage them with deadly stealth and reduce their number. We should create fear and dissent among the enemy before your army arrives."

The Emir frowned and sighed but agreed. "So be it," he said.

CHAPTER 48
1243 A.D.
A Gathering of Intelligence

Night was drawing in. The three commando units looked down from their high vantage point that overlooked the enemy camp. Arslan headed one of the units. His right-hand man, a fellow Mamluk called Mehmet took control of another, and a highly experienced Saracen soldier named Abu Tariq led the third. The seven crusaders were divided among them. Jawad and Reza joined Arslan's group and Hassan followed Abu Tariq. Abdul-Qadoos took overall control of all three groups. They were located about a hundred yards from each other. Each man was well-armed and well-nourished, with plenty of food for the entire group to feast on for several days.

Jawad sat near a crate containing carrier pigeons. Reza, who had joined the commandos en route, had 'borrowed' the birds from an old man in Jerusalem. The Persian himself was nearby, armed with a bow and watching the pathways that led away from their camp, northerly towards the Syrian Citadel.

"How many soldiers do you think there are?" Abdul Qadoos asked Jawad.

"I can't be sure, but there will be too many for twenty-seven of us to handle."

Abdul Qadoos nodded. "We'll gather intelligence, find their weak spots and send the information back to Jerusalem. Hit quickly and efficiently and we'll crush them before they can get any strategic advantage."

Jawad sent a messenger to the other two units and the intelligence gathering began in earnest. When the scouting parties returned to their camp, they relayed all the information they had gathered, to their group leaders, who met with Abdul-Qadoos immediately afterwards.

Several days later, Abdul-Qadoos and his commandos knew that the Emir's army was just two days ride away. He knew the army would be visible to the enemy long before it reached the desired battle area. He also knew that his men, and the six crusaders, would have to make some raids, but the timing of those raids had to be perfect. Chaos and fear had to be induced to distract the enemy.

The following morning, he sent Arslan's unit to attack an assassin group that was on a reconnaissance mission to the south of the main Syrian encampment. Along with his five soldiers, he had Bohemond and a rather fresh-faced English archer, named Owun Tyler. They came upon the five Assassins as dawn broke and Tyler was the first to draw blood. An arrow, fired from his longbow, whistled through a set of trees, and anchored itself into an assassin's chest. The man fell to his knees, clutching at the shaft, unable to move it and feeling his life draining away. It alerted the four remaining enemy soldiers, but they could not see beyond the trees. The sun was high in the sky and the trees were casting exaggerated shadows.

Suddenly, another arrow materialised, striking a second man, this time in the thigh. He let out a scream of pain and his comrades, swords at the ready, scattered.

Arslan came upon the wounded assassin, who had managed to break the shaft of the arrow in his leg but could not pull it free. The Turk's sword slashed across the man's arm, tearing his tunic and the muscle that lay beneath it. He reached for a knife but Arslan's blade came thundering down again. The assassin's hand, knife still gripped in its fingers, was severed at the wrist. He turned white, his bowels opened, and he vomited. It was his final act on earth. Arslan picked up his hand, the knife still held fast within it, and pushed the blade into the man's throat. Gurgling, as the blood filled his windpipe and mouth, he collapsed. Arslan left him where he lay, his dead body looking quite surreal, with his own hand fastened to his neck.

Before long, all the Assassins were dead. Arslan knew that it would take some time before Sieffuddeen became concerned over their overdue return. By then, the Emir's army would arrive, and the defence of Jerusalem could commence. The Turkish officer ordered his group of commandos back.

Back at their makeshift camp, Arslan, Owun and Bohemond talked. Culturally, they had little in common. Even Owun and Bohemond were like chalk and cheese and both were in complete contrast to their new Muslim ally.

"You fight well, Turk." Bohemond said, slapping Arslan on the back.

Arslan smiled and responded in kind. "Strange, the twists and turns fate brings to our lives, don't you think?" He added. "One day we're enemies, full of enmity for each other; now we stand as brothers. You know, the Arabs have a saying that goes 'my enemy's enemy is my friend' and I suppose it applies here, no?"

Tyler placed his bow on the ground, dropped his quiver of arrows alongside it and then sat himself down.

"I don't understand why we've been fighting each other anyway. Ever since I came to the Holy Land, I've found the religion of the Turk and Arab not much different from the religion of the Christians." He said.

Arslan was confused by this statement. "You sound as if you don't subscribe to either of these philosophies Owun," he said.

Tyler looked nervously at Bohemond before replying.

"I'm only here because I was starving and needed a way to make money. I thought there would be rich pickings on a crusade. Boy, was I wrong? Rich pickings, but not for foot soldiers, eh Bohemond?"

The Frenchman said nothing, and Tyler continued.

"As for theology, I'm still a bit of a pagan. Forests like this one are where my gods are." He paused, wondering if he'd said too much, and then added "I know that you lot, the monotheists, are likely to want to crucify me or something for such heresy, but what good would that do? All you'd do is lose yourselves a good archer."

Bohemond laughed and held out his hand, which Tyler grabbed hold of. The big Norman lifted his English associate to his feet and the three of them reformed with their comrades and settled down for a good night's sleep. Within thirty-six hours, ten thousand soldiers from Jerusalem would join them. The fighting would be fierce, and they needed to be alert.

Meanwhile, the spies reported to Abdul-Qadoos.

"Sieffuddeen has clearly taken the advice of his Templar paymasters sir," Arslan said. "They're using heavy horses and a lot of armour.

222

They're forming up in serried ranks, so hit-and-run tactics should be very effective against them."

Abdul-Qadoos nodded and took in a deep breath, as if he had been deprived of air for some time. "These heavy horses," he said, "are they stallions?"

"Oh yes. The Europeans love their stallions."

"Good. Send a messenger back to the Emir, to round up twenty Arab mares on heat. Just before the main attack, we'll send them through the enemy ranks."

He nodded to Reza who tied a red chord to one of the pigeon's legs, before releasing it into the air. The bird circled twice and then made off in the direction of Jerusalem, where the message would be taken by a horseman to the Emir's main force. The two men prayed for the bird's safe journey, but then they heard shouting from among their men. Sieffuddeen's army had arrived. Abdul-Qadoos found Jawad and together they watched the approaching forces.

"We will have to fight them, hold them in this place until your father's reinforcements arrive", Abdul-Qadoos whispered.

Some hours later, the pigeon arrived in Jerusalem. The old man knew what to do once his birds returned. He rushed to the palace and notified the guards of the red chord signal. A horseman carried the message at great speed to the Emir, who knew time was of the essence. He ordered his army to pick up the pace.

They moved quickly, stopping only to collect the horses that Abdul-Qadoos also requested in his message. Many of these were taken from the garrison, but more were commandeered from farms and homes en route. At one farm, there was resistance, the farmer being a horse breeder, who did not want to hand over his prize mares to an army. Initially, this resistance was dealt with brutally by the Emir's troops, but he knew they needed the support of these people once war took hold. Speedily, he ordered them to stop and offered the farmer a princely sum of money, far greater than the horses were worth. The farmer acquiesced, and the army moved on, bringing with it, at the rear, about forty in-heat mares.

CHAPTER 49
1243 A.D.
Trickery

There was a period of virtual calm, as both sides waited for the other side to act. Jawad scanned the opposing army's ranks, trying to identify some point of weakness, while all the time feeling the fear rising within him. He turned to his left and looked at Reza, who was staring, almost mindlessly, at his sword. He was whispering to himself, or maybe to the sword. Perhaps it was a prayer that he was muttering. Whatever it was, he did not notice Jawad's gaze.

Jawad could hear his own breathing; the silence had become so intent. Then, without warning, a horn blew. *Not one of his*, he thought, and realisation hit him like a spear from nowhere. The enemy were charging. The noise of thundering hooves, of screaming men, of swords being struck rhythmically against shields, exploded into the air. Dust rose on the plain as Sieffuddeen's army roared forward.

Seconds felt like hours as Abu Tariq's group, in which Hassan had been placed, waited for the order to engage the enemy. Hidden, out of sight, Arslan led a troop of fighters that would attack the enemy's left flank, while Al-Afdal's forces prepared to do the same on the right flank. Finally, the order from Abdul-Qadoos came, and Abu Tariq's small band of horse-mounted men hurtled towards the enemy horsemen. The plain was shrouded in dust and then the noise of the clashing of metal against metal filled the air as the two horse units met.

Hassan was at the helm of this cavalry force and he struck the first blow against an advancing rider, slicing through muscle and bone, severing the man's sword arm completely. It fell, obscenely, to the ground, but Hassan had already moved on, slicing at as many men and horses as he could, feeling blow upon blow land on his own shield and sensing the occasional sword blade narrowly miss him.

Then, once he and the men around him had devastated the enemy horse soldiers, Abu Tariq gave the order to retreat. Jawad and the remaining troops from his group separated, opening a thoroughfare, to allow their horsemen and Abu Tariq's to ride through to the rear of the army. Now was the time for the archers to execute their role with efficiency and murderous consequences. They struck before the remnants of Sieffuddeen's cavalry had reached safety. Horses and men fell like fruit toppling from the branches of trees. Many of the men were crushed by their own horses or trampled by others. Owun Tyler's archers continued to fire, using English longbows, for these were English archers. Days before, Bohemond had sent for them and ten had taken up the call to battle, at great financial cost to Bohemond. Their range gave them immense advantage, while Sieffuddeen's crossbowmen were forced to wait for Abu Tariq's troops to move closer. They did not move. They waited until the artillery barrage from the longbowmen had done the greatest amount of damage. Then, finally, the surge forward came. Men, shrieking, full of fear and bravado, the contradiction of emotions that came with battle.

They struck the centre of Sieffuddeen's army and Jawad saw Reza scything his way through the enemy with the utmost efficiency. A sword swung past Jawad's head, missing him by a whisker, but he thrust his own weapon into the assailant's chest, the sound of ribs breaking and the sight of blood spurting, hardly noticed by Jawad, as he continued to run onwards, into the melee. The united smells of shit, piss, blood and sweat quickly clouded both the air and each soldier's judgement. Bloodlust drove them on, and they could smell a small victory above all else.

Apart from the other unit that had been divided to cover each flank, Abdul-Qadoos's forces were completely committed. Even the archers had discarded their bows and taken up swords before running, almost aimlessly, into the midst of the battle. Owun, leading them onwards, lost his footing on a slimy mixture of faeces and blood. He fell backwards, landing cumbersomely upon the corpse of a soldier. There was no telling whose army the fallen warrior was from, but that body saved Owun's life. An approaching swordsman, weapon swinging wildly at the fallen archer, tripped over the corpse and landed, flat on his face, in front of Tyler who, without a second thought, thrust his sword through the man's face and head. Then, still sliding on the slimy ground, he managed to make it to his feet, assisted by a comrade. The fight continued but his side were losing. Now was the time for the flanking troops to bear down on the enemy.

A signal was given, and they moved in. But it was a trap. Sieffuddeen had not committed his main force. His army was so much larger than the estimates Jawad and Abdul-Qadoos had received from their spies and now this fact dawned on them.

Once all of Abdul-Qadoos's forces were fully engaged, hordes of enemy cavalry descended upon them, screaming like hell hounds, kicking dust high into the warm air, and ripping into their outnumbered, isolated opponents. Finally, Sieffuddeen appeared. Jawad saw him, seated upon a white stallion, some distance beyond the mayhem of this battleground, behind his infantry forces which lay in eager expectancy, awaiting the command to move forward.

Abdul-Qadoos ordered the retreat and all of his army, those who were still alive and able to escape, moved hastily away. Jawad took one glance back; he looked, firstly at his side's decimated soldiers, then at the victorious enemy cavalry, waving their swords in the air and shouting insults at the retreating army. Finally, he looked at his brother, sitting proud at the rear of his troops. *It's over*, Jawad thought to himself, expecting his brother to order the advance of his infantry, who would inflict the final blow. *We have lost.* But the army did not advance and the deflated, retreating force was watched by Sieffuddeen and his troops from a distance.

Abdul-Qadoos spurred his horse forward until he was alongside Jawad, who was still gazing behind him.

"Why aren't they advancing?" Jawad asked. "They could finish us."

"Look," replied Abdul-Qadoos, pointing ahead of them.

Jawad turned and saw his father, with an army that must have numbered more than fifty thousand souls. The fight was not over. The fight had only just begun.

CHAPTER 50
1243 A.D.
An Equine Tactic

At precisely one o'clock on the day the Emir and his troops arrived, the fertile mares stampeded towards the Templar and Syrian army. The stallions went wild, their riders lost control and chaos rang through their ranks. Many of the horses charged away from the relative safety of the high ground their riders had hoped to occupy before the fighting began, soaring down the hill sides and into the exposed valley below. Some then found themselves mired in marsh, too heavy to manoeuvre.

A rain of arrows fell upon them from their southern flank, followed by a cavalry charge into their midst. Within minutes, Sieffuddeen's cavalry had been cut to pieces and he was forced to commit his infantry, not as an initial assault backed up by horsemen, but as a futile attempt to rescue the men on horseback, and their horses.

Some forty minutes had passed before the fighting reached its peak. Almost every warrior had been committed and the raging battle triggered Jawad's battle response. Adrenaline rushed through him like waters forcing their way through a broken dam. Then, as an enemy sword ripped through his side, tearing at his flesh and muscle, his brain flooded his body with endorphins, nature's painkiller hormones. His response was instinctive. His right arm brought the curved sword upwards and it sliced through the enemy's neck, his head left rolling on the floor behind him. His body slumped to the ground and Jawad, all fear quelled by the physiological reaction to this horrendous situation, stepped across it and waded deeper into the mass of fighting men.

For what seemed a lifetime, he thrust forwards, ignoring the pain from his wound. His sword was slashing into men's flesh, breaking bone, and sapping life. Then, he saw his brother. Sieffuddeen was still mounted on his horse, shouting orders while desperately fighting off his attackers.

Jawad moved towards him without hesitation, but Abdul-Qadoos reached him first. The mighty Saracen General called to Sieffuddeen and the disgraced prince spun around to face his challenger.

"Child killer, I'm going to send you to Hell!" Abdul-Qadoos shouted, as he moved in on his quarry, but the prince made no effort to prepare his defence, either verbally or with sword.

Jawad saw the reason why immediately. A crossbowman steadied his lethal weapon and took aim at Abdul-Qadoos' back. There was no chance to warn the General before the bolt thundered into his back, smashing through bone, tearing into his chest, and forcing the Saracen warrior to the ground. Sieffuddeen dismounted his horse and stepped across to Abdul-Qadoos' limp, expiring body. The prince tilted his head, scrutinising the dying man as he began choking on his own blood.

"Like father, like son," Sieffuddeen said with a smirk of satisfaction. "Now you can join him," he added before thrusting his sword deep into the General's chest, piercing his heart and extinguishing the flame of life forever. The prince stood for a moment, admiring his 'work', when suddenly he heard his brother's voice from behind. He turned.

"Brother or not, I'm going to kill you," Jawad shouted.

He broke into a run, hoping that he could reach Sieffuddeen while his mind set was focused on justice, rather than revenge, but after a few strides a giant Templar stepped in his way. The knight swung at him with his shield, which struck the prince's injured left arm, knocking him from his feet and sending shockwaves of pain through him. The Templar stepped forwards and raised his sword, point down, preparing to thrust it into the now prostrate prince. Jawad was certain he was about to die but an arrow, fired from God alone knows where, pierced the knight's mail, entering his right calf. His leg gave way and with his balance gone, he fell sideways, his sword now used as a crutch to steady himself and prevent a complete collapse. Jawad took his chance, pulled his own sword up and forced it into the Templar's groin. The knight screamed and collapsed, blood spurted from the wound, and Jawad brought himself to his feet. He looked around for his brother, only to find that he had mounted a horse and was now riding towards him. The two princes were face-to-face. Jawad thought hard. Should he run towards his brother or wait for his enemy to come to him? He decided to wait. He hoped the mystical sword would not fail him in this hour of need.

Sieffuddeen kicked his horse and charged at his younger brother, confident of victory over the Poet Prince whom he so despised. Slashing at nearby warriors with his sword as he rode over the bodies of the slain, he could almost taste the blood that he was about to shed.

Jawad waited and watched. Then, as the horse jumped the last body in its path, Jawad thrust the sword into the ground. The earth shook and Sieffuddeen's horse toppled onto its side. Jawad stepped to his right and plunged his sword deep into the animal's neck, killing it instantly. Its rider was now trapped beneath the dying beast. Sieffuddeen fought to free his right leg, panic setting in, profanities issuing forth from his now dry mouth. It was too late for him though. His leg was almost certainly broken, and he had lost his sword in the fall. He looked up one final time and the last thing he saw was Jawad's sword swinging high above him. Seconds later he was dead, his brother's sword slicing through his jugular before being returned to its scabbard.

Jawad knelt and closed his brother's eyes. He said nothing, made no prayer of forgiveness for his sibling and shed no tears. A brief look at Sieffuddeen's body and then he returned to the battle, sword drawn once more in preparation for further bloodshed.

Close by, a tall Saracen, bathed in white light, fought his way through the enemy ranks, cutting and slashing. Jawad did not recognise him, but Hassan knew his name. It was Zenith and he winked at Jawad, before continuing to engage in the carnage.

Reza, meanwhile, had fought to the point of exhaustion. He had slain many men but had miraculously escaped injury himself. As he drew his sword from yet another dying man, he paused to catch his breath, but his moment of relaxation was to be a brief one. The sky above him suddenly burst open, like silk torn by a sharp knife, and from this fissure, there appeared a warrior on horseback. He carried a lance and behind him followed a multitude of legions. Zenith broke away from the battle and rushed towards Reza, grabbing him by the shoulder and pulling him away with all his might.

"Abigor!" he shouted, a fearful tone in his voice. "You must gather all your people, Reza, and leave."

"Who is Abigor?" Reza was dazed and confused and for an instant he was frozen to the spot.

"He is the Grand Duke of Hell, a demon who knows all the secrets of warfare and of the future. He comes with sixty legions of Hell demons and only we can stop him, so GO! LEAVE, NOW!"

Reza waited no more. As if recovering from a trance, he ran towards Jawad and the others, passing on Zenith's orders as he went. As many of them that could, ran from the battle that now raged before them. Jinn fighting Jinn, the forces of Zenith matching the forces of Abigor. Human soldiers, desperate to escape, were caught between them. The sky was red, and the earth was scorched as demons and spirits fought to the death. Then, without any warning whatsoever, the fighting stopped. Abigor was gone, his soldiers were no more, but Zenith had gone too. All that remained were the armies—that of the Emir and that of Sieffuddeen— some bewildered, some running in panic and others eager to continue with the killing.

Just then, Jawad looked up and saw a man, casually strolling among the hundreds of dead and dying, analysing them, scrutinising every detail upon their faces. The few that remained alive felt the life sapped from them as soon as they looked him in the eye. He strolled through the thick of the fighting that had re-started in earnest among the humans in small pockets of the battlefield. He walked among them, apparently unnoticed by most of the humans who were present. He was dressed in a white Jelabiya, an Arab robe with long sleeves, almost dress-like in appearance. He was a young man and handsome, his dark skin tone, black hair and deep brown eyes, standing out against the white robe.

As the prince watched him, the man touched one of the Emir's young Saracen warriors on the shoulder. The soldier collapsed in a heap and Jawad, shocked, felt his heart beat faster and his brow perspire. Again, the man touched one of the Emir's warriors and again the man fell, undoubtedly dead, at his feet. He sauntered through the blood-soaked battlefield, killing with just a touch or a glance. Jawad picked a bow and arrow from the body of a dead archer, aimed it, and fired it at the stranger. Time seemed to have stopped. The arrow flew, but nothing else moved. It struck the stranger high on the chest and then vanished. The stranger stared at Jawad and smiled. Then, time ticked on again, as did the man, ignoring Jawad's feeble attempt to halt his progress.

The prince noticed others. Demons, ghouls, Jinn, moving among the Emir's army, killing and maiming, creating confusion as the soldiers tried to work out who was attacking them.

He watched his men as they continued to fight their enemies, oblivious of the stranger among them and, it seemed, oblivious of Jawad too. It was as if the two events were occurring on different plains of reality.

"Don't you see him?" Jawad called to one of the men, but there was no response.

Then, as he reached the very edge of the battleground, he came across Reza, standing tall.

"Do you seem him?"

"Yes," the Persian replied. He was armed with a bow and arrow, which he pointed menacingly towards the Demon who approached them.

"Don't do it Reza."

He heard the voice behind him, despite the softness of its tone and volume, but he never flinched, focused as he was on the approaching target.

"You can't kill him Reza, I've tried and failed."

Reza never moved, even as he responded to the prince. "Then we must try again."

Before Jawad had a chance to reply, he noticed that the stranger had reached the young Persian. He caught hold of the bow, pushed it away from the archer and smiled.

Jawad took aim with his own bow once again and was about to unleash another arrow when he felt someone, or something, placing a hand on his shoulder. For a second time in the battle, his bladder opened, uncontrollably. He felt as if his heart were about to explode, but he did not collapse; he did not die. He heard a voice—a voice that he recognised.

Behind him, Zenith watched the events. His wings were almost translucent, with the sun's rays passing right through them, before diffusing to flood the entire region with blinding light. Reza vanished and as the light dissipated, he reappeared, stunned and confused.

Jawad was also in a state of disorder. "I... I remember you, I think, but... but I don't know where from."

231

Zenith ignored his remarks. "You were right, Jawad, you cannot kill him. He is Iblis, Shaytaan, the mightiest of all demons. Leave him be. He can't hurt you while I am here, so let him go."

He stepped around Jawad and raised his right hand towards Iblis. "Your interfering must end," he shouted, "or we will end it."

Suddenly, strange beings surrounded Jawad, an army of them, equipped with swords and spears, shields, bows and arrows. Yet, they seemed without form, merging on occasion, one with another.

Iblis stepped away from Reza, withdrawing several steps as Zenith's army of Jinn moved forward, hacking and stabbing at Sieffuddeen's army as they went. Iblis frowned in anger and lowered his gaze, unable to look directly at Zenith or his soldiers.

"I have lost this one, but there will be others," he said. "My time will come! This land and other lands will drive humankind to war, and I will be there. I will be there when they plot, when they lie, when they kill and when they die. I will pull them and push them, lead them astray, trick them and possess them, causing an affray. I will create chaos, mistrust, deceit, greed and enmity among these cursed humans. That was the deal that I struck with the Creator and the one to which I am shackled until the end of time. The universe is my playground until the Day of Judgement. That is what He promised, but I will work out a way to gain the upper hand. One day I will dominate. One day, I will hold the world in my hands and call it mine. And remember, I have the child, my grandchild."

Zenith, the Angel Jinni took a slow step forward, touched Reza on his shoulder and looked straight into Iblis' eyes.

"You have the child and you may work your influence on him, but we will fight for his freedom, be sure of that." Zenith paused to watch the events unfurling behind Iblis and then flicked his head in that direction.

"Your minions are finished. They are running and it is time for you to go. I don't doubt you will continue to usurp power until the Final Day, but when that day comes, the Creator will finally rid us all of you and yours. If you do hold the world in your hands, it will be for but an instant—a moment in time for you to reflect on all your wasted years. That day will be the end of all days."

Iblis vanished, as did his Jinn supporters. The air was still and hushed, but filled with the smells of shit, piss, blood, and vomit. A battleground is no pleasant place to be. Sieffuddeen's army was scattering. Some were ruthlessly and mercilessly cut down as they ran, but within minutes the fighting had stopped, and the light faded. Reza and Jawad found themselves alone among the dead. The spirit beings were gone, and he remembered them only as a vision. For the briefest of moments, he wondered whether they were perhaps just an hallucination. Reza picked up his bow and threw it over his left arm. He replaced the arrow in its quiver and wandered around the carnage.

Jawad, meanwhile, surveyed the devastation. He had become a different man and wondered how the world would deal with what had happened here. His thoughts provoked an unexpected response—a voice spoke to him, but nobody was near him. Yet, it was a real voice, of that he had no doubt.

No man shall remember us for many decades. Even you, Jawad, for a long time, will remember only the everyday happenings of life in Jerusalem. You will, however, recall your deep love for a woman in Acre. She also, will remember you, but the circumstances of your first meeting will be distorted.

Jawad froze to the spot. "What do you mean and who are you?"

Since you will soon forget that I even exist, there is no point in telling you who I am.

The prince sighed, Reza threw a glance at him, unsettled by the prince talking to himself and the voice continued.

Over time, some of you will find yourselves with vague memories of the Jinn, but you will not have a firm grasp of the whole truth until the destined time is nigh. Your scholars and your holy men will record nothing of the past two years, but your stories will live on as myths and legends. History, my friend, will be written without a single mention of what has happened here since Hassan and his friends plunged into our world.

"And what of this battle, and Abbas? What of him?"

The voice softened. *People died in battle and that will be recalled, but which battle and how? That will become a vague distortion of reality.*

Abbas, my friend, is lost—at least for now. You will remember him as a child and although for some years there may be a hope of his return, ultimately, you'll accept that his fate may have been to die, although you'll not know for sure whether he did, or how.

We will strive to release him from Shaytaan's grasp, but already he is in the boy's mind. Before long, he may be lost to Shaytaan forever.

For a moment, the prince appeared to black out, but the feeling passed and, returning to full consciousness, he was overwhelmed with a determination to ride to Acre and find Marie. He ran to the nearest horse and, as he mounted her, he surveyed the dead and dying. Already, he had no recollection of the battle. He took one last look at the devastation and felt a hand nestling upon his shoulder and a strong, but tender voice reassured him.

"Trust in God for we have won this day."

It was Sami. The prince turned and hugged his friend. They shook hands, hugged each other, surveyed the scene, and shook their heads, in unison.

"Assad said you were dead. What...?"

"He left me for dead, it's true, but I was saved by an angel. I drifted from this life, from this world, to another where a spirit being spoke to me. I can't remember his words or what happened to me next. Dying one minute, alive the next—a miracle my prince."

Jawad nodded and grasped his friend's arm in friendship, gratitude, and solidarity. "There are great mysteries that we may never fully understand, my friend, but magical forces are supporting us, while others offer succour to our enemies."

"Most definitely," Sami replied and then he glanced around. "Now, where is that traitor Assad?" He asked.

"He's dead," replied Jawad, "and I doubt any angel will waste any effort reviving him."

The prince smiled, Sami reciprocated, and they looked out at the two armies on the plain below, Sieffuddeen's troops running or riding away, the Emir's troops chasing, hacking at them as they ran.

"Acre?" Sami asked.

Pondering, Jawad looked out in the direction of the coast. He nodded. "Yes, my friend, Acre. We will travel with the Franj who fought with us this day, to make our passage into the city easy."

They walked to their horses and Jawad was startled to find Marie waiting there for him. She ran to the prince, hugged him, and kissed him passionately on the lips. It was a kiss that she wanted to linger but Jawad gently pushed her away.

"Marie. What are you doing? This is not our way for ones not married."

Marie was annoyed at first but then stopped before she said something that would create even greater tension. "I am sorry, Jawad, but since we went our different ways after Syria, I have done nothing but think of you and when I do, my heart beats uncontrollably."

Jawad smiled. "I too have missed you, Marie but I am concerned that you are here, so close to such a brutal battle."

"I insisted and I'm adept at getting what I want," she replied. Then, she smiled. "And on that note, why don't you marry me if that is what your religion requires? I will even take your religion if I must."

Jawad smiled again. "It would make me the happiest man in the world to marry you, for you are the beauty that lights my life and of course it would be wonderful for you to become Muslim, but…"

His pause was met with a frown on Marie's face.

"… but, you do not need to change religion for the Quran tells us that we can marry those from among the People of the Book, and that is the Jews and Christians and you are Christian, are you not?"

She nodded. "Yes, yes, I am, but does this mean you will marry me?"

Jawad sighed and nodded. "With your father's approval, yes."

She hugged him again, realised his discomfort and pulled away. "Sorry," she said.

Embarrassed, Jawad glanced at Sami, who was laughing.

Then, he noticed the frown on Marie's face. "What is it?" He asked.

"My father may not give his permission for me to marry a Saracen, prince or not." She sighed, then shook her head. "Regardless, I will approach him and, er, persuade him."

CHAPTER 51
1243 A.D.
Departure from the Holy Land

Jerusalem remained in the hands of the Saracens, while Acre remained a Crusader town, for the time being anyway. The truce would last for several years, but eventually the Europeans would leave. The Holy Land would never be a peaceful land though. Army upon army, wave upon wave of settlers, invaders, travellers, would tread its holy soil, for centuries to come.

Already, the seeds of conquest were being fermented in the Steppes, where Mongol hordes desired new trophies, new lands to plunder. Yet, within the lands yoked by the Mongols, Turkish tribes began to dissent, and in due course, these too would set their sights on Jerusalem. Already, in Egypt, Mamluk slaves, trained as warriors, converted to Islam and given great power and responsibility, were beginning to take control.

For now, though, all was quiet. The sun's rays bathed the town of Acre in its warmth and light as Marie stood at the dockside, her father's roughened hands tenderly wrapped around her own delicate fingers. A tear welled up in her eye, but she smiled. Raymond hugged his daughter for a while, then stood back and nodded. It was a nod of resigned acceptance, for she had decided to stay in Palestine with Jawad and her father had given his approval for their marriage.

He, however, was headed home to France. He was tired of war on foreign soil and matters of great urgency summoned him home.

"I am happy for you, my daughter," he had said to her. "I, however, must return to France. Cedric, the man I sent to resolve our problem there, is a traitor and I must deal with him."

Marie looked confused. "What has he done?"

Raymond stared out over the sea and sighed. "It seems he was in league with our enemies, having made a pact to gain control of Acre, had they won. At the very least, I do not want him anywhere near my estate or my family, so I will challenge him for the truth and remove him."

"Kill him, you mean."

"Not unless it is absolutely necessary."

Marie hugged him and wandered over to Jawad.

For one last time Raymond looked at his daughter, standing now at the dockside with Jawad's arm around her waist. Raymond waved. Marie waved back. Then, she turned and walked away, her new home awaiting her—Jerusalem.

Robin was preparing to board the ship too. He would sail with them to France and then on to England. He bade farewell to his new comrades in arms, lifted his meagre belongings over his left shoulder, threw his bow and quiver over his right, and walked toward the ship.

"Let me take that for you," a voice from behind shouted.

Unaware that the voice was speaking to him, Robin continued, but found his progress halted by someone pulling on the rope that bound his clothes in a canvass sack.

"I'm coming with you Robin. It is time I saw the world."

"Sami? You're most welcome, but be warned, in England, the people will view you as a very strange creature indeed".

They boarded the ship, the crew worked hard to prepare it for sailing and Robin, with his unexpected travelling companion, talked in Robin's quarters. Despite being moored at the dock, the ship swayed with the lapping tide and the strong wind that blew across the face of the port. Sami was struggling to focus clearly on what Robin was saying, and eventually rushed to the deck and threw up overboard. Upon his return to the cabin, his brown skin had turned decidedly pale. Robin tried to explain European ways to the Saracen, although he doubted very much anything had been taken in. Eventually, he suggested that Sami go to his own cabin and keep a very large bowl, perhaps even a barrel, nearby.

Half an hour later, the ship set sail, for Cyprus, then Spain, France and England.

CHAPTER 52
1253 A.D.
Hulegu

Several thousand miles away from Jerusalem, a nomadic warrior was tending to his horse on the Asian Steppes. His name was Hulegu, grandson of Genghis Khan, whose real name was Temujin. The Great Khan's people had once been scattered throughout Mongolia and the Steppes, divided into warring tribes, but Temujin had united them all and built an Empire of ruthless warriors. They had spread, like a plague, into China, where Hulegu's older brother, Kublai had begun to build a magnificent city, Xanadu, in the lands of the Chin that had now become part of what was the Mongol Empire. Within a decade, Kublai would become ruler of the whole of China and founder of the Yuan Dynasty. The Mongols had forged West too, bringing with them death and destruction. To some they were the Gog and Magog spoken of in the Bible and the Quran and here, alone with his most favoured horse, stood Hulegu. Battle-hardened and scarred, he was a terrifying sight to behold, even though he appeared to be alone. His pony had picked up a sharp stone in one of its hooves and, although his bondsmen had insisted that they stay with him while he removed it, he ordered them to continue to their camp, some two miles north.

Once the stone was removed, he checked the pony's hoof thoroughly for cuts. There were none and there was no sign that the animal was lame, so Hulegu retrieved his saddle and threw it over the pony's back. It was a Mongolian pony, small and very fast. It snorted and shifted slightly to the left, as the saddle touched it. Hulegu was distracted, however. He felt as if he were not alone and, for a moment, he glanced all around him, but saw no-one. There was also nowhere for anyone to hide, at least not in the immediate vicinity. This was a vast open savannah, dusty, with little vegetation present. He sighed and continued to prepare his pony.

He was strapping his saddle on, when he was startled by a voice behind him. He drew his sword and turned to face two strangers, who seemed unarmed but calm.

"Who are you? Talk or I will take your lives!"

The older of the strangers smiled. "My name is Abigor and you, I know, are Hulegu Khan, grandson of Genghis and soon to be first Khan of Persia."

The Mongol continued to hold his sword in readiness. He seemed unsure but intrigued and allowed the stranger to continue. All the while, however, he was scrutinizing the two strangers, calculating ways of killing them in case the need arose.

The older stranger continued to speak. "Our Master has sent us to make a suggestion to you Hulegu," he said.

As Abigor spoke, the younger of the two strangers stepped out from behind him, causing Hulegu to take a step forward, his sword gripped tightly in his right hand.

"How is it you have appeared here, when only minutes ago I saw no presence of any living thing here in this area?" Hulegu's eyes flitted from one of the strangers to the other and back. "Answer me, stranger, or I will take your head." He showed bravado and mistrust, rather than fear, but Abigor seemed disinterested in Hulegu's reaction. He laughed and waved a conciliatory hand towards Hulegu before continuing.

"Fear not, my Mongol friend," he said. "Simply heed my instructions. Ride south and take this youth with you. His name is Abbas and you will train him in the ways of war. Ride south Hulegu, for Persia awaits your arrival."

The young Mongol warrior blinked and Abigor was gone. Hulegu's face now revealed fear. He was a superstitious man, reliant on the Shamans for advice and fearful of the spirit world. The magical appearance and disappearance of a man, right in front of him, set him on edge. Cautiously, he stepped towards Abbas and, realising the boy was now alone, recovered his senses and took control of the situation. He took a deep breath and walked away.

"I cannot ride south!" he called out. "I must first return to my camp and seek orders from my brother Mongke."

Abbas was now twenty-seven years' old but, due to his time spent in the Jinn world, he looked seven or eight years' younger. He was taller than Hulegu by several inches, and he stood, straight backed, with authority. Suddenly, he called to Hulegu, not through speech, but telepathically, triggering a cluster of neurons in the Mongol's head that registered immense pain. *You cannot resist our master's call, but we shall firstly go north, where I'm sure your brother will instruct you to ride south.*

The warrior fell to his knees and the pain ceased. Abbas walked past him.

"Come now," he said, "no need to kneel. We have an Empire to build."

He paused, watched Hulegu struggle to his feet and then added; "You will introduce me as your new Shaman and I will work miracles amongst your people, but in return you will tutor me in the ways of war."

Hulegu caught his breath and nodded, somewhat reluctantly. He mounted his horse, looked down at Abbas and, just for a moment, considered riding away. Instead, he held out his hand to the youth, who grabbed it and was hauled behind the Mongol. Hulegu thrust his legs into the animal's side, urging it forwards.

It was 1253 A.D. and a new alliance had been formed.

Part Two:
Merlin's Staff

CHAPTER 53
1255 A.D.
Jerusalem

Jerusalem, 1255, and rumours were spreading like wildfire about the Mongol Horde that had ravished the plains of Asia, Eastern Europe and much of China. It was now firmly in control of Islamic regions, such as Samarkand; lands from which the Seljuk Turks had come were now held securely in the grip of shamanist pagans. Hulegu's Tumans had conquered Persia and now they coveted Baghdad and Syria. Muslims felt shame but also guilt and the Mosques were rife with controversy and debate about God's punishment for a host of reasons.

Jerusalem, like so much of the region, had changed hands numerous times; Christians, Saracens, Khawarizmian Turks and most recently the Mamluk Turks had held dominion. The Mamluks' overall rule was established in Egypt and, from there, they controlled a region from Syria to North Africa. The Jewish population of Jerusalem, who had been so brutally treated by Jerusalem's Christian rulers, had returned to the city once it had fallen to the Mamluks. They had begun to thrive once again, holding positions of considerable influence in the city—lawyers, doctors, jewellers, bankers and even political advisers. Now, however, they feared that a new war would bring new occupiers and a repeat of earlier oppression.

One such man, from a Jewish family of great prestige, was Judah Ben Zakai, a translator who had worked on numerous texts from many parts of the Muslim-dominated world, from India to Spain. His ancestors were Khazars, who had arrived in Jerusalem during the first crusade, and settled in Jerusalem, only to find themselves attacked and uprooted during later Crusades. About the year 740 A.D., many of the Khazars, a powerful Turkish tribe occupying the steppes of southern Russia, became converts to Judaism and were often referred to as the thirteenth tribe of

Israel. They were hated by the Christians and often mistrusted by the Muslims, but under Mamluk rule, the Jewish Quarter of Jerusalem thrived and the Mamluk's Turkish cousins, the Khazari Jews, thrived with it. Ben Zakai worked closely with the Emir, translating documents, and acting as interpreter during negotiations.

The Mamluks themselves were former slaves and one irony had not been lost on Hassan, who had once been the Mamluk Atabeg or tutor to the Saracen Emir's son, Abbas. That irony was that the Mamluks had once been Genghis Khan's slaves whom he had sold to the Egyptians. Now they might be heading to war with their previous masters.

Hassan was now thirty-one years old, but still had the appearance of a young man. He had been a full-time soldier since his return from Al-Baahita and had seen many battles over the years, although memories of his youth were hazy to say the least. He was aware that he was not showing his age and wondered whether this would continue as the years passed. No detailed records of birth dates were kept by the Arabs or Turks, so only those who had known him all his life would realise that there was something unusual about this man. Most of his friends would age. They would become frail and weak; they would die while he would continue to live. While they became feeble, he would remain as strong as an ox and fearsome as a lion. This was the reason he had separated from many of those who knew him some years earlier, to prevent the whisperings of those who saw his eternal youth as demonic. He had spent many years drifting from place to place, taking command of various military units across the region.

Apart from his apparent slow aging, something else troubled him. His ward, the Emir's son, Abbas, had been lost to an enemy at some point but he could not remember why or how it had happened. His closest friends also suffered this strange memory loss. One specific phase in their lives was cloudy. There was a battle, they remembered that, and many lives were lost. Abbas' brothers were involved, and one had killed the other, but nothing clear was available to anyone. The surviving brother, Prince Jawad, had married a beautiful European noble woman, Marie, who hailed from Frankia. Jawad had given up all claims to his right to Jerusalem, choosing instead to take up farming and horse breeding. He too had separated himself from society because, like Hassan and Marie, he had hardly aged at all since Abbas' disappearance. Hassan had grown close to Jawad over the years, however, and would visit him from time to time on his land on the West Bank of the River Jordan.

Standing just outside the gates of Jerusalem, he pondered those events for a moment. The Emir's General, Abdul-Qadoos Al-Harawi, had also been killed—by Jawad's elder brother, Sieffuddeen, by all accounts. The Al-Harawi family was no more. The General's only son, Ahmed, was murdered on the orders of Sieffuddeen and his wife had fallen fatally ill soon after. Hassan also remembered the men who fought alongside him; Robin, an Englishman nicknamed 'The Hud', Reza the Persian—a spy by all accounts—and Sami, a Saracen warrior who had left for England with Robin. Everything was so hazy, so distant and so surreal. What had happened all those years ago was now written only in legend. The superstitious tales of mystics and storytellers. The reality of it would not re-enter Hassan's or Jawad's awareness for a year or so.

While he considered those stories, Hassan gazed away from Jerusalem, towards the Arab Christian town of Bethlehem, his horse beside him, a grey Arab mare with a coat like silk. His thoughts were broken, however, by the arrival of two horsemen. They approached at pace and their steeds were kicking up vast quantities of dust. Hassan caught hold of the hilt of his sword, preparing to draw it and use it if the need presented itself. He waited and as the horsemen grew closer, they slowed their pace, eventually trotting to a halt in front of him. He looked hard at them, analysing their clothing, their features and, most importantly, their weapons.

They were not Mamluks, nor were they Saracens. By their appearance, clothes and accents as they spoke to each other, Hassan took them for Kurds. He assumed they were probably from Persia, Syria or Iraq. Their Arabic was heavily accented, unusual to the ear, but understandable.

The horses snorted and shuffled as the first man spoke.

"We have urgent news for the Emir," the rider said, looking past Hassan to the City's gate.

"Is it news of the Horde?" Hassan asked, his eyes shifting from one rider to the other, monitoring their eyes, their hands and their weapons.

The second man nudged his horse forwards with a slight squeeze of his legs into the horse's ribs, until the horse's mouth was almost touching Hassan's nose. The horse snorted, and its rider placed his hand over his sword.

"If you are not the Emir, you have no need to know what the news is. Now, stand aside and let us approach the gate, or take us to him!"

Hassan studied the man intently, noticing every blemish on his face as well as his hands. They were not large or powerful looking and nor did they look like the hands of a manual worker or a warrior. The rider's voice was stern, but Hassan sensed that this was not a hardened fighter. He considered what might happen if he called the messenger's bluff and refused to move, but he thought about it only for a few seconds. He wished to know the news and since he had become a confidante of the Emir, the easiest way to hear it would be to take these messengers directly to him.

"Follow me", he said, taking a step backwards, reaching for his own horse's reins and leading his steed, and the two strangers, towards the gate.

The two riders dismounted and walked their horses through the gate. Hassan spoke to the guards on duty and the three men were waved through. They dismounted and walked towards the Emir's Palace, along a dusty road, past market traders, cafés, tanning businesses and a busy blacksmith's building. Hassan nodded towards many of the people they passed. He was popular in Jerusalem; a man of courage and power who never held himself with pride above the ordinary people who were the heart of this mighty city, and the blood that ran through its veins, keeping it alive. It took about ten minutes to reach the Palace, where more guards stopped their progress until Hassan had explained the men's presence. The guards searched them both and removed their weapons. Hassan also handed his own sword over as no weapons were allowed within the Palace, apart from those held by the Emir, his family and their personal guards.

Once inside, they were led towards the richest, most ornate quarter of the Palace. The current Emir seemed to crave wealth and luxury, unlike one of his predecessors, Jawad's father, who had largely shunned such pretentiousness. Hassan knocked on the large oak door with the hilt of his small dagger and the sound reverberated outside and within the

Emir's quarters. A servant opened the door and the Emir beckoned to Hassan to enter. He took two steps into the room and stopped.

"Two messengers bring urgent news for you Your Excellency," he said.

The Emir made him wait. He was reading something, a document of some kind, maybe the Quran, maybe poetry, and he continued to read until he was finished, or at least he made it appear that way. Finally, he put aside the book and glanced up at Hassan. His eyes were dark and piercing, and Hassan wondered what memories lay behind them. *Nobody became Emir or Sultan by being pleasant*, he thought to himself.

The Emir stroked his long, black beard and took a deep breath in through his nose, before speaking.

"Bring them in!" is all he said, and Hassan stepped to one side to allow the messengers to enter the room. They also waited, unsure of whether they should speak before being told to.

"Well? Speak fools. I'm not a mind reader!" It was an order and the Emir's voice was booming, angry. He did not have the status or power of the Sultans or Khaliphs in Cairo or Baghdad. He was more of a caretaker ruler, a vice regent, acting on behalf of the Mamluk Sultan of Egypt. Yet, his tone was harsh, strong. Strangers would be influenced by it, but Hassan knew it masked a lack of authority, rather than revealing any real power.

The first of the messengers took a step forward until he stood in the centre of the vast room. Nervously, he recited his message.

"News from Baghdad your Highness; the city is perhaps days or weeks away from falling to the Mongols, as has much of Mesopotamia and parts of Syria. The few people who have escaped the carnage have fled to Baghdad or Basra. They have reported the most horrifying tales of slaughter." He paused momentarily to take control of his emotions. "Forgive me Your Highness, but my family are in Iraq and I fear the worst for them. The message is that an army is urgently needed to force these barbarians back to whence they came, or else the entire Muslim world could become a scene of devastation and death."

The Emir said nothing for a short while and the three men before him waited silently. For a few minutes, the room felt to Hassan like a morgue, the only sound an occasional rush of air from an open window.

When he finally spoke, therefore, the Emir's voice shattered the silence like a hammer on glass.

"Why have you brought this message to me? Why not take it directly to the Khaliph in Egypt?"

The messenger cleared his throat. He was sweating and the nerves were clear in his voice when he replied.

"We have sent messengers to the Khaliph twice, but we never receive a reply and they never returned."

"Bandits," Hassan said.

The messenger glanced at him inquisitively and Hassan continued. "Bandits run ravage between here and Egypt. Even our well-armed troops have had a tough time with them, so I'm hardly surprised your messengers never succeeded in their missions."

The Emir nodded. "Who leads these Mongols?" He asked.

The second of the messengers replied. "Hulegu, one of the grandsons of the Great Khan, Genghis."

"Great Khan?" The Emir shouted the question. "You call one of these savages great? Great at what, may I ask? Killing, raping, burning, and the destruction of all things civilised and educational, that's what!" His fist struck the table as he emphasised the final word and the thud echoed around the room like the rumble of distant thunder.

The messengers said nothing. They were experienced enough to know that the Emir's question was rhetorical. Any reply would have merely directed his anger towards them, so they waited, silently and patiently. Hassan, meanwhile, smiled at their position.

"Leave us," the Emir said, sweeping his left hand at the messengers in an indication of dismissal. "Hassan, approach me."

The messengers turned and left the room, accompanied by two of the Emir's personal guard. They would be required to wait outside the Palace for a response from the Emir. Hassan, meanwhile, stepped forward and stood in front of the Emir's desk. He also said nothing. It was always better to allow the Emir to speak first. It was not out of fear. Hassan never had any qualms about telling the ruler seated before him how things really were. He would not dress things up to appear positive, if they were not, but he knew from experience that it was never advisable to offer one's opinion until it was sought. So, he waited, and the Emir took a deep breath.

"I value your opinion, Hassan. Young, though you are, you are a man of great wisdom and experience, both way beyond your years." He paused momentarily before continuing. "How long have you served as one of my aides and advisors Hassan?" He asked.

Hassan took a deep breath. "Two years my Emir and a year in the army before that."

It was the truth, for Hassan had served in various military roles since his return to Jerusalem, but it intrigued the Emir, who had not failed to notice that Hassan did not appear to be aging at all. Hassan knew that as time went by, nobody could be allowed to know how old he really was. People would never understand it and he valued his life too much to allow it to become the target of religious fanatics or demon hunters. After all, a miniscule lie could keep his head firmly upon his shoulders. He would have to leave the Emir's employ soon and move to where people did not know him. As he pondered this, the Emir continued. "What, then, is your advice to me now?"

"You must report to Sultan Qutuz, in Cairo. A Muslim army can defeat these invaders, with Allah's help, but it will take time to organise that army, so we must act now. To hesitate will result in failure."

The Emir waited, pondering the enormity of the situation. The stories of Mongol ruthlessness had reached him long before today and, after the fall of Persia, he knew it was only a matter of time before the horsemen of the north would set their sights on Baghdad. He also knew that the chances of them respecting the seats of learning there were slim. Hassan was right. He acknowledged that fact too, and he resolved to contact the sultan in Cairo. He told Hassan of that decision.

"What do we do in the meantime, Hassan?" He asked.

"With your permission, I would like to take a team of hardened and experienced fighters to Baghdad, to gather information and search for weaknesses in the enemy's position."

"Spies, you mean?"

"More than just spies, my Emir. It is important to exploit some of those weaknesses now, before they get wind of our long-term plans. My team can do this. Trust me."

The Emir did trust him, more than anyone else. He nodded, lifted himself from his chair and walked around the desk until he stood face-to-face with his trusted aide. The Emir caught hold of Hassan's arms and pulled the warrior towards him, holding him in a surprising embrace, which he held for a good twenty seconds, before releasing his hold, pushing Hassan away and smiling.

"One more thing, Your Highness", Hassan said. "Send Ben Zakai to Acre with a message for our agent there. We need to gauge the feelings of the Franj and let the Sultan know".

The Emir nodded. "Go with Allah, Hassan. May He protect you and your team and guide us all to victory over these barbarians."

They shook hands and Hassan left. He headed straight to the messengers and ordered them to return to Baghdad and inform their masters that a call for assistance will immediately be sent to Cairo. He watched them leave the City, then caught hold of his horse's reins and headed over to the Royal Stables.

"Stable boy!" He called out, as he entered.

A young stable boy came running to Hassan and waited for instructions.

"Prepare my horse boy. She needs food, water and a full groom. Have her ready for me before nightfall or you will be in trouble—understand?"

The boy nodded. "Of course, Sayed. Straight away."

Hassan smiled and then added; "Do it well and I'll reward you, handsomely". He then left to gather necessary funds, collect his sword from the guards he had left it with and find other weapons and some water. He then proceeded to a café where he called together two men and sat them down away from others who were in the building. The first of the men to take a seat was Akbar, a Mamluk Turk like Hassan, with long hair, looks that turned every woman's eyes towards him and a sword too large for most men to carry, let alone wield. He was at least a head taller than anyone else Hassan had ever met. Even the tall crusaders from northern Europe did not come close to Akbar's height but his exceptionally muscular build added to his magnificence. The second man was Abdul-Qareem Al-Rashid, a professional soldier for many years, who often participated in 'specialist' work for Hassan.

The men were informed of the plan and, after a short rest, they made their way to the stables, waiting there until the boy informed him that his steed was ready. An hour later, the three men were on the road to Jordan, heading towards Jawad's farm.

CHAPTER 54
1255 A.D.
Baghdad

The Mongol force, led by Hulegu, camped inside Iraq, and waited for a response from the Abbasid Khaliph of Baghdad, Musta'sim. Hulegu had ordered surrender from the Khaliph in exchange for Baghdad being spared. He had been ordered by his brother, Mongke, not to destroy the Iraqi capital, but Hulegu was not going to allow the continued existence of the Abbasid Khaliphate. His decision was made for him when Musta'sim sent a message refusing to submit to Mongol authority.

The order was given to march on Baghdad, a city that was not prepared for the horrors in store for it. Despite all the stories they had heard, the citizens of Baghdad were stunned by the sheer brutality of the invading Mongols.

Hulegu's army was one of the biggest ever fielded by the Mongols and included supporting forces from Armenia and Georgia, bitter towards the Muslims who had forced them to suffer humiliating defeats in the past. The force also included a sizeable number of Chinese soldiers and engineers led by Guo Kan. Some contemporary writers claimed that the Mongol-Christian joint force numbered over one hundred and fifty thousand men, and this was the force that would soon sweep into Baghdad.

In Baghdad, panic ensued. Musta'sim gathered his personal guard around him and prepared for a long siege. Stores of food were under constant guard, for fear of panic-induced looting by the city's population and fortifications were strengthened. Oil was brought to the walls, ready to be heated and dumped on anyone attacking the barricades. The gates of the city were reinforced. Greek fire, a petroleum-based, incendiary mixture that could not be extinguished with water, was prepared for use against any siege towers the Mongols might bring forward. Arrows were also doused in the mixture, for use against oncoming troops.

Then, there was the calm before the storm. The hours of waiting while Hulegu's forces prepared for the attack. Musta'sim, and most within Baghdad, expected a long and drawn out siege, sure that they would be relieved by forces from Egypt or Syria. The reinforcements never came, and the Mongol offensive began far sooner than expected. Consequently, when the attack came, it shocked everybody. The Mongols struck the walls of the city with cannon fire, using weapons they had acquired from many wars in China. Gunpowder-driven weaponry that could be carried with the troops and used with devastating force, reduced parts of the city walls and the buildings within to rubble within minutes. The people of Baghdad tried to escape but were struck down with uncaring efficiency by Mongols stationed all around the outside of the city.

The taking of Baghdad was, after all that had been said by those in power in the city, swift and ruthless. Carnage was followed by rape and the taking of slaves and Musta'sim was captured. He was about to be hacked to death when someone mentioned to Hulegu that if one drop of blood from a Khaliph touched the ground, those responsible would be cursed to eternal damnation. Hulegu was a superstitious man, as were many Mongols and he heeded the warning, instructing his men instead to wrap the Khaliph in a carpet. Once secured in place, Hulegu ordered that war horses be ridden over him, time and time again, until the Khaliph's lifeless body was crushed beyond recognition. Not a single drop of his blood touched the ground.

Baghdad was left in a state of total devastation and estimates of the numbers massacred by the invading army ranged from one hundred thousand to a million. The city was sacked and burned with nothing safe from plunder and butchery. The libraries of Baghdad, including the House of Wisdom, were ransacked and demolished by Hulegu's Ilkhanate forces, who threw priceless books into the Tigris River. According to some story tellers, there were so many books in the river that they formed a bridge for the Mongol horsemen to ride across. Baghdad would be a depopulated ruin of a city for several centuries and this single invasion brought an end to what many called the Islamic Golden Age.

Amidst this devastation, a young Iraqi boy hid in a cellar below his uncle's house. His name was Jaffer Husseini and he had been thrust below the dwelling by his mother some weeks earlier. He had heard the screams of his mother as she was raped, tortured, and finally burned alive. Some of his sisters were alive when the flames first took hold on the house above him. His father's lifeless body lay just above him. He had been cut down by a Mongol sword when the invaders entered the house. Jaffer had cried in silence, fear overcoming grief to prevent him from revealing his position, but now the tears had dried and his only thought was how he would get clear of what had now become his prison cell.

For two days, the sounds of fighting, slaughter, drunken celebrations, and victims' screams had not been heard. Jaffer knew that soon his food and water would be spent, and he would have to venture out of his hiding place to seek more. Now, he decided that this was probably the time to do that. The cellar had been cleverly designed by his uncle, a smuggler. The design was such that it could remain undiscovered without the most intensive of searches. The entrance was not from the house above, but via an underground tunnel that led to one of Baghdad's feats of engineering, the sewerage system.

Jaffer opened a door at the side of the room that had been his home and jail for many months. The door was small and opened onto a tunnel, just large enough for an average sized person to crawl along. Taking some essential supplies in a pack tied around his waist and hoisted behind him, he began the arduous trek on all fours. The tunnel was well constructed. His uncle had once been one of the city's chief engineers until he was removed from his post for attacking a soldier who had tried to interfere with his work one day. The tunnel that Jaffer found himself in was a secure, well-built passageway to freedom. Air holes, virtually invisible to the world above ground, had been skilfully woven into the structure. Nevertheless, it was a claustrophobic journey for the boy and the experience was not improved by the endless dry dirt and sand that interfered with his breathing.

It took an hour to crawl the full length of the tunnel and Jaffer was surprisingly pleased to emerge into the stinking sewer where he could walk on two legs, albeit bent almost double. He held a scarf over his nose and mouth to ward off the worst of the odours, and eventually found an exit to the outside world. Lifting a small hatch, he raised his head high enough to glance around. Then, seeing nobody in the vicinity, he hauled himself out, replaced the hatch and walked towards Baghdad's main Mosque. He believed, somewhat innocently, that a house of prayer would have been left unscathed. He was wrong. Keeping to the shadows in the hours before dawn, he arrived within half an hour at the doors of the Mosque. It was damaged beyond repair, the windows broken, the calligraphic tiles smashed and strewn all around and the inside full to the brim with the bodies of hundreds of people.

Jaffer was in shock. Never had he seen so many dead bodies. Most were skeletal, but those more recently killed were now in a state of decomposition. He retched at the smell that struck his senses. The invaders had not restricted themselves to targeting soldiers either. There were clearly bodies here of the elderly, of women, of children and even animals. He could contain himself no longer and he vomited before finally collapsing in tears, his legs giving away under him. He slumped to the floor and pleaded to God for protection.

What sort of monsters can do this? He muttered, partly to himself and partly to Allah.

Slowly, he lifted himself to his feet and was about to turn towards the space where the large wooden doors of the Mosque once stood when he felt a hand on his shoulder. Jaffer jumped and yelped like a dog. He looked to where the hand had been and saw a middle-aged Arab man. For a moment, they stared silently at each other and then the man spoke.

"Fear not child. I am a man of healing, not killing." The boy looked confused, so the man smiled and continued. "I'm a physician from outside the city. I came here in case people needed help, but I fear I have come too late."

Jaffer glanced towards the door and then back at the man. *Could he make it if he made a run for the door?* The man held out a hand, in anticipation of a handshake. Jaffer was still unsure, but something about the stranger said, 'you can trust me', so he shook his hand.

"Mohammed," the man said. "Assalamu 'alaikum."

The boy responded. "W'alaikum salaam. My name is Jaffer."

"We need to get you washed Jaffer," Mohammed said. "You smell like a sewer system."

Jaffer frowned but said nothing. He stood up and followed Muhammad to the door, clutching at his bag that was loosening its previously tight grip around his waist.

They left the Mosque and walked through narrow streets and alleys, keeping close to buildings and in the shadows. Eventually, they entered a central courtyard and passed ranks of pikes, each with a skull lodged firmly on its point. It was like a gruesome boulevard of death trees and Jaffer wondered who these people were who had ended their days on earth in such a dreadful way. Mohammed could see in Jaffer's expression that he was both repulsed and intrigued by what he saw, and he muttered something to him, so softly that Jaffer had to ask him to repeat himself.

"Imams and members of the Khaliph's family," he repeated.

Jaffer frowned.

"The heads, boy, on the pikes; that's who they are."

"How do you know?" Jaffer asked, suspiciously.

"People fleeing Baghdad came as far as Basra, which is where I'm from originally and where I had fled to when the invaders arrived. They told stories, horrific, heart-rending stories of what the horse devils did here. One man told me that Hulegu had stood at the pulpit in the Mosque and told the people he had been sent by their God to punish them for their sins."

He pulled Jaffer towards another narrow side street that headed south, towards one of the poorer areas of the city.

"Why are we going this way?" Jaffer asked.

"There is some safety there with the poor. I know a family there, and they have a way out of Baghdad. A freedom route, if you like. A route that was used by traders trying to avoid the Khaliph's taxes. It was also used by smugglers and bandits, bringing their ill-gotten gains into the city."

Jaffer never mentioned that his father was one of those smugglers. In fact, he said nothing else for almost an hour, until Mohammed led him into a run-down hovel. It was hidden behind three burned out buildings, one of which seemed to be the remnants of one of the Christian churches of the city.

"It smells here," was all he said, but he did not receive a comeback from his newfound chaperone, who simply laughed. The doctor then looked the boy up and down, screwed up his nose and shook his head.

"Not as badly as you do," he said, laughing.

He led his new young charge through a dilapidated hallway and into a large lounge, at the back of which was a bookcase, empty of any reading material, but caked in dust and dirt. The doctor stepped across to it and rapped on one of the shelves three times, waited for five seconds and tapped the shelf again, this time twice. Jaffer just stood and watched, silently and patiently waiting to see what would happen. In less than a minute, the bookcase began to move away from the wall and Mohammed took a step backwards to avoid being hit by it. It stopped at a forty-five-degree angle to the wall, revealing an entrance to another room in an adjoining building. The doctor beckoned to Jaffer to follow him and they walked through. On the other side, two young Arab men hauled on some ropes and heaved the bookcase back into position, the hidden entrance concealed once more.

The room they had entered, was clean, tidy and furnished, with low Arab chairs and small tables, upon which were trays of glasses, filled with strong, black coffee. Jaffer was impressed that neither the sound of people, nor the smell of the coffee were noticeable from the other side of the wall, even after the bookcase had been opened. The smells of decay and sewage within the first house, masked anything that could be produced from a few pots of heavily brewed Arabic coffee in this one.

One of the men, seated near one of the tables, was pouring coffee into two empty glasses. He beckoned them over.

"Assalamu 'alaikum. Ahlan wa Sahlan [Peace be upon you. Welcome]," he said, placing the coffee pot down and reaching up to shake Mohammed's hand. Mohammed reciprocated and sat down opposite his host, a middle-aged man with a face so sand and heat worn that, to Jaffer, it looked like rough leather. The boy wondered if the skin beneath the man's beard was the same. He imagined the man without a beard, where the rough, sand-roughened top half of his face would meet a smooth, baby-like lower half. As he dreamily envisioned this, he smiled, but his imaginings were suddenly interrupted by the bearded man's voice, calling him. Shaken out of his fantasy world, his smile left him in an instant and he stared in the direction of the voice.

"Don't be scared boy. Sit. Sit here," the bearded man said, tapping his hand on the seat next to him.

Nervously, with some trepidation, Jaffer walked gingerly to the seat and carefully lowered himself into it.

"Goodness," the man exclaimed, screwing up his face as he did so. "You stink boy". He turned towards a door and called a woman's name, Nadia. She came as far as the door and the old man pushed Jaffer towards her. "Give this boy a bath and a change of clothes and then send him back here," he called.

About half an hour later, Jaffer returned and was ushered back to the seat beside the old, bearded man. "Here, drink this," the man said, thrusting a glass of coffee towards the boy.

Jaffer took it, graciously, and took a sip. It was piping hot and he decided to wait for it to cool a little, so he placed it carefully on the low table before him.

Gradually, he drifted into the background, becoming virtually invisible to those around him. He was a child and to the adult men in the room, was simply ignored, apart from an occasional tussle of his hair by the old man, and new arrivals. It was not deliberate. He was simply overlooked as the conversation became heated and serious. The men discussed the Mongol invaders, the slaughter, the atrocities, the destruction of Baghdad and their plans to reach Basra.

Jaffer listened carefully to the conversation, but his interest was particularly roused when the bearded man spoke of the atrocities he had personally witnessed.

"You all know me," he said, clearly directing his remark at everyone except the boy sitting quietly beside him. "My name has been well known in Baghdad for many decades. You have all sought out Sayed ibn Taoos for judgement on issues of law and now we find ourselves in a state of absolute lawlessness."

He paused to pour himself some more coffee and took two sips from his glass. After carefully placing the glass on the table, alongside Jaffer's, he continued.

"We do not know if these invaders intend to stay and establish rule or if they are intent on raiding and running away. Only time will tell, but in the meantime, we must reach our allies. It is imperative that we remove these criminals from our lands, for I tell you this my brothers, these men are far worse than the Franj, for all their evils."

He paused again, offering the others a chance to speak. Ibn Taoos was, undoubtedly, a man of great wisdom and one who understood the importance of participation in decision making. His full name was Sayed Radhi ud-Deen Abul Qasim Ali ibn Sa'aduddin Abi IbRaheem Musa ibn Ja'far ibn Muhammad ibn Ahmad ibn Muhammad ibn Taoos. He was a famous jurist, traditionalist and historian and his ancestry reached back to the second Shi'a Imam, Imam Hassan, from his father's side, and to the third Shi'a Imam, Imam Husain from his mother's side. Shi'a Muslims widely accepted that he was one of only a few scholars in history who had met with the twelfth Shi'a Imam, Imam al-Mahdi, numerous times.

As he waited, Muhammad decided to speak. He leant forward slightly and kept his voice low, even though he knew that nobody outside could possibly hear them.

"I assume that we will take the trader's route out of the city and cross rural land to Basra. Am I right?"

Ibn Taoos nodded and took another sip of his coffee, this time keeping the glass in his hand as he spoke. Jaffer watched him intently, fascinated by the way his bushy beard rose up and down with the movement of his mouth.

"You're correct Muhammad." He glanced at Jaffer and tilted his head in the boy's direction. "Will the boy be up to the journey, do you think?"

Muhammad had no time to reply as Jaffer quickly pitched in with a response.

"The boy is sitting right next to you. The boy's name is Jaffer. The boy is nearly fourteen years' old and the boy can tell you himself that he is perfectly capable of making the journey!" Jaffer shouted it and then slumped back in the seat, his arms folded across his chest, his lips firmly pressed together in a pout.

One of the men who were standing, stepped across to Jaffer and swiped him around the head with the palm of his hand. It hurt, and Jaffer wanted to complain, but he resisted. His face was set in an obstinate stare towards his assailant and he unfolded his arms, let them drop to his side and clenched his fists until the whites of his knuckles were visible.

"Everybody; remain calm," Ibn Taoos said, firmly. He glanced at the boy, placed his hand on the boy's left fist and smiled. "The boy, er, Jaffer, will be fine. Of that I have no doubt, so you leave in the morning. Now, we pray."

The other men were silent for a moment and then Muhammad spoke, his face screwed up in confusion.

"Are you not coming with us Sayeedi?" He asked.

Ibn Taoos stood up, using a stick in his left hand to help himself to his feet. Nobody moved to assist him. They had learned from experience that he did not like to be treated as an invalid and they had learned that a swipe from his stick smarted.

"I am too old to make the journey my brothers. I will stay here and write about events in this fine city of ours. Two of my messengers have already been sent with a message to the Emir in Jerusalem. The rest of you will make your way to Basra."

Some of the men moved to speak but he held up his right hand to silence them. "I will be fine," he said, adding "now, let us pray."

CHAPTER 55
1255 A.D.
Near Al-Khalil [Hebron]

Jawad stood with his employed engineer, Abdur-Raheem, inspecting the farm's irrigation system that had been sporadically failing in recent days. Suddenly, in the distance he saw dust, driven up by horses that were moving quickly from the East. There were seven riders, not riding past his farm, but heading in his direction. So, unsure of the intention of the approaching riders and unaware of their number, Jawad called to Abdur-Raheem and another of his workers, Antonio Habash, to stand with him.

His men served as workers on his land and with his animals, but were all trained in the skills of warfare, with several years' battle experience each. Some had their families with them, living in small homes on Jawad's land. Habash was working near one of those homes when he heard the call. He hurried from his work and joined Abdur-Raheem and their employer; three armed men, facing the oncoming dust as the pounding of hooves grew in volume. The riders were close. It took just minutes for them to reach the outskirts of the farm. Once there, they dismounted before walking, quite hurriedly, towards the three men. They were waiting alongside an upside-down, half tube system that fed water to the crops around them.

Jawad took the early dismount to be a sign that these men were not a threat, but still he ensured that his men were prepared to defend themselves if necessary. The former prince's hand felt behind his neck for the hilt of his sword. Comforted that he and his men were armed and in a state of readiness, he walked towards the visitors, his men following slowly behind him. Habash was armed with a Turkish recurve bow and a full quiver of arrows, while Abdur-Raheem had both a sword and a European crossbow.

As the two groups of men came together, a smile spread across

Jawad's face as he recognised one of the visitors.

"Reza, my dear friend, assalamu 'alaikum", he said, spreading his arms wide in expectation of an embrace.

Reza passed the reins of his horse to one of his men, and held his friend for a moment, but his face revealed concern, rather than delight. Jawad, noticing the visitor's expression, held him at arms' length, a firm grip on the Persian's shoulders.

"What ails you, Reza?" He asked. "Clearly this is not a social call, my brother," he added. "So, tell me why I have the pleasure of your company."

Reza gripped Jawad's wrist and removed his friend's hands from his shoulders. He took a deep breath and looked back at his comrades, who waited with the horses.

"Events in Baghdad are worse than you can imagine, Jawad. I am sure some stories have reached you, but I bring you details that perhaps have not come this far."

Jawad nodded and looked to Reza's men. There were seven of them, all rugged and covered in dust. He knew soldiers when he saw them, and he knew killers when he saw them too. These men were both. That was clear, but they were Reza's men and that meant they were guests on his land.

"Come to the house, you and your men," he said and then, turning to his engineer, he said, "Abdur-Raheem, please take our guests' horses to the stables. Ask the stable hands to feed and water them, and then please join us in the house. Everybody else, please come into the house and out of the sun."

He walked off and called on everybody to follow him, which they did. Habash was still standing close by his employer, not fully trusting these visitors yet.

Jawad had first met Reza years' earlier when they had met in Syria and fought together against allies of Jawad's traitorous brother, Sieffuddeen. Reza was a Shi'a Muslim who came originally from Iran. The Shi'a, a minority among Muslims, even in the Mesopotamia region, were themselves divided into many groups and Reza was part of the largest of these. They were sometimes referred to as 'Twelvers' because they believed that their twelfth Imam, a descendent of the Prophet

Muhammad, had gone into hiding and would return near the Day of Judgement as The Mahdi. Jawad recalled his early meeting with Reza and was about to exchange simple niceties when he realised from Reza's expression that this was neither the time, nor place, for such small talk. He led them into the house and called out for coffee to be served.

Despite the incredible heat outside, the house was very cool inside. The interior and exterior walls were coated white and the walls themselves were incredibly thick and made of adobe, a form of mud. It gave them a thermal mass, thus keeping the worst of the heat out. Like many large houses of the region, the design included a central courtyard. Windows on external walls were kept to a minimum in number and size, but windows and doors facing onto the courtyard, which was shaded by the surrounding building, were large, letting in cool air and light but restricting heat.

Jawad led them all through to a lounge area where large cushions were arranged alongside two walls. Along the third wall was a Moroccan raised bench seat, covered with an elaborately embroidered long cushion. Jawad, with a simple wave of his hand, invited the men to sit. As they made themselves comfortable, a servant entered the room with a metal tray filled with small glasses and a pot of strong Arab coffee.

After drinks were served, Reza explained that he had come to seek assistance. Jawad nodded. Then, he asked Reza to outline the situation to everyone in the room. Reza stood. He was more comfortable moving around the room as he spoke.

"Baghdad is rubble my friends and brothers. The Mosques have been burned or violated, the great libraries have been torched or plundered and the bodies of citizens lie rotting in the streets or in their homes. We will not be able to get into Baghdad, so I suggest Basra as a destination."

Marie, who was in another room, had been listening and entered the room where the men were talking. She was wearing what were considered men's clothes. She had on a form of trousers, with a long, baggy, collarless, cotton shirt. Her hair was tied back but not covered. A few of the men stiffened and took sharp intakes of breath as she entered but Jawad glared at them and they reluctantly relaxed.

"I believe my wife has something to say," he said, a wry smile gradually spreading across his face. He knew that many of the men had quite conservative views about the place of women in Arab society, but he also knew that many of those beliefs had little foundation in Islam. His own men said nothing as she spoke. Jawad had reminded them on many occasions that the wives of the Prophet Muhammad and the wives of his companions, not only took part in debates and decision making, but also fought on the battlefields when necessary. He also knew that Reza would have reminded them all that the Prophet's daughter Fatima was a warrior in her own right, as well as being the wife of the first Shi'a Imam, Ali. So, Marie, her sun-bronzed face illuminating the room as she seated herself alongside her husband, spoke uninterrupted.

"My understanding was that these horse warriors are illiterate savages. Pray tell me, Reza, why have they plundered libraries if they do not read?"

Reza laughed a little and then replied. "Well, my lady, firstly they are not all illiterate. Many have learned the ways of the Chinese and many have come from Samarkand. Secondly, many of the warriors are Chinese and thirdly, much of the plundering of books and furniture was because Hulegu wished to build bridges to reach Syria and Persia."

Jawad's response to this statement was one of surprise and confusion and it echoed the thoughts of everyone else in the room.

"To build bridges? What do you mean?"

Reza smiled. "Oh yes, they're a resourceful people these Mongols. They pulped and hardened the books and used them to build bridges strong enough to carry their troops and horses across the rivers. Astounding isn't it? Apparently, they had thrown tens of thousands of books into the river, so many that they had formed an unintended bridge. That had given them the idea."

As everybody pondered this information there was a shout from outside. One of the younger farm hands, a boy of about 15 years' old, came running into the house, screaming about three riders approaching. Instantly, all the men and Marie, headed outside, hands reaching in unison to weapons. Once outside, they spread themselves out and waited for the approaching horsemen to arrive.

Minutes later, the horses were pulled to a halt in front of them, dust thrust up into the air and obscuring visibility for a few seconds. After it had settled, Jawad stepped forward as one of the horsemen dismounted.

He had his back to the former prince, and he held tightly to the hilt of his sword as Jawad approached.

"Who comes at this hour in such a hurry?" Jawad called out.

The man turned, and Jawad recognised him immediately.

"Hassan, my friend," Jawad shouted, loudly enough for all those behind him to hear, so that they might relax their grip on their weapons and stand down. Jawad rushed forward and embraced Hassan, who reciprocated immediately. "What brings you here at this hour my brother?"

Hassan pulled out of the embrace and glanced briefly at the people behind Jawad. He smiled.

"I come from the Emir to raise a group of fighters to ride to Iraq and fight the Mongols. We would have been here weeks ago, but we ran into bandits en route and one of my men suffered an injury that we needed to treat before continuing."

Reza laughed and walked quickly across to Hassan, shaking his hand, embracing him and then holding him at arms' length by the shoulders.

"My dear friend, it is not a group of fighters that you need, but an army. Does the Emir not realise how great this threat is? Does he think we are faced with a band of outlaws? The Mongols have come with an army the like of which I have not seen before."

Hassan caught hold of Reza's arms and pulled his friend to his side so that both men faced the rest of the group.

"The fighters are to enter Iraq, undermine the Mongol occupation, kill without being seen and gather information. My brothers, an army is being raised by the Sultan in Egypt, but it will take time before it is ready to move on the enemy. In the meantime, we must create havoc and chaos within their ranks. That is why I and my two compatriots are here." He looked at each member of Jawad's group. "And it is good to see that you have already begun to raise such a group, so praise Allah for that."

He pointed to the two horsemen.

"The big man is Akbar, a brutal but honest man, a former slave and a man of great courage and honour. The other is Mehmet, a former soldier from the Emir's army who now fights for money, unless he is fighting for me. Then, he fights for Allah, for justice, for what is right."

Jawad invited the three men to his home.

"Ahlan wa Sahlan", he said, pulling Hassan by the hand towards the door.

Inside the house, Hassan, Marie and Reza worked with Jawad on plans for their campaign. Everybody else, Jawad's workers, Hassan's mercenaries, and Reza's band of soldier spy Assassins, were allocated jobs around the farm in preparation for their long journey to Iraq. Reza was quick to point out that Baghdad was not accessible, unless they could get to Basra and find those running the smugglers' escape routes in and out of Baghdad.

After hours of debate and discussion, plans were drawn up, ranks and roles were allocated, and orders were given.

That night, in the privacy of their bed chamber, Marie sat alongside her husband and placed her hand on his. He gazed at her for a minute or two but said nothing, knowing what she was thinking. Her breathing was soft and slow and for a moment, she also remained silent, her eyes firmly fixed on their hands.

"Do you remember that day when my father left me with you at the quayside as he sailed off to France? I never saw him again after that day, Jawad. Yet, I regret nothing. I made up my mind that day to stand at your side, come what may. So, if you go, I go with you my husband." She said, almost in a whisper.

Jawad took a deep breath and then lifted her hand and kissed it.

"I would prefer it if you stayed here, habeebti. I cannot spend precious time watching out for your safety when we arrive in Iraq."

Marie stood and snatched her hand from his.

She smiled. "Why would you need to spend time watching out for me?" She said, her voice raised but not angry. "I have fought before, and I will do it again. In fact, based on my experience, husband, it will be me looking out for you, don't you think?" She smiled again.

Jawad studied her. She was glorious, he thought, so beautiful and yet so powerful. "I will love you forever," he said, and then he smiled. "I'm sorry," he said, "I'll not raise the subject again. We go together. For now, I believe our bed is calling for us."

For the next three years, Reza's team of spies travelled to and from all the territories captured by Mongke's Mongol forces which, by 1258, included the whole of Mesopotamia, Persia, most of Palestine and Syria, where the feared Assassins had been virtually eradicated. The spies' reports were as sickening as they were useful but by the winter of 1259, the group of would be fifth columnists were ready to head to Basra. One final set of plans were to be drawn up and then their journey to that town would begin.

CHAPTER 56
Iblis

Tensions were also rising in the worlds of the Jinn, parallel worlds where demons, spirits and fantastic beings had existed since long before humans appeared on Earth. The Dark One, Iblis, was known by many names but was commonly referred to as Shaytaan or Satan. He had gathered his armies against those Jinn who opposed him, and he sensed victory.

Often called a fallen angel, Shaytaan was in fact a Jinni who, unlike the pure angels, had been granted free will along with all Jinn and humankind. Seeing the chaos that his representative on Earth was sewing on his behalf, Shaytaan now saw an opportunity to wrestle power in the world of the Jinn, from those who currently held it. He knew that he needed to distract the enlightened Jinn, to stop them from preventing him from gaining control on Earth. So, his armies in the world of the Jinn, had started a war. In the meantime, he had sent a small force of Dark Jinn to Earth to hunt for the one thing that could grant him absolute supremacy; a staff of immense power that would enable him to open a permanent portal to Earth, large enough to allow all his hordes of demons to pass from his world into the world of the humans. He hoped that the Jinn of the Light Side would be forced to protect it and that would weaken their forces in this alternate universe.

Iblis' forces were strong and after many skirmishes and minor battles, his giant army now faced a depleted force of Jinn from the Light Side. Neither force was a unified group of similar beings, for the word Jinn was a name that referred to many creatures of light and dark. These included trolls, goblins, ghouls, elves and angel-like beings with almost human form.

Shaytaan's massed ranks were a mix of many types of demon and devil, led by three major warriors. Abigor was the first. He was a horseman carrying a lance, a standard, or a sceptre and he commanded sixty legions. Known as the Grand Duke of Hell, he knew many of the secrets of warfare but, more importantly for Shaytaan, Abigor had knowledge of the future. He would instruct leaders of the ways to earn their soldiers' respect. When he and Abbas had found Hulegu, they knew that the Mongol warrior was proud. He would never have accepted that he could be taught the secrets of war and discipline by someone who was not much more than a boy. So, they told him the lie that Abbas wished to learn the tactics of war that he had, in fact, already learned from Abigor.

Mounted proudly upon his steed, Abigor observed his troops, analysing their formation and assessing his tactical options. On his back, wings of a dragon spread to his sides and his demonic face twisted and contorted, his red eyes piercingly bright in the darkness.

Abigor had spent many decades with Abbas, teaching him some of his secrets and had taken the young part-human into battle, but those battles were in the world of the Jinn. Iblis, however, was concerned that Abbas' ability to kill demons would not prepare him for slaughtering humans. It was for that reason that Iblis had instructed Abigor to take his young charge to the Mongols where experience of the blood frenzy among the humans would condition the young man and complete his enslavement to the power of his grandfather, Iblis. So, Abbas had returned to Earth and Abigor prepared for war in the world of the Jinn.

The second warrior chief was Volac, a high Chieftain of Hell, who commanded 30 legions of warriors. He was a deceptive Jinni, with the appearance of a small, winged child, his innocence a mask designed to manipulate humans and Jinn alike. Riding a fearsome, two-headed dragon, he could call up the serpents of any world and order them into battle for his Master, Iblis.

The third general of the massed ranks of demon Jinn was Ronove, a Grand Count of Hell and commander of nineteen legions of Jinn. His appearance was monstrous in his Jinn form and his actions in battle were formidable.

These armies of ghouls and demons were gathering in force on the outskirts of the Kingdom of Zaydussia, ruled by Zaman the Overseer. Zaman led the Jinn who worshipped the One God and he knew full well that Iblis' forces threatened the stability of all creation. For now, those forces waited, placing Zaman's Kingdom under siege, but they could smell a victory that would open a gateway to the human world.

The world of the Jinn was usually shut off from human beings, but occasionally, temporary openings appeared. These openings sometimes occurred naturally but were most often constructed by design when an agent of the Jinn conjured a gateway to the human world. This was usually by choice, but sometimes because humans had summoned them. Visits had always been few and far between because these gateways were hard to open and limited in their usage. Within Zaydussia, however, stood a permanent and powerful gateway that opened into the human world via a place named the Ridge of Fertheron. This portal had been protected eons earlier by a powerful Jinni who, while residing on Earth, had been sealed in a hidden place by a witch. The demon Jinn had long sought to possess and control this gate, but Zaman's armies had always held them at bay, while forbidding his own followers to use it, except in cases of extreme necessity. Now, an alternative gate had been discovered, that had also once been protected but was now losing its defensive shield. Shaytaan knew that once the shield fell, his permanent path to Earth would be assured. He also knew that the staff that he sought could be used to reinstate the protection, so it was imperative, to him, that his forces find it first.

This Jinn world had been visited by Hassan many decades earlier and for a while, he had wondered whether he would ever go there again. Over the years, however, his memory of that world had faded, and he focused his will and effort on his earthly life. However, he would soon be back in the world of the Jinn, and so his progress on Earth was being studied by the aged Zaman. The Overseer was the one chosen to lead the Jinn on a path of good. His main enemy, Iblis, was the first rebellious Jinni whose only purpose in life was to lead mankind astray, to torment them, confuse them and set them against each other. However, until recently, his efforts had always been thwarted by Zaman. Now, with the biggest army he had ever built, Iblis had chosen to confront the Overseer in one last attempt to usurp power.

Zaman watched a holographic image of Hassan and periodically glanced up at a tall, translucent Jinni who stood silently before him. Zaman, short and thin, with a pale, sickly-looking face, sat in a chair so large that it gave the impression of a doll sitting precariously on a king's throne. His clothes were plain, not at all king-like, but anyone who stood before him would quickly realise that they were in the presence of immense power and authority.

He had a humanoid face but an alien body, riddled with the scars of old battles, scars of purple that throbbed now and then against his pale, yellow skin. He waved a hand over the image of Hassan, which gradually faded from view, and he looked up at a tall Jinni who stood before him.

"Zenith, my dear friend and soldier, I have been informed by a Jinni I trust that Hassan and his compatriots must travel through our world and fulfil an important quest. They must find what we need to end the influence of the half Jinni Abbas and seal the openings to Earth once more. If Abbas is returned to his fully human form again, it will make it easier for us to restore our security. Then, we can drive Iblis back to his home in the netherworld."

Zenith listened in silence and then shuffled slightly. His entire body momentarily rippled like sunlight on a stream and then it stopped, without warning, and he became human-like. He was a strong, powerful being with a giant sword hanging at his side and he wore the clothing of a Turkish soldier. He took a breath and spoke.

"You wish me to go to guide them?"

"No. I wish you to meet them. They are currently headed towards Basra and I wish you to find them and pass to them an important message from me. It is essential that they receive and understand every single word. Do you understand?"

Zenith nodded and stood in total silence as Zaman recited his instructions to his loyal servant.

After what seemed a very long time, the Jinni was sent on his task. He left Zaman's chamber; a marble hall lit brightly from crystals in the floor that had been taken from the Crystal Desert of Brillar. The rocks gave off a natural, almost blinding light in the desert, but once taken away could be used to light and heat rooms, hallways and entire towns. They could not be turned off, however, so ingenious engineers from an isolated and ancient city, had constructed dark, black marble casts that encased the crystals with the push of a button, shutting off the light of each stone, as and when required.

As Zenith looked along the corridor, he recalled the time, so long before, that Hassan had entered his world.

Hassan was the son of a Turkish Atabeg, the Atabegs being servants who acted as tutors to the children of wealthy Arabs. Hassan himself, although still only a youth in those days, was given charge over Abbas, the son of the Emir of Jerusalem and half-brother of Jawad. The two boys had hidden in a cave just outside of that city when two Crusader knights had tried to capture them. After they heard the soldiers riding away, with their very young friend Ahmed as their captive, the two boys had stepped forward inside the pitch-black cave, in what they believed was the direction of the cave doorway, but after just three steps they had found themselves falling, dropping like stones, although still in contact with something firm on all sides, like the walls of a long tunnel, full of unexpected twists and turns.

Eventually, the youngsters had found themselves in a brightly lit cavern, the ceiling of which shone with jewels and glistened with traces of gold. They had entered the world of the Jinn through a portal that two ghouls, agents for Iblis, had conjured using powerful magic, attempting to enter the human world.

It was Zenith who had rescued the boys from the ghouls and guided them through his world to the permanent gateway between the worlds at the Ridge of Fertheron. As Zenith thought about those days long past, his head dropped, and a look of sadness swept across his face. He had also recalled the fate of Abbas and Ahmed. Ahmed had been killed, shot by Templars on the orders of Jawad's half-brother, Sieffuddeen. Abbas had been taken by Iblis and his mind was turned as the Evil One explained to him that his mother had been the daughter of Iblis himself. Iblis brought forth Abbas' Jinn part and suppressed his human instincts before sending him back into the world of humans.

Zenith shook his head and walked the length of the corridor until he reached the exit from the great palace of Zaman. Once outside, he spread two wings that were rooted to his back and flew into the air. His destination, Earth.

CHAPTER 57
1260 A.D.
Cairo

The winter of 1260 had passed, and the spring brought with it the blossoming of plants, the calls of wild birds and the soft dew, reflecting the sun's rays as the early light of dawn appeared. In the Cairo Palace of Sultan Saif Al-Din Qutuz, a meeting of adversaries was underway. A Mongol emissary had delivered a letter to the Sultan, containing Hulegu's demands to the Muslim world. The letter read...

From the King of Kings of the East and West, the Great Khan. To Qutuz the Mamluk, who fled to escape our swords; you should think of what happened to other countries... and submit to us. You have heard how we have conquered a vast empire and have purified the earth of the disorders that tainted it. We have conquered vast areas, massacring all the people. You cannot escape from the terror of our armies. Where can you flee? What road will you use to escape us? Our horses are swift, our arrows sharp, our swords like thunderbolts, our hearts as hard as the mountains, our soldiers as numerous as the sand. Fortresses will not detain us, nor arms stop us. Your prayers to God will not avail against us. We are not moved by tears nor touched by lamentations. Only those who beg our protection will be safe. Hasten your reply before the fire of war is kindled... Resist and you will suffer the most terrible catastrophes. We will shatter your mosques and reveal the weakness of your God and then we will kill your children and your old men together. At present, you are the only enemy against whom we have to march.

To suggest that Qutuz was angered by the letter would be an understatement. He threw it to the floor and called for his senior ministers who arrived shortly, along with the leaders of his armed forces. Once seated and served with coffee, he informed them of the letter and highlighted the main problems they faced in getting an army to attack the

Mongols.

The gathered men sat in silence as Qutuz outlined his plans. The first of these was to unite Saracen, Turk and Kurd in a war against what he referred to as the *Infidel savages who had ravaged Muslim lands like a plague of locusts*. Then, when he had agreement to his plans, he called on one of his generals to choose a man who could carry an important message to the Christian ruler of the Crusader Kingdom of Jerusalem, which now existed in name only. Its remnants were now huddled into the town of Acre, a town run by a conglomerate of Barons.

As tensions increased between the Mongols and the Mamluks, both adversaries would look to the European Barons in Acre for support. Qutuz had no desire to side with age old enemies, and the feeling among the Barons of Acre was mutual. However, both sides felt that the Mongols were the far greater threat to their own security. The message was sent and Qutuz hoped that the Barons would decline the Mongol offer to fight against the Mamluks and would, instead, remain neutral.

The messenger chosen was a young man by the name of Mehmet and he left that same day on a trek that would last several weeks, from Alexandria to Acre.

It would be more than a month later when the messenger would return to Alexandria and, in a move that surprised the Mamluks themselves, he announced that the Barons would allow them to take their armies through territory held by the rulers of Acre. They would also allow the Turks to camp near Acre and obtain necessary supplies.

The messenger explained the reasons. He outlined to Qutuz the events that had transpired in the Crusader-held territories in recent months. A Mongol raiding party had been sent into Palestine, cutting the usual path of pillage and slaughter. The savage horsemen tore through Nablus and pushed on all the way to Gaza, but on the orders of the general in charge of this foray, Kitbuqa, the warriors did not attack the narrow strip of Crusader-held land and cities along the coast.

The Crusaders were too weak to provide any kind of resistance on their own and were entangled in a bitter debate over which of the two forces, Mongols or Mamluks, they should ally themselves with. Anno von Sangerhausen, the Grand Master of the Teutonic Knights, favoured a Christian-Mongol coalition; others vehemently disagreed. Kitbuqa had hoped that by leaving the Christian-held territories unharmed, the Crusaders would be persuaded to fall in with the Mongols. He had seriously misunderstood them. His decision was also swayed by his own Christian beliefs; beliefs that had wrought in him a profound hatred of Muslims and all things Islamic. This animosity had even led Kitbuqa to hold mass in captured Mosques and it was acts like these that cemented Muslim hatred for him and his Mongol warriors.

Two Crusader leaders, John of Beirut and Julian of Sidon, took soldiers and raided the new Mongol-held territories. Kitbuqa responded by sending a punitive expedition against Sidon. The Mongols plundered the town and massacred its citizens. Only the Castle of the Sea and its garrison held out and, as a result, Christian enthusiasm for the Mongol cause cooled significantly. It then turned exceedingly frosty when word reached the Crusaders that another Mongol army under Burundai had invaded Poland. Almost at the same time, William of Rubruck, envoy to the Mongols from French King, Louis IX, returned from Mongolia with a complete report on the invaders. After reading it Pope Alexander IV sent word throughout Christendom that the Mongols were pagan, were brutal savages and were not to be trusted. The Pope insisted that anyone forming any kind of alliance with them would be excommunicated. This settled the matter of a Mongol alliance with the Latin Christians once and for all.

In mid-February Hulegu's vast army began preparations for a march on Egypt while the Mamluks, numbering around twenty thousand, took steps to defend their country against the expected attack. It was at this point that fate seemed to intervene.

A messenger came to Hulegu with news that the Great Khan, Mongke, had died. Mongol tradition dictated that upon the death of a Great Khan, all princes, and that included Hulegu, were summoned to Mongolia to attend a Kuriltai, a Council, to elect his successor. This was not the first time that the Kuriltai had prevented the advance of the Mongolian armies. The death of the previous Khan had caused the westernmost armies to pull back after conquering the Poles.

Hulegu immediately pulled his main army back to Maragheh, leaving Kitbuqa in Syria with two *tumens* or about twenty thousand Mongols. Kitbuqa was ordered to press on to Egypt.

Meanwhile, in Egypt, the Arab Sultan, Qutuz, had allied himself with a Mamluk, Baibars, and their plan was to meet the Mongols head on. This alliance between Qutuz and Baibars, was unexpected to say the least. For Baibars to offer his allegiance to Qutuz was previously believed to be an impossibility. Yet, there it was. Nevertheless, there were many who mistrusted Baibars' intentions. Qutuz, during his rise to power, had murdered the leader of the Bahri Mamluks, Aqtay, and this had earned him the lasting hatred of both the Bahri faction and its new leader, Baibars. Immediately after Aqtay's assassination, Baibars had withdrawn with a group of supporters to Syria and he had been launching raids on Egypt ever since.

Qutuz and Baibars regarded each other with contempt, loathing, and mistrust but they both realized that a Mongol victory would mean their mutual destruction. Once Damascus fell, Baibars was quick to offer his support and Qutuz happily accepted it in early March. Once again, the driving principle was that *my enemy's enemy is my friend.*

CHAPTER 58
1260 A.D.
Acre

The city of Acre was subdued. People were scared, and the authorities were divided concerning the agreement that had been made with Qutuz in Egypt. With most people remaining secure in their homes, the streets were empty, as were most of the inns that were scattered around this Christian enclave.

In one dimly lit tavern, however, three men sat drinking and talking; three men who, like Jawad and some of his comrades, had experienced an unexplainable lack of aging. All of them bore the scars of battle and the eyes of men who had seen the horrors of war; these were battle-hardened men, two of whom sat opposite the third. Between them was a well-worn wooden table. The third man had his back to a corner wall. Penned in, like a trapped animal by two large, muscular men armed with swords and knives, one could be forgiven for expecting him to show all the signs of fear, but none were evident. His two captors were dressed in leather over chain mail, had placed their helmets on the table and were constantly scrutinising their surroundings.

The third man, the entrapped prey, was shorter but equally muscular; his enormous arms demonstrated his possession of incredible upper body strength. His shoulders were immense and callouses on the fingers of his right hand revealed that he was an archer.

He lifted a jug of ale, poured some into a roughly hewn wooden tankard, replaced the jug on the table and glugged half of his drink in one quick go. For the briefest of moments, he stared at the two men and then slammed the half empty vessel onto the table, causing ale to splash over the sides of the tankard, adding more of the liquid to the already sticky and foul-smelling piece of furniture. Then, he wiped his right sleeve across his mouth and spoke.

"So, Bohemond, Amalric, what next?"

The larger of the other men leant forwards and stared at their questioner.

"We have been ordered to take you in, Owun. Theft of a horse is punishable by death. You know that, but theft of one of the Palace horses, while escaping from guards who caught you in the bed chamber of one of de Lusignan's daughters?" Bohemond said, with a raising of his eyebrows. "Well, Mr. Tyler," he continued, "you can expect worse than death."

For an instant, there was silence as the two soldiers allowed Owun Tyler to contemplate the likely consequences of his rash actions. Edmund de Lusignan, one of the minor barons of Acre, was a ruthless and sadistic man and Tyler knew that 'worse than death' was something quite possible. He would be tortured and humiliated. His death would be slow and painful, and the now tarnished daughter of the baron would live the rest of her days in the harsh confines of a convent, run by cold hearted and sadistic nuns. In fact, whatever the outcome for Owun Tyler, Lusignon's daughter would suffer that fate and there was little if anything he could do to help her.

The archer finished the remains of his drink and, in an act of bravado, again slammed his tankard down, repeating his mouth cleaning behaviour, this time with his dry, left sleeve. At this point, Amalric spoke.

"Of course, there is another way," he said.

His colleague touched his arm. "Are you sure he's the man for this, Amalric?" he asked.

Tyler looked from one man to the other, his expression that of a man whose act of defiance had, albeit temporarily, been undermined by confusion. He waited.

"My dear friend, Bohemond, wonders whether we can trust you Tyler."

The archer made to reply but Amalric continued. As he spoke, his long, drooping moustache bobbed up and down with his lip movements. "He also wonders," he said, making a point of staring intently, purposefully, into the archer's eyes, "whether you are man enough for what we plan to do."

Tyler frowned but said nothing. He returned Amalric's stare and waited for the knight to continue.

"We three have lived some years since that battle which we all now recall with vague recognition, but void of any detail. Yet, look at us. We have hardly changed and I for one am tired of the nothingness, the emptiness which peace has brought."

He shifted slightly on his stool and then continued. "We are fighting men, are we not?" The question was rhetorical. "So, we need a fight and we hear that the Muslims are hiring mercenaries for the fight against the Mongols; swordsmen and English archers are what they are seeking, according to the reports we've heard."

He stopped, leant back from the table but maintained his imposing stare at the archer who eventually spoke up.

"Why me?"

The tavern was getting busier and the noise levels had risen but none of the three wanted to raise their voices so Bohemond stood up, moved round the table and sat down alongside Tyler, moving in close to his ear to speak. "We like you. We trust you. We have fought alongside each other, side-by-side with the Saracens that day so many years ago. Plus, you are the best exponent of the long bow we have ever seen, perhaps with the exception of that Robin fellow we once knew." he said.

Tyler pulled away slightly and turned to face Bohemond. "So, why are you unsure about me?" he asked.

Bohemond placed a friendly arm around the archer's shoulder and held his eyes with his own. Then he laughed, or rather he bellowed.

"I have to know you'll keep your dick in your trousers, Sir. There is only one type of arrow we want you firing on this mission. Do you understand?"

Tyler glanced at Amalric who was now smiling. The archer relaxed, smiled, and shook his head.

"You bastards," he mumbled, with a massive release of breath. "I thought my days were numbered." They all laughed and then Tyler added "I'm in."

The three soldiers spent the rest of the evening getting drunk and passed the night away with whores. "That's your lot, Tyler," Bohemond shouted after him as the archer slipped into an upstairs room with a young Irish girl who must have been half of Tyler's real age.

In the early hours of the following morning they slept and Amalric's dreams were filled with memories of the events of all those years before. After such a long time, with just a hazy recollection of those heady days, his mind was suddenly filled with details.

A plot had been discovered that threatened the entire region. Prince Jawad's brother, Sieffuddeen, had formed an alliance with the Ismaili Assassins and a dissident group of Knights Templar and had conspired to carve up the Middle East for their own benefit. Consequently, another unusual coalition had formed between the Emir of Jerusalem and the Christian ruler of Acre and a battle had raged between these two unlikely groupings.

One morning, a Turkish guerrilla unit, led by a formidable Turkish fighter named Arslan, was ordered to attack an assassin group that was on a reconnaissance mission to the south of the main Syrian encampment. Along with an Arab prince and Arslan's son, Bohemond, Amalric and a rather fresh-faced English archer, named Owun Tyler had fought the Assassins. They came upon the five of them as dawn broke and Tyler was the first to draw blood. An arrow fired from his longbow had whistled through a set of trees and anchored itself into an assassin's chest. The man fell to his knees, clutching at the shaft, his life draining away. It alerted the four remaining enemy soldiers, but they could not see beyond the trees.

As arrow after arrow followed, the Assassins ran, but they stumbled and one of them fell, headfirst, into a dusty clearing. He wiped the dust from his face and eyes but the last thing he had seen was Bohemond's foot. The last thing he had felt was the crusader's heavy sword plunging into his back. His spine broke, and his veins and arteries were severed.

Arslan came upon the wounded assassin, who was struggling to pull the arrow free. The Turk's sword slashed across the man's arm, but still he reached for a knife. Arslan's blade came thundering down again. The assassin's hand, knife still gripped in its fingers, was severed at the wrist. Arslan picked up his hand, the knife still held fast within it, and pushed the blade into the man's throat. Arslan left him where he lay.

Before long, all the Assassins were dead. Eventually, ten thousand soldiers from Jerusalem had joined them. The fighting was fierce and bloody but Sieffuddeen was defeated.

After just a few hours' sleep, the men mounted three Arab stallions and headed out of Acre. Their route would take them to Tyre in Lebanon and from there to Syria where their Arab and Turkish contacts would meet them to provide guides who would take them to Basra. As they were about to leave, however, a middle-aged man, dressed like an Arab, approached them.

"Get out of the way, old man," Amalric ordered.

He remained where he was and spoke softly to them.

"My name is Judah Ben Zakai and I recently delivered an important message to the commander in Acre, from the Emir in Jerusalem."

Bohemond interjected. "That is no business of ours, Jew. Now, get out of the way."

Ben Zakai smiled, but still refused to move. "I overheard your conversation in the tavern," he said. "I have family in Basra, and I would like to travel with you, if I may."

Bohemond and Amalric urged their horses forward, but Owun Tyler stopped them. "Wait. I have heard of this man. He speaks a multitude of languages and could be very useful."

Reluctantly, his comrades agreed. Bohemond looked down at Ben Zakai. "Do you have a horse?"

Zakai nodded and pointed across the road to an Arab mare.

"Then you may travel with us," Bohemond continued, "but don't expect our protection. You will be travelling alongside us, but you are not part of our group. Is that understood?"

Zakai nodded again, crossed to his horse, mounted up and nestled in behind the three soldiers.

The journey was long and tiring and, on several occasions, they encountered bandits en route who were dispatched with ferocious efficiency. Twice they almost ran into Mongol patrols, but their Syrian guides led them away from any potential conflict with the Eastern warriors. At this stage in their journey, it was not wise to alert the enemy to the presence of Christian mercenaries who were offering their services for hire to the Turks and Arabs.

After several weeks of travel, tired, dusty and filled with trepidation, the three Europeans were led into Iraq's marshlands, not far from the Persian border. Basra was a few days' ride from here and the Syrian guides had handed their wards over to some Bedouin tribesmen. They took them to their camp, disguised them as Arabs and set off towards Basra. Bohemond, fluent in Arabic after such a lengthy time in the Holy Land, pulled his horse alongside one of the Bedouin, a man seated on a well-looked-after camel, whose ride height was above the horseman.

"How can we enter Basra if the Mongols now hold it?" Bohemond asked.

The Arab guide smiled and then spat. "The Mongol force has moved to Syria and many have left our lands over some funeral or some such event in Asia. Only a small force of Eastern warriors remains in Basra now and they are never based there. They come and go. We trade often so we will be granted access to the city. Do not fear, my friend."

Bohemond was dubious. He did not trust the Bedouin, but he was too tired and too thirsty to start an argument. Amalric, too, had little trust in the tent dwellers. He felt that they were too willing to shift loyalties from one side to another as long as they survived to trade. Bohemond pulled on his horse's reins, turned to the left, spun his horse around and rode back to where his two comrades were riding, at the back of the caravan of six camels.

"Who meets us in Basra?" Amalric called out as Bohemond grew nearer to them.

Bohemond huffed. "Trying to get information from these desert gypsies is impossible when we have nothing to offer them in return. All we can do is wait and see."

In the marshes, the heat of the sun is barely any less harsh than it is in the desert and it is compounded with levels of humidity that are simply unbearable to those unused to such conditions. Even without their chain mail and leather, and dressed in Arabic jelabas, the three foreigners were soaked in sweat. Beads of it glistened in the sun like pearls shimmering in clear, fresh pools of water. As they neared Basra, a light breeze picked up and, although not cold, it was cool enough to bring some very slight relief.

Some ten or so yards from the city gates, the travellers were met by two Mongol horsemen who galloped up to them, dust exploding from their ponies' hooves and filling the air behind them. The lead Bedouin guide raised his hand, called a simple command to his camel, and stopped. The remainder of the group gradually caught up with him and followed suit. Then they waited. Seconds later, the Mongols pulled their ponies to a halt, the hooves thrusting into the dusty ground. An explosion of dry earth was fired over the Bedouin guide and then drifted, like a slow-moving cloud, towards the back of the camel caravan. For some moments, the Europeans were hidden from view. Once the dust had settled and the air had cleared, they were so road-weary, dehydrated, sun-roasted and dust-covered, that only the closest of scrutiny would reveal their racial origin. To all intents and purposes, they were Arabs.

The guide and the Mongols spoke briefly and then the two Steppe warriors turned their mounts and returned to the city. The Bedouin beckoned his caravan to proceed and Bohemond again rode up alongside the lead camel. Looking up from his horse, he called out to the Bedouin.

"What is the plan?"

The Bedouin smiled and looked at the approaching city of Basra. "No plan, Franji, no plan. We find two men; you leave with them and we go. Khallas (that's it)."

"And how do we recognise these men?" Bohemond asked, becoming increasingly irritated by the blasé attitude of the Arab.

The Bedouin laughed. "They will recognise you," He replied.

CHAPTER 59
Winter 1260 A.D.
Basra

Some months before the arrival of Bohemond and his friends, Jawad's group had arrived in Basra. It was, surprisingly, unlike a city in a country ravaged by war. The markets were bustling and very few of the Mongol invaders were evident anywhere. The residents were used to incomers from Baghdad, arriving via the escape network, but a large group of men appearing on horseback would be sure to arouse suspicions. Reza knew the city well, but he could not be sure who was collaborating with the enemy forces and the last thing he or his team of fighters needed was to draw attention to themselves. His own group of spies who had spent the past year at Jawad's house and travelled ahead of the group from Palestine, had already identified a handful of trustworthy citizens. The rest of Basra's population were to be treated with suspicion, they suggested. So, the group entered under the cover of night, horseless apart from two tired mares pulling an old wooden wagon. On it, they had loaded their weapons, covered with food supplies and animal skins, ostensibly for trading.

They settled themselves into a small lodging house on the town's outskirts, with which Reza was familiar. It was run by a cousin of his and their supplies and weapons had been locked away in an undersized outbuilding where five of the men kept watch over the equipment night and day. Reza's cousin had made sure that these visitors would be the only guests at the lodging house.

The Mongol army had largely ignored Basra, with only a few small units occasionally moving in to deal with bandits who would attack supply caravans as they passed the marshes. Consequently, the town was a place of relative safety. For most of the spring months, the group had remained confined to the lodging house, with limited excursions to local traders. As the days grew longer upon the arrival of summer, however, there were more people around and, it was during the hustle and bustle of a busy summer's day, that the group began to explore the city more thoroughly.

As the first light of dawn mystically crept into view, the team ate breakfast and decided on their roles for the day ahead. Seven would stay behind to guard the weapons and supplies while the rest of the men divided into three groups of three. Dressed as simple merchants, they planned to scatter themselves across Basra to get a feel of the lay of the land, so to speak.

At mid-morning, Jawad and Marie took one of their men-at-arms, Abdur-Raheem. Reza took two of his men, and Hassan was accompanied by Akbar and Mehmet, two of the fiercest fighters in the group.

The sun warmed the day, starting with a morning tenderness that was in stark contrast to the bite of the unusually chilly wind which weaved its way through the narrow lanes of Basra. In the marketplace, Jawad took his wife to one side and spoke to her in a soft whisper.

"Hassan is confident that Egypt's Mamluks are mobilising, finally, with a massive force of warriors. His sources have told him it is the largest Muslim force ever mustered."

"I saw the pigeon arrive," said Marie. "I assumed it would be for Reza though."

"Hassan has formed quite a network of his own, it seems," replied Jawad.

He paused momentarily and glanced around, concerned that eavesdropping ears may be close by. A few feet away he saw Abdur-Raheem, who was accompanying the married couple around Basra. Jawad signalled to him with a movement of his head and a flick of his eyes, to keep careful watch. Abdur-Raheem nodded. Marie still said nothing. She perused some dates, taking one and popping it into her mouth to taste, as is the custom in the Arab world; a kind of try-before-you-buy tradition. Then, she took another and offered it to her husband's mouth, which he opened to accept the gift. He chewed it just enough to extract the stone with his tongue. Then, he spat out the stone and swallowed the date. He caught hold of his wife's arm as he did so and moved her discretely towards the dusty path that led away from the market.

"We must find out when the Mongol force are expected to reach this region and where, precisely, they are headed," he said, quietly.

He already knew, from Reza's spies, that the Mongol army was moving from Baghdad and had already joined other Mongolian forces from Persia and Syria. Hassan expected the Egyptian and Saracen forces to reach the area of Ain Jalut, Goliath's Spring, by Ramadan the following year, perhaps seven or eight months away.

Marie nodded, but pulled away from Jawad and returned to the market stall where she purchased some of the dates before returning to her husband so that they could continue their stroll through the centre of Basra, finally heading back to their lodgings a few hours later. Abdur-Raheem was always nearby but never conspicuously connected to the married couple.

Once back at their temporary base, Jawad gathered the entire team in the outbuilding for a meeting. Small and cramped, though it was, it was the safest place for a meeting of everyone involved in these subversive activities. Reza and his men were most important to Jawad at this stage because they knew most about the Mongol movements. Jawad, however, needed to handle the whole group carefully. He could see, from the moment they all came together in Basra, that animosities between them were simmering just beneath the surface. It felt like an undersea volcano that first becomes known to the world when it erupts.

The team was made up of seventeen people in total; Jawad, Marie, Hassan and Reza were greeted upon entry to the outbuilding by two men. The first was Ali Mohamedi, Reza's younger brother. The second was Mehmet Abdul-Qareem Al-Rashid, a fierce and emotionless professional soldier from Jerusalem who had been conscripted for this mission by Hassan.

They were joined by Akbar. Like Hassan, he was a Mamluk. He was taller than anyone else in the group, with muscles to match. He kept his hair long and claimed it gave him extraordinary strength. Nobody believed his claim. Nevertheless, they called him Samson, a nickname that had been given to him by Crusaders during a brief spell in a Franj prison in Acre. Akbar was followed by Jawad's men, all of whom were originally from Bethlehem, or Bayt al-Lahm (the House of Meat) as the

Arabs called it. Two were Arab Christians who had fought bravely alongside their Muslim compatriots against the last Crusader assault on Jerusalem and other holy towns and cities. Their names were George Assad, the archer, and Antonio Habash, the crossbow man. Both had exceedingly handsome looks and could charm the anger from a crazed lion if they had to. Each had short, well-groomed, black hair and, unlike their Muslim cousins, were clean shaven.

The final members of Jawad's team were his engineer, Abdur-Raheem and Marie's maid, Amina. She could fight with the same efficiency as any of the men, while also being a great cook. Many of the men found her magnificent blend of warrior and caterer of domestic needs, very appealing. None of them would ever consider approaching her with any ill intentions, however. Not if they valued their lives.

Reza's remaining men were a mix of Persian, Syrian and Lebanese fighters, all of whom insisted on being called Ali. It was unlikely that anyone would learn their true names or identities. Jawad had asked their names many times and was always met with the same response.

"Ali."

On the journey to Basra, Jawad had taken Reza aside and asked what their real names were. "Ali," replied Reza, smiling and raising his eyebrows.

The Alis had spent the past year disappearing into the night on many occasions, only to return days, or occasionally weeks later with new and crucially valuable information. Sometimes, they would also return with stolen weapons, but the group's probing questions about their activities were always met with deathly silence. All but two of the Alis entered the outbuilding and closed the door behind them, leaving their namesakes outside to keep watch. Inside, the group discussed the impending clash of armies and one of Reza's Alis spoke up. This was a surprise to everyone as nobody had heard them speak more than a single word until now. Usually, they passed information to Reza and he passed it on to the group. Heads turned as he spoke. It was Reza's brother, although nobody knew this at the time, except Reza.

"We have heard that there was a delay in the sending of the Egyptian Mamluk army because they will be passing by lands held by the Franj."

He paused, and everybody waited for him to continue.

"Qutuz sent a messenger to the Christians in Acre and it seems that the Franj are more afraid of the Mongols than they are of the Muslims. The latest news is that they will agree to allow Muslim armies to travel here, as the only viable bulwark to Mongol expansionism.

"Of course, they could be hoping that a war between the Mongols and Muslims will deplete both forces, allowing a new crusade in the near future, but…"

Jawad interrupted before Ali could continue. "Who will lead the Muslim army and where is the meeting of forces likely to take place?" He asked.

Ali took a breath and then whispered his reply. "Baibars and Qutuz lead our forces and the plan is to destroy the Mongol army at Ain Jalut".

Hassan had guessed correctly and all those present knew that the outcome of a battle on such a massive scale at Ain Jalut, would be decided by tactics as much as the strength of the warriors.

He waited for a few minutes until everyone had taken in the news and then he stood to speak. "The barbarian horde will not have experienced this type of warfare and Qutuz will surely have his spies within the Mongol camp. With the help of Allah, this war can be won by our forces. Allahu Akbar!" He shouted.

Despite the concern about being discovered in their tenuous hideaway, all of those with him echoed his call, even the two Arab Christians. "Allahu Akbar!" they shouted in unison several times, until Jawad raised a hand to silence them.

CHAPTER 60
1260 A.D.
Abbas in Basra

The following morning, Jawad, Hassan, Marie and Amina made a further foray into Basra city to seek out locals who might have information that could help their cause. They reached the marketplace to find a unit of Mongol soldiers on horseback, attacking men, women, and children with savage intent.

The four pressed themselves into the shadows created by the closeness of the buildings and waited, unsure of what, if anything, they could do to stop the slaughter. As they waited, hearts racing, breathing heavy, someone ran around the corner and slammed into Jawad, almost knocking him off balance. Quickly composing himself, Jawad grabbed hold of the stranger, immediately realising that it was a young man. He dragged him into the shadows and held his hand over the man's mouth to keep him from calling out in fear.

Just then, the Mongols left, as if they had received a message to head elsewhere. They were like lightning on horseback, a whirlwind of savagery, leaving blood, death and misery behind them. The only sound that remained was the sobbing of the survivors and the groans and screams of pain from the wounded and dying.

Jawad removed his hand from the man's mouth and held him by his arms. "What is your name?" He asked, sternly.

"Jaffer". The man stated his name boldly. He was nineteen years' old now and hardened by his experiences.

"Do you have family here?" Jawad asked, glancing across at the bloody market square.

Jaffer shook his head and Jawad released his grip on his arms.

"Don't run," Jawad said. "Tell me who you are and where you have come from. Maybe we can help."

Jawad, Marie, and Hassan had interrogated Jaffer for what seemed to him like an eternity. In truth, the questioning had lasted less than a quarter of an hour. Finally, the captive took a deep breath to regain some control over his emotions and then told Jawad of his trip from Baghdad with the physician, so many years earlier.

"And where is this physician now?" Jawad's question was delivered with authority. In the back of his mind, he was considering how useful it would be to have a doctor with them. When no answer came immediately, Jawad shoved Jaffer lightly and prompted him for one. "Well? Answer me."

Confidently, Jaffer replied. "I can take you there."

Jawad paused momentarily, wondering if he could trust this young man but the decision was made for him. Marie caught hold of Jawad's arm and asked Jaffer to supply details of the doctor's whereabouts. Jawad turned to Amina and asked her to return to Reza and deliver him an urgent message. Based on Jaffer's description and details of location, Reza and one of the Alis could go in search of the doctor and bring him back.

"Unharmed, do you hear me?" Jawad had called out to Amina as she was leaving. "Make it very clear to Reza that I want the physician unharmed."

The other Alis had gone to the marketplace to meet with a Bedouin trader and acquire three new packages, valued at the equivalent of a half a dozen goats to be paid in gold. They had waited for well over two hours but were ordered, by Reza, not to leave until the packages arrived. Frustrated, tired and hungry, they were considering disobeying the order and heading back to base when one of them spotted the Bedouin caravan entering the city.

It took several minutes for the horses and camels to reach and pass through the crowded market. Traders were out in force following the withdrawal from Basra of most of the invader army. The few Mongol warriors that remained had lost all motivation or desire to enforce rules. They were content to pass the time with whores and fermented liquids. The Arab residents of Basra quickly realised that by allowing such behaviour without protest, they had the freedom of their city once more.

So, as the bustling market became a living creature, breathing new life into this devastated city, the travellers rode through, passing a tiny alleyway on their left. The alley was shrouded in shadows and it was within that shade that the caravan stopped. The two Alis stepped out from their own cool, shaded area and into the afternoon heat. They stepped across an open space and approached the three foreigners grouped together at the back of the caravan. Then they signalled for them to follow them. Bohemond caught hold of the Jewish interpreter and dragged him along.

Seconds later, the Bedouin were alone with their animals and the foreigners were gone, but a new leather pouch, filled with gold coins, hung from one of the now vacant horses. The Bedouin's payment had been delivered as promised and any potential for double cross from either side was gone. The three Franj and their Jewish travelling companion had disappeared like a Jinni in a puff of smoke, or so it had seemed to the Bedouin.

Back at the base building, Jawad and Marie had finally met the doctor, whom Reza himself had retrieved. They learned that his name was Muhammad, and they listened intently to his story. As he concluded his tale, the door opened, and the Alis returned with their three new recruits.

Bohemond was the first to pull away his turban and wipe some of the dust and dirt from his face. He glanced up, saw Hassan, Marie and Jawad and smiled.

"I should have guessed." He shook his head and nudged Amalric's arm. "Look who we've landed with," he said.

Amalric and Owun both looked around the group, by which time Jawad and Hassan had stood up to greet their old comrades at arms. Judah Ben Zakai was left standing in the doorway.

"Welcome my Franji friends," Jawad said, grasping hold of Bohemond's huge arms. Come, sit. We have coffee and food and water for washing."

Hassan then caught sight of Ben Zakai. "I know you." He said.

Zakai gave him a nod, and everyone's attention turned to the stranger. "And I know you, Hassan."

Hassan was confused. "You were sent to deliver a message to Acre. Why are you here?"

Ben Zakai smiled and waved towards the three Franj warriors who had been his travelling companions from Acre. "I delivered the message and then joined with these fine men to reach here, where I feel my skills could come in useful. I also have family here and would like to find them."

Jawad sighed, and Hassan's head dropped. Jawad spoke softly, warmly, and approached Ben Zakai. "I am so sorry, Judah. The Jews of Basra have all fled or been massacred by the Mongol armies." He paused to gauge the Jew's reactions. "Kitbuqa ordered the removal of all Jews from Iraq. He is a convert to Christianity with a fanatical zeal and a twisted attitude towards Muslims and Jews, but his hatred of Jews was beyond bounds."

A tear formed in Ben Zakai's eye and his head dropped. He felt his knees go weak and he looked as if he may pass out. Noticing this, Hassan rushed forward to support him. "Come, Judah. You are most welcome to remain with us. As you say, your language skills could be most useful."

For several weeks that became months, the group of insurgents carried out periodic guerrilla raids against the Mongol forces that were left in Basra and the surrounding areas. These continued until news arrived of movement of the Muslim armies. They were marching to meet the Mongols head on. By this time, most of the Mongol forces had moved on to Syria, with some forces moving through Palestine, reaching Gaza on Egypt's border. A depleted Mongol army was left in the region when Hulegu had returned to Mongolia and the handful of his troops who occasionally entered Basra were finding the increasing number of attacks on them tiresome. They decided to make an example of some of the townspeople and took about a dozen men and boys as captives, preparing them for execution near the marketplace. One of the captives was Reza's brother. The Mongols were making much noise about this 'foreign' fighter.

One of the other Alis had rushed to Reza's brother's aid against Reza's wishes. Hassan and Reza went after him and caught up with him just before he had exited a narrow, shaded alleyway, into the open area that was the marketplace. It would soon become an arena of death.

Reza's hand grabbed hold of Ali's shoulder and pulled him back, away from the alleyway's exit. Hassan helped Reza to hold the younger man and ordered him to remain silent, but their efforts were met with great resistance and eventually, they decided to let him go. As they emerged from the alleyway, they saw around twenty Mongol fighters, their swords drawn, thirty bound prisoners on their knees and a man they thought they recognised, standing apart from the rest, issuing orders. He was not a Mongol. He looked Arab and Hassan insisted they get closer. Reza nodded in agreement and the two men left Ali to move across the market square towards the prisoners. They circled around, keeping close to building walls as they did so. They crept methodically towards the stranger and, once they were within about twenty yards of him, Hassan gasped.

"Abbas," he whispered.

"Did you say something?" Reza asked.

Hassan ignored him. "We have to tell Jawad," he said, turning back towards the alley.

Reza turned with him but, as he was about to follow, a voice from behind them stopped Hassan in his tracks.

"Hassan, my tutor, so good to see you're still alive after all this time."

Hassan turned in the direction of the voice. Abbas looked older than the child he was when he disappeared all those decades earlier, but he was still young. He was smiling but his eyes were cold, emotionless and piercing. He stepped towards the two men and signalled to one of the Mongol warriors to bring someone to them. The warrior came immediately, dragging the beaten and barely alive body of Reza's brother with him. When he reached Abbas, he threw his victim to the ground at Abbas' feet and then stood over the twisted, blood-covered body with his sword in hand.

"Were you seeking this one or his friend?" Abbas asked, the smile spreading.

Reza moved towards him, but Hassan held him back.

"If either of them is dead, I'll kill you, you traitor." Reza shouted at Abbas, whose cold face remained. The cold face was something he had learned from the Mongols. Genghis Khan had always taught that to show your true feelings was weakness.

Abbas remained still. He glanced down at Hussain's battered body and then back at Reza and Hassan.

"His friend is already dead and now this one will join him."

He nodded towards the Mongol, who lifted his sword and hacked off the prisoner's head. He bent down and lifted the head above his own. The lifeless, staring eyes of his brother were directed at Reza. He could contain himself no longer. He drew his sword and rushed forward but succeeded in taking but a few strides. Abbas had lifted his left arm, held it out in front of him and closed his eyes. Suddenly, an unseen force struck the Persian, knocking him backwards and onto the ground. He landed at Hassan's feet and Abbas stepped forward.

"We will find you all, Hassan, and we will kill you, although some of you may be tortured first, for information, you see."

"Your brother will be here soon, Abbas," Hassan shouted, hoping that what he said would come true. He was about to continue when Abbas broke him off.

"Do you speak of Prince Jawad? Yes, of course you do, but he is not my brother, Hassan. He is my half-brother and, really, the wrong half. Our father was a weak human, as was Jawad's mother, but my mother was a Jinni and not just any Jinni, but the daughter of Shaytaan himself. You cannot defeat me."

His words were followed immediately by sounds of chaos, pain and slaughter as a hail of arrows seemed to appear from an empty sky, each one landing firmly in the chest of a Mongol soldier. Abbas' hypnotic control over Reza and Hassan was broken and he turned towards the market square. There, he saw Jawad and a troop of fighters, bows and swords drawn, arrows nocked and aimed at the prince's half-brother.

He turned to Jawad and shouted. "I must leave you now. You will not find me, but I will leave my seed among your people, Jawad; the seed of Satan will be spread among you for centuries and one day my people will rise amongst your people, to create chaos, death and destruction."

He took one last look at Jawad before making one final remark.

"The City of Baghdad is a curse, Hassan. It has been built and destroyed so many times and will continue to be built and destroyed. Yet, from that City will come its name in the form of a man. Many centuries from now, perhaps even a thousand years, who knows? A man with the City's name will lead my army, the army of my Grandfather, Shaytaan, in the name of your God, your religion, and we will destroy you all."

With that, he vanished. No smoke, nothing. He simply disappeared.

Reza rushed to his brother's beaten and headless body, knelt and wept. He glanced up as Jawad approached and placed a hand on his shoulder. "He was my brother. I am the last of our family now," Reza said.

CHAPTER 61
1260 A.D.
England

In England, an archer stood by an Arab horse, a rare sight in England at that time. Alongside him, his Saracen companion groomed the beast with a care and attention seldom found in many of the villages of the northern counties of the country. Yet, here he was, painstakingly preparing the horse in the same fashion as he had treated the archer's horse an hour earlier.

The Englishman looked around nervously. It was unusual for either of them to be away from his manor house and walled off land, but he was following instructions from a peculiar visitor, and seeking information from someone in the village.

The day before, the archer had been on his estate, checking on some of his livestock. He never wanted to live like this and most of his life had been spent in wars or as an enemy of the powers that be. Years had been spent on the run or hiding in forest communities with bands of outlaws. As he knelt to check on the progress of the Saracen's medical work on an injured sheep, he was felled by an incredible force that appeared from nowhere, accompanied by a blinding light.

As he recovered his senses and his vision sharpened once more, he saw a man standing before him, dressed in armour and holding a magnificent sword, the like of which had not been seen in this world at any time before. The archer pulled himself to his feet and backed sharply away from the stranger.

"Fear not," the stranger said, his voice firm, authoritative, but without threat. "I am to deliver you a message."

It was at this point that the archer was ordered to enter the dark forest with his friend and squire to seek out the old woman who resided there.

"A message she shall give to you, in a tongue unknown by those this country holds in residence. You must wait for friends of old to pass the words along or guide them to a place, hitherto unknown by you or them."

"Why could those friends not go to her themselves?" The archer queried.

The stranger took a deep breath before replying. "The lady of the forest is old and frail. She holds on to life, awaiting your visit, as per my instructions to her. She cannot hold on long enough for your friends to arrive."

The archer turned his head to glance at his Saracen companion and then sought to question the stranger further. However, when he looked to where the alien being had stood, he found him gone. He had vanished, leaving no evidence of his presence in the air or on the ground.

So here, in this forest, were the archer and the Saracen, following the seraph's orders, albeit against their better judgement. They were seeking out the healer of the forest to whom they had been sent.

After four days of travel they had entered the forest and proceeded towards the healer's house. It lay one day's journey from the manor house but now they were close. The house was minutes from where they now rested but their apprehension had forced them to wait. Now, each step towards it filled both men with a mixture of fear and excitement.

Grooming complete, they mounted their steeds and rode to the thickest part of the forest where they found a house. It was built into an enormous mound of earth and covered with moss.

With trepidation, the archer approached the small door at the side of the building and rapped hard on it. They waited, and minutes later the door opened, slowly at first, but with a wild swing as it reached its maximum arc. There was nobody there to greet them and, for a few moments, the travellers looked at each other in bewilderment. Eventually, however, they decided to enter, the Saracen insisting that he should go in first. Reluctantly, the archer agreed.

The house comprised of one, small, dark room, lighted only by three candles, strategically placed around the room to offer the most minimal of light. As they looked around and tried to adjust to the dimly lit setting they had entered, a woman's voice spoke from one corner of the chamber.

"Why do you seek me out, strangers?" She asked.

The archer stepped forward and explained why they had come but she looked past him to the Saracen.

"I appreciate your eagerness, Robert of Huntingdon, Robin of Loxley, or is it Robin the Hud? However, it is your servant to whom I must convey the information. For it is he who speaks a language which is unknown in this land."

Robin glanced briefly at his Saracen companion and then spoke to the old woman. He kept his eyes on her hands the whole time, for he did not fully trust her and was convinced, if truth be known, that she was a sorceress.

"He is not my servant. He is my friend." Said Robin, frowning as he spoke.

"It matters not how you address him," she replied. "It is still he to whom I must speak for he knows the old language of Aramaic."

Robin stepped aside and waved his companion forward. "Sami," he said.

The Saracen waited, and the old woman painstakingly conveyed her message to him in Aramaic, continually checking that he had learned it off by heart and understood its meaning clearly. Repeatedly, he recited the message and nodded to affirm that he understood its importance and, after what seemed an eternity to Robin, the woman finished her task and collapsed. Sami rushed to her, checked her pulse and breathing and then turned to Robin. He shook his head to indicate to the archer that she was no longer alive.

"What?" Confused and concerned, Robin rushed to her side and checked for himself, only to find that Sami was correct in his conclusion. The woman had died. Somewhat shocked by what had happened, the two men turned and left the house. A minute after they had headed out of the door and into the trees again, they heard an eerie sound behind them. Both turned together and found that the house was gone. For a moment, they stared at the empty space where it had stood and then they continued with their journey—a journey to destinations that only Sami knew.

For more than half an hour, neither man spoke. They knew that what they had seen was as unknown to one as it was to the other, so what could be said or asked? As they ventured deeper into the forest, however, Robin finally broke the silence between them.

"You can't tell me where we're going, my friend?" Asked Robin, annoyed that he was left out of the loop.

Sami shook his head and continued riding. "If I tell you, then I must tell you in English. Once that is done, the message is no longer secure. I'm sorry brother, but you must trust me when I say I cannot tell anyone, not even you."

Their journey continued, and night fell, shrouding the forest in darkness as black as pitch. The travellers, with no way to see any obstacles that may lie in their way, reluctantly set up camp. They tethered their horses to a large tree and wrapped themselves in coarse blankets to keep out the cold. Concerned about wild animals, especially wolves, one man slept while the other kept watch and the sounds of life gradually increased with every hour. Nocturnal beings took control of the land.

Sami was first to stand guard and he had to fight hard against the pull of sleep. The sounds began to blur into one and, within the blackened surroundings, shadows became real. Sami wondered whether they were shadows, night animals or the forest Jinn come out to play. The Jinn, he knew, were limited in their ability to travel to Earth's universe, but he also knew that many lived among us, especially in the darkness of deep, thick forests, the desert lands and the barren lands of ice and snow. Some had posed as gods throughout man's history, leading people to embark on ever-increasing sinful ways.

Unwilling to allow himself any opportunity to fall asleep, he wandered around the clearing where they had camped. He found himself becoming more alert as he did so. He had passed the point of sleepiness. His mind now focused on every sound, every movement, every breath of wind that whistled its way through the trees. The night hours passed quickly and soon he saw the first cracks of morning light piercing their way through the branches. As he had done throughout the night, he returned to where Robin slept and checked on his companion. Seeing that all was well, Sami decided to gather wood and hunt for food for their breakfast.

CHAPTER 62
1260 A.D.
Syria

The Mongols had, as the Bedouin had conveyed to Bohemond, moved south from Baghdad into Syria, where they destroyed Aleppo and occupied Damascus. The destruction the Mongols wrought was not limited merely to the cities and the townspeople. The complex irrigation systems of places like Khurasan, North of Persia, Persia itself, and Iraq (Mesopotamia), sustained far-reaching damage. Those irrigation systems had taken almost five thousand years of collective efforts to build. They had turned desert and dry grassland into probably the most productive agricultural lands on earth. In the wake of this devastation, the locust-like Mongol forces headed on to Cairo but, en route, they were met by Baibars' force of Mamluks.

On 3rd September 1260, Baibars advanced at speed, engaging Kitbuqa's force as they approached Ain Jalut, the Spring of Goliath. Jawad and his small force of men-at-arms, meanwhile, were making their journey towards Galilee, in Palestine, where Ain Jalut was located. Their plans to sabotage the Mongols in Iraq had not come to much when the Mongol forces suddenly, and without warning, moved on to Syria. Reza and his spies had quickly reassessed their position and the group had set out towards Ain Jalut, hoping to act as an advance party. Poor weather, clashes with bandits and several supernatural occurrences that Hassan was certain were instigated by Abbas, delayed their progress considerably. It was unlikely, they thought, that they would arrive in time to be of any assistance at all, let alone be an advance party.

Meanwhile, as they entered Palestine, the battle had already begun. Seeing Baibars' force, the Mongol General, Kitbuqa, mistook it for the entire Mamluk army, so he ordered his men to charge. He led the attack himself and the two armies collided, both appearing to stop in the ferocious clash that followed. Then, without warning, Baibars ordered a retreat. The Mongols, thinking that they had the enemy routed, forged forward in pursuit, shrieking triumphantly as they saw victory in their grasp.

When they reached the springs, Baibars' army wheeled to face the Mongols and it was only then that the Mongols realised they had been duped, fooled by one of their own favourite tactics—the feigned retreat. As the Mamluks re-engaged the Mongols, Qutuz ordered the reserve cavalry out from its place of concealment in the foothills and slopes. Like an unexpected sandstorm, the Mamluk reserves launched themselves against the Mongol flanks.

Realising that he was now committed to a battle with the entire Mamluk army, Kitbuqa ordered his forces to charge against the Muslim's left flank. As the two forces struck, swords hacked and stabbed in the melee and one Turkish officer thrust his way through the ranks of warriors, his own and those of the enemy. His name was Arslan. He was Hassan's father and, like his son, had experienced the same slowing down of the aging process. Arslan was one of the most formidable looking men imaginable. Bearded, but light-skinned, his dark, deep-set eyes were piercing in their intensity. His sword hung, not in the Arab fashion across the back, but purposefully at his side. His hair was short and black and from his left temple, down past his ear, ran a scar acquired in battle.

As he pushed his way through the enemy ranks a Mongol warrior ran towards him, sword in hand. The wild eyes of the opponent were suddenly tamed as Arslan's own weapon slashed down onto the Mongol's arm, severing it at the elbow. There was a scream from the wounded man, but it was short-lived. Arslan followed it up with a piercing thrust of his blade to the man's throat. The Mongol's body slumped to the floor and Arslan moved on. By this time, archers on both sides had ceased their barrage of arrow artillery, put aside their bows, taken up swords and joined the mayhem. This was the true horror of warfare, as thousands of men stood face-to-face, hacking, thrusting, stabbing, and slashing at each other's heads, faces, limbs and torsos. Blood was slick on the ground and many men fell as they fought. For some, that was when they met their end. As they lay helpless on the blood-drenched ground, an enemy sword or axe came crunching through bone and slicing through ligaments and muscle.

The smell of battle was something that brought extra fear to those new to a battlefield. It was the smell of shit and piss, of sweat and of blood and vomit. It was the smell of death. Some of the younger men on both sides froze. No fight or flight reaction for them; just absolute fear that caused their cognitive processes to fail. Many such men were slaughtered without ever lifting their weapons in anger.

Others, the battle-hardened, were experiencing feelings of ecstasy. They would say that their blood was up. They were in a blood frenzy, hacking, stabbing, slashing, and screaming their war cries. They fought for their lives like biological machines. Yet, Arslan and others who were respected as the greatest of warriors, had learned to control their passion. They were as aroused by the battle as any others, but it was controlled passion and never anger, or fear driven.

The Mamluks held, then wavered before holding again but eventually they were turned, cracks appearing under the ferociousness of the Mongol attack.

The Mamluk wing threatened to dissolve and many of its officers began to fear that the entire army could be routed. At this point, Qutuz rode to where the fiercest fighting was taking place. He threw his helmet to the ground, allowing the entire army to see and recognise his face. Then, he called out to his troops, an appeal that he hoped would rouse them to victory.

"O Muslims, O Muslims, O Muslims," he shouted. He appealed to their deep religious beliefs, reminded them of their history, of victories against other invaders in the past and ordered them to offer themselves into the hands of Allah.

His troops were shaken, but they rallied, and the flank held. As the line hardened, Qutuz led a counterattack, sweeping back the Mongol forces.

Kitbuqa was now faced with a deteriorating situation and he was unsure what to do. As he pondered this, one of his officers suggested that they should withdraw. Kitbuqa showed the cold face and his response was brief:

"We will die here and that is the end of it. May the Khan have long life and happiness."

Mamluk pressure was relentless. Mamluk archers, almost as skilled at the art of firing the bow from a galloping horse as the Mongols, again began to launch their arrows. They brought massive casualties amongst the Mongol ranks. Scores of Mongol soldiers fell from the artillery barrage of arrows, while others began to feel the full force of Qutuz's and Baibars' highly trained and deadly soldiers. Despite this, Kitbuqa continued to rally his men until his horse was struck by an arrow and he was thrown to the ground. He avoided the frightening situation of a wounded horse collapsing on top of him, but he was stunned and, while lying, helpless on the ground, his horse thrashing about nearby, he was captured by nearby Mamluk soldiers.

One of them took a sword to the horse's throat, silencing the animal and avoiding any risk of accidental harm from flailing legs. Another two Mamluks held the Mongol General down while they tied his arms and dragged him away from the battlefield.

The Mongols were commonly thought of as an invincible force, but they were outclassed by the Mamluks on the battlefield. The lightly armoured Mongol horse-archers rode small steppe ponies and carried little but 'home-made' weapons. They were designed for close combat. The heavily armoured Mamluks, on the other hand, rode much larger Arab horses, and the Mamluks matched the Mongols in their mounted archery. However, in addition to the mastery with bow and arrow, the Mamluks were also able to close in and kill with the lance, club, and sword, while protected with armour themselves. The Mongols lacked structural, organised training and found themselves facing Mamluk troops that had spent their entire lives in training. The demons from the Steppes had been defeated by their former slaves from the Steppes.

By the time the battle was almost over and Kitbuqa had been captured, the Mongol forces collapsed into anarchic chaos. The Mamluks spared few of them as they rampaged through the Mongol army.

Kitbuqa was taken to the Sultan as the battle continued to rage around them. The Mongol General was thrown to his knees before Qutuz who showed no emotion on his face as he looked down on the man who had so brutally led a swathe of destruction through Mesopotamia.

Qutuz finally smiled and spoke. "After overthrowing so many

dynasties you are caught at last, I see," he gloated.

Kitbuqa remained defiant, even insolent. "If you kill me now," he said, "when Hulegu Khan returns, all the lands from Azerbaijan to Egypt will be trampled beneath the hooves of Mongol horses."

He watched the Sultan, judging his response and hoping to add insult to the threat. "All my life I have been a slave of the khan. I am not like you. I would never murder my master"

The desired effect was achieved. Qutuz was incensed and he immediately ordered that Kitbuqa be executed. "Send his head to Cairo as proof of our victory over the unbelievers" he shouted.

The soldiers who had brought Kitbuqa to Qutuz, grabbed him unceremoniously and dragged him to one side. He was pushed onto his knees and his head was forced down onto a rock. Seconds later, he was beheaded, his lifeless eyes left staring out of an isolated head, as if looking at his own body, confused as to what had happened.

With their General gone, the remaining Mongol troops fled some ten or twelve miles to the town of Beisan where they formed up to face the pursuing Mamluk cavalry. The Muslims came like thunder into the town.

CHAPTER 63
Arslan

Jawad and his band of fighters had arrived too late to witness the devastating battle at Ain Jalut but did reach Beisan in time to join the fighting there. As the Mamluk cavalry was joined by hundreds of thousands of foot-soldiers, Jawad ordered his men into the town. The fighting was fierce, and Jawad was grateful that he had left Marie, Amina, Ben Zakai, Jaffer and the Physician out of harm's way, beyond the battle arena.

Reza entered the town with the Alis amid a large assembly of Mamluk infantry who headed for the heart of the town.

The remaining fragments of the Mongol force, the few that could escape, crossed the Euphrates River. Hassan had joined a small group of Mamluks who had chased them towards the river. As he and the others stood at the riverbank, jeering at the fleeing Mongol soldiers, he was touched on the shoulder by someone's hand. Hassan turned to see who had managed to approach him so easily and with such stealth, recognising the man immediately.

"Father," he said, before taking Arslan in an embrace.

"We have won a great victory here Hassan, a great victory over the demons from Hell, but they are not gone for good. We have to prepare for them to return another day."

Arslan showed no surprise that his son still looked so young after so much time, for Arslan had also been affected by the strange forces that had slowed down the aging process for so many that had taken part in the great mythological battle for Jerusalem. He turned in the direction that the Mongols had ridden and breathed a heavy sigh.

"This is far from over Hassan," he said, with a heavy heart. "Once a new Khan is chosen and the tribes pledge their allegiance to him, Hulegu will be back and he will be seeking revenge for what we did here today to his forces and his General."

Hassan nodded, and the two men walked together to join Jawad and the other guerrilla fighters. The town was a scene of indescribable devastation and the thought of further conflict weighed heavily on Arslan's mind. More wars, more deaths, more broken families would prey on the people of these lands for a long time to come.

The remaining Mongols, the ones who were trapped in the town, were butchered. Within days, Qutuz re-entered Damascus as triumphant victor, greeted with whoops of delight from crowds that had gathered. After a short period in Damascus, his army moved on to liberate Aleppo and the other major cities of Syria. The Mongols, for the time being, were defeated.

However, for Qutuz, the ecstasy of success was short lived. Following the re-capture of Aleppo, Baibars requested that he be made Emir of the entire region in recognition of his contributions to the victory. Qutuz refused and when the Mamluk army was just a few days' ride from its heroic return to Cairo, Baibars visited Qutuz, ostensibly on a matter of state.

"Assalamu 'alaikum my Khaliph," he said, reaching out to shake Qutuz's sword hand but, as he did so, he withdrew a dagger from his belt and drove it into Qutuz' heart. Nobody challenged him and when the army entered the Egyptian capital, Baibars, not Qutuz, rode at their head as Khaliph.

Meanwhile, in the town of Beisan the group was joined by Marie and her maid. Jawad enquired as to the whereabouts of Ben Zakai, Muhammad and Jaffer.

"We could not find them. We searched as much as we could, but they were nowhere to be found," Marie replied.

Concerned, but without the luxury of time to spend on pondering about the physician and the boy, Jawad called his assembly of mercenaries together in a deserted house they had occupied. One of the Alis was sent to find each of the group's members and, in succession, they arrived. The last to enter was Hassan and he had brought his father with him. The two men entered the house and closed the door behind them. They were met with a suspicious silence as Arslan stepped into the main room where the others were gathered. He said nothing, but he could see from the faces of those in the room that he was not going to receive an immediate welcome.

"Who is this man?" Abdur-Raheem asked, some suspicion revealed in his voice. His eyes were fixated on Hassan and his hand rested on the hilt of his sword.

Jawad smiled, stood up and walked across to the newcomer, clasped his hands upon the man's shoulders and embraced him. He then turned to the gathering and laughed.

"This is Hassan's father, Arslan, and he is as welcome here as any of the rest of us."

He pulled Arslan towards a space between his own seating space on the floor and Reza's and they sat themselves down. Bohemond and Amalric sat opposite Jawad. Gradually, the talking began. It started with exchanges of stories from the battle which they had all just experienced and slowly moved on to what was needed next.

Bohemond whispered to Amalric. "What I'd do for some ale right now." Amalric laughed and then they joined the discussion. For hours, they spoke, drank coffee, prayed and ate until exhaustion finally overtook them and they slept.

They were awoken by the sound of someone entering the house. Despite their sleepy state, all of them readied themselves with weapons within seconds and were moving towards the door. It swung open with some force and one of Reza's men entered. He was out of breath. Nobody had noticed him missing when they had been awoken from their slumber, but he had left the house at some point during the night, unable to sleep and eager to find out what was happening.

As the weapons were lowered, he spoke. "I've seen the man who ordered the killing of our two Alis in Basra."

Hassan stepped forward and grabbed the man. "You've seen Abbas? Here in Beisan?"

The spy nodded, and Hassan guided him towards a place on the floor and offered him some water. "Talk to us brother," said Hassan.

"I couldn't sleep so I went out to clear my head and get some air. I strolled across the town, finding few people around, save for some soldiers on guard at key positions around town.

"As I reached the Eastern side of town, I saw movement in some

306

shadows and my suspicions were aroused, in case there were Mongol Assassins lurking. I decided to follow. I wasn't seen, keeping myself to the shadows and remaining silent as a stalking cat.

"Then, as we reached the road that heads towards the desert, I saw him."

He paused to catch his breath, his face stern and serious. The group said nothing, though they wanted to. They knew he needed to continue uninterrupted, so they waited, and he continued.

"I'll never forget that man's face and, even in the dark, I knew it was him by his gait, but then the moonlight caught his face and my thoughts were confirmed. It was, er, Abbas you called him?"

"He skulked out of town under the cover of darkness like the dirty coward he is, and I followed him for several miles into the desert, where I lost him.

Again, he paused, a frown spreading across his forehead. "He just vanished," he said, shaking his head as if trying to wake himself. "I know it sounds crazy and maybe it is. Maybe I was more tired than I thought, and my eyes and mind deceived me, but I don't believe that. I know what I saw. One minute he was walking across the sands and, suddenly, he just disappeared."

He placed the tips of his right forefinger and thumb together and then separated them, fanning his fingers in the air as he said, "Puff... he was gone."

Silence filled the room as Ali sat himself down, exhausted. Hassan turned to Jawad. "We must find him. He is the key to locking away the evil that currently plagues us all, Jawad."

Jawad nodded in agreement, although he was unsure what they would or even could do if they caught up with him. He stood up and paced around the room for several minutes.

"Ali," he said, "in the morning, can you take us to the place where Abbas disappeared?"

Ali nodded, and his face brightened at Jawad's acceptance that Abbas had vanished.

"Then it is decided. Just before sunrise, we leave." Jawad turned to Arslan. "Will you join us Arslan?"

He got no answer and Hassan stepped forwards into the only light within the room, supplied by a small candle. "Let me tell my father all that has happened so far, and, in the morning, he can make a decision," he said, turning to Arslan, who nodded in agreement. The two men left the building and wandered to a quiet area just outside. The remaining men returned to their beds. Marie and Amina had slept through the entire meeting.

Before dawn, the group was saddling horses, cleaning and sharpening swords, preparing bow strings with beeswax and filling bags with food and containers full of water. Arslan approached Jawad and Marie as they walked their horses to the front of the line and Marie smiled at the old warrior. He nodded back out of respect and fondness for the soldier princess.

"If you agree, my prince, I will join you on this quest," Arslan said, lowering his eyes to the ground as he spoke.

Jawad placed his finger under the old Turk's chin and gently pushed his head upwards. "Look at me Arslan," he ordered and Arslan complied immediately. "There are no princes or princesses here. We are brothers and sisters and you are one with all of us. If you come, you come as a man of great honour and prowess, an equal to us all and if you agree to that, then you are welcome to ride alongside us my brother."

Arslan smiled, gave a slight nod, and moved towards his own horse. "You may not have any claim to Jerusalem, but you will always be my prince, my prince. You will always be prince to all of us."

Within minutes, they had all mounted up and begun their ride into the desert, the Ali who had seen Abbas, leading their way.

Their journey would be long and arduous, constantly avoiding or fighting with Mongol soldiers, criminal gangs and several groups of religious fanatics as they sought Abbas. They set out on a search that could take years.

CHAPTER 64
1266 A.D.
Sheffield, England

It was 1266 in a hamlet just outside the town of Sheffield, England. Four armed men sat in a tavern, drinking and laughing. They passed their time clutching at passing women and occasionally stared down anyone who dared look their way. These were sword sellers, mercenaries, men for hire and the leader of the group was a man named Omerus Nottram, formerly from Nottingham. He was at least twenty years' older than his companions with a face that showed a lifetime of hard fighting and killing.

It was as they finished their fourth tankard of ale that a young lad rushed into the tavern shouting about an attack on Sheffield. Local rebels, together with a group of noble allies, the "Disinherited", had long shown resistance to King Henry III. Now, they had attacked the city under John de Eyville. The formerly jailed, but recently freed, Robert De Ferrers, Earl of Derby, marched from his castle at Duffield to Chesterfield. There, he was joined by reinforcements from north Lincolnshire.

Then, this party of barons and rebels passed through Sheffield en route to their destination. They sacked the town, burning down both the church and the motte and bailey castle. By the time the boy arrived with his announcement, Sheffield was destroyed and King Henry's nephew, Henry of Alamaine, had arrived with loyal barons to evict the rebels. The fleeing survivors hid in the murky and dangerous Ely fens, led initially by de Eyville.

Many of the men in the tavern began streaming out, in the hope of joining the battle. They were King's men and were thrilled at an opportunity to cut the necks of some rebellious criminals. Amid the clatter of armour being grabbed, swords being belted to men and horses being prepared, the team of fighting men left the tavern. The small group of sword sellers waited for the tavern to empty and then stood. They would hang back and see which side was most likely to be victorious, before selling their services. As they gathered their weapons and kit, however, they were bowled over by an unseen but brutally powerful force. It knocked each one of them unconscious. Nobody was left in the tavern to notice this event. The women and children had run to the back rooms of the tavern, knowing how dangerous groups of angry, uncontrolled and armed men can be.

When the sword sellers came around, they found themselves facing a hideous looking demon with cat-like eyes and skin like red leather. They could not move, held immobile by the demon, which spoke in a language they should not have been able to understand. Yet they could.

"Omerus Nottram, I come to remind you of your father and how he died those many years' ago, when you were a youth at his side. Your father was the Sheriff's man in Nottingham when he was killed by the leader of a band of thieves and outlaws, a man you pledged to find and kill. Do you remember?"

Omerus felt himself released from the enchanted grip of the demon and nodded. "Of course, I remember, but that man is dead for sure. He has not been seen for many years."

The demon took a step forward. "He is not dead, but he is no longer in Nottingham. He lives under a new name on his estate not far from York. He is still assisted by his Saracen companion and I will tell you where to find him… on one condition."

Omerus said nothing so the demon continued. "In the forest, wherein resided the healing Witch of York, you will find the man you seek. You may kill him, but only after you have obtained from him the information I seek, which he has been granted by the witch."

Then, he disappeared. No warning, no further information, nothing, and the men found they could move and talk again. Omerus' breathing was rapid and sweat poured down his face and neck, settling, cold, onto his chest beneath his tunic. He thought about what he had just witnessed, and a sensible man might have taken to his horse and fled, but Omerus was absorbed by the thought that Robin the Hud may, however unlikely, still be alive. Not only that, but he was within a day's ride from where Omerus and his comrades sat. They all recovered their senses after a short while and Omerus pulled at the shirt of one of his companions.

"We travel to York." He said.

Robin and Sami were less than halfway through the forest on their return to their Estate when the weather turned for the worse. Sami suggested they find shelter and build a small fire. Robin agreed and set about building a rickety, temporary shelter, while Sami searched the forest for suitable, dry kindling and wood for a fire. A cold wind was building, and clouds formed overhead. Sami knew he needed to be quick if he wanted to get a fire burning before the rains came. Robin, meanwhile, was rushing to put together something strong enough to resist the elements.

He lifted a collection of large leaves and branches, rested them against his makeshift frame and turned to collect a second bunch. It was then that the first arrow struck him, in the left shoulder, the force pushing his body backwards, but failing to force him to the floor. Surprise was rapidly thrust to the back of his mind and he quickly dived behind the biggest tree he could reach. Then, before he could find safety, a second shaft found its way through his leather shirt and into his chest, piercing his lung and leaving him completely breathless.

He staggered backwards and slumped down on his backside, falling against his half-built shelter, and pulling the entire structure down around him. He could hardly breathe and was struggling to stay conscious but through the blurry vision he could see three men approaching him. One had a third arrow nocked in his bow, the string pulled back to his chin and the arrow pointing directly at Robin's heart. Unable to move, and leaning against the tree, he waited sullenly, hoping that Sami would return sooner, rather than later.

The first of the three men, far older than the other two, leant down and shifted the arrow that was embedded in Robin's shoulder, from side to side. Robin tried to yell, but the arrow through his lung prevented it. He gurgled and spluttered. Then, the movement of the shaft in his shoulder stopped. Some of the pain dissipated and his assailant stood upright again. He took a small step backwards.

"I'm sure you're wondering who we are and why we've decided to do what we have done, so let me put you out of, at least some of your misery and tell you," the man said.

"For years, my only purpose in life was to find the elusive Robin

Hud and kill him," he continued. He frowned and, for a moment, looked away as he thought back over the years. "I was a youngster when it happened; maybe fifteen or sixteen years old and I was travelling with my father." He glanced down at Robin, who was struggling to breathe with his punctured lung. Every breath in created a gurgling sound and every breath out brought with it trickles of blood from his mouth. His assailant smiled at that and then returned to his story.

"My name is Omerus Nottram. My father was one of the Sheriff of Nottingham's personal guard and he was sent to protect a cartload of gold that was on its way to Nottingham from London. He didn't know I was there. I had sneaked out of our house and gone into the forest. It was something I did often, and nobody knew, not my father, not even my mother. On this day, I saw you and your band of cutthroat thieves attacking the wagon and its brave protectors, my father included.

"I must say that I am amazed that you have hardly changed since that day, while I have aged considerably. Anyway, I hid in some bushes and watched as you fired an arrow straight through my father's heart, killing him instantly and I swore that one day I would make you suffer, make you die slowly for what you did.

"So, for decades I planned, I searched from town to town, village to village and then I heard the worst thing anybody could have said to me. You hadn't been seen for many years and rumours had it that you had died. Some people even told me that they had witnessed your death.

"I continued to search for many months but in the end, I gave up and became a sword seller, a mercenary to the rich and powerful."

He paused and paced around a little. His two companions were standing guard and he glanced at them, checking that they were doing their jobs correctly. Satisfied that they were, he walked back to the dying man lying, pale and sickly-looking, against the trunk of a large tree.

"Then, a few days' ago, we were visited by what could only have been a spectre, a spirit of the forest maybe. You know, the sort of beast that believers in the old religions often speak of.

"He told us you were alive and where we could find you. If it had been a man or a woman who gave me such information, I most probably would have ignored it, but this was a being of great magic. He appeared, gave me the knowledge that I had sought for so much of my adult life and disappeared, right before our eyes. So, I took it seriously and here we are.

"Now, I am going to cut pieces off you and, when I am tired of that, I am going to leave you to die here, where you will be eaten by the wild beasts of the forest."

As he told his story, Sami, having heard Robin's shout when the first arrow struck, was stalking his way through the forest towards his friend. From a vantage point, unseen by the three attackers, he monitored them carefully and listened to what Omerus was saying.

Omerus leaned forwards, putting his face right up against Robin's and he whispered in the dying man's ear.

"Before I let you die, I need the information you obtained from the healing witch. If you give it to me, I will make your death quick and painless."

Robin gurgled a reply that was barely audible. "I don't have it. My companion has it," he said and then forced a twisted smile.

Omerus suddenly remembered that the demon had mentioned Robin's Saracen companion. "My god," he shouted to his men. "He's not alone. There is another…" His words were cut off sharply as a cross bow bolt flew from the forest into the clearing, striking his bow man in the throat. The force of it drove the bolt through the man's neck, smashing his spinal cord. The man suffered immediate paralysis. He dropped his bow and his body slumped to the ground. Blood poured from his throat and the third man's attention was, briefly, directed towards his friend.

Meanwhile, Robin had managed to reach out to one of his arrows that was lying, spilled from its quiver, on the ground alongside him. Omerus turned back to him and again moved in close.

"You bastard. We'll kill your man and then rip your body, limb from…" The force of the arrow, thrust into the side of his neck by Robin, tore open his artery and shut off his sentence before he could complete it. Omerus reached, instinctively to his neck in a vain attempt to halt the bleeding, but Robin knew he was now looking at a dead man. Within seconds, he would bleed to death.

As Omerus slumped backwards, blood gushing onto the ground around him, the third attacker regained his focus and began running towards Robin. He considered that holding a knife against the dying man might be a way of bargaining his way out of this with the unseen crossbow man, but he was too slow. Sami rushed into the clearing and, before the man could get halfway towards Robin, Sami's sword swung in a wide arc and removed head from body.

The Saracen wasted no time and ran across to Robin, inspected his wounds and began a very basic treatment with herbs and leaves.

"You need proper help, my friend," he said. "I am going to make a rough stretcher and pull you to the Priory we passed on our way here."

Robin never heard him. He collapsed into a state of unconsciousness and remained so for the whole time that Sami was binding together branches, interlocking them to make them strong enough to hold Robin's weight and get pulled by a horse. He laid his friend on the stretcher, tied Robin's horse to his own, mounted up and left for the Priory.

The journey took about an hour but, as Sami glanced back at his friend, it felt like an eternity. He feared that by the time he found assistance, it would be too late. As the Priory came into sight, Sami took a sip of water and brought his horse to a canter. He knew the increased speed would shake and rattle his friend, perhaps causing further injury, but time, he felt, was of the essence.

Arriving at the Priory, he banged hard on the massive oak door with the handle of his sword and, minutes later, the door creaked open and he was greeted by two nuns. After explaining what had happened, one of the nuns rushed to bring the Prioress to help. As it turned out, she was a relative of Robin, an aunt, but while she had aged naturally, the first thing she noticed, as she scrutinised the injured man before her, was that, despite his frailty, he looked no older than when she had last seen him over a decade earlier.

"Take him to one of the guest rooms and lay him on the bed. I will treat him soon," she ordered.

Sami, with the help of the two nuns who had opened the door, carried Robin to the bed. A few minutes later, they were joined by the Prioress who scowled at the Saracen and ordered one of the nuns to wake the injured man with salts.

Barely able to see, Robin was brought round and, noticing the Prioress, asked where he was.

"Kirklees Priory," she responded. "And you are the anti-Christian

Robin Hud, who killed many priests and bishops and stole the holy church's gold, are you not?"

Robin was too weak to respond but he did stare directly into her eyes, resistance written all over his face.

"You are a sinful man, Robin of Huntingdon, and I am ashamed to be your relative. You are clearly a man who has worked with the devil to remain so young-looking all these years." She paused and inspected her wrinkled hands before continuing. "Of course, the holy among us age as God would wish us to".

She reached for a selection of blades on a large key ring. Each blade had a bulbous section, towards one end, making the blade look like a pregnant woman lying down. The Prioress grabbed the blades and brought them to her patient. She then picked up a large metal club.

"I will use the fleam for blood-letting to try to heal your wounds, but you must repent of all your sins if you wish for God's help in the healing."

She took the blade, known as a fleam, and placed the bulbous part of it over an artery. Then, she tapped the upper side of the fleam, quite hard, with the club, causing the fleam to push into the skin and open the artery. As she began to bleed him, Sami forced his way past the nuns and grabbed hold of the Prioress by the arm.

"What are you doing?" He shouted. "This is not the time for blood-letting. He is wounded, not diseased and he has lost enough blood already. You will kill him, woman!"

Without hesitation, she whipped her arm away from his grip. Swiftly, she caught hold of the wooden cross she wore around her neck and thrust it towards him. "Be gone infidel!" She screamed, her face distorted with anger and hatred. "Your blackened hand has no place touching me and your Mohammedan wickedness and magic will not work here."

Sami pushed her to one side and approached Robin. He knelt on the floor by the bed and Robin beckoned him to get closer.

"Sami, my friend, I am dying and this hideous excuse for a woman is not going to save me, but if you interfere or cause any harm in this place, soldiers will hunt you down like a rabid dog and your mission, our mission, will fail."

A tear formed in Sami's eye and he shook his head in disbelief. He made to stand up, but Robin caught his arm and pulled with what little strength he had left.

"Bring my bow and an arrow, my friend."

Confused, Sami hesitated but Robin repeated the request and smiled, and the Saracen returned to the horses to retrieve the bow. Re-entering the room a few minutes later, he saw that the bloodletting had begun and again his temper was raised.

"What sort of savage, backward work is this?" He shouted, his eyes piercing, and his fists clenched around the bow and arrow in each hand, so that his knuckles were white, and his face was red with rage. "Our doctors would be shocked at the use of such archaic tools as these, all rusted and unclean."

"Your doctors are not here, are they Saracen?" The Prioress asked, spitefully. "Now leave this room and let me continue with my work."

Sami stood his ground. His reply was firm. "I must fulfil Robin's request and give him his bow and arrow."

Reluctantly, she nodded agreement and Robin again pulled his friend hear to him. "Sami. Help me to pull this string and fire the arrow through that window. Where the arrow lands, is where you must bury me, a simple grave saying only that here lies Robert of Huntingdon. Nothing more. Do you agree?"

Sami nodded and a single tear rolled down his left cheek. He tied a yellow ribbon to the arrow and then nocked it onto the string, before placing the weapon in Robin's hand. Then, he assisted his friend to pull back the bowstring and the arrow was released. It soared through the window and into the nearby forest edge, onto land owned by the De Lacy family.

"Now go, Sami. Let this bitch do what she must. Then bury me and leave this place. You have the message from the healer of the forest. You know of our destination, so go there."

Sami left the room, exited the building and waited for word from the nuns. Meanwhile, at Robin's bedside, the Prioress again insisted on Robin's repentance for his sins but he refused to say a word and so she gave the order for him to be left to bleed to death.

CHAPTER 65
1266 A.D.
Sister Cecelia

Some two hours later, Sami was called to collect Robin's body. As he walked past the Prioress, he had a strong desire to separate her head from her body, but he remembered what his friend had advised. So, reluctantly, he ignored her. He carried Robin's body in his arms to where the arrow had fallen, tears streaming down his face as he took the weight of his dead friend to the arrow-marked burial spot. Once there, he dug a grave, placed Robin's body within it, spoke prayers to the Almighty and placed, at the head of the grave, a wooden stake on which he burned the words *Here Lies Robert of Huntingdon*. Then he returned to the horses where he found one of the young nuns waiting for him.

"The Prioress says your name is Little John. Is that true? Strange name if it is," she said.

Sami looked closely at her. She couldn't have been older than twenty and there was great beauty radiating from her face.

"If she wants to think that is my name, then so be it," he said, scowling as he thought of the Prioress.

He reached for the reins of his horse and was about to mount up when the nun caught hold of his arm and stopped him in his tracks.

"Take me with you," she whispered, looking back over her shoulder to see if anyone was watching them.

Sami let go of the reins and looked her straight in the eyes. "You are a nun. Why would a nun wish to leave the security of the Priory to ride alongside a man like me?"

Her eyes moved slowly to face the ground and she sighed heavily. "It was never my choice to live in the Priory or be a nun. I was ordered here for my indiscretions a year ago; and the Prioress..." she hesitated.

Sami filled the pause. "The Prioress, dear girl, is a wicked and evil woman, hiding behind the Church and her religion. You don't need to say anything more about her, for I have seen the devil in that twisted soul of hers, but I cannot take you with me."

Sami began to turn away towards his horse once more but heard the girl's sobbing and could not ignore it. He caught hold of her arm and led her around the horses, out of sight of the Priory windows and doors. Then, he sat her down on a rock and sat down beside her. His accent was an unusual amalgamation of Arab and English Midlands, which she found quite engaging.

"I will tell you a story that I have never told a soul and I trust you to never repeat it, but once told I will ask you to make your decision about leaving with me. Do you agree to these terms?"

She wiped her eyes and held his gaze. "Yes," she said, nodding her head in agreement.

"First, tell me your name," Sami instructed.

"They call me Sister Cecelia and, if truth be known, I prefer it to my real name because that name reminds me of what I used to be. So, pray tell me your story and I will judge your worth as a travelling companion and protector."

So, Sami began. "Almost a decade ago, Robin and I left the Holy Land and came to England and, for several years we fought the oppression and corruption of the Sheriff of Nottingham, with several companion thieves and robbers. They included a man whom people called Little John. Like me, he was a big man, but death eventually took him, as it did the others whom we called our friends."

"I know of the stories of Robin Hood and Little John. They are common tales across Britain," Cecelia said, before allowing Sami to continue. "But that was long ago and neither you nor Robin look old enough to have been those people."

Sami smiled and nodded. "Robin and I never aged the way ordinary men do and this takes me to an earlier part of my story. We had taken part in an enormous battle that had led to the safety of Jerusalem, the Holy Land and the surrounding countries."

He paused to catch his breath, wondering whether he should continue. He thought cautiously about what he was about to tell her. He wondered whether she would simply think him crazed, but, eventually, after seeing the expectation in her face, he proceeded.

"We fought alongside each other, not just Robin and me, but Muslims with Christians. We fought against the corrupted leaders of other Christians and Muslims who were working with the spirits of evil to destroy everything that was Holy in the land.

"Now, please don't interrupt me as I tell you what happened when we were there. During the battle, the enemy enlisted the work of demons. We Muslims believe that Allah, God, created Angels, Jinn, humans and all living things in stages and in separation. The Jinn, like humans, are divided into those who uphold what is right and just, who work for Allah, and those who work for the evil one. We call him Shaytaan or Iblis and you call him Satan, Lucifer, the Devil.

"So, the enemy were assisted by Shaytaan's Jinn, but we found ourselves helped by Jinn who were fighting for what is good for their world and ours. We found out later that some men and women among our forces, a prince of Jerusalem included, had visited the world of the Jinn and there were many tales we heard from them that I cannot go into now.

"And the battle was won, and the evil ones were vanquished but for decades afterwards, none of us had clear memories of what had taken place. We knew something had happened, a battle, a victory but nothing more. As the years passed, we noticed that we were not aging, or at least not as quickly as people around us."

He paused again and took a deep breath before continuing. "Recently, for some unknown reason, our memories returned. Of course, by now, the battle in which we fought has become legend and mythology in the minds of ordinary people but for us it was as real as you or me."

He reached to his horse and took a flask of water from a saddle bag, removed the lid, and drank before offering it to Cecelia, who took it and drank also. Then, Sami continued.

"Robin was my friend and I had pledged to stay with him until one or other of us died. This whole time I have shunned relationships with any woman. Why? Largely because of what I saw Robin go through.

"Before embarking on his quest to the Holy Land, he had met a lady, Marian. She was a woman of noble birth and they had fallen crazily in love. Upon his return to England, he found her again and she fought with us for many years, against the Sheriff and his men.

"At first, all was well, but we found ourselves, year on year, surrounded by men and women who were looking older while we stayed the same. It was finally decided that our band of outlaws be disbanded. Robin told Marian everything that I'm now telling you and more and she had an idea. Robin was already in his forties but looked several years younger than Marian. Before she grew too old, they married and then we left and moved north.

"They went under the name de Lille and bought land and property near Leeds. I acted as their servant and lived apart from them and, for many years, Robin did not venture beyond his own land into the world of people.

"Of course, there were two reasons for this. Firstly, he was a wanted man and secondly, they did not want to arouse the suspicions of people who might wonder why he remained young while his wife grew old. Then, Marian got sick. So, they announced themselves to local people, via the doctor, as aunt and nephew, but in the privacy of their home continued to live as man and wife."

Sami stopped talking and listened to the shouts from the Priory. People were calling for Cecelia and he glanced at her to gauge her reaction.

"Ignore their shouts and continue with your story sir," she said, and so he did.

"When Marian died, Robin almost fell to pieces and it took all my effort to keep him sane. We buried her, and I knew that I had done the right thing in keeping separate and celibate. We worked the land until, some weeks ago, a Jinni came to us with orders to attend the healer in the forest. She gave me information, instructions in an ancient Semitic tongue and now I am on a new quest."

Cecelia's eyebrows raised at the mention of the forest witch, but she said nothing, and Sami proceeded to tell her of all that had led them to where they were now.

"So, Cecelia, I now ask you, having heard my story, do you still wish to come with me?"

She smiled and gripped his hand tightly. "My dear sir, perhaps what you have told me is true or perhaps you are affected in the head, but either way, you are a storyteller of great promise and even the hope of seeing what you have seen would be enough for me to leave this stinking Priory. So, yes, I do still wish to travel with you."

Sami smiled. "Can you ride, my lady?" he asked.

"I was riding long before I could walk," she replied, and she immediately leapt to her feet, lifted her cassock, and mounted Robin's horse as a man would, legs astride the beast. Then, she began to remove the part of her nun's habit that covered her face and head. Sami shook his head.

"Leave it! He half demanded, and half requested. "There is less chance of us being hassled on our journey if people believe you are a nun, travelling to new pastures and protected by a personal guard. Perhaps when we get closer to our destination you can remove it if you wish, although I find it strangely appealing."

She smiled, and he added; "You might also want to sit side-saddled, as a woman does, so as not to arouse any suspicion." She nodded and shifted herself in the saddle, so that both legs dangled over the left side of the horse. Sami mounted his own horse, untethered it from Cecelia's and asked her what it was about her past that led her to being placed in the Priory.

Her head dropped, a look of shame on her face but she took a deep breath, lifted her head, and looked Sami in the eye.

"I was a whore," she whispered, waiting for a response from Sami, but none came. So, she continued; "My parents were killed by marauders who took me as a slave and used me as a whore. For ten years, I was used this way, until my twentieth year when the camp was destroyed by the King's army and the captives were rescued." She paused briefly and collected herself, stopping her desire to cry. "I was not rescued, however. I was condemned for being weak, for not resisting, for becoming a whore. My punishment was the Priory, so here I am."

Sami gently touched her hand and spoke quietly to her. "Allah knows what is in your heart so fear not. You are no whore, my lady."

She smiled, he pulled on his horse's reins, and they began their journey.

"And where is our destination, er, what is your name really if it is not Little John?"

"Sameer but most people call me Sami, my lady, and we are going to the land of the Scots."

"I've not been that far North for many a year," she said, adding "and please stop calling me your lady."

CHAPTER 66
1266 A.D.
The Journey North

From Yorkshire, Sami and Cecelia travelled for several weeks towards the border area and, for the most part, their journey was uneventful, most people taking them at their word when they spoke of the Nun's task of taking the word of Christ to remote parts of the land of the Scots. Many were wary of her Saracen guard, but few made an issue of it, until they entered a small hamlet near the Cumbrian border.

A priest in the village challenged the story the travellers had told and insisted on knowing why a Nun was permitted to travel with just one foreign guard. Where had she come from? Which Abbey had sent her? Who was this guard? Was he Christian or an Infidel?

Sami grew impatient with the questioning and, as villagers began to show an interest and call for answers, he became increasingly nervous. They rode past the crowd, ignoring their shouts until they reached the centre of the village. The crowd dispersed. They had not followed the two riders and that raised Sami's levels of caution considerably.

"We cannot stay here," he whispered in Cecelia's ear and she nodded. So, they mounted their horses and rode towards the edge of the village, only to find a group of its inhabitants, armed with pitchforks, shovels and even a few knives and swords, waiting for them by a bridge across a small river. Cecelia suggested that they go a different way, but Sami knew there would be others waiting for them, whichever way they went.

"Stay here!" He ordered.

"Why? What are you going to do? If you are to talk to them, I am better positioned to do that, don't you think?"

"There will be no talking and, when I am done, you must ride like the wind behind me. Is that clear?"

"Sami, if you kill them, we'll…"

He heard nothing after that, for he was already charging his horse towards the bridge.

As expected, the farmers panicked. They failed to hold any kind of line against the charging Saracen who, by now, had his sword drawn and was yelling a battle cry in a strange foreign tongue. It was not that his intention was to kill or maim anyone. It was just to frighten them away, but as he neared the bridge, he saw one man standing his ground. He immediately recognised him for a warrior. His stance, his eyes and the way he held a sword, revealed that this man was a soldier. It was the priest. The priest was a soldier and Sami knew exactly what that meant. The priest was or had been, a Templar knight. So, he aimed straight for him.

As Sami's horse approached him, the priest's sword swung. As Sami suspected, it was a heavy crusader sword, unsuited for use against a highly trained, highly experienced Saracen warrior on a nimble horse, bred from the Arab line. Sami's mare was from the direct line of one that had experienced battle in the Holy Land. It was a horse which Sami was too fond of to leave that land without. He whispered into the animal's ear and pulled on the reins, the horse swerving away from the blow. The priest's sword missed, and Sami's blade struck home. It sliced its way through the priest's neck, cutting through blood vessels and unleashing a gush of dark red blood.

For a moment, time stood still, and the priest seemed to be unaffected by the blow. He stood his ground for several seconds, his eyes wide, his face growing paler with every second, blood pouring from the open wound in his neck. Finally, his lifeless body slumped to the ground and a pool of thick blood spread around him.

Sami pulled his horse to a halt and faced the crowd. "We wanted no trouble," he called out, "but your priest, this Templar knight, this man who belongs to a sect deemed illegal in this land, wanted otherwise. You saw that he incited you, provoked me and swung his blade first."

The crowd murmured briefly. Then, one elderly, grey-haired, portly gentleman stepped forward.

"Our apologies sir to both yourself and the lady you guard. I am councilman of this hamlet and we will stand by the truth of what happened here. And we bid you God's protection on the rest of your journey."

Sami bowed, unsure whether the councilman would stand by the truth, but the Saracen was in no position to call the claim into question. Cecelia had not ridden away as Sami had ordered her. Instead, she had stayed to watch. Her eyes revealed a steely determination, but also a sense of vulnerability that Sami found exceedingly attractive. This, he thought, was a woman who had suffered the most awful emotional wounds, mainly but not always, at the hands of men. Yet, she had forged a way through it, without loss of her humanity, her kindness, her warmth. He called her to follow and together they headed over the bridge towards the borderlands.

Several hours later they were close to entering Scotland and they decided to rest by Haltwhistle Burn, an estuary of the River South Tyne. They camped in a secluded place and Cecelia decided it was private enough for her to bathe in the nearby water while Sami went to find food.

He spent almost half an hour tracking small animals but was unable to catch anything, so he decided that fish would be their meal and headed towards the river. As he approached, he spotted Cecelia emerging naked from the water and found himself captivated by her beauty. She stood on the riverbank, water glistening on her fair skin as the sunlight caught it. Sami, without realising, stared like an adolescent seeing an undressed female for the first time. He was shaken from his mesmerised state, however, when she looked up and saw him watching her. He turned away, briefly, but like someone bewitched he could not resist the urge to look again, only to be surprised that she had not reached for her clothes. In fact, she was walking towards him, her firm breasts virtually unmoving as she made her way up the gentle slope to where he stood. Again, he looked away, but Cecelia touched him lightly on the cheek and encouraged him to turn his head around until their eyes met. He was stirred, and when she glanced down, that fact became very apparent to her.

"Are you attracted to me?" She asked but did not wait for a reply. "Oh, I think you are, Sami." She said, smiling.

Sami stuttered with nerves. "Er, I'll fetch your robes," he said, attempting to move past her towards her clothes at the bottom of the sloped track.

"Leave them."

Sami hesitated but then looked once more into her eyes. "Cecelia, you are a woman of immense beauty and, yes, I find myself stirred by that beauty and attracted to you, but I cannot do what I believe you wish me to do."

He touched her softly on the cheek and headed down the track to retrieve her clothes, while she remained static, a frown of confusion forming on her forehead. Then, she turned and called out to him, partly in anger.

"You stare but you reject me? What sort of a man are you?" She shouted.

Sami picked up her clothes and walked back up the path. He held them out to her, and she snatched them from him, her eyes burning into his.

"Explain yourself to me, Sami," she said, adding "please."

Sami asked her to dress and then called her to sit beside him on a large boulder.

"Remember what I said about Robin and Marian?" She nodded, and he continued. "I'm not a man who involves himself in shallow relationships, Cecelia. For me, it is all or nothing and I fear being in Robin's position—of falling in love and marrying, only to lose because I will live well beyond my wife's years on earth. I'm not sure I could deal with watching you grow old as I do not."

Cecelia noticed the use of the word 'you' but listened without interrupting as Sami spoke of his feelings and his beliefs.

"I am a Muslim, Cecelia, and as such I cannot engage in sexual relations outside of a marital contract. I believe I could quite easily slip into sin with you, so I must resist, with all my might."

After speaking at some length, he finally fell silent. For a few moments Cecelia said nothing. Then, she took hold of his hand and looked him straight in the eye.

"Do you not believe that God brings people together?" She asked.

He nodded. "Yes. Allah knows what is best for us. I believe that, and that marriage is made in Heaven. That does not quell my fears, however."

Cecelia lifted Sami's hand and placed his palm flat against her cheek. "Fear is to be conquered and no-one knows what they can cope with, unless they put it to the test."

Sami began to speak again, but Cecelia pressed her finger against his lips. "Say nothing, Sami. Think and feel and when you are ready to speak of this again, I will be ready to listen."

He pulled her finger from his lips, leant forward and kissed her palm. Then, shaking himself out of the haze of thought he was experiencing, he stood up and strode off towards the horses. He caught hold of his own horse and leant in close to its head.

"Time to ride again, Samira," he whispered. "There is much work to do for both of us and much thinking for me to face."

Cecelia had shuffled up behind him and her voice surprised him.

"You talk to your horse?"

"She understands me more than any person, Cecelia and she is a great listener."

"She?" Cecelia frowned, and Sami turned to face her. "Most of our fighting men ride stallions, not mares."

Sami laughed and patted his horse's neck. "Yes, they do, and that is why we beat them so easily. We brought to the battle mares on heat and the Frank stallions, already tired, hot and sick from being so large and heavy in such a hot and arid land, became aroused. To be honest, they became like things possessed with a sickness of the mind. Your knights lost control of their horses and we carved through them like a knife through well-cooked lamb."

He watched her smile and his heart raced. There was no doubt that he wanted this woman. *Was he bewitched? Was she a witch? Surely, were she a witch, she would never have been placed in a priory, unless nobody knew she was a witch*, he thought. He shook his head to clear it. Now was not the time to dwell on that. Now was the time to travel on through the land of the Scots.

CHAPTER 67
1266 A.D.
Return to Al-Khalil

In the desert, as Jawad and his group hunted for Abbas, who had fled the battle at Ain Jalut, a sandstorm had begun. The group were huddled together, with their horses. They were covered with cloaks and other fabrics, to shield themselves from the sand. The noise of the storm was deafening, so none of them heard the arrival of the Jinni, Zenith. He emerged from the storm like a wraith, appearing at first as if he were part of the storm. He spoke before his form was visible and the group was startled. Many of them reached for their weapons. Then, suddenly, a tornado of sand, broke free of the wall of sand before transforming into the translucent, angel-like figure that Jawad and Hassan recognised. As he walked towards them, the storm died down and the sky cleared.

One of the Alis stood, sword in hand, and approached the Jinni. "Cursed Jinni of the desert, I seek refuge in Allah from you and your wickedness," he shouted. Zenith stood, statue-like, silently waiting. Then, Jawad touched the Ali on his arm and gently persuaded him to lower his sword.

"It is fine," Jawad said, softly. "This Jinni is one who follows Allah and he is here to help us. We know him. Hassan and I know him."

The rest in the group, all standing now, muttered to each other, but Reza stepped forward and sought to calm their nerves. "I also know him," he said, "so let him speak."

Zenith asked them all to sit so that he could explain the situation to them. He informed them that Abbas had left Iraq and was travelling to Spain via Cyprus, taking with him a fortune in gold and the Mongol's knowledge of gunpowder, which they themselves had acquired from the Chinese. Abbas' intention, however, was not to remain in Spain. He was gathering fletchers, bow-makers, ship builders and engineers and was already preparing passage for them all to France and then on to England.

"But the world is changing," Zenith said. "One of the Mongol Khans, Berke, has converted to Islam and was angered by Hulegu's destruction of Baghdad and the death of so many Muslims. He heard that Hulegu was planning to bring a mighty army to crush the Muslims as revenge for Ain Jalut. So, Berke attacked Hulegu's forces, diverting them from this region. The terror of the Mongols here is on the wane."

Jawad spoke first, a look of intense inquisitiveness on his face. "But how is that relevant to what Abbas is doing? What is he up to? What is it you're not telling us, Zenith?" He asked.

Zenith hesitated, and the group thought he was going to refuse to answer. He looked away momentarily but finally decided to give them the information they requested. As he moved, sunlight caught him from many angles, reflecting beams of light in all directions. His angel-like appearance was emphasised further as a result of this.

"I will tell you what I can," the Jinni said. "The armies of Iblis are warring as we speak, against the armies of Zaman the Overseer. Their aim, their wish, is to take all the worlds of the Jinn under their control. Alas, that is not the whole of what they want". He glanced at each person individually before continuing. "Iblis, Shaytaan, Satan, that most evil of creatures, wants dominion over this world. He wants complete authority, rather than just the ability to interfere, periodically, in human affairs.

"However, to do that Iblis and his forces require a permanent gateway to Earth, accessible from the many worlds the Jinn occupy. There is one such opening that was sealed with a Master Jinni's staff a long time ago. The spell is wearing off and the staff, hidden from human view for hundreds of years, is required to re-seal it. Eager to retain some control, he enchanted his staff and trapped, within it, a potion. We believe that Abbas knows the location of that staff, or if not will soon find out.

"As I speak to you, I have no knowledge of that location but, since word has it that Abbas heads for the North of England, or possibly to the land of the Scots, we must assume that that is where the staff resides.

"The Mongol threat here has gone. They are pursuing conquest in the Western lands instead. That means that Abbas will be seeking new allies and new wars to make himself rich. Well, even more rich."

He paused and sighed. "Some of my master's agents search, even now, for the staff's location or people who know of it, but they can only remain on Earth temporarily, making their task almost impossible. The staff's enchantment prevents all but two people from handling it. Its creator, its enchanter, or one other. That other is a man, descended from the ancient people of this land, chosen and named so many hundreds of years' ago, by that master magician, someone pure. So, once they have a location, they will be conveying that information to Robin and Sami."

The mention of those names caused Hassan, Jawad and Reza to look at each other. Reza mouthed *They are alive?*

Zenith paused and studied the reactions of the newcomers to the group. They were dazed and confused but none showed any fear. *An excellent group, Jawad and Hassan has pulled together*, he thought.

"One more thing," he continued. "The potion must either be destroyed or used, so you must find that master Jinni. For, while anyone can use the potion, only one of you can handle the staff and only one who is chosen by the master Jinni can destroy the potion. Both the staff and the potion are needed if you are to remove all traces of Jinn within Abbas and return him to wholly human form. So, if you wish for Abbas to return to your family as he was before he left you, it is essential that you find the staff. Find the master Jinni and do all that is necessary for him to seal the portal between the worlds. Allowing the potion to be destroyed must be a last resort.

"And so, it is to the lands of the Britons or the Scots that you must go," Zenith told the group.

Reza's almost instantaneous reply was tinged with concern.

"It could take months for us to reach there," he said, turning to each member of the group in turn. His eyes eventually returned to the Jinni and then he continued. "Surely, you can get us there more quickly."

Everyone looked to Zenith for his response and for a brief twinkling of time, silence hung over them like a canopy. The Jinni took a deep breath and spoke softly and deliberately. His eyes fell upon each person present in turn, as if he were willing his words to settle firmly in their minds.

"You are right. There is another way, via The Ridge of Fertheron, from which Hassan and Abbas emerged those many decades ago. It is the way that you must go if you are to find the Master Jinni and locate his staff."

He paused and took another deep breath. For a second his eyes fell to the floor before returning to fix his gaze upon Jawad and Marie. "Iblis has an army fighting to gain control of that gateway, which my master has guarded at all times and that means that for you to pass through my world there will be a fight; a fight in which we would assist you, but you must be under no illusion my friends. It will be a hard fight and even then, only the beginning of a serious trial of courage and faith."

Jawad looked at his wife and then at the other members of the group in turn. Each of them nodded a silent approval and he, in turn, nodded agreement to Zenith. The Jinni stood, and the others followed suit.

"It will be a difficult journey for you," Zenith said. "And you must leave here immediately. Head back to Jerusalem where you will find the boy, Jaffer, the physician, Muhammad and the Jewish translator, Judah. I sent them there some weeks ago, after you had left Basra. From there, Hassan will guide you to the place where he and Abbas emerged from our world before." He waited for a response but there was none, so he continued. "Bohemond, Amalric and Owun must go with you. So should all the others who have fought so hard for you Jawad."

The Jinni began to walk away, his wings closed but visible as the sun's rays reflected off his back. As the group watched him, in awe, Reza decided to call out to him. Zenith stopped and turned to face them again. He realised, from their expressions, that they were waiting for more. He smiled and spoke again.

"Bohemond is a Frank and it is a form of the Frankish language that is still spoken by those in power in England. You may need him. Owun Tyler speaks the Saxon and Celtic tongues and may be useful in finding the whereabouts of your old friends, Robin and Sami when you arrive in the land of the Britons."

Jawad placed one arm around Reza's shoulder, pulling him to one side. "Reza, my trusty friend and spy," he said, with a smile. "We will ride to my farm. I have more men there and Hassan will guide us from there to the passageway that will lead us to the Ridge."

Reza agreed, and Jawad turned to speak to Zenith. "We will go to Jerusalem but first we must..." The Jinni, however, had gone. No thunderbolt, no flash of light, no smoke or dust. There one second, gone the next. Such was the way of the Jinn.

After a moment of stunned silence, each member of the group began to clasp each other's arms in bonding, before mounting horses and riding off.

The journey to the farm went quietly and safely enough, with only one or two stops for the horses to drink and for the men to hunt. However, as they approached the farm, Marie's heart sank. The barn was burned down, and the house had clearly been looted and vandalised. Crops in the field had been ripped up or burned and some of the locals who had been tending to the horses that had been left there, were nowhere to be seen.

Jawad kicked his horse into a gallop and raced towards his home, Marie and their employed men following right behind. They remained on their horses as they approached the damaged house and Marie began to cry at the sight of the theft and destruction of everything they had built over the years. Jawad, however, was more concerned about the whereabouts of his workers and the families of the men who were with him. While Marie sat staring at the destruction before her, he kicked his horse forward. He rode out towards the burned out, charred and blackened barn. Pulling his horse to a halt, he dismounted a few yards in front of the soot-covered stakes that were all that was left of what had once been the barn. For a moment, he just stared in disbelief at what was left of the building. Nothing but charcoal, soot and ash. As he did so, he was joined by Hassan, Antonio, George and Abdur-Raheem.

"Who do you think would have done this?" Hassan asked, clearly angry at what he saw.

It was Abdur-Raheem who answered. "Bandits. Thieves." He said, softly.

Jawad had already begun walking onto the burnt ground with George and Antonio, both of whom had family on the farm. "Murderers!" Came a shout from Jawad. The other two men ran to join him and were shocked at the scene on the far side of the burned barn ground. They had found the farmworkers. All of them had been herded into the barn and burned to death. There were bodies of men, women and children inside and Jawad caught hold of Hassan and Abdur-Raheem, leading them back to their horses.

"Abdur-Raheem, take care of George and Antonio. Their wives and children are among the dead." Abdur-Raheem nodded and bit his lip in an effort not to break down himself.

Jawad turned to Hassan. "There is no need for the others to see this. We return to the house, gather together anything of use that we can salvage and then we leave here," he said.

When they reached the rest of the group, Jawad announced that nothing was found in the barn and asked everybody to gather anything that could be easily carried and was of use to them. They searched through the house, but most things had already been looted and carried away by whoever carried out the attack on the farm. They retrieved some clothing, a few knives, and some scraps of dried meat in a container that had obviously been overlooked by the bandits. Jawad was informed by Abdur-Raheem that George and Antonio were determined to find those who killed their families. Jawad nodded in acknowledgement.

"Tell them that we will do that first, before proceeding to Jerusalem."

After loading all the gathered goods onto horses, they headed off in the direction of Jerusalem, while Reza's men scouted the surrounding area for signs of bandits. They had travelled less than five miles before they happened upon an encampment about a mile ahead of the group of travellers. They rode back as fast as they could and informed Jawad.

"Soldiers?" Jawad enquired.

Reza rode up alongside him, reached across and tugged on Jawad's reins to bring him to a stop.

"I don't think soldiers would be camped out here my friend. The Franj would never venture this far away from Acre and most of our armies are chasing down Mongols in Syria. So, unless these are deserters, I think we may have found our bandits."

They continued their journey, until they were close to the encampment. From a concealed position, Jawad glanced at the camp. Smoke from its fires were barely visible but, as light dissipated later in the day, the glow of the fires would reveal the size of the camp and allow estimation of possible numbers. Jawad, however, was not entirely convinced by Reza's logic.

"Many soldiers are returning to Jerusalem and to Egypt, Reza. They would come this way, would they not?"

Reza nodded. "That is true but why would they set up camp here, during the day, with Jerusalem just a few days' ride away and many villages en route for them to find lodgings and food?" He glanced across at the camp. "No, my friend, these people do not wish to encounter civilisation. They are deserters or bandits... or perhaps both."

Reluctantly, Jawad found himself having to agree with him. "We will find a safer place than this and wait until nightfall. Can you send in one of your men to gather intelligence for us?" He asked Reza.

The spy nodded and smiled, turned in his saddle and called to one of the Alis, who kicked his horse into a slow and silent walk until he was between the other two men.

"I need you to scout that camp. We need to know numbers and who they are, but don't be seen and don't get caught."

Ali agreed. "I will leave my horse with the other men and head off on foot straightaway," he said, dismounting and pulling his horse's reins to turn the animal and guide him towards the other Alis. Just then, Reza caught him by the arm, forcing him to stop instantly.

"You have two hours. After that we will assume the worst and attack the camp and that is something I would rather only do after we have the information you are being sent to collect. So, I repeat, don't be seen and don't get caught. Return here within two hours and report everything you have found out. Is that clear Ali?"

"Crystal clear," he replied before leading his horse back to his comrades.

CHAPTER 68
1266 A.D.
Scotland

It was December in the year 1266 and Scotland was cold, wet and windy from the moment Sami and Cecelia crossed the border. It grew progressively worse the further north they went, towards the Highlands and Islands. The environment of the Scottish Highlands was savage. The landscape was laden with rocky soil, heather-covered hills and haunting mountains. The weather was harsh. Fog could appear without warning and just as suddenly shift to rain. Sami had heard stories of the snow sweeping across the land in blizzards in winter but what they were greeted with was no less uncomfortable and dangerous. Hail stones struck their faces for hours as they hunted for a place of shelter. It brought agonising pain that was exacerbated by the sudden drop in temperature and the fierce winds.

The pair of unlikely travelling companions tried their utmost to avoid people, not wanting to provoke the clans. However, moving through this virtually unknown and unexplored region, they could not possibly know if the land they were riding through was common land or owned by one of the many landowners, the Lairds.

"What exactly, is a Laird?" Sami asked, with genuine interest.

"Well, most people from England would not be able to answer that, Sami, but you are fortunate, in that my mother's side of the family came from Inverness, on the Eastern side of the Highlands."

Sami was taken aback somewhat by this. "Really?" He remarked, inquisitively. "Why did you not mention this, knowing that we were heading this way?"

Cecelia stopped her horse and looked back at Sami, who was riding just behind her. "My dear Sami, you refused to tell me where we were going. Until we crossed the border, all I knew was that we were riding north."

Sami nodded, accepting her response, but now he was intrigued. "Do you speak the tongue of the Scots?"

She smiled. "As a matter of fact, I do. Would you like me to use it as we travel through this harsh country?"

Sami laughed in amused disbelief. "It would mean we could travel less covertly; do you not think?" He asked. Cecelia kicked her horse forward again, but Sami called her to wait so she pulled to a halt again. "You did not answer my initial question. What is a Laird?"

Cecelia waited for him to ride alongside her, caught hold of his arm and then touched his face. "A Laird, my dear Sami, is a landowner. The Laird, being owner of large tracts of land, becomes head of a clan."

Sami nodded to indicate that he now understood. "A little like a Sultan, I suppose... so, let us continue, but let us head towards a town and see if we can seek out someone who can introduce us to one of these Lairds so that we can seek their aid in our quest. We will most likely have to find work with one of them, if that is possible. We don't know how long we will need to wait for my next instruction from the Jinn."

"All right," replied Cecelia, continuing "but let us tread with caution."

It was an hour later that the couple came across the region of Badenoch. There, they came across a small town, about 30 miles from the Moray Firth, the opening to the North Sea. Like many small towns in Europe, there were no roads to speak of; just tracks of mud, mixed with the excrement of a variety of animals and humans. The buildings were mainly single-storey stone and wood structures and the people looked poor. They were, however, full of the strong will needed to survive in the harsh environment of the Highlands. Sami and Cecelia approached the location where they could meet the most people in one place and seek out information about the local Laird. The Inn.

Sami thought he couldn't be surprised by anything he saw in the strange British Isles, but here in the Scottish Highlands, he felt like he had stepped back a hundred years. Ordinary people here were poor, far poorer than the English. Houses were small, often dug into hills, villages and towns were simple and bleak and the clothes people wore were unusual.

Highland Scots stuck to their Gaelic roots so both men and women wore a shirt or tunic known as a leine. The men wore a mid-length version, while the women dressed in a full-length garment. Some, those who had a little more income, would wear trousers called Braies, but poorer peasants would simply coat their leine in grease to waterproof them. Some Scots also wore woollen hose, a type of tights that were toeless.

They also sported a belted plaid, a wraparound cloak that they used as an outer garment to keep them warm. These were not worn in battle, however, where they would wear only their leines. Men would also wear hats or hoods in the Highlands, but their shoes were made of thin leather and offered little defence against the elements.

As they entered the village, Cecelia swiftly and skilfully switched to riding side saddle. They passed some of the villagers, and Sami tried to ignore their whisperings but clearly the presence of a dark-skinned man and a nun was raising eyebrows among the locals. Nobody was openly antagonistic, but Sami remained cautious and prepared, just in case. Nevertheless, the two travellers rode on until they found what seemed to be a rudimentary Inn; a small hovel serving drinks, and so they entered.

Almost immediately, a few men stepped forward as if to challenge the strangers who had entered their domain. One, a particularly large man, walked up to Sami and barred his way. He was a little taller than Sami and much bigger in build. At his side, hung a Claidheamh-mor, or Claymore, an exceptionally long sword and a rare item in the 13th Century. He looked Sami straight in the eye and spoke to him in the Scottish tongue. The other men moved around the strangers, each of them with their hands-on small knives in their belts. Cecelia knew this could easily turn nasty, so she stepped forwards and spoke in Scottish Gaelic, hoping that someone in the room might understand her. It had been many years since she had used this language.

"Please, we mean nobody any harm and this man is my protector."

The men stepped back a pace when they saw a nun before them and, for a moment, the room fell eerily silent. Finally, the man with the Claymore spoke.

"Our apologies, sister. We don't see many strangers this far north. I hope you'll forgive our abruptness and accept our hospitality". He gave a nod of his head towards Sami and then opened his arms in a welcoming gesture, inviting them to find somewhere to sit.

"Are you hungry, sister?" The man asked before adding, "by the way, my name is Duncan Carrik".

"Thank you," Cecelia replied, "we are famished, and please would you call me Cecelia. My protector is named Sami. Would you mind if we used English from now on, as Sami does not speak our tongue?"

Duncan nodded and smiled. He led them to a table, sweeping his arm across its surface to remove empty jugs and plates onto the floor. Cecelia invited him to sit and dine with them and he seated himself opposite Sami, clearly scrutinising the dark-skinned warrior meticulously. He seemed particularly intrigued by the Saracen's swords, mounted upon his back. To the Scotsman, they did not look strong enough to be of any use in battle. *I must ask him about those, when the time is right,* he thought.

Once some food had arrived, they began to discuss with Carrik their needs and asked him if there was any way they could get an introduction to the Laird of the local Clan, which Duncan informed them was Clan Comyn.

The two travellers managed to obtain a vast amount of information about the Clan Comyn, their Laird and their castle base. Lochindorb was a castle that had been built in the centre of Loch nan Doirb, the loch of the minnows. It was about six miles from this small town. The Clan Comyn, like many of the families that came to power under King David I of Scotland, was most likely of Norman descent. The surname was a place-name, possibly derived from Bosc-Bénard-Commin, near Rouen in the Duchy of Normandy.

John the Black Comyn, Lord of Badenoch and Lochaber, was the son of John I Comyn, Lord of Badenoch, and Alice de Ros of Helmsley in Yorkshire. Richard Comyn, the nephew of the Bishop of Durham and chancellor to King Henry I of England, had established the Comyn family in Scotland. The clan rose to be one of the most powerful in Scotland, owning land in Buchan and Speyside.

The Comyns were close to King Alexander of Scotland who, in 1263, had attempted to recover the Hebridean Islands from the Norwegians. He had launched raids against them after King Haakon of

Norway had gathered a fleet in the summer of that year and sailed for Scotland. Alexander had acted craftily, delaying engaging in battle until October of that year. He achieved this by entering negotiations with the Norwegian King. As he had planned, autumn storms had then battered the Norwegian flotilla as it lay in the Firth of Clyde. The Norwegians were then defeated at the Battle of Largs.

Three successive Comyn Lords of Badenoch and Earls of Buchan had been justiciars of Scotia since 1205, so both Cecelia and Sami quickly realised the importance of gaining access to this powerful family.

Sami, Cecelia and Duncan sat at a table in the far Eastern corner of the inn. The Scotsman narrated the history of the clan for whom he worked. Duncan was an officer in the Laird's personal guard and was intrigued to know why these two visitors wished to meet with the Clan leader. Their explanation was vague to say the least, neither of them wishing to speak of demons or Jinn and be herded out of the town as crazy people. So, they spoke of information they had gained in England that was crucial to preserve the future for the Highland way of life.

They all fell silent as food was brought to them. It appeared to be a bird of some description, but Cecelia decided not to enquire as to what it was. Sami claimed he was feeling unwell and decided not to eat anything. As Cecelia pulled some meat off a bone, and placed it daintily in her mouth, Duncan spoke.

"And why would an English nun and her dark guardian concern themselves with our way of life?" Duncan's question revealed more than just a little suspicion.

Cecelia looked him in the eye and replied. "I am not English. Despite my poor use of Gaelic, my grandmother came from Inverness. She married a man from Edinburgh who had moved to the Highlands. It was in Inverness that I was born, my friend. As for Sami, he is concerned for my welfare above all else." She paused for a second, pondering Duncan's reaction. When the Highlander said nothing, she continued. "We urgently need to speak to the Laird himself, so who can make such an introduction on our behalf?"

Before Duncan had a chance to respond, a cheer went up as a drunk man near the rickety old wooden bar, lost his footing and fell flat on his backside. A second cheer went up when he held his drink aloft, showing everyone that he had managed to avoid spilling a single drop of ale.

Cecelia smiled at the event but soon turned back to Duncan, who was laughing along with everyone else in the building.

"Duncan," she said, bringing his attention back to the matter in hand. "Who can make such an introduction?"

Duncan looked across the room and nodded at the drunk who was back on his feet but staggering towards a nearby table.

"He can."

"Him?" Sami's tone of voice revealed derision, but Duncan smiled.

"That, sir, is the Laird's cousin. A strong, young man and great in a fight, but a little too keen on the ale and the women. He is somewhat of an embarrassment to his father and to the Laird, but I like him. He could certainly get you the audience you seek."

Duncan stood up and called out to the drunk. "Malcolm, I have some people here that I'd like you to meet."

With a little help from a woman who had attached herself to his arm, the Laird's cousin made his way to Duncan's table. He was still staggering, and the woman had to keep him from falling over. Once there, they pulled up chairs and sat down. Duncan, realising the drunken Malcolm may not remember everything, knew that in his inebriated state, this was an ideal time to request a favour from him. So, he explained the situation and, after many more drinks, was greeted with an agreement from Malcolm. He would introduce the two travellers to his cousin, the Laird, John the Black Comyn.

CHAPTER 69
1266 A.D.
The Bandit Camp and the Ridge of Fertheron

From the information supplied by Reza's spy, Jawad now knew the numbers they would face. Ali had returned well within the two hours Jawad had given him and his information was detailed. They armed themselves, mounted up and prepared themselves mentally for what was to come. Jawad led the attack on the bandit encampment. It was a savage and brutal attack and none of the criminal gang were left alive. Goods were taken by Jawad and his group, including many of the items stolen from his home. Captured horses were laden with captured property and the camp was burned. Then, they headed off towards the area where they would find the portal to what Zenith had called the Ridge of Fertheron. It was an area known only by Hassan, who had emerged from one of the worlds of the Jinn there many decades earlier. Reza had proposed sending two of his spies to Jerusalem to collect Muhammad, Judah and Jaffer. Jawad, however, decided that they did not have the time for such a trip.

By now, they were halfway to their destination. Marie rode her horse alongside her husband. For many minutes neither of them said a word but, when Jawad saw his wife crying, he drew his horse to a halt and placed his hand on hers.

"Do you cry for our home?"

Her tears stopped abruptly, and she looked him straight in the eye.

"No, my husband, I cry for those who worked for us and who now lie dead in our burned-out barn. I cry for George and Antonio whose families were murdered so brutally." Jawad tried to interject, but she cut him off with a finger to her lips and a glare with her wide, blue eyes. "Do not deny it, husband, for I know the smell of burning flesh. I know they

340

are dead, and it is saddening to know that innocent men, women and children were butchered by those demonic thieves and murderers back there. Were the women and girls raped too?"

Jawad said nothing. He nodded, squeezed her hand and looked up at the rest of their group, who had continued to ride ahead of them.

"What is done is done. We must hold back our grief and continue with our quest."

Marie forced a smile, nodded and kicked her horse on. Jawad followed.

Up ahead of them, Bohemond and Amalric glanced back. "Aren't you glad we're not tied to a woman's needs, my friend?" Amalric asked, laughing as he did so.

"Glad I'm not tied, yes, but happy to be without a woman's touch? No, my friend, not at all and by all accounts we may be starved of such a thing for an awfully long time, so maybe your laughter is misplaced."

Amalric blew air from his mouth in a sign of frustrated agreement with his friend, just as Jawad and Marie drew level with them. "And no ale either," he said with a hefty sigh.

Some hours later they arrived at the spot Hassan had led them to, but the group were confused. There was nothing there, not even a tree, but what they had not known was that the Ridge of Fertheron stood in the Jinn world. It was the edge of a cliff that overlooked a small descent to a creek below but, as the men approached it, they could see nothing but dry, open countryside and a well-worn, Jerusalem-bound road. None of them could see the entrance to the Jinn domain. There was nothing here that would ever attract the attention of anyone who had no knowledge of what it was. To Hassan, however, it was a clear opening to another realm.

Bohemond was the first of the group to dismount. He walked into the empty space of dirt and patches of dry grass that Hassan had said was the meeting point and huffed. Then, he reached for a flask that he had found at the bandit camp. It now hung from his belt. He removed the stopper and took a swig of strong ale. Amalric joined him and Bohemond handed him the flask.

"There is nothing here, my friend," Bohemond said. I think we should just get drunk."

Amalric laughed, took a few gulps of ale and handed the flask back.

"I think you're right. It could be quite some time before we come across anymore alcohol. This place is dry in more ways than one."

As they drank, the remaining group members gathered, some still mounted, others leading their horses towards Bohemond and Amalric. Minutes later, they were all together, discussing their situation, shaking their heads and questioning Hassan's mind. The fearsome Turk kicked his horse forward, drew level with the two Franj warriors and dismounted. The other mounted men leapt from their horses and the women joined them all. They stood in the open patch of ground, bemused. Only Hassan looked pleased with what they had found but he was the only one who had spent some time in the Jinn world and emerged. He and Abbas, all those years before, had exited into their own world via the Ridge, at this very spot.

"We should wait." He was speaking to Jawad and Reza who were leading their horses to where the others had been corralled. Jawad glanced around but said nothing. Hassan knew he could continue to speak.

"This is the place, but I'm not sure how to enter. None of us are. I never entered the Jinn world from here. I exited from there to here. I can see a doorway, which evidently none of you can, but it is closed."

Reza to Hassan. "What are you suggesting?"

Hassan glanced towards the rocky area ahead of them and frowned. "Zenith will be here soon. Of that I'm sure, and when he appears, he will explain all to us. In the meantime, we set up camp and wait."

Jawad nodded in agreement and Reza called to the rest of the team to set up camp.

However, while the others prepared a fire and retrieved blankets from their horses, Hassan walked forward about seven paces, then stopped. After a brief glance at his friends, he turned in the direction of the coast and waved his hand through the air in front of him. They could hear him murmuring something, although none could make out what he was saying, and they did not have time to ask or even attempt to work it out.

Suddenly, the air shimmered and what could only be described as a doorway materialised in front of him. Several of the group, those who had not been at the events many, many years before, took a step backwards, in part through fear but partly in sheer surprise. Hassan laughed and beckoned them to approach the door but, as they began to creep, slowly forwards, a strange being appeared at the entrance way. He was muscular, tall and broad shouldered, with jet black hair that hung down his back to his waist and across his bare chest to his stomach. His face was almost pig-like and yet human-like; a confusion of features that prevented those looking at him from discerning them accurately.

"Who opens and commands?" He asked, his voice deep and somewhat haunting.

The group stood mesmerised for a fleeting moment until one of the Alis, shaking himself from his trance-like state, pulled his sword from its sheath, and stepped towards the uninvited visitor. His approach, however, was halted rapidly. The visitor pushed Hassan to one side, seemingly with no effort. He raised his right hand and sent the Ali hurtling backwards with an unseen force. At this, the whole group pulled forth their weapons and stood in defensive stances, expecting a fight.

Hassan called out to the stranger. "My name is Hassan and we have been sent by Zenith. Who are you?"

The being lowered his arm, stared inquisitively into Hassan's eyes and then let out a roaring belt of laughter. "Zenith? You say Zenith sent you?" He asked. "Why would Zenith be sending a troop of humans through the gate to the Ridge of Fertheron, may I ask?"

His question was answered by a voice from behind the group. "Since when, Ashar, do you question my decisions?"

It was Zenith and Ashar's face fell, his head bowed. He straightaway ran to Zenith and, on bended knee, he began begging for mercy.

"Get up fool! Do you not recall that I informed you of an assembly who would be travelling, with your aid, through our lands to the Egress of Light?"

"An assembly, yes, but no mention was made of that assembly being human."

"Silence!" Zenith replied. He turned to Jawad and frowned. "You did not go to Jerusalem, as I instructed, my friend." Jawad began to speak but was cut off sharply by Zenith, who held his hand up to signal the former prince to remain silent. "I told you the translator, Jaffer and the doctor were waiting for you there and you will need them all. You'll certainly need the doctor. Medicine is not what it should be in the lands of the Christian Knights and neither is cleanliness, so disease is a risk for you who have no immunity to many of their illnesses. You will also need a man who knows the ancient languages and Jaffer has his own destiny to reach on this journey."

Jawad looked back at the entrance that Hassan had conjured and at Ashar, the formidable Jinni who had returned to stand guard over it. Then he turned back to Zenith and spoke. "How can we get them now?" He asked.

Zenith took a step forward and called the gatekeeper, Ashar, towards him. "Bring them!" he ordered, and in an instant Ashar vanished, reappearing moments later with a frightened, shocked trio, Jaffer clinging with all his might to the doctor, and Judah clinging to both of the others.

Their shock, their fear, subsided when they saw Jawad and the rest of the group. Jaffer released his grip on the doctor and strolled over to where Reza and his men were gathered. For some reason he felt comfortable with them. The doctor and the translator, however, stood in silent disbelief, waiting for an explanation without requesting one.

Jawad approached them, slowly, and whispered to them. "Trust me, Muhammad, trust me Judah. You are all safe, so fear not, but be prepared for many things that fall beyond our earthly comprehension. You will have many questions, some which we can answer and some that we may never know the answer to. I will take you through as much as I can in the next few minutes, but then we must go through that portal. Expect fighting on the other side and keep an eye on Jaffer. He is the youngest of us and Zenith seems to think he has a destiny to fulfil on the other side."

He explained as much as he could in the time that he had available and then patted the physician on the back. "Are you ready?"

He nodded, nervously, and Jawad added one more piece of information. "Stay close to Hassan. He has been in the Jinn world before. He was there as a child, when he was a little younger than Jaffer is now. He will keep you safe."

As he walked the physician to the rest of the group, Zenith approached him, caught hold of his arm and pulled him, gently, to one side. In a soft voice, he whispered "Ashar will guide you and fight for you but warn your comrades to take care around him. He is a Wishmaster and will offer you wishes. Don't accept his offer but, should you succumb to temptation, always be careful what you wish for."

Without warning, Zenith vanished. Reza told Jawad that two of the Alis had decided to return to Baghdad and Jawad nodded. Now, they were twenty-one. Hassan and his warriors, Arslan, Akbar and Mehmet; Reza and his four remaining Assassins; Jawad, Marie, Abdur-Raheem, Amina, Assad and Habash; Muhammad, the physician; Jaffer; Judah Ben Zakai, the translator; Bohemond, Amalric and Owun Tyler.

Moments later, the group, led by Ashar, stepped through the gateway and into a different world.

The experience of shifting worlds left many of the group disorientated and nauseous for a few minutes. As they gathered their senses and looked around, they saw before them a plain stretching far into the distance. Behind them, the entrance to the human world was gone, replaced by a cliff edge, a ridge above a drop into darkness.

Ashar stood alone, none of the humans fully trusting him. They were all wary of approaching him by themselves and this did not go unnoticed by the Jinni. His eyes passed along the line of humans, until they fell upon Jawad.

"Jawad, I understand you lead this group of humans. Please, approach me so that we may discuss the journey ahead."

Jawad hesitated, but only for a moment, concerned about offending the Jinni. He walked slowly towards him, until he was standing alongside. The Jinni turned to look at the land beyond.

"We have several weeks of travel ahead of us, human, and many battles with the forces of Iblis."

Jawad said nothing, sensing that the Jinni was not finished.

"I'm worried about the youth," he continued, turning to look at Jaffer.

Jawad also glanced at him and then back to Ashar. He had not really noticed before just how huge the Jinni was. He was not fat, but bulky and tall. He stood a good shoulder and head above Jawad and, dressed only in loose trousers, his torso rippled with muscles. In his right hand he held an enormous, curved sword which he occasionally swished from side to side. His eyes were red and, according to Zenith, this could be seen in all Jinn, if the light caught them right. It was an indication that, like all Jinn, he was a fire creature.

Jawad glanced again at Jaffer. "The, er, youth is our concern, not yours," he said. "We will protect him."

Ashar grunted and then lifted the sword to point at the vast expanse of open, dried grassland ahead of them.

"That is where we are going, human. We will leave the Ridge of Fertheron and will not be near another exit to your world for many weeks, maybe months. This is my world and your lives depend on you following my instructions, my guidance. Is that understood?"

Jawad considered this and chose his words carefully. "We rely on you to guide us well, Ashar, but I am in command here. I believe Zenith made that very clear, did he not? So, is that understood?"

Ashar grunted again, Jawad smiled and then signalled his group to join him. As they hesitantly walked towards him, Ashar walked away, shouting back that they should follow him.

There was a bright sun above them as they trekked across the open grassland and everyone covered their heads with scarves, made from some of their clothing. On his previous visit to the Jinn world, Hassan had not seen a sun or any stars in a night sky, or clouds above. Yet, here they were, with a burning sun above them and a smattering of flimsy clouds in the distance. He wondered why the environment here, so close to the Ridge of Fertheron, was so different from how it had been before. Attempts to get an answer from Ashar on this matter were met with more grunts and so he finally gave up asking. Hassan decided that this world was simply not explainable in human terms and, while pondering this, Ashar turned to him and spoke.

"If you…wish," he whispered, emphasising the word 'wish', "I can tell you."

Hassan glanced at Jawad who was walking alongside him, and the former prince subtly shook his head.

"Well, human, is it your wish that I explain to you and enlighten you?" Ashar's voice was full of mischief and his red eyes, accompanied by a most disturbing smile, sent shivers down Hassan's spine.

"No!" Both men said, together.

Ashar laughed and walked on, increasing his stride and calling on the group of humans to keep up. Everyone muttered their grievances at being ordered around by this obnoxious and arrogant creature, but to a man they did as he said and picked up the pace.

Several hours later, exhausted and with thirst and heat taking their toll on the weaker members of the group, Jawad called a halt to their journey.

"Is it your wish that we stop?" Ashar asked.

"It is my order, Jinni, not my wish. We need to find water and to rest and my order is Zenith's order, so remember that."

Ashar's smirk evaporated and he led them to a dried-up stream nearby. Once there, he plunged his sword into the bed of dust and dirt. The sword entered up to its hilt and the ground shook, causing the humans to stumble and fall. As they lay upon the ground, the Jinni began to mutter words in a language none of them had heard before and, minutes later, the stream began to fill with clear, fresh water. Jaffer was amazed, the fighters were suspicious, and the doctor was curious. Only Hassan, Reza, Jawad and Marie took the event in their stride and they were the first to drink. The others followed suit.

CHAPTER 70
The Dry Lands of the Jinn

Refreshed and rested, the group of humans, led by the untrusted Jinni, Ashar, continued their journey across the dry lands. Within a few hours, the sun's power had dissipated, and a cool breeze gently blew across the alien savannah, to the great relief of the weary travellers.

As night fell and they found themselves immersed in darkness, they decided to rest again. Jawad took this as an opportunity to question Ashar on their intended route and destination. The Jinni was lying on the ground, his hands clasped together behind his head, his eyes closed. His long, black hair lay dispersed upon the dusty ground like a blanket that partly covered his well-developed shoulders. Jawad assumed he was not yet asleep, so he approached and sat down beside him.

"What do you wish from me?" Ashar asked, again with menace in his voice as he emphasised the word 'wish', elongating its ending.

Jawad did not look at the Jinni. Rather, he inhaled deeply and said, "I wish for nothing, but I am intrigued about our journey and our destination."

Ashar opened his eyes and smiled. Then, sitting up, he caught hold of Jawad's right hand. The Jinni's hair flopped over both hands as he did so. Jawad wanted to pull himself away, but he decided to wait and see what Ashar's intentions were.

"I will show you, human, what you desire to know."

Suddenly, the scene before them changed. They were no longer on the dusty plain, in the company of the group of humans. They were in a dark, wet forest, surrounded by the tallest trees Jawad had ever set eyes on. There was nobody else with them and the forest was eerily quiet. It was, simultaneously, obviously teeming with life and yet apparently void of it. It took a moment for Jawad to realise that the only sound he could hear was Ashar's voice, narrating their intended journey as they passed, like spirits, through this alien world of trees and thick vegetation and onwards, to the foothills of a mighty mountain range, the mountains of Alghamud.

Here, they floated upwards, over and above the snow-capped peaks to a sea of blue, which lay beyond them on the other side. There, he saw for the first time, some of the dark forces that lay in wait. A section of the army of Iblis stretched across a beach at the foothills of the mountains. Mighty ships, made from some purple, Jinn-world material, shimmered from solid to translucent with the changing intensity of light from two heavenly suns. *Why had we not seen the second sun before?* he thought.

Jawad, shocked at the size of the force below, then wondered about the mission ahead of them. *If this menacing foe before me, numbering thousands of Jinn warriors, was but a small part of Shaytaan's military might, what hope would Zaman's forces have? And where are Zaman's forces that we were told protected the portal at the Ridge?*

Before he could find an answer to his self-directed question, Ashar squeezed Jawad's hand tighter and they flew along the beach to a cave. "We will enter a hidden cave at the foothills of the mountains. From here we will emerge," the Jinni said, "but as you see, it will not be an easy task to do so without being seen."

Suddenly, a flash of bright light blinded Jawad for an instant. He felt the Jinni release the grip on his hand. They were back in the dry lands.

"I can show you no more," Ashar whispered. "I cannot show you what might never happen, but it seems we will make it to the cave and the beach beyond. The fact that I could show you that, confirms it. We will make it to the beach. From there, it is hoped that we will be successful in reaching the exit place where you will re-enter your own world."

Jawad, breathing heavily, glanced across the bed of dusty land that lay ahead of them and enquired, "why can't we travel as you and I just did?"

Ashar laughed. "We were not travelling. We were merely seeing. Ask your friends. They will tell you that we never left this spot."

Jawad did ask his friends and they confirmed what the Jinni had said. Neither Ashar nor Jawad had left. They had remained still as a frozen pond, Ashar's hand firmly gripping Jawad's arm. The others had spoken to them but got no response but within a few minutes, the two statue-like figures had become animated once more.

Jawad gathered the group together and told them what the Jinni had shown him. Plans were begun for the journey ahead.

"The dry lands are barren of any signs of life, but the forest has the potential to be somewhere that we could re-stock supplies. However, it is also the most likely location for confrontation with the Dark One's soldiers," Jawad said. "There are places where they can hide in that forest."

Reza sighed. "And the cave and tunnels?" he asked. "Aren't they a risk also?"

Jawad was unsure, and he looked to Ashar for his opinion.

"The cave is unseen, protected by Zaman from any who do not know the words to reveal it. I know those words. Once into the cave and tunnels, we will be safe until we reach the portal," the Jinni replied.

There was a moment of chatter between the group members until Hassan spoke up. "What lies at the portal, Ashar?" he asked.

The Jinni took a deep breath before responding. He stood to his full height. "It is surrounded by the forces of darkness who are defending it from Zaman's attacks. Shaytaan's Jinn are working hard to find a way through to Earth, but the ancient one who closed the cosmic gate, made sure that there are only two ways for it to be opened. Either by Zaman himself from this side, or from the Earth side by one who is chosen. Hence, the reason why Shaytaan sends Jinn to Earth whenever a temporary portal has opened. "They await his orders and some may already be tracking down your friends on the other side."

More murmuring began among the group and Marie stepped forward. She spoke to Ashar. "You look concerned, Ashar. What is it that worries you so?"

The Jinni, head stooped, muttered his response softly. "The ancient one's protection over the gate is weakening. If you don't find him soon and persuade him to restore his defences over the portal, all will be for nought and…"

Marie, confused and concerned, interrupted. "So, Zaman must beat the defenders and open the portal to let us through? Then what?"

Ashar shook his head. "I do not know," he replied. "I am not privy to that information, but my understanding is that you will know once you get there."

More chatter followed for a while, until Jawad called them to move on. Weapons, bags and food were packed, and they set off again across the dry lands. For several days, they walked. Their journey was slow, however, continually being interrupted for rest breaks. Then, as the forest came into sight, they were delayed further when one of the group collapsed.

Unexpectedly, it was not Jaffer, perceived to be the weakest of the group, but one of the Alis. Heat exhaustion, the physician said, as the fallen man's brother rushed to his aid. Delirious and dehydrated, the exhausted man would need treatment and rest before they could consider moving on to the forest. The physician set to work with herbs and vinegar to bring down the sick man's temperature. He also instructed Jaffer to continually provide the ailing man with small sips of water.

Two days would pass before the fever faded and some sign of strength returned to the sick man. It was a delay that they could ill afford. So, as soon as the man insisted that he was fit enough to continue, they moved on towards the forest.

It was about a mile away and took them just under an hour to reach it. At its outskirts, Ashar called them to a halt and advised them of the dangers which lay ahead.

"Stay alert and maintain your weapons in good order," he said, before leading them into the forest.

From the ground, the giant trees appeared even more daunting to Jawad than they had in his vision. They seemed to stretch upwards forever, casting the entire forest into an unrelenting gloom, as if the entire world were covered in a dark shroud. The surroundings were filled with a cacophony of sounds, unlike the deep silence Jawad experienced during his vision. Some of the sounds were animal-like, while others were haunting, evoking feelings of dread among the travellers. Jaffer remained close to Muhammad, the Physician. He was not a warrior and was shaking with fright. The doctor held him tightly to his side as they walked and, though Jaffer clung fiercely to his friend, it offered little comfort to the youth.

Bohemond turned to Amalric and frowned. "You know what I really want right now? An ale. No damned alcohol in this forsaken world and we're surrounded by Muslims who don't drink anyway."

Amalric laughed. "To be honest, friend, I don't miss it and I feel better for not having it."

Bohemond grunted and shook his head. "First opportunity, and I'm going to get so drunk, I'll pass out and stay out for days."

Amalric laughed again and nodded towards Jaffer. "Now he, on the other hand, looks like he needs a drink."

The two men laughed and joked together in French while most of the group wondered what they were finding so amusing.

Reza, meanwhile, asked Ashar if he could send two of the Alis ahead. Once the Jinni agreed, with a proviso that they should stick to the path and not go too far ahead, he gave the task to the two brothers, Zahir and Hussain. They had revealed their names when Zahir had been suffering with heat exhaustion. In a delirious state, he had mumbled his brother's name. Hussain had prayed that Allah would protect his brother, Zahir. Within seconds of being asked to scout ahead, they were gone.

The air in the forest was damp. Combined with the sodden earth that was covered with a compost of tree leaves and other foliage, walking was made difficult. The realisation was beginning to dawn on many in the group, that it could take them several weeks to reach the foothills of the mountain range. It could take many more weeks to climb the mountain and reach the beach on the other side.

The two bowmen, Owun Tyler and Antonio Habash, positioned themselves at the front and rear of the company of travellers. Everyone remained alert. Being constantly on the lookout for danger, however, added to their fatigue. So, within hours, they began seeking a suitable rest place again. They had just found it when they heard a yell, followed by shouting. The noise emanated from just ahead of them. Realising that Zahir and Hussain were in trouble, all thoughts of rest were cast aside and, en masse, they ran to where the shouts had emanated. The sound of their approach must have scared off the attackers. When they reached the two scouts, they found only Hussain alive. He was cradling the lifeless body of his brother. Alongside them lay the body of a hideous, wart-covered, ape-like Jinni, its chest sliced open, the bloody work of Hussain's sword.

Amalric, Bohemond and the other soldiers stood guard in preparation for another attack. Reza approached Hussain, placing a comforting hand on the tearful man's shoulder.

"We must bury your brother," Reza said, softly, as he and Hassan carefully helped the distraught man to his feet. They moved him away to enable Muhammad and Jawad to prepare the body for burial. Zahir's heart had been pierced by a single arrow which had struck with such force that it had driven its way right through, exited his back and come to rest in a nearby tree.

As the two men began to remove the dead man's clothes, so that they could wash the body, as was the Islamic tradition, Hussain was overcome with grief. "Why?" he shouted. "I wish the arrow had struck my heart, for Zahir was a better man than I am, and I want only for us to be together again."

As Hussain wailed his grief-filled wishes, the arrow began to burrow its way through the tree trunk until it was deep inside. It was now completely out of sight. Only Jaffer had seen it happen and he called out to the others, who turned to stare at the trunk of the enormous plant. They were confused and perplexed. Hussain heard the shouting and stood to see what the commotion was about. He took a step away from his brother's body but stumbled when his foot got caught on a protruding tree root. His arms instinctively reached out to break his fall, but he managed to keep his balance and remain on his feet. After a swift glance at the stump behind him, he laughed off his embarrassment and continued to move towards the others.

Reza was about to say that Jaffer was mistaken and that the arrow must have fallen into the deep undergrowth when, suddenly, it emerged from the other side of the tree. Its trajectory took it in the direction of Hussain, and everyone turned to warn him. It was too late. The dart shot through the air and embedded itself deep in his chest. He died instantly, his body slumping to the ground, just yards away from his brother.

The other men rushed to his side, but Marie turned to Ashar, her face red with anger. "You did that!" she shouted, a combination of animosity and disbelief in her voice.

The others looked at the Jinni and Reza pulled his sword. He began to march towards Ashar, but Jawad took hold of his friend's sword arm and called for him to wait.

"Is this true, Jinni? Did you kill Hussain?" Jawad asked.

The Jinni nodded. "It is my nature, human, to grant wishes and your friend there wished for that arrow to pierce his heart so that he may be reunited with his brother. Once wished, there is no return, but I am sorry."

Reza jerked his arm free from Jawad's grip and approached Ashar, shouting at him and waving the tip of his sword in front of the Jinni's face.

"Don't kill him Reza. We need him alive," Jawad called out.

Reza pushed the sword tip towards Ashar's bare chest, until the blade touched skin. "Perhaps I should pierce your heart with my sword, Jinni. That is, if you have a heart. Or, perhaps I should wish you dead."

The Jinni remained impressively calm and replied, "you could but, like your friend there, you should be careful what you wish for. Without me, you will all die in this place."

Reza drew the sword across the Jinni's chest, drawing blood, and then sheathed the weapon, before returning to the bodies of his two fallen men.

"They know we're here now," Jawad called out to everyone. "Be on your guard at all times."

Once Hussain and Zahir were buried, the group moved on. They were now fully aware of what they faced from the forces of Iblis. They were also keenly aware that there was a terrifying threat within their midst; a threat that matched the external one. They would be far more careful around Ashar from this moment on.

CHAPTER 71
Early 1267 A.D.
Cyprus

Abbas, having taken cartloads of gold and jewels from Damascus, recruited a group of hardened Arab mercenaries to accompany him, as bodyguards, to Europe. He would pose as a rich businessman, who made his fortune selling weapons. He had also recruited a small team of Chinese engineers who would craft the advanced weaponry the Europeans craved. His aim, ultimately, was to reach the gate to the Jinn world before Jawad and his people got there.

Meanwhile, Jawad's excursion through that world, was unknown to Abbas, who was unable to find a way in himself. He would travel through Europe, building alliances, gaining influence and securing power, in preparation for what would be a mighty war, once the Dark One's forces broke their way through to Earth. Those forces, combined with his own, would crush the armies of Zaman, once and for all.

Abbas led his men across land to the Lebanese coast and crossed from there to Cyprus, where he bought vast swathes of land and property. From there, he planned to travel to Spain, then France and on to England. He employed many farmers, engineers, soldiers and skilled tradesmen in Cyprus, all on generous wages. He sponsored the arts and paid for the building of a hospital and several schools. The people loved him, and for a while, he wondered why he needed to move on. Months had passed and, as he looked from the balcony of his villa, across the water to Greece, he considered staying right where he was. That is when it happened.

The ground shook, the building moved, and the villa was immersed in the most brilliant, yellow light, before being plunged into total darkness. Abbas gripped the windowsill tightly. Slowly, he turned away from the window and observed the gradual appearance of a figure, swathed in yellow clothing and holding a diamond-studded, golden shield. Abbas attempted to reach the intruder's mind, a task he found supremely easy with humans, but found this creature's mind sealed. There was no way in and, for the first time in decades, Abbas felt fear. Sweating and hot, his heart pumping, his breathing short, and his body shaking, he glanced around, desperately seeking a means of escape. There was none. He slumped to the floor; his back was pressed firmly against the cold stone wall of the villa.

The creature took two steps forward, but its face was void of all form. Featureless, it shifted like water in a moving container, and yet it spoke. It was not a man, as Abbas had assumed. It was female.

"Our Master knows of your thoughts to remain here, Abbas, but time is short. The humans have entered our world now and are attempting to reach the gate from there. There are some among them who have the power to stop our plans. Jawad is one of those and only you have the power to stop him, for you are tied by blood."

There was a pause and Abbas noticed, for the first time, that there was a complete absence of sound around him. When the creature moved, she made no sound. The birds outside the villa had fallen silent and even his own, heavy breathing, was inaudible. The creature's voice pierced the darkness like lightning in a night sky.

"You will leave here," she said. "Follow me and we will travel to a new place. I will leave you there. It is then your responsibility to reach the country where we believe the gate emerges."

Although unsure why, Abbas stood up and followed her.

"Who are you and where is that country?" His question was asked nervously, his voice cracking.

She stopped and turned to face him. "I am Meztli, Queen of the Night, and I will explain more once we arrive at our destination," she replied. Then she moved on, with Abbas following as they stepped farther into the blackness, into oblivion.

Abbas could neither see, nor hear, anything. This sensory loss left his mind free to wander, aimlessly at first, but gradually focusing on key moments in his life. As his mind was cast back to his childhood, the darkness around him changed and he found himself surrounded by those he once knew and loved.

He remembered his ordeal with Hassan, his Mamluk tutor. They had been trapped in the world of the Jinn, and his life had been saved many times by the older boy. Then, his mind was cast back further, and he saw himself standing in the main hall of the palace in Jerusalem, the Emir introducing him to Hassan. They walked to the garden where they decided to play hide and seek. Abbas was poor at it and Hassan often found himself sitting behind a bush for what seemed like a lifetime.

Abbas smiled at the memories but was pulled from his dream as Meztli's voice once again thrust itself into his mind.

"We have arrived," she said, as the blackness transformed instantly into light.

As his eyes adjusted to the brightness of the midday sun, Abbas blinked and rubbed them. Gradually, he took in his surroundings. He was on a wide-open plain of dirt and green foliage and it was beginning to rain.

"Where are we?" he asked, gazing around him to try to find an answer to his own question.

Meztli's voice entered his mind, although she was no longer visibly present. "You are in Spain. Here, you must gather your forces, Abbas. Before you, stands a castle. Your castle. All of your wealth and weapons have been transported there and your men are waiting for you inside."

Abbas was confused. "You transport them into the castle but me onto a rainy, dirt-covered field?"

"The others were brought here in a sleep state and I do not wish them to see me as they awake, but I need to give you more instructions, Abbas.

"After I leave, you must go to your men. They will be disorientated, confused, fearful. Put them at ease. They know of your powers, so you should be able to calm their nerves quickly.

"Then, proceed through France to England. Our enemies are destined to travel to the land of the Scots. They will move to the North of that country, to what they call the Highlands. They will be heading to the West Coast.

"Go alone to England, Abbas. There, you will be contacted. Establish yourself, get close to the people in power in England. Then, call your men to your side and they will come."

"Contacted? By whom?" Abbas enquired, but she was gone, and he was alone.

He spent several months in Spain, training, preparing and building his army. Then, towards the end of spring, he left his men behind and travelled to France. He made contacts with agents he had fostered in Cyprus. He issued orders and left them in the summer, sailing to England. As the summer months were dying, and winter months awoke, this land was somewhat of a shock to him. Unfamiliar with the language, he made his way North through some of the wildest and poorest parts of the country, avoiding people at all costs. He hunted small animals and took water from streams. He knew that, eventually, he would have to get word to his people in France and Spain. He needed assistance, he needed fighters and, more than anything else, he needed gold. He could pass as a foreign nobleman with gold. Without it, however, he was just foreign and, in a country as wild as this one, that was a dangerous thing to be. He thought for a moment.

"I speak Arabic, Latin, French and Greek," he muttered to himself. "Where could I find someone who speaks…?" Then, it dawned on him. He needed to find a Church, a Priest, someone who knew Greek, French or Latin.

Bedraggled, tired and hungry, having trekked for days, he came across a remote Church. It was early one evening when he found it on the outskirts of a small village. It looked deserted, but there was candlelight visible through one of the windows. He knew that he must take the risk and seek assistance. A few minutes later, he approached the Church door, but found it locked. In two minds whether to leave or not, he decided to bang on the door. In Latin, he called for help and almost immediately, he heard the lock turning and the door creaking open. Before him stood an elderly Priest with a look of astonishment on his face. Was he surprised at what he saw before him or that this vagrant had spoken in Latin? Abbas did not wait to find out. He pushed his way into the Church and began to talk, not giving the Priest an opportunity to respond, until he was finished.

"I need your help," Abbas said, in French. "I am a Greek nobleman, patron to many Churches and poor houses in Cyprus. I have business interests in Spain and France. I was here on business, with two of my employees, when we were attacked, and I was left for dead in this God

358

forsaken country. Can you get a message to someone in France?"

The priest shrugged. "Where in France?"

Abbas thought for a moment. *Who would be the best to contact?* He wondered. He took a deep breath. "I have a representative in Normandy. How long to get him a message?"

"From here? At least a week. I can send a courier to the nearest port and he can take a ship to Normandy with the authorisation of the Church."

Abbas considered the irony of the grandson of Shaytaan, receiving assistance from a Priest who could deliver a message with the 'authorisation of the Church'. He smiled and then said, "I will write the message and seal it. Can you call your messenger to collect it within the hour?"

The Priest, who gave his name as Peter, nodded. Within an hour the communication was written, and a courier was on his way to the coast. Abbas knew that it was more likely that it would take up to two weeks for the message to arrive. His agent in Normandy would then need to organise a shipment of gold to be transported to the Church. The agent would also need to contact Abbas' men-at-arms in Spain and find a way for them to reach Scotland unnoticed. That could take months.

In the meantime, Abbas asked the Priest for some clean clothes and an opportunity to bathe, thinking he might be directed to an Inn in a nearby town or village. The Priest, however, insisted that he stay with him, at his home on the Church grounds. Reluctantly, Abbas agreed.

CHAPTER 72
The Mountains of Alghamud

The group of weary humans had trudged through the thick, dank forest, finally reaching the formidable mountain range. They looked up. The mountains seemed to rise without end and there was concern in the faces of the travellers. *How can we possibly ascend and cross this?* Hassan thought to himself. He voiced his concern to Jawad, who smiled.

"Fear not, my friend. Ashar has assured me that there is a cave, leading to a tunnel, which will take us through the mountains."

Hassan glanced at Ashar. "I still do not trust that Jinni, Jawad," he said. "The sooner we are rid of him, the better."

Jawad stepped closer to Hassan to avoid being overheard. "We have no choice but to follow his guidance, brother. Just take care around him and keep a watchful eye on him. As soon as we can continue without him, we will."

Jawad called the group together and asked Ashar to explain the next part of the expedition. The Jinni stepped forward and pointed to an area of rock at the base of the steepest part of the mountain nearest to them. The mountain face shimmered and a gaping hole appeared where once there was solid rock. It was large enough for horses and carts to enter, had they had any, but it was also immersed in darkness. Ashar stepped into the cave first, followed by Jawad. After a brief pause, the others followed. To everybody's amazement, they found the cave lighting up in their vicinity. The light travelled with them as they began their journey through the cave and connected tunnel. Ahead of them was also illuminated but as Hassan, who had entered the cave last, glanced behind, he found only darkness. A darkness so black that for a moment he paused. Suddenly, a wall of stone appeared before him. The tunnel was closing behind them. He moved forward, through the group, until he was level with Jawad.

"There's no way back, Jawad." He said. "Look behind us."

Jawad stopped and saw the shaft closing behind the group. He nodded and continued to walk forwards. "If we succeed in our quest, Hassan, we won't need to return. If we fail, we won't be alive to return."

So, they journeyed on, for miles, the extra-terrestrial light leading their way and lighting them up, like beacons. Taking up the rear now was Abdur-Raheem, the replenishing cave wall following his every step. He paused for a moment and the light left him. It continued with the group. *Is it linked to them or the Jinni?* He wondered. He glanced behind at the wall, then turned back towards the group. He stepped forward and, in the darkness, felt a blade being thrust into his chest. He tried to call out, but a hand covered his mouth. Pushed against the wall, he felt the life draining out of him and, within seconds, he was dead. His lifeless body slumped to the tunnel floor.

Several yards ahead, the group came to a halt as Jaffer asked for a rest. He was exhausted, and Jawad called to Ashar to wait. Clearly unhappy at this request, Ashar struck the tunnel wall with his giant fist, causing the walls around them to shake. He wanted to continue but could see that Jawad was not going to comply. They stopped. They all took the opportunity to sit and rest, but it was several minutes before anyone noticed that Abdur-Raheem was absent.

"Where is Abdur-Raheem?" A voice shouted. It was Assad. He was furthest back, and Jawad became increasingly anxious when he saw the wall was directly behind Assad. Abdur-Raheem was absent, and the wall had closed in. Jawad stood up and turned to the group.

"Did anyone see what happened to Abdur-Raheem?"

They all shook their heads and Jawad marched to where Ashar remained standing. "Can you bring him back?" He asked the Jinni.

"Is that what you wisssh… massster?"

Jawad almost said yes but stopped himself. He looked again at the wall. "How? The wall has kept pace with us the whole time. How could it? Why would it suddenly roll over one of us now?" He was pleading for an explanation and the Jinni supplied one.

"It could not, massster. Not if he were alive."

"You're saying he died back there?"

The Jinni nodded, and Jawad now had a new problem.

How did his friend die? He asked himself. *Did he fall and hit his head? Did someone kill him? Was there a traitor amongst them?*

Hassan and Reza had wondered the same things and, quietly, they let him know.

"Who do you think is the traitor in our midst?" Reza was looking at Jawad but talking to both the prince and Hassan.

Jawad glanced at the group beyond them. "I trust my men, my wife and her maid," he said. "And I'm sure you would both vouch for your men, so that leaves the doctor, the Jinni, Judah or Jaffer."

Hassan shook his head. "The Jinni was ahead of us at the time and he can only grant wishes. Plus, I doubt he would defy Zenith."

"Both the doctor and the youth were at the rear," said Reza. "I doubt Jaffer could overpower Abdur-Raheem. So, I would put my money on it being the doctor. I'll watch him closely."

For now, the three of them would keep their suspicions to themselves, but they would watch the group carefully. At least, they would watch closely those who were not fully known to them, particularly the doctor.

Now, they were eighteen. Hassan and his warriors, Arslan, Akbar and Mehmet; Reza and his two remaining Assassins; Jawad, Marie, Amina, Assad and Habash; Muhammad, the physician; the youth, Jaffer; Judah Ben Zakai, the translator; Bohemond, Amalric and Owun Tyler.

CHAPTER 73
1305 A.D.
Sami Continues to Wait

While the travellers in the world of the Jinn had spent just a few months' journey to reach the final trek to the portal, Sami and Cecelia had waited many years. John 'The Black' had died and his son, John III 'The Red' Comyn, had become Laird. Sami and John III had become close over the years and Sami had soon taken charge of the Laird's personal guards. Cecelia, meanwhile, was working as a midwife. They had both formed friendships with an assorted number of locals and Sami had learned some of the local language and customs.

As the year 1305 was moving towards its end, he joined one of many hunting expeditions the Laird held. Noble Scots at this time would often eat swans, geese, pheasants and even peacocks, but this day they were hunting hare and deer. Sami had accompanied the Laird many times before on hunts. A bird of prey was used for small animal prey, such as hare, rabbits or pigeon and the Laird's favourite bird was a peregrine falcon. Larger animals were hunted on horseback, with bows, spears and crossbows. On this day, the hunting parties were split into two. The Laird's son took the horsemen to the East, to hunt for deer. The Laird went West, on foot. Sami, already familiar with the use of falcons for hunting, was given charge over the Laird's bird. A third group, mainly made up of serfs, were sent to the loch to fish, as the church forbade the eating of meat on Wednesdays, Fridays and Saturdays.

Depending on your station in life, what you wore was a given rule. Peasants wore simple clothing. The rich and regal population would dress in more colourful elegant clothing. Sami, having gained the trust and respect of the Laird, wore a colourful, mid-length leine, which he had grown quite accustomed to. It bore some resemblance to the long Jelabiya he would have worn in the Arab lands and he felt comfortable wearing it.

The Scots were predominantly Christian, who customarily went on pilgrimages to holy sites, such as tombs of Saints but, having gained a position of importance within the Laird's clan, a blind eye was turned to Sami's Muslim belief. He spent many hours discussing religion with those around him, explaining how Jesus and Mary were held in high esteem in Islam and that seemed to satisfy his Christian comrades. The passion for the Crusades had not been as great among the Scots as it was for the English and French. Scottish priorities lay with keeping invaders at bay, particularly the Vikings in the 9th Century and, more recently, the English.

When not working, Sami immersed himself in many Scottish sports and pastimes, from hawking and hunting to bowling and wrestling. A common weapon at the time was the Bowis and dorlochis—a bow and quiver of arrows. While Sami's archery skills were unmatched when he used his own bow, he found the longbow used by the Scots a difficult weapon to handle. Consequently, in competitions, he failed in his numerous attempts to gain any mastery with it.

It was on this latest hawking expedition that he was visited by a stranger. It was nightfall and Sami had just finished greasing his bowstring with bees' wax. He placed his bow and quiver of arrows on the ground, checked the falcon and joined the other men, when the stranger appeared. He appeared other-worldly to the Saracen warrior. He was tall; far taller than Sami or any of the Scottish clansmen with him. He strolled into their camp without a care in the world, somehow passing those who had been posted on guard without being noticed. Sami and half a dozen others were sitting around a campfire, the Scots singing traditional songs and drinking whisky. Sami was enjoying their company and smiling at their joyous celebrations, following a good hunt.

Without warning, one of the Scotsmen grabbed his sword and leapt to his feet. "Stop right where you are, or I'll have your head," he shouted.

Sami and the others turned to see who had appeared, each of them reaching for their own weapons. One by one, they came to their feet, gradually encircling the man. He was dressed in a long, black cloak, a hood covering his head and hiding his face in the darkness. The light from the fire reflected off him in spurts, creating an eerie vision for the men. At first, he said nothing, and Sami noticed that the stranger's attention was focused on him. He was staring at Sami, ignoring all the others. So, the Saracen decided to speak.

"Who are you stranger and what do you want?"

The visitor took a step towards Sami and the Scotsman who had first seen him took two steps forward. "Stop where you are, or I swear I'll cut your balls from your body and feed them to our hawk," he said.

He meant every word. He, and many of the others with him, had fought with William Wallace against the English, until Wallace's capture and execution some months' earlier. They were hardened, experienced fighters.

Sami, however, held up his hand to stop his friend. "Wait Stuart," he said, firmly. "I don't know why, but I don't think he's here to cause us any harm."

Stuart stopped but glared at Sami as if to question his sanity. Sami slowly waved his hand up and down, signalling to the men to lower their weapons. They complied, although Stuart mumbled under his breath "on your head be it, Saracen."

Sami waved an inviting hand before the visitor. "Speak sir," he said.

The stranger pulled the hood from his head, revealing his face, the firelight reflecting on it revealed a form unlike that of any human and the men stepped back, with a gasp. Sami saw them clutching the hilts of their swords tightly and again signalled them to relax. Reluctantly, they placed the points of the swords against the ground and waited.

"What demon are you?" asked one of the clansmen.

"Despite his appearance, I do not believe this is a demon, my friends," Sami said in response. "So, tell us who you are and what you want, visitor."

When the creature spoke, his voice was deep, his speech slow and deliberate.

"I have been sent here by my Master, Zaman, with instructions on how you should proceed." As he spoke, his body transformed. Before their eyes, the group's visitor took on the female form. Its immense proportions reduced. Before them stood a woman of utmost beauty. The Scotsmen began to mutter prayers to ward off evil. Some made the sign of the cross and even Sami sought refuge in Allah from what he now believed was a kind of demon.

He wanted to speak. He wanted to turn and run. He wanted to stay and fight. He was flooded with conflicting thoughts and feelings, but he remained rooted to the spot, and silent. The woman smiled and spoke.

"My name is Amira and I am a Silah, a shape-shifting Jinni, sent by Zaman, who is the servant of Allah. I am here to assist you Sami. You have waited patiently here as the lady of the forest had ordered. Now, it is time to move."

The others in the group glared at Sami. Some whispered questions to each other regarding the foreigner whom they had taken as a friend and equal, but they too found themselves unable to move. It was as though they were frozen in time and fear was rising within each of them.

"Your friends, who have been travelling through my world from Palestine, are due to arrive in your world soon, Sami. They will be here by the end of the year. So, you have a few months of your time to prepare horses, fighting men and women, scouts and provisions." Said Amira.

Then, without warning, she began to speak in Aramaic. These words were for Sami alone. "In two months, your friends will arrive. They will find you. Then, you must go to the Loch to find a tree that is twisted into the shape of a man on horseback. They will tell you what to do next." It was the message the old lady in the woods had given him, so many years before.

He was about to question her when, without warning, she vanished. The surroundings were still and silent, but the men found they could move again. As if a switch had been flicked, the conversations began in earnest. Some of them jostled Sami, interrogating him and one man drew his sword. In response, Sami drew his own and pleaded for calm. "I will explain everything," he said, "if you would allow me."

For several hours he narrated all that had happened, not just recently, but as far back as the war against Sieffuddeen so many years before. As he enlightened them, he watched their faces change from suspicion to concern to intrigue and, for most of them, to acceptance. Perhaps even an understanding. They were drinking a distilled brew and, as Sami related his tale, the Scotsmen became increasingly intoxicated. Eventually, they gave him their support. He had his first recruits.

CHAPTER 74
1305 A.D.
Cecelia's Love

The women within the Laird's stronghold were busy with a range of duties and Cecelia was helping in the kitchen. Workers were preparing for the end-of-hunt meal and celebration that would take place that evening. As she prepared vegetables, the matron sidled over to her and leaned against the table.

"So, Cecelia, how did you come to have a Saracen protector?"

Cecelia was slightly taken aback by the approach and the question, but when she glanced at the matron, she saw the woman smiling. It was one of those naughty smiles that said *tell me more about you and this man. Are you more than just nun and protector?*

Cecelia placed her knife on the table and gave the matron a curious glance. Then, she told her how she had met Sami and about his quest to find his friends. The matron nodded throughout but said nothing until Cecelia had finished.

"You know that's not what I meant?" the matron finally said. "I've seen the way he looks at you, and you at him when you think nobody is watching."

Cecelia blushed and looked around, hoping that nobody was watching or listening at this time. "I don't know what you mean, matron," she said, shaking her head.

"He is a handsome man and strong too, intelligent and, by all accounts, a gentleman. I would fully understand why a beautiful young lady like yourself would fall for him."

The matron was a middle-aged woman, married with six children, all sons. She was always very proper in her manner, her speech and her behaviour, but Cecelia could see she had a mischievous side to her. She wanted to tell her how she felt but something was preventing her. Her mind drifted back to the time near the stream when she had revealed her naked body to him. She wanted him then. She wanted him to take her and make love to her. But he had poured cold water on such desires. That thought shook her out of her daze.

"I'm a nun, matron. I cannot think about men or relationships," she whispered, moving in close to the matron to keep the conversation between the two of them.

The matron chuckled and slapped Cecelia on the shoulder. "Lassie, you're about as much a nun as I am a saint," she said. "I have no doubt you *were* a nun, but you have already told me that was foisted upon you. When you left the priory with Sami, you left the life of a nun."

She could see the concern on Cecelia's face. "Worry not, my dear. Your secret is safe with me." She smiled and started to move away. Then, she stopped. "But I will want to know more about your feelings for Sami," she added. "And you, lassie, need to do something about it." She smiled and walked away.

Cecelia knew she was right. She did need to do something about it. Every time she was near him, her heartbeat rose, and she experienced a hot flush. She wanted him. Of that, there was no doubt, but Sami's warning about their different lifespans rattled around her mind like a pebble in a pot. For a moment, her mind wandered. How could she bring the subject up again with Sami? Should she? When? Then, she was startled out of her thoughts by the sound of horses. *Could it be the men returning from their hunting expedition early?* she wondered. The women would be busy now, plucking, skinning, gutting, cutting and preparing. She would have to put off thoughts of Sami until later.

She walked to the doorway, only to find a unit of soldiers, all in chainmail, heavily armed and filthy. They bore the signs of months of travel but their leader beamed authority.

"Where is your Laird?" He shouted. When there was no reply, he dismounted and walked towards Cecelia. His face, lined, rough and sun-tarnished, showed him to be a very old man, perhaps 70 years or older. But he was muscular and straight-backed, almost as if he had the well-toned body of a younger man. This was someone who had spent his entire life fighting. *A hard man. A brutal man, judging by his eyes,* Cecelia thought, *and either very lucky or a magnificent fighter to have lived so long.*

"My name is Cedric. I and my men are in this land at the request of Scotland's King and we have been directed here. I'd like our horses to be taken care of and some food for us all."

"And baths, sir?" Cecelia said, sarcastically.

He looked her up and down, intrigued by the nun's habit she was wearing.

"For a nun, you have rather a free-talking tongue. I suggest you lock it away in that pretty mouth of yours, or I will take it from you, sister," Cedric replied, his blue eyes piercing and still. His threat was serious. Of that, she was sure.

She bowed slightly. "I will send squires to care for your horses, a maid to fetch the Laird for you, sir, and the cooks to prepare food."

Cedric grunted and Cecelia left to find the squires and make the preparations for these new arrivals. She sent one squire as a messenger to the laird and the rest to lead the horses to the stables. Then, she led the men to the dining area, where food was already being laid out for them.

"Did you come directly to Scotland from France?" She enquired, adding, "er, your accents, sir. You have come from France, have you not?"

Cedric never looked at her once. Staring at the food, he answered her. "Not that it is any of your business, sister, we came from France to England to meet with a trader and purchase supplies, before making our way North to Scotland. We kept ahead of the English King's army and spoke only in Latin to those we encountered."

"You're mercenaries." She said. It was not a question.

Cedric took a deep breath and finally turned to face her. "I warn you again, woman, to keep your prying and bold attitude in check."

Cecelia nodded and left the hall. As she made her way towards the kitchen, she saw Sami and his men returning from their hunt. She rushed out of the building and, without a thought, held the Saracen in a warm embrace. Sami, somewhat embarrassed and surprised, glanced around to see his men smirking or smiling.

"What are you all gawking at?" He asked. "Take the horses to the stables and the prey to the kitchens." Their grins disappeared. They nodded and went about following his orders.

Cecelia stepped back from Sami and glanced at the house. "Men have arrived from France. Mercenaries. Rough. They are in the hall."

Sami began to walk towards the house, when Cecelia caught him by the arm. "They are French, but came north from England, Sami. Their leader, a man called Cedric, said he was in England buying supplies, but…"

"But you doubt him."

She nodded.

"Let me greet them. Has the Laird been informed?"

"I sent a squire to fetch him as soon as they arrived. I'm sure he will be in the hall with them already."

CHAPTER 75
1306 A.D.
Abbas Establishes Himself in England

The years had passed for Abbas too. He had taken the name Alarico, meaning 'rules all', and the family name Sanchez, from the Latin, Sanctus, meaning sanctified. He felt they were both appropriate names for the grandson of the Dark Lord and it would be difficult for anyone to investigate their authenticity.

He had amassed a small army of Arab, Spanish and French mercenaries and purchased a large building in Carlisle. Carlisle was a former Scottish town in the region of Cumberland, which had been held by the English for several centuries. Most of the town's citizens were trades people, working with leather and wool, but Alarico decided to produce luxury sauces, based on Mediterranean recipes. Within a very short time, his industry was supplying sauces to the English Royal Family.

Carlisle was a small town with a population of no more than two thousand. By the standards of the time it was a fair-sized market town, but Cumbria was a deprived area of England and there was little trade or commerce in the region.

Nevertheless, Carlisle, with its location near the Scottish border, was strategically important. In the 12th century, stone walls had been erected around the town and the castle was rebuilt in stone. It was strengthened at a time when the town was in the hands of the Scots. The English had regained possession of Carlisle and managed to repel the Scots, who had laid siege to it for 3 months in 1173. The Scots were again repelled in 1315.

In 1122 a priory had been built in the town and in 1133 Carlisle was made the seat of a bishop. Then, in 1223, friars arrived. Unlike monks, friars did not withdraw from the world. They went out to preach. There were 2 orders of friars in Carlisle, Dominicans (called Blackfriars because of their black costumes) and Franciscans (Grey friars).

The main industries in Carlisle were wool and leather, both of which were exported to Ireland and the town had a weekly market, plus an annual fair. The different trades were organised into guilds, designed to safeguard the interests of their members. There were guilds for merchants, butchers, skinners, shoemakers, tanners, tailors, smiths and weavers. It was said that Carlisle was nicknamed The Sauceries because the land there belonged to the man who made the king's sauces. Although unrecorded as such, this man was Alarico.

His wealth already exceeded most people in England before his industrious undertakings began earning more. Now, he mingled with Royalty and nobles on both sides of the border, strengthening his position, while building himself an army. Once word arrived of the whereabouts of the travellers from his homeland, he would move north, into Scotland, but that would be a risky undertaking. His current operations involved making his route through the harsh Scottish lands an easy one by building alliances throughout that country. The trick was to do so without arousing the suspicion of the English or their new King.

Commerce, including a trade in arms for the Scottish clans, enabled Alarico to gain inroads relatively quickly, paving a way through the country when the time should arrive. Meanwhile, in Carlisle, training of his troops had begun alongside some English units. Alarico was, to all intents and purposes, an ally of the English, preparing to assist in their future war against the Scots.

Meanwhile, using his alluring looks, his charm and his wealth, he had taken a succession of women to his bed. Most were servants. He used them, captivated them, showered them with gifts and warm words, before discarding them like an unwanted dog. Many, he managed to impregnate before removing them from his household. Their shame and their fear, he knew, would hold their tongues and his money would keep them in a life of comfort. This, he knew, was all part of his grandfather's plan. The seed of Satan was spread throughout the known world, through his amorous antics.

It was during one of these affairs, that he discovered something that would be of great use to him. The one he had seduced was an Irish girl who had travelled to England in the hope of improving her life. Within weeks of arriving, she had found that the streets of England's cities were not paved with gold. They were covered in piss and shit. The only work she could find put her just one rung up on the ladder from that shit. Alarico was certain she was spying for the Scots but that was not important to him. He cared little for the English. He needed them and would use them to his advantage.

The girl's name was Siobhan and one thing her occupation allowed, was the opportunity to listen to the drunken ravings of tavern goers and purveyors of her services. Traders, Lords, Knights of the realm and soldiers, would openly reveal information that they thought would remain with her. Alarico, however, let her do all the talking. And he listened to every word she said. It was during one of these monologues that she mentioned talk from some traders who had crossed from Scotland. Talk of a Saracen who was training the Scottish fighting men in a different form of fighting.

From his time as Abbas, Alarico knew exactly what this meant. An Arab warrior was training the Scots in guerrilla warfare; something that the Arabs had used to great effect for hundreds of years. They used it against the Persians, against the Egyptians, against the Franj crusaders. And, more recently, their Turkish overlords, the Mamluks, had used it in a most deadly way against his former allies, the Mongols. He considered passing this information onto the English, but that thought was brief. He knew that such tactics would hurt the English. They were, after all, used to defeating weaker armies in face-to-face battlefield engagements. He smiled at the thought of the English being hurt. He did not like them very much and had no care for England's problems. He cared about his own troops and his quest to prevent the closing of the barrier between his grandfather's world and this one. This information would be used to enable this to happen. And he cared about chaos and anarchy. These were among his tools.

In Scotland, events were occurring that would shake the foundations of the British Isles. Sir John Comyn, 'The Red', was murdered. Reports received by the English King stated that he had been cut down by Robert de Bruce in a Church. De Bruce was claiming his right to the Scottish Crown and Edward was outraged. With the Welsh now conquered and subdued, the English King turned to his 'Scottish problem' with a fanatical obsession.

In Scotland, Sami and Cecelia found themselves with a new Laird, one granted the land by Robert de Bruce. He was Thomas Randolph, 1st Earl of Moray. Initially, Sami tried to protest but the Scots, both house work force and soldiers, advised him to accept this as fate. The truth was that most of them were pleased with the demise of the Comyns, known by the English as the Cummings. Their reputation as a ruthless and untrustworthy clan, was known far and wide. Their treachery, including their desertion when fighting with William Wallace, had even appeared in a Highlands proverb. "Fhad bhitheas craobh 'sa choill, Bithidli foill 'sna Cuiminich." ["While in the wood there is a tree, a Cumming will deceitful be."].

"Times change, my friend, and life moves on," his second-in-command, Stuart, had said to him.

Times did change but Sami found his loyalty to the new Laird was greeted with the same level of support and favour that the previous Laird had provided.

Alarico also saw opportunities in every new event, every turn of fate. A war, thousands upon thousands of English troops travelling through Carlisle, opened doors for him. He smiled, satisfied that fate was on his side.

CHAPTER 76
Odinike, Fighting Amid Deception

The human travellers and their Jinni guide reached the end of the tunnel and were shocked to see the open expanse beyond. A wide beach, swarming with Jinn soldiers, and workers loading weapons and food onto other-worldly ships. There was no visible sign of cover for the emerging troupe. Concern about exposure, together with the obvious problem of being grossly outnumbered, caused them to pause within the tunnel and discuss their predicament.

"We will sleep here for now and make plans in a few hours," Jawad said. The others nodded and prepared areas of relative comfort where they could get much needed rest.

Reza found it difficult to sleep. He was lying near the tunnel exit and the noise from the Jinn forces outside was distracting him. Nevertheless, he covered himself up and laid his head on his pack. After what felt like an hour or so, he heard movement within the tunnel. Someone was moving towards the exit from the rear of the group. Keeping himself covered, Reza kept watch and saw one of the men inching, quietly, towards the exit. He could not identify him but knew he should find out what he was doing. He waited until the man had left and then followed him. Outside the tunnel, it was dark. There were no stars, no moon and no torches, just a thick sheet of gloom. Yet, the man he was following moved with agility over rocks that led down to the beach below. Reza struggled to keep him in sight and, after a few stumbles, decided to wait in case the man returned. He still could not make out who it was and did not want to arouse the others yet. He wanted to question this person himself.

He crouched behind a small cluster of rocks and waited. Sometime later, the man returned. He walked past where Reza was hiding and began to enter the tunnel entrance. Reza moved quickly, rushing up behind him.

He charged the man into the wall of the tunnel, causing his victim to shriek, partly in pain, partly in shock.

One-by-one, the others stirred. Torches were lit, and they approached the two men near the tunnel opening. Hassan arrived first and found the doctor, lying flat on the ground, Reza's sword held threateningly to his throat.

"What is this, Reza?"

"He left the tunnel and scampered down to the beach. He, I believe, is our traitor."

By now, everyone was awake. Whispers began to ripple throughout the assembly of travellers but they were silenced when Jawad spoke to the doctor.

"Explain yourself, doctor!" He was greeted with silence and raised his voice; "Now!"

Reza pressed the tip of his sword into the doctor's throat and drew blood, but the doctor merely smiled.

"You've lost, Jawad. Your quest is over. They know where you are and are on their way here. Here, trapped in this tunnel, a tunnel that will be your grave." The doctor's voice was surprisingly calm.

"Why?" Marie called out. "We took you in and helped you. Why would you do this?"

The doctor glanced at the sword and Jawad signalled to Reza to put it away. The Persian was reluctant to do so but did not argue. As the weapon slid back into its sheath, the doctor continued.

"I was sent to join your group. When I found Jaffer, I could not believe my luck. I knew that someone so young would melt your hearts and make you less cautious about me. It worked and the Dark Lord will undoubtedly repay me well."

Jawad turned away from the man in disgust. "Tie him up," he called out to nobody in particular, "and for the sake of Allah, gag him. I don't want to hear another word from him."

He walked towards his wife, seeking some solace and advice, when Hassan caught hold of his arm. Jawad stopped and looked at his friend.

"When I was in this world before," Hassan said, "I met a Jinni, the last of his kind. His name was Odinike and he is a mighty warrior. We need his help if we are to defeat the enemy we face here."

Jawad pondered on this but asked, "How? How do we find this creature?"

The answer came from a voice behind them and both men turned to face Ashar, the Wishmaster.

"I can find him. If it is your wisssh."

Jawad stared long and hard at the Jinni and sighed. One look at the former prince and Hassan knew that he was considering making the wish.

"Don't do it," he said. "You know that there will be unwanted consequences."

"I have no choice, Hassan. You said yourself, we need this Odinike to win the fight and I know of no other way of getting him here, do you?"

Hassan shook his head, despondently. "No" he said. "I don't."

Jawad took a deep breath and made his request to the Jinni. "I wish you to bring Odinike here to us, Ashar."

The Jinni smiled. "Your wish. My command." He clapped his hands and Odinike appeared before them at the entrance of the tunnel. He truly was a giant. He stood twice the height of Bohemond, the tallest of the human group, and taller even than Ashar. His head, shoulders and chest had crashed through the tunnel roof, bringing debris down around his feet. For a moment the others feared the tunnel might collapse, but it held, and they stared, in awe, at this behemoth that stood before them.

Odinike roared, a warning to whoever had brought him to this place, and he swung an enormous club. It missed the men but crashed into the tunnel wall, shaking the structure to its foundations. An enormous crack stretched from the tunnel roof to the floor beneath his feet. The tunnel creaked for a moment and then settled, easing the fear of the group. Realising that none of the humans were threatening him, he calmed himself. He stepped back and held his club out before him, threateningly, but then he heard a voice he recognised.

"Odinike, it is I, Hassan. Do you remember me?"

The giant stepped forwards and glared at Hassan, scrutinising his face. Then he laughed, his booming voice echoing throughout the chamber. "Hassan," he eventually said. "Did you fail to return to your earthly home?"

Hassan smiled and explained the situation to his formidable friend and the giant agreed to help. They led him to the tunnel entrance and were planning to take him outside, far enough to see the enemy below, but he came to a sudden halt. For the first time, Hassan witnessed fear on the giant's face.

"What is it, my friend?" He asked.

Odinike took a deep breath and forced a smile. "Nothing. We will go to meet your enemy."

Owun Tyler was tasked, along with George Assad and two of the Alis, with firing an artillery barrage of arrows into the Jinn force at the beachhead. Each man could unleash between ten and twelve arrows every minute, which would force the Jinn forces to run for cover. Then, Odinike and the rest of the fighters would surge forward to finish them off. Owun and the other archers left the security of the tunnel and skirted around the hill, securing themselves in a range of boulders. They waited for Jawad's signal and, when it came, their first attack began. Lighted arrows whistled through the sky, some landing on the boats, others into the unloaded cargo that sat on the sandy beach and some piercing the Jinn through countless parts of their bodies.

The screams and shouts of the Jinn could be heard all the way to the tunnel itself and, as predicted, the survivors ran for cover. It was then that the group, led by the fearsome Odinike, rushed down the hill towards the panicked enemy below. The giant arrived before any of the others, amid the mayhem caused by the arrow assault. He swung his club wildly at the frightened Jinn force, crushing bones, smashing heads and killing instantly. He thrust through the enemy forces like a hurricane, leaving bodies in his wake, but some of the Jinn managed to recover their senses. Led by a pig-like creature, they organised a response. They split up and moved to outflank the giant. That, however, was a mistake. A retreat to the boats and formation of a shield wall would have offered them greater protection. Now, they had divided their forces, those on the right being dealt with by Odinike, those on the left finding themselves attacked from the rear by Jawad's forces.

Hassan arrived in the thick of the battle first, swinging his sword at any Jinni who dared to stand in his way. The first of them lost his sword arm in an instant, blood flying in all directions. Two more ran towards the now blood-crazed Turk. He lunged at the first, his sword skewering the Jinni's neck, a spurt of brown blood striking Hassan's face, making him appear even more wild.

The second Jinni hesitated and that was a mistake. Without pausing for breath, Hassan kicked the first one away to release his sword. He swung it to his right, taking the head of the second Jinni in an instant.

Meanwhile, the remainder of his group arrived and threw themselves into the melee. Amina had remained behind with Jaffer and Judah Ben Zakai to guard their prisoner. The rest, including Marie, tore into the thick of the battle, slashing, stabbing, punching, kicking and gouging the enemy troops. The Jinn were disorganised, caught by surprise and virtually decimated by Odinike and the battle was over quickly. Everyone was drenched in blood and went to the water to wash much of it away. As they rejoiced at their victory, however, they heard a loud crash and felt the ground shake. Turning in the direction of the noise, they saw Odinike lying on his back on the ground. At first, they thought he was resting, but soon noticed there was little movement from the giant. His enormous chest barely rose. His breathing was restricted.

They rushed from the water to his side and saw that his skin had turned a sickly yellow, his eyes a bloodshot red. As if out of nowhere, Ashar appeared before them.

"He is dying," he said.

The humans looked at the Jinni and waited for him to explain. Ashar stepped forward. "I'm sorry but you know my nature and you made the wish."

Hassan marched towards the Jinni, his sword outstretched, threateningly before him.

"What have you done, Ashar?" He shouted.

The Jinni stood his ground and replied. "I did only what you wished for me to do, but the air in this region is poisonous to Odinike. He is dying and even if you wish for his return home, it is too late. His body is too badly damaged. He has been here too long."

Hassan returned to the giant who was gasping but whispering the Turk's name.

"Don't try to talk my friend," Hassan said. "I am so sorry. We didn't know. If I'd known, I would never have…"

Odinike lifted his arm, wearily, in the air and placed his enormous finger over Hassan's mouth. "What is done, my friend, is done. I am the last of my people and I am proud to die assisting you," he said, his rasping voice barely audible. "Now, bring Ashar to me please."

The Jinni was called over and he leant down to listen to Odinike's last words. The giant fought against death to speak them. "I wish to die in my own land, Ashar."

The Jinni nodded, waved his hand and blinked and Odinike was gone. Then, Ashar returned to the tunnel.

Many of the group had tears in their eyes. Even the most hardened of warriors were touched by the death of this last of a race of the greatest warriors ever seen. Some prayed for a moment, before they all made their way to the tunnel.

As they approached, they were met by Amina, running towards them, the signs of panic on her face. "Jawad, Jawad," she called out and he ran towards her.

"What's wrong, Amina?"

"The doctor. He's gone."

"What? What do you mean gone?"

By now, the rest of the group had caught up.

"What is it?" Hassan asked.

Jawad ignored the question and caught hold of Amina. "Tell me what happened as we walk," he said, pulling her towards the tunnel.

Amina took a deep breath before speaking again. "We were in the tunnel. The doctor was tied up, but I had removed his gag to give him some water." She paused to calm herself. "Ashar arrived and the doctor shouted to him. He wished himself to be with his master, the Dark Lord and he vanished, right before our eyes."

Upon arrival at the tunnel's mouth, they found Ashar waiting for them. He shrugged. "I can only do what is in my nature. He wished. I granted."

Reza rushed towards the Jinni holding a dagger but his men held him back as Jawad stepped towards Ashar. The former prince was holding back his anger. That was evident from the look in his eyes.

"I would let Reza kill you, Ashar. I may yet do so, but for now we need you to guide us through this strange land. Our friends, in our world, have been waiting several months for us and I can't afford to lose more time so, for now, you have a reprieve."

"Years," replied Ashar.

"What?"

"Your friends have been waiting many years for you."

"What are you talking about? We have been in this world only a few months, not years."

Ashar smiled, his expression that of someone who is enjoying possession of knowledge that others do not have. "Here, we have been travelling for months, but in your world years have passed."

Jawad could control his anger no longer. He grabbed the Jinni by his tunic and thrust him up against the wall. Reza joined them and held his dagger firmly against the Jinni's neck. Hassan and one of the Alis held Ashar's arms.

"Explain your words, Jinni or die right here, right now." Jawad spat the words at Ashar.

The Jinni showed no fear. Calmly, he replied. "As I said, time here is not as time is in your world. Why do you think you have not aged as other humans have?"

"Then, why did Zenith tell us this would save time?"

Ashar laughed. "You asked him for a quicker way. He told you to pass through our world. He never once said this would be faster. He said it was necessary."

Jawad tried to recall what Zenith had said to them and realised that Ashar was right. He had never said this would save time. "Now what?" He asked Ashar.

"Now, we go down river to the estuary."

Unfortunately, the boats were all burned or sunk, bar one which lacked a sail and another with a broken mast. For the next few hours, they worked on repairing the mast and salvaging some sails from the sunken boats. It was approaching evening by the time they had a boat in a fit enough state to sail. The journey, they knew, would be difficult. Nevertheless, they set off down river.

CHAPTER 77
The Doctor and the Dark Lord

The doctor, dazed and confused, found himself in a bright red chamber that felt as if it was deep underground. As his eyes adjusted to the low light, realisation struck him. He was in the chamber of his Master, the Evil One, Shaytaan. The doctor stared momentarily at the ground, trying to focus, but snapped his head upwards upon hearing a rumbling voice talking to him.

"Welcome Doctor, to my humble home."

The man before him, for it was a man, or seemed so in every way, was smiling. This was not what the doctor expected. *Is this Shaytaan?* he asked himself.

The man, dressed in the silk fineries of a pampered prince or king, stared unblinkingly at the doctor.

"Yes. I am he." His voice was deep, but soothing, confusing the doctor further. Confusing him so much that he failed to notice that this man was replying to what was merely a thought in his head.

"Did you complete your task, doctor?"

Dizziness began to overcome the doctor. The chamber was disorientating. The walls seemed to be moving, like jelly in a bowl. Before he could reply, he fainted.

When he came around, the man before him had changed clothes, to the chainmail of a western knight. No helmet on his head. No gloves. His hair was long and fair. It hung over his face like a veil and his head stooped forward slightly. Muhammad, the doctor, was lying on the ground, shaking. He was not sure if it was fear or cold making him shiver, for the chamber was now decorated with icicles. He was surrounded by sheets of ice, stalactites and stalagmites.

"Get up doctor." The man's voice seemed deeper this time. It was more commanding, more authoritative. Without hesitation, the doctor struggled to his feet and stood, watching the figure sitting before him. For a moment, the man did not move. Then, slowly and deliberately, he raised his head, parting the long hair away from his face with his hands. For the first time, the doctor noticed his fingernails. Long and sharp. "Did you complete your task?" The man asked, his voice echoing around the chamber.

Nervously, the doctor replied. "My Lord, I tried. I, er, warned the Jinn at the beach and they were prepared for the human attack, but I was discovered." His voice was cracking.

"FOOL!" The man shouted, his face contorting, his skin turning bright red, his eyes aflame like torchlights. He stood and grew as he did so, reaching the height of the cavern itself. Behind him, two wings appeared, not feathered like a bird's wings, but stretched skin, like those on a bat. They flapped once and then receded. The doctor felt piss running down his legs and wanted to vomit. He was shaking uncontrollably, but the man sat back down, shifting once more to a human-like form.

"Be still, doctor. You know who I am." His voice was soft, calming, even friendly and the doctor took a deep breath.

"You are Iblis, the Dark Lord, Shaytaan." His voice was still unsteady.

"I am, and I am disappointed that you could not complete the task but tell me what happened after you were found out."

The doctor took another deep breath.

"They tied me up and summoned a mighty Jinni called Odinike, a giant the like of which I have never seen before.

"He fought for them and helped them to win, but I don't know what happened to him.

"I knew I had to get away, so I called to the Wishmaster, Ashar, their Jinni guide and wished myself here."

Shaytaan tapped the nail of the index finger of his right hand on the arm of the enormous wooden chair, upon which he sat.

"You speak the truth, doctor. Thank you for that."

The realisation that this was a test took the doctor by surprise, but he said nothing.

"Odinike died," Shaytaan continued. "The humans defeated my

forces at the beach and are now continuing their journey. I and my armies are tied up in this damnable war against Zaman and I cannot impede the humans' progress. For the time being, they are free to journey onwards."

He tapped his fingernail on the chair again. "As for you, it was your wish to come here to do what?"

"To, er, be with you Master. To, to, er, be with you, by your side forever."

Shaytaan leaned back in the skull-covered chair, his hands resting on the cranial remains of two trolls. "Let me tell you about Ashar. He is a Wishmaster, no doubt, but his nature is to be mischievous for he is one of mine."

The doctor's frown revealed his confusion. He wanted to ask how this could be, when he was helping the human travellers, but he was overcome with fear. Shaytaan continued, his speech slow and deliberate with continual pauses that showed his own roguish nature.

"I see your confusion. Ashar was taken from us. Zaman cast a spell, of sorts. He controls the Wishmaster's behaviour. But he can't control his nature.

"You surely knew that Ashar's wishes have additional consequences, undesired, unforeseen consequences. You saw that yourself, did you not?"

The doctor nodded.

"Still, you wished to be with me, forever."

The doctor nodded again.

Shaytaan smiled. "Then it shall be so," he said, and with a wave of his hand, the doctor began to transform.

He screamed in agony as his body contorted and shrank, until finally he became trapped in a small pebble.

Shaytaan held up his hand and the pebble flew from the ground to his open palm. Inside, the doctor was motionless, but alive. His eyes were open. Shaytaan held the pebble in front of his face and spoke.

"You will remain alongside me here forever, hearing, seeing smelling, feeling everything, but unable to move. A prisoner of your wish."

He paused for a moment and then smiled, a smile of sadistic pleasure. "I almost forgot," he said. "When first we met, you wished to be with your family again and so you will."

He waved his hand and the dead bodies of the doctor's wife and children appeared with him inside the world within the pebble.

"For eternity, you shall live in that world with your dead family, until I need your services once more."

Shaytaan placed the pebble in a transparent locket that hung around his neck, then leaned back and called for Abigor, who appeared before him in a cloud of smoke.

"What do you see, Abigor?"

"They are almost at the river's end, my Lord. I feel the presence of the White Wolf. She awaits them there."

"Keep monitoring their movements and keep me informed."

Abigor nodded and vanished.

"Guards!" Shaytaan shouted.

Two troll soldiers ran towards him, heads bowed.

"Gather all our remaining troops. We join the fight for Zaydussia. Zaman must be defeated."

With that, he rose from the chair and shifted into his natural form of deep red skin, eyes of fire and claws like those of a bear. He rose to his full height. At fourteen feet tall, he dwarfed Abigor and the guards and, once clothed in armour, he would strike dread in the hearts of any who saw him. As he walked out to his troops, the chamber fell into darkness.

CHAPTER 78
The Master Jinni

The travelling humans had almost reached the end of the river when Ashar approached Jawad.

"Prince Jawad," he said. Without waiting for Jawad to point out that he was no longer a prince, he continued. "It is almost time for me to leave you. Anchor the boat here and swim to the shore there", he said, pointing to the Port side of the boat. "I will join you in a moment and explain your next task."

Jawad wanted to ask why Ashar was leaving but did not. He was glad that they would finally be rid of the mischievous Jinni. So, he conveyed the instructions to the remainder of the group and the swim to shore began. Jaffer and Amina, neither of whom could swim, were assisted by Hassan and Marie.

Later, in a small glade within a wooded area, Owun Tyler sat in the shade of a large oak tree, treating his bow string with bee's wax and replacing some of the feathers on his arrows. He glanced across at Hassan and Jawad, who were standing nearby, discussing the quest for the Master Jinni that lay ahead of them; a quest that none of them fully understood. For a moment, the discussion ended and as silence fell, Owun called out to the group.

"Merlin's staff!"

Jawad turned towards the young archer. "What was that?" He asked.

Owun placed his bow on the ground beside him, stood up and strolled across to his two compatriots.

"The thing you're looking for is Merlin's staff and on its own it will not remove the threat of your half-demon relative."

Sami frowned. "What do you mean Owun?"

Tyler heaved a long, drawn out sigh, glanced at both men and then nodded.

"OK, I'll tell you about it but know that this could take some time and you may not believe it."

He tapped his palm on the ground and all three men sat in a triangle of sorts. Tyler began to explain.

"Merlin's staff was taken from the wizard before he was imprisoned by Morgana, the Witch, on the Isle of Avalon. It was taken to a safe place by Merlin's apprentice, in the hope that one day a man of true character would be able to find it and use it to revive him."

"Whoa," said Bohemond, who had been listening to the conversation while relieving himself behind a nearby tree, his frown growing deeper with every word he heard. "Revive him?" he said, as he wiped his hands on his trousers and wandered across to the group. After sitting with them, he continued; "Merlin is just legend, Myth, my friend and even legend states that he is dead."

Tyler shook his head and continued. "Merlin was made myth by your Christian forefathers, Bohemond. The idea that a wizard, a shaman, a man of majik could possibly have been a confidante of a great English King could not be allowed to be accepted as truth."

Hassan was about to interrupt, but Jawad held his friend's wrist and silently shook his head, a request for them to allow the archer to continue.

"Merlin was real, my friends, and he did not die. Tricked by the Lady of the Lake, an enchantress that Merlin himself had taught, he was taken and imprisoned in a hidden world. Only his staff can release him and only by a man of good character. I believe it is one from this group, but I cannot be sure of that."

Jawad looked sceptical, but he continued to humour the archer. "Why do we need to revive him?" He asked.

Owun shifted his position to get more comfortable. "Only Merlin can show you how to return Abbas to his human form. Only Merlin can instruct us on how to reseal the portal. Find Merlin or lose Abbas forever. Find Merlin or lose everything."

"And where do we go to find this wizard and his staff?" Asked Jawad.

As they sat in silence, pondering Jawad's question, Ashar spoke. "I can answer that. I am leaving now. My task is over. Wait here in this clearing and you will be met by a White Wolf. She will guide you to the wizard." With that, the Jinni disappeared.

They waited for several hours, made camp, lit a fire and ate a kind of fish they had caught from the boat. Wondering whether this White Wolf would ever arrive, their peace was suddenly disturbed by a howl. Everyone reached for a weapon and focused their attention in the direction from which the noise had emanated. Minutes passed before a magnificent white wolf emerged from the surrounding woodland. Its eyes were red, and it scanned the group, as if analysing every one of their features.

Without warning, she spoke.

"I am your guide from this point onwards. We will journey overland to Zaydussia. There is little chance of meeting enemy Jinn in any great force but be on your guard for occasional attacks from insurgents. Shaytaan has all his forces tied up fighting those of Zaman and it is on the outskirts of Zaydussia that we will face the greatest threat. He will stop at nothing to stop you entering the city. So, are you ready for what may come?"

Jawad replied on behalf of the rest. "We are ready for whatever may greet us."

"Then sleep and once you are rested, we shall proceed. I must, however, correct young Owun Tyler on one thing. Merlin and Morgana were and still are Jinn. They took human form and Merlin served King Arthur, knowing that Arthur was the only man who could lead the forces of good against Morgana, the Black Knight and their Master, Shaytaan."

As the darkness faded and the light of an alien purple dawn materialised, the team of humans awoke, gathered their belongings and put their trust in their new guide.

The journey took them first through a brief wooded area that soon opened into an expanse of ice.

"There, before you, lies the Isle of Avalon. To cross, you must demonstrate faith and follow me without question. Are you ready and willing to do that?"

Tentatively, each member of the group nodded, and the white wolf stepped from the shore of the lake onto the water. She did not sink. She walked on water, or so it seemed. Reza turned to Jawad. Others in the group turned to each other and muttered concern, awe, confusion.

Hassan, however, stepped forwards and followed the wolf. Miraculously, he also walked on the water. He took several steps, stopped and turned. The others remained hesitant.

"It is all right," Hassan called out to them. "There is an unseen platform, just below the water's surface. It's safe. Come on."

They followed, and like a line of ants, they walked across the lake to the small island that lay in the water's centre. Once they had all arrived safely, the White Wolf spoke again.

"The witch's cave is there, before you. It is in there that you will find the Master Jinni; the one you call Merlin.

With Jawad taking the lead, they entered the cave, surprised to find it bathed in bright light. At the cavern's centre stood a man, dressed all in black, his long silver-coloured hair hanging well below his shoulders, almost to his waist. Nervously, the humans approached but, when they were a few yards from him, he shouted a command.

"Stop! That is as far as you can go, for I am trapped within a chamber of energy. If you touch the barrier between us, you will most certainly die. Stand where you are, and I will explain all."

After a brief pause, he began to relate his story.

"As you are most probably aware by now, my name is Emrys, although in Earthly legend, I have become known as Merlin. I am not human, but a Jinni and I have lived for thousands of years."

He continued for some time, relating his story and that of the legend King, Arthur of the Britons. His audience was captivated.

Merlin explained that Morgana, also a Jinni, enticed him to the lake and stole him away to Avalon, where she trapped him. She hid Avalon and sealed it in the dimension of the Jinn, using a collection of words in a foreign language, Aramaic. The words were from the gospels and related to the sealing of the tomb of Jesus. Finally, he asked if they had questions and it was Owun Tyler who spoke up.

"Why are we here and what is it we are expected to do?"

Merlin took a deep breath and glanced to his right.

"Hidden within the rockface there," he said, pointing, "is my staff and you will need it to seal the portal currently being guarded by Zaman. However, you cannot reach it in this world. You must find the Isle of Avalon from the Earthly plain."

"That draws me back to my original question. Why are we *here*?" Tyler asked.

The wizard smiled. "When you find your way back here from your world, I will not be here. At least, I will be here, but you will not be able to see me. You had to find me in this world to receive my instructions, but you must return in your world to fetch the staff."

He went on to explain that freeing him would require celestial magic that was beyond the understanding of anyone alive in either realm.

"However," he added, "the staff can be released from its prison by reciting the Biblical verses relating to the discovery of Jesus' empty tomb. This is exactly as it was for young Arthur, when he pulled the sword from the stone; a sword that I had placed there."

He laughed. "I placed it there and then taught him the words and how to say them. His destiny was ensured, by me."

Jawad glanced at Hassan, who simultaneously looked at Jawad, who raised an eyebrow. "Crazy," he whispered.

"Not crazy at all, Jawad," Merlin said, taking the former prince by surprise.

"Oh, I did not mean to offend, but…"

"Offend? I am not offended. I am amused. Now, where was I? Oh yes, once again, the recitation will have to be in Aramaic.

"Who knows Aramaic?" Reza asked. "It is a dead language."

Once again, Merlin smiled. "Your friend, Sami, who awaits you in the earthly realm. He knows Aramaic, as does your Jewish friend. Is he not a translator?"

Judah muttered something under his breath about his knowledge of Greek, Latin, Arabic and Hebrew, but not Aramaic, but nobody heard. Merlin continued to relate the instructions for the group.

"However, in order to reach the Isle of Avalon in the earthly dimension, the first chapter of the Quran, Al-Fatihah, 'The Opening' must be recited, in Arabic.

"Only the recital of those words by a person of truth and good character can open a gateway to the hidden Isle. That will be a person who has never taken another's life, a person chosen for this task."

He paused as they muttered to each other and then continued.

"That person is among you." He looked directly at the youngest of the group, who was mesmerised by the wizard. "Jaffer is the key with which you will unlock the gateway to Avalon."

There was more muttering among the group, some discussing Jaffer's apparent position of privilege and others discussing Sami. Hassan leant towards Jawad.

"Did you know that Sami speaks Aramaic?"

Jawad smiled. "I did. He came from a wealthy family in Syria and had a private tutor who taught him Greek, Latin, Arabic, Hebrew and Aramaic. Other tutors guided him in mathematics."

Hassan looked stunned. "I never would have guessed. He is such a formidable fighter, a natural soldier. I would have never believed he was anything other than a lifelong man of war."

Jawad's expression was solemn. He took a deep breath and whispered to his friend. "During internal strife in Syria, the palace where Sami's family lived was attacked. Everyone was slaughtered. His parents, his sister, his younger brother, all the servants. Sami hid and was missed. He was fourteen years' old and the experience set him on a military course."

Their conversation was interrupted as they realised Merlin was speaking again.

"Now, White Wolf will lead you on to Zaydussia and the portal home. She will follow you into your world to guide you to Sami but know this; once in your world, she will not speak.

"Once the staff is acquired, you will then need to travel through dangerous regions to Tintagel in Cornwall, for that is where the portal is situated. Be advised, however, that the Cornish are an unusual people, obsessed with their own culture and land. They dislike the English, the Welsh; in fact, anyone seen as an outsider and you will be outsiders. So, you must find a Cornish guide, called Bennath. She will keep you safe."

"What about my half-brother, Abbas?" Jawad called out.

"What of him?" Merlin replied, frowning.

"He is part Jinni, the grandson of the Dark Lord, Iblis, Shaytaan, and I must free him. We thought you would help us in this endeavour."

Merlin smiled and took a deep breath. "Atop the staff is the potion which you, Jawad, or someone you choose, must administer to your half-brother without his knowledge."

He paused and sighed. "It is not guaranteed that it will free him from the grip that Satan has on him, but it is the best I can offer, I'm afraid."

With that, the cave fell into absolute darkness and White Wolf entered.

"We must go," she said.

CHAPTER 79
The Battle for Zaydussia

From the group's vantage point on a hill at the edge of the Kingdom of Zaydussia, Hassan could see the grassy plain where he had stood once before with Zaman and Abbas. Beyond the plain, he could see where there had once been trees and birds, a stream of pure water and a bright, blue sky. All of these, however, and the illuminating light of day that had encircled them all those years before were gone. Now, the plain was shrouded in darkness. Zaydussia no longer reminded him of Lebanon. It filled his soul with dread. The armies of Iblis had brought death and destruction; Hell was encroaching on the Kingdom of Life.

Above them, floating in the air like a gigantic balloon, was Zaman's castle, exactly as Hassan remembered it. Untarnished, unharmed. It stood magnificently over them, a powerful symbol of justice and morality. But it was under attack, from the ground and from the air. Shaytaan's ground troops were goblin-like creatures, short, bent over, but muscular and hairy. Hassan recognised them immediately. He had seen them before, the day that he and Abbas had fallen into this world.

"I know how to defeat the little goblins there," he said, pointing in their direction. "When here before, Abbas had cried and one of his tears fell onto one of those creatures. It burned."

Bohemond laughed. "Are you suggesting we cry our tears on them? There are hundreds of them."

Hassan smiled. "No, my Christian friend. I'm suggesting it was the salt in the tears that burned them. We need salt. Lots of it."

White Wolf stepped forward. "There are salt mines beyond the plain, but what are you proposing?"

"Make a sticky, salty solution to tip our spears, swords and arrows with."

The others were clearly sceptical, but it was decided that they should at least try, so for what felt like days, they mined salt, made glue and coated their weapons. Once ready, they returned to their hillside position to survey the scene.

"What about the flying Jinn?" It was Marie who asked. "How do we stop them from turning their attacks from the castle to us, once we move on the ground troops?"

"Don't concern yourself with them," White Wolf replied. "Zaman and Zenith, with their castle forces, can handle them if we force the rest to stop their assaults."

They discussed tactics and strategy for what seemed like hours and White Wolf informed them of the weaknesses of the ghouls they would be fighting.

"Our salt-infused weapons and salt-dipped rocks in slings will help, of course," she said, "but it will not be enough to destroy them.

"The ghoul is a nocturnal creature. It is repelled by both sunlight and artificial light. Hence the reason for the darkness in Zaydussia. Yet, neither of these will cause them any lasting harm. However, they are vulnerable to fire. Like all Jinn, they are fire-based creatures, but for ghouls, the fire consumes them, traps them and, over time, forces them into non-existence. Fire is the only way to destroy these beasts."

The heads of all the humans dropped. They were defeated before they had even begun. Reza shook his head.

"We have nothing to burn and certainly cannot find enough fuel for an army that size," he said.

Hassan sighed. He looked, long and hard at the army of ghouls on the plain below and a silence fell as the fighting came to a natural pause. Zaman's troops had retreated but the ghoul numbers had been diminished. Time was available for both sides to recuperate.

"There is a way," said White Wolf. Her voice pierced the silence and shook the group from their thoughts. "But it is perilous."

"Tell us," said Jawad.

White Wolf slowly glanced at each person in turn before continuing.

"Wadjet. The Ancient Egyptians viewed her as a goddess. Of course, like all the gods of mythology, she was a Jinni. Legend has it that she served as nurse to Horus and her symbol is the sun. She often appears as a snake with a woman's head but her normal form is the human form.

When identified as the protector of Ra, she was said to be able to spit fire onto her enemies. Like a cobra, which spits poison into the eyes of those whom it perceives as a threat."

"And how does this help us? She is not here." Judah's annoyance was evident from his tone.

"We summon her, or at least I summon her," replied White Wolf, "but herein lies the peril. She will demand something in return that you may not wish to grant."

"And that would be what?" Marie asked.

"A year on Earth. She will demand a year on Earth, free to roam, free to influence and she will expect you to take her there."

"Never!" Reza stood and thumped his fist against the hillside. "There must be another way."

"There is no other way," White Wolf replied, waiting patiently for a response while the others pondered this precarious situation.

"We need to sleep on this and discuss it upon awaking," Jawad said.

Later, Jawad found Reza sharpening his sword. Owun was with him, checking arrow flights and waxing his bow string. Jawad took some dried food from a sack and offered some to the other two.

"Where did you get this from?" Owun asked.

"White Wolf sneaked off and stole it from the Jinn encampment," Jawad replied.

Sitting alongside Reza, Jawad glanced around as the rest of the group lay on their blankets, some of them drifting off to sleep.

"I often wonder why none of us have children," he said.

Reza stopped working on his blade and looked up, enquiringly.

"Marie and I are not celibate, but we have no children," Jawad continued. "I know that Hassan has had a throng of women over the years but, to my knowledge, has no children. Bohemond, Amalric and even you two. No children. Don't you think it strange?"

"I have a son."

Reza's response startled Jawad but before he could reply, Reza continued. "Or should I say I had a son."

"What? Why have you never mentioned this before?" Jawad asked. He waited and then added, "and what do you mean 'had'?"

Reza sheathed his sword and Owun, intrigued, placed his bow and arrows on the ground. Reza sighed.

"I was married and living in Qum in Persia. My son was born about nineteen or twenty years' ago, but I never really got to know him. Four years later, while I was away fighting, bandits attacked my home. They killed my wife, then burned the house down. When I returned home, I feared that my son had died in the fire, but a neighbour said they had found him hiding in an outhouse. He was too young and too shaken to tell anyone what had happened, but they guessed my wife had sent him outside when she saw her killers arrive.

"When I looked at the poor child, I found myself feeling very little. Don't ask me why. My thoughts were filled with images of what had happened to my wife and how much I craved revenge.

"I told the neighbours I could not care for a child and they also said they were unable to take him. But the local Imam suggested a good family in Baghdad who would adopt him. They had been trying for children for many years to no avail and were desperate to have a son."

Reza paused, swallowed and shed a small tear. Both Owun and Jawad, realising he had more to say, waited silently for him to continue.

"Days later, the arrangement was made, and my son was given away. That was the last time I saw him."

As he reached again for his bow, Jaffer wandered past them to fetch some food from the sack. Jawad's eyes followed the young man and he asked Reza; "What was your son's name?"

Reza glanced up and saw Jawad looking at Jaffer.

"No. No, Jawad. He is not my son."

"He is from Baghdad; he is nineteen years' old and something brought us all together. Zenith was adamant that he and the doctor join us."

"Leave it be Jawad. He is not my son." Reza's piercing eyes were focused on Jawad. Not once did he glance at Jaffer.

"What was your son's name?" Jawad repeated.

"I told you to leave it, Jawad!" Reza shouted, as he stood up and turned to walk away from his friend.

"What was his name, Reza?"

"JAFFER!" Reza's shout echoed through the hills. For a moment everyone fell absolutely silent, fearful that the sleeping Jinn on the plain below may have heard.

No movement was observed among the enemy and the group let out a collective sigh of relief. Reza walked to Jawad and, in a low voice, repeated his son's name. "Jaffer. My son's name was Jaffer."

Jawad looked again at Jaffer, who was now staring at Reza, wondering why he had called his name.

"He looks like you Reza."

Through gritted teeth, Reza replied. "I swear to God, Jawad, if you were not my friend, I would kill you to shut you up."

Jawad remained calm and smiled. "You must have wondered though, when this lad named Jaffer suddenly arrived among us."

Reza took a deep breath and glanced across at Jaffer. "Yes, I wondered for a moment but then I dismissed the idea, as should you."

Deep within, however, he wondered again. Could this be his son? His eyes fell to the ground at his feet and his thoughts were disturbed by Jaffer's voice. "Did you want me, Reza?"

"What?" In that moment, Reza feared that the youngster was his son. He considered it again and now felt sure that he was. The feelings he was experiencing were uncomfortable and he began questioning his decision to give him away.

"You called my name just now," Jaffer replied.

Reza contemplated dismissing the incident as nothing and waving Jaffer away, but something was pushing him to find out who this boy was. He stared at Jaffer, scrutinising his features.

"What were your parents' names, Jaffer?"

The boy seemed confused and frowned. "Er, my father was Shaikh Abdullah bin Salman al-Araf. He was Baghdad's chief engineer for many years. My mother's name was…"

Samira, Reza thought.

"…Samira," Jaffer said.

Reza felt his legs weaken and he stumbled backwards, reaching for something to hold onto. Owun saw him and caught him before he fell. "My God," Reza whispered. "Subhana Allah, Jawad, he is my son."

This was something else that they would need to sleep on, and it was agreed that, for the time being, Jawad, Tyler and Reza would keep it to themselves.

The plain below remained calm and quiet and now the group, wrapped in blankets against the increasing cold, gradually drifted off to sleep.

CHAPTER 80
Wadjet the Fire Jinni

It took a while before Reza managed to fall asleep. His mind was filled with thoughts of Jaffer and how he would approach the issue with him. He already felt more protective towards him and he knew that sooner rather than later, he would have to have a conversation with him. He also knew that such a conversation would be one of the hardest things he had ever done.

He closed his eyes, attempting to visualise how the dialogue would proceed, but at some point, he dozed off. He soon found himself immersed in a vivid dream. He was standing on the plain below, surrounded by the charred, burning, smoking remains of thousands of ghouls. The air was putrid, and he heaved, trying his hardest not to empty the contents of his stomach onto the blackened earth. He had not noticed before, but White Wolf was there with him. So was Wadjet. She had the appearance of a complete human woman, her normal form according to White Wolf in the dream.

White Wolf introduced Wadjet to Reza as if they were meeting at an elaborate conference or a dinner party, but Reza found this to be perfectly normal; such is the nature of dreams. The party continued and, after a brief conversation, Reza took them to meet the group.

Within this surreal fantasy world, the move from the battleground of dead ghouls, to the group on the hillside, was instantaneous. Wadjet was introduced to the group and she promised not to disrupt the human world, except to gain some influence. Nobody questioned what gaining some influence meant and, slowly, the dream evaporated.

They awoke and Reza, keen to relay his dream to the rest, was shocked to discover that all of them had experienced the same dream.

"Are we all agreed, then, that we should allow the summoning? Jawad's question was answered instantly in the affirmative, but White

Wolf interjected.

"To summon Wadjet, each one of you needs to sign your name on the rock that protrudes from the hillside."

They all agreed and headed towards the rock, trying to remain quiet and hidden from the view of the ghouls below. One-by-one they scratched their names into the rock. Reza was last to make his mark and Jaffer's attention was drawn to the name and the handwriting.

"Your full name is Reza Ahvazi?" Jaffer asked.

"Yes, why?"

"I was adopted," Jaffer replied. "My true father had given me away. He clearly did not want me... did you?"

Reza opened his mouth to speak but the words stuck in his throat like a chicken bone.

"You are my father, are you not? Reza Ahvazi, the man who threw his only son into the arms of strangers. I know this to be true for my parents, those who cared for me all my life, told me so."

Jawad, Hassan and Marie had overheard the conversation and waited, wondering how Reza would respond. The Persian sighed and stepped towards Jaffer.

"Keep away from me. Just tell me why you rejected me!" Jaffer's voice revealed his anger and sadness and Reza shed a tear. Whether it was noticed by Jaffer, he could not tell, but he wiped his face with his sleeve and looked his son straight in the eye.

"I only found out yesterday that you are my son, but you are wrong to assume I did not want you."

"Don't lie to me. Just answer my question and tell me why!"

Reza sighed. "I need you to understand. When your mother died, I was distraught and away fighting. I cast my soul into every battle to rid myself of the melancholy I was experiencing.

"When I found out you were alive, my thoughts were not for me but for you."

Jaffer huffed with disdain, but Reza continued. "It is true. My immediate thought was what sort of life would you have with me? I know nothing about caring or providing for a child and most of the time I would be away, leaving those tasks to others. So, I decided to find you another who would love you and care for you as their own; care for you as I could not."

He paused briefly when Jaffer shook his head.

"Did you not have a fine life until your adoptive parents were taken from you?"

"They were not 'taken' from me. They were butchered!" Jaffer was crying. He wiped the tears from his face and looked away.

Reza repeated his question. "But was your life not fine before that day?"

"Yes but…" Jaffer's voice broke as emotion gripped him harder. He looked hard at Reza and took a deep breath. "You're all I have left, and I don't even know you," he added, finally breaking into a flood of tears.

"That is not entirely true, Jaffer," Reza said, waving his hand in the direction of the others. "We are all your family now and you know me fairly well by now." He watched his son's crying stop and stepped forward. Jaffer's head was down, his eyes focusing on the ground and Reza gently lifted his chin with his finger until their eyes met again. He expected greater resistance from a youth of his age, but there was none. "I promise, Jaffer, to protect you for the rest of my life and to try to be a father to you. That is all I can do now, and I hope you will accept it."

Jaffer walked away. "I need time," he called back.

Jaffer was yet to add his name to the rock and Jawad asked him to do so. The boy, full of a young boy's anger, huffed and marched over to the rock. Taking a dagger from the ground, he carved his name, with all of his anger directed to the carving.

Suddenly, an explosion occurred on the plain below and an immense light bathed the area white. Wadjet appeared among the ghouls while most of them still slept. She spat fire so powerful that it was as if the sun itself had fallen to the plain and killed them. As the plain fell silent and the light dissipated, the group walked cautiously across the crematorium of ghouls.

The other-worldly sounds and smells that the humans had experienced since arriving in the Jinn world, were now masked. The smell of burned bodies attacked the humans' senses like a wave striking a rocky shoreline. The silence seemed to enhance their sense of smell and some members of the group heaved. Others vomited. Wadjet had incinerated every one of the ghouls that had, earlier, filled the plain. As they burned, their screams and the odour of singed hair and flesh had become so intense that the humans had covered their noses and ears, but still the odour fought its way through. The intensity of the screams could easily have sent a person insane if it had been prolonged, but it was not. The mass execution had lasted less than a minute.

Now, having taken the female human form, Wadjet stood at the centre of her devastation, a conflicting image of vicious devastation with incredible beauty at its centre.

The humans walked across the plain, their feet trampling the charred bodies as they went. Wadjet greeted them with a smile but nobody reciprocated. They stood, stone-faced, eyeing her with suspicion. Finally, Jawad spoke. "What do you seek in return for this favour you have afforded us?" He asked.

Wadjet continued to smile and glanced towards Zaydussia. "You know the answer to your own question, Jawad," she said. "For all of you met me in your dreams and my demands were made clear to you then. To take me to the earthly world where I may gain some influence."

"And what," interjected Hassan, "do you mean by 'some influence'?"

"Enough to free me from this world, remove my ties to those who seek to summon me and enough to make me a ruler over others. Nothing more."

"In the dream, your wish was to spend a year in our world. Has that changed?"

She fluttered her eyelids flirtatiously and Hassan cleared his throat. "All right," he said. "A deal is a deal. I don't trust you, but I know we have no option now. You have helped us immensely and now we should grant you what you want. So, let us go."

"I'm not sure about this deal we've made with Wadjet," Reza said.

"I feel the same way," replied Jawad, "but what choice did we have? Now, we must enter Zaydussia, find Zaman and enter the portal he will create for us."

The trek to the city took longer than they thought it would. None of them had noticed how exhausted they were when they began the relatively short walk. They climbed the invisible staircase and arrived in the city bedraggled, dusty and weak. They were confronted at the gates by two formidable Jinn guards. Two mighty warriors, each one at least nine feet tall, dressed in suits of metal that covered their entire bodies from head to foot. They were armed with huge swords and sunlight glinted off the blades into the faces of the arriving group of travellers.

"Halt!" The order was given by both guards, simultaneously. Their voices boomed across the plain below.

The group stopped in their tracks and Jawad began to speak.

"We have come to…"

"Silence!" The guards' order stopped Jawad dead and the guards continued. "We know who you are and why you are here. What we don't understand is why you have brought that creature with you." There was a moment of silence before the guards spoke again. "You may reply, Jawad," they said.

He turned to glance at White Wolf, somewhat confused as to why she would not be permitted entry. The guards saw his glance and spoke again.

"Not the wolf, that thing there," they said, both pointing at Wadjet.

Nervously, Jawad explained what had happened and asked that the guards seek permission from Zaman to bring Wadjet with them.

"Wait here," said one of the guards, speaking alone for the first time. He sheathed his sword, turned and banged his enormous fist on the vast metal doors that sat snugly within the surrounding walls of the city. A moment later, the doors opened, and the guard entered the city.

"May I ask you a question?" Hassan asked the remaining guard.

The guard nodded and Hassan continued; "I have noticed that while you have been negotiating, this castle has left its position in the sky and settled on the plain. Why is that?"

The guard's expression did not shift at all and his response was blunt. "Too much power is needed to sustain the city's flight and we need all our remaining power to fight the Evil One's minions."

As he stopped talking, the great doors behind him opened again and the second guard re-emerged. He stood alongside his companion and once again drew his sword.

"You may enter," they said, simultaneously, before standing aside to allow the travellers to walk into the city.

Inside, Zenith was waiting for them. After greetings were over, the

Jinni approached Wadjet and whispered something into her ear. Then, he led the group to Zaman in the citadel. The Overseer was seated on his oversized throne, a holographic image before him that showed the Scottish Highlands. Zenith brought the group to the hologram and stopped.

"In a moment, you will step into the portal and enter the land of the Scots. With White Wolf's help, you must find your friend Sami and together you will fit the pieces of your stories together to calculate your next move."

Jawad was confused. He glanced at Reza and Hassan and saw the same look on their faces that he was displaying. "Friend? Singular? What of Robin?" he asked.

"Sami will explain all when you arrive. Now, you must go."

Zenith stepped aside to allow the group to move towards the hologram, but Hassan stopped to speak to the Jinni. "What did you say to Wadjet?" he whispered.

"A warning. Now, you must go," Zenith replied, pointing at the hologram.

CHAPTER 81
January 1314 A.D.
The Travellers Emerge

One-by-one, the human travellers emerged from the Jinn realm into their own world. They stepped, cautiously, into the land of the Scots. They were followed by White Wolf and Wadjet and, upon treading onto the Earthly plain, the wolf Jinni immediately fell silent. Wadjet looked around and smiled. She hurried to get alongside Jawad and touched him on the shoulder.

"I will leave you now, Jawad, but I'm certain our paths will cross again before long."

Jawad frowned but said nothing. He watched her walk away, in the opposite direction to his own. The group walked on, eventually arriving in a small village. There, they conversed with locals to gain information about the lay of the land; physical and political.

They soon discovered that England had a new king, and that he had already secured his authority over the English barons and over the Welsh. He was Edward I, known as Longshanks and his efforts were, for the time being, firmly fixed on maintaining the new Kingdom of England and Wales. Soon, however, the Scots too would come under his iron fist. Political tensions were high. The Scots had staged many rebellions and besieged the town of Carlisle several times. Edward was determined to crush the Scots once and for all and was now marching armies to Scotland.

Meanwhile, Scotland had crowned their own King, Robert de Bruce, a year earlier, much to the indignation of Longshanks.

As the travellers left the village, they could see the English campfires in the distance. The army was impressively large and, glancing at the Scottish landscape, Hassan wondered why such a huge force was necessary to take a barren country such as this.

What the villagers did not know and, thus, what the travellers had also not realised, was that Longshanks had died on the journey north. His son, Edward II, was now leading this vast army against the Scots.

Hassan silently recalled the many similar such armies he had seen and faced in battle over the decades. He shook his head, sighed and then turned to Jawad and Reza. "I understand why my aging process has altered, Jawad. I was there, in the world of the Jinn before but I don't understand why it has happened to you or Reza or Sami."

"I was there, Hassan," Jawad replied. "Granted, it was a fleeting visit, but I was there, and you saw me."

"Ah Yes," Hassan said. "The dream, and Marie was also there in a dream, but Sami and Reza?"

"We were also there," Reza replied. Zenith and the angels moved us there for our protection, but surely everyone dreams. Why did the dream state only affect Jawad and Marie?"

Hassan smiled. "I remember Zenith telling me that some people enter the land of the Jinn in their dreams; but not all people." He paused and shook his head. "I don't really understand it all. I suppose some things are beyond our understanding and maybe should never be questioned."

The others nodded their agreement and their journey continued. For the next two days, White Wolf led them across the rugged terrain of the Highlands, until they arrived at the town in Badenoch where Sami and Cecelia had arrived some time before. They found a lodging house and Amalric suggested that all but he, Bohemond and Marie, remain inside. They were from France and France was allied with Scotland. Owun, however, was ostensibly an Englishman. Although he had Celtic roots on his mother's side, he spoke only English and a smattering of French. He would immediately raise suspicion among the Scots, as would the darker skinned foreigners in the group.

The trio left the Inn. It had not taken them long, before drunken soldiers began wagging their tongues uncontrollably. Within the hour, they returned to the rest of the group, to inform them that a man fitting Sami's description had arrived some time ago with a nun and that they had been residing at the Laird's manor ever since.

"Nobody could confirm seeing Robin. Just Sami and the nun," said

Bohemond. "And it seems that our Syrian friend has secured himself a powerful position as leader of the Laird's private army."

Jawad smiled at this. "That's Sami. He is a very resourceful man indeed." He paused for a moment and then added, "In the morning, I want Amalric and Marie to find a way of meeting with the Laird. Let people know that you are friends of Sami. Soldiers should be good sources of information. Speak to them."

The room went quiet and Amalric spoke again. "There is a problem. A group of French mercenaries arrived at the Laird's manor some time ago, led by a man named Cedric." He cleared his throat and then continued. "The description fits a man that Bohemond and I know... er, knew well. He is now an old man but, by all accounts, still a formidable presence."

Jawad interrupted. "What is the problem? Isn't this a good thing?"

Bohemond stepped forward. "No. Apart from the fact that neither of us trust Cedric, there is the issue of his obvious old age; he must be 60 at least and will look it. Compare that with our relatively young appearance. He will be suspicious of us and he may already have the ear of the Laird."

Jawad sighed. "Who then?"

"I can go with your wife." It was the Jewish translator. "We both speak French. We simply tell people that we have journeyed through parts of Europe, since leaving the Holy Land, and that I have been the lady's personal interpreter."

Jawad pondered this for a moment and then looked to his wife for advice. She nodded. "It makes sense, Jawad. In fact, it is our only option."

"But, did you not tell me that it was this Cedric who found you on the Spanish ship when you arrived, as a stowaway in Acre? Surely, he will recognise you too?"

Marie smiled. "My dear husband, I may still look very young, considering my age, but when Cedric last saw me, I was a girl who looked like a boy, dressed in rags with my hair cut very short. I don't think he will see that person when he sees me now, so fear not." She paused before adding, "besides, we will take White Wolf with us. As protection."

So, it was agreed and within the hour, the pair had headed off to the

Laird's manor.

As they walked towards the Laird's manor, Judah began to talk. At first, Marie thought he was muttering to himself, but then she realised he was speaking to her.

"Sorry, what did you say?" She asked.

"What we experienced, in that other world. Does it not leave you in shock, wondering about everything we thought we knew?"

"I suppose it does, although it isn't the first time I have come in contact with the Jinn or visited their world, so maybe I have become used to it." She paused for a moment. "It is as much a part of life as those trees," she said, pointing ahead of them.

"But it challenges everything I was taught; everything I believed. How do you go back to anything normal after that?"

Marie smiled. "This is normal, for us. We are privileged, don't you think? To know what we know while the world is shrouded in ignorance."

Judah nodded and sighed. "It may take some time before I am as relaxed about this as you are. My biggest problem is that I want to shout about it from the rooftops, but I know that people would call me crazy or possessed."

The remainder of the walk to the Laird's home was completed in silence. An hour had passed since they left the group in the town, and now they approached the outskirts of the Laird's walled home. A guard stopped them and asked their business. They explained that they were seeking Sami, a friend of theirs.

"Your names?"

Marie cleared her throat. "Tell him it is Marie, wife of Jawad."

The guard looked at Judah and assumed he was the husband she mentioned. He seemed suspicious but he called over a young boy, who was seated on the grass behind him. He asked the boy to find Sami and inform him that two people, claiming to be friends of his, were at the gate.

"Marie and Jawad are their names, apparently, and a wolf," he added, rather sarcastically.

Marie was about to say that Judah was not her husband but thought better of it. It would raise further questions from the guard, so she remained silent and watched the boy run off with his message.

Minutes later, Sami arrived at the gate and hugged Marie as soon as he saw her. After a warm embrace, he turned to Judah, but spoke to Marie. "And this is?"

"Judah Ben Zakai, a translator from Palestine," she replied.

The guard stared at Marie, clearly irritated at what he saw as her deception, but he said nothing.

Sami looked down at White Wolf. "And who is this gorgeous beast?" He asked, carefully holding the back of his hand towards the animal's mouth.

White Wolf sniffed Sami's hand and allowed him to stroke her behind the ears.

"This is White Wolf. She has served as our guide and protector for many months," Marie replied.

Sami eyed the beast with curiosity and led them towards the house, away from the guard. "Is she from the world of the Jinn?" He asked.

"Yes, and there she could talk, a skill that seems unavailable to her here, I'm afraid."

Sami smiled, held his arm out for Marie to lean on, and led them through a large garden and into the house.

"Come. We have much to discuss," Sami said. "I'll arrange quarters for you where you can bathe and pray."

He called for some maid servants and instructed them to prepare two rooms, with bathtubs and fresh clothes. One of the maids led them up a set of stairs and as they ascended, an old and grizzled soldier approached them on his way down. He glanced briefly at Marie but did not show any recognition. Then, he held out his hand to Sami.

"You must be the Saracen I've heard so much about, er Sami, isn't it?"

Sami shook the man's hand and nodded.

"My name is Cedric. I've been meaning to find you as I understand you oversee the Laird's troops."

Sami said nothing, realising that Cedric had more to say. "My men and I have offered our services to the Laird, so if you tell us what you wish us to do, we will oblige." He held out his hand again and Sami shook it for a second time. Cedric's grip was strong, and he held on far longer than Sami cared for, a clear attempt to appear imposing.

Sami smiled and pulled his hand away. "I will be in touch Cedric, but right now I must escort my guests to their rooms."

Cedric glanced again at Marie, smiled and slightly bowed his head. "Of course, my apologies for the imposition," he said.

Sami asked the maid to lead on and then he followed behind Marie and Judah. Marie looked back at Cedric. He seemed to be staring at her, his eyes piercing and cold. *Has he recognised me?* She wondered.

The thought passed as she reached the top of the staircase and followed the maid along a dimly lit corridor to two rooms at the end.

"I will send someone to fetch you both in an hour", said Sami, as Judah and Marie entered their respective rooms, each with a maid servant.

CHAPTER 82
January 1314 A.D.
The Group are Re-united

Marie explained the problem that the presence of Cedric could pose. Sami considered the situation and decided to send the mercenary and his men on a scouting mission. That way, he could introduce the rest of the travelling group to the Laird. He needed to get permission to use some of the Laird's fighters on the quest ahead of them.

A few hours after the departure of Cedric and his company, Jawad's group arrived. They met first with Sami, a meeting that was long awaited and full of emotion. They were introduced to Cecelia and then they discussed everything they knew so far. Sadness settled on the visitors when they heard of the death of Robin and, for a while, nobody spoke. The silence was eventually broken by Hassan, who explained everything Merlin had told them. Sami and Cecelia listened intently and then nodded.

"We will leave in two days," he said. "I can't leave the Laird unguarded, so we will have to wait for Cedric and his men to return."

Bohemond was about to protest, but Sami cut him short. "I understand everything you have told me, Bohemond. Nevertheless, we will have to take the risk and hope his suspicions don't create unwanted tension between us."

Marie stepped forward. "I think his curiosity, if not suspicion, is already aroused. I am sure he recognised me yesterday, Sami," she said. "The way he stared as we passed on the stairs. I'm not sure if he knows yet who I am, but he knows that he has seen me before."

"Then that settles it," replied Sami. We wait for Cedric, treat him with much caution and leave after he has agreed to guard the Laird while we are away."

As he considered the group's tale of Merlin and how they must once again enter the world of the Jinn, a realisation dawned on Sami. *Once Cecelia enters the Jinn world, she will experience the same effect on her longevity as he and the others had,* he thought to himself. He came to a decision that he never believed he would. He would propose to her.

Cedric returned the following day and made his way to the Great Hall, where Sami and his friends were planning their next move. Cedric surveyed the group, his eyes resting temporarily on Marie. Once again, he showed some recognition, but he shook his head, clearly unable to place where he had seen this woman before. He continued to scan the room until he caught sight of Bohemond and then Amalric.

"What is this witchcraft?" He shouted.

Sami replied. "Of what do you speak, sir?"

"Of what do I speak?" He pointed at Bohemond. "Of that." He then pointed at Bohemond and Amalric. "I knew these men when we were far younger, but they have hardly aged while I have grown old. Explain yourselves!"

Bohemond stood and stared directly into Cedric's eyes. "You would not believe us if we told you. Something has happened and we have found ourselves growing older at a far slower rate than you. That is all I can say."

Cedric huffed. "There is evil at work here and, by God, I will find out what it is."

Suddenly, a flash of acknowledgement struck him, and he turned to Marie. "You!" He shouted, pointing at her. "You are Raymond's daughter, that filthy urchin I dragged from the ship, but you too do not show the signs of the passing years on your face."

Amalric stood and took hold of the hilt of his sword. He was ready for a fight, but Marie crossed the room and placed a gentle hand on his arm.

"Keep calm," she said and his grip on the sword relaxed.

White Wolf, however, stood up and snarled at Cedric. For a moment, Cedric's attention was divided between Amalric and the wolf.

"Keep that creature quiet, woman, or it will feel my blade across its neck." Cedric's anger was evident, but his bravado faded as White Wolf took two steps towards him. Cedric took a step back, and fear showed on his perspiring face.

Marie stood, and walked around a chair to Cedric. She touched White Wolf gently and told her to sit. The wolf obeyed and Marie stepped towards Cedric, until she was a few feet away from him.

"Yes, we have aged differently from you and yes, it is something magical," she said. "But it is not Witchcraft and we need your silence on this, sir, for we have an important mission to complete."

She stared into his eyes, but he could not meet her gaze, focused as he was on Amalric and the wolf.

"Failure to do so," Marie continued, "could have untold, catastrophic consequences for all of us."

Cedric kicked out at the chair, stared intently at Marie for a few seconds and then at Amalric and Bohemond in turn. He huffed again and pushed past Bohemond. After one last look back at the wolf, he left the room, slamming the enormous wooden door behind him. Once the thunderous sound it produced had dissipated, for a few moments the group remained silent. Finally, Sami spoke.

"Cedric may become a problem but a problem that will have to be dealt with as and when it arises. For now, we have a mission to plan."

As they began their discussions again, there was a knock at the door. Jawad raised a hand to request silence and then shouted "Come in."

A young boy entered nervously and stood, head down, sweat upon his brow.

"Well? Head up and speak up boy!" Amalric shouted in French.

The boy raised his head slowly and looked at Marie. "I am sorry to disturb you my lady, but your maid has fallen ill and has asked for you."

Marie nodded and waved the boy away. "I will be there soon," she said, before turning to Jawad. "If Amina is ill, I must stay here with her."

Jawad's face revealed his unhappiness with this suggestion. To leave her here, with Cedric roaming around in anger, was not something he could countenance. He was particularly concerned that much of Cedric's anger was directed at her. He made to say so to her, but she raised her hand to stop him.

"I know what you are going to say, but my decision has been made. If Amina needs me here, I will stay."

Reza stepped forward and spoke. "Then my remaining men will stay here with you, for protection. I don't trust that Cedric either."

White Wolf stepped forward and sat, faithfully, at Marie's feet. She stroked the animal's head and smiled. "It seems I have plenty of protection." She said to Jawad.

It was agreed and Marie returned to her quarters. She was accompanied by White Wolf and the two remaining Alis, all of whom stood guard outside the room while she helped tend to her maid.

Meanwhile, Sami brought some of his Scottish warriors to the gate that led from the Laird's land to a track that weaved its way towards the Loch. He crossed to Jawad and informed him that he was bringing these men to stay on the Loch's shoreline and wait for their return from the island. Jawad was concerned that they would react badly if they saw the mystical events that were due to unfold. Sami calmed his fears.

"I have explained all to these men and they have witnessed a Jinni in person. They will remain strong and loyal until our return. Fear not. They have sworn an oath on that to me."

Jawad took a deep breath and nodded. He then ordered their walk to the Loch.

CHAPTER 83
May 1314 A.D.
The Meeting Place

On the bank of the Loch, the group of travellers had found the tree that was twisted into the shape of a man on horseback. For a moment, they stood in silence, watching the still waters. There was no wind, but the winter air had numbed their hands and faces. Each of them shuffled their feet and rubbed their hands in a vain attempt to warm themselves up and the sniffs and coughs were increasing the longer they stood in that one spot.

"Are you ready Jaffer?" Jawad asked, placing a comforting hand on the boy's shoulder.

"I'm ready," Jaffer replied, stepping forward to the water's edge. He then took a deep breath and closed his eyes before reciting what Merlin had instructed him to recite. "Bismillaahir Rahmaanir Raheem. Alhamdu lillaahi Rabbil 'aalameen. Ar-Rahmaanir-Raheem. Maaliki Yawmid-Deen. Iyyaaka na'budu wa Iyyaaka nasta'een. Ihdinas-Siraatal-Mustaqeem. Siraatal-lazeena an'amta 'alaihim ghayril-maghdoobi 'alaihim wa lad-daaalleen." He said and the water began to shimmer.

The entire area was suddenly cloaked by a haze and, right before their eyes, an island materialised at the centre of the loch. A path then appeared that led from the loch edge to the island. Cautiously, Jawad stepped onto it, followed by the rest of the group. Sami's men marvelled at what they had witnessed, but they did as he had asked and took positions on the shore. That enabled them to keep a lookout for anyone approaching from any direction.

As the group crossed, Owun turned to Reza and asked him what the verse was in English. Reza smiled and relayed it to him. "In the name of Allah, Most Gracious, Most Merciful. Praise be to Allah, the Cherisher and Lord of the worlds; Most Gracious, Most Merciful; King of the Day of Judgment. Thee do we worship, and Thine aid we seek. Show us the straight path, the way of those on whom Thou hast bestowed Thy Grace, those whose (portion) is not wrath, and who go not astray," he said, before adding "It is a chapter, not a verse and it is called Al-Fatihah, The Opening".

Owun nodded. "It was beautiful," he said.

Arriving on the island, Sami pulled Cecelia to one side.

"Now that we are in the world of the Jinn, I must speak to you," he said.

She stopped. He took hold of her hand and bowed to kiss it. "Will you marry me, Cecelia?"

Stunned, Cecelia struggled to answer for a moment and Sami began to regret his decision to ask her. He released her hand and stood upright again. He was about to apologise and seek forgiveness for his impudence, when she replied.

"Yes," she said. "Yes, absolutely, yes." Her smile was bright enough to light a room and Sami released a deep breath he had been unconsciously holding in. He reached for her hand again, but she moved past it and took him in an embrace.

"Thank you," he said.

"Sami, Cecelia, stop dawdling." The shout came from Hassan. Cecelia bit her upper lip and then laughed. Sami smiled and they half ran to catch up.

From the shoreline, the Scottish soldiers watched as the island shimmered, then faded and vanished. The Loch returned to its calm state and birds, that had fallen silent during the island's materialisation, began to sing again.

Some of the soldiers made the sign of a cross. All of them were visibly shaken but they soon regained control of their senses. They took up strategic positions to guard the area and waited.

Meanwhile, on the mysterious Isle of Avalon, the quest for the staff of Merlin continued. The group, led by Jawad and Jaffer, trekked through woodland until they reached the location where they had previously met with Merlin. Where he had stood before, there was now an empty space in the rockface, but to the right stood the staff. It was not elaborate. In fact, it was unexceptionally plain; the sort of staff a simple shepherd might fashion from the branch of a tree. A long piece of oiled ash, at the tip of which was a glass orb encased in an iron 'claw'.

Jawad brought Jaffer forward and called Sami to his side.

"It's your time to shine, Sami. Merlin told us that to retrieve the staff, the Biblical verses relating to the discovery of Jesus' empty tomb, must be recited in Aramaic."

Sami shook his head. "I can't."

There was an intake of breath from everyone.

"What do you mean, you can't?" Jawad asked. "Merlin said that you know Aramaic."

Sami nodded. "Yes, I speak Aramaic, but I don't know those Biblical verses."

Jawad glanced at the staff, so near yet out of reach. As he pondered their predicament, Judah stepped forward and touched Sami on the shoulder. "I know them in Greek," he said. "Can you translate them from Greek to Aramaic? Do you speak Greek?"

Sami nodded. "Yes, I do, but which verses are we supposed to use? Doesn't the story of the empty tomb appear in different gospels, worded slightly differently?"

Judah merely smiled. "Shall we try?" he asked.

Sami took a deep breath and nodded. He turned to Jawad.

"This may take some time and we may have to make several attempts at translating until we find the precise wording needed to release the staff.

"I suggest you all rest. Judah and I will find a quiet spot to work."

CHAPTER 84
May 1314 A.D.
Abduction

At the Laird's castle, a messenger arrived for Cedric. The French mercenary ushered the man, surreptitiously, into the house and to his quarters. He was handed a letter and immediately recognised its seal. It was from his paymaster in England. He broke the wax seal and opened the letter, which read:

My eyes and ears from a world beyond this world, have informed me that my half-brother and his band of criminals are housed in the very place where you and your men are stationed. His wife is with him, I am reliably informed. Bring her to me.

It was signed *Alarico*.

Cedric took the note to the fire that illuminated the room. He tossed it into the roaring flames, collected his sword and headed off to gather four of his men. After explaining to them the task they had been set by their employer, they skirted around the areas of the home where people were gathered. They headed upstairs to Marie's quarters and from the end of the landing, they could see two guards and the wolf.

He instructed two of his men to tackle the Wolf, while he and the others would handle the guards. One of the mercenaries kept hidden behind a wall at the end of the dimly lit corridor. He raised a crossbow to his shoulder, took aim and fired. In the relative darkness, the silent instrument of death soared through the air and struck White Wolf just behind the front shoulder blade. She yelped and fell onto her side.

The Alis turned in the direction from which the bolt had come and saw movement. Two men were running towards them, swords in hands. The Alis acted swiftly, drawing their own weapons in an instant and engaging the enemy ferociously. As swords clashed, White Wolf fought through the pain and rushed past the fighting men, launching herself at the men at the end of the corridor. Before the crossbowman could reload, he found his arm locked between the massive jaws of the angry white beast. He screamed and his comrades tried to rush to his aid, but they were too late. White Wolf wrenched at the arm and pulled it from his body. Blood spurted, geyser-like, into the faces of the other men, giving White Wolf time to turn her attentions to them.

Her speed was immense, and the men stood no chance. Their sword swings missed the target and within seconds, all three men were dead. White Wolf, in pain and weakened by the fight, turned her attention to Cedric and the other fighter. She had lost a great deal of blood and, as she glanced down the corridor, her vision blurred. The last thing she saw before passing out, was Cedric manhandling Marie out of her room.

She came around an hour later to find herself in Marie's room. Amina, her face badly bruised where Cedric or the other soldier had struck her several times, had removed the crossbow bolt and was tending to White Wolf's wound.

"He took her. Cedric took my lady, Marie, and I couldn't stop them", Amina whispered as she placed an herb poultice on the wolf's injured shoulder.

White Wolf thought to herself, *I also failed*. Then, she passed out again.

Meanwhile, Cedric had gathered the rest of his men and left the Laird's land. By the time White Wolf had regained consciousness, the mercenaries were well on their way towards England. To avoid unwanted attention from anyone they met on the way, they had gagged Marie, wrapped her in sheets and placed her on a horse. She was, to all intents and purpose, part of a mixture of goods that they would allege were to be traded.

By the time they reached the border, the troop of mercenaries had encountered only one person, a hunter. They had chatted, joked with each other and drunk a great deal of ale, before leaving him in a drunken stupor by the side of the road.

Within a day, they had arrived in Carlisle. Upon arrival at Alarico's land, they were led by guards to the house. It had been enlarged significantly since Cedric was there last. Alarico's leading employee exited the house and handed Cedric a sack. Cedric peered inside. It was filled with gold coins and a note, signed and sealed by Alarico. In the note, he agreed to hand over to Cedric, a hectare of land, South of Carlisle.

Cedric thanked the man before signalling to his men to hand over Marie. They pulled the sheet-covered bundle from the horse, carried it to the guards and dropped it on the ground.

The guards unwrapped the bundle and dragged the semi-conscious Marie to the house. She was taken to a bedroom at the far end of the house and tied to a large four poster bed. Her gag remained in place and her hands remained tied up. There, she was left, alone, for several hours. When the door finally opened, she saw Abbas enter. She froze. The awareness that Cedric had kidnapped her and handed her over to someone else, paled into insignificance, compared with the revelation that she was now in the hands of this half Jinn monster.

She felt the sweat running down her forehead and into her eyes, as he approached her. Frightened beyond belief, she found herself unable to make a sound, even after he ripped the gag from her mouth. She had to pluck up some courage from somewhere. She had to show no fear. She prayed for protection, prayed for courage and finally managed to speak.

"Is this how low you have got, Abbas? Kidnapping. What next? Do you wish to control my mind? Find out where my husband has gone?"

Her captor laughed. "Abbas is no more. I go by the name Alarico now. I am a wealthy, respected, Spanish businessman and I have other plans for you."

Marie tried to glance around the room, to find a way of escape, but there was none. She could see no windows and the door was solid oak, guarded outside. She wanted to say something but could not find words of any significance, so she waited silently for Abbas to continue.

"Oh, and I could control you with my mind, but where is the excitement in that? No. A physical engagement brings far more pleasure." His voice was cold, unemotional.

"My half-brother has not been man enough to afford you with a child, I see. I can remedy that. Correction. I will remedy that. And I will destroy Jawad's life. So much more satisfying than just killing him, don't you think? He will be unable to even look at you or the child, for therein he will always see me."

He paced around her as he spoke. "And you will be unable to give the child away or remove it from your previously barren womb. No, after so long a time without a child, you could never face losing the only one you may ever bear. And thus, I will cut you all without a knife in sight."

Then, he set upon her and she tried to resist him but with her hands and feet tied, there was little she could do. For some time, she wriggled and screamed. She even tried to bite him, but to no avail. The fear subsided, as did her fight. His strength and aggression had beaten her into submission. She cried as he entered her and became virtually paralysed with shame as he ravaged her. *It must have been like humping a corpse*, she thought, but he showed no desire for her to be animated in anyway. When he was finished, he pulled away and she could feel the warmth of his semen, dripping from her onto the bed.

He stood, adjusted his clothes and ran his fingers through his hair. Then, he smirked at her, but the smirk turned to a look of anger and frustration when there was a knock at the door.

"I said I was not to be disturbed." He shouted.

There was a pause and then a nervous voice replied. "I beg your forgiveness Lord, but the English King has arrived and requests your attendance."

Alarico struck one of the bed posts and then turned to leave. As he passed through the door, he called back to her. "I will return later. You may resist me if you wish. It will give me great pleasure if you do."

He left the room and the door slammed shut. The key turned in the lock and Marie began to cry. She found it impossible to stop the tears and finally she cried herself to sleep. At some point, she had slipped into a dream in which she was back in Palestine making love to Jawad on a warm afternoon. There was the click of a door being closed carefully and Jawad pulled from within her to see what was there. Then, the dream changed, and she was alone in the room, staring at the closed door, when she suddenly felt Jawad pulling on her arm and calling her name.

"My Lady, My Lady." Why was he calling her 'My Lady'?

Then, she awoke and saw one of Abbas's maids shaking her to bring her out of her slumber.

"My Lady. I could not bear to hear your suffering any longer and I am going to help you escape."

She was a young woman, maybe twenty-four years old. Marie looked into her eyes, unsure at first whether this was a genuine offer of help or part of Abbas' trickery and games.

"We must go now," the woman said, as she untied Marie.

Marie massaged her wrists and ankles and came to her feet. Then, noticing her nakedness, she began searching around for some clothes.

"I have clothes for you, my Lady." The woman handed her a bag and Marie emptied it of its clothes and got dressed.

"What is your name?" She asked.

"Isabelle, my Lady."

"You are risking your life. Abbas, er, Alarico is a despicable man, capable of the most evil acts. Why are you helping me?"

The woman opened the door slowly and peeked out to check that the coast was clear. Whispering, she replied to Marie. "I know what sort of man he is. I have suffered at his hands. We are poor and he uses that to control us."

"We?"

"I have two children, a boy aged eight and a girl aged five. He has abused me on many occasions, my Lady, with threats to take my children or evict us with nothing but the clothes on our backs. He has even threatened to reveal our times together to the other women and that would kill my reputation forever." She paused and waved to Marie to follow her.

They tiptoed along the corridor and down the stairs, to a door that led to the rear of the building. "I feel that you are someone who can stop him, my Lady, but only if you can leave this place."

Marie touched Isabelle on the shoulder to both comfort and thank her. "Please, don't call me Lady. Call me Marie."

As they left the building and made their way towards the stables, they failed to see the figure standing in the shadows, watching them. Upon reaching the stables, Marie saddled a horse, hugged her saviour and set off, at a quiet walk initially, out of the compound and onto the road north.

Isabelle watched her leave, sighed and turned to head back to the house but as she stepped out of the stables she was grabbed from behind. A strong arm wrapped around her neck. She tried to struggle and was about to scream when a second assailant stepped out of the shadows. It was Alarico. He held a finger to his lips, an instruction for her to remain silent. Her heart was pounding and a bead of sweat ran down her temple. She held back her scream.

"Isabelle, oh, Isabelle, my dear servant. I am so disappointed with you." Alarico's voice was cold and threatening. He stepped towards her and stared into her eyes. "I'm sure you're wondering about the King. Is he here? Does he know what I'm doing?" He laughed and shook his head. "My dear woman, the King's arrival was a ruse. He is not here. Not yet anyway, but he is on his way, so I must conclude our business now, before he arrives."

"Please Lord. I know I have done wrong but please don't kill me. I have children to care for."

Alarico's expression did not change. Nor did his tone. "Not anymore."

Hearing this, Isabelle's body fell limp and she became a dead weight in the arms of the man restraining her. Alarico stepped away from her, crossing the yard to a cart. He pulled back a tarpaulin and revealed the bodies of Isabelle's children. She could restrain herself no longer and her scream pierced the air like an arrow through flesh.

Alarico smiled. "Do you think I care that you let the woman go? No. It is what I had hoped. I had seen you taking an interest in things that do not concern you. I saw you lingering near her room and I wanted you to help her. She carries my child. Of that, I am certain, and now she will take it back to her husband, that interfering half-brother of mine."

He approached her again, his face almost touching her own. His finger poked into her forehead and he forced her head backwards. "Yet, still I am disappointed with you. I promised you that if you challenge me your children will suffer. As you can see, they have."

He paused for a second and then continued. "And suffer they did. I'm surprised you didn't hear their screams. Delightful, it was."

She found her voice, feeling now that she had nothing more to lose. "You bastard!" She shouted. "May God's curse be upon you, you wicked man." And then she broke down and sobbed.

"God? Do you think such a curse is something I care about? Foolish woman. And do you think I can do nothing to you that will cause more pain than you are already feeling?"

He grabbed her face and squeezed it. "I am giving you to my men, to do with you whatever they please. That is your fate. Enjoy or not, I don't care." He glanced at the man who held her. "Take her away."

CHAPTER 85
The Words

After several hours and multiple attempts at releasing the staff, Sami slumped to the ground, exhausted and disillusioned. They had one more translation to use but his confidence was drained.

"Maybe you should rest," said Judah. "A fresh mind will help us to find the answer that a tired mind is shrouding in fog."

Sami shook his head and forced himself to his feet again. "No. This one must work. We have tried every possible translation of the Greek words into Aramaic, with a variety of possible Aramaic words that could replace the Greek ones. This is the last possible structure. It has to work."

He walked, unsteadily, to the staff and recited the words. Initially, nothing happened, and his head dropped in disappointment, but as he turned to walk away, the staff began to emerge from the rockface. Illuminated, it floated silently towards Sami and stopped an arm's length from his face. He looked at Judah, then Jawad, asking without speaking what he should do.

Jawad shrugged. "Reach out and take it."

Sami reached out his right arm and caught hold of the staff. He tried to move it to where the others were gathered, but it would not budge.

"I can't move it," he said.

Jawad called out to Jaffer. "You need to take it. You are the one that Merlin said has been chosen for the task."

Jaffer crossed the cave and caught hold of the staff. The illumination surrounding it dissipated and he rested its point upon the ground, leaning on it as if it were a crutch. Everyone shouted in excitement and congratulated Sami and Judah for their hard work.

"Now rest Sami." Jawad was insistent so Sami walked to the other side of the cavern, slumped to the floor and quickly fell into a deep sleep.

A few hours had passed when he awoke to find the rest of the group discussing the journey from Scotland, through England to Tintagel in Cornwall. The conversation he joined was becoming quite heated, with Bohemond and Owun in disagreement about the route to take.

"If we go overland, we risk encountering King Edward's forces and either explaining why such a diverse group is moving South through England, clearly away from Scotland, or fighting them." Owun was drawing an invisible line on the ground with his finger as he spoke.

"What, then, do you suggest?" Asked Bohemond.

"Ship, through the Irish sea to Cornwall. We can work our passage on board."

"And what of the women?" Asked Jawad.

There was a pause in the discussion and Sami moved across the cave and sat down between Owun and Cecelia, placing one hand on the archer's shoulder and the other on Cecelia's hand.

"The women are being sent to Cornwall for their safety. Sent away from the fighting that is inevitable. We are their bodyguard. Nobody will question our different appearances or languages as many foreign mercenaries are used as soldiers and bodyguards." Sami said. "Owun is right. The sea route is the way to go."

"I'm not sure I can handle another ship," Hassan called out.

"Isn't it worth suffering a bit of seasickness, if it gets us to Tintagel faster and more safely?" Bohemond asked.

Hassan shrugged. "I suppose so," he replied.

"Then it is agreed," said Jawad. "But first we must return to the town and pick up Marie, Amina, the Alis and White Wolf."

As they headed to the walkway across the lake, Reza turned to his son. "I hate boats too," he whispered. His son smiled but said nothing.

As they neared the water's edge, they spotted Amina and White Wolf with the troops they had left behind. Stepping onto the land, Jawad went straight to Amina. "Why are you here?" He asked. "Are you better?"

Her face was forlorn. Something was wrong. "What is it Amina? Where is Marie?"

She sighed and began to cry. Jawad caught hold of her shoulders and made her look him in the eye. "What has happened, Amina?" His voice revealed his concern and some impatience.

"Cedric and his men took her. They killed the Alis and wounded

White Wolf. I treated her for the last few days but all I could think of is the Lady Marie."

Jawad stroked her hair. "It isn't your fault. Tell me what happened."

As she related the events of the day when Marie was snatched, the rest of the group chatted with the soldiers, informing them of what they had seen and showing them the staff.

"But I heard Cedric mention Carlisle, and someone called Alarico. He called him their paymaster," Amina said.

"Then, we must go to Carlisle." Jawad said. Then, he called to the others; "We must travel to Carlisle first, so it seems we will be journeying overland after all. We will undoubtedly meet the English on our way, so let us first go to the Laird and gather his forces."

He approached the unit of the Laird's soldiers, some of whom appeared shaken, even suspicious, about what they had witnessed. Walking up to their unit commander, he spoke. "Is there a problem?"

The commander shifted, awkwardly, shuffling his feet as if he were about to start a kind of ritualistic dance.

"Well?" Jawad asked, more forcefully.

The commander glanced at his men and then at the floor.

"Look at me Stuart," Jawad said, assertively. "Tell me what is wrong."

The commander took a deep breath, glanced again at his men and then looked Jawad in the eye. "They're worried that if anyone finds out what happened here, well, er…"

Jawad interrupted. "The Church, you mean. The priests. If they find out. Is that it?"

The commander nodded, still shuffling, uncomfortably.

"Then don't mention it to anyone, ever. What you have seen goes no further. We came to the Loch to find a clue and we found it."

The commander nodded and proceeded to instruct his men. Satisfied, the entire group headed back through town to the Laird's manor house. Upon arrival, Sami found the Laird standing with a man he had not seen before. Not dressed in fineries, the man nevertheless had the air of someone with power, influence and authority. He wore his hair quite long, but he was by no stretch of the imagination a handsome man. Sami walked towards the Laird, who held out a hand to his Saracen warrior.

"Sami let me introduce you. This is Robert de Bruce, King of Scotland. I have told him about you and your friends, and he has been keen to meet with you all and discuss the situation regarding the English forces."

Sami nodded, rather than bowed. "It is an honour, your Majesty," he said.

The Scottish King took him by the arm and led him to the Great Hall. "Dispense with these formalities," he said. "I am not your King, after all, Sami and I understand your religious rules regarding bowing. We must talk."

He turned to the Laird. "Bring them in when you have concluded your business," he said.

The Laird beckoned to Jawad and Reza to join him. "I am so sorry about your wife, Jawad, and for your loss, Reza. If there is anything I can do to help, don't hesitate to ask. And Reza, your men were given an Islamic burial, as instructed to us by the maid, Amina. I hope that does not cause any offence."

Reza nodded. "Thank you. That is very kind of you."

"And how is Amina now? She was unwell, I hear."

Jawad sighed. "She had a fever, which has passed, praise Allah."

The Laird nodded. "Come now," he said. "Let us not keep the King waiting."

In the Hall, Robert de Bruce sat at the end of the large oak table, two of his advisers either side of him. He looked up as the Laird and his companions entered the room. The Laird and most of the others bowed as they entered but Jawad, Sami, Reza, Jaffer and Amina remained upright.

"Do you not bow to the King?" De Bruce asked, teasingly.

Jawad replied. "Our religion forbids us to bow to anyone other than God."

The Scottish King stared long and hard at him and then laughed. He banged his right hand on the table. "Muhammadans, eh?" He asked.

"We prefer to be called Muslims, but yes." Replied Jawad.

The King laughed. "Well, I wish some of our Scottish barons took that view when in the presence of the English royals." He waved his hand to the seats. "Please, join us. I am only fooling around with you. I fully understand your customs and I understand you are a prince, Jawad."

"Former prince. Now I am just Jawad."

The King nodded and invited them all to be seated.

As they took their seats, Sami noticed De Bruce was scowling at Cecelia and Amina. "Is the presence of our women a problem?" He asked.

The Laird leant over and whispered to Sami. "You must address the King as 'Your Majesty'."

De Bruce placed a hand on the Laird's arm and winked. "It is fine, my friend. The Muhamma... er, Muslims, believe only God can be afforded such titles and I must say I find some appeal to their view." He turned to Sami. "I apologise if my face appears stern. It is how I am, even when I'm joyous. No, sir, these beautiful women are not a problem, just a surprise. If you include them, then so shall I. Now, let us discuss the impending war with the English."

After lengthy discussion, it was decided that they would move south, straight into the path of Edward's approaching forces. King Robert de Bruce would deploy them as an advanced party, with a troop of the Laird's men. Following Sami's advice, they would confront the English at Bannockburn.

Meanwhile, Marie's journey north was delayed as she made every effort to avoid the English forces. For days, she was forced to hide out in wooded land, taking to the roads only after dark. By the time she reached the Scottish border, an advanced guard of the English Army was approaching close behind her. The remaining English troops had stayed in Carlisle. She took shelter within the thick undergrowth and waited for the troops to pass. Suddenly, as she listened to the sound of marching boots resound in the quiet of the desolate surroundings, she heard a voice.

"They are many, for an advanced troop, don't you think?" It was a female voice and Marie jumped slightly in shock. "Don't move and don't speak," the voice continued.

Marie was desperate to look, to see who this person was but was concerned about attracting the attention of the troops. *Is this woman standing?* She thought to herself. *And, if so, why hasn't she been seen?*

"Stay quiet," the voice said. "They cannot see me, but you can, so turn your head, Marie."

How does she know my name? It isn't Isabelle. This voice was different, more haunting, deeper. Nervously, cautiously, she turned.

"Wadjet? What…"

The Jinni placed a finger to her lips to keep Marie silent. "They can hear you. They can't hear me, so let me speak."

Marie nodded and waited.

"I was planning on travelling through this world, but I crave excitement and realised that you, your husband, your friends are magnets for adventure, for fighting, for exhilaration. So, I stayed close by and saw you being taken. I followed you to Carlisle and then I saw him. Shaytaan's grandson, bold as brass, with wealth and power."

She smiled. "I cannot lie. A part of me was tempted to approach him, join him, but I saw what he was doing to you and realised I had to help."

She paused and glanced at the troops, most of whom had now passed them. "I had a plan to free you but then the servant woman stepped in. Such a brave woman. Foolish, but brave." Another pause and a sigh. "He killed her children, you know. And handed her over to his men. Poor woman. I suppose I could have helped, but that would have involved a direct challenge to Abbas and that would have been a fight I could not win. So, I followed you instead."

She glanced once more at the troops as the last few passed by. "We must get you back to your husband and that means these advanced troops must die. I will return momentarily. Do not move."

Wadjet moved swiftly and silently through the wooded area until she was in line with the middle of the troop of soldiers. She took on the appearance of an old beggar man and shuffled onto the road, stumbling into some of the men. Fearful of attack, they stopped their march and drew their swords. One of them shouted to pass on to the head of the line that they were under attack, but then stopped once he realised it was an old beggar.

"Fuck off, you smelly bastard, before I take your head," he shouted at the old man, who transformed before their eyes into something unearthly.

More shouts went up from the soldiers and those at the front and rear of the line began to converge on the middle, weapons at the ready. Wadjet smiled. For these men it was too late.

As the soldiers burned, their screams carried on the air, like evil banshees in the night. The smell of burning flesh drifted with the wind and Marie wondered if she would ever rid herself of that nauseating odour. Within minutes, the road was charred black and the soldiers were gone. Wadjet returned to Marie, now in her womanly form. She reached down and Marie caught hold of her hand. She lifted her to her feet as if she was light as a feather and their trek North began in earnest. As they travelled, Wadjet began to relate her activities over the past months.

"I spent some time spying on King Edward's army, taking many different forms. I was there when his father died. Poison, some say," she said, with a smile. "I know their plans, their troop numbers, their weapon stockpiles. I know much that I need to pass on to your husband, but we must make haste."

CHAPTER 86
June 1314 A.D.
Carlisle

Several days later, Wadjet and Marie arrived at Loch Tay, about 50 miles North of Bannockburn. They found Jawad and the others camped there with Robert de Bruce. A Scottish army had been besieging Stirling for several months and de Bruce had brought a small troop to the Loch to plan their defences against the English army that was making its preparations in Carlisle. After some lengthy explanation for Wadjet's presence, Jawad took the Jinni to the Scottish King, where she supplied a mass of information about Edward's troop numbers, plans and movements. Asked how she managed to acquire such detailed material, Wadjet simply said that a good spy never reveals their secrets. The King, while intrigued, did not press her on this and was clearly interested in her suggestion that Bannockburn, South of Sterling, was an ideal conflict point. It was something that Sami had already recommended.

Meanwhile, in Carlisle, Alarico was feigning illness to avoid being conscripted to the English King's army. He lay in his sick bed, while servants took care of him. His personal guard protected him, and his workers spread the word that a contagion had begun at the Sauceries.

King Edward was meeting with those Scottish barons who had allied themselves with the English. Also present were another group of England's allies, the Welsh chieftains.

"Have we heard anything yet from our advanced guard?" The King asked, but his question was greeted with shakes of the head and deep sighs.

Then, one man spoke up. "It has been two days Sire, so I sent a scout to obtain information about the whereabouts of the advanced guard. He should return soon."

The King was an angry man and it came as no surprise to those around him that he would lose his temper upon hearing that the whereabouts of the advanced guard was unknown by his commanders. He slammed his fist onto the table, called his chief adviser and stormed out of the room.

"I don't trust these Scottish barons," he said, after they were far enough away to be out of earshot. "I know we need them, but what sort of people fight with their enemy against their own people? Anyone willing to do that cannot be trusted. Keep a close eye on them."

The adviser nodded and the King continued. "Who was sent in the advanced guard?"

The adviser coughed and shuffled, clearly uncomfortable with the question.

"Speak up man. Who made up the advanced guard?"

"Er, mainly Scottish troops, Sire. Some Welsh troops and some English, but mainly Scots."

The King was about to storm off when a man arrived on a horse at great speed. Coming to a halt in front of the two men, he jumped from the horse and ran towards the Hall, almost knocking the King over as he tried to hurry past him.

"You man!" Edward shouted. "Who do you seek in such a hurried state?"

The man stopped and looked at the King. "I am so sorry, Your Majesty. I was in such haste that I did not notice it was you standing here." He bowed.

"Never mind. What word do you have? I take it you were the one sent to find the advanced guard?"

"Er, yes Sire. I, er."

"Well, out with it, man. Where are they?"

"I don't know Sire."

"Don't know? What on earth does that mean?" The King was red in the face now and the messenger was growing increasingly nervous.

"They have gone. Vanished. There is a patch of road that is scorched black and there is armour that has melted into the soot-covered ground, but no bodies and no living soul in sight."

The King dragged the man by the arm back into the Hall and ordered him to repeat what he just said. There was stunned silence on hearing the news, which was gradually broken by mutterings from the men inside the Hall. The King raised his voice above the escalating murmurings.

"It seems to me that either the Scots crossed the border, murdered our men, dragged away the bodies for some inexplicable reason and torched their equipment, or…" He paused and looked at each of the Scottish barons in turn. "Or, the Scottish soldiers in the advanced guard have turned, have taken the few English and Welsh hostage, burned whatever they could not carry and fled across the border."

The muttering began again and a few of the Scottish barons tried to protest but were shouted down by the King. In the backs of their minds, they too wondered if their men had deserted.

The King pondered the situation for a moment, calmed himself and sat down at the large oak table.

"I will not wait for the Scots to come here. I will not wait inside these walls and endure a lengthy siege. Too often, that has happened in the past. Just look at Sterling, for God's sake."

Carlisle, the King knew, was a vital stronghold for whoever controlled it. This was due to its strategic position on the border between England and Scotland, offering the perfect border defence. However, this also made it a town that was continually a focus of Anglo-Scots relations.

When the Scots had made an alliance with France and attacked Carlisle, the former King, Edward I, had sent his army north. He made an example of the people of Berwick, laying siege to the town before sacking it and slaughtering around 8000, which was almost the entire population of the town.

Then, in 1296, the English army defeated the Scots at Dunbar. The Scottish nobles were led away to English prisons and John Balliol, the Scottish King, was stripped of his kingship and incarcerated in the Tower of London. Edward Longshanks had taken Scotland. An English parliament sat in Berwick to govern and tax the Scots and Edward's troops held castles across Scotland. Longshanks' brutality against the Scottish clans had earned him the nickname, the Hammer of the Scots.

Edward I, however, had died on July 7, 1307 near Carlisle, and now his son was leading an English force that would once again attempt to crush yet another Scot calling himself King. Robert de Bruce.

Edward II was a very different type of man from his father, however.

Lacking any patriotic or royal ambition, the young Edward cared only about his amusements. He surrounded himself with sycophantic and wealthy favourites, rather than by efficient men who were instruments for executing his orders.

So, instead of carrying out his father's plans, Edward II had, for far too long, contented himself with military parades. He gave up all thoughts of a conquest of Scotland and left that country's government in the charge of the Earl of Pembroke. The King had retired to England.

So, de Bruce continued to raid. He was only held in check by the numerous castles the first Edward had occupied with English garrisons. The hostility of nobles opposed to de Bruce also kept the new Scottish King at bay. These were nobles who were either with the Comyns during de Bruce's blood-feud with that clan, or, for various reasons, were irreversibly committed to the English side.

The fall of Stirling would remove the last fragment of Edward I's subjugation of Scotland. Even Edward II could not ignore that. The siege of Stirling awoke the new King to the need for action. Without the express sanction of Parliament, he had led this mighty army north and, within a week, in June 1314, he would lead it across the border. Vast quantities of the most advanced equipment had been hauled north and had been attended by a vast baggage train consisting of hundreds of heavy horses and carriages. In one week, his advisers told him, Stirling was pledged to surrender to the Scots unless it received assistance.

"In one week, we move north." The King said, firmly.

So, the mighty English Army prepared to roll to the north-west in what was a hasty and badly organised march.

CHAPTER 87
1314 A.D.
Blàr Allt a' Bhonnaich: The Prelude

On 23rd and 24th June 1314, King Robert knew that the decisive hour had arrived. He dispatched his relatively small force to the shrewdly designated location, the field of Blàr Allt a' Bhonnaich [Bannockburn]. This enabled the Scots to guard the immediate approach to Stirling.

De Bruce turned to his senior commanders, including the French-speaking knights. "I remember our defeat at the hands of this English King's father, when William Wallace banked everything on the field of Falkirk."

He pointed at Falkirk on a map as he spoke. "That battle should have been a decisive victory for us, and it almost was, but Edward had turned it, instead, into a crushing English victory."

Standing upright and looking each man in the eye in turn, he breathed in deeply and continued. "Falkirk will not be repeated at Bannockburn. The English army is void of any commander with the extensive experience of Edward I. My spies tell me that Edward, the son, also lacks the loyalty of his troops that his father possessed."

He asked for the latest information from spies and scouts. The head of Clan MacDonald, one of de Bruce's most important allies, spoke up.

"The English force has left Carlisle and mustered at Falkirk. I believe they expect us to repeat the mistakes of the past and meet them there."

De Bruce nodded. "How many?"

"The English force is estimated to be in the region of thirteen thousand strong Sire," MacDonald continued. "That includes two thousand heavy cavalry and an indefinite number of Welsh and English archers."

This was a substantial force, compared with the estimated six thousand that made up the Scottish army. The English also possessed state-of-the-art equipment, but de Bruce did not seem perturbed. If anything, he seemed pleased.

"Thirteen thousand men is a significant number, but it is at least seven thousand short, of what Edward was seeking in his original summons," he said.

Another of the Clan leaders responded to this. "Yes, Sire. Apparently, Thomas, the Earl of Lancaster has failed to provide any support." He laughed. "He is, by all accounts, dissatisfied with Edward's leadership."

MacDonald added, "There is more good news, Sire."

"Go on." De Bruce said.

"Well, we understand that the English force is attempting to operate with a protracted logistical chain that stretches all the way back to Berwick-upon-Tweed. This will create considerable command problems for them.

"There are also tensions within the army. It appears that Humphrey de Bohun, the Earl of Hereford, and Gilbert de Clare, the Earl of Gloucester both assert that it is their right to lead the Vanguard. Edward, however, was unable to make a decisive choice between them." He laughed again. "So, instead, he appointed them joint commanders."

All the men present in this briefing laughed. "The man is clueless," one of them shouted.

"Perhaps he fucks his wife, daughters and sisters because he can't make a decision," another barked.

The laughing continued for some time before de Bruce interrupted the merriment to focus again on their battle plans. He knew men preparing to fight, to kill, to die, needed this release. However, he still had concerns. His army was half the size of the English force and the bulk of his troops were poorly trained militia men armed only with long spears. Planning would have to be flawless and perfectly executed and the input from experienced, battle-hardened warriors, such as Sami, Hassan, Arslan, Jawad and Reza, would be crucial.

It was decided to divide the Scottish Army into three divisions. Bruce's division included Walter Stewart and James Douglas. There was a small detachment of around 500 cavalry, but they were lightly armed.

However, they were highly manoeuvrable in stark contrast to the English equivalent. They had received training from the Saracen knights in their midst. The Saracens had, after all, used rapid horse attacks efficiently and effectively against the European knights in the Holy Land.

It was evident that the English, with their vast force of men-at-arms, would rely upon customary medieval tactics. Their aim would be to crush the Scottish infantry using the shock of charging regiments. Bruce had to rely upon the stubborn bravery of his footmen. Like Wallace, de Bruce had no masses of horse soldiers and very few archers. What he did have, however, was a group of advisers who had been part of the defeat of the Mongols by a numerically smaller Arab and Turkish force. Their advice would be decisive.

He spoke to Sami as the meeting was being wound up. "The young Edward is nowhere near as sharp as his father. When Longshanks took Wales, the Welsh were adamant that they wanted no English speakers ruling them. Edward promised them that he would give them a prince who spoke no English. He then held up the baby, Edward, his son. "Here is the prince," he announced.

Sami laughed. "Clever bastard".

"Yes, but fortunately for us, his son has not progressed far since that time when he was a babe in arms."

As everyone began to leave the hall, Hassan looked at his father. Arslan was pale and grimacing, clearly in pain.

"What ails you father?" Hassan asked as he approached Arslan, who was pressing his hand against his chest and wincing.

"I'm fine," he replied, through gritted teeth, as he straightened himself up and attempted a smile.

Hassan stepped in closer to allow them to speak in low whispers and not be overheard. "The Mongols call it the cold face. Did you know that?"

Arslan frowned. "What? What are you jabbering on about?"

Hassan sighed. "This attempt to seem as if nothing ails you, worries you or frightens you. They call it the cold face and you're not very good at it."

Arslan, agitated, began to reply but started to cough. He turned away, not wanting to be seen by his son or anyone else in the room. Hassan stepped around him and, as Arslan coughed into an old rag, Hassan caught a glimpse of blood.

"You're coughing up blood, father." He was angry now. "So, tell me what is wrong with you!"

"Keep your voice down," replied Arslan. He glanced over and saw that nobody in the room was paying them any interest. He relented, tried to take a deep breath, felt his lungs struggling and thought better of it.

"I have a canker on my lungs, or at least that is what Doctor Muhammad said, before he went rogue." He shook his head. "He probably lied. It is nothing. It will pass. It is most likely this miserable, cold, damp country we're stuck in."

The coughing started again, and more blood appeared. Weakened, Arslan became unsteady on his feet and Hassan led him to a chair.

"You sit this fight out, father, and get help. There are healers here."

"Pah! Healers? These barbarians know less about human ailments than my horse does." He stopped, glanced around the room and pulled his son towards him. "Tell no-one. You hear me? No-one. Not even Jawad." Hassan was unhappy with this request but nodded in agreement and Arslan continued. "My time is near, and I will die fighting, not tucked up in a warm bed." He laughed, which made him cough again. Then, he rubbed his arm. "Mind you," he added, "a warm bed would be welcome in this bitterly cold land. My bones hurt as much as my chest."

Reluctantly, Hassan agreed not to reveal his father's state to anyone but deep own he felt this would be Arslan's last fight. He pledged to himself to try his best to keep his father alive once the fighting commenced.

CHAPTER 88
1314 A.D.
Blàr Allt a' Bhonnaich: The Battle

De Bruce had to guard against having his flank turned. He also had to avoid a repetition of the English archery tactics that had been so effective against the battle led by Wallace at Falkirk. It was for these reasons that de Bruce had chosen Bannockburn as the battleground. It gave him precisely what he needed. It was a narrow front. His soldiers could be massed there, with fragmented and boggy ground on the flanks. That protected them from being turned.

Where there was boggy ground on the front itself, the shock of the charge would be minimised. Where there was no bog, de Bruce ordered his troops to carefully prepare the ground with iron spikes called calthrops. He also ordered the digging of covered pits that would serve a similar purpose to the calthrops. The bulk of the Scottish cavalry would be dismounted and would be used to strengthen the line of infantry. Only a hand-picked unit of men would be held back, ready to strike rapidly and without warning, once the time was right. De Bruce was unconcerned about being severely outnumbered because he knew that, on the field of battle, the English would be unable to bring their numbers into play.

De Bruce's force of around 600 light horsemen, commanded by Sir Robert Keith, would have far greater opportunity for success, than the heavy cavalry deployed by the English.

For the English, the most important element was the mounted knighthood of Angevin, England. A fully equipped knight wore chain mail, but this was re-enforced with plate armour. They wore steel helmets and carried a shield, a long lance, a sword and, in some cases, an axe or club and a dagger.

The knights' heavy horses were strong enough to carry a fully equipped rider at speed but, as the crusades had shown, these horses were not suited to all environments. De Bruce knew this.

For the Arabs, Turks and Persians in the Scottish ranks, the thought of fighting and killing the Franj knights was welcome. The heraldic designs of the knights were emblazoned on their shields and surcoats, making them an easy target to find.

The surcoats, long cloth garments worn over the armour, were also designed to cover the horse. Soldiers from lower social ranks, such as men-at-arms, wore less armour but did carry a shield. They were armed with short lances, swords, axes, clubs and daggers. These men rode lighter horses, but there were very few among the ranks of Edward's army.

The foot soldiers on both sides had to fight with whatever weapons they had or could find on the field of battle. These could be bows, spears, swords, daggers, bill hooks, or anything else capable of inflicting injury. If they were lucky enough to get them, they would wear metal helmets and quilted garments. The poorer the soldier, the less protection they had from the enemy's weapons.

Edward cast an eye over his army and settled his sight on the knights. As far as he, and most of the upper classes, were concerned, battles were won or lost by the knights. The common men were there to support the knights. He breathed in and smiled.

"Impressive, don't you think?"

His adviser assumed the King was commenting on the size of the army. "Would have been nice if it were bigger," he said.

For a moment, the King was confused. Then, it dawned on him that his adviser was referring to numbers. "Not the size, sir. The knights. They are impressive, are they not?" He did not wait for an answer. Instead, he looked across at the archers. "And our bowmen too. They will be a scourge on the enemy, with arrows like a plague of locusts, reigning down on their barbaric heads."

Two officers had joined them and decided to appeal for caution.

"We must not get over-confident, Sire. The Scots have learned much since we crushed the revolt of Wallace."

"Nonsense, sir. We have our knights and our archers. We will be victorious."

The officers looked at each other and then the one who had spoken, dared to contradict the King again.

"Sire, they have chosen their positions well and they too have knights. Their knights and our knights are predominantly French. They trained together. They know each other and that swampy land will not favour our heavy horses, weighed down with ironclad knights."

The King blew air and waved the men away. As they left, they remarked on the King's naivety and arrogance.

On the Scottish side, it was not long before de Bruce and his army had a foretaste of the coming fight.

"On our flank," a voice shouted. "A detachment of cavalry has made a dash around our flank."

De Bruce saw what the English riders were attempting. They were trying to reach Stirling to relieve the besieged army there. The Scottish King, however, had no need to issue orders. From his vantage point, he watched as a detachment of Scottish infantry intercepted the cavalry attack just in time. The horsemen were routed, driven back. However, one English knight, Henry de Bohun, noticed that the Scottish king was riding, virtually unarmed, along the Scottish line. De Bohun charged towards De Bruce but, as he reached him, the King swerved his horse. De Bohun galloped past the King who smashed open the English knight's skull with a battle-axe.

The remainder of the first day consisted of a few attempted minor incursions by the English, each one being driven back.

Jawad, Hassan and Reza, mounted on light horses on the Scottish left flank watched as masses of mail-clad English knights hurled themselves against the Scottish front. The horses, weighed down by their own bulk and the weighty knights on their backs, were unable to keep their footing in the boggy ground. Many broke legs as their feet stumbled over the pits that the Scots had dug. Those that got through crashed hopelessly onto the lines of Scottish spears. Many of these horsemen were struck by spears. Others fell into the swampy ground when their steeds were attacked with spears or fell in the pits. This was the point at which unmounted knights would move in to finish them off.

Amalric and Bohemond rushed forwards, swords and daggers swinging, thrusting and chopping at the floundering English knights.

Bohemond's sword struck one knight's helmet, causing little damage to the enemy cavalryman. The sword slid off the metal and lodged instead in the neck of the knight's horse. It bucked in pain and panic and the knight fell into the filthy swamp. Bohemond noticed the heraldic imagery on the knight's surcoats. He immediately realised he was fighting against a fellow Frenchman from Normandy, but he did not seem to care. Lifting his sword again, he swung it with two hands, removing the knight's head with a single blow.

Amalric, meanwhile, was engaged in a close-quarter knife fight with an English knight, the two of them writhing in the mud as others fought around them. Bodies of horses and men began to pile high and the stench of battle filled the air. The smell of excrement and urine mingled with the iron odour of spilled blood, which spurred soldiers on to survive. Amalric was holding the knight's arm away from him, keeping the blade he was holding at a safe distance. But the knight was strong and almost twice the size of Amalric, who was growing tired. Just as he thought he would have to release the knight's arm he saw the horseman's face contort. Amalric released his hold on the knight when he saw Bohemond's sword blade appear through the man's chest. Bohemond stood above him laughing, as he used his foot to push the knight's lifeless body away, while pulling his sword towards him.

"Must I keep saving your skin, sir?" He asked, holding out his hand to Amalric. The hand was clasped and Bohemond lifted his former senior officer out of the boggy earth.

Some of the Scottish archers, led by Owun Tyler, were firing over the heads of the main Scottish force, into any attempted advance by the English infantry. It delayed their progress, giving the Scottish force even greater advantage on the battlefield.

"I can't believe we agreed to follow you, Sassenach," one of the Scottish archers said to Owun. The Englishman smiled. "Sassenach I may be," he said, "but you know I'm no friend of those Christian fanatics over there."

The Scotsman laughed. "We're Christians too." He said.

"Yes, but you've not threatened to whip the skin off my bones unless I convert, have you?"

"They did that?"

"Yes, and it would have been more than a threat if I hadn't run off to the Holy Land. Another mistake of mine, fleeing one bunch of crazy Christians to fight alongside an even crazier mob."

"Well, I don't care who you worship, as long as you're fighting with us against the English," the Scotsman replied before unleashing another arrow towards the English infantry.

Jaffer watched the melee from the rear and remembered the Mongols massacring his family and others in Baghdad. He stared at the English army and saw just another imperialist oppressor, trying to subdue people in order to steal their land. His blood boiled and he decided it was time to fight against the enemy. Sword in hand, he ran from the rear of the Scottish forces to the front where the fighting continued in earnest. He saw an English soldier swinging a sword haphazardly but relentlessly at anyone around him. Jaffer ran at him, parried the Englishman's swinging sword to the left and brought his own sword down on the soldier's neck and shoulder. He cringed when he heard breaking bones and went lightheaded at the sight of the blood. Nevertheless, he pulled back his sword and struck again. This time, his weapon pierced the soldier's chainmail and thrust through his stomach. The soldier fell, blood pouring from his wounds and from his mouth.

Jaffer looked down and noticed he was just a boy. He looked no more than fourteen years' old and was screaming for his mother. Jaffer felt sick. He turned away and vomited, but then decided that it would be less cruel to kill the boy outright. He turned back towards his victim and sliced off his head. Then, he vomited again. He wanted to cry. He wanted to run away, but other Englishmen were moving towards him, so he had no choice but to continue fighting.

Meanwhile, the English archers were ordered forward on the Scottish left flank. They moved cautiously and unleashed the first flight of arrows towards the Scottish foot soldiers, but no knights or men-at-arms had been sent with them. With no cover, they were exposed, and a small squadron of Scottish horsemen burst upon their flank and cut them to pieces. Leading the charge was Sami, followed by Jawad and Reza.

Without archers, the English heavy cavalry was unprotected. All they could do was carry out repeated charges into the melee and they very quickly became a huddled, unruly mass. The Scottish infantry rolled forward in unbroken line, led by spearmen. Those knights that were not cut down from their trapped horses, dismounted and charged forward on foot to meet the oncoming Scottish soldiers. Hassan had tried to keep close to his father, but in the melee, they were parted. A knight ran towards Hassan, armed only with a bludgeon. He was swinging it wildly like a man possessed. Hassan remained calm and when the knight was almost upon him, he dropped to the ground and thrust his sword upwards into the knight's groin. A scream of pain cut through the battlefield noise and the man slumped to the ground, clutching his groin and bleeding out.

Hassan looked around to find his father and spotted him some yards away, fighting off a group of four knights. Hassan ran to reach him, jumping over or stamping on dead bodies and fighting off attackers as he went. He was within touching distance of his father when he saw the axe, wielded by a man-at-arms, smash into Arslan's back. It was swung with such a force that the blade became completely embedded in the Turk's back, his spine broken instantly. Hassan launched himself at the axeman and slashed at his arms as he was attempting to pull the axe from Arslan's back. The man screamed in pain, but it was short lived. Hassan whipped a dagger from his belt and stabbed the man in the side of the neck. He bent down to his father, but it was too late. Arslan was dead.

As the battle raged, a band of camp followers descended the neighbouring Gillies' Hill carrying supplies or just to be witnesses to the battle. The English army mistook them for Scottish reinforcements and the vast English army panicked, broke ranks and ran. What followed was a rout.

"Where are they going?" Edward shouted, pointing at the fleeing troops. "Force them back. Force them back!"

The officer made no attempt to stop them. He sighed. "It's over Your Majesty."

"It is not over. We outnumber them. We are English. We can't run from a pack of Scottish savages."

Some of his own Scottish troops overheard him. They turned and left, as did most of the Welsh who had not been slaughtered during their failed archery assault. The Officer watched as the defeated troops fled the battle. He shook his head. "Sire, these 'savages', as you call them, are battle hardened men. Most of our troops are farmers who would normally do very little because our knights would crush the enemy. That has failed, dismally, this time. It is over and we must go before de Bruce pushes on to our position."

Edward, still angry, resigned himself to the fact that he had been defeated. For a moment he was glad his father had not witnessed this humiliation. He turned his horse and followed the departing troops.

This was the worst defeat the English had experienced. Never, since the time of Alfred the Great, had they suffered such an overwhelming disaster. Edward and his senior officers, with the remaining cavalry knights escaped, but vast numbers of the fugitives, leaving the battle on foot, were slain. Their bodies lay in heaps. Many others became prisoners and the Scottish conquerors took possession of enormous spoils of war.

On the field of Bannockburn, the Scots had won their independence and that victory was decisive. The English, however, refused to acknowledge that fact and it would take nearly two decades before they would. It would finally be declared in the Treaty of Northampton. At this moment, however, England's failure to accept Scotland's freedom stirred further anger.

"If they refuse to accept Scotland as an independent country, with its own King," de Bruce said to his clan leaders. "We will become the aggressors."

"We will march on Berwick, the last piece of Scottish soil the English still hold. Douglas and Randolph, you will harry the north of England.

"The English will be in disarray. Their King is weak and his unfailing misrule in the South will mean they are unable to muster any organised attempt to regain what they have lost."

CHAPTER 89
1314 A.D.
Alarico in Carlisle

With the Battle of Bannockburn won and de Bruce forging an aggressive war against a weakened and unstable England, Jawad and his compatriots were released from the Scottish King's service. They decided to journey to Carlisle where, as far as they knew, Abbas, Alarico, still resided.

Approximately ten miles from the town, they camped as night fell. Owun Tyler separated himself from the group and sat in a small clearing, waxing his bowstring. A rustle in the bushes nearby made him stop and reach for his sword, but he relaxed when he realised it was Reza. The Persian did not seem to notice the English archer. He stopped, gazed up at the stars and then stood facing South East. He began to pray, a fixed ritualistic series of patterns that involved bowing and prostrating. During each sequence there were two prostrations, his head touching the dry, dusty soil. Owun was fascinated and watched the entire ceremony in silence.

When Reza was finished, he sat on his heels, knees out in front of him and raised his hands three times. He called out "Allahu Akbar, Allahu Akbar, Allahu Akbar", each call synchronised with the raising of his hands. Once completed, he stood and made to return to the group.

"Reza!" Owun called out.

Startled, Reza turned in the direction of the shout. He had recognised Owun's voice and knew there was no threat. He was somewhat annoyed with himself, however, that the archer had gone unnoticed when he had arrived in the clearing. *Careless,* he thought.

"Owun, what are you doing here?"

"I like to work on my bow alone. I find it more relaxing."

Reza smiled. "Well, I won't disturb you further," he said, beginning to walk away.

"Reza. Please join me," Owun replied, patting the ground with his hand. "I have questions to ask."

Reza sat down on the ground beside the archer. "Go ahead, friend." The air was cold, and Reza rubbed his hands together to make himself feel warm.

"Well, I have to admit, this religion of yours intrigues me." Owun said. "You have no statues, no relics, no symbols, no Mosque here either. Yet, you stop, you pray to an unseen God, with no desire to give that god form or shape. No attempt to make god human. Why is that?"

Reza smiled. "Allah is not human, my friend and, strictly speaking, Allah is neither male nor female. The term 'He' is used to simplify for humans. And He is beyond the confines of time, of life as we understand it. We need no building to pray, to worship what we cannot see."

Owun was frowning, not from confusion but out of thoughtfulness, as he pondered Reza's words. Reza realised this and allowed him time to think.

"You will need to leave that philosophical notion with me Reza so I will ask a different question. I have watched you pray on many occasions. I have watched the others too. They often place a mat down for prayer, but you do not. You place your head in the dirt."

He paused for a moment, collecting his thoughts, choosing his words carefully. "And when indoors, you put your head on a small stone. The others do not and…"

Reza interrupted. "I see you have many questions but let's deal with one for now. We Shi'a believe the Muslim at prayer should place himself in the lowliest of positions when prostrating to Allah. Our head should touch the earth, the dirt as you call it. What you call a stone is in fact a tablet of clay—the earth, brought indoors."

He smiled again and then stood up. He reached for Owun's hand and pulled him to his feet. "Let us return to the others."

"I want to learn Arabic," Owun said suddenly, taking Reza by surprise.

"Well, I was not expecting that. Why?" He asked.

"So that I can read your Quran."

Reza raised his eyebrows but thought Owun's request would soon be forgotten once their mission continued.

With the rising of the sun, the group's quest continued. Most of them had rested well and now they prepared to enter Carlisle, disguised as merchants. There were no Scots among them, so they did not believe their arrival would raise any suspicions. They walked their horses, rather than arriving at the town on horseback, which some might see as a threat. The women had gathered blankets to sell and the men were planning to pose as purchasers of goods.

As they walked slowly along the main road into town, Alarico was within the secure confines of his home, trying to relax. He was, however, plagued with thoughts of lost influence; thoughts that had begun as the town witnessed the bedraggled and defeated English army making its way back home.

"I should have sold more arms to them." He muttered to himself, thinking about the wealth that the town's other providers of swords and other weaponry had built up by selling to both sides.

"Yes, you should."

The voice startled Alarico. He jumped from his seat and reached for a sword lying on the table before him. He leaped across his bed, but before he could catch hold of it, the weapon flew from the table and lodged itself into the wall behind him.

"You don't need that," the voice said. It was a man's voice, deep and gravelly, full of menace.

Alarico turned in its direction and saw a being that was human-like but not quite a man. The creature's facial features were unlike anything he had seen before and kept shifting, as if this creature's form lacked permanence.

"Who, what are you?" Alarico was nervous. Was this one of his grandfather's emissaries, a demon of the Dark Lord, or was it from his enemies?

The creature gradually took the form of a human man and stepped forward to within touching distance of Alarico. Then, it laughed. "Sauces. Huh. Sauces? What in hell were you thinking? Weapons and war, Abbas. That is how we break God's hold on this world. Have you learned nothing?"

Alarico was taken aback by the visitor's use of his real name, but he said nothing. Waiting seemed to be the appropriate thing to do.

So, the visitor continued. "Your half-brother is on his way to find you and there is nothing we can do to help you. I doubt, somehow, that your sauces will be of much assistance and we cannot permit you to leave the town."

Abbas stood. "Then what do you expect, and I ask again, who are you?"

The visitor sat. Behaving differently from Abbas to let it be known who had the authority and power in this meeting. "Who am I? I am Murrah al-Abyad Abu al-Harith, The White One, father of the Light, Malik al-Abyad, the White King, the lord of the Moon. I am closest to our Master, Shaytaan, so you must heed my words."

He waved his hand up and down, indicating that Abbas should sit. For a moment, Jawad's half-brother considered refusing the request, but if this really was the White King, he would be a fool to resist. So, he sat and Murrah stood. Then, he continued.

"You and your men must stop your half-brother and his troublesome band of followers. They must not be permitted to reach the gateway, over which we are so close to gaining control.

"They have the Jinni's staff and will seal our entrance to this world for more than a thousand years if they can. So, you must stop them, even if it costs you your life. Do you understand?"

Abbas nodded.

"One more thing," continued Murrah. "Your half-brother is also in possession of a potion which would transform you from what you are back to human form. Your power, your influence, your ability to force change in this world, will be gone forever. So, be on your guard."

Without warning, Murrah collapsed into a puddle of water on the floor, which evaporated instantly. He was gone and Abbas was alone once more.

The room fell silent and Abbas' heart rate fell. Briefly, he felt relaxed, but his sense of serenity was broken by a loud knock at the door.

"Enter!" He shouted.

A servant entered and bowed slightly.

"Well? Speak up boy!" Abbas said, his voice raised.

"Lord, there is a group of people entering the town and one is the woman who fled from here several weeks' ago."

448

Abbas called to his personal guard and together they followed the boy. The messenger was known to all of them, but they had been fooled. Wadjet had taken the boy's form and she led them away from the safety of the main house into a quiet corner of the town. The men grew nervous as they approached an empty square, lit only by the reflection from the moon.

"Here?" Abbas called out. "Why have you brought us here boy?"

All the guards had drawn their swords, aware that this was a trap. They looked around, trying to discern movement in the blackened nooks and crannies surrounding them, but it was too dark. Abbas reached for the boy, ready to strike him down but the child's face shifted, like water rippling in a pond. It changed to that of a woman and the body followed soon after.

"What is this?" Abbas cried out. "You have come this time as a woman? Explain yourself, Jinni!" His anger was rising, but his men were wary.

As Wadjet took the form of a fully developed adult female, the men began to panic. They were all Christians and they crossed themselves repeatedly, while muttering about witchcraft. Some reached for hip flasks of alcohol to calm their nerves and remove their fear.

"Silence you fools!" Shouted Abbas, as he stepped forward towards Wadjet.

She remained still and the silence was abruptly shattered by the sound of men screaming in pain as swords penetrated their flesh. Abbas turned to see his men lying dead before him. He glanced up from their bodies until his eyes met those of his half-brother. His shoulders slumped. He could easily outwit the humans, he knew for sure, but this Jinni was now standing behind him and he did not know what its powers were.

As he pondered his next move, he heard someone running behind him. Thinking it to be the Jinni, he turned and threw a streak of fire from his hands in her direction. However, she was no longer there, and by the time Abbas realised, Jawad had rushed up to him and thrown the potion from the staff, into his face. He felt burning and a smell of sulphur. Then, weakened, he fell to his knees. A red coloured mist lifted from him, settled on the ground, and vanished.

Jawad walked around him and stood in front of him, towering over the defeated half-Jinni. "Get up, brother," he said. "It is over. You are no longer enslaved by Shaytaan."

Abbas stood and Jawad stepped forwards to hug him. Then, he held him at arm's length and explained everything that had happened since they last crossed paths, in Basra.

As Abbas stood talking to his brother, and unseen by either of them, Isabelle came rushing towards Abbas. She was holding a knife in her right hand. Jawad saw her at the last moment and shouted to her to stop, but it was too late. On hearing his brother shout, Abbas turned but could not stop the inevitable now that his powers were gone. She thrust the knife into his heart and then let go of the handle. Abbas slumped to the ground and Isabelle walked around him, like a cat admiring its defeated, but not quite dead, prey. Finally, she stopped by his head, leaned down and spat in his face.

Jawad knelt alongside his brother. Abbas mumbled something and Jawad leaned in closer to hear what his brother was saying.

"I have done so many things that I regret, brother. You know much of what I have been responsible for, but I must warn you. I have placed my seed in hundreds of women in different parts of this world. Even your wife carries my child."

Jawad's heart rate increased. He could feel the pain and the anger rising as he heard these words. He glanced across at Marie and she bowed her head. *Had she heard Abbas? Was it shame that caused her to avert her eyes from me?* He thought to himself. *Or was it genuine concern for my feelings?*

When he turned back to Abbas, his brother was dead, eyes staring lifelessly at the sky. He stood, drew his sword and marched towards Isabelle. "You will die, woman, for murdering my kin," he shouted.

"Wait!" The shout came from Marie. "She saved me from Abbas. She freed me and she has good cause to want him dead after the way he treated her."

Jawad stopped but held his sword in front of Isabelle's throat. "Speak woman. Why did you kill him?"

"He raped me many times and beat me, but he also murdered my children. He murdered them and then displayed their bodies for me to see. He was a monster and deserved to die."

"Husband," Marie said, softly.

"Do not speak to me wife. We will have words later."

Jawad stared at Isabelle, who was crying and shaking. He was prepared to slice his sword into her neck, when Hassan placed a hand on the sword, forcing it to be lowered. "Let it be Jawad. What is done is done. We have a greater mission to accomplish and time is passing."

Jawad took a deep breath, sheathed his sword and called two men to his side. "Take my brother's body and prepare him for burial. Leave the others." he said. Then, he walked away, passing Marie without comment and without meeting her eyes. She reached out to touch his arm, but he brushed her hand aside.

Oh my God, he knows. She thought, and then the tears came.

CHAPTER 90
1315 A.D.
The Siege of Carlisle

Following his success at Bannockburn, De Bruce was invigorated with a renewed energy and a desire to capture, among other English towns, Carlisle. Sir Andrew Harclay, Earl of Carlisle, was the man appointed by King Edward to rule over the town in his absence. It was the morning that the siege by the Scottish army began, that some of Harclay's men found the bodies of the guards belonging to the owner of the Sauceries. Harclay was informed of the discovery and he feigned surprise, although he had already been informed of the bodies by an unearthly ally. It was the reason why his men were searching Carlisle for Alarico in the first place.

"What of the man they call Alarico? You know he supplies us with arms as well as sauces, don't you?"

The two soldiers said nothing. They knew the question was rhetorical.

"Fine," Harclay continued, "I assume Alarico was taken by the brigands who murdered his men. We need him back, especially at a time like this. He seems to have contacts and skills that we require at this perilous time."

He turned to the Officer in the room and said, "Gather a troop of as many fighting men as you can. Don't leave us short of real soldiers, though. Take men who can fight. Perhaps that is what I should have said, rather than fighting men. Report back here to me when you have them and I will give you instructions. I think I know where they are headed."

The officer and the two soldiers with him left the room and Harclay sat down in a large wooden and leather armchair. Before him, the shape of a woman began to take form. She appeared out of nothing, like dust becoming visible in a stream of sunlight that has pierced through the clouds. Once fully formed the woman smiled.

"As I told you yesterday, they are headed to Cornwall. To be precise, they are en route to a place called Tintagel. Your men will need to stop them from reaching the Castle. Do that and our Master will repay you in riches beyond your imagination."

Then, she vanished and while Harclay considered the promise of wealth and maybe power, she materialised outside the town walls. *I am so sorry, Jawad, she whispered into the air. Iblis made me do this, with the threat of eternal agony. He would trap me within a box of horrors of his making.* Then, she disappeared again.

Inside the town, the officer, an experienced soldier named Ligart, had mustered forty men, including himself. Most were farmers and labourers who had done some fighting. This was expected, given the need to leave soldiers to defend the town from the Scots. Four of Ligart's men, including Ligart himself, were trained, experienced, battle-hardened warriors. One, his son, was barely fifteen years' old and had no experience of war at all.

They saddled forty horses for riding and loaded two more as pack horses and Ligart handed his son a long spear, at the top of which was the flag of King Edward. "Your job, boy, is to keep this flag flying at all times. If it falls to the ground, I'll give you a whipping you'll remember until you're my age.

"Yes sir," replied the boy, as he mounted his horse before grasping the spear and flag with both hands.

In the weeks leading up to this, Harclay had been preparing to defend Carlisle. He had every blacksmith, fletcher and wood-turner in the city working all the hours of every day. Arrows and javelins were made in their thousands in the weeks before the Scottish army arrived, and boulders were set every few yards around the bulwark behind the city walls. Those walls were only fifteen feet high, so once the Scots reached them, the English defenders would be relying on those stones and javelins to repel them.

Harclay had engines of war, including springalds, which would fire long darts. Stones could also be launched at the enemy.

Once the siege began, it was noticeable that the Scots were not, initially, setting up any siege machines, so Harclay concluded that his enemy was expecting to take the city by escalade, scaling ladders to breach the walls.

The weather was typical of a Northern summer in England. There were a few dry days intermingled with very wet ones. 1315 was also the first of many famine years. Bad weather wreaked havoc on harvests all over England. Regular torrents of rain meant that the ground around the city was swampy, making it difficult for the Scots to attack the walls. The rain would also make it virtually impossible for them to burn the gates as they had successfully done during other sieges.

Harclay was satisfied that even with one of his senior officers absent, they could successfully defend the city. This was especially true because he retained the services of a bold, intelligent knight,

Sir James of Douglas.

Harclay smiled to himself. He was, after all, a minor knight from Hartley, one of the poorest and smallest manors in England. His father had been Sheriff of Cumberland for many years, but the family was not one of any note. In fact, many would have called his family notorious, rather than notable. His brother Michael had been accused, but acquitted, of being an accessory to murder in 1292. As for Andrew Harclay, many condemned him as nothing more than a brute. They felt he had been lucky enough to be in the right place at the right time. If he could protect Carlisle, if he could drive the Scots back, he would wipe the self-satisfying smile from their faces. He could establish a reputation for himself as the man who stopped the Scottish invasion.

Nevertheless, he feared the consequences of not being able to stop the fleeing group who had, apparently, kidnapped his ally, Alarico. The demon had told him they were Scottish spies and now they were heading south. Harclay had signed a pact with the demon that tied him, body and soul, to Satan. It would give him some success in this world. He was confident of that, but what would happen if his men failed to stop the spies?

He pushed the thought away. His only concern right now was the defence of Carlisle.

CHAPTER 91
1315 A.D.
The Journey to Tintagel

Following the death of Abbas and his dying words, Jawad was distraught. The day after the group had left Carlisle, they found a brief resting place in an abandoned Hall, several miles outside of the town. Jawad had kept himself apart from them much of the time. He even slept away from his wife for the first time in decades. *How could she allow him to do this?* He kept saying to himself, although occasionally he would remind himself of what Abbas had been. *Could he have forced himself on her? Would she have been able to fight him off if he had?* That was the most likely scenario. He knew that, but the worst thoughts kept surfacing, feeding on his pride, his jealousy, his basic animal nature. They niggled at him, and he could not put them away. On one occasion, he had confided in Amina, occasionally unleashing his anger in her direction. She never shied from his verbal attacks, but calmly told him that Marie would have never willingly paired with Abbas.

"It is Shaytaan," she said, "whispering in your ear, and you must snap out of this Jawad. I have seen this before in people. You will turn yourself inside out with these thoughts that pollute your very soul and we all need you alert and free of the grip this has on you."

He knew she was right, and he asked her to bring Marie to him.

Marie tried to talk to Jawad about what had happened, but his mood was resistant, obstinate. Within minutes of her arrival, they begin to argue.

"You are carrying his child?" Jawad shouted. "Keep away from me!"

"He raped me! He tied me up and forced himself on me, just as he did with Isabelle. I didn't choose this. Why are you punishing me while mourning him? I never took you to be this kind of man, Jawad. Never!"

Her words were filtering through his defences and he sat down, his head slumped forward, eyes staring at the ground. He said nothing, but the silence seemed to calm the situation. Marie knelt on the floor at his feet and looked up at his face until their eyes met. She touched his hand and he let her.

"You are my husband and I love you. I have never loved anyone else and never will. I don't believe you really blame me for this."

Jawad made to reply, but she placed a finger to his lips, and he stopped himself short.

"My beloved Jawad, if Odinike were here now and you were defenceless, unarmed, and if he forced himself on you, could you stop him? With all his strength, could you prevent the inevitable?"

Jawad took a deep breath and shook his head. "No," he replied. "No, I could not."

A tear fell from his eye and Marie reached out to embrace him. Then, the grief, the anger, the pain all melted into sobbing. Marie cried too, but she had more to say.

"He raped me, but that does not mean this child I carry is his. We made love the night before I was taken, did we not? So, why not believe that this is your child?"

Jawad nodded and, releasing himself from her grasp, stood up. "We must prepare to leave. Please could you call the group together for me?"

A little taken aback by the abrupt change in tone and subject, Marie stuttered her response. "Er, er, of course." She moved towards the door but regained her composure before leaving the room. Turning back to Jawad, she said, "I would like Isabelle to join us on the journey. She has begged to be allowed to join us on the journey south."

"Absolutely not." Jawad's response was firm but lacked the anger he had displayed earlier.

"Please, put it to the group. Her children were murdered by Abbas and he abused her as he abused me. She did what any of us would have done in her position." She waited for a response, but Jawad said nothing, so she continued. "She did what I was intending to do."

He looked up sharply, clearly shocked by that admission, but still he said nothing.

"Please, let the group decide," Marie asked again. Jawad sighed and waved her away. She left to convene a meeting of the group and Jawad met them in the Hall. They discussed plans for the journey to Tintagel in Cornwall and, finally, they debated Isabelle's request. After much argument, thought and discussion, and despite Jawad's initial opposition, the group agreed to take Isabelle with them.

They left the Hall and bumped into one of Sami's Scottish soldiers outside.

"Sami," he called out, as he walked hurriedly towards them.

The Syrian left the group and strolled over to his Scottish comrade, a man in his mid-fifties, leathered, wind-beaten skin, a bushy grey beard and long red hair. He was a huge man, larger even than Bohemond, and armed with a two-handed broadsword. "Stuart, what are you doing here? Is there a problem?" Sami asked.

Stuart shook his head. "Not really. Er, I don't understand everything we've seen recently, especially down at the Loch, but I want to understand."

"We're leaving here soon, Stuart. I'm sorry, but there's no time to explain right now." He paused for a moment and looked around. "I don't know how you managed to reach us, but it isn't safe for you here."

Stuart sighed. "I want to come with you to wherever you're going," he said.

Sami's surprise was etched on his face, along with his concern. He glanced back at Jawad. "You're a Scot, Stuart, and we're headed into the heart of England. It would be dangerous for you to come with us."

"Laddie, in case you've not noticed, you're as Scottish now as I am. Your accent, when you speak English, will betray you as a Scot."

Sami laughed. "Aye, you're right, but I'm not the pale, sickly-looking, red-haired beast that you are. I'm not a man mountain who would find it hard to conceal himself. I can say my accent is Greek or Spanish or anything and most people in England would not know any different, but you? Oh, you'd be like a beacon in the dark, my friend."

"I can dye my hair and stay silent," Stuart replied.

Sami laughed, then hesitated for a moment, but eventually headed back to the group to seek permission for his man to join them. Jawad was talking to Owun, the only one among them who knew England well and had experience of travelling through Cornwall. Sami apologised for interrupting and made his request. Jawad was unsure and kept glancing across at the Scottish warrior.

"He's a tough fighter and loyal, Jawad. We may need him. We don't know what dangers lie ahead of us." Sami was passionate in his plea.

Before Jawad could answer him, Owun spoke up. "I know what dangers lie ahead, not only with the English but also with the Cornishmen. We'll need every hand we can get, Jawad."

Jawad squinted and raised his hand over his eyes against the sudden burst of sunlight that had forced its way through the clouds. "He joins us. Go and tell him, Sami, but you're responsible for him."

Sami collected his friend, who still refused to explain how he got from the Scottish siege, past the English to arrive here in an abandoned Hall on a lonely stretch of road in England. Sami shook his head and smiled. "Resourceful bastard," he muttered to himself.

As they all gathered themselves together, Wadjet suddenly materialised before them.

"Where have you been, Jinni?" Hassan asked.

"I needed rest," she lied, feeling, perhaps for the first time in her life, a sense of guilt. *I am so sorry, Jawad,* she thought to herself. *Perhaps I can redeem myself without him ever having to know that I betrayed him.*

They were nineteen. Hassan and his warriors, Akbar and Mehmet; Reza and his son, Jaffer; Jawad, Marie, Amina, White Wolf, Assad and Antonio Habash; The interpreter, Judah Ben Zakai; Bohemond, Amalric, Isabelle, Stuart MacDonald, Owun Tyler and Wadjet.

They set out at dawn the following day. The sun's light, peering through the sheet of darkness, triggered bird songs and the crowing of cockerels. The farmers were already up, tending to livestock, but most of the town was quiet. Abbas' body was carried on the back of a horse-drawn cart to a neglected area of woodland a few miles outside of town. There, he was buried before the group moved on.

Several miles into the journey, Bohemond struck up a conversation with Isabelle, although he did most of the talking. She never once made eye contact with the tall Frenchman, but occasionally responded to a question, often with a one-word answer or a head nod. Her attention was focused straight ahead at the front of the travelling pack. Bohemond did not seem to notice and Amalric, walking just behind shook his head and smiled. For at least an hour he left Bohemond alone, but finally he felt he had to pull his friend to one side. He pulled on Bohemond's arm and eased him away from Isabelle, noticing that she seemed relieved to be rid of the huge Frenchman.

"What?" Asked the larger man.

"Bohemond, my friend, you seem to be taken by our latest recruit."

Bohemond smiled. "Was it that obvious?" He asked.

Amalric laughed. "The problem, my friend, is that she seems to be smitten with someone else."

Bohemond looked at Isabelle. "What do you mean? Who?"

"Look where she is looking. Believe me, she has not taken her eyes off him since we left Carlisle."

Bohemond followed Isabelle's eyes and he saw Reza, striding ahead of the group. He had separated himself from the rest, so it was certain that he was the focus of her attention. He sighed. "Damn".

Free of Bohemond and no longer needing to find an excuse to move away, Isabelle hastened towards Reza. She caught up with him and struck up a conversation and they seemed to gel immediately. She asked him about his home country, and he inquired about her life. He raised the issue of her children and she was surprised to find that she was able to talk freely with him about them. She was comfortable around him and Reza felt the same.

It was many days until they were in sight of the Cornish region. The trek across the Moor had been arduous and difficult to navigate, with clouds constantly shutting off their view of the stars. Nevertheless, they had made it to the unmarked border with Cornwall. They decided to rest and had no sooner settled into a makeshift camp when Hassan's scouts, Assad and Habash, came riding towards them at speed. They dismounted and ran to Hassan and Jawad.

"There is a small force of armed men following us." Assad said, breathing heavily and having to stop to catch his breath before continuing. "They have stopped and made camp, so it should give us time to discuss our next move."

"Are they soldiers or brigands?" Jawad asked.

"Soldiers," replied Assad, "in uniform, although not very disciplined."

Jawad looked at Owun. "Any thoughts?"

Owun turned to face the Cornish border, where many armed men had gathered. "We're at risk of being squeezed like a fruit in a fist but what we must avoid is a fight with the Cornishmen. We need ease of passage to Tintagel and, if possible, their help too."

He paused and looked back in the direction of the English force, gaining on them, the longer they waited here. "We draw the English closer to the Cornishmen and then we fight them, the English, kill most and take some as prisoners. The Cornishmen have no love for the English, and we would be held high in their eyes if we crush an English force that is approaching the Cornish border. They'll love us even more if we hand the prisoners over to them."

As Jawad pondered their position, Owun decided to explain the political and military situation to the group. What was happening now in Cornwall, was directly affected by what had occurred at Bannockburn. After Edward II became King of England, he immediately recalled his favourite, Piers Gaveston from exile. Longshanks had banished Gaveston to France for being a bad influence on his son. Rumours of a homosexual relationship between young Edward and Gaveston, were rife.

Edward gave Gaveston, a non-royal, the Earldom of Cornwall. It was a title normally conferred on royalty. However, opposition to the king and his favourite had begun almost immediately. In 1311 the nobles issued 'Ordinances', as an attempt to limit royal control of finance and appointments. Gaveston was twice exiled on the orders of the barons, but each time returned to England shortly afterwards. In 1312, however, he was captured and executed by the barons.

Following Edward's defeat by Robert de Bruce at Bannockburn, power fell into the hands of the barons headed by Edward's cousin Thomas of Lancaster. By 1315, Lancaster had made himself the real ruler of England but did little to initiate reform. Ultimately, large parts of the country collapsed into anarchy, including Cornwall, where family-based gangs each vied for power in the region.

Jawad and Hassan discussed their next move and decided that a trap had to be laid for the English. Hassan called to Assad and Habash to join them.

"How many are there?" He asked.

"Forty," replied Assad. "Only one officer, in brightly coloured attire over mail."

"Most of them do not have mail or armour," added Habash. Commoners, recruited at short notice, I would say. Perhaps de Bruce is occupying the English forces in the North and this is all they could spare to chase us down."

Hassan looked around. "I have an idea. How many horses do we have, including the pack horses and those ridden by the women?"

Assad counted them in his head. "Twenty," he replied.

"So, what is your idea, Hassan?" Asked Jawad.

"We cut some branches and build fake people, dress them in clothing, seat some on horses and place them in two places. One group over there to the West and another several yards that way, to the East. We entice the English to divide their numbers. Meanwhile, we wait, out of sight and attack the divided troops separately."

Jawad pondered the idea for a moment. He stroked his beard and mumbled to himself. Then, in a flash, he pushed past Hassan and looked at the two proposed positions. Then, he glanced at the sky.

"It could work, especially with the cloud cover and the light rain that is beginning to fall. They won't spot the deception until they're very close.

"We'll place four horses to the West and three to the East. Then, we'll build the fake soldiers and ask the women to gather some clothing."

He paced around, nodding his head repeatedly. "If it goes well, the English will attack what they see as the smaller group first. The officer and the flag bearer will wait with the professional soldiers and will attack once they see our first group defeated. Or, at least, that is what I hope will happen."

"Call everyone together," Hassan said to Assad and Habash.

Once gathered, Jawad outlined the plan to them, and everyone approved.

"Hassan's idea, not mine, but I think it will work," he said. "We will attack the group that approaches our decoy in the East. They'll realise, once they get close, that they are approaching dummies. By then it will be too late for them. When they hesitate, and they will hesitate, we attack. We hit them hard and we hit them fast and we kill them all."

461

There was some muttering among the group, but Jawad continued. "We must kill them all. A slaughter will force the second group to re-think. By then, they will also have realised that they have been deceived. They will be in two minds. Their numbers advantage will be significantly reduced, and they will be unsure whether to fight us or turn and run."

He paused again, took a deep breath and continued. "Whatever they choose, we chase them down and kill them, except for the officer. I want him alive and I want that flag. Understood?"

Everyone grunted agreement.

They dispersed and began to prepare. They worked quickly, knowing that time was not on their side and the English force was close and would be on the move again very soon. Eventually, the work was done, and the decoys were in place. Jawad's force waited some distance away, shielded by a cluster of trees, a rare sight in the moorlands.

CHAPTER 92
Abigor and the Sand Jinni

In the dark chamber of Jahanam that was Iblis' place of confinement, the Jinni-turned-fallen-Angel paced up and down. His grandson, Abbas, was lost forever with repentance on his lips as he drew his last breath. Iblis' form shifted, like the ripples of water, from the attractive, but deceptive charmer to the hideous, almost reptilian, horned devil that revealed his true nature. He was naked, for shame was not one of his attributes. Yet, none of his minions, except Abigor, dared look. They stood in serried ranks behind Iblis, their eyes firmly fixed on the floor. For his anger could be cast on any one of them in an instant. While the others stood in humility, however, Abigor kept a keen and careful eye on his Master. He waited patiently for the anger to subside and then, he spoke.

"Master, the humans approach the portal. Your servant has persuaded the English to send troops after them, but those troops are few. The English have a siege in Carlisle to deal with."

Iblis turned and glared at his most loyal of servants and spat his words. His skin, red like blood, his hair like the flames of a roaring fire, illuminated the chamber. His eyes, black as night, stared through Abigor and, for a moment, the seer froze in terror. Rarely, did Abigor show fear, but he had not seen his Master like this for centuries.

"Do you think I don't know that, Abigor? Have you not told me this already? Do you think me old and forgetful?"

Abigor's voice shook as he spoke. "Of course not, Master, but..."

"Silence! We must stop them from sealing the portal with that damned staff. The Sand Jinni can assist us. Find him and task him with taking possession of Jawad and..." Suddenly, he stopped. His form changed again, to that of the handsome man he liked to portray himself as—the being he had once been, before he was cursed to live out his days in the depths of Jahanam. He laughed.

"No, not Jawad," he said. "One of the others. One that they all hold dear. One who is loved by, perhaps a son and a woman." Another pause gave Abigor respite. His breathing returned to normal, his heart slowed, and he waited for Iblis to finish. "Reza. He should possess Reza and present them with a choice. He will understand."

"Yes, Master."

Iblis looked at him and his human-like skin began to redden again.

"I will go now, Master," Abigor said, before leaving the chamber for a journey that would take him to a part of this Jinn world that touched a desert in the human world. It was one of very few places where occasional rifts between the worlds appear quite regularly. A Jinni or two could cross worlds for short periods, or longer if they could take possession of a human or an animal.

The journey was quick and Abigor found the favourite of the Sand Jinn, an Ifrit whose name was Marash. Made of fire, the Afarit dwell in deserts, caves and beneath the surface of the Earth, but are usually trapped unless or until they are released. Humans can call on them or they can be temporarily released by Shaytaan or his emissaries. Marash was summoned by Abigor and appeared in a swirl of desert sand. He stood at least fifteen feet tall, was swathed in dust and smoke. His eyes lit up when he spoke and when he appeared, it was with his back to Abigor.

"Who summons me?" His voice was deep and loud, filling the desert air.

Abigor remained calm. His own powers far superseded those of the ifrit. "I did." He said.

Marash turned sharply and looked down at Shaytaan's envoy. The ifrit's boldness had evaporated at the sight of Abigor. "Forgive me, my lord. How can I be of assistance to you?"

Abigor gave instructions for Marash to journey, urgently, to where Jawad's band of travellers were. He told him to take possession the one named Reza. He presented him with the details of Shaytaan's order and then he left. Marash surveyed the barren desert for a moment and then, in a waft of smoke and a swirl of sand, disappeared.

CHAPTER 93
1315 A.D.
The Trap is Set

As planned, Jawad and his men placed four horses to the West and three to the east. They sat some dummies in the saddles and others in positions around them. As Jawad and his small crew prepared the Western trap, he glanced across at the one on the Eastern side. "They look real enough to me, from here," he said, and the others agreed after looking for themselves.

Their hopes were fulfilled when Ligart arrived, surveyed the scene and split his force. He sent half of his soldiers to the Western flank. Twenty horses, riding at a gallop across the Moor, kicked up masses of dirt and mud and could be seen for miles. Jawad's forces watched and waited. He looked up at the sky. Cloud cover was intensifying, and it was beginning to rain. He nodded to himself.

"We will attack when they are twenty yards away from the dummies," he said.

The second group of English horsemen had also started to move on the Eastern flank, but at a canter. It was clear that Ligart believed his opponents would think he had sent his entire company against one flank. Within minutes, the first group of attackers had reached the twenty-yard mark. They slowed to a halt as they saw the deception and Jawad gave the order to attack.

"Remember," he said, "hit them hard and hit them with speed."

He led the charge and they came out of nowhere. The English cavalry tried to turn their horses when they realised a force almost as large as theirs was charging at them with ferocity. However, as their horses wheeled around, Owun and two other archers hit them with a hail of arrows. Half their number died as the shafts struck and then Jawad's force tore through the remaining horsemen with ease. They struck hard, with no mercy, and the enemy panicked. Most of the English fighters were not soldiers. They had never experienced anything like this before. Some kicked their horses in an attempt to make a run for it, but they were too slow. Swords sliced through flesh and bone, and in minutes, the fight was over. A swathe of bloody, butchered bodies lay on the ground. Frightened horses fled the scene, leaving their riders where they had fallen.

By this time, Ligart had witnessed the slaughter at the Eastern flank. They turned towards the fighting, but halfway across the space between them, his fighters realised their men had been massacred. Some of Ligart's men fled in fear, but he and his soldiers continued. "Death before the shame of returning to Carlisle in defeat!" He shouted, pointing his sword towards Jawad's force.

They swung their horses towards the Eastern flank and kicked them into a gallop, but Jawad's force was waiting. Again, arrows struck first. Then, the scream in a foreign language as Hassan and the other Turks thrust their way through the handful of remaining Englishmen. "Take the officer alive and take that damned flag too," he called out.

Ligart was knocked to the ground by an arrow that struck his shoulder. As he struggled to get to his feet, the hilt of a sword struck his head, knocking him unconscious. The only other English fighter left alive was the flag bearer. Seeing how young he was, neither Hassan nor his men had the heart to kill him. Both the boy and the revived officer were eventually dragged to Jawad.

"Please, don't harm the boy," begged the officer. "Do what you will with me, but please let the boy go."

Jawad glanced back at the youth and nodded. His gaze returned to Ligart. "He is important to you? Is he your son?" he asked.

Ligart nodded. His eyes were pleading, and Jawad understood why. He took a deep breath. "You and your flag will be handed over to the Cornish rebels and they will hold you for ransom. Your son can leave, but only if he tells of your capture, informs your family of the ransom amount and swears not to mention us. As far as anyone is concerned, you have been taken by the rebels. Is that understood?"

Ligart nodded again. Then, looking around at Jawad's group, he frowned. "Do you have a captive from Carlisle? A man named Alarico?"

Jawad showed no emotion as he replied. "The man you call Alarico, was in fact named Abbas. He was my brother and now he is dead. There is nothing more about him that you need to know. Now, do I have your word on what I have demanded for the release of your son?"

Ligart looked nervous, perhaps even frightened. "He cannot return to Carlisle. The sole survivor, a flag-bearer, without the flag. He would be executed for cowardice."

Jawad shook his head. "I am sorry, but I cannot let him take the flag." He thought for a moment. "Is your family in Carlisle?"

"My two older sons are there, defending the town against the Scots, but my wife is in London."

"Then your son should go to London and inform your wife of the Cornish demands. She can send a messenger to Carlisle who can say he came across some injured soldiers, fleeing from a fight. He can say they gave him the message before succumbing to their wounds."

Ligart nodded his agreement. "Swear to me. Voice your agreement and we will proceed," Jawad demanded, and Ligart did as he was asked.

He was then taken, with the flag, to the Cornish rebels, who were confused at first, but grateful once Jawad had explained the situation to them. He asked Ligart his name, informed the Cornishmen, agreed terms for a guide to travel with them to Tintagel and then left, leaving Ligart and the flag, and watching the boy begin his long journey to London.

Their Cornish guide was a woman called Bennath. "She will keep you safe and guide you well," the Cornish leader had said. About twenty years of age, she was short and stocky, with callouses on both hands. *Probably a farm girl*, thought Jawad. She certainly knew her way around Cornwall, knew the terrain and knew where to travel to avoid other people. She also knew which farms they could steal food from, and which were guarded well. As a result, the journey to Tintagel was swift and safe. She was accompanied, at the head of the trek, by White Wolf, with whom she had quickly developed a relationship.

CHAPTER 94
1315 A.D.
Tintagel

By the time they reached Tintagel, the relationship between Reza and Isabelle had flourished and blossomed.

As they neared the location of the castle ruins, Amalric sidled up alongside his friend, Bohemond. "She seems happy," he said.

Bohemond nodded. "And I'm happy for them both. Plenty more women around." He paused and smiled. "In fact, I'm getting close to Jawad's maid, Amina. Beautiful woman. She knows how to cook too."

Amalric laughed and pondered his own life briefly, but the thought passed as quickly as it had appeared, and his mind returned to the mission. Ever the professional soldier.

From their vantage point on the hill above the ruins of Tintagel Castle, they could see the sea stretching into the distance. This was despite the rain that had been falling since they arrived. The fierce waves crashed against the rocks below and, for a while, they rested. However, as warm air hit moisture, a fog began rolling in from the West. Within minutes, it had reached them. Suddenly, visibility was virtually zero. Neither the sea, nor the ruins could be seen anymore, and the rocky hillside on which the tide was crashing, had disappeared.

"How long does a fog like this last?" Jawad's question was to Owun, who shrugged. Jawad sighed and sat on the ground.

Bennath had heard his question and answered. "We will have to sit and wait it out. We'll end up toppling off the cliff if we try to go anywhere in this," she said.

Reza had been standing at the cliff-edge when the fog hit and cautiously sat, feeling for the border between land and sky as he did so. As he looked in the direction of the sea, he thought he saw something in the fog. He looked around but his companions were out of sight, so he looked again into the haze. At first, there was nothing, but then he saw it again. A swirl of dust, dirt and sand rising from the beach below. He stared at it and almost fell from the cliff as he was startled by a face appearing in the mist. His heart beating and beads of sweat running down his temples, he shuffled backwards, and the face disappeared. The fog returned to its normal state and he began to wonder whether he had really seen what he thought he had.

An hour later, the fog dissipated, and the ruins of Tintagel were visible once more. Bennath left them, after giving White Wolf a long lasting hug.

"We need to go down there. The portal is located within those ruins somewhere," Jawad said, calling everyone together with a wave of his hand.

"It is rumoured to be the site of Camelot, you know." Owun Tyler smiled as he spoke. "I know, you don't believe it, but consider this. You met Merlin."

The others laughed and Amalric slapped him on the back. "Not much of a castle. It is tiny. If that was Camelot, my friend, King Arthur's Kingdom couldn't have covered much further than where we are standing."

The laughter continued but Reza had once again separated himself from the group. He was already making his way down the cliff to the small beach below. Once there, he stood looking around as if expecting to see the apparition he had witnessed earlier. At first, there was nothing, but then he heard a voice calling his name. He turned, thinking the rest of the group had caught up with him, but they were still at the top of the cliff. Their progress down the precarious path that Reza had taken, was slow.

"Who's there?" He asked and was shocked to receive a reply.

A haunting voice seemed to enter his entire being, as if it were emanating from within his head, rather than from outside. "I cannot tell you who I am or show my face until you welcome me, Reza."

I'm going mad, the Persian said to himself.

"Not at all, my friend. I am here and I can help you in your quest, but first you must welcome me, invite me to join you."

"How?"

"With a traditional desert welcome, of course, for I am from the desert."

Reza thought for a moment and then decided it could not hurt to welcome this thing, although he struggled to understand why he had no reservations. He took a deep breath and said "Marhaba. Ahlan wa Sahlan."

Suddenly, the dust and sand at Reza's feet began to rise and swirl until it reached the height of a tall man. Within a second, it began to transform into a human, a man. Reza stepped back, almost tripping over a rock behind him. As if emerging from a trance, he realised his predicament. He had welcomed a Jinni. Steadying himself, he turned to run back up the path towards his friends, but it was too late. The man vaporised and the smoky mist darted towards Reza. It flew up Reza's nose and the Persian fell, semi-conscious, to the ground.

The others found him, lying face-down on the rocks, his eyes open but glassy, as if he were transfixed, in a trance. Hassan rushed to his side and shook him. Reza blinked and looked up. Hassan helped him to his feet. Isabelle took hold of his arm and walked him, gingerly, across the rocky beach to a dry patch against the cliff. There, she comforted him and checked for any external injuries but, aside from a bruised arm and grazed leg, he seemed in good health.

"He may have lost his footing and hit his head," Hassan said.

"There is no indication of a head injury," Isabelle replied.

They took him to an area above the Tintagel ruins where they had made camp. Amina treated wounds on his arms and leg with antiseptic ointments she had made from plants, gathered on their journey. Isabelle stayed with him for the rest of the day and throughout the night, while Jawad and Hassan investigated the ruins and the rest of the group took the opportunity to rest.

"I'm not sure what we're looking for, exactly," Jawad said, as he and Hassan entered the castle ruins.

"Merlin's Cave." The voice came from behind them. It was Owun and he was pointing down to a gaping black hole in the cliff face below them. "That's what the locals call that cave there. Given that it was Merlin who sent us here, I would wager that it is there we should be looking, not here."

Jawad nodded. "You're right, Owun. We'll wait for Reza to recover and then we'll investigate."

It was high tide when Reza came around and re-joined the group. Merlin's cave was now inaccessible as the beach leading to it was submerged in sea water. As they waited for the waters to retreat, they tried to ascertain from Reza what had happened to him.

"I'm not sure. My memory is hazy," he said. "One minute I was standing down there on the rocky shore and the next I was waking up here with all of you."

Despite his ordeal, he seemed physically well, apart from the minor injuries he had suffered when he collapsed. He was upbeat and ready to investigate the cave below. However, Isabelle was unsure. "Something about Reza seems different, not quite right," she whispered to Bohemond. "Can you keep a close eye on him please?" She asked.

Bohemond smiled and nodded. "I'm sure you're concerning yourself over nothing, but I will stay close to him for you," he replied.

It took a couple of days for Reza to fully recover and, once everyone was satisfied that he was ready to participate, they set off down to the shoreline at low tide. Leaving White Wolf to guard their camp, they descended the cliff above Merlin's cave, lit torches once they were at the cave opening, and headed in, cautiously. Bohemond walked behind Reza and watched him closely, becoming increasingly alarmed at the Persian's behaviour. He kept looking around and was blinking rapidly. Every so often he smiled, apparently at nothing. The tall French Knight was about to push ahead to speak to Jawad of his concerns, when Hassan yelled out that they had reached an impasse. As the group assembled, it was clear there was nothing here but a solid wall. The cavern went nowhere.

"What is this?" Marie asked. "Where is the portal?"

Jawad sighed and touched the wall of the cave, just in case the solidity was a kind of mirage.

"It is solid," he said. "We have several hours before high tide, but I don't want to spend them hunting for the portal." Then, turning to Wadjet, he added; "Any ideas?"

The Jinni asked for silence as she approached the wall. She touched it and closed her eyes. "It is here, and the protection Merlin placed on it is weakening. The staff must be used to reveal it and then seal it permanently. If you fail to seal it, and Shaytaan's forces overcome Zaman's army, they will enter this world as a horde."

Jawad was about to step towards the wall with the staff when Marie let out a scream. The prince turned to see his wife pinned against the roof of the cave by some unseen force. He rushed towards Marie and then heard laughter, a chilling cackle that reached his bones. Looking toward the source of the laughter, he frowned in shock. "Reza!" He shouted. "What are you doing? How are you doing it? Why?"

The rest of the group turned in Reza's direction. His right arm was pointing up towards Marie, his eyes were red, and his continuous laugh echoed throughout the cave.

Bohemond stepped towards the Persian. "If you come near me, you hulking great fool, I will crush her against the cave ceiling and then I will do the same to you." Reza was speaking in a stranger's voice, gravelly, deep and eerie.

"He is possessed," said Amalric.

"Yes," replied Wadjet, "by a Jinni. I sense a Sand Jinni."

Reza turned his head slowly to face Wadjet, his red eyes occasionally illuminating. "Oh, Wadjet, what has become of you? You have become almost human. You have spent too much time with these inferior creatures. Join me and our master's forces will take this world."

Wadjet shook her head. "He is no longer my Master, Sand Jinni, and I advise you to release the human whom you have possessed."

"Or what? You will burn me to death?" The Sand Jinni laughed again. "In doing so you will kill your human friend."

"Please, release my wife," Jawad pleaded.

"I do not think so, hyoooooman," the Jinni replied. "Now, you are in a quandary. You see, the staff you hold can only be used once. You have a choice, use it to remove me from this creature and send me back to my home, or use it to seal the portal." He laughed again. "Save your friend or save the world. Some choice, huh?"

Isabelle was distraught. She screamed at Jawad to help Reza and Jaffer joined her in a chorus of pleas. Jawad shook his head, his face cold and stern. "I'm sorry, but the fate of the world outweighs the fate of one man, albeit a man who is one of my closest friends and allies."

"No!" Jaffer screamed at the prince and then rushed him, grabbing the staff and running at Reza.

The Sand Jinni, realising what was happening, tried to stop Jaffer in his tracks, but to do so, he had to release Marie. She fell to the ground, her arm twisting and breaking beneath her. Jawad, concerned for his wife and the unborn child she was carrying, ignored Jaffer and rushed to Marie.

The Jinni turned his attention to Jaffer, but it was too late. Jaffer jabbed the staff into Reza's chest and the Persian howled, an ear-piercing, blood-curdling scream that was not of his making. His face contorted and he slumped to the ground. Then, the Jinni left him in a plume of smoke that transformed into sand, fell to the earth and disappeared.

Jaffer and Isabelle rushed to Reza's side and began to comfort him. Jawad was doing the same for Marie. "I'm fine," she said. "And the baby is kicking. Also, fine, I believe."

Reza was dazed and confused, asking what had happened, but before there was time to reply, the portal was revealed. After using the staff on his father, Jaffer had held it against the wall. The gateway was unfolding. Eventually, it was fully opened. Suddenly, there was an influx of Jinn of all shapes and sizes, all forms, flooding the cave and passing the group of humans with ease. Bohemond, Amalric and Hassan managed to draw their swords and began swiping at the Jinn, striking some, but missing most. The horde of unearthly beings stormed to the cave exit and, within seconds, they materialised into the human world. However, the incursion was not over. More came from the Jinn world. The rest of the humans were now striving to fight them off but to no avail. The Jinn, however, were not fighting back. They seemed intent only on fleeing their world and escaping from the cave into which they had emerged.

Realising the futility of their task, the humans backed themselves against the cave wall and watched the swarm of alien beasts pass them by.

CHAPTER 95
1315 A.D.
Zenith the Saviour

Just as they thought all was lost, Zenith and an army of Jinn soldiers stepped through the portal. They were hacking at the next force of Jinn that were trying to escape their world and Zenith called out to Jaffer.

"The staff, the staff! Throw it to Jawad now!"

Jaffer did as he was commanded and, as Zenith's troops were virtually overcome, Zenith caught hold of Jawad and tugged him towards the portal. Jawad struck at it with the staff and, suddenly, the entire cave was filled with light. The sound of Jinn being incinerated by the portal as it closed, was ear-splitting.

Covering their ears, and keeping their eyes closed, the humans cowered. Then, without warning, the light was extinguished, and the banshee-like sound ceased.

Immersed in an eerie silence, the group of humans looked to Zenith for guidance and an explanation. He sensed this immediately and, patting Jawad on the back, spoke to them of what had happened.

"The Sand Jinni lied to you when he said the staff could only be used once. Meanwhile, a multitude of Jinn, the servants of the Evil One, Iblis, Shaytaan, managed to enter your world." Seeing the shock and regret on their faces, he paused momentarily, then sighed. "Fret not. You weren't to know. As for the Jinn who have passed into this world, there is little we can do about them, except to continue to hunt them down."

"How? We don't even know where they are." It was Hassan who spoke, and the others looked at him, shaken from their dazed mood by his voice.

Zenith continued: "Some of you will continue the fight here on Earth and you must pass on the secrets of your tribulations and experiences to your descendants, so they might carry on after you have gone.

"As for how, you will know them by the actions of the humans they are influencing and controlling. They will target the most powerful among you, corrupting them, exploiting their greed and their lust for power and, while you may not stop them, you can hinder them." He glanced at each member of the group before him.

"They will be working hard to destroy everything; not just humans, but the world itself. Your job is to delay them at every opportunity for the time is not yet near for that to happen."

"You said some of us will continue the fight. Why not all of us?" Marie's voice was shaky, and her breathing was accelerated.

"Calm yourself, Marie. I need all of you to continue the fight, but only some of you in this world."

The group began muttering to each other. "So, you want some of us to return to the Jinn world?" asked Reza.

"Yes, and those have already been chosen, by Zaman."

"Zaman's alive? Not defeated?" Hassan queried, excitedly.

"He lives and continues to hold back the bulk of Shaytaan's forces, but an even greater threat has been discovered in my world and that is why we need some of you to return with me."

"Who?" All of them asked the question simultaneously.

"Before I tell you who, let me explain something to you all. You know of the time lapse that occurs when you are in my world?" They nodded and he continued. "Well, there is something, not now, but in the future of your world that needs to be stopped, but it can only be stopped in my world. If we can find the threat, defeating it, sealing it up in the place from which it has escaped, could take decades. So, those who return with me may live for centuries, but those left behind here will eventually pass away. By the time you return here, your friends may be gone."

There was more murmuring from the group, but Zenith continued. "I cannot force any of you to come with me, but shortly I will name names and I hope you will agree to make this journey."

They all waited in silence and Zenith looked at each one in turn, stopping at those who had been selected to go with him.

"Jawad, Marie, Hassan, Bohemond, Amalric and Isabelle. You have been chosen. Do you consent to come with me?"

"Can we have a moment to discuss this?" Jawad asked.

"Certainly," replied the Jinni.

The five chosen to re-enter the world of the Jinn, moved to one side and began to discuss Zenith's request.

Marie spoke first. "Husband," she said, "I am with child and my arm will take time to heal. Is our baby to be born in the Jinn world and live there for God Knows how long? And who will help me with the child while my arm heals?"

Jawad was sorely tempted to question her use of the words 'our baby' but restrained himself. "I understand your reservations and I can't make any promises about the child's safety or well-being, but nor can any of us make such promises were we to stay here either."

Marie began to cry and whispered a prayer before replying to her husband. "After all we have seen and done, Jawad, I am yet still afraid, but not for myself. I am afraid for our child and for our love for each other."

Again, the reference to 'our child' made Jawad shiver with thoughts of his half-brother. Nevertheless, he knew he loved his wife as deeply as ever and he convinced himself that he could love this child too. It was hers, after all, even if he was not the father.

The discussion continued for over an hour, with arguments and counter arguments from all five of them. Finally, Jawad approached Zenith alone. "Marie has concerns about her baby," he said, and Zenith frowned in surprise at the way Jawad had phrased the statement.

"Her baby? Your baby too, Jawad."

"But we don't know that, do we? She was raped by Abbas."

"That is true, and you may not know who the father is, but I do. The child is yours, Jawad. Believe this truth and ease your mind."

Jawad returned to the group and took Marie to one side. "The baby is mine."

"What? Did Zenith tell you that?"

"Yes."

"And, does it make things any different?"

Jawad took a deep breath before replying. "I know it shouldn't. I had all but convinced myself that it would not, but knowing now that the baby is mine, affected me. So, yes, it does make things different."

Marie shook her head and began to cry, looking away from Jawad. He caught hold of her and hugged her tightly.

"I love you more than I have ever loved in my life, Marie. I will love you for eternity and I will protect our child with my life. However, I see no difference in the risks for all of us here or there, you included. The world is not safe, especially after the influx of Jinn that we witnessed. Please, come with us."

She nodded, they returned to the four others who had been chosen to return to the Jinn world and the discussion continued. Another hour passed before they finally granted Zenith their consent. Isabelle offered her apologies to the group. She had chosen to travel with Reza to Syria. She then approached Amina and asked if she would continue as Marie's maid on the journey to the Jinn world. Isabelle knew that Marie could not ask for a better nanny for the child, once born. Amina agreed and Isabelle told Jawad and Marie. Satisfied that they had made the right decision, Jawad informed Zenith. Upon receiving his approval, the group spent the night together. They prepared themselves for what lay ahead of them.

As they all sat around a fire, Owun again asked Reza to teach him Arabic and pleaded to return with him to the Middle East. "My friend, I am a Persian. I speak Farsi although my Arabic is just about good enough to communicate with Jawad and the other Arabs here. I have a better idea. I will teach you Farsi and educate you on the Shi'a school. My son will teach you Arabic and all about the Sunni school. He was brought up by Sunni Arabs."

"If Jaffer agrees, then I accept the offer," replied Owun.

The following morning, Reza and those remaining on Earth, packed their bags and horses, bade their friends goodbye and left Tintagel. Reza, Jaffer, Isabelle and Owun decided to travel with Sami and Cecelia to Syria. Stuart MacDonald bade them all farewell and headed North to Scotland. He was joined by the Jewish translator, Judah, who desired to spend more time in this strange land. The remaining men began their journey to Jawad's farm near Jerusalem.

As his friends rode away, Wadjet approached Zenith. She had taken her most well-known form—that of a woman of ancient Egypt and she lowered her gaze in the presence of the Angel Jinni, Zenith.

"My Lord Zenith, may I ask something of you?"

Zenith frowned and snorted. Jawad approached and saw anger on the Jinni's face that he had not seen before.

"You may not," Zenith replied to Wadjet.

"I wish to return to our world with you and your volunteers and White Wolf also wishes to return."

Zenith's eyes turned red and he stepped forwards, lifted her head up with his finger and placed his face against hers. "Do you think that I am not aware of the betrayal you engaged in; a betrayal that could have cost these brave humans their lives?"

She closed her eyes and replied so quietly, her voice was barely audible. "I asked Allah for forgiveness. I was threatened by Shaytaan, by Iblis himself and I was afraid, but I made amends." Her voice cracked with emotion as she repeated "I made amends."

"And if you betray us again, if you return with us to our world? What should I do then? Kill you?"

"If you think it necessary, then yes, but I won't betray any of you again and you will need my powers, will you not?"

At this point, Jawad chipped in. "Doesn't Allah know all things, including the future?" He asked.

"Of course," Zenith replied.

"So, doesn't He know already whether Wadjet will come with us and whether she will betray us or not?"

Zenith hesitated for a moment. "Yes."

"Therefore, it is not our choice to make, is it? It is not our role to decide on a future we cannot see, surely."

Zenith nodded, the red in his eyes faded to a pale green and he looked at Wadjet. "You may join us, as may White Wolf."

Jawad then continued. "Does Allah not know whether our mission will be successful or not?"

"Yes."

"Here is where I struggle to understand. Let us assume that the mission is destined to fail. Why would He permit it to continue? Why would He not stop us from wasting our time and maybe our lives?"

"Perhaps He knows it will be a success or perhaps what we deem to be failure, He will deem to be a success. We do not know His plans."

"But we're not passive zombies. You told us we have free will. We can choose to go on this mission or not. We can choose to take Wadjet, even if there is a risk that she might betray us. What if the future He has seen, therefore, is not the future that comes to pass? What if we choose, now, to discontinue this mission?"

"Then, that is already known to Him. You see, there are multiple choices, each leading to a different outcome and He knows them all."

Zenith bends down and picks two mushrooms from the ground and calls Bohemond over. "Bohemond, I have two mushrooms here. One may be poisonous, or they may both be poisonous, or neither of them could be poisonous. If either of them is poisonous, it might or might not be deadly. You have four main choices. Take the one on the left, take the one on the right, take both or reject both." The Jinni then whispered something in Jawad's ear and turned back to Bohemond. "Choose."

Bohemond replied, "I choose neither."

"Jawad, what did I whisper in your ear?"

"You said he would choose neither."

"Bohemond, did I give you a free choice? I did not prevent you from choosing any of the four options, did I?"

"You did not prevent me. I made my own, individual choice."

"But I know you hate mushrooms. I gave you a free choice but, because I know you very well, I knew which choice you would make, before you made it. And that, my friends, is how Allah can present you with free choices, while knowing exactly what choices you will make before you make them. He knows you better than you know yourselves."

He waited while they digested the philosophical idea that had been presented to them and then continued: "You will choose to embark on this mission. That has already been determined by your own characters, personalities, beliefs."

Part Three:
Dajjal

CHAPTER 96
1315 A.D.
Return to the Jinn World

Zenith asked Jawad to use the staff to open the portal enough to see through it. Surrounded by his Jinn soldiers, prepared in case there was another breach, he peered through to the other side.

"It seems clear," he said. "Zaman's forces must have defended the citadel and pushed the armies of Shaytaan back. We can go now."

Jawad tapped the staff and read the Chapter of the Quran, al-Fatihah, and the portal opened wide. Half of the Jinn soldiers went through first, along with Wadjet and White Wolf. Once through, they signalled to the others that it was safe to follow. Zenith went through next, followed by his human companions, their horses, and finally the remaining Jinn soldiers.

As the last one stepped through, the portal closed.

They found themselves in an environment consisting of a deep red-brown desert, dotted sporadically with rocks the height of a minaret, of the same hue. It was hot; far hotter than the Earthly land they had come from. Bohemond pulled off his thick, woollen cloak and wiped his perspiring brow. After rolling it up, he tied it securely to his horse. The other humans followed suit.

"We have a lengthy journey ahead and it will be fraught with many perils," Zenith said. "Stay close together at all times and follow any instructions I give, to the letter."

Hassan stared at the red desert for a while before glancing up at the cloudless sky. "When we first entered your world, Zenith, we found ourselves in a cave system, through which you led us to a great cliff. From there, we trekked through a forest and a desert of crystal. When we entered more recently, the environment had changed and now we find ourselves in yet another place."

"What is your question, Hassan?" The Jinni asked.

"Well, every visit we have made has taken us to a very different place, but we are always not far from Zaman's castle in Zaydussia. How is that possible?"

Zenith smiled. "Do you not recall the physical location of Zaydussia?"

Hassan frowned and Zenith looked up. Hassan's eyes followed the Jinni's and he stared at the empty sky above them. Then, he smiled and nodded. "It is in the air." There was a pause before he continued. "You're saying it moves? Zaydussia moves?"

Zenith nodded. "Now, let me explain what is happening. Hundreds of thousands of Jinn got through before the portal was closed and they will create chaos and harm for many centuries, before they start to age and die.

"They may have children with humans. They will build very rich elites around the world and gradually destroy the Earth, sacrificing people and animals to Shaytaan.

"However, the bigger threat is that which is posed by Abigor. He has discovered the whereabouts of Merlin's arch enemy, the Jinni, Morgana and she has a way of opening a new portal, one which could unleash many millions of Jinn into the Earthly realm.

"The worst of these will be Masih al-Dajjal, a demon who, when released into the Earthly plain, will be the cause of the final extinction of humans and the end of time itself.

"We must hunt for Abigor and Morgana in the Jinn world and destroy them both before they can release Dajjal. So, let us proceed."

The Arabs, used to the desert heat, gave advice to Amalric and Bohemond on how to dress for protection and comfort, but still this heat was greater than anything the two former Crusaders had ever experienced. Within an hour they had each depleted their personal supplies of water and were asking Jawad to speak to Zenith about finding fresh water sources.

The prince handed his own water bottle to Bohemond. "Take this for now. Share it with Amalric and I will speak to Zenith."

He caught up with the Jinni, who was walking ahead of the group. "Zenith, we need water. Our supplies are almost exhausted," he said.

Zenith continued to walk and did not look at Jawad. "We will find water soon, but be warned, you will have to fight to take it from those who occupy its source."

"What sort of enemy will we be faced with?" Jawad asked, wiping his brow with a turban he had wrapped around his head when they first entered the desert.

Zenith finally stopped walking and turned to face Jawad, waiting for the rest of the group to catch up. His eyes rested on Jawad's for a moment, then moved to Marie. "Your wife will have to be hidden when we encounter them, Jawad."

"Excuse me?" Marie said. "What decisions about me are being made without my voice being heard?"

Jawad looked at her and shook his head, hoping she would stay silent, but she ignored him.

"Well, Jinni? I'm waiting," she said, sternly.

Zenith sighed, then spoke to the whole group. "There is a source of water not far from here, a natural spring, but the spring and its source are held by a tribe of very powerful, extremely dangerous Jinn. None of you have experienced these beasts before, so I must warn you that they are formidable warriors.

"They are often referred to as the Babylonian Lilitu, blood-drinking, female demons that roam during the hours of darkness."

He glanced at Jawad. "I see you carry the sword the Angels gave you many years ago. You will need it and you will need great courage, but also strategy."

He turned to Bohemond now. "If you blunder in, they will kill you all. Even with the right tactics and an intelligent, cautious approach, this will be a very risky encounter."

The Jinni turned back to Marie. "My dearest Marie, you carry a child. I have no doubts about your skills in battle. I have seen them for myself, but you are by no means fighting fit in your current state."

"I will make that decision, Zen…"

"The decision is made. You will agree to hang back or I will restrain you."

Shocked, Marie looked at her husband, whose head was bowed, his eyes fixed upon the desert sand. She glanced at the others, but they turned away.

Zenith then continued; "The Lilitu use the night for hunting and they enjoy nothing more than killing new-born babies and pregnant women. It is too great a risk to take, for you to join the fight. Instead, I will secure you somewhere that the demons won't find you."

"Fine!" She huffed and shook her head, reluctantly agreeing to hang back of her own accord.

"Tell us more of this enemy, Zenith," Amalric called out.

"In daylight, they go underground, away from the rays of the sun, which are lethal to them. Then, at night, they come out and hunt. Some will stay near the water source, because beasts, Jinn and, occasionally, humans, will stray into their path as they search for water.

"Once anything reaches the source, they will attack, shrieking at high pitch, a call to those who are roaming and hunting, to return. Some will kill their prey instantly, drinking the body dry of all its blood. Others will drink without killing, leaving the victim in a half dead state—neither alive, nor dead. These victims will too seek the sustenance of blood, but they will be slaves to their Lilitu Queens.

"We must tempt them away from the water supply, for it is near to their underground lair. If we can pull them from their secure base, then we become the hunters."

Amalric, shaken by the description of this enemy, stuttered as he spoke up with a question of his own. "You say the sun can kill them, er, c-can Wadjet's f-fire kill them too?"

"Yes, and an arrow or spear through their hearts, but we must fight from a distance. Get too close and they will overcome you, their strength far exceeding yours. Then, they would either kill you or turn you."

CHAPTER 97
1320 A.D.
Damascus

Sami and most of his entourage arrived, tired and dusty, in the region in which the city of Damascus was situated. They arrived, however, with enough wealth between them to purchase a reasonably large estate on the City's outskirts. Sami had sold the land that was left to him by Robin and their journey to Syria had included a stopover in Malta, where Reza had a fortune in gold stored with bankers that he trusted. Jaffer and Owun had gone into the city of Damascus to find a scholar who could assist Owun in his desire to learn Arabic and understand the Quran. They would most likely remain in the city for several weeks, while Reza, Sami and their wives organised the house and estate.

It was summer and the air was hot and humid. A well on the estate provided adequate water for both people and horses, but for Cecelia and Isabelle, unaccustomed as they were to this climate, it was quite unbearable. Both women were sitting under the shade of an awning, built on the Northern side of the house. Cecelia was wearing traditional Arab clothing and her head was covered with a light, thin scarf. She wafted a slender wooden board in front of her face as a fan and occasionally wiped her forehead with a piece of fabric.

Isabelle, still wearing European clothes that were wholly unsuited to the weather, had untied her hair to allow it to flow more freely. It was a rather vain attempt to allow what breeze there was to flow freely across her head and neck. It was not working. Clearly uncomfortable, she blew air from her mouth, as if expelling a creature that had been inadvertently swallowed.

"How can you stand wearing that scarf on your head?" She asked Cecelia.

The latter laughed. "I wore far worse when I was a nun," she said.

"Besides, you're feeling the heat more because of all those tight, thick garments you're wearing.

Isabelle grunted and waved her hand at a fly that was hovering near her face.

"Damned heat, damned flies and I've been bitten by something too," she said, angrily.

"Take off that top layer," Cecelia suggested. "Just don't show too much to the Muslim men. They'll pretend to be offended."

"Pretend? What do you mean?"

"Isabelle, my dear, they are men. They love to see what we have, but they are socially obliged to keep up a certain level of decorum; to follow a social and religious guideline, so to speak." She smiled and gave Isabelle a mischievous glance. "It wouldn't do for them to be criticised by the other men, so they all act prim and proper around each other, don't they?"

Isabelle nodded. "I suppose so."

Cecelia laughed again. "But look at how they are with us, their wives, in the bedroom. Like animals, they are. Nice animals mind you. And, do you think, if they caught a glimpse of either of us naked, they would not have a good look if they thought they wouldn't get caught? I know from my years with nuns and priests, that most piety is pretence."

Isabelle giggled then, but that only intensified her discomfort in the heat. "I'm going to change. Do you have anything suitable for me to wear?"

"As it happens, I do. Come inside."

From around the side of the house, Sami had overheard their conversation and chuckled to himself. *They know us far too well,* he thought. With a broad smile on his face, he turned to find Reza standing behind him.

"Women are trouble," Reza said.

Sami stopped smiling and cleared his throat. "Er, yes they are, but beautiful trouble just the same." For a moment, neither man said anything. Then, Sami clapped Reza on the shoulder. "So, how is married life, Reza?" He asked.

"Very good. Very good indeed, mostly, but Isabelle refuses to become a Muslim."

Sami squeezed his friend's shoulder. "And why should she? There is no reason why she should, is there? She is of the People of the Book and the Quran permits marriage to a woman who is Christian or Jewish. And remember, the Quran also says, "there is no compulsion in religion"."

Reza nodded, reluctantly, his lips pursed, and his forehead etched with the lines of a frown. "True," he replied, "but I don't understand her resistance. Cecelia converted." He paused, thoughtfully. "Do you know what Isabelle asked me?" He did not wait for a reply to this question. "She asked me if Muslim women can marry non-Muslim men; men who are from the People of the Book. I told her no, but can you believe it, she began quoting the Quran to me, in Arabic!"

Sami smiled. "Really? Well I would have thought you would be happy that she is reading the Quran. What did she say?"

Reza frowned and sat down on the seat the women had vacated. Sami joined him. The breeze was intensifying, and the air was cooling as the day wore on towards evening.

"She asked me why it doesn't say in the Quran that Muslim women can't marry non-Muslims. I said that it doesn't say they can either. Then, she threw my own words back at her. 'You told me', she said, 'that paradise lies at the feet of the mother, because she does most of the child-rearing'. I nodded and then she said, 'then surely, it would make more sense for a Muslim woman to marry a non-Muslim man, than the other way around, because she would rear the child as a Muslim'.

"I didn't know what to say, but it made me realise that she will be teaching our children Christianity, so maybe she has a point."

Sami watched the beginning of the setting of the sun and sighed. "I'm not a scholar, my friend, but I don't think we can say that something is forbidden, just because it *isn't* mentioned in the Quran."

He looked around, as if checking that nobody was nearby and listening. "I would never say that publicly, though, but think about it. Are catapults and those Mongol explosive sticks forbidden? They're not mentioned in the Quran, are they?"

Reza shook his head, his frown deepening. "As you say, you're not a scholar, and nor am I. This is too much for me to consider. I am just a soldier and a spy."

Sami shivered a little and stared at the setting sun, the sky around it turning a deep, dark red. "It will be a fine day tomorrow, my friend."

Then, he turned to face Reza. "Did you hear the women talking?" He asked, and Reza shook his head, so Sami told him what Cecelia had said about men. "And she is right, is she not? We concern ourselves too much with what other people will think. Let me tell you something, Reza. I spent many years with the Scots, and I was far more comfortable with life and religion there, than I am here. I didn't have to worry about what people thought. What I mean is, they didn't know whether my behaviour was in accordance to what the Muslim scholars say or not. As long as I was doing right in the sight of Allah, as long as I followed the Quran, I was at peace with myself."

"What are you saying?"

"I'm saying that maybe the Scholars are not always right. I'm saying that men fear that a Muslim woman marrying a non-Muslim, will succumb to his power and authority—that women are that weak; that they do whatever we tell them to do and that isn't true is it?"

Reza hesitated for a moment, so Sami continued. "If it were true, my friend, your wife would be a Muslim by now, wouldn't she?" He laughed, slapped Reza on the back and then stood.

Reza nodded. "They will be calling you a heretic, if you're not careful, Sami."

Sami laughed, a loud and bellowing chuckle. "They already call *you* that, my Shi'a friend."

Reza smiled and changed the subject. "The night will be a cold one," he said, "and tomorrow, we must consider our task. It is a pity Zenith didn't make it clear for us; our purpose, I mean."

"Let's retire for the night and pray that tomorrow will be a fine day. Look at the sky, so red and calm."

CHAPTER 98
The Water Source

Zenith gathered the group to discuss their plans further but before he could speak, Bohemond staggered over, carrying an earthenware flask in his left hand. He was unsteady on his feet and kept spilling liquid from the flask all over himself and those he leaned on to keep his balance.

"What is the point of all this?" His speech was slurred, his eyes bloodshot.

He took a swig from the flask and, as his head tipped back, he lost his balance, collapsing in a heap, his backside striking the ground with a thud. He laughed raucously. "That's going to hurt in the morning," he shouted, unaware of how loud he was. He laughed again at his own attempt at humour, but the others did not share his jovial mood.

"You're drunk!" Hassan shouted, marching across to Bohemond and swiping the flask from his hand. "Where did you get this filth from?" He poured the remaining contents of the flask onto the ground, much to Bohemond's annoyance.

"Hey, I was going to finish that, you Arab donkey." He laughed again and turned to Amalric. "They hate being called donkeys," he said, smiling like an imbecile. He made a futile attempt to stand but fell back to the ground. Then, he fumbled for his sword before realising he had left it with his horse.

"He brought it through with him," Amalric said. "We both did." He saw Jawad and Hassan shaking their heads, which annoyed him. "Look, we're not Muslims. We don't have to forsake drinking alcohol to satisfy your holier-than-thou, self-righteous attitudes. Since teaming up with you we have either not had access to it, or we have abstained out of respect for you. Now, we've decided that if we're going to fight some blood-drinking horde of demons and either die or get stuck in this God-forsaken world forever, we're not going to do it sober."

Jawad stepped forward to face Amalric. "You're not drunk," he said.

"Bohemond had a bit more than I did. Maybe I should have stopped him, but to be honest, I didn't care."

Hassan threw the flask to the ground and it shattered into several pieces. "You didn't care? I should beat some sense into both of you. Look at the state of him. How is he in any fit state to fight?"

Amalric took a deep breath to calm himself. "He'll be ready when we are. You have my word on that."

Hassan huffed and walked away. "Your word?" He mumbled, before stopping and turning back to face Amalric once more. "Where did you get this from?" He pointed at the shattered pottery at Amalric's feet.

"The Cornishmen. They make it from fermented apples. You might like it. At least it might take some of that edginess away from you."

"You insult me, Christian," Hassan replied, his face red with anger, his hand reaching for his sword.

Amalric, however, still relatively sober and still armed, was faster. In the blink of an eye he unsheathed his own sword and held it out, pointed in Hassan's direction.

"STOP! Stop this at once!" It was Zenith who called out. Once again, his eyes had turned red. He stormed past Hassan and stood between the two men. "Amalric, take Bohemond and sober him up. Hassan, back away. We will continue our planning. Amalric and Bohemond can join us once our resident drunkard is in a fit state to participate constructively."

For a moment, nobody moved.

"Now!" Zenith shouted, his voice resonating, piercing the minds of everyone present—everyone except Bohemond, that is. He had passed out. Amalric reacted quickly. He dragged the dead weight of his unconscious friend to the horses where there was some water and bread. The rest of the group sat in a circle to discuss their next moves.

Zenith returned to his normal, calm demeanour. Seated in the shade of a canopy that Jawad had erected with cloaks and blankets, the Jinni began to speak. "We cannot risk getting close to the Lilitu. Their ability to entrance those they encounter, is daunting.

"We have no skilled bowmen with us," Hassan interjected.

"No," continued Zenith, "but we do have Wadjet and White Wolf, the presence of whom, I confess, I opposed."

He turned to Wadjet and sighed. "I remain reluctant to entrust you with something this important," he said, glancing briefly at Jawad, before returning his gaze to the female Jinni. "You are able to take a male form, are you not?" He asked and she nodded. "Then you can enter their camp. They will lust after a human male. Once among them, you can burn them all."

Wadjet smiled. "I can do better than that. I can take on their form and blend in as one of them." She paused and patted White Wolf on the head. "I don't think White Wolf should accompany me, however. They would rip her apart and drink her blood the minute they set eyes upon her."

The sun was sliding gracefully beyond the horizon and, as it did so, the temperature dropped. Marie shivered, as if someone or something had walked through her and Jawad took his coat from the ground and placed it around her shoulders. She smiled and he kissed her on the cheek. "I agree with Wadjet," she called out. "It is too risky for White Wolf to go."

Zenith was clearly agitated but agreed to send Wadjet alone.

Almost from relief, one-by-one each person reached for a cloak or a blanket from the canopy and wrapped themselves in them to shield themselves from the cold. Jawad looked around to see if there was anything with which to light a fire, but there was nothing available to them. As he shivered, Wadjet stepped forward, pointed at the ground and smiled at him. A burst of flame shot forth from her fingertips and struck the dry, desert earth, igniting it instantly. They had their fire and Jawad was left grateful, but also awestruck, witnessing her power at such close range.

"This is someone we need to keep on our side," he whispered to Marie and she nodded.

As the group huddled around the fire, they were joined by Amalric.

"How is our resident inebriate?" Asked Hassan, a mischievous smile on his face.

"A couple of hours sleep, and he will be right as rain," replied Amalric, as he sat down alongside Hassan. He reached out a hand to the Turkish warrior, who took it and shook it. "My apologies," Amalric said.

"I am also sorry, my friend."

Everyone spoke French to each other most of the time, as it was the lingua franca in the group, but occasionally they would speak Arabic, a language of which Bohemond and Amalric had just a rudimentary understanding. As they settled into clusters of conversations, Amalric asked Hassan, in Arabic, what the plan was.

Jawad, seated to Amalric's left, laughed. "Eager to practice your Arabic, eh?"

"Me too," Marie said.

So, they spoke in Arabic and, although the conversation was somewhat laboured, they did manage to communicate for about half an hour, before Amalric finally said, "All right. French now."

They laughed, explained the plans again and then, gradually, eased into general conversation. As the evening wore on and the two moons lit up the night sky, Bohemond joined them. He looked the worse for wear and continually rubbed his temples in a futile attempt to ease his headache, but his speech was no longer slurred.

"I would like to apologise for my behaviour earlier," he said, pain etched on his face. "However, my concerns remain. We never win. This fight just goes on and on, so what is the point of it all? How long must we fight for?"

Zenith heaved a big sigh. "Until the end of time," he said.

Amalric glanced around to see if others were as bemused as he was by that response. "What does that even mean, Zenith? How can time end and, if it can, if it does, when will that be?"

Zenith stood up and walked across to Amalric, placing a hand on the French knight's shoulder. "I don't have that information. All I know is that before the Universe existed, time did not. Without our fight, the Universe and time itself will end sooner, rather than later. That's what I know."

Bohemond laughed. "Are you going to tell us that God knows, or Allah knows, or whatever you want to call him, because I don't think I believe that anymore."

Hassan was about to challenge Bohemond, but Zenith raised a hand in the air to stop him.

"Calm yourself, Hassan," he said. "This is neither the time, nor the place, for us to debate, argue or fight over philosophical matters such as these. I suggest we rest, and, in the morning, we will capture the water source."

"I will capture the water source," Wadjet added.

"Very well," replied Zenith, "*you* will capture it."

CHAPTER 99
The Blood Drinkers

During the daylight hours, Wadjet waited on the outskirts of the Lilitu camp. There was no movement there, as the blood drinkers, fearing the sunlight, were securely housed underground. She considered her strategy, ensuring her transformation would be convincing. However, the Lilitu were a hive, connected to each other psychically, communicating mentally. If Wadjet was unable to connect to the hive mind, she would be discovered immediately and, despite her power, could easily be overcome. Surprise was essential for her attack to succeed.

During this waiting period, she practised her psychic skills, by reaching into the creatures' minds while they were dormant. By the time night began to fall, she was satisfied that joining the hive would be possible. She was confident that she would not be detected as an enemy.

It was as the sun slipped beyond the horizon that Wadjet made the decision to move. However, as she approached the water source, she saw a small group of the Lilitu leaving their camp and flying out across the cold, dark desert. Wadjet needed to find out where they were headed but she did not want to risk joining the hive mind again until she was deep undercover. Physically, her transformation was complete. Her face and body were covered in hair, her canine teeth were extended, her eyes were black with tiny pupils and, extending from her back, were two leathery, bat-like wings. She walked into the camp as discreetly as she could. Then, she immersed herself among the Lilitu before, finally, linking to the hive mind.

The saturation of her mind with the multitude of telepathic voices made her wince. She was tempted to cover her ears with her hands, in a vain attempt to silence the bedlam, but she resisted. The last thing she wanted to do was to draw attention to herself. She forced herself to filter the voices, focussing on any that seemed helpful. It was crucial that she discover where the party of Lilitu she saw leaving were headed, and why.

As she reached the heart of the Lilitu hive, close to the water source, she stumbled upon a small collection of voices. They were discussing the 'hunting party'.

Damn, she thought, *they're hunting.*

Then, she caught herself, quickly becoming unsettled as she remembered that her thoughts were no longer her own. There was no time to waste. She knew that. The destruction of the hive had to be carried out immediately. As this decision entered her mind, the hive turned to face her, en masse. *Caught* she thought, and her hands raised, as if in surrender. The hive moved towards her, but it was too late for them. Wadjet took on her true form and the fire, the burning power within her, was thrust out towards those closest to her. Their screams, their pain, was felt by the rest of the hive, all of whom buckled and tensed in agony. Wadjet spun like a dancer. She began to twist in circles, the flames from her outreached hands scorching and scarring all around her.

Some of the Lilitu, those furthest from her, broke from the hive mind. They released themselves from the grip of the group pain. They turned and fled to the water, the pool of dark blue liquid that seemed black as pitch in the darkness of the night. At first, they hesitated, but finally they threw themselves in. As they struck the water, they screamed and squirmed, thrashing about in apparent agony.

Wadjet sensed them but did not see them. She continued her slaughter of the rest, until not a single Lilitu remained alive, or so she thought. As the fire subsided and she returned to a calm state, she heard voices and animal sounds emanating from the pool. Realising these were external sounds, she rushed towards the water. Stunned for a moment, she shook her head in disbelief. Emerging from the water were five humans, two horses and two Jinn. *The water has returned them to their original form,* she thought.

Not wishing to startle them unnecessarily, she approached them in the form of a human woman. Her arms were bare, as were her legs, and her brown skin shone and shimmered. Her brown eyes glowed and her face was framed by jet black hair that flowed past her shoulders all the way to her waist. Her figure was stark and pronounced by the tight-fitting vest and skirt she was wearing. She stood at least six feet tall and, as she walked towards the stunned survivors, they appeared mesmerised by her presence. She looked to them like an ancient goddess and she knew this. She used it to her advantage, just as she had in Ancient Egypt some millennia before.

"Fear not," she said, her voice like a soft breeze to the survivors' ears. "I am not going to harm you."

The horses had panicked but two, tall, unusual-looking Jinn had calmed them and now held them close. One human, a woman, stepped from the group of humans who were huddled together, shock and fear etched on their faces.

"Where are we and who are you?" She asked.

Wadjet explained where they were and asked if they could remember how they got there.

A woman answered. "I remember falling. I was out riding, and the horse lost a shoe. She tripped on some rocks and we fell off the edge of a seaside cliff. That's all I can recall."

The other humans muttered that they had had similar experiences. The second woman had fallen with her horse into a sinkhole in the desert. There were similar incidents related by the children, but none could recall what happened after their fall. The only man among them, however, related a confused tale of being confronted by a desert spirit. The two Jinn said they had been thrown from the roof of a tall building by the agents of Iblis, but again remembered nothing more. A handful of humans and two Jinn, all seeking answers.

"How do we get back home?"

"Is this real?"

"Who are you?"

"Are you an angel?"

"And who are those two with the horses?"

Wadjet held up her hands for them to stop and, gradually, the questioning subsided, and she lowered her arms.

"I don't know how to get you back."

Voices began to shout at her, all at once, and she held her hands up again.

"Please, please, I can bring someone who can answer all of your questions, but you must remain here." This brought further muttering and complaints, but she continued; "I'm sorry, but I have to stop something terrible from happening. I will return, with others like you, in just a few hours."

Reluctantly, and after some half-hearted protests, they agreed to wait, so Wadjet left. Once out of view of the survivors, she took the form of a Lilitu once more, which enabled her to fly back to Zenith and his human followers. She knew that was where the Lilitu hunting party was headed and she needed to stop them.

CHAPTER 100
1325 A.D.
Abigor Visits Reza

Reza awoke from a nightmare. He was sweating and let out a shout as he entered an awakened state. It brought Isabelle into consciousness too and she placed a comforting hand on her husband's arm.

"Bad dream?" She asked.

Reza sat up and rubbed the sleep from his eyes. Then stared, vacantly ahead of him. "More than just a dream, I fear," he replied.

He swivelled himself out of bed and prepared for the morning prayer. Isabelle dressed and left the room. When Reza was dressed and his prayers were completed, he headed through the cooking area of the vast house, past Isabelle and out into the empty courtyard.

"Come out here, all of you!" He shouted and was instantly greeted with opening window shutters, clattering and banging against the walls of the house. "Come, please, we need to talk," he said to Sami who poked his head out of the window.

Cecelia and Sami joined Reza and Isabelle in the courtyard, which was just beginning to feel the warmth of the rising sun. Reza began to explain his dream, or vision as he called it.

"It was our world," he said, "but not as we know it. There were billions of people, living in every part of the world. And there were wars, the like of which we have never seen, with weapons of indescribable destructive power and ferocity. Weapons that could wipe out entire cities with a single strike and I mean cities that are forty, fifty times larger than Damascus is now."

He paused to control his emotions and the others waited for him to continue.

"Damascus, in fact most of Syria, Yemen, Iraq, were a wasteland of death, destruction and disease and there were some people, a small number compared with the total world population, who were so rich that they owned more, between them, than all the rest of the people of world put together." He paused again and caught his breath.

"In my vision, I was approached by Zaman and he told me I was seeing a possible future, but one that was becoming increasingly more likely since the horde of Jinn entered our world

"He told me what our mission is. To kill those Jinn. They are controlling, advising and, in some cases, possessing that rich elite. Zaman told me where to find them, how to identify them and how to kill them."

Sami took a deep breath and spoke up. "If these people are so rich and so powerful, how can we hope to stop them?"

Reza shook his head. "You misunderstand, my friend. They are not here yet, although their ancestors are. Our role is not to stop them, but to delay their rise to power. And to kill the Jinn who are advising and empowering them."

He frowned and for a moment his eyes wandered, as if he were imagining something. "Jawad and the others have another role," he said. "Their job is to stop the one who will one day bring to humanity the knowledge of how to build those weapons. He will also teach strange means of control that will enslave the world."

He sighed. Sami looked dubious. "I understand your hesitation, Sami, but please trust me."

Isabelle touched him on the arm. "We do trust you," she said, and turning to Sami and Cecelia, added "don't we?"

"Of course," they replied in unison.

"But this is a great deal to take in, Reza, especially based on a dream," Sami added.

"Not a dream, Sami, a vision," came Reza's quick reply.

"All right, a vision, but I wish we had more information." He glanced around and added "and more people with us."

"We will gather more people, Sami," said Reza. He looked up at the cloudless sky and added, "it is growing hot out here. Let us retire to the shade."

"I'll fetch some coffee," Isabelle said as she headed to the kitchen.

"I'll help you," added Cecelia.

The two men strolled over to a bench and an elaborately decorated copper table that had discoloured over time. They were placed beneath a veranda, designed to provide shade in the immense heat, especially in the summer months. Once seated, Sami rubbed his fingers through his thick, dark hair and said, "this is a nice place, and it will be a beautiful day. It's a shame we'll soon have to leave, won't it?"

Reza sighed. "In my vision, Zaman told me to wait for notification of our first task, so I think we can relax here for the time being, my friend."

Sami was about to respond but the women returned with two small pots of the thick, strong, dark coffee the Arabs love so much. Cecelia placed the pots on the table and Isabelle did the same with a tray, containing four tiny cups. As she let go, however, the ground beneath them began to shake and the tremor grew increasingly violent very quickly. The table toppled over, the cups smashed on the hard ground and the pots of coffee spilled. Cecelia and Isabelle instinctively reached out for something to hold on to and the men called to them to lie on the ground. Suspecting an earthquake, they were aghast when their surroundings were bathed in bright light and grey smoke. Isabelle let out a scream.

As quickly as they began, the tremors died away. The smoke dissipated and the light faded. They found themselves confronted by a huge Jinni, horns protruding from his head, red eyes, dark reddish-brown skin and two bat-like wings protruding from his back.

"Preserve us from the accursed Shaytaan and from the Jinn," Sami shouted, but the figure did not move. He looked at Reza and smirked.

"I am Abigor, Grand Duke of Hell," the creature said. "I know the secrets of warfare and have knowledge of the future and my Master has sent me to issue you all with a warning."

Reza stood, but was less than half the height of Abigor. Still, he was adamant that no servant of Shaytaan would be allowed to issue a warning without a reaction. "You do not frighten us, Abigor. I, for one, remember you from the battlefield a long time ago and I saw you flee in the face of Zenith, the coward that you are."

"Silence, foolish human. I'm sure you have noticed that Zenith is not here. Just you four." He paused and laughed. "And me." He paused and smiled. "But I will not stay long."

Sami reached for his sword, then realised it was still in the house. Resigned to their position of weakness, but determined to show resistance, he also stood and took three steps towards Abigor. The Jinni was enormous, not just in height but overall physique. Muscular, with vast arms and legs. Sami's eyes were in line with the base of the Jinni's chest and so he looked up to meet Abigor's eyes.

"Speak then, Jinni! And afterwards, be gone!" He said, unblinkingly.

Abigor sneered and closed his eyes for several seconds. When he opened them again, his red irises were aglow. The surrounding air had cooled since his arrival and Marie shivered. Abigor's grin faded and he took a step away from Sami.

"I have seen the future and your mission here is pointless, as is that of your friends in our realm. The Master's army has dispersed around the globe, reaching lands known to you as well as those which are, hitherto, unknown. Abbas performed his duties exceedingly well and our plans are in motion."

"Abbas is dead," Sami called out, "so your plans have not fully succeeded, have they? What can he do to assist you now?"

Abigor grinned again. "Abbas sired many children. Shaytaan's descendants will continue to wreak havoc in the Muslim world and beyond for generations to come."

Sami looked up and stared directly into Abigor's eyes. "The future has many possible outcomes. You have seen only one, Demon. Maybe the future you saw is not the one that will come to pass."

Abigor ignored Sami's comment. He blinked and turned to view the green acres that surrounded the estate. "In the future I saw, this land will be laid bare in a war so devastating, you will not be able to imagine its ferocity and the Muslims will be a weak, subjugated mass of ignorance." He paused, looked back at Sami and his nose twitched. "You may be right, of course. The future I saw may not come to pass, but can you risk ignoring the fact that it might?"

Sami was sceptical, but Reza was concerned. Abigor's prophecy matched his own vision. He remained silent, but anxious and Abigor continued.

"You know that my Master's servants now walk the Earth; those who came through the gate and those who are the offspring of Abbas.

"And you know they are already beginning to influence those with power or assist those who strive for it. That is why you are here, and I am here to warn you of the consequences if you try to interfere."

"And what might those consequences be?" Asked Sami.

Abigor laughed. "I have found a great Jinni witch, who knows how to release the Dajjal, the demon so feared by so many of you Muslims. The Christians called him the beast, the anti-Christ and in my world your friends' attempts to prevent his escape are already being delayed."

He waved his hand at the scenery around them. "We will release him, and we will send him through to this world and he will bring about the end of all things. Mark my words. I need not say anymore, for you know what is coming."

Isabelle spoke out at this point. "And Jesus will destroy him. That is the Prophecy."

"That is correct," Reza said. "That is foretold in our religion too. The Mahdi will come and then Jesus will return and the Dajjal and all his followers will be defeated. Did your vision fail to foresee that?"

Abigor grinned again. "No, it did not but perhaps the stories you have been told are incorrect." He paused, momentarily and then added, "As Sami rightly said, there are a multitude of possible futures. So, stay here, give up on your quest and you will be safe. Continue on this path you have chosen, however, and you will be annihilated."

"We could kill you now, Demon," shouted Reza.

"Ha! Puny humans. I have fought more fearsome enemies than you and they are all dust now. You are no match for me, and I am nothing compared with Shaytaan or Dajjal. You will see death, torture, the slaughter of the innocent, disease, famine, hunger and the extinction of life and you will beg for help, but your God will not hear you. Nor will he help you."

Then, he was gone. No burst of light, no smoke, no sound. None of the drama that greeted them when he appeared. One moment he was standing before them and the next moment he was gone.

CHAPTER 101
The Hunting Party

The attack came without warning. Out of the night sky, fell a dozen or so Lilitu, shrieking like banshees as they rocketed towards Jawad and his companions. Quickly, Zenith ordered them to stand together, in a tight huddle. He then ordered Amalric to arm himself with a bow and the French knight did as he was told, without question.

He placed his arrow on the bow, pulled back the string, aimed and fired. The arrow whizzed over the heads of the oncoming Lilitu. Then, they landed and rushed the group. Jawad and the remaining humans already had their swords drawn and Zenith's Jinn were armed with pikes. The Lilitu were not armed, but their fingers, with long claw-like nails, were attempting to rip at least one of the group away from the huddle. They stepped forward, clawed at the group and then, retreated as the swords swung and the pikes were thrust towards them. Hassan felt they could hold them off for some time but doubted they could keep them at bay until dawn, when the sun would become their saviour. He said as much to Bohemond. The Frenchman nodded and then, without warning, left the huddle and rushed at the Lilitu.

Swinging his sword like a berserker and shouting a war cry at the top of his voice, he hacked at the first Lilitu, slicing its head clean off. The others, joined telepathically, turned towards him in one synchronised movement. Then, they rushed him. He continued to hack at them with his sword, but it was a futile action. One of them grabbed him and sunk its teeth into his neck. Once subdued, Bohemond was lifted into the air, like a rat being hoisted aloft by a bird of prey.

Amalric took aim at the Lilitu holding Bohemond and unleashed an arrow. It soared, almost unseen, through the air and lodged itself in the Lilitu's heart. The creature screamed in pain and released Bohemond, but by now they were high in the air and the knight crashed to the ground legs first. The sound of breaking bones echoed around the empty desert and Jawad, the others following, sprinted to assist their fallen companion.

The Lilitu, seeing the defensive huddle was broken, reacted instantly, making a beeline towards Jawad. He looked up and saw the approaching onslaught and then he watched as a bolt of fire propelled from behind the Lilitu, destroyed them all instantly. It was another Lilitu and even Zenith was confused by this intervention. It landed on the ground before Jawad, who held out his sword in defence, but the creature's appearance changed and Wadjet revealed herself.

Jawad let out a long breath in relief and sheathed his sword. He rushed to Bohemond, followed by the rest of the group and Wadjet.

Bohemond was unconscious and his legs were broken in multiple places. His companions were shocked by the injuries and knew, in their hearts, that if he survived, he may not walk again. Hassan shook his head. "By Allah, this is serious. May Allah heal his wounds or comfort him through the changes."

Marie was more constructive. "Pray by all means, Hassan, but also get to work. I need something to use as splints and something to use as bandages. You men are going to have to use your strength to try to reset the bones."

Hassan nodded. "Absolutely," he said, but as he was about to go to the horses to find the materials Marie needed, Amina shrieked.

"Ya Allah [Oh God], look at his legs."

They all watched, partly in awe, partly with anxiety as Bohemond's wounds began to heal themselves. Cuts sealed over, leaving no scar, bones fused back in place and bruises vanished.

"A miracle," Amalric whispered. "Your prayers answered, Hassan," he added.

Wadjet, however, did not agree. She pushed herself past the others and looked at Bohemond's healing process. "This is no miracle. This is a curse. He has been bitten and he is turning."

"Turning?" Jawad looked, inquisitively at Wadjet.

"She means he is becoming Lilitu, Jawad," Zenith added. "You know what has to be done and it is safer for all of us if it is done before he has fully turned."

A sense of loss and sadness descended upon the group, but Amalric stepped forwards, his sword in hand. "Tell me what to do," he said, but before anyone could answer, Wadjet caught hold of his sword arm.

"Wait!" She called out. "There is a cure."

She explained what had happened to the Lilitu that had plunged into the freshwater oasis during her attack.

"The Lilitu weren't holed up at that water source only because they knew it would attract their prey to them. They were guarding their treasured secret. The water changes them back to their original form." She paused while everyone digested what she was saying. "I don't know if it is something about that particular source of water, or if it is all water, or any source of fresh water, but I know what I saw."

Zenith stepped forward and looked her in the eye. "It appears I misjudged you, Wadjet, and I believe your story, but where are the Lilitu who transformed back?"

"I left them at the oasis and told them I would bring you all to them. If we hurry, we can get Bohemond into the water before he becomes a threat to any of us."

Amalric huffed. "She may be lying, leading us into a trap."

"Why?" She replied. "Why would I do that?"

"What would stop you? That is a better question," Amalric asked.

Wadjet, to the astonishment of those around her, began to cry. "What would stop me? Bohemond."

Amalric scoffed at her. "What are you talking about? You are not making any sense. You…"

"I love him!" Wadjet shouted, stunning everyone into silence. "He doesn't know this, and I don't want any of you to tell him, because I know what a shock it would be for him, but I really do love him. I have loved him from the moment I first joined your group." She glanced down at Bohemond, still lying unconscious on the ground. "We must save him."

When she looked up again and saw the faces of the humans, she sighed. "That look. The one you're all giving me. That's the reason why I have never told anyone how I feel."

Jawad approached her and laid a gentle hand upon her arm. "Wadjet, we cannot help who we love and I, for one, will not judge you."

Amalric, however, was not as appeasing. He huffed and waved his hand towards Wadjet. "This thing cannot have any kind of relationship with Bohemond. How can a human and a demon ever form any kind of bond, let alone one of love?" He shook his head and Wadjet slumped to her knees.

"I am sad to hear that Amalric. I have always liked you and respected you and to hear that you see me as a demon, well, it hurts."

Amalric walked away, alone, and made his way back to the horses. Jawad watched him go and then spoke to Wadjet. "He'll come around. In time. Now, let us get Bohemond to the oasis."

As he began to issue orders to load up and prepare to move, Wadjet stopped him. "There isn't the time to take him overland, Jawad. His transformation will be complete soon, so I will become Lilitu again and fly him there. Meet me at the oasis in a day or two. Maybe speak to Amalric. I don't want to be his enemy."

Jawad nodded, Wadjet's appearance shifted, then she lifted Bohemond up and flew away.

White Wolf ran after her and the others gathered the horses and supplies and followed. Zenith unleashed his enormous wings and flew into the air, determined to arrive at the water source with Wadjet. Jawad and Marie took the horses and the others set out on foot.

CHAPTER 102
Wadjet and Bohemond

The water source was eerily quiet. None of the shrieking and chattering that was present when the Lilitu were there. It was also empty of life, except for a handful of humans a single horse and two, tall, slender Jinn, one male and one female. Their features were human-like, but their heads were oversized, relative to their bodies. Their arms were long and thin, ending with bony hands, each with just three fingers and an opposable thumb. Their mouths were small, and their bodies were translucent. In fact, they were see-through, with internal organs on display to the world.

As Zenith touched down nearby, he could see Wadjet talking to the humans and pointing away in the direction from which she had just arrived. He walked over to them and heard her explaining the situation. Bohemond's limp, unconscious body held up by her unnaturally strong arms. As Zenith reached them, the humans took a step back, but he had not noticed. He was focused on Wadjet. He watched in surprise as she kissed Bohemond on the forehead and then breathed into his mouth, bringing him back into consciousness. It was clear that he was turning at an increasing rate. His skin colour was changing, and his eyes were red. Without waiting any longer, Wadjet threw him into the water. He landed on his back with a loud splash and then began to scream, his arms and legs thrashing about in the water.

Zenith rushed forward, anxious that the water could be doing more harm than good, but Wadjet held up a hand and asked him to wait. Against his better judgement, he waited and, seconds later, Bohemond, returned to his normal, human self, emerged from the water. He was dazed, confused, but perked up when he recognised the familiar faces of Zenith and Wadjet.

He was squinting against the rising sun and staggered slightly as his feet met the desert sand. Wadjet stepped forward to help steady him and led him, gingerly to Zenith.

"What happened?" he asked, his voice raspy and his speech slow.

Zenith explained what had occurred and then Wadjet took Bohemond to one side and helped him to lie on a soft patch of grass, near the waterline. He was still dazed and was not sure who this beautiful woman was. She smiled and he smiled back, or at least he thought he had smiled. Actually, it appeared more like a grimace. Wadjet touched his cheek and spoke softly to him, asking him to rest and regain his strength. She sat next to him and, after he dozed off, she watched him as he slept.

Two days' later, the others arrived. Wadjet had remained with Bohemond the whole time, nursing him back to full strength. There was no doubt in her mind that she was in love with this man. She smiled again, but when she glanced up, her eyes met Amalric, who was glaring at her, anger in his eyes.

Why do you hate me so? She asked silently. *I know you will tell your friend. How will Bohemond react when you do? Will he hate me too? I don't know if I can bear that.*

She sighed and considered what she would have done to Amalric in the past, before the enlightenment she had experienced since travelling with these humans. Then, she returned to watching Bohemond, a look of true peace on his face.

Zenith turned to the human survivors, a man, two women and two children. "What can you remember?" He asked, in French.

The woman answered first but spoke Spanish. "I don't understand what you are saying," she said.

As Zenith pondered this latest predicament, a voice from behind him spoke in Spanish. It was Amalric. "He asked what you remember."

Zenith looked around at the European knight, clearly surprised, but impressed, and Amalric spoke to him. "We dealt with a Spanish sea captain; a man named Miguel. He only spoke Spanish, so we learned it," he said. Then, he repeated Zenith's question to the woman again.

She looked down, as if trying to pull some memory from the well of her mind. "Not much. I remember walking my horse through a field. I was picking berries and then I fell into a gully and hit my head. The next thing I remember is being here, surrounded by those creatures. Beyond that, my mind is blank, up to the point where I emerged from the water and saw her." She pointed at Wadjet.

"You are Spanish. What year was it when this happened?"

She frowned. "I can't recall, but the Moors had arrived and had taken control of all of our lands."

Zenith pulled Amalric to one side. "The Moors invaded Spain from Morocco early in the 8th Century, more than six hundred years' ago."

"You're saying she has been here for six hundred years? My God, her homeland would be totally alien to her now."

Zenith asked Amalric not to break this news to her too suddenly. Gradually, he explained where she was, how she most likely ended up here, what had happened to her since she arrived on this world and what had happened in Spain since she left there. Initially, she was in denial. Her demeanour flipped, constantly, between anger and sadness, her behaviour sometimes aggressive and at other times, depressed. She cried, she laughed, she shouted, she lashed out, until Marie and Amina finally took her to one side and calmed her down.

The second woman said her name was Zahara. She explained how she had been in the Arabian desert when a sandstorm appeared out of nowhere. She remembered being on horseback and accompanied by men at arms. One of them, she said, carried a hawk so she assumed they were hunting. The last thing she could recall was sand spirits emerging from the storm, a whirlpool of sand appearing at her horse's feet and then falling. She and her horse, tumbling into the pool of sand.

Amalric asked the man and the children what they could remember but they stared at him, blankly. He realised they did not speak Spanish, so tried French. The man, an African, spoke up but in a language that nobody who was present understood. Frustrated, he began looking around for something and, unable to find what he sought, knelt and began to draw in the sand with his finger. He built a picture of what had happened to him. He was from a small village somewhere in Africa, although nobody could determine from his pictures where, precisely, he had lived. One day, he said, a spirit had come to him in the night and dragged him from his bed. He was taken from the village and into the jungle to where a large, hollow tree had stood. The demon pulled him into the tree, and like the woman, he had emerged here, surrounded by the Lilitu. The next thing he remembered was leaving the water. He had no idea of when that had happened as his tribe did not track time with any form of calendar. He was, he said, two hundred and forty moons old. That would be twenty years, mused Zenith, although he looked much older. His name, he said, was Lungelo.

As they pondered the man's story, one of the children spoke, in Greek. "We are brother and sister," she said, pointing to the young boy beside her. I am the oldest. I'm fifteen. He is twelve."

Amalric asked her the same question as he had asked the others. "What can you remember about how you got here?"

"We were playing," she said. "There was a hole in the ground. It wasn't there the day before and we wanted to see what was there, so we jumped in. Well, I jumped in. He cried and wanted to go home, but I pulled him in with me. Then, a strong wind appeared from nowhere and began swirling around us until we were spinning, round and round and round. Now we're here. That's it."

"What are your names?" Amalric asked.

"My name is Serene," she replied, "and my brother is Alcander. We're worried about our parents."

Amalric knelt alongside the children, so that he was at their height. "What year was it when you went into that hole?" he asked.

"I don't know," Serene answered.

Marie approached and took the children with her to join the woman who was still being comforted by Amina. "The Spanish woman's name is Rositta," she said, as she led the children away.

Zenith called the men together and shook his head. "Returning these people to a world that is no longer the one they left is not advisable and may even be cruel, but if we take them with us, we will be faced with a host of problems, not least the fact that we do not have one single, unifying language between us all. I can't decide on this. Jawad, you must agree among yourselves."

After some discussion, they agreed to take the newcomers with them. They also agreed that everyone should learn French as a common tongue between them. They spent several weeks camped out at the oasis until Zenith was confident that they were ready to proceed. Then, one morning, very early, he called them all together.

CHAPTER 103
The Nature of Dajjal

Zenith informed them he had gathered them together to notify them of their destination. The original group had now been joined by the humans who had been turned back after a lengthy time as Lilitu. The Jinn who had undergone that same transformation had chosen to leave, hopeful that they could track down their people, a nomadic race of Jinn from the South of this world.

Seated along the edge of the water source, the group listened as Zenith outlined, in far greater detail, their mission henceforth.

"Beyond the desert," he said, "lies a city, more advanced than anything seen on Earth or in any of the Jinn worlds at this time in history." He pointed South, to a hazy horizon in the distance.

"The city was built by a company of genius scientists, engineers and mathematicians. They have machines that run all aspects of the city's services."

"Machines? You mean like our siege machines?" Asked Amalric.

Zenith chuckled. "Well, in as much as they are technical devices, then yes, but that is as far as the similarity goes. These machines are operated by codes, by algorithms, by numbers."

He went on to explain that the city's society was the most powerful of any in the Jinn worlds. It possessed deadly, protective defence systems but it was isolated.

"They're not interested in the conflicts and wars among the rest of the Jinn. They have advanced weapons, including ships that fly at tremendous speeds, but they are solely for defence of their city," Zenith continued.

He answered some questions about the location of the city, indicating that it was several weeks' journey from where they were currently. Then, he continued.

"It is inevitable that, one day, this advanced knowledge will reach earth and humans. Perhaps it will be Jinn who will help the humans to acquire this learning. The important thing, however, is that this should not happen too soon. Humanity is not ready for it. Most Jinn are not ready for it."

Jawad interjected. "Are you saying these Jinn in the city are more advanced, more powerful than Zaman or Shaytaan?"

"Very much so, but they are not Jinn. They are human, or at least their origin was human."

"What does that mean and how can a human city be here?"

"All of that will be explained in good time." Zenith replied.

"So, who is this person we are searching for?" Asked Marie.

"Not who. What? We are searching for Dajjal, a devious, destructive Jinni who suddenly appeared in the code of the city's machines and, like a virus, began to take control of the system. It failed, but had it succeeded, the city's defences would have been shut down. That would have left it vulnerable to an attack by Shaytaan's forces."

"So, this Dajjal was defeated?" Asked Amalric.

"It was. The machine's programmers, the operators, found it hidden in their code. They removed it and imprisoned it in a penitentiary, a vault, also built from code. They believed the vault was impenetrable but Abigor found a way in."

He took a deep breath and looked at the confusion on his audience's faces. "Abigor found Morgana, the Jinn witch whom Merlin had sealed in a separate dimension, just as she sealed him in the cave on the Isle of Avalon. The name of the city is Madinah al-Taqnia and both Morgana and Merlin lived there. This was a privilege that the owners of the city afforded only to the brightest and trustworthy Jinn. However, Morgana was not as trustworthy as the city folk had believed. She was eventually expelled centuries ago for revealing some of the city's secrets to outsiders."

He waited while they digested his words and then asked Wadjet about Bohemond's recovery.

"He is improving, although he remembers very little of what happened to him," she replied.

"Probably just as well," said Zenith. "Now, where was I? Ah, yes.

Morgana has been found, by Abigor, and she has the ability to release Dajjal. As we were delayed by the Lilitu, it is quite possible that she has already succeeded in releasing him."

"Why is this Dajjal such a threat?" Amalric's question was one that many in the group wanted to ask.

Zenith inhaled deeply before continuing. "While in the City's systems, Dajjal obtained knowledge of how they work. His knowledge is not complete, but is extensive and if he is freed, he will undoubtedly flee to Earth."

Amalric chipped in. "I thought you said it wasn't a he, wasn't a person."

"We're getting to that and you will see why it wasn't but now he is." Zenith stated it in a matter of fact way but could see his listeners were very confused.

"But we don't have these systems you speak of, Zenith," said Hassan. "This code-based system. We have no idea what it is."

"True, you don't have those systems," Zenith replied, and paused. "Yet," he added. "But Earth is not ready for the wonders of the City and will not be ready for many millennia. It is feared that Dajjal will introduce rapid advances in stages and in less than six hundred years, the first major shift will occur.

"It will give humans knowledge that they will not be prepared to receive. It will give them great power, without the wisdom needed to control it and once that shift occurs, more will follow as Dajjal reveals the ways and means for building systems like those of the Madinah al-Taqnia. He must be stopped, or at the very least, delayed."

Jawad frowned. "Dajjal is mentioned in our religion, so isn't it inevitable that he reaches Earth?"

Zenith nodded. "Absolutely, but he shouldn't arrive for many millennia. Abigor and Morgana are altering the future; taking us all down a path that should never have been chosen."

"You said his knowledge is not complete. Isn't that a good thing?" Marie asked.

Zenith tilted his head sideways, left to right. "It may be, it may not be. Only Allah knows. We know that Dajjal is missing the most crucial part of the information; how to control the systems. That is what is so dangerous, for without the ability to control them, the risk is that they could bring about Earth's destruction."

The Jinni pointed to the West. "Taqnia lies many weeks away in that direction. The City's leaders sought the assistance of Zaman, as none of Taqnia's citizens are permitted to leave the City. Since the incident with Morgana, it has been a rule that non-residents are forbidden to enter. We, however, have been given special consideration. You will see things beyond your imagination. Try to stay level-headed and the Taqnians will advise us on how to track down Dajjal. They will show us what to look for, should he escape to Earth."

CHAPTER 104
1325 A.D.
A Dilemma

Once Abigor had left, Reza stormed indoors, angry that the Jinni had had the gall to approach them here. "I will kill that demon one day!" He shouted as he threw a glass across the kitchen, smashing it against the wall. He kicked a chair and cursed Abigor and Shaytaan. "I swear this sword of mine will pierce that Jinni's heart and remove his head."

"And we will help you in that effort, Reza, but for now you should store this anger for that time." It was Sami and his intervention had startled Reza. He looked at the pieces of shattered glass on the floor and the turned over chair that had nestled itself in the doorway. He calmed himself and nodded.

"Of course, as usual Sami, you're right, but I am tired of all this waiting. We should be acting, not idling our lives away here. There must be something we can do."

Sami walked to the chair, picked it up and placed it back in its original place. Isabelle entered and began clearing up the broken glass. She looked at Sami, wondering what he could say that would calm her husband. She had never seen such anger from him before.

Sami's eyes met Reza's. "We could try to find some of these descendants of Abbas."

Reza huffed. "How? How do we even begin? And, even if we find them, what do we do? Kill them? Kill people who have done nothing wrong?"

Sami bit his lip. "We could watch them, see who they meet, determine what they are doing. Anything is better than this, Reza, don't you think?"

"OK, but how do we find them? We don't know who Abbas gave children to?"

Isabelle, who had been listening, called out to the two men. "I do," she said.

Both men turned to face her.

"As you both know, Abbas spent a great deal of time with me, and though none of it was pleasant, he liked to talk, to boast. I know some countries, some cities, some people's names; those he bedded." She cocked her head sideways and smiled.

Cecelia came to join them but did not look very happy. "You're leaving us here, aren't you?"

Isabelle glanced at her and then at her husband. "No, we'll all go, isn't that right?" She asked.

Reza took a deep breath and frowned. "It is better that you stay here."

"Because we're women?" Isabelle enquired.

"Not at all. Because, if Zenith sends a messenger, someone needs to be here."

Cecelia shook her head. "And if Abigor returns?"

Sami chewed his lip for a moment and turned his head towards Reza. "She has a point."

"Damn," Reza responded. "We're trapped here, waiting for a message that may never come. Isabelle has the information we need to begin tracking down Abbas' little offspring, each one a descendant of Shaytaan himself. Yet, here we sit, doing nothing."

"We can all go," said Isabelle, "and leave a note here for any messenger."

"No. I don't want to go." Cecelia began to cry and stormed back to the house. Stopping briefly in the doorway, she turned and shouted back at them. "I'm settled. We have a home here."

"All right," said Sami. "We all wait a little longer for a messenger to arrive and, if Abigor returns, we will all be here, together, but know this; we are not settled here. When the messenger arrives, we will be moving on."

Cecelia stormed to her room and slammed the door.

"She'll come around," Sami whispered to Reza.

"And how long are we going to wait?"

Sami thought for a moment and then said; "Jaffer and the others are due to join us here soon. Unless they've got themselves into some trouble, their stay in Damascus will be over next week. We can't really do anything until they get here. So, we'll give it another two weeks and then we go."

CHAPTER 105
Al-Madinah al-Taqnia

As they travelled to Taqnia, Zenith continued to explain the City and its inhabitants to them all. He explained that the beings that occupied the City were human-like in appearance and that most Jinn believed they were humans; and originally, they were. They were humans who had been brought here by some unknown power. Most believed that they were most likely the descendants of humans who had fallen into the Jinn world thousands of years before. Some, however, believed that they were the very same people who came here originally. If that were the case, they had most definitely changed over time.

He told the group that the Taqnians' technological advances had led them to build artificial people, initially with mathematical codes, like the Dajjal code. More recently, however, they had been working with biological codes and a combination of both types of coding. They had perfected cloning a thousand years earlier but had more recently built a person from scratch by using the biological building blocks they had discovered.

"So, Taqnia is an example of perfection then? A utopia?" Asked Hassan.

Zenith huffed and smiled. "Not at all. Their insulation from the outside world led to physical and mental defects that were rapidly destroying the society. It is the reason why they created copies, clones, and now original versions of their race." He took a deep breath before continuing. "But even these creations presented them with problems. The clones and other artificial people could not breed and, even if they could, would still be restricted to a small population, tucked up inside the City."

"And that would produce, in time, the same defects or worse." Jawad said.

"Yes. There was another problem with the clones, however. Each clone is a copy of a copy and each time one is made, quality is lost."

Zenith then frowned and hesitated slightly before continuing. "Consequently, they have demands in exchange for allowing entry to their City to strangers and the sharing of their knowledge." He said.

"What kind of demands?" Asked Amalric.

"Unfortunately, they will not inform me of what those demands are, until we reach the outskirts of the City," Zenith said.

"Sex I hope," Amalric muttered under his breath. Amina heard him and giggled. Marie frowned.

The city outskirts were now in sight and they could see that the city was vast, spreading out from the desert into a lush, green wilderness, beyond which lay a colossal sea. Even from a distance, the city's scale, and the height of many of its buildings, were awe-inspiring. Most of them were glass structures but tinted and there were flying objects travelling across the air around them. As the travellers got nearer, they could see a shimmer in the air surrounding the city.

CHAPTER 106
The Taqnian Demands

The group of humans, with their Jinni guide Zenith, his Jinn warriors and the group's Jinni companion Wadjet, were met and greeted outside the city. The person who met them was, to all intents and purposes, human. However, he was at least a yard taller than the tallest people on Earth. He was slim but muscular and was wearing a skin-tight body suit that left little to the imagination in terms of his physique. Marie and Amina cast their eyes away in embarrassment, although neither could resist the occasional peek, for this was most definitely a well-endowed man.

His head was shaven and, judging by his hands, neck and what could be seen of his lower arms, he was most likely completely hairless. His eyes were dark brown and his facial features handsome to the point of being too perfect. It was as if he had been engineered this way, with all imperfections removed.

Is this a clone? Jawad wondered, *or one of their created originals?*

Hassan eased closer to the prince and whispered in his ear. "Clones? Manufactured people? Allah forgive them for this is not natural."

"And yet Allah has not stopped it from happening," Jawad replied.

Hassan shook his head. "Zenith said they have breeding problems. Are they not the detrimental effects of this biological manipulation?" He asked.

Jawad puckered his lips and shrugged his shoulders. "Maybe. Or maybe their community has shrunk so much that their breeding circle was not large enough." He looked at the Taqnian and continued. "Let's not pass judgement until we know more and try not to disrespect our hosts, Hassan."

Hassan huffed. "For now," he said.

The Taqnian waved for them to approach, stopping them before they reached the city itself. When he spoke, it was in French, but nobody

521

seemed surprised by that.

"We have agreed with Zaman, to allow you to enter. We need your help to track down Dajjal and to put a stop to that Jinni's plans for Earth and for this world. However, we also need your help in other matters."

He looked embarrassed for what he was about to say, and it took him a moment to compose himself. "We instituted a law on all our people not to breed, because our genetic sample is too small and there were deformities appearing."

"Genetic sample? What is a genetic sample?" Amalric asked.

The alien man continued. "All life is made up of biological code. We call the codes genetic markers. Humans will discover this eventually, or Dajjal will leak the information to someone if he reaches your world. For adaptive, healthy offspring, the breeding of a species should be with those far from their own family or tribe. We call this genetic variation. It is what is missing from our society here."

"So, you want us to fuck some of your women then," Amalric called out. "Good. Let's get on with it. I've been celibate since leaving Acre and my hand is hurting from so much self-gratification."

Jawad closed his eyes, partly out of embarrassment and partly annoyance, thinking Amalric may have disrespected their hosts with such course talk. The Taqnian, however, laughed.

"A rather crude way of saying it, but yes. That is what we need. I'm glad you are willing. And able. Now, let us proceed to the city."

He led them into the metropolis, which had no protective walls. Hassan wondered how this could be such a safe and secure haven when it seemed so open to attack. He would add that thought to a growing list of questions he had for the city's occupants.

As they approached the first buildings, they stepped from the desert sand onto a smooth path that ran alongside an equally smooth road. Both were made of a material the humans had never seen before and Amalric, curious, bent down and placed his hand on the path.

"It's so smooth," he said. Then he rapped it with his knuckles, "and yet so hard."

"Which is what their women will be saying to me, once we meet them!" Amalric called out.

His comment was met with laughter from Bohemond and a few of the others, but Jawad gave him a stern, reprimanding look.

Hassan logged the issue of the paving in his memory too, for later.

The streets were busy. Flying objects shot over their heads. Coaches without horses glided past them, silently. Amalric leaned over to Bohemond, placed a finger below his chin and gently closed his gaping mouth.

"Zenith wasn't wrong when he said this was beyond our wildest imagination. Is this what the future holds for our world, do you think?"

Bohemond let out a long breath. "I'm stunned," was all he said.

They all walked on, following their Taqnian guide, who led them to a long coach and invited them to climb aboard. They embarked, finding the inside as luxurious as many castles and manor houses in their own world. Thirty seats, in rows of four, with a gangway down the centre. They sat down and watched in awe as the door closed, apparently on its own. Their guide sat at the front and issued verbal commands. The vehicle moved off without a sound. Hassan's list of questions was growing longer by the minute.

Other vehicles moved aside to allow the coach free passage across town. The sounds outside were muted and, while the outside temperature was uncomfortably high, the air within the vehicle was cool. Within minutes they arrived at an enormous, glass edifice in the city's centre. The guide and his visitors disembarked and made their way on foot into the building. They went through a glass door that opened as they approached it and entered a vast open area. They turned right, walked across a smooth, shiny floor and were shown into a small chamber, just big enough to hold the guide and the visitors. A sliding door closed behind them, the visitor said something in an unknown language and the room shot upwards until it arrived at the top of the structure. The doors opened and they stepped out into a vast room that overlooked the entire city.

The guide beckoned them to a huge, circular, glass table situated in the middle of the room and they sat down in comfortable, padded seats. Through the windows that encircled them, they could see flying machines, whizzing past. The sky was clear and bright, and it soon became clear why. The clouds were floating beneath them.

Hassan could wait no longer. "I have many questions sir." He said.

The guide smiled, sat down among them and nodded. "Be my guest Hassan."

The surprise Hassan experienced at hearing his name spoken, was written all over his face. "Well, firstly, how do you know my name? Secondly, what is your name?"

The Taqnian glanced at Zenith momentarily and the Jinni blinked and nodded to indicate that it was time to explain all. Their host then informed them that his name was Vander. He explained that Zaman had notified them of many facts about the group that was visiting, but some of the group had not been mentioned by the Overseer. Zenith explained the incident with the Lilitu and how these people had been cured of the Lilitu disease that had inflicted them.

Hassan went on to ask about the City, the roads, the coaches that ran without horses, the flying machines and the Taqnians themselves.

Vander spoke in length about the different theories related to the origins of his people and explained how they harnessed the power of the sun, wind and tides to produce something he called electricity. They used this energy to power everything from homes to flying machines to artificial people.

"We came from Earth," he said. "From very far in your future." He paused as they digested what he had said and he waited for a response, but when none came, he continued.

"We have existed here for hundreds of thousands of years. As I said, we come from so far into your future, that we had already begun working on several experimental ideas, including cloning, long before we ended up here.

"Our technological advances had led us, not only to produce artificial intelligence that was close to the workings of the human mind, but also to combine mathematical coding with biological coding. Our work was leading to a theoretical breakthrough regarding the creation of enhanced biological entities, using microscopic machines called nanites. We thought we could advance humanity beyond our dreams." He paused and took a deep breath before continuing. "It was at that point that our research centre and the surrounding city, were transported here."

He paused momentarily to monitor their reaction and found their expressions to be those of the confused. He smiled and then continued.

"You see, one of our co-workers had been experimenting with spatial and temporal wormholes. One of his experiments, however, must have gone catastrophically wrong. We were transported here, to this world. We had crossed both time and space. Our time-travelling experimenter colleague did not arrive here, however."

He noticed that the confusion of his audience had turned to disbelief and he waited for a response. After a minute or so, it was Hassan who spoke up. "I don't know about the rest of our group, but I don't really understand most of what you've told us so far. Maybe we never will, but are you saying that you did not just cross from Earth to this world, but also crossed time? How can that be?"

"We come from your future, but this world is parallel to yours in terms of time and we have been here for hundreds of thousands of years. Thus, we must have travelled through time, don't you agree?"

"Yes, but... Please continue." Hassan replied, shaking his head.

Vander took a deep breath and resumed his explanation. "Just before the, let's call it 'jump', the man working on his own, on time travel, came to my notice. I had discovered that he was using a false name. He was not who he was claiming to be, but that's not all. I found evidence that hc existed in the past as well as the present."

"How?" Hassan asked.

"Unfortunately, before I could find out, we ended up here. The man who sent us here, because that's what I now believe, had left the city before it vanished from Earth.

"We could not return to our own world and time as the man had gone and his laboratory, with all of his research, had been destroyed. Whatever happened in that lab, it generated power beyond anything even we could have imagined."

Jawad frowned. "Who rules here? Do you have a king?"

Vander laughed. "We were a business community before the jump, all competing with each other, to achieve personal fulfilment. Praise from our employers, money for work done well."

He sighed and, for a moment, glanced out of the window before returning his gaze to his guests. "Once here, it quickly became obvious that there was no use for our money, there was nobody to trade with and that competition between us was pointless. So, we formed a co-operative.

We work in co-operation with each other and make joint decisions."

"But you seem to hold an ambassadorial role, which surely gives you a level of importance, status, above others in your community, doesn't it?" Asked Jawad.

"We had a vote to decide which of us would greet and guide our visitors and who would serve food. Once you are gone, we will return to our normal roles. If other visitors arrive, others may be chosen for these official roles."

Jawad was about to speak again, when Hassan interrupted. "You mentioned enhanced beings and combining technology with biology. As I said, I don't understand the details of what you're saying. Can you show us? Show us one of these enhanced humans, or a clone or one of your artificial beings."

Vander stood up and took a step back. "I am an enhanced human," he said. "Millions of microscopic machines course through my body, augmenting my mental abilities, keeping me free from sickness and healing injuries. They are now biologically-based machines, fully integrated with my own biology."

He sat back down. "Dajjal, a unique type of Jinni, took the form of mathematical code and worked his way into our systems, attempting to destroy them from within. It was a stroke of luck that we discovered him. He was extracted and sealed up in a virtual vault.

"Unfortunately, Abigor found the Jinni, Morgana, and she knew of Dajjal's whereabouts. She freed him, enabling him to enter a supply of nanites, which she had stolen from us. Our fear was she would implant those into a human. Our fear became reality, I'm afraid and Dajjal now has physical form. That makes it possible for him to travel to Earth." He paused and rubbed his hand over his bald head.

He then told them a location where Dajjal was last reported to have been seen. He was, they were informed, heading to the Ocean of Infinity, the largest ocean on this world. He suggested that, accompanied by Morgana, Dajjal was most likely planning to open a portal to Earth.

"You must try to stop him, but without killing him," Vander said. "His destiny is to one day reach Earth, for he will trigger the final battle and the end of days."

Jawad considered this. *How will we ever find Dajjal if he implanted himself into a biological human?* he thought and was about to ask this when Hassan jumped in.

"What of Morgana?" He asked.

Vander waved a hand to Jawad. "Your prince has Merlin's staff. If you find her, all you need do is point it at her heart and recite the following: *centum carcere animam millennia.* Then, she will return to her prison and it will be sealed for a hundred thousand years."

There was quiet reflection for a while and Vander allowed his guests to digest all that he had told them. After a few minutes, he broke the silence.

"Later", he continued, "I will show you the other developments we have made. For now, do you have other questions? We have about half an hour before food is served and then I will take you to your accommodation. Amalric, I will send some ladies to keep you company. If anyone else wishes to partake, please let me know."

Bohemond began to raise his hand to volunteer, but a look from Wadjet forced him to lower it very quickly. He did not understand why she had that effect on him.

Hassan then asked about the roads, the power sources for the vehicles and the lighting of buildings and all was explained, in detail. Vander then explained why the city had become so isolationist, separating itself from the Jinn world beyond the city limits and Jawad asked why they didn't use one of the many temporary gateways to re-enter Earth.

"Our aim has always been to find our way back home, but only to our time. To enter in any other time would disrupt human history severely and that brings us to the problem that you are here to help us resolve. Dajjal. For now, however, we shall eat and then you will rest. Tomorrow, I will show you around the city and our laboratories and explain why Dajjal must be stopped."

CHAPTER 107
The Wonders of Taqnia

Having eaten and rested, the band of human travellers, together with Wadjet and White Wolf, were taken on a lengthy tour of the great city of Taqnia. It was wondrous beyond any expectations they might have had and Wadjet felt privileged to be the first of her kind to be granted entry. The streets were bustling with people. Just like on Earth, they came in many shapes, sizes, colours, but it was impossible to distinguish artificial beings, from enhanced biological entities. They were intrigued by the change in ambient temperature between the buildings where they met and were accommodated and the outside. Here in the streets it was hot; not as hot as it was in the desert, but far warmer than any of the buildings they entered. Vander tried to explain the air conditioning systems that were used throughout the city, but eventually settled on just saying the air was cooled using technology beyond their understanding.

They spent several hours touring the City, learning more about these beings from the future. They scrutinised the laboratories where both the artificial beings, which Vander called Artificial Intelligence Humanoids, and the biologically enhanced humans, were created. Then, exhausted, both mentally and physically, they returned to their accommodation, ate, rested and prepared for a final meeting with Vander back in the glass room.

As they clambered into three flying vehicles to return to base, Jawad looked at the staff he carried everywhere. He considered their task. Unsure that they could successfully prevent Dajjal from reaching Earth, he questioned his host.

"What if Dajjal gets through?" He asked.

Vander sighed. "Then we will have to hope and pray that the world is neither mentally nor technologically ready for everything he has to offer."

Back in the glass room at the top of the sky-scraping building, Vander mentioned Jawad's earlier question. He was stood by the windows and looked over the city streets below. "The time when humans are mentally and technologically advanced enough to understand our knowledge, should be far into the future, beyond even the time my people came from. However, he can still cause mayhem and chaos, even in your undeveloped world."

The humans shuffled and huffed upon hearing their world described in such a derogatory way, but nobody said anything. They knew, of course, from what they had seen in Taqnia, that he was right.

Vander smiled, as if he knew what they were thinking, and then continued. "Dajjal will provide humans with knowledge they should not have. They will take leaps and strides in development that would not be possible without his help. If that happens, it will be unfortunate, but not..." He laughed and added "not the end of the world, for as I said, that is for a much later time."

He paused and looked back at the group. "You would have to return to Earth if Dajjal breaks through. You would need to meet up with your allies there and resist the oppression, the greed, the hatred, the indignity, the killing and the worldwide destruction that Dajjal will bring about.

"He will begin recruiting and rewarding servants with whatever they desire, from the moment he reaches Earth. To many, that will be wealth, power and influence. To others, it will be other things. Over time, people will sleepwalk into slavery."

He waited for a moment while they digested the information and he called for refreshments for the group, which were duly brought through.

"Your job will be to disrupt, oppose, educate the masses, be charitable and offer hope. You will need to recruit too, but only a select few, chosen by you, can ever be told the whole truth of who the enemy is. Those few should be your descendants. Keep it in the families, so to speak. Is that understood?"

With some hesitation, they all nodded, slowly, but Amalric wanted further clarification. "You want us to form some kind of secret network, like the Templars?" He asked.

"Yes and no," Vander replied. "A network, yes. Secretive, yes, but not secret. Like the Templars? No. You are to tackle, head on, those who abuse their power; those who, with Dajjal's support, seek to rule absolutely, viciously, tyrannically, deceitfully, while using the masses as tools to achieve their evil ends."

He took a deep breath. "How you do that, is down to you," he said.

Marie had been silent throughout the discussion but felt it was time to raise a point. She coughed gently, to attract attention and Vander waved a hand, indicating that she should speak. She took a deep breath.

"Our allies on Earth may show the signs of age that we do not. How can we be sure they're fit enough to help, or even if they are still alive?"

"They live," Zenith said. "They have been trying to track down Abbas' descendants, but they have been blundering around with no direction or purpose. They have decided to wait for either your return or a message from me."

"And the wives", Vander added, "now each with children, are tired of the months their husbands would spend journeying the world in search of people they don't even know."

Vander sighed and paused, as another of his kind entered the room with food and beverages. She laid a tray onto the table. As she did so, her female form was fully visible to Amalric, sitting where she placed the tray. The skin-tight clothing the Taqnians wore, was shocking to most of the humans who were present, but Amalric had spent many a night with whores in Acre and was not as prudish as his comrades. As he stared at the Taqnian's breasts and nipples, the shape of both being stark and close to Amalric's face, he felt the sharp prod of Bohemond's elbow in his ribs. Amalric looked up to find everyone staring at him, some smiling, others frowning, the women shaking their heads.

The Taqnian woman glanced at Amalric and smiled. She then laid the food and drink out on the table, grabbed the tray and left. Amalric could not resist peeking at her as she walked to the door, her hips gliding from side to side and the shape of her behind, so round yet so firm. He sighed.

Vander winked at Amalric and Zenith cleared his throat. "If I may say something?" The group nodded and mumbled their approval. "Jaffer and Owun, unfortunately, have found themselves thrown into a Damascus prison for fighting. You may have to free them before embarking on any other tasks."

"Fighting who?" Hassan asked.

"That, you must find out from them. All I know from Zaman is that blood was shed, and men almost died."

Vander stood up and, for a second, gazed out of the window at the slowly setting sun. "Now," he said, "you must rest, except for Fenrir. I need her to take a message to your friends on Earth."

The group of humans looked at each other and shrugged, clearly confused by Vander's comment. He noticed but continued anyway. "She is fast and can reach the portal quickly; hopefully, before Dajjal."

"Fenrir?" It was Bohemond who interrupted. "Fenrir is from Viking mythology. We know of no Fenrir among us."

"Fenrir is your wolf," Vander explained.

Bohemond frowned. "Are you saying the Viking gods were real, but were Jinn?"

White Wolf said nothing. She left further explanation to Vander and Zenith and it was the Angel Jinn, Zenith, who spoke next. He stood and took a position front and centre, with his audience remaining seated.

"Of course. They were real, in as much as they existed, but they were not gods. They had powers, as all Jinn do. They knew that humans tend to be superstitious. Human are easily impressed. However, these Jinn grew arrogant. They told the humans they were gods."

"But Christianity overpowered them, is that it?" Bohemond asked.

Vander laughed, a haughty bellow of a laugh that belied his slim physique. "Oh no. The rise of Christianity and the demise of the Norse Jinn was coincidental. In the same way, the fall of the Pharaohs and the rise of the Hebrew faith under Moses, occurred at the same time by chance."

Bohemond shook his head. "I'm confused. Coincidence?"

"Lights on", said Vander. The lights in the room came on just as darkness fell outside. Some were distracted, but Bohemond persisted. He cleared his throat and Vander smiled. "According to legend, the forces of Zaman, the Overseer, the primary Jinn agent of the Creator of worlds, of life, of time, a man whom some of you know well, was involved.

"Zaman and his troops destroyed the Norse Jinns' powers and they did so just as forces among the humans subdued the Norse Jinns' human followers."

531

"So, you're saying that Thor, Odin, Loki are dead?"

"Not dead. Weakened."

Suddenly, a light flashed outside, illuminating the city and the room for a moment. Everyone turned to look out of the wall of windows.

"Fear not," said Vander. "That was merely our defences warding off an ill-advised attack by a foolish assailant. It happens occasionally. Jinn always think their magic will eventually win the day for them, but our science is hundreds of thousands of years beyond their magic. We have been here a very long time."

Heads turned back from the windows to Vander. Hassan leaned forwards, resting his muscular arms on the table. "White Wolf," he said before correcting himself. "Er, Fenrir. She has no speech in our world. How can she convey a message to Sami and the others?"

Zenith intervened. "Fenrir has speech wherever she goes. It was merely that she chose not to use it when on Earth before. Too many people were present who would not have taken kindly to a talking wolf. It will be different with your friends. They are living in isolation, many miles outside of the main inhabited areas in Syria."

The room fell silent and, as its occupants considered the task which lay ahead, another Taqnian entered. He hurried to Vander and whispered in his ear. Then he left. Vander waited until the door had closed before speaking again.

"It is time for you to get some rest. I have some work to do. I will send Fenrir and will meet again with you in the morning."

CHAPTER 108
A Matter of Urgency

Jawad and his group were woken in the early hours by a Taqnian. He called them, as a matter of urgency, to the meeting room. When they arrived, Vander and Zenith were already seated at the table. Vander had an anxious look on his face.

"Please, sit down," he said, waving a hand toward the other seats. "It seems we must speed up your departure. When I was called away last night, I was informed that Dajjal is nearing the portal sooner than we expected and with an army of Jinn. I believe Fenrir should have made it through before Dajjal was anywhere near the portal, but now it seems you will have a fight on your hands to stop him from going through the portal. The alternative, if you can't stop him, is to follow him through."

Bohemond found himself sitting with Wadjet. He glanced at her and she smiled. He placed his hand on hers and whispered something to her.

"I can't hear you," she replied. He looked at Vander, let his eyes scan the others and realised nobody was paying him any attention, so he leant in closer to the Jinni.

"I said Amalric has told me about your feelings."

Surprised, her initial reaction was to pull her hand away, more out of embarrassment than annoyance.

"I'm sorry, is he wrong?" Bohemond asked, his eyes focused on Wadjet's hand.

"This isn't the time or the place, Bohemond, but no he is not wrong. Can we talk later?"

Bohemond nodded and tried to pay attention to the discussion that had begun in earnest.

"What type of Jinn are they?" Wadjet suddenly asked, taking the others by surprise because the conversation had moved on since Vander's initial announcement.

"Er, well, many are like Ashar, the Jinni who guided you on your previous journey," replied Zenith. "They are Wishmasters. However, others are shapeshifters, like yourself. There are also several Zao Tarsan demons. They often harm pregnant women, but they also enjoy frightening people to death—literally."

"And what of Dajjal? What does he look like? How do we recognise him?" Asked Jawad.

Hassan chipped in before Zenith or Vander could respond. "Is he blind? Does he have one eye like a floating grape? Can he speak to the whole world at once?"

Vander seemed confused but Zenith knew that Hassan was referring to a hadith, a saying of the Prophet Muhammad, which described Dajjal in these terms. He explained this to Vander, whose face lit up. "That is an interesting analogy," he said, "for in the future that we are from, the entire world communicates through devices that fit your terms. A machine records moving and still images through a lens that looks a bit like a floating grape. Those images are shown to people via another machine, a screen or monitor, that cannot see. Dajjal is basically code and could one day nestle himself within this technology to communicate globally."

He stood up. "As for his appearance, we don't know, exactly. Now, as I was saying, Fenrir should have reached the portal before Dajjal and his Jinn Militia. She will get her message to your friends on Earth. The rest of you, however, must leave now. Zenith has a unit of Jinn soldiers beyond our city limits who are waiting to assist you in your endeavour. I have also arranged for some volunteer Taqnians to guide you and fight with you. For, my friends, there will most certainly be a fight."

He paused and appeared quite sombre. "We can give you weapons that can inflict enormous casualties on your enemy, but there remains great risk nevertheless." Another pause and a deep breath, before he continued. "You must not take our weapons through the portal and cannot leave them behind intact. You must leave them with the Taqnians accompanying you. However, should they die, each weapon has a self-destruct mechanism. You will be shown how to set it and you must do so before you step into the portal or..."

Again, he paused and seemed reluctant to continue. He cleared his throat and added; "if you look likely to be overrun and defeated." At that, he lowered his head for a second. Then, he asked if they were ready and whether they agreed to the terms. They did and the next stage of their journey began in earnest.

CHAPTER 109
1326 A.D.
The Messenger arrives

Sami was awoken by scratching at the door of the house and an occasional howl. Fearing an emboldened wolf pack, he pulled some trousers on and snatched up his sword. He rushed to the window that looked out onto the courtyard, expecting to see several hungry wolves outside. Instead, he witnessed just one. White Wolf.

"Are you going to stand there with your mouth wide open or will you let me enter?" Fenrir asked.

"You're talking."

"You're observant. Now, may I come in?"

Sami opened the door and let her in. "Sorry," he said, "of course you may enter." He paused and frowned. "But how are you talking and why are you here? Are you alone? What has happened to the others? Are they in trouble?"

Fenrir growled to silence the human with his incessant questioning and then she spoke again. "I come with an urgent message. Your questions will be answered in good time, but first I must give you the message. All of you. Bring the others to me please."

The women hugged Fenrir, who explained her true identity and why she had not spoken on Earth last time she was there. Then, she advised them of Dajjal's entry to their world, with a troop of Jinn. The four humans listened attentively and mentioned Owun and Jaffer.

"We have not heard from them and nobody seems to know anything about them," Cecelia said. "Sami rode into Damascus some months ago and he heard there was a fight. A witness said that two men fitting their descriptions were arrested, but there is no way of confirming his story, or finding out where they are being held."

Fenrir explained that both men were imprisoned in the fortress-like

535

prison in Damascus, but that Jawad and his ever-growing unit of followers would release them.

"So, what else do we need to know?" Asked Reza. "What are we supposed to be doing?"

Fenrir scratched behind her ear with her back leg and sat. She sniffed the air and panted briefly. "Is that food I smell?"

Cecelia laughed. "Would you like some? Of course you would. I will bring a bowl for you."

Fenrir sniffed again. "Smells good. Now, your mission is to do what you have been doing. Track down the likely whereabouts of Abbas' offspring, but remain here for the time being. Do not reveal yourself to any of them. Once Jawad and the others arrive, they will explain everything."

She paused and looked long and hard at the humans. "You've aged since I saw you last."

Cecelia arrived with food, for Fenrir and the humans. For the time being, they would wait.

CHAPTER 110
Into the Dark Realm

As the forces of Jinn and humans gathered beyond the outskirts of the City of Taqnia, Zenith gave them one more piece of information. The portal to which they were headed was situated in an area called the Dark Realm. Shaytaan was strong there and visibility would be extremely difficult, if not impossible. One of Zenith's Jinn, a night spirit, had full nocturnal sight and an ability to link her mind with everyone in the group, enabling all of them to see what she could see. This was going to be crucial once they arrived in the Dark Realm, but it also meant that keeping this Jinni safe from harm was high on their list of priorities.

They set off across the remainder of the desert, towards the sea. Navigating dunes of sand, some as tall as oak trees, the travellers grew weary and, by the time they reached the desert's end, several days since leaving Taqnia, their water supplies were almost depleted. They began noticing patches of green that gradually became thicker and more numerous until, exhausted and dehydrated, they found themselves surrounded by acres of lush, green foliage. A freshwater watercourse spread itself into a river that ran wild to the sea. However, it was what lay before them, across the river, that concerned them. A wall of black nothingness. It looked terrifying, as if life suddenly stopped and oblivion began.

Zenith stopped them to allow them to drink and rest, pointing out that they were safer this side of the river than they would be once they crossed it. They took containers to the river, filled them and drank the surprisingly cold, clean water. Then, their thirst quenched, they settled themselves down in the shade of a small cluster of palm-type trees. Eventually, they drifted off. They slept for several hours before being shaken from their slumber by Zenith.

Once they had rubbed the emulsified sleep from their eyes, they gathered around Zenith. He was waiting by the riverbank with an unknown man who looked almost like Zenith's double. Zenith introduced him as Jibreel, an Angel. The Arabs immediately related the name to that of the Angel who revealed the Quran to the Prophet Muhammad. Jawad whispered to Bohemond that Jibreel was Arabic for Gabriel and Bohemond, ever the religious sceptic, appeared somewhat shocked. Nevertheless, he passed on that information to the other non-Muslims.

"Jibreel is able to pass between worlds at ease, with the permission of Allah," Zenith said. "And he will help you on Earth, although most of the time you will not see him. Unfortunately, he comes with unwelcome news. Dajjal has definitely made it through the portal to Earth with his Jinn supporters."

A new day was dawning. Even alongside the flowing river, with a soft breeze reaching them from the nearby sea, it was growing warmer. Zenith's news that Dajjal had escaped their grasp was greeted with muttering and the wiping of brows. Hassan pulled his shirt from his skin and wafted it to draw air underneath. "How has it got this hot in such a short time?" He asked.

Zenith turned towards the region of darkness beyond the opposite bank of the river. The heat was not what he would expect from a warming day and it was emanating from the black region. Something was coming but before he could say anything, Hassan spoke again.

"If Dajjal has reached Earth, we've failed," he said, with some resignation.

"Not at all," replied Zenith. Dajjal was always going to reach Earth one day. That is prophesied. It is destined. We hoped that the moment of his emergence on Earth could be delayed, but it is not so bad that we failed to do that."

The others looked confused, so Zenith continued. "Dajjal cannot achieve what he hopes to achieve on Earth in this time period. Neither the technology, nor the knowledge, exist for that. He will be forced to spend his time influencing, coercing, bribing, controlling, manipulating, until the time of his revelation is right."

Once again, Zenith looked at the black realm beyond the river. The light of a roaring fire was now visible from within and he knew what, or who, was coming. He wanted to convey information about their future tasks and convince them that their quest was not a futile one. However, he worried about the approaching visitor. After a long and deep sigh, he turned back to the group. They had seen what he had seen. They stood, aghast, staring at the ever-brightening light emanating from the blackness beyond. A fire was on its way, or something extremely powerful, made from fire.

Zenith called out to them and, momentarily, broke the spell that was being cast over them.

"Listen to me!" He said. "I must inform you of your task, of the future, of the end of days before that thing that you see emerging before you, finally arrives."

They continued to stare, mouths open, eyes unblinking, breathing erratic. "Now!" He shouted. "Listen!"

They all shook their heads, blinked and turned towards the Jinni.

"Dajjal will make people powerful; those who serve his aims. Then, far into the future, when Earth reaches the advanced level of the Taqnians, he will reveal himself as a saviour, a Messiah. But he will be the false Messiah, al-Dajjal al-Masih. Even so, people will follow him. He will perform miracles; he will give the people what they want.

"Those who do not follow him will be oppressed, enslaved, slaughtered. Dajjal will think he has won. He will open a gateway as a signal to his master, Shaytaan. Then, the Evil One, Shaytaan, Iblis, Lucifer will arrive with his hordes of Jinn followers. Their aim? To reclaim Earth which once was theirs before Allah gave it to humankind.

"However, the true Messiah will end Shaytaan's campaign, but until that time, you must fight the oppressors, fight for the oppressed, hinder Dajjal at every opportunity."

As he ended, the Dark Realm behind him exploded with the light of a fire as bright as a sun. Everyone covered their eyes and looked away. The sky burned red and a living form burst forth. Unclothed, the form was part human in appearance, with dark red skin, like newly tanned leather. He was muscular and fierce looking. His feet were cloven hooves, his hands claw-like, his eyes completely black and upon his head were two, goat-like horns. He stepped closer and his height soon became apparent. He stood at a good eight feet tall but as he neared them his form shifted and changed. By the time he was standing before them, he had taken on the form of a handsome man, dressed all in purple. His skin was pale, but his features were not unlike Hassan's. His hair was short and slick. It was jet black but full of sheen and his eyes were blue.

The bright red fire that had pre-empted his arrival dissipated, and the light faded. The world went black. The gloom of the Dark Realm had stretched across the river and smothered the travellers like a blanket. They were immersed in a night of silent emptiness, a void. The night spirit quickly enabled everyone in the group to see in the depressing darkness that seemed to reach into their very souls. Some shivered, partly from the sudden coldness that accompanied the lack of daylight, but partly out of fear.

Zenith spoke first. "Be careful Shaytaan. You are far from your home in Hell," he said.

The group of humans whispered.

"Shaytaan? Isn't that what you Arabs call Lucifer, the Devil?" Bohemond asked Jawad, who nodded but remained silent.

Amalric heard this, noted the look of fear on Jawad's face, and huffed. "I'm tired of all this nonsense. Lucifer? Gods? Illusion, all of it. The Taqnians explained it all to us in terms of science and knowledge. This is a clever enemy, with greater knowledge than us, who has convinced you all that he is the Devil, to frighten us. Remember what Vander told us? The Jinn tricked humans into believing they were gods."

He stared at the man in purple. "I don't believe you're the Devil and to prove it, I will take your stinking head, warlock!" He shouted, pulling his sword from its sheath and charging towards the stranger.

"No, Amalric!" The shout came from Jawad, but it was too late.

Shaytaan lifted a hand and Amalric was stopped in his tracks. "Foolish human," Shaytaan said. "Now, your friends will watch as you bleed out."

At that moment, Amalric's sword hand ripped itself away from his arm and fell to the ground, still gripping the sword. Blood began to gush from Amalric's arm, and he shrieked in pain. Bohemond began to rush to his friend's aid, but he was pulled back by Wadjet.

"No, Bohemond," She said. "You will suffer the same fate if you intercede."

Shaytaan smiled at Wadjet. "Ah, my dear Wadjet," he said. "What a pleasure to see you again."

"I am no longer in thrall to you. My Master is now He who made you."

Shaytaan laughed and Bohemond moved again towards Amalric who was bleeding profusely and turning pale with blood loss. "Oh, Bohemond. Do you really wish to do that?" Shaytaan asked.

Bohemond stopped in his tracks, hesitating between helping his friend and staying still to avoid a similar plight. Shaytaan laughed again. "Has Wadjet made her feelings known to you yet?" He asked. "It would break her heart were you to suffer your friend's fate, for he is destined to die. Be sure of that."

He paused and held a hand up towards Amalric, who had passed out. Suddenly, one by one, the fingers on Amalric's other hand began to pull away from his hand, each falling to the ground before him.

"I wonder if Wadjet will rush to attack me, to save you. That would be exciting, wouldn't it? I could watch all three of you die in agony, and it would be so needless."

"Needless?" Bohemond yelled. "You will kill us all anyway to stop us from chasing Dajjal into my world."

The smile disappeared from Shaytaan's face and he shook his head, slowly. "On the contrary. I have no intention of killing you all, unless you challenge me. I don't even intend to stop you from following Dajjal to Earth."

"Liar!" Shouted Jawad. "Why would you allow us to pursue Dajjal? You are the arch deceiver, Shaytaan and we seek refuge with Allah against you and all of your followers."

"Why would I let you go? It amuses me. I enjoy watching your feeble attempts to thwart me, to thwart destiny. I have been watching your stumbling about like blind men in a marsh pit. Besides, your destiny is to meet Dajjal and his force of Afaarit and Wishmasters. You see, Jawad, I am the cat and you are the mice. I toy with you and every day that you survive, your confidence increases, but sooner or later the mice are caught."

Wadjet again pulled Bohemond back. This time, she stepped in front of him. "Let me at least cauterise Amalric's wounds and allow us to help him to live."

Shaytaan waved a hand and Amalric's limp and lifeless body

slumped to the ground. "I think not, Wadjet. I think he should die." He waved his hand again and, to the shock and horror of those gathered, Amalric's head was torn away from his body. Bohemond, Jawad and Marie rushed forwards, yelling in grief and anger but they were thrown backwards by an unseen force emanating from Shaytaan's hand.

Zenith and Jibreel stepped to the front of the group and formed an invisible shield against further attacks from Shaytaan, but they knew this was a temporary measure. "We must go," Zenith said. "We are not strong enough to fight him."

Shaytaan cackled so loudly that the sound echoed throughout the area surrounding them. "I cannot be killed. I was promised reprieve until the end of time and that moment is a very long way off. So begone, all of you."

He glanced down at Amalric's abused and bleeding body. "But leave this cadaver, for I will take his soul with me and feed his flesh to my minions. Meanwhile, I bid you all farewell, until we meet again." With that he waved an arm and produced a grey mist which drifted into the warm air and vanished. Suddenly, they found themselves surrounded by a swirling circus of faces and the sound of banshees. Their high-pitched screams were so piercing that they could split ear drums. Jawad and his troop covered their ears and fell to their knees, but the sound was clawing its way to their brains. They began to wonder if this was the end but remembered that Shaytaan had said he did not want to kill them. *But he is the deceiver,* Jawad thought to himself.

Then, as suddenly as it had begun, the sights and sounds ended, and the Dark Realm receded back across the river. Shaytaan's Jinn troops, those that had not gone with Dajjal, turned into swirls of dust that faded into nothingness.

Jibreel, anxious not to dally any longer, called on them to follow him. He waved farewell to Zenith, who had headed off in the direction of Taqnia. Jibreel, followed by the troop of humans and their friend, Wadjet, gathered the Taqnian weapons. Unused, they were set to self-destruct and thrown in a pile some distance from the portal. Then, reluctantly, they followed Jibreel through the gateway to Earth. Bohemond turned to look back at Amalric just before going through but the body of his friend was gone, snatched away by Shaytaan and his Jinn forces to God knows where.

CHAPTER 111
1326 A.D.
Return

Upon their arrival back on Earth, the group of human and Jinn travellers were initially disorientated. Unsure where they were, they all looked around, attempting to find some recognisable landmark or anything familiar. It was the middle of a hot summer's day and they blinked as the sunlight struck them. It took a few minutes for their eyes to fully adjust to the brightness after being immersed in the Dark Realm and travelling through the portal. Eventually, things came into focus. Jawad, Hassan, Marie and Amina quickly realised they were on the outskirts of Damascus. Jawad and Marie both recalled what had happened not far from here many years earlier. Marie put her arms around her husband, rested her head on his chest and listened to the beating of his heart.

"The memories are within you, as they are within me," she said.

He sighed and kissed her on her forehead. Then, turning to Jibreel, he asked why they had come through so close to Damascus.

Bohemond, waiting for the reply, did not notice at first that Wadjet was holding his hand. Suddenly, her touch became apparent, but he did not pull away. "I am so sorry about Amalric," she said.

He sighed, pulled her closer and held her tightly. His strong, muscular arms wrapped around her, giving her comfort. For the first time in an age, she felt safe and loved. They kissed, a long, lingering kiss that only ended when Bohemond was nudged in the back by Hassan. He had missed Jibreel's reply, but Hassan filled him in. They were to enter Damascus, break into the prison and free Jaffer and Owun.

"Here we go again," Bohemond thought. Then he resumed his passionate engagement with Wadjet.

Later, they sat in a circle and discussed ways to free their compatriots. Everyone had an opinion. Everyone had an idea, but nobody could agree on the best way to execute the escape. Jibreel had told them he could create mystical diversions for them inside the prison, but they needed to find a way in. They came to realise that it was probably more difficult to break into a prison than it was to break out. *Quite ironic, really,* thought Hassan.

Finally, they agreed to go with a plan proposed by Wadjet. Jibreel would create a chaotic disturbance within the prison to distract as many prison personnel as possible. Meanwhile, Wadjet would shapeshift, taking on the form of one of the Sultan's senior military officers. She would be accompanied by Jawad, Hassan and Lungelo. All would be dressed in the clothing that suited military personnel of such high standing. Wadjet would acquire suitable clothing in the Damascus marketplace, through deceit and persuasion.

Together, they would inform whoever stood guard at the main gate of the prison, that the Sultan has requested the transfer of two prisoners, Owun and Jaffer. Wadjet would offer as little information as possible to the guards. She would, however, state that the two men have knowledge crucial to the security of Damascus.

"With so many people distracted by Jibreel, the guards should be unable to seek permission from senior officers," Wadjet explained. "A few well-placed threats, given with the authority of one of the Sultan's senior officers, should frighten them into complying with my orders."

It took her an hour to acquire the clothing necessary for the deception. Once dressed and clear on their duties, she and her three human associates began the walk to the prison gate. Jibreel, meanwhile, vanished. He re-materialised inside the prison and began to create a multitude of mystical events. Guards were thrust into the air and left floating and helpless. Objects were moved around, apparently on their own. Eerie sounds were produced around the prison and, in one section, cell doors were opened. Prisoners ran from their cells, forcing guards to confront them to force them back under lock and key.

Wadjet, Hassan, Jawad and Lungelo approached the two guards at the gate. Seeing four of the Sultan's elite guard made the guards nervous and Wadjet's orders were authoritative and convincing. One of the guards unlocked the door. He left to find someone senior for permission and his colleague relocked the door. His colleague returned moments later, disappointed.

"The prison is overrun by Jinn. Everyone else is occupied dealing with an attempted prison break," he said to his fellow guard.

"We cannot wait!" Wadjet, in her male form, dressed as she was, spoke with certainty and confidence. "If you cannot find your superiors, you must follow my orders and bring the two prisoners to us immediately."

The guards hesitated, so Wadjet took two steps forwards until she stood inches from them. "NOW!" She shouted.

The guard who had remained at the gate before, barely out of boyhood, snapped to attention and then fumbled for his keys. He dropped them, retrieved them and then struggled to unlock the door. Finally, the lock clicked, he opened the door and ran to fetch the two prisoners.

Several minutes later, he returned. His fellow guard unlocked and opened the door and the prisoners were shoved through. They looked weak and tired. Their clothes and their long hair and beards were matted and filthy. Their skin was pallid and their lips were dry and chapped. Owun almost collapsed in front of Wadjet, as he was pushed forwards by the guard, but she managed to catch hold of him.

"Your treatment of these men will be conveyed to the Sultan," Wadjet said. "Have you not fed and watered them? Have you tortured them? For what purpose? What possible reason could you have for torturing two men imprisoned for a street brawl? And why are they still here?" She was livid. She passed Owun to Hassan as Jawad caught hold of Jaffer and walked him slowly behind Wadjet.

"Admit it. They were left to rot and used by some sadistic bastard as toys to torture. Isn't that so?" She pushed the younger guard as she spoke and he nodded, a nod of shame and regret.

"The Sultan will, I am sure, be sending forces to inspect this prison. This is not how Muslims should treat anyone, even criminals."

She turned and stormed off, followed by the others, Owun being supported by Hassan and Lungelo. Once out of view of the guards, they headed as quickly as they could to the City's gate where they waited for Jibreel. He arrived moments later with a rickety cart, drawn by an aging carthorse. After loading the now passed out Owun onto the cart, the rest climbed on. Wadjet, now transformed into an elderly trader, with a long, shaggy grey beard, sat up front and drove the horse forward. Jibreel sat with her and gave directions to the villa where they would find Sami and the others.

CHAPTER 112
1326 A.D.
Reunion

It was nearing twilight when they arrived. They were greeted first by Fenrir. She bounded up to Marie, a clear and lasting bond having been formed between them, when they were in Scotland.

"There is much to discuss now you are all here. Come into the house."

She swivelled around and headed back to the house without noticing the newcomers with the travellers. The two sibling children had the broadest smiles on their faces. Almost in unison they expressed their awe and wonder in words. "The talking wolf. The beautiful talking wolf. We missed you."

Amina squinted at them. "Do you always say the same thing at the same time?" She said.

"Not at the same time," replied Serene. "He copies me but does it so quickly that it seems as if we're saying things together."

It happened again. Amina smiled and put her hands on the children's shoulders, guiding them gently towards the house. Once everyone was inside, Jawad, helped by his fellow travellers, explained Zenith's and Vander's instructions. They were to establish a secretive society that would fight Dajjal at every opportunity. For as long as it would take, they would seek out Dajjal's agents and thwart them, undermine them and even attack them if necessary. They would pass on their duties to their children and so the Society would operate throughout the world, perhaps for centuries to come.

Once everyone understood and they were all willing to take part, they relaxed and chatted. Owun was treated by Amina and the men discussed building quarters for everyone to live on the estate. Jawad turned to Reza.

"You look older, but not by much my friend."

Reza laughed. "I'm not sure if that is because I was left on Earth, or because I'm married," he quipped.

Jawad laughed and called Bohemond and Wadjet over. He explained about their relationship and spoke of Amalric's death at the hand of Shaytaan.

Reza sighed. "A sad loss for sure, but Shaytaan will not keep him long. Amalric was a good man, despite his faults. His soul will not remain with Iblis. Of that, I'm sure."

Bohemond thanked him for his words and sat alongside him. Wadjet gave her apologies and left the men to join the women.

"Interesting relationship, Bohemond. How is it working out?"

Bohemond glanced at Wadjet, whose hips swayed as she walked away. "I'm happy. She's happy. What more could we ask for?"

"Can I ask a question?" Sami said, as he sat down with them. "What happens about children between you and the Jinni?"

Bohemond bit his bottom lip. "According to Zenith, there is nothing to stop it happening. After all, Abbas was part Jinni, was he not?"

"But will the child have Wadjet's powers?"

"Only God knows the answer to that my friend. We will have to wait and see."

As the conversations continued through the day and evening, they were visited by Jibreel. The Jinni had been gathering intelligence from several parts of the world. He had also been tracking down some of Abbas' multitude of progeny. He appeared out of nowhere in the middle of the main room. Everyone was present and expectant, and they waited quietly for him to speak. Reza and Sami, having waited so long, were eager to hear what the Angel had to say. They were hopeful that it would be a clear plan.

Jibreel was dressed in a Jellaba, a long Arab dress-like garment. His wings were not present, and his translucent appearance was absent. He looked like any other man of the region, with a long, brown beard and shoulder length hair. He took a moment to prepare himself and then addressed his audience.

"May I begin by apologising to those of you who remained here on Earth, for keeping you waiting so long. May I also ask you to permit entry to your comrades, whom I have gathered and brought here. They are waiting outside, somewhat confused."

They nodded in acknowledgement and acceptance. He nodded back and opened the door, inviting Stuart, Judah and the others who had formed part of this group before, into the house. Then, he began to explain.

"All of you here today, who fought and travelled alongside each other, are the beginnings of a secretive organisation. Henceforth, it will be known as The Society. The aim of this organisation is to disrupt Dajjal and his master, Shaytaan, whenever and wherever they engage in their machinations."

He began to circulate the room, taking in each person as he approached them. "All of you, the children included, must protect what is good, what is morally right in the world and fight against corruption, oppression, unjust wars and anything that damages the world or its life forms."

He invited them all to sit before continuing.

"The followers, willingly or unknowingly, will harm children, animals, women, the elderly and the natural world for no reasons other than those which are self-serving. Over the coming millennia wars will evolve into the most destructive events the world has known. The planet Earth will be polluted and will cry out in pain, but the destruction will continue, virtually unabated.

"You will find yourselves, at times, fighting on one side, only to find yourselves, later, fighting against those you once fought for. Why? Because your fight is against all that is wrong, on whichever side it occurs. Consequently, most of The Society's work will be revelation. Revealing the corruption of the wrongdoers to the world. This, however, must be done with caution. Subtlety will be the order of the day and, under no circumstances can any member of The Society reveal the presence of Dajjal on Earth until he reveals himself. Is that clear?"

He waited for a response and his audience nodded, but Jaffer posed a question that was on everybody's mind. "Why? Why can we not reveal his presence now? Why must we wait for him to reveal himself?"

Jibreel frowned. "Dajjal's people will have control of numerous means of communication. They will be in positions of power and influence. They will convince the masses that your message is false and that will undermine everything The Society is doing."

"And how will they convince the masses that our message is false?"

Asked Jawad.

Jibreel sighed and, for a moment, sat deep in thought, considering how to explain this to the people of this time period. Finally, he inhaled deeply and replied.

"In this age, you will be said to be possessed. That view will last for some centuries. In later ages, you will be called crazy, insane, having a sickness of the mind. Once Dajjal reveals himself, your criticisms of him will seem to be the logical, sensible, rational, sane position. And if you push hard enough, his true nature will emerge for all the world to see. That will be the beginning of the end."

The group began muttering to each other, considering what they had been told. Sami, who had remained silent throughout, suddenly turned to Jibreel and spoke.

"What are we to do now? This group. What is our mission?"

Jibreel opened his hands, palms upwards and a blue, holographic image appeared before him. It was a box and he leant forward to rest it on the table that sat between him and several of the group. When he pulled his hands away, the blue box remained, but now in solid form.

"Everything you do, everything you say and everything you find out must be recorded. This box will become invisible after use, but can be made manifest and opened with a word that I will teach you all before I leave. Inside there is another, smaller box made from a material which has not yet been discovered on Earth. When you speak to that box, all will be recorded for future reference. Next to the small box, is a cube. Using another word, you can retrieve everything that has been recorded in the form of a hologram like the one I presented to you a few minutes ago."

He tapped the large blue box on its lid. "You can also summon Zenith or me, using this box. Don't do that unless it is absolutely necessary.

"The box must be held by the leaders of The Society and passed down from one generation to the next. As time passes, the information stored in this..." He tapped the box lid again, "... will help The Society to establish the identity of Dajjal."

The Jinni told everyone present the code words for opening the box and operating the equipment inside. He explained that the scientists at Taqnia had produced it for The Society. Then, he asked them to rest, assuring them that in the morning he would tell them their first mission.

CHAPTER 113
1326 A.D.
The Society's First Mission

Jibreel woke everyone early and called a meeting in the main room of the house again.

"Already, armies are on the move again, land expansion is occurring, and ordinary people are caught in the middle, as usual. Since Osman I, the nomadic Turkish ruler, began his conquests, we have seen the Byzantine Empire crushed, together with Bulgaria and Serbia. This year, Bursa fell. This Ottoman empire will continue to expand, into Europe, into the lands of the Arabs and into Persia, for centuries to come."

Owun, recovered from his prison ordeal, entered the room. "Excuse me for interrupting, Jibreel," he said. "I have been listening. Is it not the case that empires bring great wealth and security to the people they envelop?"

"Of course, but at what cost? Didn't your own countrymen throw out the Romans?"

"Yes, but..."

"Why?" Jibreel interrupted. "The Romans brought knowledge of buildings that your people lost for centuries. They brought knowledge of mathematics and military tactics, did they not?"

Owun took a moment before replying. "Yes, but they destroyed our culture, our beliefs and our way of life. They forced young men to fight for their Empire. They took goods and money from hardworking Britons, to fund their armies and..."

Jibreel interrupted again. "I think you have answered your own question, Owun. Empires do bring advancements, but these are often less favourable to the occupied than to the occupier. They are often physical advantages, not spiritual or social ones. There is more to life than just an improvement in living standards."

Owun was about to speak again but Jibreel held up a hand to stop him. The Ottomans will hold Palestine for many centuries, until they are removed by another Empire, one from your country, Owun. And, thus, the occupation of this land comes full circle. How? The Turks will align themselves with the wrong side in a massive, global war."

He waited for comments, but none came. "This is but one example of the corruption that power brings. Power provided by Dajjal and Shaytaan. I cannot tell you the specifics of the wrongs done by these people of power. You will see them for yourselves. You will feel them, experience them, know them. As will your descendants. Thus, The Society will take action when it is needed and when it can act."

The room was suddenly filled with a multitude of mutterings, as each person present began to talk about Jibreel's revelations. They were so engrossed in their conversations that none of them noticed when Jibreel left the house. They did notice, however, when he returned with a baby in his arms. The room fell silent as, one by one, each person turned towards the Jinni.

"This is Amalric's child, from Taqnia. I cannot tell you why, but for his safety I have brought him here. I need you to take care of him and name him. Please, do not question me regarding this, as I do not have the answers you may seek."

Amina stepped forward and held out her arms to receive the infant. Jibreel handed him to her and she drew him close, kissing the top of his head. "We will need a wet nurse," she said.

Owun drew alongside her. "You cannot take care of the child alone," he said. "I will take care of him with you. I'm sure Cecelia or Isabelle can find a wet nurse for us in one of the local villages."

He looked back at the two women and Cecelia nodded. "Of course."

"The child will live beyond the length of any of your lives," Jibreel added. "He will lead The Society eventually and will be a constant for millennia."

"I will call him Yusuf," Amina said.

CHAPTER 114
In the Future in The Netherlands

A group of three men and a teenage girl sat in a warehouse just outside Amsterdam. They were a collection of people of varying ethnicities, ages and beliefs, political and religious. They were part of a much wider organisation, a secretive, global cartel of protesters, hackers, political agitators, resistance fighters and environmentalists, called The Society.

"We've had an email from Alan, our guy in Tech City. You guys are gonna want to see this." The speaker was a young man, maybe twenty years' old. His hair was long. It was tied in a ponytail and he sported a plaited beard. His skin was a bronze colour, hinting at his mixed racial background. His mother was Dutch, but his father was from Turkey.

"Put it up on the screen, Daniel," someone said.

They sat together at the front of the warehouse and the email was projected to a big screen on the wall.

Guys, I've been doing a lot of research, while working here, and some of what I've found out is gonna blow your minds. The work on AI and nanotech is way beyond anything I've seen before, but that's not all. They're also working on genetic engineering. They've been combining computer coding with biological coding [genes].

That isn't what I'm writing about, though. There's a guy working here—goes by the name of Radawan Cilic. He comes and goes, works in isolation and never talks to any of us. Rumours are that he is the greatest programmer the world has ever had but has also never heard of. He is said to be the originator of much of the research and work going on here, but he is obsessed. His obsession? Time travel.

He is very elusive. I've only seen him once, in a corridor yesterday. I sneaked a photo of him [see attached].

They opened the picture. It was a young man with a tidily trimmed beard, dark, short hair and designer glasses. They shrugged and returned to the email.

Anyway, I started doing some digging. I wanted to find out more about him. This is where things get pretty spooky. His name isn't Radawan Cilic at all. It is Jalal Mashad Jali and he is the owner of... yep, you guessed it—Tech City. He owns the whole fucking place. But that's not all. Photos of him keep coming up in different places, at different times throughout history.

The Ottoman's massacre of Armenians. He was there. Nazi Germany, alongside Goering. He was there. The massacre of Native Americans at Wounded Knee. In the background at a press conference about the dropping of nukes on Japan. At the massacres of Palestinian civilians at Deir Yassin, at Sabra and Shattilla. And, the conspiracy shit that went around during the coronavirus pandemic all that time ago? Yep, he was behind the fake stories—even ran a Media outlet pushing all sorts of crap about 5G, as if an electronic system could possibly create a biological virus. It goes on and on. The man is a fucking monster and, either he has solved the issue of time travel, or he has lived for a very, very long time.

I'll let you have more if I get it.

It ended *Alan Van der Meer.*

There was a moment of silence once everyone had read the email. It was shattered by a female voice. A teenage girl, sitting behind the rest of the group, her hair dyed purple, her clothes 'designer scruff' mixed with skater rock chick style. She was staring at her phone and had headphones on. Extremely gifted, she would have read the email in its entirety in seconds. From then on, she had been scrolling through the Internet looking for something on anyone using the names Alan mentioned.

"Guys, have you seen the News?" She spoke English with a Dutch accent.

There was no response, so he continued.

"Tech City has vanished. Nobody can explain it. It's all over the news."

They turned on the Television and, sure enough, the News programmes were full of the mysterious disappearance of the world's foremost technology centre. Tech City, a specialist city in the Netherlands where Alan Van der Meer worked, had vanished. As they watched the TV, one of the gathered group mentioned the email.

"He must have sent it just before the City disappeared."

The teenage girl who had directed them to the breaking news, sniffed and spoke again.

"It's reported that this Jali guy vanished from public life after being publicly humiliated over his obsession with time travel."

Another of the group, an Arab man in his thirties, got up and began wandering around the room.

"Do you all remember the stories of our ancestors, our predecessors? Didn't they include a story about Madinah al-Taqnia in one of the worlds of the Jinn?"

The others nodded but seemed confused by this question.

"Well, Madinah al-Taqnia is City of Technology in English." The others stared blankly at him and he grew increasingly excited. "City of Technology. Tech City."

A sudden reaction of awareness greeted him from the others, so he continued. "Well, we know what has happened to Tech City, don't we? It has been sent back in time hundreds of thousands of years and to another dimension; to one of the Jinn worlds."

Daniel leapt to his feet and interjected. "Of course. You're right, Yusuf. There was a guy there called Vander. The man who guided our ancestors around Taqnia and helped them in their quest. Vander? Van der Meer? Alan Van der Meer? Do you think it is possible that our Alan, was their Vander?"

"Daniel, I think you're right, but who is this Cilic guy or Jali or whatever his name is?"

"Don't you see?" Daniel replied. He is Dajjal. Cilic is Dajjal. Jalal Mashad Jali is an anagram of Al-Masih al-Dajjal. He didn't disappear with the City, but he needed it to go. Without the hundreds of thousands of years of research and progress in the Jinn world, the code that is Dajjal would not have been created. The progress on genetic engineering would never have happened. Dajjal owes his creation to the existence of Taqnia in the Jinn realm."

A man with a Northern Irish accent, leaned back in his chair. Despondently, he said: "And now he has gone again. We had him, or at least Alan had him in his sights, but we've lost him again."

"Not necessarily, Aidan," replied the teenage girl, staring at her phone. "Take a look at this."

"Is it more news about Tech City, Amy?" Yusuf asked.

"Just take a look," she replied, shoving the phone across the table to him.

Daniel and Aiden joined him, and he clicked play.

In the video, the man known as Jali was shown performing a host of what many would call miracles. The first of these occurred at a road traffic accident on an autobahn in Germany. The video showed him placing his hands on seriously injured people and, as the image zoomed in closer, it was clear that gashes, cuts and broken bones were being instantly healed. The video jumped to another incident where Jali seemed to appear from nowhere among insurgents in a bleak country somewhere in Asia, possibly Afghanistan. He waved a hand and the electronic systems controlling an anti-aircraft missile unit, suddenly shut down. The missile was made instantly inoperable.

This was followed by Jali apparently materialising in a drone control room, much to the shock of the American drone operators there. A subtitle boldly announced that this section of the video was leaked by someone at the Pentagon. Jali held his hands in front of him, palms facing the two drone operators. Their eyes closed and they collapsed on the floor. He then waved a hand, just as he had done among the insurgents, and the drone operating equipment immediately turned off.

The video, with over an hour's worth of compilation footage from security cameras and phones, was filled with unnatural occurrences, all involving Jali.

"The false Messiah. Al-Masih al-Dajjal." Yusuf whispered the words, as if he feared being heard by Shaytaan or his agents. "We are going to need help."

CHAPTER 115
The Summoning

Amy was shaking her head. She kept restarting the video and watching it repeatedly. She was mumbling and Daniel asked her to share her concerns, her thoughts. She took a deep breath, paused the video and put down her phone.

"I never believed any of the myths and legends surrounding what we do. I just thought Daniel and Yusuf were a couple of science fiction and fantasy geeks, who loved to embellish what they did with stories." She stopped, looked up at Yusuf and shook her head. "Even when you showed me the box with all that fancy tech in it. That shit was at least a hundred years ahead of anything we use. But I just thought that Tech City was like every other Tech company, with research miles ahead of what they release. I thought it was just another money-making scam. Release upgrades and new tech bit by bit to keep the profits rolling in."

"You believed me when I said the box came from Tech City though?" Yusuf asked.

Amy took a deep breath before replying. "Yes, but I never believed all that time travel shit." She glanced at the screen on the wall. "Until today, when we saw that news story about Tech City and then the email from Alan and now this!" She pointed at the video of Dajjal on her phone.

"Fuck!" She shouted. "Fuck yes, we need fucking help. The hacking, the protests, the activism, I've loved it all, but this shit is too much."

She stopped talking and the room fell silent, save for the humming of computers and other technology. Daniel broke the silence when he addressed Yusuf. "What sort of help?"

Yusuf did not answer. He walked to the end of the warehouse where a fingerprint and eye scanner was situated. Pressing his whole hand on the flat screen, while positioning his eye on a small lens above it, he spoke the word 'Iftar'. An electronic voice responded. "Voice, print and iris scans accepted." A section of the wall moved backwards some three feet and then slid sideways to the right. Yusuf entered the hidden room behind the wall and returned seconds later with the box. After carrying it to the table where the others were gathered, he shoved it against a computer to move the machine out of the way. Then, he settled the box onto the table, spoke the code word and stood back as the box opened.

"What's your plan then, Yusuf?" Aiden asked.

"We summon the Jinni, Zenith."

It took half an hour to fathom the procedure for summoning Zenith and a further ten minutes to carry out the summoning. Zenith appeared behind them as all their attention was directed at the box, as if they expected him to appear from there in a wisp of smoke. The Jinni entered the room, unseen and unheard, the only sounds coming from the computers and the box. The latter emitted a sonorous hum that they found entrancing. In their semi-mesmerised state, they failed to hear Zenith's first attempt to attract their attention. So, he tried again. With a wave of his hand, all noise in the room was muted, except for a low drone, similar to that made by bagpipes. The humans turned, stunned when their eyes saw the Jinni. Standing about seven feet tall, dressed all in black leather, with long, wavy, black hair and with two angel-like wings spread out behind him, he was an awesome sight.

"Your heartbeats race. Do you fear me, humans?" He asked, his voice firm but simultaneously comforting.

They said nothing, but Daniel and Aiden backed away.

"Who summoned me?" The Jinni asked, his eyes lighting up as he spoke.

Nervously, Yusuf replied. "Er, we did, I er, I think. Are you Zenith?"

"I am. Who are you?" He teased with them for he knew very well who they were, but he wanted them to say it. He had been watching them for some time in Zaman's holographic image-maker and had heard Amy's reservations. Now, he wanted to hear her say that she believed. He waited. Slowly, Amy stepped forward.

"We are The Society, or at least the leaders of that anonymous group. I can't believe you're here, and yet, here you are. You are Zenith, aren't you?"

The Jinni's eyes transformed from the beacons that they had been to blue, human-like eyes. He smiled.

"You believe, Amy? Your scepticism has gone?"

"I would like to touch your hand, to feel that you are real. May I?" She asked.

Zenith stepped forward and held out his hand to her. "Of course, you may. But should I call you Thomas?"

She looked confused and turned to her friends, seeking explanation. Aiden responded. "Doubting Thomas. In the Bible, Thomas doubted that Jesus had risen and was only convinced when he put his hand on Jesus' wounds."

He smiled and Amy nodded. Then, she reached out and touched the Jinni's hand. She nodded again. "He's real," she said, turning to the others.

The mood in the room became calm and contemplative. The humans relaxed. The Jinni wrapped his hand around Amy's, smiled and led her to a seat at the table. The others, feeling more comfortable in his presence, also sat down and the Jinni joined them.

"I am Zenith and I understand you are seeking my help. Is that so?"

Yusuf cleared his throat and replied. "We have identified Dajjal as a man called Jalal Mashad Jali, who also goes by the name of Radawan Cilic. However, he has come into the open under just the name Jali, and is performing what appear to be miracles."

"I am aware, Yusuf," replied Zenith, who placed his palms together and brought his fingertips to his lips as he thought about what to say next. Suddenly, his hands dropped away from his face and he continued. "As you know, Dajjal is a Jinni who takes the form of electronic code. He is utilising a biological body together with highly technical embellishments. His Jinn powers, along with his enhanced biology and technical additions, enable him to perform what appear to you as miracles. He is a trickster, like his master."

"I've had a thought," interjected Amy.

"Feel free to share," Zenith replied.

"Well, Tech City, er, Taqnia, was thrown into the past on one of the Jinn worlds, yes?

"Yes."

"And they spent hundreds of thousands of years growing in

knowledge of biology and electronics. Dajjal himself emerged from that city, didn't he?"

Zenith nodded and she continued. "Surely, Tech City still exists and has had a further thousand years or more of learning and research. Why can't they assist us?"

Zenith's expression turned sullen. His head dropped for a moment and he sighed deeply. "That is not possible, I'm afraid."

"Why not?" The humans asked, almost in unison.

Zenith sighed again. "I should have considered this at the time and so should the Taqnians." He paused, trying to find the best way of saying what he needed to say. "When your ancestors entered Taqnia, they took with them a multitude of bacteria, viruses, illnesses that they had become immune to over time. We Jinn are not affected by human diseases, but the Taqnians were. At least, those rooted in biology were. They had no defence, no immunity against the illnesses your ancestors brought to them. Within weeks of Jawad and his group leaving our world, the Taqnians began to get sick and die. In fact, every biological entity in the city fell prey to these hidden attackers. Taqnia no longer exists, my friends."

Daniel frowned. "What about the artificial intelligence entities? They would not have been affected, so wouldn't they have continued the work Taqnia was engaged in?"

Zenith shook his head. "The reason Taqnia was working so hard on biological enhancements, genetic engineering, was that they had found the resources needed to produce and maintain machines were limited on our worlds."

"So, the machines started to fail?" Asked Yusuf.

"Yes, and so did the City's shield. Months passed after Jawad and his people returned to Earth and the Jinn realised that Taqnia was vulnerable. Shaytaan sent an army of Jinn to the city. It was looted and destroyed. I'm afraid, you are to handle this yourselves."

"But how?" Amy asked.

"Continue with your hacking, protests, research and social media campaigning. Keep recruiting soldiers in our cause but never tell them everything, unless they are fully fledged members of The Society. Monitor Dajjal carefully. Watch his movements, scrutinise his actions and undermine him at every opportunity.

"Don't confront him. Continue to work anonymously. Create doubt about him online. Organise protests. Find links between him and any immoral or criminal people or activities. Bring them to the public's attention. Harass and delay. That is your job. We are in the final phase, my friends. Others will come soon to challenge Dajjal. In the meantime, follow Yusuf's lead. Now, you have work to do."

BIBLIOGRAPHY

Although this is a work of fiction, I have tried to ensure that much of the context in which it is set is accurate. To do this, various sources were accessed, the most used being listed below.

Battlefields of Britain
http://www.battlefieldsofbritain.co.uk/battle_bannockburn_1314.html

Crawford, Paul (1997) "The Crusades." Online Reference Book for Medieval Studies.

Dafoe, Stephen (1998) The Battle Of Hattin—July 4th, 1187.
http://www.templarhistory.com/hattin.html

Grousse, Renee (1970) "The Epic of the Crusades." Orion Press. Translated from the French by Noel Lindsay.
http://www.templarhistory.com/saladin.html

Dere Militari. http://www.deremilitari.org/resources/sources/ctit2.htm

History of war (logistics)
http://www.historyofwar.org/articles/concepts_logistics.html

Islamicity http://www.islamicity.com/mosque/ihame/Sec11.htm

Maalouf, Amin (1984) "The Crusades Through Arab Eyes." Al Saqi books. First published as Les croisades vues par les Arabes by Edition J.-C. Lattés, Paris (1983).

Middle Ages http://www.middleages.org.uk/life-in-scotland-in-the-middle-ages.html

"Richard The Lionheart Massacres The Saracens, 1191," EyeWitness to History, www.eyewitnesstohistory.com (2001).

Scaruffi, Piero (1999) A timeline of the Mongols
http://www.scaruffi.com/

The way of truth online.
http://www.thewaytotruth.org/prophetmuhammad/achievements.html

Velagoni, L. http://www.transoxiana.org/Eran/Articles/venegoni.html

Waterson, James | Published 05 September 2018
https://www.historytoday.com/miscellanies/who-were-mamluks